"The best book about Leonard Coh⟨en⟩" — ⟨Jean-Luc Porquet,⟩
Canard enchainé

"Combining scholarly biography, luminous exegesis, and metaphysics of the broken heart, this is the Summa Cohenia we needed. With Gilles Tordjman's book, this is the best homage to the work of the Christ-loving Jewish poet." — Bernard Loupias, *Le Nouvel Observateur*

"An erudite and amorous page-turner on the wandering Canadian, that reaches beyond dates and facts." — Emmanuel Dosda, *Poly*

"An extraordinary piece of work, at every level . . . It's the biographical denouement that Leonard deserves. . . . Takes Cohenian biography to another level." — Michael Posner, author of *Leonard Cohen, Untold Stories: The Early Years*

"Cohen ceaselessly questions the world, as Christophe Lebold brilliantly demonstrates in *Leonard Cohen : L'Homme qui voyait tomber les anges*, a learned, vibrant, and inspired study devoted to the immortal creator of 'Hallelujah.'" — Myriam Perfetti, *Marianne*

"With wide-angle shots of the Cohen constellation and clever close-ups on this loved woman or that inhabited place. This work is a treasure: the wind of rock has blown there and vibration rhymes with erudition." — Vincent Dussol, *Transatlantica*

"Cohen under the surgeon's scalpel: a book that retraces Leonard Cohen's unique poetic odyssey, and combines liveliness and passion with a scholarly twist. The inspired biographer crystallizes the different avatars of 'the man who saw the angels fall' and takes us along on the poet's existential quest." — *Dernières Nouvelles d'Alsace*

"It's marvelous and highly recommended. Crammed with photos, footnotes, a blizzard of evidence, of fantastic research and opinion: this is ESSENTIAL." — Jim Devlin, author of *Leonard Cohen: In His Own Words* and *In Every Style of Passion: The Works of Leonard Cohen*

"Christophe Lebold devotes to the poet a marvelous volume, which opens with a triptych on gravity, wandering, and the broken heart." — Daniel Bougnoux, *La Croix*

"An impressive piece of work: Christophe Lebold has chosen a literary form for his homage and succeeds. The book rises to the level of its subject and that is not saying little." — Eric Naulleau, literary critic

"A great and very stylish book that makes you feel the poet's soul." — Pierre Charpilloz, *Réservoir* (culture)

"I am deeply respectful of the mind that has produced this book." — Leonard Cohen, private email

LEONARD COHEN

THE MAN
WHO SAW THE
ANGELS FALL

CHRISTOPHE LEBOLD

Published by ECW Press
665 Gerrard Street East
Toronto, Ontario, Canada M4M 1Y2
416-694-3348 / info@ecwpress.com

The first edition was published in French by Camion Blanc
in 2013. A second revised edition was published in 2018.
Translated into English by the author.

Cover design: Caroline Suzuki
Cover photo: Dominique Issermann

LIBRARY AND ARCHIVES CANADA CATALOGUING
IN PUBLICATION

Title: Leonard Cohen : the man who saw the angels
fall / Christophe Lebold.

Other titles: Leonard Cohen. English

Names: Lebold, Christophe, author.

Description: Translation of: Leonard Cohen :
l'homme qui voyait tomber les anges. | Includes
bibliographical references and index. | Translated
from the French.

Identifiers: Canadiana (print) 20240280741 |
Canadiana (ebook) 20240281209

ISBN 978-1-77041-744-1 (softcover)
ISBN 978-1-77852-271-0 (PDF)
ISBN 978-1-77852-270-3 (ePub)

Subjects: LCSH: Cohen, Leonard, 1934-
2016—Criticism and interpretation. | LCSH:
Composers—Canada—Biography. | LCSH: Poets,
Canadian—20th century—Biography. | LCSH:
Singers—Canada—Biography. | LCSH: Lyricists—
Canada—Biography. | LCGFT: Biographies.

Classification: LCC ML410.C69 L4413 2024 | DDC
782.42164092—dc23

We gratefully acknowledge the financial support of the French Embassy in Canada and the Research Unit 2325 SEARCH
at the University of Strasbourg. *Nous tenons à remercier l'Ambassade de France au Canada et l'Unité de recherche 2325
SEARCH de l'université de Strasbourg pour leur soutien financier.*

AMBASSADE
DE FRANCE
AU CANADA
*Liberté
Égalité
Fraternité*

Laboratoire
Savoirs dans l'**espace anglophone :
représentations, cultures, histoire**
SEARCH | UR 2325
Université de Strasbourg

PRINTED AND BOUND IN CHINA

PRINTING: C&C OFFSET PRINTING CO.

5 4 3 2 1

MIX
Paper | Supporting
responsible forestry
FSC® C008047
www.fsc.org

Every heart to love will come,
But like a refugee.

— LEONARD COHEN, "ANTHEM"

To Leonard Cohen and Yoshin David Radin,
For their immense hearts and infinite kindness.
With my gratitude and a thousand *gasshos*.

TABLE OF CONTENTS

PROLOGUE

THREE PORTRAITS OF LEONARD COHEN

This prologue presents three portraits of Leonard Cohen, each a point of entry into his universe. They can be read in sequence as appetizers or separately as the reader peruses the book.

FIRST POINT OF ENTRY

THE MAN WHO SAW THE ANGELS FALL

But love is strong as gravity
And everyone must fall
At first it's from the apple tree
Then from the western wall.

— LEONARD COHEN, "GRAVITY"[1]

Leonard Cohen, Barcelona, May 1993

eonard Cohen's art derives from a very specific visual acuity: he sees men fall. And, with them, women, saints, and angels. Hence, a fascination for falling bodies and a career devoted to a methodical and quasi-amorous exploration of the laws of gravity. His subject: how and why we fall, from what heights, along what trajectories. His stated goal: to assert, with the required rigor, the unfathomable beauty of falling bodies and to explain why men — unremittingly — fall.

Operating first as a poet and novelist, then as an international troubadour, Cohen observed everywhere — in Montreal, on the Greek island of Hydra, in New York hotels, and the Luberon vine-yards — the infinite variations of gravity at work: tragic downfalls here, jumps into inner abysses there, and in all places, slapstick slips on the banana peels of life. Armed with the visionary force that alone makes you see the world exactly as it is, he sharpened his tools along the way — a voice so deep it leaves us charred; a terse and increasingly lethal writing style; and his unique combination of angst, Jewish mysticism, and Christian and Buddhist flirtations. Along the way, he fashioned a world that is uniquely his own yet a lot like ours: the world of Leonard Cohen, where men step into avalanches and saints fall in love with Fire.

Quite predictably, the result is ferocious: songs that comfort us with little waltzes but are also spiritual weapons that aim for the heart and never miss. What do they say? What we already know — the invincible gravity of existence. That we die. That our heart cooks and sizzles like shish kebab in our breasts. That the apoca-lypse has begun and the Flood has already happened. That God has summoned us for a game of hide-and-seek that He clearly intends to win. That men and women are forever attracted to each other but that their embrace is a fire that leaves only ashes behind. In a word: that we hang dangerously between gravity and grace. Our fate: to fall from high. Our patron saint: Icarus. *The gospel according to Leonard.*

THE PROPHET OF GRAVITY

Leonard had felt the grip of gravity early on in his life and he soon discovered that he had a great talent for falling. First, for falling in love, which he did ceaselessly. Sometimes for the night, sometimes for a decade and most often with saints. With Saint Kateri Tekakwitha, a seventeenth-century Iroquois Virgin. With Saint Suzanne, to whom he wrote a famous ode. With Saint Nico of Köln, whose iciness he endured. With Joan of Arc, who was burnt at the stake. And with a thousand others. "Men have hearts of puppies," he once told a Swedish TV sexologist interviewing him in bed; "they fall in love every second."[2]

In adolescence, Cohen also started falling into abysses, with the bouts of depression that initiated him into what is blackest in life and later earned him his reputation as a great poet of personal doom. A few times also, he simply fell down, quite literally. In Tony Palmer's documentary *Bird on a Wire*, he can be seen lying flat on the stage of Frankfurt's Jahrhunderthalle on April 7, 1972, huddled in the arms of spectators in the first row. It was the last day of Passover, as Jews around the world were celebrating the parting of the Red Sea, a parting that had obviously not happened for him. His filmed comment the next day was eloquent: "I disgraced myself." In other words, "I fell from grace."[3] Another fall occurred to the audience's great panic almost four decades later, during a concert in Valencia, Spain, on September 18, 2009, three days before the singer's seventy-fifth birthday. The footage is painful to watch: a few minutes into the show, Leonard Cohen collapses. First on his knees, then flat on his face — defeated by gravity.[4] And, seven years later, when the poet died peacefully in his sleep, it was after a fall in his apartment, his last taste of gravity.

So, at some point, in a life spent collecting and studying falls, as he wrote book after book about the fall of man (like *Beautiful Losers*) or impossible elevations (like *Parasites of Heaven*) or songs that say, "I fell with my angel down the chain of command,"[5] things — necessarily — must have gotten clearer. At some unspecified point, Leonard Cohen must have understood — maybe after observing once more through his hotel room window what was falling from the sky (rain, snow, or angels) — that essential truth: that gravity is the absolute law that rules our lives, but also the only place where those lives can truly be lived. That it is only in our falls that we can truly enjoy having a weight.

Hence an improbable wager — arguably more dangerous than Pascal's — the great Cohenian wager: that frivolity bores us and eventually cheapens life but that a great joy awaits us in the heart of gravity. In other words, he bets that gravity is grace.

It is impossible, of course, to tell when that wager was made: like all conversions, that type of event happens silently and deep in the soul. But at some point, his mission as a poet must have stood clear in front of him: to take our falls seriously.

> We don't want a frivolous life. We don't want a super-
> ficial life. [. . .] Seriousness is something voluptuous
> that we are deeply hungry for, and very few people
> allow themselves the luxury of it. So life becomes
> shallow and the heart tends to shut down in a kind
> of despair that is intolerable.[6]

In other words, frivolity sucks; gravity heals. Hence the poet's mission: to be the prophet and pedagogue of gravity, to write "manuals for living with defeat" that will help us locate in ourselves a centre of gravity that will sanctify our lives. Now, what better place for that than four-minute pop songs?

THE ART OF FALLING FROM HIGH

Late 1968. Arpeggios on a Spanish guitar, a waltz melody, discreet strings, and female voices that rise like angels: Leonard Cohen kicks off his singing career with "Suzanne," a song whose celestial beauty seems to launch an assault on Heaven. The lyrics, however, are about falling angels and how poignant and beautiful all things — an afternoon, a sunbeam, a lover — become when they disappear.

We know the story: Suzanne is half-crazy; she feeds you tea and oranges and sees heroes in the seaweed. You want to travel with her but eventually you won't, and Jesus sinks beneath your wisdom like a stone. In the context of LSD, student rebellion, and Jimi Hendrix's guitar solos, Leonard Cohen uses "Suzanne" as a triple reminder to the youth of 1968: sainthood, he warns, has a price; it can be attained only through falling; and the laws of gravity are not negotiable. In the next decade, most of his songs will be concerned in some way with the art of falling, and in one of them a choir of children asks:

> Wasn't it a long way down?
> Wasn't it a strange way down?[7]

This is the first phase of the singer's career, a phase of diagnosis. Its metaphysical conclusion is Leonard's first teaching: no one escapes gravity. We are not Homo sapiens, but Homo cadens — falling men.

Fifteen years later, the setting has changed: Leonard had relocated to Los Angeles — the City of Angels, where else? — and he wore double-breasted pinstriped suits, mafioso style. His idea of fantasy: charcoal grey. His favourite leisure: to quit smoking. His idea of a prophet's job: to sing deeper every year. The year was 1992. After twenty years of Zen practice, the singer has gained in humour and vocal depth. In a voice now so low it can cause minor seismic incidents, he dispensed instructions on the proper conduct after falling on the highway, namely: stay put, don't complain, and wait "for the miracle."[8] That's his second lesson in metaphysics: our falls must be fully accepted and even loved — and with good reason: they are the doorways to our true lives.

It's still 1992: against a backdrop of gospel singers, Leonard announced that he has seen the future, that the future is murder and that this improbable Christian concept — repentance — was actually never clear to him. In the video that comes with the song (aptly named "The Future"), the deadpan prophet can be seen to improvise a few ironic dance steps — a funky little boogie — in the hall of a luxury hotel, where (strangely enough) it has started to rain. Behind him, images of falling bodies in slow motion: elegant women drowning in water, men in dinner jackets with their heads upside down, some pulled down by the weight of a suitcase, others grabbing a passing ankle, all of them sinking, drawn to the bottom, drowning in the Flood. The beauty of falling bodies once more.[9]

Of course, this may remind some readers of the philosophical parable that closed Cohen's first novel, *The Favourite Game*, in 1963. The page in question describes a winter game that the narrator, Lawrence Breavman, used to play as a child. A friend clutches your arm, you spin him fast until he's lifted from the ground and, at the crucial moment, you let him go. He is cast out by kinetic energy and tries to fall in the snow in some unpredictable position, preferably with his legs and arms outstretched. Then comes the nice bit: you admire the beauty of the silhouettes imprinted in the snow. Those kids may not be aware of it, but they give us a third metaphysical lesson: our falls are beautiful and you can play with God's laws. In the process, Breavman and his pals invent the poetics that will inform most of Cohen's work: to turn our falls into works of art, and to inscribe the Fall of Man in the snow.[10]

BODHISATTVA, ACT 1

Genius, they say, is the ability to see things exactly as they are, and the public has recognized Leonard Cohen's vision for what it is: absolute realism. Our hearts are irretrievably broken, our thirst for love cannot be quenched, and our lives are filled with undetectable falls that only saints, holy losers, and angels can see. That's reality itself, verifiable by all. Paradoxically, there's something uplifting about this and even good news here: Cohen's secret gospel of gravity.

His work restores to us the precious things that the dominant culture of infotainment and feel-good psychology had denied: our broken hearts and the true weight of our lives. In Buddhism, awakening your fellow men to their true nature is the task of the bodhisattva.[11] It's an act of empowerment and emancipation:

Cohen frees us from the false dreams of perfect lives and from the chore of having to pretend we are not broken. A first significant step towards a lighter, freer life.

THIS HIGH AND NO HIGHER

Of course, gravity is also a property of the singer's voice and, as a singer, Cohen has often played with the limits imposed by his timbre. Interestingly, he opened his 1984 collection of psalms, *Book of Mercy*, with a portrait of himself as an angel placed in one of the remote choirs of the celestial court — very far from the divine throne. There he is

> A singer in the lower choirs
> born fifty years ago
> to raise my voice this high and no higher.[12]

Four years later, he was only half-joking when he declared in "Tower of Song" that:

> I was born like this, I had no choice
> I was born with the gift of a golden voice.

For yes, indeed, for what Leonard Cohen meant to say (that our lives are broken), his voice was indeed golden, and no, he had no choice: with that timbre, he could only engage with the gravity of the most solemn truths.

That voice has a history, however, a history that features a spectacular drop — almost two octaves — into gravity. On his first record, *Songs of Leonard Cohen* (1967), Cohen's voice was still a fragile and delicate baritone that said goodbye to women with a slight trembling and a delicate combination of serenity and angst: a poet's voice. In the '80s, toughened by a very strict diet of cigarettes, whisky, and looking into the abyss, the voice had become a seismic bass, vibrant with authority and depth: a prophet's voice, sometimes used for crooning, sometimes to announce the apocalypse. And at the end of his life, a third, elegantly broken voice invented something that came from beyond the grave: a weightless gravity that was both aerial (it belonged to the sky) and telluric (it shook the earth): an archangel's voice.

All three voices tell about our exile, very far from Eden, in the world of the Fall, where people and plans crash and fail, but each also asserts the secret pleasures of gravity. As every crooner knows, gravity is a tool for seduction; it is something you can play with. And it is secretly hilarious.

THE COSMIC JOKE

That's the best news of all, probably. Falling can be fun and gravity voluptuous. Gravity is a game that God plays with us: it is a cosmic joke, and Cohen — obviously — wants us in on it.

So often, when he embodies gravity, he does it like a comedian whose irony warns us that none of the identities he presents — the unrepenting seducer vanquished by Love, the Zen master teaching the dharma, the prophet announcing the Flood, or the ironic crooner that says our hearts are in flame — should be taken entirely seriously. And that's perhaps the heart of the singer's artistic gesture: to teach us not to take the tragic too tragically. Gravity is a sacred space where our lives are sanctified, but it is also the place where you can enjoy life to the fullest and laugh with God because we get the joke.

That's why Leonard reinvented the metaphysical poet in an Armani suit, the troubadour as rock star, and the ironic crooner as gnostic high priest of the heart. His underhand message: things are grave, but that's an excellent reason to find them funny.

SECOND POINT OF ENTRY

ETERNAL PILGRIM, PERFECT JEW

But the true voyagers set out to sea
Just for the leaving's sake.

— CHARLES BAUDELAIRE, "VOYAGING"

Leonard Cohen, Toulouse, November 1980

UNTRACED JOURNEYS

That's how the Jesuit thinker Michel de Certeau designated lives that are determined by a calling: "untraced journeys." Journeys towards an unnamed thing that awaits at the end of the road and calls.[13] Journeys that transform lives into trajectories and men into pilgrims. And with only three words ("calling," "trajectory," and "pilgrim"), that is already an almost sufficient portrait of Leonard Cohen.

Mapping out Cohen's peregrinations is a hard task. After a first exile in New York in 1956, a second one in London in 1959, and a third on a Greek island the following spring, he became a professional passerby, someone who, like the heroes of his favourite folk song, was "only passing through."[14] In the '60s, he journeyed back and forth between Greece and Canada and, when he became a singer, he adopted the peripatetic life of the troubadours, with concert tours that kept him on the road for more than seven years in cumulative time. Seven years, therefore, of airports and anonymous rooms. Seven years of the eternal return of the same cities: London, New York, Berlin, Paris, Rome — the world is a hotel and a taxi ride.

Of course, the tours were interrupted by new exiles (in Nashville, the Luberon, or Los Angeles), incessant returns (to Hydra, London, Montreal, and Toronto), regular retreats (in recording studios or monasteries), new itineraries (to Mexico, Morocco, Israel, and India), and by a civilian life that was equally restless.

With the notable exception of six years spent in a monk's cabin up a mountain northwest of Los Angeles (in the 1990s), it therefore seems that Leonard Cohen never spent more than six months of his adult life in the same place. Which is probably how he found that balance between gravity and grace: he kept moving and offset the vertical axis of the Fall with the horizontal lines that French philosopher Gilles Deleuze called "lines of flight." His friend Leon Wieseltier called it an "art of wandering,"[15] and he was right: Leonard made travelling an art form, and his life grew lighter with every move.

PROFESSION: WANDERING JEW

As many documentaries attest, Leonard Cohen was always a great urban explorer. He can be seen pacing the streets of Montreal in *Ladies and Gentlemen . . . Mr. Leonard Cohen* (1965), the streets of Paris and Berlin in *Hallelujah in Moll* (1985), of Manhattan in *Songs from the Life of Leonard Cohen* (1988), and he explored Jerusalem and various European cities in *Bird on a Wire* (1974). As if he only ever put down his suitcases to hit the streets and start walking again.

Leonard actually combined three types of wanderers. To the flâneur that Baudelaire defined as the quintessential man of modernity, at home in constantly renewed crowds and unknown cities and open to every possibility,[16] he added a more tragic figure: the existentialist stranger. Inspired by Albert Camus (and featured in songs like "The Stranger Song"), that character is fundamentally alienated: from himself, from others, from the world. In exile, so to speak, from his own life. Dressed in a raincoat, the existentialist stranger is like a metaphysical private eye looking for the meaning of existence, a heroic figure of considerable masculine charm.

The third type of wanderer is of course the wandering Jew, whose task is to roam the world and remain a stranger everywhere. As philosopher and Talmudic scholar André Neher reminds us, a Jew is both a Hebrew — that is an offspring of Abraham (i.e., someone who practises the art of wandering) — and an Israelite, i.e., someone who, like Jacob/Israel, struggles with an angel. An expert in contests and dialectics.[17] With his incessant travelling and constant dialogues with women, God, and avalanches, Leonard was therefore an exemplary Jew. But Neher added that, after the first diaspora, Jews had also become exiles and living away from home — as we know — was one of Leonard's favourite hobbies.[18] No wonder, therefore, that he tried his whole life to embody the two paradoxes of the wandering Jew: to stay on the move but never seem lost and to multiply havens but remain a stranger everywhere.

And indeed, Leonard Cohen almost never seemed lost. Perhaps the many callings that set him on his way were so clear that getting lost was impossible to begin with. And perhaps he carried in his suitcase a copy of the *Guide for the Perplexed* that Moses Maimonides wrote in the twelfth century for all lost Jews. But mostly, you cannot get lost if you don't have a specific destination in mind. And Leonard actually never had one. His art of wandering was more like a philosophical exercise, an attempt (in his way) to be free, a way of re-attuning himself to the world and to life through constantly encountering new cities, new climates, and new crowds. Hence, a motto that could have been his: veni, vidi, ivi. I came, I saw, I left.

HOST OF HOTELS, HOST OF EMPTINESS

Of course, the easiest way to never appear lost is to feel at home everywhere and for that, multiplying havens is not a bad idea. Which is why hotels were so central in Cohen's life and imagination. The list of hotels mentioned in his work is impressive. There's the Penn Terminal, the Henry Hudson, the Royalton, the Algonquin, the Chelsea in New York; the Cluny Square, the Raphael, the Prince de Galles, the Napoleon in Paris; the Regent's and the Savoy in London; the Hotel de France in Montreal; the Windsor Arms and the King Edward in Toronto; the Landmark and the Chateau Marmont in Los Angeles; the Kemps Corner in Mumbai; the Takawana Prince Hotel in Tokyo; and the Hotel Sainte-Anne in Roussillon. As he explained in 1965:

> The hotel room is a temporary sanctuary and therefore all the more delicious. [. . .] In a hotel room, you always have a feeling that you are on the lam, and it's one of the safe moments in the escape: the door is shut [. . .] and you're going to have a drink, light a cigarette and take a long time shaving.[19]

Years on the road had turned Cohen into an expert in hotels: a great connoisseur of rooms and of the activities that rooms are conducive to — writing, courting, and introspection.

And what ultimately matters is what those places had taught Leonard: that we are but hosts in this life. That's the humble wisdom of travellers: to know that the task of making the world hospitable must be started afresh every day with every new room. Being at home is every man's responsibility. No wonder, therefore, that a grateful Cohen wished, with the movie *I Am a Hotel* (1983), to draw his self-portrait as a hotel the way Dylan Thomas drew his as a young dog.

There were also more permanent anchorage points in Cohen's life: houses rather than hotels, four of which were often featured in photographs and documentaries. His parents' house in Westmount (where he spent his childhood) looms large in his legend, as do the iconic white house in Hydra (bought at the age of twenty-six), the photogenic grey house in Montreal (bought at the age of thirty-eight), and the anonymous pavilion in Mid-Wilshire, Los Angeles (bought at the age of forty-five).[20] There were also lesser-known places where he only stopped over: a cabin surrounded by forests and pheasants twenty miles south of Franklin, Tennessee (he lived there on and off from 1969 to 1971), a monk's cabin up Mount Baldy in a Mountain Zen centre (where he lived for six years in the 1990s), a caravan in the vineyards in the south of France (where he wrote a book of psalms), and a friend's house in the fourteenth arrondissement of Paris. And of course, there was an even more secret point of anchorage, which never failed him: the sitting posture in zazen.

All those places were inhabited with the lightness of someone who is about to leave. And if the various lodgings have struck observers by their simplicity — bare rooms, bare walls — it's mostly because Leonard never intended to stay anywhere long (uncluttered spaces are easier to leave) and because he wanted to live at home as though he was travelling still. His ideal: to be everywhere just the guest of an empty room.[21]

Many photographs have immortalized the singer *in situ* and *intra muros* and the intensity and ascetic strength that emanates from those pictures of Leonard in his various houses is quite striking. We see a man in dark suits surrounded by white walls, but also a very precise way of inhabiting the world. Like a perfect host, with an intense lightness.[22] A cleverly edited sequence in the CBC documentary *Summer Festival* shows Leonard in his Montreal house in the winter of 1989. We follow him from room to room: he prepares a working table, plays his guitar, looks out of a window. Several successive fade-outs make the poet disappear and reappear in another corner of the room. What is filmed, of course, is a metaphysical operation: *intra muros poeta evanescit*. Between four walls, the poet disappears. How light can life get?

QUO VADIS, LEONARD? THE TRIPLE CALLING OF THE WORLD

Of course, leaving places is easier when something calls you. In this regard, Leonard was lucky: like Abraham, he was called three times. First, by his own name, which defined a very clear mission. Then by the women that he pursued everywhere, and of course, by the life that he wanted to live. But the first calling was in the name. As we know, *kohen* (*kohanim* in the plural form) means priest in Hebrew and the priest's role is to bless the community and serve as an intercessor. The priest reconnects us to our hearts and to the mysteries lodged inside those hearts called "God" or "Love." With that patronym (which he took very seriously), Cohen inherited a fundamental rabbinical disposition: the desire to assert the meaning of existence and our irrepressible thirst for gravity.

Equally urgent — as we will see — was the calling of a life asking to be lived and an oeuvre asking to be written. Cohen had decided early on that his life would be a poet's life, and since his grandfather, a Talmudist, had been the "Prince of Grammarians," he could not just be the poet next door: he had to be the prince of poets and the absolute bohemian. Hence, a very precise life and a specific program: writing books and igniting souls, following impulses and following masters, collecting cities, women, and passports.

The third calling, of course, was what would transform Leonard into the professional romantic that seduced the world: the calling of the beauty of women, a form of beauty he could never resist.

ALL JEWISH HEROES AT ONCE

That triple calling determined a triple career: that of high-priest, ladies' man, and poet. The result is a life whose hero is Leonard Cohen. A life that was of course improvised (like all lives) but one that was so naturally dramatic that it seems to have been scripted. Nothing is missing from the plot of that life, not even the necessary obstacle, namely the incessant struggle with that abyss which William Styron (quoting Milton) had called — in a forceful essay on depression — "darkness visible."[23]

Along his comings and goings, Cohen indeed enjoyed the privilege of being the protagonist of four simultaneous novels and all Jewish heroes at once. Like Abraham, he travelled the world and tried to be at home everywhere — that was the first novel: Leonard's wanderings. Like King David, he sang psalms to heaven and burnt for all women — the novel of desire and irrepressible attractions. Like Jonas, he engaged in a game of hide-and-seek with his Creator but was never closer to Him than when he thought himself perfectly hidden — the (sometimes comical) novel of Leonard's spiritual quest. And like Jacob, he struggled with an angel (the black angel of melancholy) hoping not to win but to be blessed in the morning, wounded but not vanquished — the epic novel of Leonard's struggle with darkness.

With a thousand twists and turns, with women and angels at every corner, that quadruple novel is the blueprint of Cohen's life and the matrix of his whole work. At the heart of it, an undercover poet who tried to revive mass culture and rock music with the art of King David. An exemplary Jew.

THIRD POINT OF ENTRY

LEONARD COHEN, METAPHYSICIAN OF THE BROKEN HEART

ALBERTO MANZANO

Leonard Cohen and his daughter, Lorca, in Hydra, January 1981

KAMASUTRAS AND RAZOR BLADES

In the late '70s, when punk was at its height, the name Leonard Cohen (as the singer knew full well) was used essentially for comic relief.[24] The punks — who obviously had not read *Beautiful Losers* — had decreed that any work sustained by a strong poetical vision involved a denial of reality. And yet, in some respects, Leonard was a closet punk, who could give pogo dancers lessons in realism. Five years before safety pins became de rigueur on leather jackets, he had published a poetry book called *The Energy of Slaves*, which sought lyricism in hatred and featured a silhouetted razor blade on every page — Johnny Rotten must have taken notes.[25] And five years before that (as flower power was in full swing), he claimed to be "cold as a new razor blade"[26] and made explicit his project of de-sentimentalizing the love song with *Songs of Love and Hate* — Sid Vicious was listening.

The razor blade is a recurring motif in Cohen's late '60s work and it could be seen as a metaphor for a poetical vision so sharp that it cuts through appearances to the core of reality.[27] It just so happens that for Cohen, reality is ultimately metaphysical. Beneath the social and psychological surface of our lives, interior dramas are silently played out, weaving the thread of a second, "secret" life that no one can escape: the life of the heart.[28]

Cohen's work is essentially an exploration of that secret life and for more than six decades, he documented it in hundreds of black notebooks. The result is 140 songs, two novels, and more than a thousand pages of uncompromising poetry. Taken together, that oeuvre — a vast inquiry into the heart — contains (among other things) a fragmented spiritual autobiography, a seducer's diary, an *Ars Amatoria* in the tradition of Ovid, several Kamasutras, and a modern *Anatomy of Melancholy*. Its central theme concerns us all, whether we are punks or not: what to do with that heart of ours, with its infinite aptitude for despair and its constant hunger for love.[29]

THE SCIENCE OF THE HEART

But you cannot just ad-lib your way into being a "prophet of the heart."[30] To actually simply look at what is inside — to just look at the fire within and determine what exactly is burning — takes courage and lucidity, but also method and patience. And method and patience (as well as scalpels and razor blades) is what Leonard Cohen proceeded with — like a scientist. As we know, modern science is based on observation, experimentation, and hypothesis and in that respect, Leonard was very modern.[31]

So for years, he observed the heart — that thing that burns in our chest, the mind — a restless monkey who jumps from branch to branch, and the ego — a fragile thing that dissolves ten times a day. For years, he put every twinge of our inner life (every desire or attraction, every pang of pain, hope, or despair) to the test of various esoteric traditions: Jewish Kabbalah, Sufi poetry, Christian mysticism, Scientology, the *I Ching*, Zen Buddhism, and — when nothing else had worked — Kamasutras of all kinds. For years, he practised prayer and courtship like exact sciences, seduced women, angels, and God, and betrayed them all. In his love life, he multiplied both victories and failures and explored all facets of love: short idylls and long enslavements, adulterine triangles and unilateral passions, irrepressible desires and chaste alliances, and, of course, solitudes of all kinds. The ones that drive you mad, the ones that bring you bliss.

His conclusion? Never overlook the obvious. For the obvious is true: men and women are indeed each other's joy and their union is the dark centre of the divine plan (that's the very story of Adam and Eve[32]). Sparks of light will ignite in our hearts at any moment and set our lives on fire (a central idea in Lurianic Kabbalah). And in the amorous triangle formed by man, woman, and God, there is indeed always a cuckold and a loser. All of which are easily observable facts that can be confirmed by all.

GROUNDWORK FOR A METAPHYSICS OF THE HEART

The result is Cohen's poetic theology of love, which rests on just a handful of principles. The first is a simple truth and the foundational axiom in Cohen's metaphysics: we are all broken. The heart's function is to break and, until it does, it "cooks and sizzles like shish kebab in our breast" on a furnace called love.[33] Love — that's Cohen's second axiom — is therefore no fortuitous accident but our true condition, and therefore without remedy (ergo: *there ain't no cure for love*). The third principle — famously featured in "Anthem" —

THIRD POINT OF ENTRY   XXIX

is that light gets into our lives only through cracks and that our broken hearts are therefore vehicles of grace. In other words, only losers are beautiful.[34] And that's pretty much it.

Of course, there are a few weirder observations — a quantum physics of love — which claim that matter turns into light when it manifests in the body of a naked woman. That lovers disappear in the erotic embrace and reappear only after kisses have ceased. And that the attracting centre of all desires is an empty centre and the locus of an absent God. Nothing much beyond that. Three axioms and a few observations. Just enough for Cohen to build — via four-minute pop songs — a humble but very luminous literature of spiritual instruction. What it teaches us: the thousand ways in which love is a fall and in which falls bring salvation.

THE SONGWRITER AS KABBALIST

Last question: why do that in songs? Why did the song form become Cohen's vehicle of choice? The answer is of course biographical: Leonard has always sung. As a child in the synagogue, as a teenager in the Montreal cafés, as a student in a country music band, and as a young poet whenever someone listened. He was therefore always aware of the multi-layered redemptive power of songs.

But to really understand the deeper mystical resonance that songs took on for the teenager Cohen, a small detour is necessary. A detour via the sixteenth century and the provocative theology of the father of contemporary Kabbalah, Isaac Luria (1534–1572).

Luria contended that Creation was in part a catastrophe. After retiring "from himself into himself" to generate a void where Creation could fit in (the so-called tsimtsum theory), God immediately reinvested that void with the light beams of His love. But that light — originally contained in clay vases — exploded these vessels and flung back to its source, leaving countless sparks scattered in the world. Since then, gathering the sparks (and thus re-assembling the light of God) has been every Jew's task — an act called tikkun or great reparation.[35] Now, with its insistence on brokenness and on a love so strong it destroys everything, its explosion of God, and its quest around the world, Luria's theology seems tailor-made for Leonard Cohen. Especially when we know that Hasidism — to a great extent a popular tradition derived from Lurianic Kabbalah — later granted a special role to songs and singing in the accomplishment of the tikkun.

Those ideas — familiar to Leonard since Hebrew school[36] — were confirmed in the early '50s on the jukeboxes of Montreal, when the teenage Cohen discovered the country-and-western songs of Hank Williams and the lamentations of a black Orpheus called Ray Charles who seemed, with his suave swing and the fire in his voice, eager to bring solace to the whole universe. And every crooner of the day (including Leonard's favourite Frankie Lane) actually tried the same thing. So, on these jukeboxes, the young Cohen must have understood the singer's true mission: to accomplish single-handedly and unilaterally (at least for the duration of the song) the great tikkun, the impossible redemption of our lives and of the world. In other words, to be the metaphysician of the broken heart. All it takes, as Leonard would explain later, is three or four chords and a "golden voice."

> A good song exists in modest and in Himalayan terms. It's a modest thing that gets you through the dishes or provides a soundtrack for your courting or your solitude. But it also provides deep solace and courage and stimulation. [. . .] Songs are for deep things. For summoning Love. For healing broken nights.[37]

So a song can bring salvation. How is that done? It's a simple process: the melody connects you to your emotions, enabling you to enjoy even the sad ones. The singer's voice speaks to you directly and dissolves your solitude. The lyrics say in three or four minutes all there is to say: we live, we love, we burn, we die. And throughout, the sonic harmony makes you forget everything that alienates you from the world.

And the whole of Leonard Cohen's songwriting career rests on that fundamental belief: songs are spiritual weapons that break open our hearts but also immaterial talismans that we carry with us everywhere we go. And sanctuaries where we stand consoled — spaces of deep and true consolation.

It's clear in the dark flamenco waltzes of the singer's early career and in the electro songs of wisdom he composed later: songs have healing powers and can accomplish our salvation. At least for four minutes.

All we need to do now is to show how Leonard's life made him such a great a master in that art.

CHAPTER 1

GENESIS

AUTOPSY OF LEONARD COHEN THE YOUNGER

I know this can't be me
Must be my double.

— LEONARD COHEN, "I CAN'T FORGET"

Leonard Cohen, self-portrait, 2003

LEONARD COHEN'S FACE BEFORE HE WAS BORN

"What was your face before your parents were born?" You can trust Zen koans to ask questions that nobody was asking just to dissolve everything you thought you knew, offering nothing in exchange but the infinite mystery of things. The koan above — often called the koan of the "original face" — can forever change your relationship to mirrors and seriously impede their ability to confirm every morning that you are still yourself. For if you had a face before you were born, whose face exactly is looking back right now? Certainly not your "true" face for, as the question implies, there is no origin to "identity" and nothing stable to call "me" to begin with. So, like a mirror, the koan confronts us with the only thing that we are not: what we think we are. Which is more or less what Zen master Joshu Sasaki Roshi told Leonard in his pidgin English the first time they met as master and disciple: "Me not Japanese, you not Jewish."

For Leonard Cohen, this idea of the face as enigma was always concrete. As she aged, his mother Masha often repeated that it was no longer her true face looking back in the mirror, that she had left her face in Russia when she was young. Leonard himself often said that he distrusted mirrors: he warned us in a poem that they wear out when "overused," just as he sometimes explained to journalists (via Jim Harrison's novel *Dalva*) that some Native American tribes refused mirrors because your face is not for you but for others to look at.[1] And yet, in the early 2000s, Cohen often started the day in front of a mirror for a self-portrait done on his computer. Inspired by Zenga art — the traditional self-portraits of Zen masters — the cartoons in question (many of which have been published since) are accompanied by the poet's signature seal and a humorous comment. They expose the instability of a sixty-five-year-old face which, despite an incontestable gravitas, has its good and its bad days.[2] With wit and good humour, Cohen makes us see how aging and the laws of gravity plot against a face that is constantly on the verge of collapse (with sagging eyes and drooping cheeks) but also how the same face always rebuilds itself around glaring eyes and miens so solemn they amaze the artist himself.[3]

So every day for several years, Leonard Cohen dramatized the ravages of time and displayed his fine flair for ironic captions, but he also suggested that one's face (and therefore one's ego) is essentially a vast joke. A faithful companion, of course (it is there every morning), but fundamentally an unstable entity: never exactly the same, never really confirming the idealized vision of ourselves that re-emerges as soon as there is no mirror around. The face stubbornly resists whatever we want it to be. Another poet had warned us before: "I is another."

These remarks are necessary because, in narrating Leonard Cohen's life, we will be holding up a mirror. But what will that mirror reflect? Our own lives leave little trace: a few photographs and maybe a couple of stories. But where exactly is our teenage self or the baby we once were? And if our own past escapes us, how can we presume to recover someone else's, especially when that person is as elusive as Leonard Cohen?

Here again, it's the poet himself who suggests an answer when he describes a typical Leonard Cohen day in the song "I Can't Forget" (1988):

> I stumbled out of bed,
> I got ready for the struggle,
> I smoked a cigarette
> And I tightened up my guts.

And then everything stops because the poet has an insight:

> I know this can't be me
> Must be my double.

So Leonard Cohen warns us: he's not the one who has lived his life — his double has. And we concur: Leonard Cohen will not be present here. But we will investigate a few interesting doubles.

SYNOPSIS: THE LIFE OF THE DOUBLE

Prologue in Paradise: God said, "Let Leonard Be" and a little Eliezer Nehemias Leonard Norman Cohen was, in a family of entrepreneurs, philanthropists, and rabbis. The year is 1934, the place Montreal, and the child receives three thousand years of Judaism, an anthology of English poetry, and a very good eye for male elegance — he is well-armed for what ensues.

When his father dies (Leonard is nine), the child buries a scribbled paper in an old bowtie: his first poem and the first intuition that writing can name the things that have no name. The boy inherits a handgun and hears that his family name means "priest" in Hebrew, a fact he takes very seriously. Attracted by hypnosis and García Lorca, he devotes his teenage years to the world's mysteries: Montreal jukeboxes, the naked bodies of women, and the first attacks of black bile. After only three lessons, his flamenco teacher commits suicide, but 1954 brings Leonard the ultimate recognition: a disciple of Ezra Pound appoints him "poet." He publishes a book (*Let Us Compare Mythologies*, 1956) and things accelerate: government grants, peer recognition, and reading tours strike the end of act I — a career has begun. Leonard Cohen is ready to launch an assault on the '60s.

After another poetry book (*The Spice-Box of Earth*, 1961) and a bildungsroman partly written in London (*The Favourite Game*, 1963), Leonard settles on a Greek island where he plays Saint Francis of Assisi in a house without electricity. He speaks to daisies but meets Marianne, a "Madonna with child" of astounding beauty. From the island, he sends flowers to Hitler (*Flowers for Hitler*, 1964) and brings to Canada a second novel full of pornographic mysticism

(*Beautiful Losers*, 1966), inventing as he proceeds the concept of the "beautiful loser" — a good move for what comes next.

What comes next is New York and the Chelsea Hotel, where he will meet angels in hotel lifts and Joan of Arc in a nightclub. He quits the literary world, becomes an international troubadour, and invents existentialist folk with his first record (*Songs of Leonard Cohen*, 1968), which establishes his style: well-cut lyrics, low-key waltzes, minor chords on acoustic guitars, and celestial female voices. But the baby boomers are many and Dylan is their prophet, so Cohen becomes his generation's poet laureate. He conquers Europe on the back of "Suzanne," says "So Long" to Marianne, and the poet becomes a star (*Songs from a Room*, 1969).

Third act: Cohen steps into an avalanche, it covers up his soul and someone steals his famous blue raincoat (*Songs of Love and Hate*, 1971). Hence a depression, a quasi-marriage, two children, and the nagging suspicion that the Apocalypse has begun. He stays in Buddhist monasteries where an old Zen master hits him with a stick and with a few paradoxes. He writes anti-poems with a razor blade (*The Energy of Slaves*, 1972), enlists in the Sinai War, tries his hand at compulsive seduction, adds drums to his songs but to no avail: his record sales plummet (*New Skin for the Old Ceremony*, 1974) and his career slowly evaporates. Things get worse when a megalomaniac producer disguised as Wagner points a handgun at his head while Leonard hears his wife making love to a stranger in the hotel room next to his. The '70s come to an end, it's the *Death of a Ladies' Man* (1977).

Fourth act: adagio. A slow redemption through Zen practice, the book of psalms and ferocious melodies played on an oud (*Recent Songs*, 1979). Leonard has a breakdown in Montreal and a breakthrough in Los Angeles. With his new French girlfriend, he buys dark double-breasted suits and a Casio keyboard and spends four years writing "Hallelujah" (*Various Positions*, 1985). His record company no longer answers his phone calls, but time is on his side:

his devotees are devoted and he reaches cult status. After fifty ferocious psalms (*Book of Mercy*, 1984), he creates a clandestine spiritual order (the Order of the Unified Heart), smokes fifty thousand cigarettes, and re-reads Ezekiel. His goal: to sing two octaves deeper.

Then comes a miracle: Leonard Cohen is half a century old and has a commercial strategy. In love with sunglasses, bananas, and cool totalitarianism, he poses as the absolute playboy on ironic album covers (*I'm Your Man*, 1988) and speaks of taking world capitals with God knows what army. In between poignant prayers and tongue-in-cheek crooner songs, he gives poetry lessons to Miami Vice fans and hits the top of the charts in Norway. The following years are busy: he rewrites the Bible, brings down the Berlin Wall, gives Prozac a try, and plans the apocalypse (*The Future*, 1993). Having finally converted the Western world to his militant pessimism and seriously depressed Kurt Cobain, he retires to a monastery, defeated at last by a lengthy tour and vintage Bordeaux wine. That was the fifth act.

We find him again in the thirteenth century, drinking ginger sake on a mountain with his Zen master Joshu Sasaki Roshi. But the Roshi doesn't speak English, so they meditate on the beauty of paradox and spend a few years waiting for the miracle. An angel passes, another one does, and then a thousand invade the sky. Leonard leaves for India where he apparently starts a new life as a refugee on the other side of depression. Disguised as a very humble and elegant bodhisattva, he travels the world once more and publishes celestial synthetic songs that secretly change the listener's life (*Ten New Songs*, 2001).

After a semi-retirement comes the seventh act. Defrauded by his manager, the young poet (now aged seventy-five) spends a few years conducting spiritual experiments in the world's concert halls: every night, he reinvents the ironic crooner as a fedora-hatted high priest of the heart and becomes, for three hours, the audience's guardian angel and Zen master. He disappears once more and, while the world expects the eighth act or the final dissolution, he comes up with a string of albums (*Old Ideas*, 2012; *Popular Problems*, 2014; *You Want It Darker*, 2016) that reinvent the blues and make the spiritual sexy again, proving you can face death with your sense of humour intact. He has not been seen since November 2016.

So that's the usual story, the framework rock critics use to talk about Leonard Cohen's life. Of course, none of it is true. Rather than a neat heroic story, Cohen's life was — like all lives — caught in a web of improvisation, complexity, chance, and chaos, as we will amply see. We must therefore question the narrative and interrogate everything that is too heroic or neatly mythological about Leonard Cohen's life. And yet, there is definitely something in that life that seems determined, driven, and inherently dramatic. Something that makes that life a perfect novel. Something that touches our hearts so very deeply.

THE BIOGRAPHER'S VERTIGO

Like any portraitist, the biographer must learn to look at his model. And for this, a "theory" — in other words, a point of view — is necessary.[4] Just sticking to facts is impossible, if only because facts are elusive and opaque to begin with and besides, a life is not just made of facts.

This was actually Cohen's advice to his first systematic biographer, Ira Nadel: "Don't let the facts get in the way of the truth." Nadel therefore consulted the archives, conducted interviews, established chronologies, but his book *Various Positions* (1996) rested on a theory: Leonard is an embodied paradox, someone who devotes his life to the reconciliation of opposites: poet and rock star, ladies' man and monk, joker and melancholy. For her book *I'm Your Man* (2012), Sylvie Simmons decided to let the facts tell the story. Some readers will find her volume — and its impeccable research — a little soulless, as if the life described there had been lived in absentia, in Leonard's absence, or as if the author had chosen not to engage with the deeper dynamics that animated that life. We will not be so shy, for we have invented Leonard Cohen: he is the man we described in the prologue, who sees angels fall and restores the gravity of our lives, and it is that man's story that we are going to tell — the life of the double.

Of course, we have put that double to the test of the facts: we have consulted the archives (the public ones at the University of Toronto and the private ones that were kindly opened for us), studied the books, watched dozens of hours of sometimes unpublished films, attended concerts, ceaselessly cross-checked information, read, and reread, and read again the hundreds of interviews that the poet — an unparalleled raconteur — has used to compose an improvised oral autobiography. And when all that was not enough, we have entered Leonard's life on tiptoes. For after corresponding with him for a few years, I sat with Leonard Cohen and walked with him and talked to him in Los Angeles, where he was kind enough to let me watch him live a little and where, among other things, for a few incandescent days, we were like old friends. We spoke buddy to buddy, and Buddha to Buddha. Or perhaps we just hung out and considered together the mystery of our respective lives.

With that research came two unsurprising conclusions. First, Leonard Cohen does not escape the common rule: his life was lived by himself only and its precise unfolding is known only to him.[5] It's easy to know what day he gave a concert in Berlin, but who knows what happened after he left the stage? What woman or what loneliness did he join? And what about the silent days in Leonard Cohen's life? The many days without witnesses, the days spent writing or struggling with angels, or observing the mist on Mount Baldy or the snow in Montreal? Maybe a life truly lived is, by definition, always already lost in the moment it is lived. Maybe all that is ever available is apocryphal stories,[6] but one thing is for sure: facts and witnesses will only get you so far. To know what living that life *felt* like, to know what it felt like being Leonard C., the necessary gateway is what happened when Leonard turned that life into Logos: the songs, the poems, the novels.[7]

The second observation is that, even as a biographer, you cannot escape Leonard Cohen's masks. Already during the poet's first career in Canada, he had created an intriguing media persona, half-melancholy Don Juan, half-wandering Jew, and agent provocateur. This was both an artist's mask (to better say what he had to say) and a stand-in or a double that the poet had — perhaps unwittingly and mechanically — created as a vehicle to live his life with greater acuity.[8]

From a certain angle, charged as it was with drama and meaning, this persona, this double was more real than the man himself and, perhaps, the double is who really lived Leonard Cohen's life. Mishima had called his autobiography *Confessions of a Mask*. He knew — like Oscar Wilde before him — that a mask is required to tell the truth or maybe even to be truly oneself. Leonard knew that as well.

KOSHER PARADISE AND LEONARD'S TRICYCLE

Another question, of greater technicality, is where to start the narrative of a life. In *Various Positions*, Ira Nadel chose to begin with the great-grandfathers and their arrival on the continent in the late nineteenth century, placing Leonard Cohen in the history of the Jewish diaspora.[9] A tinge academic, perhaps, but it makes full sense. Tim Footman began another book (*Leonard Cohen: Hallelujah*) with a lie: "Leonard Cohen was born in 1949," i.e., the year he bought his first guitar, attended his first blues concert (Josh White for those keeping score), and discovered the poetry of García Lorca.[10] But is this *really* where the story begins or just a well-written sentence? I propose to resume instead our original line of questioning with the Zen koan: what was Leonard Cohen's face before he was born? Or, to rephrase the question: how far should we go back in time to speak of a poet who dreams of falling men?

Maybe to his first fall. And here, the biographer can only hypothesize. But for this data is available. For example, an eight-millimetre home movie shot at the end of the 1930s which shows a four- or five-year-old Leonard falling in Montreal. He is on skis, a little stiff, and slides down a small slope, as in slow motion, seeming unsure of what to do with his ski poles. Then things accelerate, and bang! Leonard Cohen has fallen down. A comedy scene, obviously, of the burlesque kind, but a tiny catastrophe as well: it happens to a child. Is this how it begins? In that opulent Montreal park behind the family house?[11] Or should we go back further to 1935 and imagine the young Eliezer Leonard Norman Cohen taking his first steps maybe under the watch of his great comrade, the fox terrier Kelef, and see how, like every toddler, he discovers the laws of gravity through trial and error and endless falls? Is he already attentive? Probably not. Things must have crystallized later when he saw loved ones decline and sink: his father into illness and death (Leonard is nine), his mother into depression, nostalgia, and a perpetual Jewish mother act (Leonard is seventeen), his loved grandfather into senility (Leonard is twenty). Another hypothesis involves the book of Isaiah. It is the beginning of the 1950s and the said grandfather, probably tired but still a gifted Talmudist, has moved in with his daughter for a year. A good opportunity to initiate his grandson to the Scriptures. His bar mitzvah is behind him, but it is never too late. On the menu: the grandfather's favourite prophet — Isaiah. Cohen has often told how the old man would fall asleep during the lesson, how he would wake up and start over, again fall asleep, and begin once more. The eternal recurrence of the same commentary. Is it too much to imagine that this fateful page in Isaiah may have been the lamentation on the fall of kings and stars in chapter 14: "How art thou fallen from Heaven, O Lucifer, how art thou cut down to the ground which didst weaken the nations?" (Isaiah 14:12). Is this how Leonard Cohen learnt to see men fall?

It is, of course, impossible to know, but the answer to our original question now seems obvious. How far should we go back in time to speak of a poet in love with the Fall of Man? To the Garden of Eden. And for Leonard, that garden has a name: Westmount,

Montreal. It is an anglophone district on a hill to the western side of the city where, much later, mailboxes will explode during the "Quiet Revolution." And for Leonard, that paradise is kosher. In a poem published in 1979, he declared his firm intention "not to go back to the Garden" but thanks to his father we can go back for him.[12] An amateur photographer with a passion for images, Nathan Cohen had bought an eight-millimetre Kodak camera in the mid-'30s. With it, he filmed his children and family on holidays in three-minute film spools. Around the same time, Eva Braun did the same on the other side of the Atlantic. With the same jerky and slightly accelerated flow of images, the same grainy quality so typical of pre-war home movies. On one side, Adolf Hitler in a tweed jacket relaxing on his terrace at Berchtesgaden with his henchmen and innocent blond children. On the other, a tiny future poet who will later throw flowers at the Nazi leader with *Flowers for Hitler*, but who for now simply discovers the pleasures of a paradise that will soon be lost: Westmount, Montreal.

A second film from Paradise appears in various documentaries. A smiling little cutie pedals like a madman on his tricycle, with the energy of a little boy who knows he is being filmed. He runs past the camera with a smile bigger than himself. An explosion of joy: Leonard Cohen is four years old and he is wearing a tie. Little does he know that sixty years later, he will interview his Zen master for a Buddhist magazine called *Tricycle*.[13]

Another well-known image, reproduced in several books and magazines, shows what must be a five-year-old Leonard Cohen posing with his sister, two years his senior, at the end of the 1930s.[14] Standing side by side, the two children are beaming with elegance and joy. The Cohen family is in the clothing industry and you can tell: the coats are well-cut, their leather shoes are shined, and anyone can guess these kids will never like what's cheap. The young Leonard wears short trousers. He is laughing, his face slightly turned to the ground with one eye almost closed, as if blinded by the sun. His sister, who is laughing as well, is staring at the camera, very steadily but evidently happy to have her picture taken with her brother. A touching detail: Leonard wears a small Band-Aid crosswise on his knee — one of childhood's innumerable wounds. The Second World War is about to begin; his father (who probably takes the picture) will die soon and the five-year-old Leonard does not know it. What matters right now is having his picture taken with his sister.

So, all it takes to imagine Leonard Cohen happy is to go back to Paradise. Salman Rushdie said, "The past is a country from which we have all emigrated and its loss is part of our common humanity."[15] In other words, we are all refugees from the lost paradise of childhood. We have all lived in Westmount, Montreal.

A PROPHET'S CHILDHOOD: DRAMATIS PERSONAE

After the images, the facts. Inevitably less universal. Leonard's childhood, as we know, was rather well-off. The Montreal Cohens were a line of philanthropic industrialists typical of the late nineteenth century: "Victorian gentlemen of Hebrew persuasion," as the singer would later describe them.[16] With his rabbi brother, the great-grandfather Lazarus had emigrated from Lithuania in 1869, making his fortune in river drainage and the coal trade. He later founded W.R. Cuthbert and Co., a brass foundry which he passed on to his sons and the Shaar Hashomayim synagogue in Montreal, the first Ashkenazi temple in Canada. It was there, under the high ceiling, that his great-grandson Leonard would later shudder from the third row when the rabbi held up the Torah scrolls high above the assembly. Leonard would learn to pray (or, as he preferred to say, "speak to the boss"[17]) in Hebrew there and receive his bar mitzvah. There again — or perhaps in the adjoining building — he provocatively declared to the community in 1963 that there were no prophets left among Montreal Jews and that their God was "the horrible distortion of a great idea," provoking the next day one of those hilariously concise headlines cherished by the Anglo-Saxon press: "Poet Novelist Says Judaism Betrayed."[18] There also, a tree was planted in his honour in the early 1960s to celebrate the birth of a Jewish poet.

The grandfather, Lyon Cohen, was an equally extraordinary man: a community leader and business tycoon. He took over his father's foundry and bought the Freedman Company (1906), which he quickly turned into one of the largest clothing corporations in Quebec (its specialty: the manufacture and shipment of men's suits and coats). He did not know, of course, that fifty years later, his grandson, then a budding poet, would briefly work in the two family factories (by day in the textile business, by night in the foundry) nor that he would (much later still) give sartorial lessons to three generations of rock fans.

A charismatic man and a tireless philanthropist, Lyon was indeed a pillar of the Montreal Jewish community: the president of the synagogue founded by his father, he also created a Hebrew school, the first Jewish newspaper in the country (*The Jewish Times*), a free loan company, and a sanatorium. He helped found and often presided over several national Jewish and Zionist institutions, like the local branch of the Baron de Hirsch Institute or the Canadian Jewish Congress.[19] Between 1900 and the 1930s, as the Jewish population of Canada was multiplied by ten, he was a key member in many networks that helped Jewish immigrants and often welcomed them on the Montreal docks.[20] His grandson once described the man to me as the "local Jewish Don Corleone, someone people would go to."

But Lyon Cohen was also a patriotic Canadian and a passionate anglophone, very proud when his two eldest sons Nathan and Horace (respectively Leonard's father and uncle) joined the Canadian Army to serve in the First World War. He narrowly missed being presented to the Pope and, in his later years, was invited to join the race for Parliament, but he declined: he had worked hard already and was eager to retire in his house on Rosemont Avenue, a house adorned with a Star of David. His three sons took over: the two eldest in the textile corporation (Nathan in the factory office and Horace at public relations) and the youngest, Lawrence, in the foundry. All of them (as well as their sister Sylvia) had sons and daughters: Leonard's countless cousins whom he saw every Friday night at the synagogue and every Saturday afternoon at the grand-father's house and soon (after Lyon died when the boy was three) at his grandmother's apartment, on high-class Sherbrooke Street.

As we know, the poet will abandon that world of Montreal businessmen to become a bohemian. But he was highly aware of (and grateful for) his lineage, as is evidenced in a 1961 poem where he reclaimed all Jewish stereotypes:

> For you
> I will be a banker Jew
> and bring to ruin
> a proud old hunting king
> and end his line.[21]

A PROPHET'S CHILDHOOD: SETTING AND CHARACTERS

What does a house look like in Westmount, Paradise? With two storeys and a beautiful porch, the father's house (later the mother's house) was large enough for the paterfamilias to have his private study, but small enough for that study to be converted into a bedroom when Leonard's young sister-in-law moved in after the mother remarried in the 1950s. The house adjoined Murray Hill Park — then known as George VI Park — which Leonard wrote about in his first novel and in which he can be seen to roam wistfully in the 1965 docu-mentary *Ladies and Gentlemen . . . Mr. Leonard Cohen*. As a child, Welsh poet Dylan Thomas had declared himself "the prince of the apple towns"; Leonard Cohen would be the more urban monarch of Murray Hill Park, a place that will witness his many debuts in life: as a Jewish mother's only son, as a brooding orphan, as a solitary poet, and — one imagines — as a Westmount teenage Casanova. It is also here that he will later meet the Spanish musician who taught him the rudiments of flamenco that got him through much of his songwriting career. A rich child's territory is a small place indeed: the father's house, the park, the school two blocks away, the synagogue just down the street, and the stage is set. Enter the characters.

First comes the father, Nathaniel Bernard Cohen, a.k.a. Nathan, who will stay only for the first act. In spite of his fragile health (a heart complaint made worse by his weight problems), he was a bit of a dandy, his elegance slightly old-fashioned: a tail-coat and a monocle for evenings out and, in case of rain or snow, spats for the office. In the available photographs, Nathan has thick jowls and his son's anxious eyes. In *The Favourite Game*, Leonard described his hero's father as "the persecuted brother, the near-poet, [. . .] the sighing judge who listens but does not sentence," a description confirmed by what comes across in the photographs: kindness, stiffness, fatigue.[22] Leonard would see this sick father struggle every day: struggling to finish the Sunday afternoon walks, struggling to make it upstairs to his room, struggling to make it to the end of the books he read. A struggling father. As the son retrospectively observed, somewhat cruelly: "When he was up and walking, he lied."[23]

If you ask for the mother in the Cohen family, a Chekhovian character appears: Masha, freshly arrived from Lithuania with a Russian accent and a heart filled with nostalgia. Nathan had married below his social class, to a nurse sixteen years his junior. As for Masha, she simply married the son of her father's bene-factor. Perhaps she even fell in love with Nathan for a minute.[24] She later sank into chronic depression, wild mood swings, unstoppable monologues, and a hysterical relationship with her son, and is described at least by one witness as "raving mad."[25] But she was the daughter of Rabbi Solomon Klonitzki-Kline, the brilliant author of a dictionary of Talmudic interpretations and the head of a Yeshiva in Kovno, who soon made a name for himself in the Yiddish world of New York. He belonged to a very old world, that of the Ashkenazi shtetl. Said Leonard, ready to take over from the Talmudist:

> For you
> I will be a ghetto Jew
> and dance
> and put white stockings
> on my twisted limbs
> and poison wells
> across the town.[26]

This double lineage is a strange mixture. On one side, the Cohens of Montreal — the local Rockefellers: integrated, patriotic, liberal. On the other, the world of Chagall: rabbis flying over the snow with angels, violins, and singing brides — the Klonitzki-Klines of Kovno. The name of the crossbreed: Leonard Cohen.

THE DOG KELEF AND BUDDHA NATURE

Enter also Esther, the older, wiser, and complicit sister (she will be later become a librarian and marry a New York businessman also called Cohen) and — for a while — two servants: a tall Black chauffeur and gardener called Kerry (visibly adored by the children, to judge by the home movies) and a maid (actually several successive maids, one of whom later taught Leonard ukulele and — probably — more intimate arts as well[27]). When the children were small, there was also an Irish nanny who would take them to the Catholic churches of Montreal. A fateful discovery for little Leonard: Jesus on the cross, the statues of saints, the poignant kitsch of popular piety, the mineral sensuality of the churches, and each footstep — including his own — filling the whole space with echo. The future poet thereby fell in love with Catholicism and there were few women that he was more faithful to than the Virgin Mary. When I visited him in Los Angeles seventy years later, he invited me to offer the Virgin incense (he had a little statuette in his study) and he also showed me a secret shrine to her and to other saints in one of his kitchen cupboards. But in the late '30s, no one could imagine that the mischievous-looking little boy with a neat side-part would one day write about Christ sinking beneath the wisdom of men, nor that he would invent a world where desperate seekers want to "fuck" a seventeenth-century Iroquois saint. But it starts here, with the nanny, in the churches of Montreal.[28]

Perhaps the greatest heroes of that childhood were the dogs. First, a white fox terrier called Kelef, who is shown on the lawn in an adorable photograph next to a baby Leonard in diapers. It is summer; the day seems very hot and the dog is exactly the same size as the future poet. They are friends and you can tell — preparing for a life where he will be photographed a lot, Leonard looks straight at the lens while the dog looks at the ball laid in front of his little master. He seems to be pondering the famous question asked by a monk to Master Zhaozhou in a thirteenth-century book of koans known as *The Gateless Gate*: "Does a dog have Buddha-nature?"[29]

Kelef is soon replaced by Tomavitch, a.k.a. Tinkie, another fox terrier — a black one this time — who will follow his young master to school every day and sleep under his bed every night for fifteen years. No doubt the animal felt that Leonard's heroic life could begin at any moment, and that constant watching over was therefore required. He was the four-legged La Boétie of the little Jewish Montaigne of Westmount: together they discovered the power of elective affinities and the eloquence of shared silence. Cohen has spoken at length about this dog's death in the early 1950s, a moment he has always presented as a lesson in dignity and compassion. One winter evening, the poor sick animal went out and died under the piles of the house next door to reappear only when the snow had melted the following spring, as everyone, including his young master (who was away from town), was ready for the unacceptable. So, does a dog have Buddha-nature? In the *Gateless Gate*, Master Zhaozhou's answer is "Mu!" — a great negation which literally means "no" in Japanese, but which in fact dissolves the question and transforms the Buddha who utters it into a barking dog that goes "Mu! Mu! Mu!" It is a "no" that means "yes" and that transcends dualist thinking. In any case, twenty-five years before he met Sasaki Roshi, Leonard took his first Zen lesson as he left childhood — a lesson given by a dog: know how to disappear with grace. Later, the poet would greatly admire Saint Francis of Assisi for preaching to birds, and when singer Rufus Wainwright first met him, Leonard was in his underpants, feeding a wounded bird. The lessons in compassion had been well learnt.[30]

JEWISH DIALECTICS AND DOUBLE-BREASTED SUITS

By cross-checking the interviews and Leonard's novel, we get a good idea of the tempo of his childhood: an endless parade of family parties, Ashkenazi synagogues, well-cut clothes, Russian songs, and American comics. With the book of Isaiah as guest star. That childhood raises a question that is crucial for the future: what do you learn when you are brought up like Leonard Cohen?

The first thing you learn is that you were not born on September 21, 1934, at 6:45 a.m., but on a Shabbat in the month of Tishri in the year 5695. In other words, you learn that you are Jewish, that Judaism belongs to you, and that you can — should you wish to — avail yourself of a whole liturgy of daily life, a grammar of rites, gestures, and words that gives your existence a structure called the practice of Judaism.

For the time being, Leonard (a.k.a. Eliezer Ben Nissan Cohen) is just a child, but he finds himself trembling in the third row of the synagogue when the Torah is lifted or when he is told that, by virtue of his name, he is the heir of the high priests of the Temple. He discovers a collection of stories and motifs that he instantly recognizes as his own: a world created by God's Word, a Flood sent to destroy it, a burning bush and sparks of light scattered in the universe, not to mention life itself defined as a metaphysical game of hide-and-seek with the Creator. The boy immediately saw that this was not just a legacy connecting him to the past, but also a crucible of living parables that could boost your inner life. We said above that Leonard Cohen inherited Judaism, and that is correct: three thousand years of Judaism were placed in his hands so that he could play with it and transform Jewish mythologies into a poetic vision available to all. His claim fifty-five years later that he was "the little Jew who wrote the Bible" may have been a wee bit exaggerated, but the fact remains that a tradition exists only when you keep it alive, which means you have to reinvent that tradition every day.

So like all Jews, Leonard Cohen is not so much the heir as the author of Judaism. His initiation to Talmudic practice and exegesis in Hebrew school taught him exactly that: to "make the Torah sing" and to put every text, every belief, and even the Law into question.[31] Hence the ease with which Leonard later passed from one master to the next, hence also that biographical truth which he loved to recall: that he never rebelled against tradition because no tradition was ever imposed on him. So, for most of his life, every Friday night, Leonard lit the menorah candles (except when he did not), he recited the prayers (unless he forgot), and he observed a day of rest (unless he chose to work). He did this dressed as a beatnik, as an Orthodox Jew, as a Zen monk, or as a rock star and was always eager to see if the menorah candles shone with extra brilliance somewhere else — in Greece, Paris or Los Angeles, or in a Buddhist monastery in the mountains. As early as 1961, he had predicted his many apostasies:

> For you
> I will be an apostate Jew
> and tell the Spanish priest
> of the blood vow
> in the Talmud
> and where the bones
> of the child are hid.[32]

The second thing you learn when you are raised like Leonard Cohen is *discipline* — a term the singer has pronounced with unconcealed delight his whole life. In the Cohen household, jackets were worn at dinner, children were quiet at table, and their shoes were neatly lined up under the bed. Leonard escaped the military school his father had in mind for him, but he discovered the virtues of work and order. So that it later seemed natural to him to work on song lyrics for years, just as he was immune to the cheapest clichés of rock rebellion. His childhood had taught him that you never really were the Lizard King who "can do anything" and that when you jump off Rimbaud's drunken boat, there is a price to pay. To the Swedish journalist Stina Dabrowski he would later explain that his education brought him something even more precious than discipline: good manners. It taught him life could also be lived in the minor mode without endlessly hammering your ego against the world.

And of course, when you are raised like Leonard Cohen, you learn to dress. "I was born in a suit" is what he later told Sylvie Simmons,[33] but it's almost as if the suits brought him up. The 1930s' religion of well-cut tailored clothes and his visits to the family factory taught the poet that in matters of dress as in all things important, precision is king. How a jacket fits, the exact width of a lapel, how the crease of trousers breaks on the shoe are details that will make your presence luminous. Or not. Cohen frequented tailors his whole life and — as countless pictures attest — he knew that a well-cut bespoke suit envelops the wearer in the joyful majesty of the right form.[34] His elegance, which started in childhood, was not the extravagant elegance of dandies, but a humble elegance, almost a philosophical exercise, and a virtuous practice that affirms, in the face of the disordered and chaotic character of our lives, our dignity and the inalienable beauty of the right form. In a famous poem, Baudelaire invites us to a kingdom (that we must rebuild every day) where "all is order and beauty / calm, voluptuousness and luxury."[35] For Leonard Cohen, the double-breasted tailored suit is that kingdom: a realized utopia and every man's best friend.

Judaism as a structure of daily life and the classic double-breasted suit are therefore two "forms" (to which he would later add the sitting posture in zazen) that Leonard will explore his whole adult life to try to inhabit the world as precisely as possible. As a poet of course, he cherished another form: the poetic system of classicism (the stanza-rhyme-meter system), which he always used like a tailor uses scissors: to give his thoughts a clean, precise, and frank form. And perhaps that's the only thing that Leonard Cohen inherited as a child: a love of form.

But, as a good Zen student, Cohen knew that forms are not ends in themselves: they are by nature empty and valuable only for their ability to concentrate and clarify life, as tools to make all things sharp — your looks, your thoughts, your days.[36]

So Leonard began his apprenticeship of the virtues of form as a child in Westmount, Montreal. In paradise, so to speak. But paradise is a place we all have to leave.

NINE YEARS OLD

January 1944: when his father dies, Leonard suddenly leaves paradise to plunge into ice-cold water. Fifty years later, he began the narration of a CBC documentary on the *Tibetan Book of the Dead* with these ominous words: "Death is real, it strikes without warning and it cannot be escaped."[37]

Back in 1944, death seemed to have given fair warning with Nathan Cohen's prolonged ill health, but a father's coffin remains a violent incursion of reality into the life of a nine-year-old boy and Leonard was deeply affected by the funeral.[38] And since incursions of reality call for symbolic responses, the little boy invents a ritual that, perhaps, did seal his fate. Some time after the funeral, he wrote a message for his dead father, slipped it into the seam of one of Nathan's bow ties, and buried the tie in the garden. It was not exactly the *Tibetan Book of the Dead* and no one noted it then, but in 1944 in a Montreal garden, a little genius reinvented the elegy, the act of mourning, and death itself, which he had transformed into a buried butterfly.

Later, when he told the tale of that first poetic act, he always specified two things: first, that had he decided to climb a mountain, he would have become a mountaineer; second, that his whole oeuvre was perhaps just the extension of that first poetic gesture: a symbolical attempt to exhume that first poem. What is certain is that this buried butterfly established a secret covenant between little Leonard and the Logos: the recognition that mysterious circumstances require acts and words that are stronger in impact and more charged with meaning than ordinary speech or behaviour. "Heightened speech" is what he often called it.

Twenty-five years later, Leonard would write a song about Genesis 22, the sacrifice of Isaac. The biblical story is well known. God says to Abraham, "Kill me a Son," preferably in a ritual offering, and preferably now. But at the crucial moment, God sends an angel to stop old Abe, thereon forbidding human sacrifices. Cohen's song presented the episode from the son's point of view, who saw his father enter his bedroom:

> The door it opened slowly
> My father he came in
> I was nine years old
> And he stood so tall above me
> His blue eyes they were shining
> and his voice was very cold
> he said "I've had a vision
> and you know I'm strong and holy
> I must do what I've been told."

In the context of Leonard's life, the episode takes on a different resonance. Is the father who appears at the door — suddenly so tall and cold — the father who has just died? Was dying his holy mission? The equation seems quite simple: Isaac is nine years old, like Leonard in January 1944. Ergo: the death of the father is Leonard's great sacrifice and only voices of angels will be able to console him: of female angels, if possible. Hence, the innumerable future girlfriends, the female voices on his records, and the backing singers that always stood beside him on stage.

For the moment, however, the consequences of Nathan's death are more immediate: after 1944, Leonard, not yet ten years old, is the man of the household. He will now cut the meat at the table, inherit his father's gun[39] and his poetry books (he will read them all), and get a pension from his uncles. And since the book of Ecclesiastes promises "woe to the city whose king is a child," he stops being one. Another consequence, of course, is that he will never have to explain to a father that he will not take over the family factory and that he will be a poet instead. He is now also surrounded by the mystery that blossoms where death has passed (a fact not entirely lost on his schoolfellows, especially girls). When death took his father away, it actually offered Leonard something in return: it made him understand that the past exists, that it lives within us, and that some things — a dead father, for example — must be remembered.

The following year brought a second fall from grace and the definitive exit from Paradise. Leonard is ten years old and stumbles on the sealed photographic insert that a Montreal newspaper had devoted to Auschwitz. Around the same time, he hears a familiar religious term in a new context, a word he will no longer be able to forget: *holocaust*. He thus discovers that the Jews are (as he would later put it) "the professionals of suffering" and his inner life becomes a little clearer.[40] In *The Favourite Game*, the hero and his little friends liked to play Nazis during the war, because Nazis were the perfect villains. We know what will follow: countless poems about the camps, flowers sent to Hitler, a cover of a French resistance song, and a scathing "Wolt Ihr den Totallen Krieg?" thrown to the Berlin Sportpalast public in April 1972, exactly twenty-eight years after the same question had been asked from the same stage by a certain Joseph Goebbels. In his poem about Jewish masks, Leonard concluded:

> For you
> I will be a Dachau Jew
> and lie down in lime
> with twisted limbs
> and bloated pain
> no mind can understand.[41]

He has just lost his innocence.

HYPNOSIS AND FLAMENCO: NOTHING SPECIAL

But Holocaust and death of father aside, all is well. As they say in Zen: nothing special, life itself. Leonard's youth is a normal, almost exquisite youth by some aspects: he lives with his dog in a small bedroom with a view on the park. He attends Roslyn School a few hundred yards from his home, the Hebrew school three times a week, and Westmount High not much further. He is very popular at high school and is elected president of the student council. Big deal. In the summer, he usually goes to Jewish summer camps in the Laurentian Mountains, first as a camper and then, from the age of sixteen, as a counsellor.

There, he meets Morton Rosengarten and makes a friend for life, with whom he soon begins to scour the city's bars and the Catholic nightclubs.[42] True, the young man is not very tall: he allegedly needs a stool to be able to read the Torah for his bar mitzvah. That small size is his first hang-up: he slips Kleenexes in his shoes for parties and, for a while, considers hormonal treatment.[43] In adolescence, things get trickier. As evidenced by many photographs, the teenager's weight varies a lot: he gets plump, starves himself, loses weight, gets plump again. Not exactly an Adonis. Hence the idea that hypnosis might be a safer way to seduce girls. And lo and behold, he has just stumbled on a Victorian manual on the subject: *25 Lessons in Hypnotism or How to Become an Expert*. Soon, he practises on everything that moves (his dog, his friends, his sister, the maid), apparently with some success. When he hypnotizes the maid, he allegedly asks her to undress and touches her body.[44]

Around the same time, the fourteen-year-old Cohen — probably tired of his piano and clarinet lessons — decides that he should not enter the '50s without a guitar. So he buys one second-hand for twelve dollars. The crime scene: Craig Street, Montreal. The year: 1949. The same year, his mother remarries, with a pharmacist who soon develops multiple sclerosis and begins a series of depression.

Nothing extraordinary, therefore; nothing that seems decisive: the average youth of an offspring of the local Jewish bourgeoisie. Perhaps somewhere, the father's death brews in, perhaps a sharper sense of beauty, but nothing yet that predicts the immensity of what is to come. No running away à la Rimbaud, no great Baudelairian storms, no electric shocks à la Lou Reed. With Mort and his good friend Robert Hershorn, Leonard cobbles together a semblance of bohemia: he hangs out in cafés at night and flirts with the waitresses among jukeboxes and junkies. He also tries busking on street corners and he sits in bistros in the afternoon writing. At night, he and Morton drive in and around Montreal in a borrowed car looking for girls and, like all teenagers, they talk each other blind. Nothing decisive. The quasi-ordinary adolescence of a gifted boy with a bit of the poet in him.

In many artist biographies, the question of vocation is seriously underrated. Something highly enigmatic — a calling — becomes something banal and predictable: just an inclination, a taste that gradually asserts itself and leads to a choice of lifestyle. Leonard

Cohen buys a guitar, he receives an anthology of poetry, starts a country music band, and becomes a poet rather than a lawyer.

But we're talking about far more urgent calls, about lives that are ripped open, about departures with no way back. We're talking about Isaiah, who sees an angel fly down from God's throne to purify his lips with a burning coal so that he may answer: "Here I am — Hineni — send me!" (Isaiah 6:6–8). We're talking about Ezekiel who, after seeing the Lord's face (apparently made of pure light), is made to eat a scroll of Scripture that tastes sweeter than honey, and then hears God say to him: "Son of Man, fill thy bowels [and] go to the house of Israel and speak" (Ezekiel 3:1–4). We're talking about Jeremiah who argues that he is "too young" but has no choice: God touches his mouth and — bang! — he is a prophet (Jeremiah 1:6–10).

Of course, in Leonard Cohen's teenage years, the heavens were not ripped open by the divine chariot — or if they were, he never said so, which would be very out of character. But that's simply because outside the Bible, the calls are more discreet. But they are just as precise, and just as strong. Like many artists, Leonard's adolescence was an echo chamber where solemn calls resounded — some in tune with the career plan (law studies, the uncle's factories, a ready-made career as the family lawyer), others pulling towards the uncharted path, the untraced journey. It's not very hard to imagine which calls Leonard — a future disciple of Joan of Arc — chose to follow.

EVERY INCH OF YOU

There are two stages in every vocation: first, a revelation tells you something exists, then the actual calling tells you the thing exists for you. And for a poet, the thing that calls is always the infinite mystery of the world.

In Leonard's case that mystery, as we saw, made a violent intrusion with his father's coffin. It then manifested in sweeter ways in

From the video "Moments of Old Ideas" (2012)

the magnetic attraction that female bodies started to exert on him. Whether this started with the little girls with whom he climbed trees as a child, with the female counsellors at summer camp, or with his first high-school flirts, is of course impossible to say. He once told a friend that the first woman he fell in love with was the "Sun-Maid girl" in a 1916 California advertisement for a brand of raisins, obviously modelled on the iconography of the Virgin Mary. We know that he had high-school flirts and that one was a dancer; another, the "blondest and tallest girl" of class.[45] We know that the girl who "initiated" him was probably the maid from Alberta who also taught him ukulele. And we know that his first "official" fiancée was the art student and left-wing activist Freda Guttman, who had "God knows how long" legs and with whom he formed the hippest couple at college.[46]

But the calling happened much before that. Pampered by an angst-ridden mother, a loving sister and a retinue of nannies and maids, that fatherless young man must have perceived very early on a mystery he could not resist in the voices, gestures, and moods of women. As he started getting intimate with girls, he discovered in the female naked body — whether that nakedness was just fantasized, accidentally glimpsed at, or amorously revealed — a miracle and an epiphany of light. And of course an urgent invitation to poetry. Hair strewn upon the pillow? No, a "sleepy golden storm." The curve of an unveiled breast? No, the "upturned bellies of fallen sparrows."[47]

During Leonard's late teenage years, women became an obsession but also muses, playmates, and allies on the path to knowledge. When they let themselves be kissed or touched by him, they became the embodied *Song of Songs* and taught him everything he would later read about in the Kabbalah: that a kiss on the mouth is an exchange of souls, that you can touch a perfect body with your mind, that beauty is an unfathomable mystery and a necessary nourishment of the soul, that the union of man and woman is a joyful alchemical dissolution. Hence the following statement, in an unpublished early essay on love:

> The important thing is not to approach anyone too close because the next day you may have become pure light.[48]

That sentence sounds like the heretic proposition of a Father of the Church intent on making the contemplation of naked women a philosophical exercise. As the teenager Cohen soon found out, the lover is by nature a philosopher (he interprets signs and bodies) just as philosophy — the art of looking at naked truth — is an erotic science. And that is indeed the task the young man set out for himself in those early years: to be a lover and a philosopher. If possible a great one. To contemplate all things in general — and female bodies in particular — in their nakedness. Several decades later, he would put it like this: "I'll examine every inch of you."[49] He once explained that scopic obsession:

> I don't think a man ever gets over that first sight of the naked woman. That's Eve standing over him,

that's the dawn, and the dew on her skin. And I think that's the major content of every man's imagination. All the sad adventures in pornography and love and song are just steps on the path towards that holy vision.[50]

Back in his teenage years, it must have happened like this: an empty room, a girl with no clothes on (most likely the house maid), and the irreducible mystery of the divine plan that created Man "male and female" (Genesis 1:27).[51] And, immediately, Leonard must have known. That women would be the main topic of his forthcoming oeuvre. That he would therefore have to pursue in secret a second career beside his career as a poet, one he has often downplayed in later life: that of a "ladies' man." This was no mean task. It meant collecting ladies (in bedrooms, in notebooks, in memories) and earnestly and honestly studying what really happens when men and women have to meet without their clothes.

And soon — with the *Song of Songs* and the Kabbalah as reference — he would develop a mystical vision of sexual union where the lovers initiate a "divine episode" that reconciles opposites and actually brings God into existence, a vision he would stick to his whole life.[52] But all mysticism aside, there was also a strongly neurotic element in Cohen's attraction to women, his need to have them all, which made him, for most of his adult life, sometimes a regular Lothario, sometimes a poet of love and Platonician worshipper, and sometimes just a cynical skirt-chaser. With time, he would learn — though not too quickly — that, try as he might, what he will once call "the magic of womanhood"[53] would always partly escape him. Women and love have a habit of escaping and, consequently, there really can never be such a thing as a "great lover." But for the moment, a great lover is exactly what the teenager Cohen wants to be.[54]

Of course, something in the way he idealized women and their beauty connects Leonard to twelfth-century troubadours and their conception of love as an initiatory experience.[55] Throughout the early '90s, Cohen kept repeating in interviews that he drank only for professional reasons (the concerts, he claimed, made the wine necessary). He could have made the same joke about women: he approached them only for professional reasons. Because it was his job to reinvent the great poetry of Love, the great tradition of courtly mysticism initiated by the Sufis and the Western troubadours. Except that, in his case, it was more than a job: it was a calling.

So, in the late '40s, Leonard started to form alliances with women. They were sometimes platonic, sometimes fiery and dangerous, but always temporary. The list of his many girlfriends unfolds a whole geography of love. With Freda, Madeleine, and Erica in Montreal, Anne in New York, Marianne from Oslo, Nico from Köln, Janis from Texas, Joni from the Prairies, Despina in Greece, Suzanne from Miami, Dominique in Paris, Rebecca from California, and Anjani from Honolulu. Not to mention a hundred anonymous others, one in every port and harbour.[56]

IN THE BEGINNING WAS THE JUKEBOX

After that, it's just a matter of finding his own weapons to approach the great mystery. As is often the case with Leonard, it all began in the synagogue. There, the little boy discovered, in the prayers and songs of the liturgy, a type of speech that touched him deeply. It seemed to promise something about language itself. That it can achieve our redemption. That it is the appropriate response to our fall.[57]

Next came the discovery of poetry in the leather-bound books left by his father. Soon, the teenager Cohen carried around an anthology of English poetry, memorizing poems by George Herbert, Lord Byron, Keats, Yeats, and Blake, and reciting them on command — his little party piece. In the process, he discovered that great poems are alive, sometimes very much so. You carry them inside you and they renew your life with the never-before-heard, the never-before-seen, the never-before-felt.[58] Cohen has told the story of his true birth to poetry a thousand times. He is fifteen years old, he walks into a second-hand bookstore in Montreal, he randomly picks up a volume and reads these lines by Federico García Lorca:

> Cover me up at dawn,
> because dawn will throw fistfuls of ants at me.

The Kabbalah says that whenever we feel that a text is really addressing us personally, we give birth to an angel.[59] It is not known whether wings were heard flapping in the bookstore that day, but for Leonard, this was what Zen Buddhists call a satori, a sudden moment of awakening. The book threw a handful of ants at him, and the itch to write lasted for the next sixty-seven years. During a concert in Spain in 1988, the singer summarized the García Lorca episode in one sentence: "The guy destroyed my life."

And then came the songs. It may have started with the Jewish tradition that some prayers must be sung by the eldest son. But more central probably were his mother's Russian songs, which she sang in the kitchen by day and in restaurants at night, when she sometimes accompanied her teenage son's retinue of friends for joyful late-night dinners. Before that came the radio, with American country music stations available only at night, and of course the folk songs played by the fire at summer camp.[60] Flamenco came later, when Cohen was famously given three guitar lessons by a young Spaniard who decided, before the fourth lesson, to go and play matador with this black bull called Death, committing suicide in his boarding house in Montreal.[61] But throughout the poet's adolescence, songs mostly meant jukeboxes. And apparently, as a teenager, Cohen had an encyclopedic knowledge of all the jukeboxes in Montreal: what songs were in what machine, in what bar, what the number was. The thing is, he loved them all. The doo-wop tunes, the blues and country ballads, the crooner numbers, the boogies, and the early rock and roll. Fats Domino, Frankie Laine, Pat Boone. And of course, his all-time favourites. On his right, a cowboy escaped from a Greek tragedy, a rock-and-roll hero before rock and roll, the author of "Lost Highway," and the first Elvis: Hank Williams, killed by loneliness and amphetamines in the back of a taxicab one cold morning in 1953 (Leonard was sixteen). On his left, a blind cotton-picking Orpheus, whose warm voice sang the great lament buried in everybody's heart: Ray Charles, more real to him than Keats or Byron. Both will accompany Leonard his whole life and he will often compare them to his third-favourite songwriter: King David.[62] Every day, Buddhist monks around the world pronounce four vows, the third of which goes: "Sentient beings are numberless, I vow to save them all." That is exactly what Ray Charles and his colleagues seemed to be doing. In the secret of his heart, Leonard vowed to do the same, hence his pledge to uphold yet another Jewish identity: that of the mad Kabbalist intent on mending Creation, even if that means doing it every which way:

> For you
> I will be a doctor Jew
> and search
> in all the garbage cans for foreskins
> to sew back on again.[63]

Like Ray Charles and King David, Leonard Cohen vows to save the world. In slots of four minutes.

THIS BROKEN FEELING

With prayer, poetry, and song, Leonard Cohen discovered the forms he will work with. He began to spend his nights writing and he learnt from Irish poet Yeats that that activity consists essentially in the humble task of ceaselessly visiting "the rag-and-bone shop of the heart."[64] One of the young man's first poems was entitled "Midnight Song" and it may well be his first prayer as well. It was apparently a staple of his early repertoire. He performed a slow version of it for a CBC Radio program in 1958 and a faster one six years later for *Ladies and Gentlemen . . . Mr. Leonard Cohen*. The lyrics (published in his second volume of poetry[65]) mention giving yourself to a "bright light," or to a "black light" — the great Cohenian temptation already:

> Hold me hard light, soft light hold me
> Moonlight in your mountains fold me [. . .]
> Death light in your darkness wield me.

As the '50s began, with no Elvis, no Kerouac, and no James Dean in sight on the Canadian horizon, Leonard — as the song attests — began what sixteenth-century alchemists called "nigredo": a slow infusion of darkness. He was still in high school, but he discovered he had inherited a dark and painful condition from his parents: depression.

Around the same time, he began to see loved ones fall and disappear. As we said, the first to go was his dog, and it took Leonard decades to understand that the grief he felt then was actually universal:

> Everybody's got this broken feeling
> Like their father or their dog just died.[66]

The German romantics call that feeling "Weltschmerz" — the pain of the world — and a great classic of the Kabbalah (the *Book of Splendor* or *Sepher El-Zohar*) claims in the chapter devoted to Jeremiah's Lamentations that singing the pain of the world is the task of the Jews.[67] Of course, in the early '50s, Cohen had not read that book but its message was already understood. Ray Charles (who was not Jewish at all) was delivering it on every jukebox in town.

BIRTH OF A POET

What does that mean? That Leonard Cohen is born? That Leonard Cohen is ready? That this is the end of Genesis? Not quite. But surely with "Midnight Song," the poet's artistic journey had indeed started. One more step was necessary however, and uncharacteristically, it would take place in university.

On February 21, 1951, Leonard, aged seventeen, enrolled at McGill University to have literature, law, and business classes to skip, debating clubs to join, and fraternity presidencies to run for. In 1953, after two years of sneaking out of his mother's house every night, he finally took a room downtown — on Stanley Street near the campus — with his friend Morton for a life of wine, guitars, poetry, and girls. He was nineteen years old and he had finally left his mother's house. And she was not too happy about it. She wanted to give him all the silverware, plus the tablecloths and the curtains. She would never ever need them again, "not in an empty house."[68] Yet, things were in place for true bohemia to begin and Leonard spent most nights in the downtown bars. In the Mansfield Town at the entrance to the campus. In the Café André (a.k.a. The Shrine). In Dunn's on Sainte-Catherine (with its jazz club upstairs). In the Swiss Hutt on Sherbrooke, and of course, in every bohemian's favourite: The Bistro or Chez Lou-Lou where Leonard would later scribble that famous supplication on a wall:

Marita,
please find me,
I am almost thirty.

In addition, there was the Pann-Pann and Ben's All Night Deli with its "poets' corner." That's a lot of zinc-topped counters, a lot of drinks, a lot of early morning Pekinese soups, and, presumably, a lot of one-night stands.

The student Cohen, still 50 percent Westmount Square, soon formed a 100 percent beatnik couple with Freda Guttman, a beautiful arts student and active member of a communist group. They would love each other on campus, in summer camps, and in rundown hotels, and, if we go by *The Favourite Game*, they would quarrel a lot, ceaselessly betray each other, and cause one another quite a lot of pain. With two comrades, Terry Davis and Mike Doddman, Leonard also formed the Buckskin Boys, a country-music band that played at high-school dances, fraternity parties, and village fairs. They wore cowboy hats and buckskin jackets and played Appalachian tunes and square dance music (which was all the rage). Do-si-do, do-si-do, do-si-do. It's far from the blues, far from *folk*, and very, very far from rock and roll, which has not yet spread to Quebec. It's not Broadway, of course, but it's already show business, as Leonard announced in his programmatic poem:

> For you
> I will be a Broadway Jew
> and cry in theatres
> for my mother
> and sell bargain goods
> beneath the counter.[69]

Then came that day in 1953 or 1954 when Leonard decided to submit one of his poems to Louis Dudek, his literature professor. A bigwig of local Canadian modernism, he edited magazines, published books, and was in contact with Ezra Pound: an ally of choice. But Dudek was not impressed by his student's efforts. Cohen persisted, however, and his second poem "The Sparrows" (later published by Dudek) caught the professor's attention. In the corridor, he allegedly asked the young man to kneel and used the manuscript as a sceptre to declare him "poet" in a mock knighthood ceremony (so the story goes). From then on, Leonard would be invited to the soirées where the Montreal poetic avant-garde (a very small group) met and worked. If he could bring along a pretty student or two, so much the better. The poet stood up. His eyes were wide open. It's official: he was no longer a civilian.[70]

CHAPTER 2

THE POET AND COLLECTOR OF EXILES

LEONARD'S FIRST CAREERS
1956–1964

Dunn's Delicatessen, Sainte-Catherine Street, Montreal,
early 1960s

SAINTS AND AVANT-GARDES

The '50s. In the United States, girls' skirts are pleated and avant-gardes triumph. Led by Jackson Pollock, the abstract expressionists invent action painting: they throw paint on the canvas while the Black Mountain poets throw rhythmic shocks at their readers. Happenings invite violence into art galleries, and jazz, with its poetics of improvisation and its mythologies of hard drugs and lost Africa, is everywhere. A hundred years after Baudelaire's trial for *Flowers of Evil*, history repeats itself as Allen Ginsberg is sued for obscenity for his great epic poem *Howl*, an evocation of his generation's quest for hallucinated holiness. He begins with a famous panoramic vision of the forces at play:

> I saw the best minds of my generation destroyed by madness starving hysterical naked

And he concludes with the holiness of everything:

> Holy! Holy! Holy! Holy! Holy! Holy! Everything is holy! Everybody's holy! [. . .] Everyman's an angel![1]

Obsessed with holiness, the beat generation was looking for saints among the drug addicts, the mad, and the deviants.[2] This was why Kerouac crossed the United States in a 1949 Hudson Commodore, with a "saint" on Benzedrine at the wheel. *On the Road* was of course the great success of 1957, a few months after the confidential publication of *Let Us Compare Mythologies* on the other side of the border, the first volume by an unknown young poet named Leonard Cohen.

In the Greenwich Village cellars, middle-class kids listened to folk ballads and very old blues. They hated the A-bomb and would soon protest against segregation. Down in the South, a fop from Tennessee with made-up eyes and a strange lock of hair had apparently decided to desegregate America all by himself. He undulated his pelvis to a strange battle-cry ("Awopbopaloobop Alopbamboom!"), sang like a Black man, danced like a stripper, and definitely disrupted the barriers between entertainment and juvenile delinquency. Meet Elvis, the American Prometheus, who stole the sacred fire of rock and roll from Black people to free white America from the FBI and conformist sleep.

The '50s, then. America is the centre of the world, and its artists claim that freedom lies in gestural art and open form. It's actually an old American credo: as early as 1855, Walt Whitman had invented free verse to sing Manhattan and its crowds, and in 1919, a New Jersey doctor named William Carlos Williams had developed a short, clipped line inspired by cubism to sing the machine age. Later generations had tested the limits of both forms, but the result was there — American verse had been liberated and the new forms were alive and well. Up in Canada? Not so much.

MONTREAL POETS/A STYLIST IS BORN

In Canada, poets worked in similar directions, but they did not hit the road with junkies; they stayed on campus. In Montreal in particular, poetry was very much an intellectual and academic affair, as was the circle Cohen joins around 1954 — an informal group of poets, novelists, painters, and sculptors gathered around the moral authority of Louis Dudek, a teacher, poet, and soon the editor of two avant-garde magazines: *CIV/n* and *Delta*. Informal poetry workshops took place at his house on Thursday nights. Usually present were Eli Mandel, Hugh MacLennan, Phyllis Webb, Doug Jones, Raymond Souster, and F.R. Scott, and of course, Dudek's best friend and arch-enemy, loudmouth poet Irving Layton.

The group's project, as Cohen would later recall, was revolutionary: to be Montreal's avant-garde.

> Every time we saw each other, we thought it was a summit meeting, a historic moment. We thought we were the avant-garde, creating the spirit of our country, but we were the only garde![3]

For Dudek, what mattered was to be absolutely modern, and to get rid of traditional forms with a language "that awakes the reader to see the world as it is."[4] Writing epic poems about Indians and the railway line junction was definitely *out*. Gathering three poets to write experimental texts and calling the result Cerberus was definitely *in*.[5] The ultimate reference was American modernist Ezra Pound, who had indeed given Dudek lessons in concision and rhythmic invention while demanding that we read old Chinese poets and twelfth-century troubadours as if they were our modern brothers.[6]

In this group, Leonard, who was still a student, was in many ways the odd one out. He was fifteen to twenty years younger than everyone, he owned a guitar, set some of his poems to music, and professed an almost heretical attachment to the Bible and the great lyrical tradition. He also had a nasty habit of saying "I" in every text — not exactly what modernists were supposed to do. Yet here he was, surrounded by artists for whom poetry was the laboratory where language is renewed. Whoever read a text at the group's parties must be prepared to defend it and criticism was very harsh:

> We would stay on the poem until we discovered its code, until we knew exactly what it said, how the author had constructed it. Verse by verse, word by word. It was our life. Life was poetry.[7]

In this permanent writing workshop (alcoholic beverages were welcome), Cohen began to hone his style and that was the first advantage of frequenting the Montreal Poets. His imagination, of course, needed no teachers: pebbles that dream of themselves, sex toys with a will of their own, men who wish to deceive God and give birth to monkeys — all of this would be invented without help.[8] What Leonard learnt from the Montreal Poets was an ethics: to dig deep and to absolutely refuse slogans and easy ways out. There was only one method: chain yourself to your worktable and pay your rent every day with a tribute of blackened pages. An asceticism called "poetic labor" that is practised with — as Leonard will soon find out — "the energy of slaves." His poet friends repeated it tirelessly: beware of first drafts and quick probing of the heart. The poet is a craftsman of depth, a coal miner who has to find, by successive rewritings, the absolutely new, the absolutely right, the absolutely surprising. As a bonus, the young Cohen acquired a few literary virtues: economy, accuracy, and concreteness in expression.

The result was that Leonard soon knew his craft. Economic narrations, razor-sharp quatrains, and perfect metrics — that is the edge that Leonard would always have on the future Tim Hardin, Jim Morrison, and Phil Ochs.

ENTER IRVING L.

The second benefit of attending Montreal Poets gatherings is that you meet a few friends who can advance your career. Like the poet, activist, and legal luminary F.R. Scott (1899–1985) who will later support Leonard's grant applications and occasionally provide a summer cabin to write in. But mostly, you meet Irving Layton. With him affinities were deeper, and Leonard had sensed from day one (when he invited the poet to speak at the Zeta Beta Thau fraternity he presided over) that he and Irving had escaped from the same biblical landscape.

With his loud, boisterous, macho persona, Layton was the discordant voice in the poetry scene, a man able to challenge Dudek at handball to find out who the better poet is. Hyperbolically in love with life and sex, but mostly with himself, he was the flamboyant son of Hasidism and Friedrich Nietzsche, as well as an indefatigable creator on his way to a Governor General's Award. In 1955, he had already published ten volumes of poetry and thirty more would follow. Ardently engaged with the modern nightmare and the Holocaust in particular, Layton loudly professed to anyone who would listen (and much louder to anyone who wouldn't) that the whole world had become Jewish in the twentieth century. Inevitably, he recognized in that young poet from Westmount who — like him — liked to have a few drinks after readings, not a spiritual son, but a kindred soul. He opened a few doors for Leonard, but mostly, he reminded him that "arrogance and inexperience" were the major qualities of young poets, just as he taught him to submit each career choice to a crucial test: "Are you sure you're doing the wrong thing?" Quite amused, Leonard was taking notes, and Layton may have inspired the character called F. in *Beautiful Losers.* "I taught him to dress; he taught me to live forever," is how he later summed up their rapport. As for Irving, he saw Cohen's art as "seducing women with words and vice versa."

Flash-forward to eternity. First stop: Toronto, a television studio, ten years later. October 27, 1964. Layton and Cohen are guests on *The Pierre Berton Show.* The host has decided to push the leather-jacketed Leonard out of his con act. With the aloofness of a popish Dorian Gray, the poet has just explained that the problems of the world did not concern him. Quoth Berton, "How can you be a poet and not care about anything?" Leonard answers (not too convincingly) with prepared lines (soon to be published in his next novel) about holiness and the state of grace. Quoth Berton, "Oh, you lost me there." And Layton comes to his protégé's rescue: "What Leonard means is . . ." A thousand examples will follow where the older poet will publicly defend his friend against the critics who are shocked by his work, against the leftists who do not forgive him not being a communist, against jealous colleagues who do not forgive him for being Leonard Cohen.

Flash-forward, second stop: Montreal, late summer 1979. Leonard keeps a bust of Irving Layton in his kitchen. Filmmaker Harry Rasky is shooting a documentary at Leonard's home as his career takes a more confidential turn after years of great success. Surprise arrival of Layton, with a blonde companion. The singer is delighted, brings out a couple of bottles and a cassette machine to play his old mentor a track of the yet unreleased niggunim-flavoured *Recent Songs.* Moved to tears, Layton spends the next fifteen minutes expounding on Leonard's poetic gesture. To sum up, he is the best balladeer since the thirteenth century.[9]

Flash-forward, third stop: Los Angeles, early '90s. Leonard Cohen never gives an interview without referring to "the greatest

Canadian poet, Irving Layton." One quote he likes to feed the press is his elder's opinion that "Leonard has never been contaminated by a single idea." A continent away, Layton (who has also called Cohen "the Jeremiah of show business") still makes him laugh.[10]

Flash-forward, last stop: Montreal, the mid-2000s. Cohen visits his old friend in hospital and watches him eat the almond cake he has brought for him. But the friend doesn't recognize him. He has forgotten Leonard and everything else. At his cremation, Cohen (a pallbearer) proclaims that "Alzheimer's couldn't silence [Irving]. Death will not be any more successful."

LET US COMPARE MYTHOLOGIES (1956)

To be a writer is fine; to get published is better. And this is the third benefit of hanging out with the Montreal Poets: Cohen gets published. Despite deepening aesthetic differences with Dudek, the professor invites the young man to inaugurate the Poetry Series he plans to edit with the local university press. As if on cue, Leonard delivers a volume entitled *Let Us Compare Mythologies*, forty-four poems for the twenty-two-year-old poet, complete with illustrations by his fiancée, Freda Guttman. A handful of favourable reviews will praise its candidness, its elaborate imagery, and the syncretic ambition of a volume that connects contemporary Montreal streets with ancient mythology and Hasidic motifs. One critic deplores a "reductio ad absurdum of the Folies Bergères and Madame Tussaud's Museum of Horrors" (in other words, an abundance of sexual ecstasies, crude words, and scenes of torture[11]), but to no avail: a career is launched and, in May 1956, Leonard Cohen, who has sold no less than 300 copies, is world-famous on the McGill campus. The critics are not entirely wrong, though: the forty-four texts have their strengths — among which the clarity with which certain Cohenian themes (like the secret glory of defeat or the sacredness of sex) already emerge[12] — but, with classical elegies, evocations of Renaissance painting, parodies of John

Donne, allusions to T.S. Eliot, and decadent influences, the volume seems quite artificial in retrospect and perhaps a little immature in sentiment, especially when compared to what his beat colleagues or the American confessional poets were publishing across the border. What is obvious, however, is the power of Cohen's imagination. From one page to the next, the reader encounters a Montreal golem made of grass, children blowing up frogs, suicidal lepers floating on the St. Lawrence, Jewish lovers kissing while burning in a crematory oven, a young girl mutilated in a boarding room, soldiers planting flowers in the wounds of Christ, a moon dangling in the sky like an eye out of its socket, and a vast field of honour where a host of biblical heroes — Moses, Job, David et al. — hang crucified side by side.[13] Not exactly the sobriety favoured by the Montreal modernists, however, and Dudek disavows the book in private.

But the following year, together with A.M. Klein, Dudek, and Layton, Leonard is invited to read his poems for a spoken word record called *Six Montreal Poets*, co-produced by the Canadian Broadcasting Corporation and the hip US label Folkways.[14] Though not exactly electrifying, his performance of eight poems is not without charm: the tone — closer (one imagines) to Oscar Wilde than to Jack Kerouac — is declamatory and the voice still very young, but at least, here is someone who reads out his poems as though they were the best ever written. The fact that he is the only poet of his generation on the record makes it sort of official: he is the new wave.

NEW YORK, NEW YORK

What follows is two uncertain years, during which Cohen (as he later declared) had "no goals,"[15] as though an ingredient was still missing. As though he was not ready yet. After abandoning his law studies at McGill a few weeks into the first semester in 1955, Leonard registers at Columbia University the following year, this time for a master's degree in law. His aim was probably just to delay his enrollment in the family business and drop out soon. In New York, he takes a room on campus:

> New York City. He lived in the tower of World Student House. His window overlooked the Hudson River. He was relieved that it wasn't his city and he didn't have to record its ugly magnificence. He walked on whatever streets he wanted and he didn't have to put their names in stories. New York had already been sung. And by great voices.[16]

Almost unknown at university, Leonard scours the city, noting his insignificance in the face of skyscrapers, and attempting the impossible: getting lost in Manhattan. Chinatown is his favourite destination. He hangs out in the fish market at night and asks the name of each species, fascinated by the endless variations of silver on the crushed ice. He also hangs out in the Greenwich Village folk cafés and jazz clubs, where he sees Kerouac the Great declaim his poems to a background of very cool jazz piano at the Village Vanguard. He takes notes for the future and crashes a couple of beatnik parties, where he also meets Ginsberg, but the hip crowd snubs him and denies entry into their magazines. Not hip enough, too bourgeois, too square.[17] Leonard takes his revenge by living a great passion with Anne Sherman, a very beautiful Yankee divorcee, to whom he writes so many poems that she asks for a break. He answers in verse that silence would just be another poem.[18]

Employed for a while as an elevator boy, he finds it amusing to answer "Charon" when passengers ask for his name, in homage to the ferryman of Hades who took the dead souls to the other shore. There's black humour there, but also a ring of truth: the young man seems in a bit of a limbo. Maybe because he has adopted very high standards that make his life difficult. With three unbreakable rules: always be a saint, always leave the women you love, never resist the ones you don't. Enough to test anyone's limits.

And indeed, to be a saint is his great obsession. Fascinated by Christian martyrs and Hasidism, Leonard longs for the clarity of those close to God and for the state of grace that comes when you stop struggling with the world. But like all 1950s bohemians, Cohen read *Howl* and aspired to a holiness that reaches beyond good and evil, one that is attained (if necessary) through excess. And besides, isn't sexual pleasure a privileged path to God?

Hence, the first rule in the ethics of Cohenian sainthood: never resist women. And yet, believing as he did that women could dissolve you in their light, Cohen was also afraid of female power — and probably unable to commit and actually *receive* love. Hence, the second rule: to systematically leave the women you love, a rule he would live by for a very long time. Nobody had told him yet that *there is no cure for love.*

December 1956. Back in Montreal, there is no way to escape: Leonard has to find a job. It will be summer camp counselling in summer and a go at his uncle's factories the rest of the time. For a few months, the snowy city sees the advent of Leonard Cohen the shop and office boy in the textile factory once run by his father, and of Leonard Cohen the unskilled worker in his uncle's brass foundry. There, the recurrent sight of molten iron — "the colour gold should be" — offers an intimation of true alchemy and of the absolute beauty he has not yet attained in art.[19] At nights and on his days off, it's a three-word program: bistro, bohemia, and poetry readings. He reads his poems in Montreal coffee houses, in the Eastern Townships, and — when Layton takes him with him — in Toronto art galleries, where (as a witness attests) Cohen was the man who always left with "the most interesting woman."[20] He would later sum up that life to a French journalist:

> Drinking and trying to find girls — Montreal was
> ideal for that, with a few cafés where you could bring

your guitar and sing. Living the life that the poems were about: freedom, love, that kind of things. [. . .] Poetry was the Holy Scripture, the Law — you had to live by the Law.[21]

Along the way, he develops three hobbies that will become habits for life: to write every day (at least five hours), to methodically derange the senses with every available intoxicant (wine and hashish among them[22]), and to complexify his sentimental life as much as possible with a multitude of girlfriends. The objective: to uncover the secrets of the heart and suffer less. Or suffer more — he is never sure.

So he writes. In furnished apartments. In countless cold-water flats. In a log cabin surrounded by crickets. He writes poems and short stories[23] but also (more surprisingly) essays. On literature. On the nature of love and on the ways to resist it. On women's tits and their magic. And he writes a short novel with fine dramatic tension, *A Ballet of Lepers*, turned down at the time by several publishers. A novel about a young department store employee who lives alone in furnished rooms with a senile grandfather.

Two failed projects teach him he is not entirely equipped for classic bohemia. The first was the ill-titled *The Phoenix*, a literary magazine that never made it to its second issue. The second was an art gallery called the Four Penny that Cohen opened with fellow bohemians Leonore Schwartzman and Mort Rosengarten. There, openings were very *hip* and very *chic* for a very short time — until the gallery burnt down, that is, joining *The Phoenix* in ashes it would never rise from. It is probably a coincidence, but Cohen will repeatedly portray himself in poems as an arsonist, as in:

One night I burned the house I loved
It lit a perfect ring.[24]

More about this later (Leonard is not done with fire), but to be fair, it was hard to imagine the young man as the integrated bohemian who runs groups and edits magazines. His demon (in the Socratic sense of daimon or personal genius) clearly pulled him in the opposite direction: away from all institutions. He would have to be — as he soon found out — the eternal foreigner who is only passing through. What is more, he has family business to attend to. All is not well in the Cohen household in 1957. An increasingly senile Rabbi Klonitzki-Kline has come to live in the Westmount family house for a while and this quickly turned Masha's life into a nightmare. Overwhelmed by the decline of a man whose teaching once attracted crowds from all over Lithuania, she is hospitalized for several months for clinical depression.

JAZZ POET

The following year, first success: from February to June 1958, Cohen puts on a cabaret act with pianist Maury Kaye (and sometimes with the musician's jazz trio). The crime scene is the Birdland club, on the third floor of the fashionable Dunn's Steak House, a landmark of Montreal nightlife on Sainte-Catherine. Looking cool in his suit and tie, the poet hits the stage around midnight — after the concerts, the dance numbers, and striptease shows — to recite poems to a background of jazz piano improvisations:

> Go by brooks, love
> where fish stare
> Go by brooks
> I will pass there
> Go by rivers,
> where eels throng,
> Rivers, love
> I won't be long.

Again, it's very hip and very beat, and the available recording shows that Cohen is not a bad performer at all — relaxed, lyrical, and almost funny. He has definitely found a tone, a clever mix of oratory and swing. À la Kerouac. The students love it, so does a local radio channel, and his writer colleagues are intrigued — like Morley Callaghan, the hard-boiled Irish novelist who once knocked out Hemingway. He finds the young prodigy "sensational."[25] Little by little, Leonard Cohen — who does not yet have a publishing contract — creates a persona as the "in" poet of Montreal, a quasi-beat who smuggles the literary experience into a jazz club, offering it to the hip world and to the anti-heroes of the night — the boozers and all those who refuse to go to bed. It's not the general public yet, but it's getting closer.[26] Of course, these serious breaches of the modernist ethic (which spurns popular success) have Dudek disavow his former pupil, this time publicly in a magazine appropriately named *Culture*.[27] But poet Raymond Souster defends the young jazz poet and, thinking perhaps of French surrealist boxer-poet Arthur Cravan, he encourages him:

> Sock it into 'em, Leonard,
> grind it,
> bump it out, boy!
> Make that old bitch poetry
> shake her rusty ass![28]

Leonard was obviously listening.

THE HEIST AND THE GREAT ESCAPE

His elder's disavowal was almost timely. Cohen was indeed beginning to discover the great disadvantage of being a Montreal Poet: you have to stay in Montreal. But the world was calling, and the poet was itching to move on. After a last self-promoting stunt, he would depart for Europe and its age-old parapets.

The stunt is actually a heist. Still galvanized by Layton's advice on the active practice of arrogance, Cohen had decided that

McClelland & Stewart, one of the country's leading publishers, would publish him and, with a hundred poems under his arm, he storms into the publisher's office, determined not to leave until his book is accepted. Under the spell of a young man who could explain in one breath that he was "the Jewish Keats of Canada" and that he was addressing "disappointed Platonists and pornography lovers," Jack McClelland did the unthinkable: he accepted the manuscript of *The Spice-Box of Earth* without reading the volume.[29] A good move for the businessman: Leonard Cohen will sell quite a few books in the coming decades and, although he never signed a binding contract, he will remain faithful to the publisher even after Jack McClelland's death in 2005.

Second phase of the heist: money. Arguing that he had a novel to write and that he needed to write it in the great capitals of Antiquity, and aware that Canada was very determined to exist culturally alongside the American giant (and therefore was very generous with promising young artists), Cohen obtains a grant of $4,000 (worth about $36,000 today) from the newly created Canada Council for the Arts as well as an open pass on Canadian airlines. Since the plan was to visit Rome, Athens, and Jerusalem, he first settles in London. There's that Japanese proverb, you see: "If you are in a hurry, make a detour."

LONDON 1960: "TOO EARLY FOR THE RAINBOW"

First stop: London. Leonard Cohen drops his bags in December 1959, ready to assail the '60s. He knocks at the door of Mrs. Pullman's pension on 19b Hampstead High Street, where his childhood friend, dancer and future filmmaker Nancy Bacal, has preceded him. There is no vacant room, but Cohen insists and finds himself sharing the living room with a cat. He is required by the landlady to vacate the premises every morning and write at least three pages a day. No problem for the poet — he loves neatly made beds and getting up early.

The first day he goes shopping (this is London after all), and, for forty pounds, buys an olive-green typewriter (an Olivetti Lettera model 22) that will accompany him for twenty-six years. On that machine, he will write two novels and hundreds of poems, not to mention the lyrics of some of the songs that will make his reputation. He will smash it against a wall, try to use it under water (in his bath), get it repaired several times, carry it across a thousand borders. It was famously immortalized on the back of his second album, *Songs from a Room*.

We know the picture: sitting in front of the Olivetti, a luminous blonde damsel is wrapped in the tiniest bath towel you have ever seen. She smiles from the back of an austere room. On a coffee table in the foreground lie a sun-bleached goat's skull and a chessboard. And that's everything a modern poet needs: a muse, a typewriter, and the reminder that death is among us. Countless memento mori and quite a few carpe diem are waiting in the wings.[30]

On that first day in London, Cohen also buys the blue Burberry raincoat that he will make one of the most famous overcoats in rock music. He can be seen wearing it in the sleet and snow of Montreal in 1965 (in *Ladies and Gentlemen . . . Mr. Leonard Cohen*) and, six years later, it reappears in "Famous Blue Raincoat" (1971), possibly the saddest ballad of all times. A side benefit to being a great poet: you can immortalize your wardrobe. Oscar Wilde would be proud.

For the moment, the raincoat (which will be stolen from Marianne's loft in New York, probably in 1970) protects the poet from the English weather. For Leonard's daily life is indeed made of rain, fog, and hard work. He has been at work on a semi-autobiographical novel for two years now and he constantly fills notebooks with poems. The remaining time is devoted to chasing girls and a long, bored wait for a Swinging London that is arguably slow in coming.

Surrounded by a few Canadian expatriates, by Jacob Rothschild (a future Lord), and by a girlfriend named Elizabeth (there's nothing like local colour[31]), Leonard explores the margins of the capital and the niches where the counterculture is hidden. It's a small affair, indeed: a few folk pubs and a Caribbean club called the All-Nighter, where you can dance to proto-ska and talk about the revolution in the smoke of Jamaican weed. A few dealers work the place, but there is mostly Michael X, an apologist of armed rebellion and disciple of Malcolm X. He prepares the fall of Trinidad in that nightclub and finds the Jewish poet who comes from the cold so funny he offers him a job in his future government, the only one suitable for a white man: permanent adviser to the Ministry of Tourism.[32]

Leonard works hard, though: four months after his arrival, he sends McClelland & Stewart a complete version of *The Spice-Box of Earth* and the first draft of his novel (only the third will get published, two years later). Defeated by a climate that he finds more pernicious than the Canadian winter, he was ready (after an extended pub crawl in the land of Yeats) to hit the road again. The anecdote is famous and he has told it many times.

April 1960. Rain and fog. Bank Street, London. Leonard Cohen has just had a tooth pulled out and he is in the financial district. To cash a cheque, he enters the Bank of Greece. There, he sees a clerk who is wearing improbable sunglasses "as a sign of silent protest against the weather." A brief dialogue between the poet and the cashier ensues:

> *The poet:* What is the weather like in Greece?
> *Tiresias the cashier (Greek accent):* It's spring.

Three words are enough to seal the poet's fate and three days later, Leonard Cohen is on his way to Athens. On the morning of the fifth day, he boards a ferry on the Aegean Sea. His destination: Hydra Island. After a five-hour ride, he disembarks eight centuries earlier in the land of gods.

HAPPY AS LEONARD IN HYDRA/THE GREEK MIRACLE

Anything that moves is white
a gull, a wave, a sail
and moves too purely to be aped.

— LEONARD COHEN, "HYDRA 1960"[33]

Hydra, a view of the town and harbour

Second stop: Hydra. The Greek word for "water." Even today it isn't hard to imagine the purity of the experience that the island offered a visitor in April 1960. Especially if that visitor was a poet fleeing the foggy greyness of London. The purity was — quite literally — elemental, for elements are what the island puts you in contact with: light, water, wind, and stone. Twenty-five years earlier Henry Miller had spoken of the "wild and naked perfection" of the island in *The Colossus of Maroussi*, and the expression rings true. The city of Hydra is a cubist proposal: a complex layout of white cubes of various sizes — the houses — on the side of a hill, like an amphitheatre facing the harbour. Everywhere you look, you see clear lines and intense colours. The whitewashed walls: white. The sea and the sky: blue. The poppies and roofs: red. For Leonard, it's love at first sight.

> The people, the architecture, the sky, the mules, the smells, life itself: everything you could see was beautiful.[34]

Very quickly, he will discover "a philosophical quality of the light" and claim that the island has purged him of his "Gothic insincerities."[35] We are inclined to believe him.

> It's white, you know. In Hydra everything is white. [. . .] Whitewashed walls, especially when they were illuminated by oil-lamps, give a pale light that makes everybody look great [with the] soft brilliance of billions of little crystals.[36]

A small detail: when Leonard Cohen took up residence there in April 1960 (first lodging with Australian authors George Johnston and Charmian Clift), nothing had been built on the island for a century, and half of the houses were abandoned or unoccupied. Tourism hardly existed, swimming pools and the jet-set crowd were almost unheard of. An inventory of Hydra in 1960 was therefore brief: two thousand inhabitants, a few dozen donkeys, cats galore, a couple of hotels, five or six bistros, a few grocery stores, countless wells, a handful of telephones, and only two hours of electricity per day — one in the morning, one in the evening. There was also a small sponge factory, but Hydra was mostly an island of fishermen and therefore of widows, black silhouettes that were hard to tell apart from popes or nuns. For there was a convent on Hydra (the convent of the Assumption of the Virgin) as well as several monasteries, among which (on the hilltop above the city) the monastery of

Profitis Ilias where the prophet Elijah had been waiting for Leonard Cohen since the eighteenth century. If you came from a metropolis, nights in Hydra were quite a shock. They engulfed you in darkness. Unless the moon was there, of course, in which case, everything was covered in white light. And everywhere, of course, was silence. The silence of the sea, obviously. The silence of the passing sails and of the grazing donkeys. The silence of the wind and of the crickets. And, at night, the more aggressive silence of cats in heat. "My Franciscan dream" is what Cohen would later call the island and, indeed, in places like Hydra, it is tempting to picture yourself as Saint Francis and, like him, to call the sun and the wind "brothers" and the moon "sister."[37]

Of course, on Hydra, the poet also met brothers and sisters of flesh and bones: the local bohemians and expatriate artists, often here for the cheap life or tax reasons. A happy crowd: Australian and Scandinavian novelists, English painters and Irish poets, Buddhist enthusiasts, former ballet dancers, gay couples and local eccentrics. The right people with whom to have a drink or two and talk art and redemption. Along with a contingent of wives, lovers, favourites, and mistresses, they all lived in houses without running water, enjoying a village life of sorts around the three cafés in the harbour — a very small world that Leonard had just joined with his Olivetti, his guitar, and a few letters of recommendation. In a matter of days, "Leonardos," as the locals would soon call him, was friends with the expatriate and with the local aristocracy, finding for example a friend for life in the eccentric millionaire George Lialios. He happily adopted the local daily routine of writing, sea-bathing, and assiduous hanging out in the Katsikas grocery store, but soon discovered he was also expected to join the elaborate game of musical chairs through which the couples were regularly rearranged. Flirtation in the land of Zeus — not a problem for the Don Juan of Montreal.

One of the first Jews on the island (and probably the first Canadian), Leonard also set up a simplified form of the Shabbat

Mitzvot: he lit candles on Friday nights, pronounced the blessings over his meal, and rested the following day. Unless he forgot of course. In the first few years, Hydra would thus be synonymous with a constant sanctification of life:

> Every corner, every lamp, everything was in its right place. Without running water, you had to mind every drop of water [. . .]. Every time you used the lamp, you knew it would have to be refilled and cleaned the next day.[38]

After enjoying the hospitality of George Johnston and Charmian Clift (the Australian godfathers of the expat crowd), Leonard soon rented his own house for four dollars a week. Five months after his arrival, convinced that his forefathers had made a "terrible mistake" in their choice of Canada, he took the dive and purchased a two-century-old house (house #764) on the Kamini hillside: three storeys, a dilapidated garden surrounded by high walls (not unlike the enclosed gardens where late medieval artists liked to place the Virgin Mary[39]), and a terrace overlooking a chapel devoted to Saint Tykhon. The price of the operation: $1,500 — less than ten times that sum in today's money. The date: September 19, 1960, two days before Leonard's twenty-sixth birthday. He now owned a little acre in the land of gods. Not bad for an unknown poet who had yet sold less than 500 books.[40]

MARIANNE OR THE NECESSARY ANGEL[41]

After sixty days on the island, a subtle transformation took place:

> I had never been warm before. I remember lying on a rock after I'd been there two months and feeling some interior sliver of ice melt from inside my bones. And I thought: God, the universe is benign![42]

As Lord Byron knew full well, the Greek sun cheers up even diehard romantics. In Hydra, a revigorated Cohen therefore felt he was in the right place to launch his great offensive against Hitler with *Flowers for Hitler* and an even greater one against his inner demons with *Beautiful Losers*. But before that, he had to set up a modus vivendi, which would basically last for the next five years: six to eight months in Greece (usually from spring to fall) followed by a long winter in Montreal to make a few bucks and "renew his neurotic affiliations" with Canada, the literary world and — incidentally — his mother. If we judge by Cohen's private correspondence, Masha had a thousand ways in those years of letting her son know that while he "lived it up in the pleasure spots of the modish world," she was — as Leonard ironically put it — "lonely, abandoned, depressed, persecuted, unloved, forgotten, ignored and penniless."[43] It's true that every year when Cohen came home, he wasn't sure whether he would simply find Masha's usual Jewish-mother act, or nurses in the house looking after her, or the house empty and his mother in the Allan Memorial Institute, receiving electric shock treatment.

But in Hydra, the magic of the island dissolved everything. In the first few months, however, an essential element was still missing: an angel. Cohen finds it in the person of Marianna Ihlen Jensen, a Norwegian model and young mother who has just been abandoned with her four-month-old son by her husband, novelist Axel Jensen, off schmoozing with an American painter ("So Long Marianne," act 1, so to speak). For Leonard, falling in love with a Scandinavian goddess by the Mediterranean Sea was too tempting a paradox to resist. His courtship was astute: he first played the saint. The first time he saw her alone, he invited the Virgin and Child (after seeing her in the Katsikas grocery store) to join his group of friends for a glass of wine on the terrace. That day — as she later confided to her biographer — Marianne danced her way back home, up the hill of Kala Pigada. Because the girl had to live alone with a baby, Leonard temporarily moved into her house. Like a knight servant, almost. And that fall, he took her to Oslo in the Karmann Ghia sports convertible that the young woman loved to drive very fast, and that Leonard liked to drive very slowly. Although a romance of sorts had already begun, they became an "official" couple only a year later when Marianne finally decided, at Leonard's insistence, to join the poet (who still had a girlfriend in Montreal) first to London, then back on Hydra, in the spring of 1962 for a delicate and actually fragile union that, according to Leonard, was always more like an amorous cohabitation than a husband-and-wife type relationship. At least that's how *he* saw it.

So a new story begins: Leonard, Marianne, and little Axel are in a white house on a beautiful island far, far away. In front of them: the sky, the sea, and the sun. Serious work can begin. But the shy angel Marianne loves to dance Greek dances and drinking retsina sometimes transforms her into a more daring angel. Not a problem at first for Leonard: he loves to watch blonde angels dance. It's a nice change from angels that fall.[44]

Leonard often extolled Marianne's beauty, so evident in the photographs, but he also praised "the infinite grace with which [she] inhabited a house," as though she carried within her a spiritual force that made their Hydra home a consecrated place. She placed a gardenia on the poet's table every morning, brought lamps in the evening and a snack at noon. As Catholic theologians explain, angels have no will of their own — their mission is to serve. Here, the angel doubles as muse and she takes it to heart to make the poet work. American feminists must have gnashed their teeth and they still do, perhaps with reason. But in 1962, on a Greek island, America and women's lib seemed very far away, and we can imagine that the muse and the poet were actually in love. Some of Leonard's poems and a couple of songs hint that the angel did not necessarily come home every night and that she occasionally became the muse of other poets, just as Leonard often disappeared with a passing model or a local beauty. But two decades later, the angels will take their revenge: twenty-seven of them will tie the poet to his table to make him pay his rent in song. It will then be his turn to serve.[45]

Leonard will later sum up that early life in Hydra in one sentence: "Everyone was beautiful, young, full of talent and covered with a kind of gold dust."[46] A photograph taken by James Burke on the terrace of the Douskos tavern in the fall of 1960 confirms that impression.[47] Among other things, it captures the bond that united Marianne and Leonard in the early stages of their relationship. Under a tree, a group of expatriates. Among them, Leonard Cohen, playing the guitar in an impeccable shirt with rolled up sleeves: the exemplary beatnik. To his right, a brunette (the novelist Charmian Clift), beautiful and intense: she is singing. To his left, a young man (the poet Michael W. Heckstall) impeccably styled — perfect khaki pants, suede desert boots, and Malcolm X horn-rimmed glasses: he is singing. A few steps away, a Germanic Adonis (photographer Klaus Merkel) wistfully looks into the distance while an oddball with a crazy beard and a well-tailored suit (painter David Groschen) is talking to a young woman sitting on the floor. At the surrounding tables, a dozen more people are enjoying drinks, among them the New Zealand novelist Bim Wallis in a suit and tie. A very elegant blonde is sitting on a low wall with her knees huddled against her and her eyes are fixed on Leonard, beaming with joy: Marianne. Whenever I see the picture, what comes to mind is Greek names — Aeolus, Ulysses, Achilles — not the actual names of the expatriate artists, and there's only one thing I want: to be able to join that Greek night and sing with them in the golden dust. In Hydra. In 1960.

Of course, the Hydra mystique, the songs that Marianne later inspired, and the woman's stunning beauty make it easy to idealize the couple, especially as Leonard himself had spread in early interviews an idyllic and somewhat sanitized version of their love affair. But careful examination of the evidence now available — among which are Leonard's very revealing private letters to Marianne (made public when auctioned at Christie's in June 2019) and Nick Broomfield's documentary *Marianne & Leonard: Words of Love* (2019)[48] — allows for a more realistic vision both of Marianne as a person (to a great extent a tragic figure, beset by depression and deep insecurity) and of her relationship with Leonard. Obviously, the couple's love was authentic and led to an immense tenderness that lasted a lifetime, but the intensity of their feelings varied and was rarely synchronous. After a couple of happy (though sometimes stormy) years, their relationship was plagued by what would now be called a classic case of codependency, with depressive and insecure personality traits on both sides, frequent infidelities (with the jealousy, humiliation, and pain that usually come with them), not to mention a series of abortions (illegal at the time). To a great extent, the main problem seems to have been Leonard's inability to either really commit or really leave. Whoever said the course of true love never did run smooth must have lived in Hydra — and probably knew Marianne and Leonard.

YOU SAY YOU WANT A REVOLUTION

Segue to an intense winter spent in Montreal to write plays with Layton for CBC TV (the project aborts) followed by a picaresque interlude in the Caribbean. It is the third stop on Cohen's journey: six weeks in Cuba from April to May 1961. Let us recall the context: *The Spice-Box of Earth*, announced almost a year before, is about to be published and Jack McClelland has high hopes that the volume will receive the country's most prestigious literary prize, the much-coveted Governor General's Award. But once a romantic poet, always a romantic poet, and Cohen apparently thinks that nothing can bring him more publicity than dying heroically. Lord Byron had gone to liberate Greece, García Lorca had fought in Spain, and in 1944 Hemingway had freed the Ritz bar from German occupation. It was Leonard's turn to follow those examples. "I wanted to kill or be killed" is how he explained it later.[49] After hundreds of hours spent in Montreal bars or on the terraces of Hydra arguing with bohemian colleagues about what socialist revolutions should or shouldn't be, it just so happened that a real one had occurred in Cuba. And bam! Leonard was in La Havana, ready for six weeks of political tourism, secretly persuaded that the events were unfolding for the sole benefit of his personal instruction.[50] Once on the island, he grows a beard, writes poems and a parody of Raymond Chandler. For local colour, he also wears army fatigues and a military beret. À la Fidel Castro — not a very good idea. Every night, in bars, brothels, and the last open casinos, he discusses the vices and virtues of communism with the local artists and a few American leftists that are still around. Not a very good idea, either: an American invasion seems imminent and everyone is getting very nervous. Soon, el gringo gets arrested by a Castroist patrol who, quite understandably, takes him for an American spy. He knows only three words in Spanish ("Amigo del Pueblo"), but repeats them a lot, so he ends up fraternizing with the patrol over a bottle of rum. The following day, he is summoned to the Canadian embassy where his mother has left a message. She is very worried. In the wake of this, the inevitable happens: the famous Bay of Pigs Invasion. A fiasco for Kennedy, a triumph for Castro, and a point of no return for the population, half of which suddenly wants to leave the island. Leonard understands that this is no longer the best time to discuss politics in bars, but at the airport, the police think he has a fake passport and Leonard is arrested again. During an unrelated scuffle, he escapes surveillance, jumps on a plane to Miami, then another one to Montreal, where he lands just in time for his new book's launching party. The Cuban interlude is over, and Leonard has a thousand stories to tell.

In La Havana, he had written a mock-political manifesto for a Canadian revolution called "The Only Tourist in Havana Turns His Thoughts Homewards." His program? To export snow to Third World countries, to bomb the White House with asbestos, and be extremely nice to Black people because they will soon seize power.[51] Not exactly realpolitik, and Leonard has not exactly converted to socialism, either. But he has made secret appointments for further occasions to hear bullets fly, namely the Yom Kippur War in October 1973 and the recording of his fifth album in February 1977 with a decidedly ill-mooded Phil Spector. Right now, he has a book to promote.

CHAPTER 3

TV TZADIK AND POP POETRY

PORTRAIT OF LEONARD AS A MODERN SAINT
1961–1966

Leonard Cohen, Montreal, November 1964

RIMBAUD AND THE RABBIS: THE SPICE-BOX OF EARTH

While still an amateur in politics, Cohen joins the rank of professionals of literature with *The Spice-Box of Earth*. In this soberly
written but admirably manufactured second book, the poet seeks
to carry out in poetry the task that rabbi Marc-Alain Ouaknin
considers the mission of the Kabbalist: to see the invisible and hear
the ineffable.[1] Throughout the volume, the poems — surrounded
by typographical quirks in red, gold, and blue and by thirteen delicate illustrations by the Canadian designer Frank Newfeld — try to
capture the most delicate and the lightest things: the bonds of love

and slavery that unite a man and a kite, the grace of a morning prayer that makes a butterfly follow you all day, the lightness of Hasidic dance, and (of course) the thousand ways in which undressing a woman is a major victory over darkness.[2] Everywhere, the poet tries to unravel the riddle of the impalpable, as in the nine words of this delicate haiku:

> Silence
> and a deeper silence
> when the crickets hesitate.[3]

Nine words. Nine words to remind us that it's fundamentally impossible to pursue one thing without catching the opposite: the crickets' song is an entry into silence and silence an entry into the crickets' song. Nine words also to help us perceive that when the crickets hesitate, the world hesitates with them. A cool little poem.

Elsewhere, Cohen speculates about the meeting of mist and hill, of breeze and hawk, of lover and lover, and ten years before his first serious forays into Buddhism, he comes up with a Zen-like answer to all queries: nothing to grasp.[4] Everywhere, the volume explores the paradoxical sensuality of the immaterial world and, for this, *The Spice-Box of Earth* proposes a new poetic persona, very different from the decadent romantic of the first volume: the poet is now a saint who embraces the energies of the world without trying to appropriate them. Hence the beautiful title of the collection, and its reference to the Jewish ritual that closes the Sabbath. After the dinner, observant Jews pass around a box filled with spices so that each guest returns to the secular world fully aware of the fragrant richness of Heaven and the benevolence of God. If Cohen's spice box is not made of silver (as is customary), but of "earth," it may be to suggest that what is most precious is what isn't worth a thing: the ground beneath our feet.[5]

OPIUM AND THE SHAPE OF CLOUDS

But the volume is not awarded the Governor General's Award that Cohen and his publisher expected, and Leonard feels betrayed. He leaves the country again after a brief reading tour on the East Coast and a stay in Oslo with Marianne. But not before crossing paths with a sulfurous Scottish junkie novelist, the quasi-beat Alexander Trocchi. In May 1961, the author of *Cain's Book* happened to be on the run from the American police (he had sold heroin to teenagers) and he had to be smuggled into Canada and out to Europe. Layton and Leonard gave him shelter for a couple of rocky days that will include Cohen's first contact with opium. After sampling the drug left behind by the junkie novelist, he suddenly went blind and collapsed in the middle of traffic in downtown Montreal. Very impressed by the way Trocchi took out his syringes in public places (he had just shot up heroin live on American TV), Cohen saw in him the inverted image of the saint and wrote a poem in the form of a prayer to Trocchi that made the holy drug addict an intercessor and dispenser of graces like the Virgin Mary. Its title:

> Alexander Trocchi,
> Public Junkie,
> Priez pour nous![6]

Back in Greece, drugs were present as well, but they were used in a gentler way. A light opiate tea was made with poppy petals and there was always someone who smuggled in a chunk of hashish from Turkey, where Leonard had travelled in the summer of 1960. The two most addictive substances, however, were bought over the counter in Athens pharmacies: one was Dexedrine (an amphetamine that kills your appetite and helps you work for days without sleep), the other Mandrax (a barbiturate that slows down your system). For at least a decade, Cohen would use both — as well as many other substances, from pot to acid to opiates — with a thousand goals: to regulate his moods, stimulate his imagination, work without end, or just clear his mind. As he often explained, a delicate stomach cut short all prolonged experimentation with heroin, so he never had the credentials of a true junkie. He later paid a heavy price, however, when he stopped taking amphetamines.[7]

For the time being, it's the summer of 1961 and Leonard returns to live an apparently idyllic life on the island (Marianne joins him only the following spring) around a trinity of sea bathing, bouzouki, and bohemia. Several poems celebrate the infinite lightness of the days spent on the island around 1962: one evokes butterflies and wasps, the wind playing in lemon trees, and an "army of ants" around the bare feet of his muse, as well as ringing bells that sanctify the space.[8] And, across the street from his terrace, Leonard could indeed see the Agios Tychon chapel and even hear the popes singing when the popes were there and smell their incense if the wind blew in the right direction. In such circumstances, how could every day not be an invitation to sainthood? Youth, beauty, and love must have made a victory over the gravity of things seem possible and, definitely tempted by the lighter side, the poet introduced regular periods of fasting into his daily regime, no doubt facilitated by the appetite suppressant he was taking, as well as a joyful vegetarianism that will later make him say he was "the kind of vegetarian that only eats roses."[9]

With a few friends, among whom were Steve Sanfield, George Lialios, and Axel Jensen, he also created an informal esoteric Abbey of Thelema where the divinatory book of ancient China called *I Ching* was studied alongside the Kabbalah and the *Tibetan Book of the Dead*, often considered at the time as a gnostic manual for living the great inner experience. Thanks to a (still legal) vial of LSD brought from the Sandoz laboratories, the disciples added practice to theory and it's fair to say that both the *I Ching* and the acid had a great impact on Leonard.[10] According to orientalist Thomas Cleary, the divinatory book of ancient China helps you "to read the universe, to tame the chaos and to marry universal harmony: opening the book is opening the world."[11]

For almost fifteen years, Leonard would use the book to guide him in small and big decisions, with the hope it might free him from ego-based living. But with its poetical Taoist answers, perhaps what the *I Ching* mostly taught him is to pay attention to what is most subtle in life: the constant tiny changes that characterize all phenomena. Combined with LSD, sky observation, and its ever-changing clouds, Chinese wisdom may indeed (one imagines) have enabled exciting forays into the visible world and the invisible one, and soon, Leonard would claim to feel "the molecules dancing on the hill."[12]

But work was what really gave Leonard's life its tempo. Despite many visits (Ginsberg and Harry Rasky dropped by in 1960, as did beat poets Harold Norse and Kenneth Koch, followed by Masha Cohen — who visited her son in 1962 — and Irving Layton, not to mention an endless retinue of friends and cousins), Leonard put in a minimum of four hours of work every day. The core and kernel of his days on Hydra was therefore spent tied to his Olivetti (in intense periods, from morning to night). And the discipline paid off: the poet completed *The Favourite Game* in 1963 and *Flowers for Hitler* the following year. He wrote *Beautiful Losers* over two eight-month periods in 1964 and 1965, and by late 1966 a new volume, *Parasites of Heaven*, was in bookstores. Not bad for a vegetarian expatriate. As though the Greek gods did not hold it against Leonardos to write so little about Greece and so much about Montreal.

PORTRAIT OF THE ARTIST AS A YOUNG EGOIST: *THE FAVOURITE GAME* (1963)

Completed after three years of labour during a short return to London at the height of the "twist" dance craze in the winter of 1962, *The Favourite Game* is indeed set in Canada and, in many ways, it is Leonard's farewell to Westmount. The book chronicles the formative years of Lawrence Breavman, a young Jewish poet whose life seems very similar to Leonard's with a sheltered childhood, an overprotective mother, a dead father, and a taste for hypnosis and women. Feminine first names abound (Bertha, Lisa, Tamara, and Shell) and the hero's aspirations are the same as Leonard's: to charm the world, make the poet a sacred figure again and contemplate the naked body of every woman he meets.

It is therefore tempting to read the book as a roman à clef; we can easily recognize Mort Rosengarten here, Anne Sherman and Freda Guttman there. We can also enjoy how artfully the novel resurrects the past with the feel of lived experience and can see *The Favourite Game*, as contemporary critics had done, as the '60s equivalent of James Joyce's *A Portrait of the Artist as a Young Man*. But to leave it at that would be to miss the point.

The strength of the book, which gives its enduring freshness, is the impression on every page of plunging into the very heart of life, an impression given because of the original novelistic form — a rapid succession of short scenes that erupt before our eyes — and a vigorous writing that captures existence as it occurs: sensual, surprising, and always concrete. The result? Some of Cohen's most beautiful pages.[13]

There is also the central but hidden theme of the book: election. All through the book, Breavman keeps discovering that he is chosen because, firstly, he is Jewish and has received the Law, but mostly because he is an artist and has a certain power over the Logos. He speaks, and things happen: a little girl falls from a tree, people stop and listen, women take off their clothes. The hero remains suspended, however, between the thrill of that election, the constant temptation to exploit it for selfish purposes, and a growing sense of complete failure. In the story, the talented young man accumulates mistakes: he betrays himself, disrupts everybody's life and the narrator, leaning over his shoulder like a disappointed but compassionate angel, cannot stop the waste. It's only at the end of the book that we understand the title's double meaning: we have seen a seducer play his "favourite game," seduction, but also a hunter pursuing his favourite "game," women, himself becoming a prey in the process — the prey of karma.

To the question "Is Leonard a good student?" asked thirty-two years later by a French journalist to Joshu Sasaki Roshi, eighty-first patriarch in the lineage of Rinzai Zen, the master answered, with a glass of ginger brandy in his hand, "An excellent student, because he embraces both the negative and the positive."[14] This is the very basis of Zen: refusing the illusion that life is a buffet table where we may take what we like and leave what we don't. *The Favourite Game* already illustrates this idea, reminding us that each moment of existence, whether banal or glorious, demands our full attention and our courageous assent. Each moment is the moment of our election, something the hero never learns.

Despite a few good reviews, the novel sells moderately (a thousand copies in Canada and only four times that number in the United States) and — in line with a still prevalent Canadian prudery — was chastised for its explicit sex scenes.[15] Angered by the condescension of some critics, a nicely besuited Leonard, with a quasi mop-top haircut, put on a show for CBC Television where he denounced an "ignorance as vast as the country," reminding that success is "obscene" and redefining the poet's role as "to spread trouble and chaos and depress everyone."[16] He simply could not understand why people didn't get the humour in scenes like the one in which an autistic genius-child gets crushed by a combine-harvester while he's off killing mosquitoes in a marsh.[17] Leonard is a joker, all right. It's just not always easy to appreciate the thousand hilarious ways in which he's not funny.

POET OF THE MASS MEDIA

In 1964, the novel wins the Prix littéraire du Québec ($4,000). One of the country's most influential critics explains that:

> Cohen is potentially the most important writer Canadian poetry has produced since 1950 — not merely the most talented, but also the most professionally committed to making the most of his talent.[18]

It is true that, unlike many writers, Leonard enthusiastically accepted the society of the spectacle and its challenges. He saw mass media (particularly TV and radio) as allies in his career plan and as a kind of modern agora, where the collective imagination is forged and the Zeitgeist made visible. Like Oscar Wilde before him, he wanted to assail the public space and be a trickster-poet — one that would speak to and for his time and hold up a mirror to it. His yearly visits to Canada were always moments of performance where, with a little help from the CBC, his publishers, and various cultural institutions, he created a public persona: "Leonard Cohen," a televised poet and agent provocateur, the eternal enfant terrible of Canadian letters. It should be noted that in the early '60s, perhaps due to the beat generation, poets were fashionable creatures that got interviewed in *Playboy* and TV talk shows.

When he was invited to symposiums or conferences — for example a government-sponsored conference on the arts (Toronto, May 1961), a CBC conference on the culture crisis with Romain Gary (Paris, November 1962), a symposium on the poet status in Quebec (October 1963), a Jewish Public Library symposium on the future of Judaism (Montreal, December 1963), or on Jewish writers and the English language (June 1964) — Leonard made sure he always held the most outrageous position.[19] On television, he was the ideal guest on talk shows who openly flirted with female hosts and always threw in a couple of shock phrases to keep things entertaining and launch a few cultural wars. Wars against the pusillanimity of his peers and the narrow moralism of the critics ("nobody in this country can judge my work"). Wars against the sterility of academism and the provincialism of Canada ("Canada is a dying animal; I will not be attached to a dying animal"). Wars against the spiritual poverty of contemporary synagogues ("In any junkie's kitchen, there is a greater contact with the spiritual than in any given synagogue of the North American continent"). Wars against a community that doesn't make the sacred the centre of all concerns ("The God that we venerate is the ugly distortion of a sublime idea. It must be attacked and destroyed"). And of course, wars against this all-too-mundane world where everyone is not called Leonard Cohen ("today more than ever, I want enemies").[20] So much so that each time the poet visited Canada, it was literally impossible not to have heard of him, especially if you hung out in the right Montreal bars.

The poet was also backed by a very efficient publicity machine: his back cover blurbs praised "the most shocking novelist of his generation" and promised "great sexual frankness" and, like Oscar Wilde allegedly declaring "his genius" at the American customs, Leonard never shied away from singing his own praise, as on the back of *Flowers for Hitler*:

> I say that no book like this has ever been written in Canada, either in prose or in verse. I ask only that this volume be placed in the hands of my generation. It will be recognized.

The volume covers had cool designs, and often exploited (and fed) the author's public image as romantic hero and pop poet, hence a triple portrait of Leonard on the cover of *Selected Poems* (to better show his hollowed face and hip haircut); hence a Lord Byronish Leonard caught in suave melancholy on the cover of *Parasites of Heaven* or a young girl undressing on a bright orange background (on the softcover US edition of *The Favourite Game*). An outré project (thankfully cancelled) for the cover of *Flowers for Hitler* (1964) was a naked woman's breast with two photos of Cohen as nipples.[21]

Each time, the books were launched with a lot of promotion and publicity (interviews, lavish launch cocktails, advertising posters, excerpts published in men's magazines). In five years, Cohen crossed the country four times for reading tours: for *The Spice-Box of Earth* in May 1961; for *The Favourite Game* in November 1963; in February 1964 with a jazz trio on West Coast campuses and nightclubs; and in November of the same year for *Flowers for Hitler* (this time followed by a camera). The winter of 1966 saw one last tour of bookstores, coffee houses, and nightclubs in Alberta, and this time Cohen had also brought his acoustic guitar. Each reading tour was a foretaste of rock-and-roll life, with train stations, hotel rooms, taxi rides, late-night cafés, and — presumably — quite a lot of one-night stands. To boost his fame, the National Film Board of Canada financed a one-hour documentary (shown first on television in 1965, then in theatres) and Leonard was present on a second collective record (*Canadian Poets 1*, 1966) which billed him as "one of the most sensual and lyrical love poets of our time." The result was that, by the mid-'60s, Leonard was a national celebrity and a pop poet, what a critic then called a "Jet-Set Mahatma," who claimed in poems that he "had loved more than a hundred women but never told the same lie twice" and sometimes, on stage, invited the women in the audience to join him in his hotel room (as he did in Vancouver in 1966[22]). That reputation as a seducer was quickly integrated into his public persona and, soon enough, the poet had groupies waiting everywhere he went. But that was only fair — the poet was a star.[23]

MR. COOL COHEN & CO.

Filmed in black and white with a cool jazz soundtrack, *Ladies and Gentlemen . . . Mr. Leonard Cohen* follows the poet during his October 1964 reading tour in Montreal, Ottawa, and Toronto, and in his "civilian" life the following month. The goal is to inform Canada: a poet-hero in a dark raincoat circulates among them, and he adds a *beat* edge to a unrepentant practice of romanticism.[24] We see him walk through Montreal in the snow, write in hotel rooms, look pensive in taxicabs, sign books for smiling girls, question the *I Ching*, play the harmonica to a dog, and seek shelter in trendy cafés where, half metaphysical poet, half private eye, he defines late-night drinking as a courageous act of protest against sleep.

We also see the great performer the poet has become. The opening scene, filmed on Sunday, October 30, 1966, in the main auditorium at McGill University, shows how Leonard turns a poetry reading into a countercultural stand-up comedy act. À la Lenny Bruce.

He enters the stage to audience applause, *Flowers for Hitler* in his hand. He is stylish if nothing else: a leather jacket, what *Time* called a "Julius Caesar" haircut,[25] and a tie and shirt in clever disagreement. He faces the crowd and speaks: "The other time I was in corridors such as these was in the Verdun mental hospital in Montreal." Laughter in the audience. A silence. "I was visiting." Laughter again.

A story follows, in deadpan voice, that doesn't seem entirely fictional[26]: in search of the cafeteria, the poet, who is visiting a friend, gets lost in the corridors and finds himself face to face with two male nurses who mistake him for an escaped patient and chase him through the establishment. Interrupted thirteen times by laughter, the story closes with Leonard returning to his friend, who has eaten his jacket.[27]

With expert timing and just the right mix of insolence and self-deprecation, Cohen's act is quite good indeed and, beneath its obvious humour, culturally resonant. In the budding days of anti-psychiatry, it all comes across as a comment on the asylum as an institution and the social role of the madman.[28] The story blurs barriers between madness and sanity when the supposedly sane guards behave like madmen, while the supposedly mad friend is reasonable enough to prefer the asylum to college (but mad enough to eat a jacket). As for the poet, Cohen makes him a kind of go-between between madness and wisdom. He thus leads the audience exactly where he wants to take them: into the universe of alienation and tyranny of his new volume, *Flowers for Hitler*. Three minutes into the reading, the score is 1–0 for the Broadway Jew.

At the end of the film, however, Leonard warns us against the showman in him. A sequence shows him in the editing room, watching the rushes of the documentary. On the screen, his filmed self is taking a bath in a hotel bathroom and traces a Latin formula on the tiled bathroom wall, a distant memory from his classes in business law: "Caveat emptor" (i.e., Buyer, beware!). In the editing room, Leonard explains that, for a brief moment, he wanted to be a double agent, both the ally of the filmmakers in their construction of the poet as romantic hero and modern saint, and the ally of the viewer, whom he warns against that fabricated image. The scene, he said, was "not entirely devoid of the con." Or "of the Cohen." Or what you will. Not that anyone was taking a Jew who gives flowers to Hitler entirely seriously.

FLOWERS FOR HITLER

An inverted image of the previous collection, *Flowers for Hitler* proposes a descent into hell after the magic of Hasidism. It is hard to believe that this consistently dark book was written on a terrace near the Aegean Sea. Leonard evokes the death camps, but also the grip that Hitler and the Nazi mythology have taken on his mind. As he explained to Eli Mandel, those poems were written with a view to freeing himself from the inner concentration camp that the awareness of the Holocaust had created in him. There, he was being tortured and devoured by Nazi devils:

> Hitler the brain mole looks out of my eyes
> Goering boils ingots of gold in my bowels.[29]

So Cohen confesses: his body is in pain and his soul contaminated by evil. The Third Reich has inflicted metaphysical damage on our souls and we are now condemned to see the world through the eyes of Hitler the brain mole, whose kingdom is within us. The collection ceaselessly returns to the most atrocious evocations: human soap, lampshades made of human skin, and the poet declares his mind "stuffed with bodies tangled closer than snakes."[30]

Let us recall the context: it's only two decades after the Shoah, the Eichmann trial is still in the news as well as Hannah Arendt's concept of "the banality of evil" and, a few years before, Adorno had famously declared that writing poetry after Auschwitz was "barbaric."[31] In that context, Cohen's book is transgressive in many ways — not only is it poetry after Auschwitz but also poetry *about* Auschwitz and, in one of the pieces, Cohen even perversely rhymes "Rimbaud" and "Dachau."[32] The volume recurrently argues that there was nothing special about the inhumanity of the Nazis, who were in many respects profoundly like us.[33] What is more, the Nazis were now everywhere, having established a regime of universal guilt: a Third Reich in our souls. Hence, at the onset of the book, a Baudelairian interpellation of the "hypocritical reader," fellow, and brother of the torturers who is asked to imitate the poet and confess that evil is lodged in him as well:

> I do not know if the world has lied
> I have lied
> I do not know if the world has conspired against love
> I have conspired against love
> The atmosphere of torture is no comfort
> I have tortured
> Even without the mushroom cloud
> Still I would have hated.[34]

On the opening page of the collection, a "Note on the Title" explains why the poet wrote the book: to use poetry as a weapon against political evil — to find "sunshine for Napoleon," "walls for Genghis Khan," and "flowers for Hitler." But the project goes awry and, quite predictably, the flowers offered to Hitler become flowers of evil as the disgust of concentration camps spreads to all spheres of existence. The book itself actually seems in a bad mood, and disgust (at Canadian politics, cancer-eaten bodies, eels smashed against rocks, hard drugs, mysterious fat women shaking their bodies to terrorize thin girls) is a recurring theme. Values are reversed — fair is foul, the sinister is funny, and the coarse is poetic. Men admire their reflection in bowls of soup, women hate their bodies, and the poet himself wishes to annihilate his style. He is portrayed burning his own books, "happy as a Gestapo Brute."[35]

Three years later, in one of the first academic responses to his work, Cohen will be placed by Sandra Djwa among what she calls the "black romantics" alongside Baudelaire, Lautréamont, and Jean Genet,[36] and surely, the blackness of the volume is undeniable, although what is darkest is often just Cohen's humour. With hindsight, the book seems to indicate that the poet's inner landscape was indeed darkening and, from one poem to the next, Cohen often seems trapped in suffering, something also apparent in his private correspondence of those years. Overuse of amphetamines as well as his flirtation with opium may not necessarily be unconnected to that mood. Of course, this is not the last time he flirts with an abyss.

POP POETRY AND TV TZADIK

A question remains: what is this early poetic work really worth in retrospect? Arguably, in the mid-'60s, Cohen had not yet decided what kind of poet he wanted to be. In the meantime, he often seemed to be embracing the field of all possible poetries, fluctuating from one poem to the next between exquisite lyricism, prosaic confession, black humour, and satire. Which means that those early collections are not easy to read from cover to cover and may seem to lack coherence to the untrained eye. And yet, between 1961 and 1964, a few key themes emerge with increasing clarity, forming the kernel of Cohen's future vision: sacred sexuality, failure as a moment of grace, the necessary struggle with darkness, and the sanctity of the poet. The author also already uses two very authentic voices: that of the provocateur poet, who sings drugs, sex, the Self, and the Holocaust (sometimes in the same poem),[37] and that of the practical theologian of love. Both voices are saintly: the holy blasphemer versus the holy lover and although some critics considered the first voice amoral and off limits (while others encouraged it[38]), everyone praised the second voice, which undoubtedly gave birth to some of Leonard's most beautiful poems. The incantatory "Two Went to Sleep," a list of the dreams made by two sleeping lovers who sleep side by side but cannot meet in their dreams, is a good example, as is "You Have the Lovers," an allegorical presentation of physical love as a century-long ritual during which two lovers locked in a room join the purity of vegetal life.[39]

As for the gesture that underlies the work, Leonard seems at this stage to have a triple program that somehow connects him to *beat* poetry or to the future Liverpool poets: 1) to extract the poem from avant-garde magazines and throw it back into the world; 2) to speak again (after the parenthesis of modernism) of the ordinary life of the heart; 3) to re-enchant the social space and make the poet a saint. But in the mid-'60s, after existentialism and the Holocaust and with the reign of mass media, the question seemed pertinent: how can you be a saint in the era of the spectacle? Rimbaud wants poets to be seers, television wants soundbites. So Cohen chose to obey both injunctions: to be a seer and a clown. To do this, he turns to a very old way of pouring holiness into the world: that of the Tzadik, the Hasidic saint who danced in public and practised healing through joy.[40] And Leonard's many provocations can indeed be seen as stemming from a similar logic: the transgression of taboos was the poet's shock tactic to disrupt the seriousness that still permeated official culture. His aim: to awaken the audience and bring a smile to their face.

When advocating LSD in a mainstream magazine or proclaiming his wish to take over a small country to conduct life-size poetic experiments on television, Cohen is not that different from the tzadiks of old: he dances in public to re-enchant social space. He invents the TV Tzadik and creates scandals to re-awaken our sense of the sacred.[41]

Another conceptual figure that seems to have inspired Leonard at the time is the Nietzschean hero who declares wars and inverts values. Nietzsche famously philosophized with a hammer; Leonard applies the technique to poetry: he uses poetical hammers — his poems and media interventions — to check how hollow the Canadian poetic doxa rings, blaspheming as he did against a series of orthodoxies: the modernist retreat into impersonality, the highbrow respectability of Canadian letters, the moral severity of post-Holocaust Judaism . . . For blasphemy, as Leonard quickly found out, was often the most direct way to awaken the dozing sanctity of things.

And sanctity was indeed Leonard's obsession in the mid-'60s. Still in a TV interview, he explained that during his nocturnal peregrinations, when he was not in the right mood to bless the entire city, he sometimes stood in front of buildings and declared the inhabitants divorced. On certain evenings (so he claimed), he saw men and women run out of houses. The poet as diabolus in the literal sense: he who disjoins. He had warned in *The Favourite Game*, "There's something special about my voice. When I speak, things happen." They will no longer stop happening.[42]

WELL LOOKS AT DONKEY, DONKEY LOOKS AT WELL

Playing the saint in Montreal and the hermit in Hydra: such was Leonard's binary rhythm in the early to mid-'60s. Now, on Hydra there were donkeys, there were wells, and there was Steve Sanfield

Douskos Taverna in Hydra

who was not yet the "master of American haiku" nor the disciple of Joshu Sazaki Roshi he would become later, but already a friend of Leonard's and a student of eastern philosophies and modified states of consciousness. It just so happened that a donkey, a well, and a thirst for the absolute were the exact ingredients of a famous koan recorded nine centuries earlier in the *Shoyoroku* or "Book of Serenity," which Sanfield showed Leonard.[43] The koan in question consisted of a dialogue between the Chinese master Sozan and a disciple about a donkey looking at the bottom of a well, an image in no way exotic on Hydra. Of course, Zen teaches you are both the donkey *and* the well. What the animal sees at the bottom (his reflection? a black hole? Buddha nature?) matters little as long as it peers down long enough for the well to look back. That's the lesson of all koans: look at the abyss of your true nature long enough for your ego to dissolve, and stop being as stubborn as a donkey.

Now, during that last year in Greece — 1965 — Leonard was a little like that Zen donkey. He was considering the enigma of a career that he could not decide was successful or a failure. Now thirty, he began to make appraisals. On the one hand, he owned a very good blue raincoat, an excellent typewriter, and a house with whitewashed walls. He had adopted an angel, waged wars against critics, and worked hard to inform Canada that it had an exiled son, and that this son was a Jewish poet named Leonard Cohen. On the other hand, he sold at best a few thousand volumes of each publication, not nearly enough to live the kind of life he aspired to. Every year he had to apply for grants, get his books into competitions, borrow money from his uncles, accept media appearances, or sell his manuscripts to university archives (as he then began to do).

After five years like this, he is now tired and discovers that something painful gnaws at him. The appetites that have driven him to become a poet — the hunger for love and applause, for beauty and spiritual enlightenment — do not abate, but intensify. Through a series of inexhaustible questions (is this the right island? the right companion? the right profession? the right life?), the flipside of existence is again revealed to him. The obscure part that lurks beneath the alibi of the golden poet covered in golden dust: the first intuition of something he would later call his "invincible defeat."[44] In plain words, he has a nervous breakdown.

So back to the donkey, the well, and the answers that must be found in the black holes that yawn inside you. Cohen knows from the Torah (from the story of Balaam in the Book of Numbers, to be precise) that donkeys have a special talent for seeing angels.[45] Day after day on the island, the poet must have wondered what angels exactly these donkeys of Hydra could see when they stayed for hours peering into the bottom of the wells. Perhaps this is how he decided to imitate them and bend over his own well (an inner well, of course) so as to hasten an angelic revelation, which explains his next move: to write a novel about beautiful losers.

THE HALLUCINATED MASTERPIECE: *BEAUTIFUL LOSERS* (1966)

Leonard began that second novel in the midst of a violent attack of black bile, probably in the early summer of 1964. The Beatles had just charmed the world when he settled on his terrace with his Olivetti, his transistor radio tuned to a country-and-western station, and a firm intention to fight back. Also close at hand were a rare book about a seventeenth-century Iroquois saint called Kateri Tekakwitha (borrowed from an Indigenous friend) and a 1940s superhero comic book called *Blue Beetle*:

> I had to write that book. I was at the end. I hated myself. I said if I couldn't even write, it wasn't worth living. So I sat down at my desk and said I would use only the books that were in front of me.[46]

Cohen apparently worked on the book from May to December 1964, eight months for a first draft. After the ritual winter stay in Canada, revisions took eight more months and Leonard grew a moustache that made him look like a Greek shopkeeper. By May 1965, after the sun had melted his only Ray Charles record and the wind had blown a first version of the manuscript into the streets of Hydra, the books in front of him had indeed turned into a strange literary object that would soon make Jack McClelland fear censorship. Leonard himself later reclaimed its baroque quality on the cover blurb:

> A love story, a psalm, a Black Mass, a monument, a satire, a prayer, a shriek, a road map through the wilderness, a joke, a tasteless affront, an hallucination, a bore, an irrelevant display of diseased virtuosity, a Jesuitical tract, an Orange sneer, a scatological Lutheran extravagance, in short a disagreeable religious epic of incomparable beauty.

Beautiful Losers is all those things and more, but first and foremost, it is a great novel that grips the reader and opened new territory for Canadian fiction — something that Canadian critics took a while (actually, a couple of decades) to notice.

Set in the Montreal of seedy movie theatres, pinball arcades, and Greek restaurants, *Beautiful Losers* is about a triangle of hallucinated characters: a constipated, cuckolded historian locked in his underground apartment, his young hypersexual Indian wife Edith (who eventually commits suicide by sitting under the elevator the husband uses to go home), and their guru and shared lover, a very Nietzschean Québécois separatist MNA called F. The book follows this trio's tribulations and their fascination with the seventeenth-century Iroquois virgin-martyr Saint Kateri Tekakwitha. As the story proceeds, we discover how the three friends interpret their torn lives in the light of the martyr's passion and how, driven by the iconoclastic desire to "fuck a saint," they write the hagiography of the Virgin Kateri. To a great extent, the novel is the narrative of an initiation that shows how the mentor and quasi-Zen master

F. guides his disciple (even after his death) through an astounding spiritual and erotic crisis.

Divided into three sections, the novel begins with the historian's diary that chronicles his growing love for the Iroquois Virgin and the progress of his madness. Section Two is F.'s spiritual will, written in the psychiatric hospital where he is confined after setting off bombs in Montreal, and a short third part merges all the characters into an allegorical and hallucinatory finale where the goddess Isis disguised as a Hollywood starlet invades the sky and dissolves the whole of Montreal into a vast mystical epiphany. The book also contains an embedded second novel: the fragmented narrative in thirty-four episodes of the life, passion, and miracles of Saint Kateri, both a historical account and a religious fable that mixes Christian hagiography and the aesthetics of cruelty.[47]

Two forces compete in the text: one is centrifugal and works at exploding the novel — it ceaselessly interrupts the narration with advertisements, comic strips, or excerpts from Greek phrase books;[48] the other is centripetal and constantly refocuses our attention on religious motifs: miracles, apparitions of saints, and goddesses taken from Christian, Iroquois, or Pop mythologies.[49] Thanks to genuine dramatic suspense and captivating dialogue, the book is gripping and wonderfully written throughout. In short, a very good novel.

In the spring of 1966, the book release (once again a superbly designed volume[50]) came with a vast promotional operation: interviews in the press and on television, a string of public readings, and a giant launch cocktail party where three hundred guests from the literary and media elite had cocktails and schmoozed between immense posters of the poet.

Most of the publicity, however, was generated by the outraged reviews. While American critics praised a novel they often compared to James Joyce and William Burroughs, and interpreted it in the context of pop art and psychedelic drugs, Canadian reviewers were (for a change) shocked and strangely blind to the book's humour. To be sure, some scenes were not to everyone's taste. A sadomasochistic orgy with Hitler and a flying Danish vibrator? The historian exploding a whole box of fireworks in his underground apartment for his own private apocalypse? Detailed evocations of Kateri's rapes and of the martyr's mortifications? Surely Mr. Cohen was kidding. Hence a lapse into hyperbole: "the most repulsive book ever written in Canada," "verbal masturbation," "excremental vision," or, in more nuanced fashion, a "failure" that is also "the most interesting book of the year."[51]

Why critics failed to acknowledge or even notice the book's mysticism, its magnificent prayers,[52] or exquisite poetical scenes like the banquet where Saint Kateri spills a glass of wine and the stain spreads to the entire tablecloth, the guests' bodies, and the whole landscape, even the moon, remains a mystery to this day. Unless, of course, we remember how morally self-righteous Canadian institutions still are. With today's dark reign of woke hypocrisy, the book would not even get published.

A Nietzschean novel in many ways, *Beautiful Losers* confronts its heroes with the absolute, and insists that all absolutes (God included) are always abysses of sorts. And in front of an abyss, of course, there are only two solutions: to jump or to step back. Nietzsche, as we know, chose to jump, as did Cohen's heroes in the novel. As for Leonard, his response to his own novel will be Nietzschean, too. Soon, he will follow the injunction that the German philosopher had stolen from the Greek poet Pindar: "Become what you are." In 1966, Cohen will indeed start bringing his guitar to poetry readings. More radical changes will follow. But before that, one last miracle must take place.

LEONARD PLAYS ICARUS

Before he left Greece, Leonard — like Icarus before him — had to confront the sun. Weakened by long periods of fasting, extensive amphetamine use, and eight months of intense work of often fifteen to twenty hours a day, the novelist was hit by a severe sunstroke, probably in May or early June of 1965.

A sunstroke is a commonplace occurrence in a Mediterranean country, but it's still an encounter with an element: the fire in the sky. It's just a matter of scale: Greek heroes and philosophers fall into the Etna or burn their wings when they fly too close to the Sun — expatriate poets have sunstrokes.

May 1965. In London, the Beatles have just finished shooting *Help!* and they spend an evening smoking pot with Bob Dylan at the Savoy Hotel. The prophet is on tour and everywhere he goes, D.A. Pennebaker films what happens: Dylan at work; Dylan at play. We see him in taxicabs, in hotel rooms, in Victorian concert halls, and in streets that still look insanely Dickensian. The resulting footage (released two years later in *Don't Look Back*) is breathtaking: we see the Zeitgeist in person — the one Hegel had seen on horseback the day Napoleon zoomed by him near Austerlitz. In May 1965, the Zeitgeist wears no bicorn, but he looks like Rimbaud in sunglasses and Chelsea boots. By cross-fertilizing the blues with surrealism and the theatre of the absurd, he has just invented rock poetry on a series of incredible LPs. But Leonard Cohen (eight years Dylan's senior) is hardly aware of that. Stranded like Ulysses on a Greek island, he has just completed the corrections of his new book and, musically, he sticks to Ray Charles. For the moment.

It's late May or perhaps early June. The poet, who has been fasting for the last twelve days, decides to take a trip to a nearby island to celebrate the end of his ordeal. *Hubris* plays a part, obviously, as it should in any tragedy: he refuses to wear a hat. Phoebus does his job and the sun strikes down the man who has just written such a scandalous novel. Leonard collapses, becomes delirious, and is confined to bed for over a week and perhaps hospitalized.[53] Then comes the miracle, often told since (and perhaps apocryphal): one evening, the domes of all the island churches are covered with hundreds of cranes for their yearly stopover on Hydra as they return from Africa. The next day, the birds are gone and so is Leonard's fever: he is cured and on his feet. Leonard is a poet: he knows how to decode signs. In this case, it's time for a new beginning — the birds have told him so. Of course, it's not the last time that he is given instructions by winged beings.

CAN I BORROW YOUR WINGS?

With hindsight, the need to leave Hydra would seem obvious: the island was rapidly turning into the local Saint-Tropez. Movies were shot on the beach, yachts were seen in greater number, and Jackie Kennedy danced in the harbour cafés. Plus, Leonard had reached the end of an artistic cycle. He dimly knew that his latest effort would remain the masterpiece of his first career and that a third novel would necessarily be a step backwards.

Back to Nietzsche's word, then: "Become what you are." But what exactly is this thing that Leonard Cohen already was, that maybe he had always been, and that will now help him start anew? It couldn't have taken that long to find out. He has always loved the spotlight and, for seventeen years, has not attended a party without his guitar. He had even taken those famous flamenco lessons in Montreal three years earlier and, more recently, he gave a concert or two in the back-room of Katsikas. What is more, he has been adding his own songs to his repertoire of traditional folk tunes for some time now. He is still at work on one of them. Inspired by existentialism and by a famous film noir with Frank Sinatra, it deals with a professional card dealer who abandons the woman he loves for the "holy game of poker," pursuing the card that will free him. The title "The Stranger Song" is nicked from Albert Camus's famous novel, but the song (yet unfinished) is Cohen's best self-portrait since *The Favourite Game*.[54]

It seems that all signs point to a major departure. For a little while now, Cohen has been considering recording a country-and-western record, maybe in Nashville. Or writing songs for others. Actually, he has just discovered Bob Dylan — maybe during a short stay in London in early 1965 — two years after everybody else. This resulted in a famous episode on January 8, 1966. The place? F.R. Scott's apartment, 451 Clark Street, Montreal. There's a literary party going on and Leonard has taken it upon himself to educate his colleagues about the future of poetry. He insists until he gets his host to put on a Bob Dylan record (most likely *Highway 61 Revisited*), which causes a new secession among the Montreal Poets. Half of them start dancing and want the volume turned up; the other half seek refuge in the kitchen. Some say Cohen was very vocal that day in his support of the rock-and-roll poet and others even claim they heard him say he would be the Canadian Dylan. Not that anyone took him seriously. He had a new fad every time he came home: sainthood, Cuba, LSD, Hitler, Bob Dylan. But the following month, Leonard takes Layton to see Mr. Zimmerman and his electric band at Place des Arts in Montreal. Part of the audience booed but Leonard saw the future. And it wasn't murder yet.

So, there are several reasons why that particular stay in Montreal, which begins in December 1965, is special. First, it is not followed by a return to Greece. For a few years, Hydra will be a place for short breaks only, not extended stays. Second, in addition to his outrageous novel, Leonard had another product to sell: a new persona. He was now an existentialist troubadour. Invited on the set of the CBC program *Take 30* on May 26, he insisted that he would sing "The Stranger Song." The producers indulged him, thinking it's just another whim. Five months later, his new book of poems, *Parasites of Heaven*, contained lyrics about a certain "Suzanne" who takes you down to the river, an "Avalanche" that covers up your soul, and a "Master" that takes you travelling.[55] That whole year of 1966, Leonard travelled back and forth between Canada, where he was still the subversive poet, and New York, where he tried to establish himself as a songwriter.[56]

To make sure everybody gets the message, he teams up with a Canadian pop band whose Rickenbacker guitars are reminiscent of the Beatles and the Byrds: the Stormy Clovers. The singer, Susan

Jains, is so sexy that, in the words of the *Toronto Star*, she does not smoke like an average person but organizes "love stories between her lips and the cigarettes."[57] The band, featured that July on the cover of *Hoot!* magazine, is playing its delicious folk-rock repertoire on campuses and in trendy cafés: the Penny Farthing in Toronto, the Venus de Milo in Montreal, and Le Hibou in Ottawa. They sing the songs Leonard composes, more or less as he completes them, and this is how "Hey, That's No Way to Say Goodbye," "Sisters of Mercy," and "Suzanne" were born in delightful folk-pop versions sung by Susan Jains.[58]

When not in New York, the future singer sometimes joins the Clovers on stage but, for the time being, it's winter again in Montreal and Leonard becomes an actor for a short avant-garde movie (*Angel* by his friend Derek May). In many ways, this will be a temporary farewell to his hometown. The film shows a man — played by Leonard — and his female companion pretending to be angels (or maybe they are angels in human form — we're not sure). They are running in a field of snow, accompanied by a dog, laughing and chasing each other. They alternately wear a pair of wings that eventually end up on the animal's back. The dazzling overexposed whiteness of the images (it's an *art* movie) makes us think we are facing real luminous angels but at the end of the film, the couple sit on a bed and close the door to engage (as we suspect) in an activity that angels are not well equipped for.

In retrospect, *Angel* fits in Leonard's trajectory very organically: it seems to announce that he has wings, that he will soon leave to become a troubadour who whispers to the ears of flower children and angels. The soundtrack — dark guitar chords based on the flamenco tremolo that will soon become his signature sound — is already incredibly "Cohenian," and Leonard's only line of dialogue ("Please miss, can I borrow your wings?") seems to announce the future. In the weeks that follow the shooting, Leonard leaves for New York where he takes a room in the Penn Terminal Hotel on Thirty-Fourth Street. A bad name for a new beginning.

CHAPTER 4

ANGELS IN EMBER AND SNOW

NEW YORK
1966–1967

Aerial view of Manhattan

THE HOWLING CITY

New York, fall of 1966. A long travelling shot captured by a US Army helicopter shows the city as Leonard must have seen it: huge and frightening. First comes a tiny island with a big statue of oxidized copper, then a seemingly endless parade of stone buildings. Block after block after block. Just brown stone and endless windswept avenues. Here and there, of course, you see groves of giant skyscrapers in the fog but, in that footage, New York is certainly not a tourist destination; it is more like a gigantic mineral

chessboard or the howling, uninhabitable stone monster that Allen
Ginsberg had described in "Moloch," the second part of *Howl*:

> Moloch, whose eyes are thousands of blind windows,
> where skyscrapers stand in the streets like infinite
> Jehovahs . . .

In the mid-'60s, the city was still a large harbour and a small
industrial centre with a few remaining factories and textile mills.
But in Harlem, Brooklyn, the Lower East Side, the Bronx, whole
neighbourhoods were decrepit and in disarray. Soho was a string of
empty warehouses and lofts, and everywhere rents were very low.
Every year, the city — which was only a few dollars away from
bankruptcy — reminded its inhabitants that all it took for chaos
to break loose was a single incident: in 1965, the great twenty-
four-hour blackout; in 1966, a twelve-day transportation strike and
the Great Smog; in 1968, a series of race riots and a ten-day garbage
worker strike. Each time was like a dress rehearsal for the apocalypse: New York was an Atlantis that had not yet sunk.

For a few years, Cohen will hit the streets of Manhattan and
move from one hotel to the next to reinvent the twelfth-century
troubadour as a poet of failed love affairs and great solitudes. A few
movies give a glimpse of the decrepit beauty — a beauty made of
stone — of the city in those years: there's of course Andy Warhol's
Chelsea Girls (1966), a trashy evocation of the underground shot in
a hotel that Leonard will inhabit for a long time; there's *Midnight
Cowboy* (1969) with an ailing, black-coated Dustin Hoffman (then
a spitting image of Cohen); and *The Panic in Needle Park* (1971), a
hyper-realistic elegy for the city's junkies. *Rosemary's Baby* (1968)
reveals the gothic potential of the Manhattan buildings, and of
course, *The French Connection* (1971) shows the city, then still ripped
open by the elevated subway, for what it partly was: a parade of
dilapidated facades, seedy bars, and abandoned vacant lots.

Such is the setting Leonard Cohen enters in 1966. He will transform it into the world of ember and snow on his first three records. A world that an absent God seems to have plunged into the night, where orphaned creatures (men, women, and demobilized soldiers) wander in empty streets and eternal snowstorms while angels, saints, and lovers try to restore the lost hospitality of the universe in hotel rooms.

That world undoubtedly owes much to the heroic and forlorn moods often aroused by New York. For like many metropolises, the city has this ability to amplify solitudes and make you lose your centre of gravity. As though life was happening out there, without you, and you didn't really exist. As he gazed out into the night from his hotel room window, the thirty-two-year-old poet must have often thought of that poem he wrote five years earlier, after a first stay in Manhattan:

> I wonder how many people in this city
> live in furnished rooms.
> Late at night, when I look at the buildings
> I swear I see a face in every window
> looking back at me,
> and when I turn away
> I wonder how many go back to their desks
> and write this down.[1]

We can picture the scene. Late 1966, the Penn Terminal Hotel, near Macy's. Across the street, a train station that is being demolished and the greatest hole you can imagine. Plus horns and sirens, of course, echoing in the endless avenues: Pascalian moods in Manhattan. At this stage, however, Leonard plans to stay in New York for a short time only.[2] He doesn't know yet that the city that had overcome him ten years earlier will challenge him again, nor that he will replace here the loving angel Marianne with a vast solitude and an inner collapse. He doesn't know, either, that after a few short years, he will have become an international rock star, the darling of European radios and magazines, nor that he will provoke a few riots during a triumphant tour in Europe and Israel.

His plan in 1966 is humble: to stop in the Big Apple long enough to find an agent, pitch a few songs, and quickly move on to what he thought was his real destination: Nashville, Tennessee, the Capital of Country Music, where he plans to record the album that will solve his financial problems. He has everything he needs in his pocket: a few hundred dollars borrowed from his friend Robert Hershorn, a reputation as a melancholy poet, and a series of contacts provided by his new agent, Mary Martin, the Canadian assistant to Bob Dylan's manager, as well as a couple of demos recorded in her bathroom. But Atropos, Clotho, and Lachesis, the three daughters of Zeus who weave the destinies of men, are not from Canada. Probably annoyed that a poet may choose to leave Greece, they decide that Leonard will be trapped in New York and that it will take him almost three years to reach his destination. Ulysses had taken ten, but the Canadian's ordeal is no less cruel. He will be held back in Manhattan by the comet tail of the folk revival movement and an underground scene of which he was barely aware, but mostly by the type of circumstances he could not resist: an unrequited love affair and the prospect of a vast suffering. He will indeed fall in love here with a haughty Germanic goddess. But first, he needs a good hotel.

THE POET, HIS WOMEN, HIS ROOMS

Armed with the songs he has already completed, Cohen first settles in the gloomily named Penn Terminal Hotel on Thirty-Fourth Street, across from the bus depot.[3] He pins a portrait of the Virgin Mary on his wardrobe and starts work on a song called "Hey, That's No Way to Say Goodbye," his first farewell to Marianne, one of many in a cycle of aubades (the troubadours' songs of parting).[4] Cohen has just signed a managing contract with Mary Martin, who is also the agent of the Stormy Clovers — a first woman at the service of his career. In literary studies, the characters who help the hero on his quest are designated as "adjuvants" and, in Cohen's case, "adjuvantes" will often be women, which seems only fair: he is obsessed with their bodies and tirelessly celebrates their magic. The agent introduces Leonard to Judy Collins, a Joan Baez–style folksinger with an acoustic guitar, a crystalline voice, and a lyrical twist. Her hair is long, her smile irresistible and, with five LPs under her belt, she is a prominent figure in Greenwich Village. She will soon make "Suzanne" a hit song, but, for the moment, there is nothing in the poet's catalogue that she thinks she can sing. They stay in touch and here is a second "adjuvante" for Leonard's career: a blue-eyed brunette.

In the meantime, the poet has changed hotels. The Penn Terminal was so gloomy that the singer would still complain in interviews decades later: the dark corridors, the leaking faucets, the windows that just wouldn't close, the hot water pipes that made sleep impossible, and, of course, that lugubrious name that reminded everyone of the ineluctable character of dead ends. His destination is Fifty-Eighth Street, the Henry Hudson Hotel, a gigantic and labyrinthine twenty-eight-storey building of "1,200 rooms, 1,200 bathtubs," as their advertisements say. He had finished "The Stranger Song" here a few months earlier, that ballad about a man who keeps train schedules in his wallet and reminds the women he leaves that they had been warned:

> I told you when I came
> I was a stranger.

But after a few weeks, discouraged by a dense retinue of junkies and prostitutes, Leonard moves again and finds refuge in the lion's den or, to be precise, in the Chelsea Hotel, where he is given a tiny room on the first floor with a window on Twenty-Third Street, from which he can observe the city and let it do its work on him.

METAPHYSICS OF THE HOTEL ROOM
(OR HOW TO BE PART OF THE FURNITURE)

That room will undoubtedly host a few embraces, but it is also by its exiguity conducive to self-examination (like the future monk-cells), and it is of course the quintessential place for writing. The title of Leonard's second disc, *Songs from a Room*, is brilliant in that it encapsulates everything that needs to be known about the songs: they come from a room. From the poet's room at the Chelsea, of course, but also from the dark room of the heart. The title is therefore a manifesto of sorts which declares that Cohen's music will, quite literally, be *chamber music*. Music that will replace the great narratives of rebellion of rock music with whispered confessions. Sometime in the late '60s, rock stars — Keith Moon and Keith Richards leading the way — famously started to systematically trash their hotel rooms and smash the furniture, perhaps overwhelmed by the slightly hostile imperturbability that hotel rooms greet you with. Leonard Cohen, on the other hand, was always happy to make these places sanctuaries and to live in them, as if they were home in their own right.

Almost twenty years after his arrival in New York, in a documentary cleverly entitled *Hallelujah in Moll* (Hallelujah in minor mode), German filmmaker Georg Stefan Troller had the brilliant idea of filming Leonard in his room, still at the Chelsea. It is January 1985, and the singer is preparing for a European tour. He is at this point rich and famous; the room is therefore larger than the one he stayed in in 1967, although it's certainly an old-fashioned room with time-worn table lamps, curtains that nobody would buy, and a couple of armchairs that struggle to still be vaguely art deco. The dark-suited poet is sitting in one of those, looking uncharacteristically relaxed, at ease, as though he hasn't moved in twenty years. A fish in water. He literally seems to be part of the furniture. Intrigued, Troller asks, "You spend a lot of time in hotel rooms. Do you enjoy that?" Leonard looks up and seems to notice the room for the first time, a room in which — as we suspect — he must have slept quite a few times. In one of those rare smiles that resuscitates the seven-year-old boy in him, he answers with an enthusiasm that will not be repeated throughout the documentary: "Yeah. It's a nice room!" The confession is actually deeper than it seems: this man is obviously very fond of rooms and of all activities that seem to be done well only in hotel rooms: writing songs, undressing women, and reinventing love. Or even better: not to do anything at all. In 1975, the cover of *Greatest Hits* featured Leonard in an Italian hotel room (complete with flowery curtains and a circle-shaped mirror) while another picture on the inner sleeve showed him sitting on the bed, making smoke rings: Leonard playing with nothing, with forms that immediately dissipate. Leonard living the smokey life and observing the disappearance of things. Leonard in a hotel room, where he belongs.

So in New York, in 1966 and 1967, Leonard does a lot of writing in a lot of hotel rooms. He writes about the fundamental alienation that isolates us from the world, from each other, and from ourselves. About the ontological condition of the stranger. About the need to always leave. About a few women that obsess him. And about the attractions that female bodies exert on the souls of men. In the Chelsea he also travels a lot, from room to room and floor to floor: the fourth, the fifth, the eighth . . . For at least ten years, the establishment will be his home in Manhattan.[5]

SAYING GOODBYE A THOUSAND TIMES

For the time being, at the Henry Hudson, he is composing his second — quite explicit — farewell to his favourite muse: a song called "So Long, Marianne."[6] So let there be the case of Marianne Ihlen Jensen, a young woman who, quite tragically, thought that she had lost her beauty in her thirtieth year (sometime around 1963). Three years later, as the poet was planning his new career, the muse had joined him in Montreal, where she found work in a trendy fashion boutique. The couple settled in the poet's Aylmer

Street apartment with the little Axel (now aged six) for a life of urban bohemia. Two years before, only a couple of streets away, a first attempt at conjugal life in Montreal had failed miserably.[7] Leonard and Marianne would not be any luckier this time around, as if the formula of their romance was lost as soon as they left the white house in Hydra. As one of Cohen's friends said: "Love born on Hydra doesn't travel."[8]

Focused on his new career and increasingly polygamous, the poet seemed determined — that year of 1966 — to live pretty much his own life, quickly leaving Marianne to feel redundant and out of place, increasingly convinced she was in the wrong town, on the wrong continent, living the wrong life.

In the extensive time the two lovers had spent apart in the intervening two years, both of them had had affairs. Marianne apparently slept with a couple of other artists and, at least once, she let herself be seduced by one of Cohen's closest friends.[9] As for Leonard, he increasingly considered it his sacred mission to wrap his sexual compassion around the souls of every lost woman he met — saints must be saints, apparently, and lovers, lovers. Of course, this was the '60s and free love was de rigueur in bohemian couples, but as her man increasingly followed the calls of new lifestyles, new cities, and new mermaids, the deeply insecure Marianne started panicking — she watched herself slowly but inexorably lose her Leonard and gradually slipped into a spiral of depression that would last many years.[10]

But for the time being, it is the winter of 1966. And as Leonard's notebooks fill with lyrics that systematically mention departures, quarrels, and lovers who no longer speak the same tongue,[11] the couple try to rekindle their love by living apart. Actually, a continent apart. After a solitary trip to Mexico for a psychedelic initiation with an American *beat* guru that left her just a little more bereft, Marianne finds herself back in an empty house on a Greek island, where she will try various forms of therapy and the occasional boyfriend. There, like a powerless Calypso, who attracts all men to her island but cannot retain a single one, she will wait for Leonard's increasingly noncommittal letters.[12]

To be fair, the poet is busy: he is reinventing his life and scouring Manhattan for the perfect hotel room, one that would protect him in his many struggles — with inspiration and dark angels, and with a thousand passing encounters, some of which will be more lethal than others.

In the meantime, notebooks fill with the valedictory songs that will appear on the first album: "Hey, That's No Way to Say Goodbye," "The Stranger Song," and (inevitably) "So Long, Marianne," about an idyllic love that has run its course:

> You know that I love to live with you
> But you make me forget so very much
> I forget to pray for the angels
> And then the angels forget to pray for us.

So obviously, Leonard is saying goodbye. If he doesn't seem determined yet to set Marianne free, it's because it's hard to let go of an angel — you don't catch one every day. So, to keep her in his life, he says goodbye over and over. A thousand times.

After 1967, the time the two lovers spend together is actually few and far between (two weeks in January 1968 and not even that in the summer), but most likely, Leonard actually never told Marianne he was leaving for good. Except in song, of course, where he said:

> So long, Marianne, it's time that we began
> To laugh and cry, and cry and laugh
> About it all again.

Decades later, as the lively chorus would routinely be sung in unison by thousands of fans in concert halls, it was easy to forget how much those lines, originally addressed to a young blonde woman on an island in the Aegean Sea, must have hurt. When she first saw the lyrics on the Olivetti (probably in Greece, in the summer of 1967, as Leonard was also writing "Bird on the Wire"), Marianne is said to have announced, quoting her real name: "I'm very happy that this song was not written for me: my name is *Marianna*." The muse's elegant answer to the poet.

THE DRUNKEN HOTEL

The Chelsea Hotel

But for the moment, it's late 1966 and Marianne is still in Montreal waiting for Leonard — and perhaps it was better like this. The Chelsea Hotel was no place for angels from Norway and certainly no place for six-year-olds.

Ten blocks away from the Empire State Building, this was indeed the hotel's equivalent to Rimbaud's drunken boat: thirteen storeys plus a basement, 400 rooms and apartments of all sizes (some with a yearly lease[13]), and a decayed beauty that perfectly mirrors that of the city. On the front, a neo-gothic façade, an iconic neon sign, and hundreds of windows. On the west side, a forest of fire escapes — the city's visual signature. Inside, traces of a past glory and the ethereal atmosphere left by eighty years of artistic bohemia. The lobby is cluttered with paintings (De Kooning, Christo, Larry Rivers) and the wrought-iron staircase takes you to eleven successive landings and to a terraced roof. Half a mile of corridors lead to superbly decayed rooms with ornamental chimneypieces and, at an infinite distance from the floors (so that angels may pass), ceilings with period mouldings.

Everywhere, there are artists at work: composers who compose, painters who paint, writers who write, and prostitutes who prostitute themselves. Arthur Miller lived here for many years (sometimes with Marilyn), and he keeps a room on the sixth floor, while the French avant-garde (sculptors Arman, Christo, and Niki de Saint Phalle) inhabit the higher floors, together with heiress Peggy Biderman and underground filmmaker Shirley Clark. When she's in town, Janis Joplin rents a room on the fourth and folk music anthologist, amateur occultist, raconteur, and conman Harry Smith occupies a tiny room (#737) with his archives. A few ghosts are rumoured to haunt the place. Dylan Thomas is said to have died here after eighteen whiskies, and former patrons Mark Twain and Sarah Bernhardt sometimes appear to drunken guests, as do a few anonymous suicides (people have a habit of jumping off the iconic staircase). That summer in 1966, Andy Warhol and Paul Morrissey have just filmed part of *Chelsea Girls* here, and in the corridors, you will always meet a drug dealer or two, a few junkies, the occasional firemen come to extinguish a fire, and — it happened once — a company rehearsing a Verdi opera and (so the legend goes) the tiger of a passing circus. A rickety elevator will take you from one circle of bohemia to the next and occasionally, its sliding door will reveal a girl in her birthday suit. Every day, of course, there are parties on the roof and in the rooms.

The manager, Stanley Bard (who inherited the hotel from his father), likes artists and makes sure that the establishment remains a bohemian academy and a buoyant Ship of Fools where artists will find just the right amount of paranoia to stay creative. He maintains the tradition of the place: if you're famous and talented, you can pay your rent with a painting or get credit. "No questions asked" is the golden rule and the owner will tolerate everything except a deficit.[14] Cohen would later recount that you could ask for your key at three o'clock in the morning with a polar bear on one arm and a naked teenage girl on the other without raising anyone's eyebrow.[15]

But behind the counter, Bard exerts power. He is both the guardian dog Cerberus and Rhadamanthus, the brother of Minos and judge of the underworld. He decides who stays and who goes, assigns rooms and weighs souls. There is always room for passing stars: Jimi Hendrix, Jim Morrison, Norman Mailer, William Burroughs, Salvador Dali, Allen Ginsberg. For his first stay, Leonard Cohen gets a broom closet with peeling paint on the first floor. Not a very good pick, but he's in. Bob Dylan has just vacated room 221 and Edie Sedgwick, the poor little rich heiress and former Warhol superstar, has installed her furs, her amphetamines, and her pearls on the same floor as Leonard, where she will soon set fire to her room.[16]

The Chelsea Hotel is like Dante's hell in thirteen circles plus one basement, with a purgatory in the adjoining bar (the adequately named El Quijote, where incurable idealists raise their glass to lost causes) and Paradise on the roof, with a full view of the Empire State Building. Some days, everything is inverted; it's heaven in the rooms and hell in the bar. But in any case, it's the ideal hotel for Leonard to observe the world in that pivotal year, although in 1967, the omnipresence of drugs makes the Chelsea a fairly dangerous place — the risk of an accidental acid trip is serious, as the singer later remembered:

> It was dangerous to accept a potato chip at a cocktail party then, I mean literally. It could be sprinkled with acid. I went to somebody's room who was having a cocktail party, had a few chips, and four days later was still trying to find my room.[17]

For a change of scene, Leonard would occasionally move back to the Henry Hudson or take a room at the YMCA further down the street, where he could swim every day. Greek habits die hard.

CELESTIAL HIERARCHIES AND ADVENTURES IN ELEVATORS

In those years, nothing made Leonard feel better than riding in elevators. Ten years before, he had briefly worked in New York as an elevator boy and he would later joke that the small elevator at the Chelsea was his favourite place, where he spent whole days going up and down aimlessly. On some level, you almost believe him. Elevators are indeed excellent places to learn to play with gravity and the perfect vehicle in modern times for mystical initiations: at the touch of a button you can travel underground like Orpheus, have a peep and come back immediately, or you can rise closer to God. In certain circumstances, you can even meet angels in elevators. At least that was Leonard's secret dream, now that his Norwegian angel had lost her precious ability to help him inhabit the world: that the elevators in New York be modern versions of Jacob's ladder where you could meet a winged being or two.

Many trips from the basement to the roof are necessary, however, to understand the celestial hierarchy described by the Christian mystic Pseudo-Dionysius the Aeropagite in his famous treatise on angelology: Messenger angels, Archangels, Seraphim (who burn to warm and illuminate us), Cherubim or Virtues (through whom miracles are performed), Dominations (who help us refuse evil), Powers (who rout diabolical forces), Principalities and Thrones (guardians of God). But how to recognize which is which? And how to invoke them?[18]

The strangest thing is probably that the expected encounters did take place, even if the angels Cohen met in lifts were angels for him only. In the Henry Hudson elevator, a mysterious ethereal blonde told the poet that he was dead and only she could bring him back. For a mere $500, he followed her tantric teaching for a few weeks and sang his new songs to her before the angel turned out to be a Swedish hooker and destitute artist who dispensed her wisdom to many clients.[19]

The most famous encounter took place a little later, in the Chelsea elevator. There, Leonard met Saint Janis, a blues singer in distress who wouldn't be walking this earth for much longer, which was perhaps why she also spent a lot of time in elevators — to get used to leaving the earth. Four years later, in memory of a dalliance that lasted half a night, Cohen wrote an elegy for the late singer, one he simply called "Chelsea Hotel." In concert, he often told the anecdote of his elevator rides with Janis: how he would see her there every night, how one day he dared ask her what she was looking for, how she replied "Kris Kristofferson," how, although he himself was looking for Lily Marlene, he pretended to be Kris Kristofferson, how, her solitude being as vast as his, she pretended to believe him, and how it all ended with a now famous oral gratification on Saint Janis's bed, as recounted in the famous opening:

> I remember you well in the Chelsea Hotel
> You were talking so brave and so sweet
> Giving me head on the unmade bed
> while the limousines wait in the street.[20]

Cohen has since publicly asked the singer's ghost to forgive him for so bluntly revealing their brief intimacy. Yet the lines are also poetically interesting. They offer a discreet back-and-forth movement between the open and the closed, the intimate and the immense as we move from the closed chamber of memory ("I remember you well") to the gigantic hotel ("in the Chelsea Hotel"), from the small open mouth of a chatting girl ("talking so brave and so sweet") to the girl's closed mouth on the lover's phallus ("giving me head") and from the open "unmade bed" to the closed limousines waiting in the open streets of an immense Manhattan. Great poetic work, therefore, and a good compendium of rock-and-roll life in the late '60s:

sex and drugs and hotel rooms. The song also delivers a beautiful portrait of Janis not so much as a heavenly angel than as a woman of flesh who re-enchants the world with her oral talents: good at small talk, good at fellatio, and (most of all) good at singing, as Cohen reminds in an early live version:

> Making your sweet little sounds, didn't you baby?
> Making your sweet little sounds.[21]

"Chelsea Hotel" ultimately shows an angel caught in an elevator that only goes down. The closing lines contain Leonard's farewell to Janis, whom he compares to a fallen bird:

> I don't mean to suggest that I loved you the best
> I can't keep track of each fallen robin
> I remember you well in the Chelsea Hotel
> That's all, I don't think of you that often.

Traditionally, in a ballad, the last four lines (the envoi) were used by the troubadours to "send" their song off into the world with a dedication to a lady or a protector. With marvellous frankness, Cohen uses his envoi to send Janis off to oblivion, dismissing her from her own elegy, seeming to confess that in the end, she was only a very touching elevator companion, a bird that fell out of the nest.

A third encounter in a third elevator, that of the luxurious Plaza Hotel on Fifth Avenue, would take place much later in the spring of 1969, as the song "Suzanne" (which Leonard wrote for an angelic woman in Montreal) was still on everybody's acoustic guitar. At that time, the singer was a part-time rock-and-roll celebrity and, that particular day, he was on his way to a meeting of the Church of Scientology when he bumped into a nineteen-year-old brunette of luminous beauty. He did not immediately foresee that she would give him two children or that he would call her "the gypsy wife," "Lilith," or "the naked angel in my heart / the woman with her legs apart."[22] But at that moment, because he saw her in an elevator, he just assumed she was an angel and asked her name. When she answered "Suzanne," he understood he must have invoked her.

SUZANNE

Back in 1966, Leonard was yet unfamiliar with the Plaza elevator and the only angel he seemed interested in was the one he was trying to put into song in Montreal. He had just spent an afternoon in the harbour district with a young woman whose aura had fascinated him since he had first seen her three years before — a dancer named Suzanne Verdal.[23] A prominent figure of the local bohemia, she's the companion of the Québécois sculptor Armand Vaillancourt with whom, as everybody agrees, she forms an immaculately graceful couple. Suzanne lives near the river, by the Notre-Dame-de-Bon-Secours Chapel, in what is not yet called a loft space, where she serves her many visitors tea with orange zest. On that particular day, Leonard and Suzanne go for a walk along the St. Lawrence banks (perhaps hand in hand), they sit in the sailors' church where Leonard likes to pray, and back at Suzanne's, they drink the famous tea.[24]

Obviously, it must have been a moment of intense beauty. Touched by Suzanne's ethereal presence and by the eccentric grace with which she inhabits the world, the poet must have felt he was indeed in the company of an angel and something had been revealed to him, as though his companion had held up a mirror reflecting the poignant beauty of all things. Angels are messengers and Suzanne's message — one she delivers to all men who watch her live — is that complete dissolution into love is the only answer to the poignancy of life. Of course, she's half-crazy, as Leonard knew full well, but that doesn't change anything. In her company, you suddenly "want to travel with her, and you want to travel blind."

So that afternoon, the theological questions examined by Leonard in New York elevators (how to recognize an angel? what are the signs of its presence?) are suddenly replaced by an equally urgent though purely aesthetic question: how to represent an angel? For Leonard knows now that this song he was writing, which until that afternoon had no title but was merely an evocation of the Montreal harbour, must finally include a portrait of Suzanne Verdal as a glorious though fallen angel. It will be a song about epiphanies and platonic embraces.[25]

But how do you represent the spiritual? Medieval artists had chosen to symbolize the incorporeal nature of the angel with various symbolical elements: androgynous beauty, elaborate drapery (angels wear luxury clothes), and, evidently, wings.[26] Leonard follows suit. When he describes Suzanne's attire as "rags and *feathers* / from Salvation Army counters," he discreetly equips her with wings and the ability to bring salvation. Of course, he also drapes her in the melody's celestial beauty and makes her an allegory of the three Christian virtues of faith, hope, and charity. Like a perfect host, she serves you "tea and oranges" and takes you to the river to teach you that beauty is everywhere. And she shows you the true nature of beings in her mirror: men are sailors and women, bringers of light. In sync with the spirit of the age, the song therefore includes Leonard's version of the feminine mystique: Christ sinks, but Suzanne — now identified with the Virgin ("Our Lady of the Harbour") — redeems our lives by channelling her light into the world.[27]

The song makes the listener actually experience the angelic. To begin with, because they are written in the second person, the lyrics make us — the listeners — Suzanne's hosts: she serves *us* tea and *we* want to follow her blind. Then there's the music. The sequence of ascending chords in the chorus together with the beauty of the successive images (the oranges that come "all the way from China," Christ in his wooden tower, the golden sunset spreading "like honey" on a statue of the Virgin) suggest the ascending movement of the soul that Saint Thomas Aquinas considered the sure sign of an angelic presence — the very movement Leonard must have felt in the presence of Suzanne.[28] For the version that the singer will record the following year with John Simon, the singer's voice will be enveloped in the counterpoint of a female soprano that never lets us forget that the celestial is actually accessible on this earth. Precisely what the song purports to teach.

HOW TO SLEEP WITH AN ANGEL

In Leonard Cohen's work, the angel is not so much an object of philosophical and theological speculation as a lived reality. Leonard has met angels; he has lived with them and they have spoken to him. Quite logically, his work contains a phenomenology of the angel (an approach to angels as a lived experience) rather than a strict angelology (a science of angels).

Which doesn't mean he shies away from theological questions. The song "Suzanne" is actually just an introduction: it approaches some of the modalities of angelic action, reminding us that angels are messengers that bring illumination. But the question remains: is Suzanne *really* an angel? Or to be clearer, are women "angels" only metaphorically? A logical extension of the question: can angels assume a corporeal nature? And an underlying question (probably the one Leonard is really interested in): is it possible to have sex with an angel?

Saint Thomas agrees with all previous theologians: the immateriality of angels is the very condition of their immortality. It's hard to disagree, for that's the very definition of spiritual beings — they are pure spirits. Yet the Book of Enoch and Book of Jubilees, two pseudo-epigraphic parts of the Old Testament supposedly dictated to Moses by an angel, mention that in ancient times, angels were united with women and begot children with them, a belief on which the Kabbalah has speculated at length. As for Saint Thomas again, he grants angels the ability to enter our world *embodied*: the angel can, so the theologian asserts, manifest a "body" by condensing air to interact with us physically. As the angelic doctor specifies, this body nevertheless is not where the angel resides; the angel moves the body from the outside, whereas our human bodies are moved by an interior soul.[29]

Cohen seems willing to test (at least poetically) a new hypothesis: that angels can borrow the bodies of women (creatures he deems by nature more spiritual than men[30]) or (a variation on the same hypothesis) that women can manifest angels. It is difficult to distinguish between the two possibilities, but he had certainly observed the phenomenon on Marianne, a few years earlier:

> Whenever you move,
> I hear the sound of falling wings,
> of closing wings.[31]

The hypothesis, whatever it's worth, enables Cohen to imagine that you can indeed deceive an angel into sleeping with you when that angel possesses a woman, or that you can just inadvertently sleep with an angel when a woman manifests one. And that obviously opens a whole new field of mystical and erotic experiments. For the time being, Leonard's hypothesis — perhaps theologically debatable, but poetically fertile — allows him to treat every woman as a potential angel (what he calls in a poem "theoretical angels").[32] So that's what girls are for him at this stage. The girls who open his eyes (like Suzanne): angels. The girls who open their arms (like Marianne): angels. The girls who open their thighs (all the others): angels.

One could, of course, be tempted to reject this erotic theology as null and void, as just another metaphor, and say women are not angels; angels do not exist. But that would be to underestimate the power of metaphors and their absolute necessity. Great poets (and Leonard is one) do not use metaphors as simple tools for poetizing reality. Metaphors have a heuristic function: they stimulate our imagination and invite us to engage with realities that are impossible to notice without the metaphor. Which means that, for Leonard Cohen, certain metaphysical and spiritual connections between man and woman make it rigorously necessary to speak of angels or angelic experience. In other words, if the "angels" of which Leonard speaks are to be considered as purely metaphorical (and that is far from obvious), the metaphors in question are necessary and operative.

One can, of course, see in this erotic approach of the angel a resurgence of the vast Cohenian paradigm of holy sexuality: the idolaters of *Beautiful Losers* wanted — as we remember — to "fuck a saint" and the cover of his fourth record would later feature a sixteenth-century engraving of an allegorical coitus between two winged beings. But the question remains: what lies in that desire to sleep with an angelic woman? Is it a desire for sainthood? And, conversely, if the desire to sleep with a woman is pure enough, could it be that one's desire might turn her into an angel? And if you join an angel in coitus, will her angelic nature rub off on you, making you what the mystical poet Johannes Scheffler (better known as Angelus Silesius) calls a "cherubinic pilgrim," an angel who walks the world? (Which was, perhaps, Leonard's goal, as we shall see.)

In many ways, the poet will indeed become that angel, or at least he will continuously strive to do that. But he is not there yet. Far from it. In 1967, quite unsure of himself, he hesitates for an hour before asking the names of waitresses of the late-night cafés on Eighth Avenue: a very shy (and probably very depressed) suitor confronting angelic waitresses.[33]

A PILGRIM IN MANHATTAN

Back in New York, winter of 1966–1967. When tired of elevators, Cohen ventures outside, usually with a black briefcase he carries around everywhere. For example, he sits in the Mexican restaurant on the ground floor of the Chelsea (you can access it from the lobby), the aptly named El Quijote. Or in case of urgency, he sits in the Twenty-Third Street Synagogue, next door to the hotel or, two blocks away, in the St. Vincent de Paul Catholic Church, where Edith Piaf got married. Cohen also becomes a regular at the Bronco Burger, a Spartan all-night diner just across the street: a room, a jukebox (where Janis likes to play her own records), hamburgers at all hours, and all the loneliness you can take at three in the morning. And, still on the same block, there is an entirely automated Horn & Hardart twenty-four-hour cafeteria which, to a certain extent, is the poet's most reliable friend in Manhattan.[34]

Not far away, an esoteric bookstore called Magic Witchcraft will provide the poet with the candles and books required for rituals to attract the love of a woman he will soon become obsessed with. But originally, New York was for Leonard a very small world organized around his sleepless nights on Twenty-Third Street.

It was therefore necessary to expand his perimeters. Faithful to the first principle of urban itinerancy — when in doubt, hit the streets — and to his conviction that night owls are the members of a secret party that conspire against sleep, Cohen starts exploring the nocturnal monster of Manhattan, an exploration that will take him in three directions and make him discover three different scenes. Somewhere down the road, his new career awaits him.

His first forays into Manhattan take him to the East Village, supposedly the "in" neighbourhood of the hippie counterculture. Although Cohen spent a Sunday afternoon there in October 1966 (in Tompkins Square, to be precise), chanting the "Hare Krishna" mantra with Swami Prabhupada and Allen Ginsberg (Marianne was also there), he was not impressed by hippie spirituality. We don't know if the Chelsea tenant, then a great advocate of hallucinogens (which must have facilitated angelic visions), attended one of Timothy Leary's happenings at the Village Theatre, where the former Harvard Don, a gnostic without a gnosis, taught his very young listeners how to destroy their ego with LSD on blotter paper and the *Tibetan Book of the Dead*, but we know that five years later, Cohen would voice in a poem his detestation of the "flabby liars of the Aquarian Age," an expression he liked so much he still used it twenty-five years later in interviews.[35] And we know that one day, he held a glorious protest against the smugness he saw around him in a coffee shop on St. Mark's Place, when he wrote the words "Kill Cool" on a tablemat and held it silently over his head without really impressing anyone.[36] Two decades later, the singer would still explain to journalists that the '60s never happened, or that they lasted only fifteen minutes, and warn with the Talmud that whoever marries the spirit of his generation will be widowed in the next.

Greenwich Village, home of the folk revival movement, was Leonard's second playground. There, the budding songwriter was soon a regular in the cafés (the Kettle of Fish, the Bitter End, the Gaslight. . .) where college kids still listened to acoustic guitars. What struck him immediately was a glaring absence: Bob Dylan. After dynamiting the folk revival in 1965 when he plugged in his guitar, the folksinger had dynamited himself the following year in a mysterious motorcycle crash. The result? Dylan was no longer there. Not at the Chelsea, not in the Village, not anywhere. Some say he was disfigured; others that he had been killed by the FBI, and as the kids still danced on the last echoes of his music, the movement had clearly lost its prophet and part of its momentum. Which meant there was a power vacuum. Good news for Mr. Cohen.

The folk world was indeed in crisis: the old guard of blues and folk purists (Dave Van Ronk, Pete Seeger, The Clancy Brothers . . .) and the hard line of protest singers (Phil Ochs, Joan Baez, Tom Paxton) were losing ground to an unassailable folk-pop crossover (Simon & Garfunkel, Tim Buckley) while the simultaneous emergence of confessional voices (Tim Hardin, David Blue, Gordon Lightfoot, Joni Mitchell) heralded the impending replacement of the protest singer (whose concern is the world) by the singer-songwriter (whose concern is the heart). In this context, Leonard's ballads about saints and his timeless waltz melodies would soon seem at the vanguard of things. Not to mention the authority that comes from being a published poet and novelist.

So quite logically, the Greenwich Village artists welcome the poet with open arms and, as early as the winter of 1967, a photograph shows a rather sullen-looking Cohen sitting on the floor in Joan Baez's Chelsea Hotel apartment, surrounded by Dave Van Ronk, Mimi Farina, and others: the local aristocracy.[37] Of course, his first asset to get his colleagues' attention was obviously his lyrical abilities, but another was that he was that rare thing — not a child of the blues, not a true child of folk: a flamenco playing troubadour. Hence the Cree singer Buffy Sainte-Marie's comments in *Sing Out* about his "disregard of old folksy musical clichés," his "outrageous modulations," and his "unguessable" but bewitching melodies.[38]

All he needed to do was hang out in the right places, meet the right people, and wait for *kairos*, the right moment. In the meantime, he was preparing demos with Montreal's Garth Hudson (Dylan's organist, no less), and began to pitch his songs to the local artists (with a little help from Mary Martin), starting of course with "Suzanne."

Sensing that perhaps Hendrix's "Foxy Lady" or the Doors' "Light My Fire" had not entirely exhausted love poetry, Leonard felt there was something in "Suzanne" that the era was hungry for. In the summer of 1966, after the song had joined the Stormy Clovers' repertoire in Montreal (name of the singer: Susan), the poet called Judy Collins and sang her the song over the phone. Like your average folk-pop Platonist, Judy fell in love with the tune and recorded it immediately (she was in a studio in London) with another ballad, the desperate "Dress Rehearsal Rag" for a record called *In My Life*, which gained "Suzanne" a lot of airplay in late 1966. Squeezed on the album between tracks by Lennon-McCartney, Kurt Weill, and Bob Dylan, the song got people's attention. Who has written that little gem? The curiosity rose a few notches when folk queen Joan Baez started singing the song live and, the following year, when a pop crooner called Noel Harrison (son of Rex) made the song a minor hit again (#54 on the pop charts) after singing it live on *The Ed Sullivan Show*.[39]

That year, as the Canadian's songs got airplay in New York coffee shops and radio stations, the singer (who was still very unsure of his voice) would make a few shaky appearances, but the best is yet to come.

For the moment, it is still late 1966, and the tireless pedestrian explores other portions of the city, looking for a "scene" that, as a Chelsea Hotel resident, he had already found: the New York underground. Along a few paths of perdition, Cohen soon discovered some of the underground's sacred places. There was of course the Forty-First Street Cinematheque where Jonas Mekas used all means necessary — overexposure, the superimposition of tapes, pornographic sequences, accelerated speed — to turn films into poems. There were the off-Broadway theatres, where the Living Theatre has just launched a great Artaudian revolution and John Cage and La Monte Young's workshops. And of course, there was the mecca: Andy Warhol's Factory on Forty-Seventh Street, both a studio and a social salon, where hard work was done during the day and parties went on at night. Everybody loved the Village Theatre, the Scene, and the Ondine nightclub, where visiting bands like the Doors or the Jimi Hendrix Experience played or, later in the night, the One-Two-Three, a swingers' club with three floors, each devoted to a different sexual proclivity.

But the ultimate place to be was the back room of Mickey Ruskin's new restaurant, Max's Kansas City, near Union Square. There, the in-crowd gathered after hard days spent impressing the bourgeois and Warhol, and his entourage held court there for the glitterati to present their nightly tribute. Virtually unknown in the art world, Leonard usually sat at the bar, near the entrance. Alone. That particular day, he was no doubt about to write "Kill Cool" on his paper mat again when a young man in dark glasses approached him. "Are you Leonard Cohen?" The deep-voiced boy had recognized him from the picture on the inner sleeve of *Beautiful Losers*, in his eyes the best novel since *The Naked Lunch*. Introducing himself as Lou Reed, he invited Leonard to join Warhol's table where the pop-art pope hung out with his transgender muses: a one-way ticket to the underground. Leonard would later appear in the odd experimental movie, but he was not the type to hang out at the Factory all day (even if he visited a few times), nor to draw penises in the socialite Brigid Polk's cock book.[40] He had songs to write and angels to chase, especially now that the legendary John Hammond of Columbia Records — the discoverer of Billie Holiday and Bob Dylan — wanted to meet him.

SISTERS OF MERCY

Hospitality: the charity that consists of taking in, lodging, and feeding the indigent and travellers free of charge in an establishment provided for this purpose.

But before that, he needs a makeover. He needs to get into the skin of a songwriter. All year, he has brought his guitar to poetry readings, adding a couple of songs to the proceedings and twice (in May and November) he has played "The Stranger Song" to TV audiences for the CBC. A few times, he has also joined the Stormy Clovers on stage. In late November, the poet was due for one last reading tour on a Canadian campus, at the University of Alberta in Edmonton. There, something happened that would never happen again: Leonard Cohen wrote a song in one go. Surely, the circumstances were exceptional: he had just met two angels.

So November 1966, Edmonton, Alberta. Invited by his friend, poet and teacher Eli Mandel, Leonard, now donning a quasi-moptop haircut and a black turtleneck, has brought his guitar again. The message is clear: forget the beatnik; meet the minstrel. Some poems will now be sung, especially as extra bookings have been arranged for performances in nightclubs. After a successful concert, he writes Marianne an ecstatic letter that must have sent a shiver down her beautiful spine:

> I was able at last to be what I must be, a singer [. . .]
> I was able to give to over a thousand people the love
> that I have never been able to place, the ungreedy
> love which I know can warm the universe. I know
> now what I must train myself for. I must work, I
> must be celibate, I must be selfless.[41]

In Alberta, Leonard also meets an Avalanche. On his way back to his hotel one night, he is caught in a blizzard and finds refuge under a porch where he discovers two penniless frozen travellers, Barbara and Lorraine.[42] In that kind of circumstance, a poet of the female mystery has no choice: he offers hospitality. What happened next has been told many times in concerts and interviews: how the young women fell asleep on the poet's hotel bed; how the poet stayed up all night at his writing table while the moonlight reflecting off the frozen Saskatchewan River filled the room; how a song called "Sisters of Mercy," about the hostility of the world and the hospitality of angels, was played for the first time in the morning.

Like all great songs, "Sisters of Mercy" is based on a simple idea. In this case, a classic metaphor: we are fallen leaves abandoned to the wind. In other words, we are not in control of our lives — unseen forces take hold of them and our need for consolation is insatiable.

The melody — a little swirling waltz that picks up our souls like dead leaves — is enough to defeat us. French philosopher Gilles Deleuze explained that the ritournelle is what the child sings to himself for reassurance in the dark, and that is exactly what "Sisters of Mercy" is: a lullaby meant to bring solace in our darkest hours.[43] On the version recorded the following year, John Simon's arrangements seem to emerge from the depths of childhood to express the vulnerability of all things: a barrel organ, the smallest accordion imaginable, tiny bells, and a glockenspiel. Over delicate guitar arpeggios, Leonard's clear, precise, and soft voice will unfold the story, almost as if he was speaking. He addresses the eternal travellers inside us, those who "must leave everything / that they cannot control" (their families, their souls) and, right on, gives them a reason to hope:

> Oh, the sisters of mercy
> They are not departed or gone.[44]

Concise like a medieval ballad, the song proceeds with Leonard's testimony: how he met the sisters, how he confessed to them, how he went away, leaving them asleep in a moonlit room. He now commends them to us and declares the night illuminated by their mere presence. A single moonbeam is now enough to see the world as it is:

> When I left they were sleeping
> I hope you run into them soon
> Don't turn on the light
> You can read their address by the moon.

Very skillfully, Leonard presents the episode both as something that happened to him and as something about to happen to us, so that his confession becomes our confession.[45] He also offers us a very concentrated vision of his universe: a frozen world plunged in darkness and tiny eruptions of grace: a moonbeam or damsels' hands blindfolding a man and tying him up with a love that is "graceful and green as a stem."

If Leonard could still sing "Sisters of Mercy" forty years later (many years after the song gave its name to a cold wave band) it is because the song contains a metaphysical statement, reminding us that should we wish to make this cold world inhabitable, even for one night, we need to form alliances, even a tenuous, temporary one. It teaches us that giving hospitality is receiving it, and that when lovers embrace (even briefly, even in their imagination), they become each other's host and each other's redeemer.[46]

Written in one sitting, the song — possibly one of Leonard's early masterpieces — confirms the poet's songwriting ambitions, and his passage in Edmonton is an important step, with a first taste of adoring crowds and star status: the climax of that year's "Leonard Cohen boom."[47] But what the song also signals is the deep and inexhaustible solitude that was haunting Leonard. The truth is the pop poet was on the verge of an inner collapse.

SHE'S A FEMME FATALE

That same winter in New York, Leonard would indeed walk into another snowstorm, one that had a female name and that would cause serious harm. Of course, walking into harm's way was one of his favourite hobbies, but this was a time of professional and personal uncertainty. After dreaming for a few years that he was a golden poet with a golden voice and a golden wife, born to shock Canada and indulge himself, he suddenly became aware, as he walked the streets of Manhattan in increasingly black moods, that he still was what he had been in Montreal fifteen years before: a creature of desire and lack, with an abyss inside him and inane levels of ambition. His hunger for recognition was gnawing at him every day. And this is when he crossed paths, probably first in late October, with a fearsome blonde who almost instantly — as the poet wrote — "captured [his] shadow."[48]

Blinded perhaps by the churches of Montreal and the luminous angelic theology of Denys the Areopagite, Leonard may have neglected to reread the more obscure *Sefer Raziel HaMalakh*, a treatise on angels compiled by his namesake rabbi Eleazar of Worms, a thirteenth-century disciple of Judas the Pious. Inspired by the abundant Babylonian demonology, Eleazar asserts that there is an angel in charge of every man's destiny (a classic position shared by

Saint Thomas Aquinas), but also that the whole universe is popu-lated by angels and demons. "No corner is empty," says the rabbi before setting up a frightful demonic typology made of invisible spirits (or *naziquim*), evil spirits (or *ruhin ra-hot*), shadows (or *telanen*), and nocturnal spirits (or *lilin*).[49] The angel that Leonard has just met in New York may well be a female incarnation of the Malakh Amawat, a.k.a. "the angel of death," from whose gaze no one escapes and that no one keeps waiting, unless she be Lilith, Adam's legendary rejected first wife, now the tormentor of men who sleep alone.[50]

In any case, in October 1966 or perhaps February 1967, between a writing session at the Chelsea and a night spent cruising the all-night cafés, Cohen commits the irreparable: he walks down the steps to the basement bar of the Polsky Dom Narodny (also known as "The Dom") on that section of Eighth Street they call St. Mark's Place, which had just been rented by Andy Warhol for his multimedia show: the Exploding Plastic Inevitable. Under a stroboscope, Gerard Malanga and Edie Sedgwick had danced there with a whip while the Velvet Underground played a loud urban rock with droning violins and detuned guitars. As for Warhol, he projected experimental movies on the band (filmed portraits, footage of the Empire State Building, and so on). With the deepest voice that ever came from a female body, the singer — a hieratic blonde beauty — was chronicling the misfortunes of a pop Cinderella:

And what costumes shall the poor girl wear
to all tomorrow's parties?

The day Leonard Cohen pushed the door and sat down at the bar, the walls were still covered in aluminum foil but the Velvet was no longer there. Warhol had moved to the basement bar, where he was sponsoring the solo act of the chanteuse, his superstar of the year and soulmate of the moment, German model Christa Paffgen, a.k.a. Nico, a stunning beauty and Köln's very own femme fatale. Together, they had just shot the movie *Chelsea Girls* and announced the end of the '60s in *Esquire* disguised as Batman and Robin. That October or February night,[51] in that cavernous voice that seemed haunted by an impalpable absence, Nico sang the pop tunes of her first opus, *Chelsea Girl*, and a few other songs of infinite sadness composed for her by the likes of Bob Dylan, Lou Reed, John Cale, Tim Hardin — a whole army of authors at her service. On stage, she was accompanied by a single instrument: a guitar played by a very young Jackson Browne, one of her many androgynous boyfriends. Behind the bar, Leonard Cohen was transformed into a statue of salt.

It's impossible to understand that moment if we don't forget for a moment the iconic Nico, rock star and junkie goddess, to see instead the woman that Leonard must have seen. For this, the fourth scene of *I, a Man*, shot by Warhol and Paul Morrissey the following summer, is the ideal tool.

I, a Man, scene 4. Six minutes filmed in static shot. A conversation between Nico and actor Tom Baker and, to close the sequence, a kiss. What do we see? First, we see irrefutable beauty. Nico's face comes straight from Plato's world of pure forms. Beneath the iconic style of the '60s (bangs and dramatic eyelashes), we see Doric perfection, classicism at its most astounding — an impeccable symmetry of features, a Roman nose, and lips by Botticelli. She is literally sculptural. Or like Baudelaire said, "fair as a dream of stone."[52]

And yet, a closer look at the sequence shows endless life on that face and in the model's gestures. Nico smiles, she lowers her eyes, looks at the sky, makes faces, seizes a glass with her huge, white, sculptural hands, brings it to her lips, swings from one leg to the other, puts a finger on her mouth, flicks back her hair. A grammar of gestures with nothing learnt, nothing that suggests posing or the "professional" cuteness of the model; just a natural sophistication and something inside her that is irreparably absent.

Then there's the voice. Beneath a strong German accent lies something like a tenor bell — the lowest bells of cathedrals —

something dark, cracked, and very low. Not so much an angelic voice as the voice of an armour-clad archangel.[53]

Nico sings at the Dom almost every weeknight from February to April and a fascinated Leonard will return dozens of times. To him, that beauty made of flesh, darkness, and ice was a signal of Nico's absolute superiority, which bestowed her the authority of a goddess. After being introduced to her by Lou Reed, he often brought songs as gifts, but Nico will ignore every single one. Being a very frank creature, she also warns him: when she visits the world of mortals, she prefers her men young and handsome: Alain Delon or Jim Morrison — the Adonis type. So, things are clear from the onset: Leonard stands no chance. But the goddess offers her friendship and the poet accepts, fully aware that he is entering a season of high turbulences and unbearable suffering.

The *Zohar*, the foundational book of the Kabbalah, describes Lilith as a winged creature with long hair who seduces men in their sleep to give birth to Nephilim, nocturnal demons that prevent their soul from ever finding rest. Nico will obsess and haunt Leonard for many months, never granting him more than just holding her hand in the back of a taxicab or looking into her eyes, forehead to forehead. He saw her unclothed once or twice, and that was it.[54] This is a new love position for the Lothario of Montreal: the slave, the humiliated one, the one howling for his mistress's love. For Nico, he will carry amulets, interrogate the *I Ching* a thousand times, and practise rituals to attract the good graces of Venus: candles shaped like naked silhouettes, cones of different incense to mix masculine and feminine smoke, prayers addressed to God on High.[55] The entry in an unpublished diary for March 15, 1967, says it all:

> Terrible day. Endless thoughts for Nico. Guitar dead, voice dead, melodies old and lying [. . .]. Nico in a terrible mood. Tried to keep her by my side for a few moments. Impossible.[56]

Possibly, Cohen then understands that terrible truth about love that the Jesuit Michel de Certeau formulates thus: "We become the guest of another who worries us, strips us of our solidities and keeps us alive: the Christian experience par excellence."[57] Whether or not that anguish had opened an access to grace is unknown, but it certainly allowed Leonard to better grasp the central tenet of the troubadours' *fin'amor*: every poet must be defeated by love. The desire for Nico that he had allowed to grow inside him is indeed reminiscent of the suffering described by thirteenth-century poet Thibaud de Champagne, who compares himself to a smitten unicorn killed by treachery after falling asleep on the bosom of its beloved virgin:

> I was killed in the same way,
> by Love and my lady — that is the truth:
> they hold my heart and I cannot take it back.[58]

So, for half a year, possibly a little more, Nico becomes Leonard's inaccessible lady. During that time, he writes many poems that describe how she lives "like a god," taking baths dressed in a heavy black dress and clipping her nails with razor blades.[59]

Of course, the fascination exerted by Nico on many men is in many ways connected to her own alienation. An opiate addict who seemed to be worshipping heroin, she undoubtedly became for Leonard a new embodiment of the junkie as holy martyr: a saint whose addiction dictated an existence that was as pure and elementary as the white powder she consumed, and a martyr because she paid her daily tribute of insanity to her invincible alienation.[60] More prosaically, Nico was deaf in one ear, something that Leonard took many months to understand. She therefore answered questions randomly with constant non sequiturs and oracle-like pronouncements. Little wonder if her many suitors, among them Brian Jones, Jim Morrison, Jackson Browne, Lou Reed, John Cale, Iggy Pop, and Tim Buckley, saw in her an embodiment of destiny or death: Medea for some; Fata Morgana for others; the definitive femme fatale for Warhol; and a Valkyrie for Leonard. Remembering French history, he later transformed that woman whose coldness reminded him of the Canadian winter into a "Winter Lady" and, in two songs, into an inaccessible Joan of Arc, with an army at her disposal:

> I met a lady, she was playing
> with her soldiers in the dark
> One by one she had to tell them
> that her name was Joan of Arc.
> I was in that army,
> yes I stayed a little while.
> I want to thank you, Joan of Arc,
> for treating me so well.[61]

Also inspired by the poetess, the darkly humorous "One of Us Cannot Be Wrong" is like a war memorial to the fallen men of Nico's wars of love. Cohen lists the casualties — a frozen Eskimo, a doctor gone mad, a saint who drowns in a pool, and a ghost who drools at her beauty — and closes the song with an imploration:

> But you stand there so nice
> in your blizzard of ice,
> O please let me come into the storm.[62]

The singer later explained that he had seen in Nico "the perfect Aryan, the queen of ice" and her Germanity obviously played a part in the hold that she exerted on the Jewish poet. For someone who had published *Flowers for Hitler* less than three years before, it must have been difficult to resist a woman he later described as "the apotheosis of a Nazi Earth Mother."[63] As though Nico was the German persecutor he had imagined five years earlier:

For you
I will be a Dachau Jew
and lie down in lime
with twisted limbs
and bloated pain
no mind can understand.[64]

In his '60s memoir, entitled *Popism*, Warhol remembers how Cohen sat fascinated, night after night, unable to take his eyes off Nico. He hypothesizes in the book that the singer was discovering the pop virtues of low-pitched voices.[65] Perhaps he was falling in love with the voice that would be his twenty years later, detecting in Nico's timbre something he deeply aspired to: the depth of gravity, a metaphysical space where Nico already lived "like a God."

Two more songs Leonard wrote for his unattainable lady are "Take This Longing" and "Winter Lady." The latter portrays a winter muse who is about to leave: she's already on the doorstep. To hold her back a minute or two, the speaker tells her that she reminds him of a former lover, one who wore her hair like her when he was a soldier. Surprisingly, few people have noted the similarities between Marianne Ihlen and Nico Paffgen, but in retrospect, how not to see Nico as Marianne's dark double? Both women are Aryan beauties; both speak with a Germanic accent; both are mothers of fatherless boys of similar age (little Axel is six and a half while Nico's son, Ari — who will soon turn out to be a spitting image of Alain Delon — is five). On the left is Marianne, a Virgin with child and discreet angel of domestic life, and on the right is Nico, a Poetic Medea and angel of death. And in the middle is Leonard Cohen. Hesitating.

"Winter Lady" seems to illustrate the infinite frailty of all things: the frailty of a love affair and of a moment (with a woman about to depart, almost already lost); the frailty of a resemblance (between the "winter lady" and the "child of snow" — Nico and Marianne); the frailty of a woman's sleep and that of the melody itself — one of Leonard's most delicate, later played on his first album on a detuned piano. And frailty was certainly something the poet was experiencing to the fullest in that winter of 1967. It was increasingly clear to him that this life in New York, and the accompanying drugs and unrequited passions, were taking their toll and weakening him. What will follow is a determining insight.

IMAGINARY SATORI: THE PHYSICAL LAWS OF THE UNIVERSE

I am with the falling snow
falling in the seas.

— LEONARD COHEN, "ON HEARING A NAME LONG UNSPOKEN"[66]

New York, winter 1966–1967. Nights and days haunted by an inner avalanche and a sense of collapse.[67] A few snapshots of his daily life will give us a further glimpse of what Leonard goes through: he destroys a Mexican twelve-string guitar by jumping on it "in a fit of important fury." He takes fifteen minutes to decide whether or not he should wear a cap when he leaves his room, and half an hour to decide if he should take it off when he comes back. He writes three songs about suicide, two that mention abortions and another two with stillborn babies. He slams his green Olivetti against a wall after a failed attempt to type in his bath. He sponsors the novels of three runaway girls and calls himself a "literary pimp." He describes the heart as "an unfathomable refrigerator," the world as a "vast monastery," and himself as "the voice of suffering that cannot be consoled." Intrigued by an inscription on a sandwich board carried by a blind man ("Please, Don't Pass Me By"), he follows him in the snow down Seventh Avenue and finds himself surrounded by dozens of cripples who are all singing that same plea, revealing to him the true pulse of the city and the depth of his own need for love.[68]

Obviously, in the last few months, Leonard has taken a lot of walks in New York City, he has sat in a lot of all-night cafeterias to blacken a lot of pages, and he has taken a lot of rides in elevators where he met angels that were not always angels. But every night out has invariably taken him back to that room at the Chelsea with a view on Twenty-Third Street, the focal point of all wanderings and the obscure centre of all circles: just a table, a window, and a bed. Hence a question: what is it that happened there that made the songs of the first album so clear, so precise, so self-evident? How did Leonard Cohen give birth to a world in his room at the Chelsea Hotel?

Here again, we can only surmise. But inevitably, Leonard must have used his hotel window for his favourite game: seeing the world as it is. It always begins with an inventory — you just name the things in front of you.[69] In the present circumstances, the hundreds of windows of the buildings across the street, a few neon signs, the record shop named Interesting Records, and the Bronco Burger. Then you name the things that pass by and never stop: yellow cabs, Cadillacs, a couple of pedestrians hurrying home, a few lost souls. The list continues with what falls from the sky: the rain, the sleet, the snow (it's the winter of 1967, an inordinately cold winter even for New York, with snowstorms till late March). And, at that moment, Leonard must have seen the first angel fall. And he must have understood. The physical laws of the universe. A Newtonian epiphany — nothing too complex, actually. Having seen from his window the falling snow, the falling angel and, in his life, the falling saints, he registers a first law. One that is elementary and inescapable: gravity. "Many men are falling," as he will soon argue in song.[70] Everything that doesn't move falls, everything that falls breaks. He notes in passing how poignantly beautiful falling bodies are but, immediately, he moves on. Having seen the pedestrians pass and the Cadillacs flash by, he understands that the world cannot be inhabited. It can only be passed through. Homelessness and exile are therefore our true condition. And that's the second law of Cohen's world: the universal gravitation of beings.

Being the logical type, he surmises that a third law is necessary to hold the universe together. Otherwise, gravity and gravitation would have destroyed it long ago. And that's when the great insight must have come. That cohesive force, the third law of the universe, is the universal attraction of bodies, the very force that attracts him right now to the Germanic goddess: Love itself.[71]

And, inevitably, several more satori — sudden moments of awakening — ensue in quick succession. These laws are not just abstract principles, or just forces at work in the world, but extensions of God that must be studied. The Talmud had warned him: a law is not just a prescription, but also a path that leads to God. And inflexible as they are, the three physical laws Leonard has just listed are indeed expressions of the Father's most benevolent pedagogy. Universal gravitation incites us to reinstate the hospitality of the world every day. The law of gravity helps us understand the true weight of our lives (and, with a little luck, the ultimate weightlessness of all things). And the law of irresistible attractions reminds us that alone we are nothing: we must dissolve into love.

The only thing that was now required of Leonard was to translate those laws poetically. A task best done bent on a table in a hotel room, possibly with an acoustic guitar and a green Olivetti at hand. For things now were self-evident. The themes of the forthcoming album? Universal homelessness. Incessant departures. The split between man and woman, between man and God, between human beings and their soul. The metaphors to be used? Avalanches that eat you alive, love as a fire that burns you to ashes, apocalypses in every heart. Also suddenly clear was the topography of the Cohenian world: a city caught in a snowstorm, a road that calls, the sanctuary of a hotel room, and, of course, that holy place where lovers meet: the embrace, the wedding, the orgy. And, right there in his room, Leonard also knew what characters should inhabit the songs: an absent God that he will never again mention so little, femmes fatales who trick you into the furnace, stray angels who attempt to mend the world even if for two hours), and every form of traveller: lovers who seek love, lovers who flee love, travelling ladies, and demobilized soldiers. His world was complete.

The poet also understood that the songs would have to be heroic as well as lyrical. Because of the fundamental discrepancy between our desires and God's laws. We want to inhabit the world; we are thrown on lines of flight. We want to rise and shine; we fall. We want to be self-sufficient; we get caught by irresistible attractions and indomitable desires. Hence, two options — the great Cohenian dilemma at this stage. We either negate the laws of the universe, get defeated, and become "beautiful losers," for who are we to contend with gravity or desire? Or we accept these laws and become saints: we become Suzanne. Whichever option we choose matters little: it's a losing game, anyway. A game that makes us all failed heroes. But the Gospel's claim that "the first will be last and the last will be first" (Matt. 20:16) was not lost on Leonard. Sitting in that hotel room on a winter night in early 1967, he surmised that our heroic task is to move from one defeat to the next, with only one certainty: "Everything that you lost, you'll never have to lose it again."[72] It isn't much, but it's a start. He had just created a world.

CHAPTER 5

A TROUBADOUR IN MANHATTAN

SONGS OF LEONARD COHEN
1967–1968

Are you a teacher of the heart?
We teach all hearts to break.

— LEONARD COHEN, "TEACHERS"

Leonard Cohen, Montreal, 1973

A TRAGICOMIC SEASON

When Leonard met John Hammond, presumably in early April 1967, Hammond, twenty-five years his senior, was the famous man. He had discovered Billie Holiday, Aretha Franklin, and Bob Dylan, and was one of the top executives at CBS. He also had the moral authority that came from his involvement with the Civil Rights Movement. After a little coaxing by Mary Martin and Judy Collins, the producer had finally seen *Ladies and Gentlemen . . . Mr. Leonard Cohen* and was impressed enough to go and meet Cohen (whom he also knew as the author of Collins's recent hit "Suzanne") at the Chelsea. He had lunch with the poet at the El Quijote, and together they went up to Leonard's room where the A&R man heard "The Stranger Song," "Master Song," "So Long, Marianne," "Winter Lady," and a few others for the first time. He knew instantly that he had the next big folk star sitting opposite him and decided to sign Cohen on the spot. His company was not so easy to convince ("A thirty-three-year-old Jewish-Canadian poet? Why not sign Moses as well?") but Hammond insisted and, less than three weeks later, Cohen did sign a recording contract. This led to the discovery of a new elevator — one leading to the recording studios on the fifth floor of the CBS building on East Fifty-Second Street, where records were made with a view of the Manhattan skyline.

Although it was a long and painful process — twenty-one sessions stretched out over six months in four different studios[1] — the recording of the album, which began on May 19, would bring a touch of comedy to the depressive turn that Leonard's life seemed to have taken. It would include several nervous breakdowns, rumours of a heart attack, many quarrels, three successive producers,[2] and the intervention of a hypnotist. But the result turned out to be one the most memorable first albums ever made. It would hit the shops in late December 1967 in the US and January 1968 in the UK — an eternity from now. Many angels will pass in between; some with a blessing, some with a chuckle.

On that first day, May 19, John Hammond, who has gathered a team of seasoned session musicians, is probably hoping for a swift operation thanks to his well-honed method: to read the newspapers, smoke a cigar, and disturb the artist as little as possible. Perhaps an encouraging word or two when necessary.

But then there was the Leonard Cohen factor. Suddenly in terra incognita, surrounded by professional musicians, with the studio clock ticking, the poet almost immediately finds himself barely able to play, let alone sing. He knows, however, that the rest of his career depends on those sessions, so the inevitable happens: he starts to panic.

The first problem is language: he doesn't speak the musicians' lingo and has to rely on Willie Ruff, the bass player, a former Dizzy Gillespie collaborator, to translate his impressionistic indications (i.e., "play greyer") to the session players. Soon he feels — probably rightly so — that everybody is laughing at him. Then, there's the issue of the studio space itself. Leonard doesn't feel quite at home at CBS (where does he?), hence a few unusual requirements. Maybe the studio could be made to replicate the exact atmosphere of his room at the Chelsea. So the lights are turned down, candles and incense sticks are lit, and — the poet being used to singing in front of his wardrobe mirror — a full-length mirror is brought in. Fifty years later, a muffled laugh or two can still be heard. A few sessions go by; a lot is recorded. Cohen feels self-conscious and unsure of his voice.[3]

So after a couple of painful sessions, the band is sent away. Work resumes with just the producer and Willie Ruff. Leonard tries on seventeen songs, not all of them good. Hammond is a busy man, and he's used to temperaments like Dylan's, who records albums in three days. He gradually loses interest, and the Cohen sessions are increasingly spaced out and sometimes rescheduled. By early summer, the inevitable happens again: the singer has lost contact with his songs and has to consult a hypnotist to get back in touch with the silent space inside him that the songs emerged from.

Meanwhile, it's July 1967, the "summer of love" and for a couple of months, the universal consciousness is relocated to San Francisco. Leonard plays a couple of festivals on the West Coast but, after a short summer break in Hydra, tragicomedy resumes in the CBS Studios: Hammond has a heart attack. Or at least, that's what the rumours then say. Most likely, the producer is using earlier health problems to hand over the Cohen sessions, which have clearly stalled, to a younger colleague. In mid-September, with no song completed so far and the album nowhere, a dejected Leonard disappears for a week of sulking at the Chelsea Hotel, where he apparently spends eight days in his room in a hashish daze, probably also doing some serious rewriting.

He relocates to a bleaker hotel (his beloved Henry Hudson) and sessions start anew in October under the direction of a twenty-four-year-old producer who has one idea a minute. His name: John Simon. The two men get on quite well and Leonard's songs about lovers bound by spider webs and golden strings inspire the producer. At some point, since Cohen refuses to use strings, he suggests female voices as ornaments. Enter his girlfriend Nancy Priddy, who adds a few "bom-bom, ba-la-la-la-las" to "Hey, That's No Way to Say Goodbye" and soaring voices to "Suzanne" and "So Long, Marianne." Hallelujah! Leonard likes the sound — a major step forward.[4]

But Simon, who is simultaneously working with Simon & Garfunkel and has just produced a major hit for the Cyrkle, wants to give the record a folk-pop twist. He is determined to use whatever means necessary: a barrel organ, bells, horns, muffled trumpets, and a detuned piano. Plus drums on "Suzanne." Which entails disagreements, discussions, and despair, finally leading to Cohen's satirical text on the back cover of the finished record:

> The songs and the arrangements were introduced. They felt some affection for each other but because of blood feud, they were forbidden to marry. The arrangements wished to throw a party nonetheless. The songs preferred to retreat behind a veil of satire.

But Simon is a gentleman: he gives in and lets Cohen get rid of some of his arrangements and mix the record himself. So early one morning in November, in an editing room called studio E, on the top floor of the CBS building, a poet warns the engineer: either they succeed in erasing some of the instruments from the mix or he commits suicide.[5] A week later Cohen is still alive. After three last-ditch sessions to add mandolin, a Turkish luth, and other Middle Eastern instruments to a few tracks, courtesy of a West Coast band called Kaleidoscope that Leonard has just recruited in a bar where Nico was playing, the album is finally complete, with the discreet presence on some tracks of another key ingredient of the early Cohen sound: a Jew's harp. After six months of work, many sleepless nights, and much more money spent than CBS had originally planned, *Songs of Leonard Cohen* is finally ready for release. Available just after Christmas in the US and two months later in Europe, it will be sent to radio stations with a press kit that mentions the "hypnotic, spellbinding" effect of "lyrical and universally poignant songs." Not exactly a lie.

A year earlier, a Canadian weekly had asked, "Is the world (or anybody) ready for Leonard Cohen?" With hindsight, it was clear that the house producers at CBS were not, but the question seems a good one: in the context of high psychedelia and acid rock à la Sgt. Pepper, was the world ready for this album? The answer is yes, of course, but it's hard to explain why. With no drums (except on "So Long, Marianne") and only traces of electric guitar, Leonard's waltz melodies and flamenco-inflected folk must have sounded resolutely untimely. But being "untimely" is perhaps the first step to becoming timeless.

SONGS OF LEONARD COHEN: AUTOPSY OF A SPELL

What strikes even today with *Songs of Leonard Cohen* is how bewitching the album is. With its nocturnal universe, its waltz melodies, the singer's haunting voice, and the endless guitar arpeggios, the record just grabs us and doesn't release its grip.

First reason: the voice. Not yet very low, but already endowed with an infinite capacity for murmurs. There's hardly a loud word on the album and the singer (who barely *sings* at all) seems to address each listener personally, as in a private confession. Recorded so close that every inflection, every inbreath, every click of the tongue can be heard, Leonard's voice, in its infinite quietness, sounds almost as if it actually came from inside ourselves, as if his confessions were actually ours, and we were the ones in cahoots with the Suzannes, the Mariannes, and the angels in hotel rooms.

The second factor of bewitchment is the quality of the story-telling. The album's effect is almost that of a novel: the first song introduces a poetic universe and opens an unspoken plot that each successive track seems to advance. A plot about male and female seekers and their quests for love and redemption in a fallen world.[6] With many encounters on the way: soldiers, saints, and madmen. It's almost like a corpus of old tales: a saintly woman shows the ulti-mate beauty of each moment in her mirror ("Suzanne"), a mistress realizes she is only a pawn in her lover's spiritual war game ("Master Song"), travelling ladies and card dealers find out they are ultimately "strangers" to each other ("The Stranger Song," "Winter Lady"), while departing lovers turn farewells into moments of grace ("Hey, That's No Way to Say Goodbye"). "Stories of the Street" condenses the suffering of a whole city into one hotel room, and another room becomes an asylum thanks to two angels and a moonbeam ("Sisters of Mercy"). The album ends when the pilgrim who sought a "teacher" in hospitals and orgies ("Teachers") finds one in the snowstorm of a woman's body ("One of Us Cannot Be Wrong"), closing our journey with the dissonant "la-la-las" sung by a frozen lover lost in the blizzard — an ironic inversion of the aerial grace of "Suzanne" that had opened the record. The circle is complete, from the saint to the femme fatale, all in the name of love.

Third factor of bewitchment: the music. Incredibly poetic in its own right, the album's soundscape introduces the prototypical early "Leonard Cohen sound": mid-tempo ballads delivered in a precise soft voice accompanied by a warm, nylon-stringed acoustic guitar. Plus the Leonard Cohen magic, of course: a clever tension between a melody — usually a very simple, almost child-like waltz (literally a ritournelle, something that goes round in a circle[7]) — and, beneath that melody — actually supporting it — the straight line of rolling arpeggios borrowed from flamenco, sometimes with a tremolo: chords repeated very fast to give the songs drive, drama, and suspense.[8] Add to this a few embellishments — discreet strings here, an isolated organ chord there — and each song takes on a strong metaphysical resonance. The ritournelle suggests an escape towards Heaven; Leonard's voice reminds us that everyone must fall and the rolling arpeggios say that time matters, and the end is near. The female voices are pure incursions of grace or (to be precise) incursions of shekinah, a Kabbalistic term that designates mercy and consolation, God in his feminine aspects.[9] And when they are evident only in their absence (as here in "Master Song," "The Stranger Song," and "Teachers"), the angelic voices evoke the exile of shekinah, a world temporarily deserted by grace.[10] So, for once, the press kit was not lying: it's spellbinding indeed.

When *Songs of Leonard Cohen* started getting airplay in America and Europe in early 1968 and made its way onto the charts, often staying for weeks or even months on people's record players, listeners probably perceived, in one way or another, that the sonic texture of these songs, the musical formula, had a "depth" of its own that located the listener in a metaphysical landscape. The Leonard Cohen magic: metaphysics for the ears.

The last vector of bewitchment is of course the writing itself — sharp, luminous, and gorged with mystery. Leonard claims that "the limpidity of certain Scottish ballads" has helped him purge his style and it's certainly true.[11] In "Teachers," the meter of medieval ballads gives his modern story of quest in psychiatric hospitals the resonance of centuries, just as the poet elsewhere concentrates what could have been a full-fledged novel into just 300 words ("Master Song"). He will repeat it for decades: a song is not intended for the page. It has to move swiftly "from lip to lip and heart to heart," which means perfect metrics and direct language.[12] And pretty soon, the music press spreads the news: there's a new poet in town; his name is Leonard Cohen; and he's the missing link between Lord Byron and Bob Dylan.

A sequence in Don Owen's feature film *The Ernie Game*, shot that winter in Montreal, illustrates the power of that first album. The movie chronicles the return to civilian life (after a stay in a psychiatric hospital) of Ernie, the anti-hero, who seems to come straight out of one of Leonard's songs. A failed writer and incorrigible womanizer, he is obsessed by sainthood but always ready to break into ex-girlfriends' apartments to disrupt their lives. The scene in question takes place in one of those huge white apartments where the Montreal bohemians seem to have spent the decade. A party is in full swing as the snow falls over the city. From the kitchen (where he tests his love rhetoric on yet another girl), Ernie makes his way to the living room, attracted by arpeggios played on a Spanish guitar. There, with his back turned to a large baroque mirror, Leonard Cohen is singing "The Stranger Song" with his eyes closed. All around him — on the sofa, on the floor, against walls — is an assembly of neo-beatniks (mostly young ladies) who seem absorbed. Everywhere, there's '60s beauty in full swing: eyelashes like black corollas, geometrical dresses, cigarettes, and feather scarves, and all manner of short and long hair. The girls all seem mesmerized by that ballad about the eternal temptation that seizes men to leave their ladies. A lovely blonde girl clutches her glass of wine and closes her eyes, as in intense contemplation. Around Leonard, for three minutes, everybody is an existentialist.[13]

That scene may remind one of the cover of Jimi Hendrix's *Electric Ladyland*: a dozen naked girls looking at the camera in a photo studio. In *The Ernie Game*, the girls are not naked, but they might as well be — they have found their Pied Piper. Only the singer looks curiously absent. With drawn features and a thin and tired face (amphetamines, perhaps), he seems to have withdrawn into the song. He is the empty centre from which the bewitchment unfolds. The black hole. The white avalanche.

THE TROUBADOUR OF '60S HEROINES

Despite its odd timelessness, *Songs of Leonard Cohen* is also a '60s classic and very much a record of its time. The universe created in the songs — a world made of orgies, hotel rooms, psychiatric hospitals, and train stations — mirrors New York in 1967. Men and women undress for each other, but never stay the night. Madmen, saints, and demobilized soldiers are lost in forlorn streets, and everybody is looking for grace. Leonard's heroines, who walk German shepherds with "collars of leather and nails" and meet their lovers in temples "where they take your clothes at the door,"[14] are evidently the liberated assertive women of the sexual revolution that adorned the covers of *Vogue* or *Harper's Bazaar*.[15]

It's a little as if Bernard de Ventadour had left the twelfth century to fall in love with Nico's mascara in the holy freedom of the Chelsea Hotel. Leonard just reconfigures the troubadour as an existentialist poet, seeking what type of courtly love can survive in the age of free love and existential despair. *Songs of Leonard Cohen* is definitely a troubadour record on which the singer declares himself — like all troubadours — a *subject* of Love: he is *subjected* to it (he falls in love all the time), serves it (the way you serve a mistress), and considers love as a spiritual path and an initiatory experience. It's just that for Cohen, loving means losing, and lovers are by nature losers.

There's no doubt that the allegorical image of feminine grace in "Winter Lady" — a woman weaving her hair on a loom "of smoke and gold and breathing," a metaphor that speaks of the frailty of all bonds — would have made Leonard's reputation in twelfth-century Languedoc. With figures like Marianne and Suzanne, it's also easy to see why the record immediately earned the singer the support of the female audience, establishing his reputation as a great poet of woman-hood and a great connoisseur of the ways of love. Less than two years before, Dylan had sung "Just Like a Woman" and "Sad-Eyed Lady of the Lowlands." Dylan has just been out-troubadoured.

As for the album cover, it is both overly romantic and secretly funny. On the front, a sepia portrait of a shy-looking poet with a nice side-parting and an intense gaze, taken in a photo booth in Grand Central Station.[16] Critic Roland Barthes explained that every face seems to be "about to speak" on a photograph, and this is clearly what that cover suggests: Leonard would like to speak to us — and he will if you buy the record.[17] On the back, however, is a widespread votive Catholic image (a postcard that Leonard bought in Mexico): the Anima Sola — literally a "solitary soul": a young naked woman caught in flames, symbolically figuring the souls of the purgatory (who need our prayers). Now, in Cohen's universe, turning things over is revealing their metaphysical side and therein lies the cover's secret joke. On the front, a bashful poet (i.e., what Leonard seems to be). On the back, what he really is: a burning soul that hopes to be purged by the flames. If this is not deadpan metaphysical humour, then I don't know what is.

Of course, *Songs of Leonard Cohen* is also where the misunder-standing begins: the supposed sadness of the songs, and the clichés about depression and the irrelevance of poetry in rock. Ideas that rock critics will soon churn out in truckloads.

THE ORIGINAL TRAUMA

Leonard had prepared for the record's release with a few concerts. His first public performance in New York took place February 22, 1967, on the Town Hall Theatre of New York stage at a benefit concert for the Vietnam Day Committee where Judy Collins had invited him to sing "Suzanne," a traumatic affair that would impact his relationship to the stage for a long time. Unable at first to tune his guitar and distraught by the sound of his own voice, the singer stopped mid-song and walked off stage. Bye-bye, guest star. Bye-bye, high priest. Bye-bye, career. Backstage, Collins coaxed the poet into returning on stage — she will sing the song with him. And there he was: defeated and (one imagines) with his trademark sheepish smile. A little boy too shy to sing without his mummy by his side. So at thirty-three, the age of Christ, Leonard found out that declaring metaphysical wars to Hitler is one thing and singing in public is another. There's something, however, that he doesn't notice that day, but that Collins mentioned every time she related the anecdote: how much the audience cheered when he came back. They had fallen in love with the trembling poet — a love story that would last for several decades.[18]

In the summer, Leonard gives five cabaret-style concerts (sometimes accompanied by the Stormy Clovers) at the Montreal World Fair, Expo 67. Of course, he refuses to sing unless a candle is lit on every table (he has to feel at home, you see). On July 16, still invited by Collins, he is paid fifty dollars to present his songs at a songwriting workshop during the Newport Folk Festival, the high point of the folk liturgical year. A considerable challenge. A photograph by David Gahr shows him backstage alongside Joan Baez, Joni Mitchell, Arlo Guthrie, and Judy Collins: everyone seems magnetized by what happens on stage (Joan even stands on tiptoe to see better). Only Leonard stands back, with a pronounced stoop, hands in pockets and guitar on his back, looking terrorized. He gives three more performances that summer — at a festival in Central Park, at the Mariposa Folk Festival near Toronto, and at Big Sur, California — hippie gatherings where the poet does not make a strong impression.[19]

But when CBS devotes its Sunday morning cultural program *Camera 3* to Leonard Cohen (his world, his songs, his women), the *New York Times* announces, "the probable future spokesman of his generation." *Songs of Leonard Cohen* is then praised in the *Village Voice, Sing Out! The Beat, Vogue, Harper's Baazar, Mademoiselle,* and

most of the music press (with a few reservations here and there[20]).
With good reviews, quite a lot of airplay, and a song on its way to
be a hit for the third time ("Suzanne"), logic would have it that the
singer did a tour of North America. But the artist says, "Nyet." He
already told his manager: he's not a singer.

ANNÉE ÉROTIQUE

Actually, the non-singer has more urgent business to attend to that
year: to get off amphetamines and take his revenge on women.[21] For
him, 1967 will indeed be the year of Eros. As 1968 will be, and 1969,
and the following two decades. He says it himself in the first version
of "Chelsea Hotel":

> My friends of that year they were all acting queer
> Me I was just getting even.[22]

So, he gets even. Increasingly frustrated by Nico and still theo-
retically engaged to Marianne (who, probably tired of waiting in
Greece, was having lovers of her own), he starts an affair with the
twenty-four-year-old Canadian songwriter Joni Mitchell. That
summer, every young folk chanteuse wants a Leonard Cohen song
(preferably a hit). Not Joni. She wants Leonard Cohen: the existentialist poet just for herself. As she will later confess, of the "holy
wine" this man is made, she could "drink a case" and still "be on her
feet."[23] Half-seduced, half-unavailable, the poet plays Pygmalion: he
gives the young singer a reading list and a restricted access to his
heart. Together, they visit his mother's house and stay in the young
woman's villa in Laurel Canyon, but she will never be Leonard's
"official" girlfriend: free love is in the air and, as many tenants have
noticed, the girls at the Chelsea are not exactly shy. In an interview
during a photo shoot with Richard Avedon two years later, Leonard
recounts what his life was like at the Chelsea:

I was very hung up on sexual truth in those days . . .
I felt like if any two people had any kind of sexual
affinity they had to sleep with each other immediately,
otherwise it was a terrible betrayal and waste . . . I
spent a lot of time trying to decipher what the feelings
I had for someone were and whether I had to sleep
with them or not . . . Fortunately, I'm relieved of those
obsessions now. It's really wonderful not feeling you
have to sleep with everybody.[24]

If we go by the poems, Leonard also has affairs with a French model, a young rich heiress's daughter, several muses and groupies, and actually pretty much any available girl who happens to come his way. In November, when journalist Paul Grescoe spends a few days with the singer in New York for a profile in *Canadian Magazine*, he sees him surrounded by Cassandra ("20 years old, a baby face, bracelets and high leather boots"), Donna (18 years old, "looks like an Egyptian Pharaoh"), Denise (16 years old, Donna's flatmate), and Louise ("his new muse"). He notes how the singer "comes alive in the company of women."[25]

Many testimonies describe the young Cohen's "knack" with girls. And undeniably, he had a few assets. As a troubadour, he seemed to professionally retain some occult knowledge on Love and his constant references to the Kabbalah, angelology, the Song of Solomon, and fin'amor surely made for a much better pick-up routine than that of your average hippie proselyte of free love. What is more, the young man was now in his mid-thirties, and he had a way of making twenty-year-old girls believe that he knew them much better than they knew themselves. In December, he declared to the *New York Times* that he was ready for matriarchy and gave the journalist the whole works: sex as a eucharist, alchemy's great work realized between sheets, the lovers' embrace as the only way to dissolve ontological solitude, women as eminently spiritual creatures.[26] A well-honed discourse that must have made a few victims at the Chelsea and the time is not far removed when the poet will ask female journalists to interview him naked.[27] But to be fair, despite its demagogical overtones, Cohen's shtick about women is at least partly sincere. As we remember, he has asserted since adolescence that the undressed body of women gives off a light that can dissolve you. Since then, he has read the works of Carl Gustav Jung and discovered that there exists in the soul of man an inaccessible feminine part called "anima" (Jung also calls it "Our Lady of the Soul"[28]) that can be reached only in the company of women or in the contemplation of their anatomy. As someone who enjoys the company of saints (he reads Saint Theresa of Avilla, collects pious images, and brings flowers to a statue of Saint Kateri on the portal of St. Patrick's Cathedral), he is convinced that for a man who comes to them with a pure heart, all women are saints and that they remain holy virgins even in the midst of lovemaking for whoever can see the Virgin in them.

In that erotic year of 1967, Leonard checks out the theories behind the Kabbalah and the Song of Solomon: in the interlockings of the flesh, in the fire of embraces, in the kisses on mouths which are exchanges of souls, men and women discover their own souls and obtain in the process "the consolation for the bitterness of life" that comes only with sex and religion.[29] Many women seemed ready to test those theories in his company and check whether erotic encounters were indeed dances of the soul and whether you can really "touch [a] perfect body with your mind."

But let us be precise. At this stage, Leonard was not yet the Casanova who would later haunt the bars of luxury hotels in Armani suits whom Anjelica Houston would describe in the mid-'90s as "part angel, part wolf."[30] In her confessional songs, Joni Mitchell described her lover of one season as a "devil wearing wings." She claims to have liked the "collected women" in his "gallery" (until she became part of the collection) and described him elsewhere as a gambler that she caught cheating "once or twice."[31] Cohen's friend Jennifer Warnes, who first met Leonard in 1972, would later evoke "a trench-coated dark angel on the prowl."[32] Which all means that women perceived both the celestial part in Leonard, and his strong desire for them. And also his talent for opacity and absence, his aptitude to remain elsewhere even in their company: partly in the avalanche; partly in the hotel room. He was the ideal man, therefore: simultaneously a father figure, a wounded child, and a professional lover — half theologian; half sex addict. How could women resist? So For Leonard, 1967 was the année érotique. As were 1968 and 1970. And a couple of decades after that.

LONDON CALLING

In rock music, 1968 is a year placed under the aegis of the letter *H*. *H* is for "Hendrix," who turns up the volume of American rock forever; for "heroin," the drug that was starting to cause serious havoc; and for "heavy," the fetish word of that year (exit "groovy"). Everything was "heavy" in 1968: sex, drugs, politics, and even Beatle songs.

As the coffins were flown in from Vietnam, the '60s lost their lightness: protests turned to riots in a climate of civil war and political assassination. For Leonard, however, 1968 was the year of international recognition. Still in New York, he struggled with depression, self-medicated with acid and Mandrax, and had at least three simultaneous romances: with Joni Mitchell, Scientology, and the El Quijote restaurant on the ground floor of the Chelsea Hotel. "Suzanne" was a hit again — this time in the author's version, which seemed to confirm that a new career was coming his way. As soon as he was ready, Leonard would be a rock-and-roll star.

For the time being, it's January and after a short and stormy stay in Greece with Marianne, the poet is heading for London to promote the record. A short performance for the BBC in a TV program hosted by a friend from Hydra, *One More Time with Julie Felix*, makes him an overnight celebrity. Wearing a velvet peacoat on a cream-coloured turtleneck, he unfolds a bewitching version of "The Stranger Song" with his eyes closed. Seven minutes of pure mystery that open a new path for English pop. The tear that runs down his cheek on the last chord is just one more sign that Lord Byron has indeed survived the swinging London and that his name was Leonard Cohen. The following summer, the singer is a guest on *Top Gear*, John Peel's trendy radio show, and he appears two Saturdays in a row on *Prime Time on the BBC*, for the two parts of a splendid and luminous radio concert.

Listening to that recording today, it is hard to understand why Cohen refused to tour: he jokes, improvises songs, makes fun of himself, charms everyone — he seems already at the top of his game. And the songs, meticulously interpreted, beam with luminous gravity. There's "Suzanne," "Sisters of Mercy," and "So Long, Marianne," of course, but also two infectious black waltzes he has just finished writing during a stay in California — "Story of Isaac" and "You Know Who I Am," plus a crooner ballad composed in Greece: "Bird on the Wire." The applause is intense, and Cohen's art appears again for what it is: a bewitchment.

The Times places the singer "halfway between Bob Dylan and Schopenhauer"[33] and *Songs of Leonard Cohen* soon reaches #10 in the UK charts, where it will stay for eighty-three weeks. Reviews for the album are occasionally ecstatic (as in *The Observer*) and across the channel, Cohen will soon become an idol. After his second album and a TV appearance courtesy of Joe Dassin (another Hydra friend) Leonard will be acclaimed in Gallic land by all sides of the political spectrum, from the new left of *Le Nouvel Observateur* to the Communist Party (who invite him to the "Fête de l'Humanité"), the countercultural *Rock & Folk*, or the conservative but poetry-loving President Georges Pompidou. Already in 1968, the solemn-voiced New Zealander Graeme Allwright had translated "Suzanne," "The Stranger Song," and a few others into French, bringing them into the local charts, beginning his "Suzanne" with a great line that Leonard would never have written: "Suzanne t'emmène écouter les sirènes."[34]

In Canada, aware that there is a new covenant between their author and youth, McClelland & Stewart publishes a Leonard Cohen anthology in May 1968 (*Selected Poems: 1956–1968*). Twenty thousand copies are sold over the summer and ten times that amount in the following months. Something has obviously changed in scale. The collection wins the Governor General's Award (missed in 1961 and 1966), but this time Leonard refuses the prize, arguing that the poems themselves "will not allow it." Tantrum? Revenge? Political protest about the situation in Québec? None of the above? We will never know and Leonard probably didn't know, either, but the refusal caused a minor scandal in Canadian letters and angered quite a few people. But it didn't matter anymore. The *bird on the wire* had flown away. Had he not just been seen in Los Angeles with chic hippie friends? Or was it Morocco? Or Paris, perhaps? At any rate, the poet was now a rock star, and the European music press was waiting for his next move. The great misunderstanding was about to begin. How do you say "melancholic" in Québécois?

CHAPTER 6

INTO THE AVALANCHE

THE PRINCE OF SAD PASSIONS, OR LEONARD THE OBSCURE
1968–1972

I'll speak of the dark.

— ROGER GILBERT-LECOMTE, *Testament*[1]

Leonard Cohen Superstar, *Montreal Gazette*, August 25, 1973

THE INFUSION OF DARKNESS:
A PORTRAIT OF LEONARD COHEN AS ALT-ROCKER

As a prologue to an ode to Leonard Cohen published in *The New Yorker*, Leon Wieseltier demonstrates the superiority of sad passions over happiness with two decisive arguments: 1) that sadness is a form of contemplative life — albeit an incomplete one; 2) that despair is an indispensable component of humour.[2] Hence a double reason to hear what sad poets have to say: they alone know the true state of the world and they alone have a true comic genius.

At the dawn of his songwriting career, Leonard Cohen was no stranger to black humour, and he certainly knew that there was a luminous potential in the colour black. Still, his initial trilogy, *Songs of Leonard Cohen* (1968), *Songs from a Room* (1969), and *Songs of Love and Hate* (1971), isn't exactly teeming with jokes and it proposed something then quite unheard of in pop music: a dive into the night.

With their recurrent references to black bile, razor blades, and sleepless nights, the first three records, when listened to in a row, could indeed be summed up with a famous pop tautology: "black is black." Hence of course the clichés ("music to slit your wrists by"), the sobriquets of a supposedly biting English music press ("Laughing Leonard," "The Prince of the Bedsits" . . .), and a public image that would stick to the singer for thirty years: that of Leonard Cohen, poet laureate of unhappy consciousness who unfolds an uninterrupted defence and illustration of melancholy — Eli, Eli, Lama Sabbactani and other delights.[3]

Clichés are impossible to refute, for the simple reason that they tell the truth. But they do so in such a crude way that what they claim to reveal becomes invisible. Hence a necessary effort: to forget the clichés and return, again and again, to the artist's original gesture and — in the present case — to remember that, in his pursuit of darkness, Leonard Cohen has objectives of light: once a Kabbalist, always a Kabbalist. But making melancholy luminous and blackness tonic is no mean task. It's an alchemical operation that was once called nigredo. The principle? You let the blackness of the world brew and macerate in you until the properties of light are isolated through fermentation and distillation.[4] A dangerous art obviously — as all alchemists know — and several decades spent exploring the dark zones of the psyche have not left Leonard unscathed. But such is the price of poetry, as French surrealist poet René Daumal reminds us: "Every poem is born from a black seed that must be made to produce fruits of light."[5]

Cohen will thus come up with decisive metaphors to describe depression: it's sexual union with the night, or being swallowed by an avalanche, or eating all your meals with a scalpel and a silver spoon.[6] Those images of course will not endear him to the many rock critics who think his vision too dark, his voice too grim, his tempos too slow. An opinion apparently shared by one of the Isle of Wight Festival organizers, who declared in 1970 that "Leonard Cohen is a boring old drone [. . .] and he should fuck off back to Canada where he belongs."[7]

And yet, Leonard's darkness was actually very much in tune with the late 1960s. After 1968, the atmosphere in the counterculture wasn't exactly carefree and, with political disillusionment, the rise of heroin, and an overall sense of fatigue, every pop idol seemed to be struggling with a dark angel. Forget the fringe jackets and coloured headbands and Jimi Hendrix appears for what he is: an electric shaman who expressed the dark side of hippie hedonism in quasi-voodoo guitar solos. And while Jim Morrison exposed his black soul in leather pants and forgot to resist his own shadow,[8] Janis Joplin seized everything that was dark in the blues to cry out with quavers and trills her despair that hippie love was not to be after all. The difference with Cohen was, of course, the mode. Rebellious as they were, Jim, Jimi, and Janis were also to some extent the obedient children of the Woodstock ideology. In full conformity with the great rock narrative of transgression, they unfolded their art and life exclusively on the epic mode, with hyperboles galore and constant challenges to society and death. In all three cases, death quickly called their bluff, giving the hippie pantheon three beautiful martyrs and sellers of posters an income for life. In that context, Cohen's great dissidence — the one that *Rolling Stone* would never be able to forgive — was to become the tireless champion of the minor mode.

Perhaps coming from somewhere else — from a Greek island, from the literary scene, from a Jewish family, from the 1930s — had taught him a few things that Jimi, Jim, and Janis didn't know. For example, that the radiant presence of death in us requires great delicacy, not drunken brawls and mud fights. You can speak to death as a sister as Saint Francis of Assisi had taught, and the black nights of the soul mostly call for great patience.

The great theatre of rock-and-roll rebellion was completely alien to Leonard. Instead, he wrote intimate folk songs with precise lyrics, whispered singing, and — to preserve the songs' ethereal quality — hardly any drumming on the first three records. So, inevitably, the tempos were slower, the record covers less exuberant, and, during concerts, Leonard Cohen did not invent melancholic stagediving. However, he invented a middle way in rock with songs that spoke to the soul and subjects that were underground by definition: the mysteries buried in our hearts.

So against all odds, in 1968, while the English press thought they were dealing with a poet lost in rock music, Leonard Cohen invented alternative rock. And it turns out he agreed with other alt-rockers in saying, "In the beginning was the darkness." Which is what alt-rocker Dante had said back in 1308 when he began his great poem with the words: "Midway along the journey of our life, I woke to find myself lost in a dark wood." Alt-rocker Saint John of the Cross agreed when he explained, three hundred years later, that in order to reach grace one must cross two very painful dark nights of the soul. And the shy alt-rocker Sylvia Plath (who invented the cold wave in London in 1960) said nothing else when she wrote: "I'm terrified by this dark thing that sleeps in me."

So, in the beginning was the darkness, and the darkness was with Leonard and the darkness was Leonard. Between 1968 and 1972, the singer turned that darkness into three luminous records which earned him a large following in Europe and his reputation as a prophet of doom. At the end of 1966, to Nico's great admiration, he had invented the "black photograph" in New York City. It's a simple technique: you prepare the composition and the lighting, you put the lid back on the lens, you take the shot. And the photograph, inevitably, is black. For a while, there was talk of an exhibition,[9] but luckily Leonard moved on to other projects, namely the first three records which, in their own way, propose a topography of darkness. And although Leonard claimed in "The Stranger Song" that he had "no secret chart to get you to the heart of this or any other matter," the public immediately felt that Leonard's maps would lead them somewhere interesting. Where exactly is what we will now find out.

REDNECK CONNECTION: IS IT ROLLING, BOB?

The story continues in Hollywood. After a first short stay in Los Angeles in 1967, when he was solicited by John Boorman for a film score he never wrote,[10] Leonard returns to the West Coast in the spring of 1968 for a project by Michael Barry called *The Second Coming of Suzanne*, a screen adaptation of the famous song. The script is about a filmmaker obsessed with the idea of a female Christ who ends up crucifying his main actress (Suzanne, of course). The project would be delayed for six years, Leonard having forgotten to specify that he no longer owned the rights of his song, but it brought the poet back to the City of Angels in late April 1968. He stayed there a couple of months, biding his time and visiting friends, lodging first at the Landmark Motel (home of penniless rock stars, where he met Janis Joplin again[11]), then in Joni Mitchell's house in Laurel

Canyon. At the Landmark, he polishes two songs he had just written in Greece and that he would first perform the following summer at a radio concert for the BBC: one is about a bird perched on a wire; the other about Isaac's sacrifice. In May, only a few days after writing a postcard to Marianne where he tells her he "has abandoned the career of singing," he spends a couple of days in a Hollywood studio working on demos for the new songs with David Crosby, of Byrds fame.[12] Unsurprisingly, he disliked both the arrangements — too poppy — and his singing — too insincere.

Meanwhile, *Songs of Leonard Cohen* was selling quite well in Europe and not so badly in the United States (where the record hit #64 in the charts). So much so that the artist's record company and manager (still Mary Martin) started to insist: could he please go on tour, make a new album, and do more public appearances? The album's reputation was actually quite phenomenal, to the point that even Beatle John and Beatle Paul had allegedly asked for a copy during a business trip to New York in May. But the singer is in no hurry. He actually enjoys his status as a reclusive songwriter.

In Los Angeles, a decisive meeting takes place when Leonard speaks to one of the *hype* producers of the time, Bob Johnston. With his shaggy beard, his suede jacket, and his crazy high-pitched laugh, Johnston was the man who had reconciled Nashville and the counterculture. In the previous two years, he had crafted the sound of Dylan's *Blonde on Blonde* and Simon & Garfunkel's *Sounds of Silence*, and recorded Johnny Cash's concerts in Folsom Prison. He can summon his army of mercenary musicians and book you a session in Columbia's mythical Studio A in three phone calls. He will also dance for you in the studio if it makes you sing better. Still paid union rates at this stage, he is the first producer to have an agent (soon to become Leonard's) and the one that all hip artists want to work with. Over drinks, Bob and the wandering Canadian have a conversation in the no-bullshit style that is the Southerner's trademark. The subject: what is good on *Songs of Leonard Cohen* and what sucks on it. After an hour, they have agreed to work together on Leonard's new songs and the singer feels he has found a musical soulmate at last. And an idyll begins between the poet and the producer. It will last for almost three years with a very strict distribution of roles. As musical director, organist, semi-manager, and friend, Johnston will be Leonard's anchor in the material world: he will produce records, set up touring bands, organize auditions, and even find the poet a house in Tennessee. As for Leonard, he will be Bob's anchor in the world of the Invisible. Which is the poets' task, as everybody knows. And that is how, between late 1968 and early 1972, the author of "Suzanne" became a kind of poet-in-residence in rural Tennessee and Johnston's Zen master in plain clothes.

For the moment, an appointment is made for the autumn of 1968 to see what could be done in the studio. So that in October, after a couple of months in New York and a short stay in Greece (his last summer with Marianne), Leonard, a star in absentia in London, finally arrives at the art deco lobby of the Noelle Hotel on Fourth Avenue, with the *Zohar* under one arm and a childhood friend — filmmaker Henry Zemel — under the other. We can imagine his reaction when he discovered, in a park just blocks away from the city's countless honky-tonk bars, a life-size replica of Athens's Parthenon. Intact and new, of course. He must have loved Nashville.

Flash forward to understand what is going to happen in the studio. First stop: three and a half years later, April 1972, Jerusalem, on the last night of a tour. The scene is captured by filmmaker Tony Palmer. For a series of reasons to which we shall return, the concert that has just ended is both a catastrophe and a miracle of grace. In the hall, the audience is singing Hebrew prayers for Leonard. They have just clapped for half an hour and they refuse to leave. Backstage, everyone (the backing singers, the poet, the roadies, and even the manager) is moved to tears and Leonard thinks his career is over. In charge of troop morale, Johnston knows he must act fast. He grabs a guitar and starts singing "Bird on the Wire," turning the song into a funny serenade that is supposed to cheer up the poet, who is struggling opposite him between laughter and tears. That sequence in Palmer's *Bird on a Wire* illustrates what all the musicians who worked with Johnston repeat: he is the sweetest guy in the world and he works miracles. Here, he is singing to Leonard to convince him to return to the stage he has left in mid-concert, but he might as well be out in the Tennessee fields, singing their song back to the crickets to get them to sing louder and console the world: Bob Johnston.

In Nashville, everything was supposed to be easy, and the producer had warned the poet: in the South, clocks don't work and the musicians love to stay late at night and get paid overtime. So, the first thing to do under the cathedral ceiling of the mythical Studio A that first night of recording (on Friday, September 26, five days after Leonard's thirty-fourth birthday) is to order beer and hamburgers and get to know the musicians. On one side, an introverted Jewish poet who knows five flamenco chords. On the other, the Nashville mercenaries: Charlie Daniels on bass, Ron Cornelius on guitar, Elkin Fowler for the rest, and Charlie McCoy as backup — Johnston's private army, with Viking looks and redneck jokes. They expected to see (as Cornelius later explained) "an intellectual who doesn't sing too well" and this is exactly who they meet.[13] Two years earlier, Johnston had brought Dylan into this very room and the city had not recovered. After keeping everyone awake for eight hours (the time it took to rewrite the song), the prophet had recorded "Sad-Eyed Lady of the Lowlands" in one take — a cultural revolution. With Cohen, the first session was not as productive. For Leonard had listened very carefully when God told Adam he shall eat his food by the sweat of his face. After dozens of takes, the singer is not satisfied. Johnston raises his hands to the sky to encourage Leonard and he becomes more and more jovial as the night progresses — a bad sign. The following sessions were not any more successful, as Cohen would later recall:

> I played with a bunch of really good musicians, but listening to the playback, I thought my voice sounded fake. I asked the guys to go home and told Bob I was

done. They couldn't squeeze me like a lemon to get another record out just because people had liked the first one. Bob said, "Okay, let's drop it," and I went back to my hotel, increasingly depressed.[14]

Perfectionism is a silly term. An artist never seeks perfection; he seeks accuracy. In Leonard's case, "limitless accuracy" as a critic later put it.[15] As he often explained, he wants his songs to be so sharp that they cut through our opinions and tastes, right to the truth of our inner lives, and he aspires to sing like how a Zen calligrapher paints: on a single impulse that is clear, alive, and true. For this, nothing must get in the way of the singing. The slightest approximation, the tiniest lie in the lyrics and the words get stuck in the singer's throat. So after a few sessions, there was only one thing to do: rewrite, cross out, clean up. The sessions resume in late October with rewritten lyrics and, this time, Leonard's friend Zemel plays the cheapest instrument in the world: a simple metal rod that you place in your mouth and strike with your finger: a Jew's harp. That instrument will kick off *Songs from a Room* and its metallic vibrations will almost single-handedly define the sonic colour of the album. Leonard always thought that the Jew's harp was the harmonica of the Jews. When he heard it that night in Nashville, he must have felt at home. Is it rolling, Bob?

NOTES FROM A BLACK SQUARE – *SONGS FROM A ROOM* (1969)

The title tells you all you need to know about the songs: they were born in a room. A hotel room probably, but also that secret chamber of the heart which Leonard has turned into a photographic dark room. There, thanks to the developing bath of his pessimism, he has isolated very precise images of his heart and of the world. His aim: to clarify despair. To give a clear vision of it.

With dry humour, the record cover hints at the dark contents: confined in a black square, Leonard Cohen's tired face stares at us, as though looking out of an abstract window. His parted lips suggest he is about to speak but, frozen in the night of his own record, he says nothing. From inside that dark room, he will sing about the subtle art of finding your way in a pitch-black night — the main theme of the album. And certainly, *Songs from a Room* crosses a threshold with a darker vision and a new sobriety.

Having defined his role as Leonard's "musical bodyguard,"[16] Bob Johnston chose to protect the artist's music from outside incursions.[17] His objective: to help us focus on the lyrics and the guitar work and make us hear the songs for what they truly are: haunting melodies that rip your heart open. *Less is more*, therefore, with just a handful of instruments: a bass that shapes out the melodies, a Jew's harp that wraps up the songs in metallic vibrations, and Johnston's Hammond organ — just a chord here and there to give the songs a vaguely sacramental colour. At the centre of it all: crystalline melodies. Around them: almost nothing — just silence put into music.

But Cohen is in Nashville and he surreptitiously adopts some of the local idioms. "Bird on the Wire" opens the record with a Ray Charles–styled crooner ballad and, strummed on a dark guitar, "The Butcher" unfurls a wicked little blues that puts God himself on trial while "Lady Midnight," "The Old Revolution," and "Tonight Will Be Fine" veer towards the upbeat end of country and western.[18] Johnston's organ plus echo on the voice transform "Seems So Long Ago, Nancy" into the funeral dirge the song aspires to be, and the only track that strays from the minimalistic recipe ("A Bunch of Lonesome Heroes") shows, with its drum breaks, its crescendos, and electric guitars, the rock balladeer that Cohen could have been. But the peak of the album is elsewhere: in three simple waltzes.

Three waltzes that remind us that when Leonard dares to be minimal and truly dark, he has a very acute melodic talent. It's the same formula for the three songs: an insistent loop of rolling guitar arpeggios kicks off the track, gives it a pulse, and fills it with tension. Then the singer lays down his vocals on that loop in a fragile waltz melody in minor mode. Already tested on "The Stranger Song" and "Master Song," that formula — the archetypal early Leonard Cohen song — finds its perfection here. With "You Know Who I Am," an intriguing dialogue with God and evil. With "Story of Isaac," Leonard's dark rewriting of a biblical episode. And, of course, with "The Partisan," a cover of a French resistance song. There, the Cohenian treatment works wonders: a relentless tremolo and a knell-like bass — ding-dong, ding-dong, ding-dong — fill the song with metaphysical suspense and off goes the gloomy waltz. In each case, there's tension and drama and grace. A film noir atmosphere that speaks to our soul.

The end result is ten sober songs and barely thirty-five minutes on the clock. The band was obviously aiming at efficiency with a simple objective: to serve the poet's vision. A successful operation.

THE EXISTENTIALIST TROUBADOUR

Hence, a first remark: the record is very different from the first one. *Songs of Leonard Cohen* was a troubadour's record, replete with worshipped ladies and erotic encounters. Here, only "Tonight Will Be Fine" (an evocation of Marianne written years before) fits that description and few women of flesh are actually even mentioned. The narrator may see his Montreal friend Nancy "everywhere" ("Seems So Long Ago, Nancy"), but the song is an elegy written after the young woman's suicide and a portrait of her as a martyr of free love.[19] "Lady Midnight" evokes an allegorical mistress whose body is "eaten by stars" and who teaches Leonard the necessity to unite with one's inner night. Not exactly a woman of flesh. And since women are Leonard's great mediators to grace, beauty, and angels, there will be little of each on the album. Instead, *Songs from a Room* examines what happens when grace is suspended and consolation withdrawn.

Of course, this is Leonard Cohen *opus 2* and there are obvious similitudes with *opus 1*. It's just that the troubadour is replaced by an existentialist philosopher who seems obsessed with a single question: what to do with the freedom that insists in us in a world where freedom is impossible? For Leonard, this is not an abstract question at all. Trapped in past relationships, pressurized by his record company, feeling dishonest as a lover, illegitimate as a singer, and unfulfilled in his spiritual ambitions, he is probably enslaved as well to a couple of drugs (opiates among them) that help him regulate his mood. Most days are actually spent struggling with anguish (sometimes desperately so) and in the midst of it all, he is indeed still trying, in his way, to be free.

To examine this dilemma, *Songs from a Room* proceeds methodically, starting with a simple observation: all hearts belong to heaven and long to be back there ("Bird on the Wire"). But the laws of the universe — gravity among them — are inescapable ("The Butcher") especially when they are backed up by the inflexible Law of the Father ("Story of Isaac"). This is called an aporia, an unresolvable contradiction: on the one hand, a freedom that insists; on the other, its programmed defeat.

Hence, the hidden thesis of *Songs from a Room* — our lives find their meaning precisely in that aporia: at the very junction point where the yearning to be free comes up against its impossible realization. In every song, Leonard puts that thesis to the test, each time with new literary form: a hymn in "Bird on the Wire," a biblical story in "Story of Isaac," allegories in "The Butcher" and "Lady Midnight," a philosophical dialogue in "You Know Who I Am," an elegy in "Seems So Long Ago, Nancy," a confession in "A Bunch of Lonesome Heroes," a political tract in "The Old Revolution," and an anthem in "The Partisan." In philosophy, reviewing all aspects of a notion is called an "anatomy," and that would actually be a good subtitle for *Songs from a Room*: "The Anatomy of Impossible Freedom."

Hence a record with strong existentialist overtones and (quite logically) a mega-hit in France. It chronicles many dangerous confrontations: with the father's axe ("Story of Isaac"), with the butcher's block ("The Butcher"), with bourgeois morality ("Seems

So Long Ago, Nancy"), with German occupation ("The Partisan"), and of course with clinical depression ("Lady Midnight"). In every song, Leonard celebrates the heroes who obey when freedom insists: the partisans who refuse oppression, the birds who refuse gravity, the girls in green stockings who choose to love whoever they want, and even the Mandrax-fuelled singers who try to get rid of despair.

With its trinity of sex, drugs, and revolution, *Songs from a Room* is also a topical album that offers an accurate picture of the late '60s. The recurrent references to smoke, sacrificed children, and butchery show the undeniable presence of Vietnam but, being who he is, Leonard approaches political issues from the metaphysical angle.[20] Like an elder brother, he tries to teach his hippie audience a couple of things he thinks they should know about politics. Namely that revolutions are systematically betrayed by revolutionaries ("The Old Revolution"). That true heroes are always lost in the dark ("A Bunch of Lonesome Heroes"). That the sons will always be sacrificed on the altars of the fathers ("Story of Isaac"). And that flowers grow where the throats of lambs have bled ("The Butcher").

This metaphysical realism earned Leonard an interesting nickname, coined by the French novelist Michel Houellebecq: the "impossible libertarian," a phrase that points out the singer's ability to celebrate our longing for freedom without succumbing to slogans or cheap utopias, as the late 1960s invited him to.[21]

So, in the era that produced *Hair* and *Jesus Christ Superstar*, Leonard sought to readjust hippie idealism with healthy doses of voluntary pessimism. Each song on the record is a little injection of black insulin to keep us sharp and lucid. The objective (as always): to help us see the world as it is. Death exists — no one can escape it. The opacity of things exists — no one can escape it. Failure exists — no one can escape it. As for love, it's a two-faced affair: it enlightens us, but sets our lives on fire. So, Leonard was indeed a "grocer of despair" (as he would soon joke) before he was a smuggler of light.

BIRD ON THE WIRE

"Bird on the Wire" is like a condensed version of the singer's pessimistic credo. We know the opening:

> Like a bird on the wire
> Like a drunk in a midnight choir
> I have tried in my way to be free.

"I have tried": that's actually an acknowledgment of failure. Flying is the privilege of birds and angels — try to imitate them and gravity soon gets back at you. Imitate an angel and you end up a brute — the principle is well known since Pascal.[22] What follows in the song is a first version of that "manual for living in defeat" that Leonard was still trying to write forty years later.[23] For the moment, he isolates three steps: you expiate your sins ("If I have been unkind . . ."), you promise the impossible and try to keep your word ("But I swear by this song . . ."), you strategically fall back on the tiniest of freedoms: that of the drunkard who sings in the night, that of the worm who wriggles on the hook. "Bird on the Wire" or the secret glories of Plan B.

There is nothing resigned about the song, however. When Cohen asserts that failure is our homeland (we live in a world where things fail), he simply invites us to a Copernican revolution: to see defeat as the place of appeasement. The place where the obligation to succeed dissolves. The place therefore where fraternity is possible. And the parade of losers in the song (a defeated knight, a stillborn baby, a cripple, a worm, a woman who is a wee bit too pretty . . .) is there to help us locate our own intimate failure so that we may, from that place, fraternize with others. Hence a liberation of sorts: no longer alone (we have brothers and sisters in defeat) and no longer ashamed, we can begin to live our lives with the tiny grace of the sparrow. Like birds on a wire.

With the full force of the crooner's toolkit — warmth in the voice, a Hammond B3 organ, jazz brush sticks, violins, and soaring musical phrases — Leonard makes us feel in the recording the sweetness of the unburdening that comes with renunciation. The song is not a prayer, but it is perhaps Leonard's first psalm and the perfect antidote to Sinatra's triumphant "My Way," released the same month.

Therefore, it's easy to understand why Cohen would soon describe his songs as "songs of personal resistance," not "protest songs" that claim to change the world, but little waltzes that comfort the soul and unify the heart. The best songs on the record ("The Partisan," "Story of Isaac," "Bird on the Wire," "You Know Who I Am") can indeed be used as immaterial talismans that we carry about in our hearts. They are also spiritual weapons that force us to explore the most desperate areas in ourselves, with the hope that the landscapes we find there are actually less bleak than we had thought.

SALVATION THROUGH DESPAIR

> *NO is my name.*
> — RENÉ DAUMAL, *Le Contre-Ciel*[24]

By choosing to stimulate our aptitude for pessimism on this record, Leonard introduces an idea that will stay with him his whole life. A scandalous idea — even more so in 1969 than today. An idea that Zen will soon enable him to specify: that despair is not necessarily desperate. Practised as a voluntary asceticism, as a radical refusal of illusions, despair can become a "non-hope" that can be a virtue and, in some cases (as Leonard seems to imply), a path to salvation.[25] It is theologically audacious and pure Leonard Cohen: salvation through despair. We are very close here to the "negation as positive act" that obsessed French surrealist poet René Daumal: an absolute and systematic NO that is so radical it becomes an act of emancipation and illumination. On *Songs from a Room*, Leonard's pessimism is indeed an asceticism, a gigantic NO, a rejection on principle of ideological consolations and cheap joys. In this sense, that NO, though dangerous, is an act of unburdening, but one bound to be largely misunderstood in the context of hippie hedonism.

What many critics failed to see at the time is the subtlety of Cohen's approach. His songs proposed a spiritual experiment: for the duration of a song (or an album or a concert), while we stand protected by the melodies and their dark beauty, not to avoid despair, but to greet it instead and look at the world from the radical perspective thus provided.

And then to note how strangely tonic the experience can be, how it makes you sharper in your appraisal of truth, how it can brace your heart, deepen your compassion, and boost your sense of inner readiness. If you're lucky, that is. If you're lucky, you return from the song sharper and better equipped cognitively and spiritually. If you're not, you've just taken a ride on a dark waltz.

Of course, voluntary pessimism is a dangerous game that requires a great leap: to refuse the crutch of ideologies and easy consolations and see if one's ability to hope survives. And that kind of wager — an inverted Pascalian wager — is never won for good: tonic pessimism, lightness in gravity, good mood in despair are *active practices* that can never be taken for granted. And for three more decades, Leonard himself, in his struggle with depression, will have countless opportunities to explore the moving borders between pessimism and despair, lucidity and hope, enlightenment and self-delusion. He will, of course, not come out of the experience unscathed, but with interesting thoughts to share. And a few songs to sing.

For the time being, he transforms "The Partisan" (the most fatalistic French resistance song, which shows freedom fighters fleeing gun in hand and counting their dead every night) into a metaphysical hymn.[26] During his first two tours, he will dedicate that song to those who struggle in the world, but surely he also meant the great inner struggle, a resistance against an inner occupation, against the darkness inside. It's very clear in the way he sings the song — with blank voice and closed eyes — during his first appearance on French television in May 1970. After four minutes and forty seconds, when he has reached (with eyes still closed) the promise of the last line ("Then we'll come from the shadows"), the wry smile on his wiry face shows that this man evidently knows a thing or two about how dark the nights can be.[27]

In the late fall of 1968, at the end of the recording sessions, Johnston knows that *Songs from a Room* will be a landmark in modern folk music and certainly a hit record. Something extraordinary has happened in the studio. A poet had stolen the Nashville idioms to sing the mystery of the world in such a compelling manner that his musicians were not just convinced; they were converted. In just two months, Johnston and Ron Cornelius have become fully fledged Cohenians who will follow the poet on the road for several years. Their future testimonies suggest that a saintly hero (perhaps King David) had briefly left the pages of the Bible to have a couple of beers and record a few psalms in Tennessee. Travelling incognito, he had taken the guise of a Canadian poet interested in Buddhism and country and western. As Cornelius would later say, "Leonard taught me to take care of my guts more than anyone else" and the confession rings true: in the topsy-turvy world of Leonard Cohen, it is indeed the poet's task to teach hard-boiled, moustachioed guitar players and seasoned, brawling rock producers how to live their lives. Percy Bysshe Shelley didn't think otherwise: poets are the "unacknowledged legislators of the world."[28]

In mid-April 1969, as Leonard (still incognito) was travelling in the desert and smoking kief in Morocco, *Songs from a Room* reached number two in the English charts and number ten in Canada, an honourable score the year of *Abbey Road*, *Nashville Skyline*, and *Led Zeppelin II*. Very soon, with the help of "The Partisan" and exquisite French covers of his songs by New Zealand folksinger Graeme Allwright, a Cohen-mania seizes Gallic land, where he was declared by the left-leaning *Le Nouvel Observateur* "folksinger of the year."[29] Likewise in Germany, where the Jewish poet was adopted by the younger generation. This time around, Leonard would not be allowed to escape; he had to go on tour. At least that's what his new agent Marty Machat was telling him.

With an office high above Forty-Second Street, Machat, a former employee of Allan Klein who had briefly managed the Rolling Stones and the Beatles, looks the part: long raincoats and unreadable smile — the ultimate éminence grise. He has taken an instant liking to his new client, with whom he shares a taste for good-looking women and well-cut suits. As for Leonard, putting himself in the hands of someone called Machat must have seemed like a natural step: Macha was his mother's first name.[30]

Before the tour, however, the balladeer tries to gain a little time: he has to pay a visit to a couple of saints. Afterwards, he swears — cross his heart — he will be available. The first saint, Francis of Assisi, is dead and Leonard (who has always adored him) travels to Italy to visit his tomb. There, another Francesco (Zeffirelli) is preparing a movie about the "juggler of God." To highlight the saint's luminous simplicity and validate his countercultural aura, the director wishes to include a few acoustic folk songs and he thinks Leonard is the man for the job. So in June 1969, the singer takes a train from Paris to Rome and from there he proceeds to Assisi with the *Brother Sun, Sister Moon* producers and another Leonard (Bernstein, also involved in the project) to visit the basilica built on Francis's tomb. There, he "takes away" a couple of metal birds, has them blessed by the abbot, but declines Zeffirelli's offer. Donovan will replace him.[31] Back in Rome, Leonard sees Nico again, who still declines his offers for sex, and returns to New York.

The second saint is alive, and Leonard has already met him. In January, at a friend's wedding in Los Angeles. The friend in question was Steve Sanfield, a veteran of Hydra's esoteric club, and the ceremony rather original: a Zen wedding, Steve and his wife Jacquie being the disciples of a continually irate-looking Japanese master called Joshu Sasaki Roshi. Leonard — who is Steve's best man — is impressed (as he would often tell) by how the holy man allegedly produced a bottle of sake at the precise moment when the bride and groom renounced all intoxicants (one of the traditional bodhisattva vows). If the scene really happened, it must have made the nine-year-old Talmudist inside Leonard smile, as was the case every time he was confronted with the beauty of paradox. This time around, he barely speaks to the roshi but he promises to come back to the roshi's dojo and give Zen practice a try. Pretty soon, he will.

ELEVATOR FOR SUZANNE

For the moment, his quest for redemption has led the poet up another path. In that spring of 1969, he had indeed been following the Church of Scientology teachings for almost a year.[32] The adventure will not last much longer, but it will bring an encounter with the category of beings that is most dangerous for Leonard: a luminous nineteen-year-old girl.

One version of the story sets the meeting in the Plaza Hotel elevator. The girl, dark-haired and of stunning beauty, is from Miami. She lives upstairs, apparently at the expense of a rich businessman and it is not unlikely that she is actually operating as a hooker. Leonard is here to attend a Scientology meeting, but his peace of mind will have to wait. The girl will see to that. Legend has it, it went like this: she gets out of the elevator, he gets in. He turns around and, before the doors close, steps out and speaks to her.[33] Banal. Except we don't know what they say. We don't know what Leonard Cohen's pick-up routine is in 1969. He's a smooth talker for sure, and can be outrageous, but presumably, there must have been an exchange of names. "Me Leonard" — it must have started like this: "Me Leonard." Then came the lady's answer: three familiar syllables. "Me Suzanne." Me Leonard, You Suzanne.

And then what? A burst of laughter? The world stopping on

its axis? Did Adam and Lorca — the couple's future children — smile from the depths of that emptiness mentioned in Zen koans about the faces of children before their parents were born? Did Leonard immediately think of the biblical Susanna, who inflamed the lust of old men when she bathed naked in a garden?[34] Did he foresee the succession of joys and sufferings — the romance, the bliss, the war in the bedroom, the flight to Israel, the infidelities, the reconciliations, the violence, the divorce — that would lead him fifteen years later to live in a trailer on the edge of the mater familias plot with a ban on entering the grounds? Did he foresee the numerous songs the affair would inspire ("There Is a War," "The Gypsy's Wife," "I Tried to Leave You" . . .) and anticipate the parts he would cast that woman in: angel, lover, gypsy, temptress, demon, shrew? Probably not. In all likelihood, nothing happens. Just Suzanne meeting a half-famous songwriter who wrote a song that she probably knows because her name's in it.[35]

One thing is certain: Suzanne breaks a cycle, the cycle of women (real or imaginary) whose names start with a "J" (Judy, Janis, Joni, Joan, and Jane) and begins another series, as Dominique Issermann would point out thirty years later[36]: the names that end with an "an" sound: Marianne, Suzanne, Issermann . . . Poets just can't help it: things have to rhyme. What we also know is that very soon after the meeting, as an attentive reading of *The Energy of Slaves* will confirm, Suzanne leaves the Plaza to take up residence in Leonard's room at the Chelsea, a few steps down in terms of comfort, from high luxury to decrepit bohemia. And in a matter of weeks, the "couple" is in Montreal — where Leonard introduces her to his circle and to his mother — and in Hydra, where Suzanne will later write a pornographic novel and hang erotic engravings beside his holy images. There's something karmic about it: he had lost the rights of "Suzanne" almost immediately after writing the song; another Suzanne is returned to him. She will prove to be a formidable adversary. Leonard doesn't know it yet, but it's the beginning of the death of a ladies' man.

JEWISH COWBOY GOES TO NASHVILLE

Meanwhile, Leonard chooses to settle in Tennessee for a while. And, while he's at it, why not real Tennessee? For example, a place known as Big East Fork, a few miles out of Franklin, twenty-five miles southwest of Nashville, where Leonard rents a log cabin in the middle of nowhere (actually 1,400 acres of wood). Three small rooms, with a skylight and a fireplace, a mattress on the floor, a table to write on, a creek a stone's throw away, and pheasants and wild peacocks as the only visitors. A pastoral paradise, where he will bring Suzanne in 1969. A million trees away from the Chelsea Hotel. For seventy-five dollars a month, what more could a poet want?

Big East Fork may seem an odd choice for a trendy folksinger at a time when hippie communes and eco-friendly villas were flourishing in California. Unless we understand what that log house was for Leonard: a new hermitage that happened to be close to the office (the Nashville studios). The word *hermitage* comes from the Greek *eremetos*, desert, and we can imagine Leonard sitting in that desert with his Olivetti and his guitar nearby, listening to the wind. In front of him, hazel trees, beech trees, black ash trees, and oak trees. There, two years in a row, he watches the Indian summer turn slowly to autumn, knowing that only two things can happen. Either God will speak to him (which is what hermitages are for) or he won't and in both cases, he will have something to write about: God's message or his silence. There's probably also the hope that the things that were so heavy in New York — the suffering, the dissatisfaction, the rain, the ego — might be a little easier to bear here. It's the principle of eremitic life: to leave everything behind and enter the other life that awaits in the great silence of things. A life that reconnects you to the invisible. "To use clouds for ballast and live in heavens with roots on the earth," is how medieval monks summed it up.[37] Leonard, as we know, loves contrasts and dialectics. After being an asphalt pilgrim for three years in New York, he had to become a hermit in Tennessee. Of course, he is not Saint Anthony in the desert, nor Thoreau at Walden. The hermit has a guitar, a rifle, a Toyota 4-wheel-drive, and — when she's not in Miami — the company of his new fiancée Suzanne ("Sue" in Southern parlance). She will later recall that she lived there "on tiptoe not to disturb the poet," sculpting masks and making pottery.[38] And the hermit takes regular breaks from hermithood: he flies to New York or Montreal, goes on tour — or simply travels on.[39] But the fact remains that when the Toyota is parked next to the creek, and all you hear is the wind in the trees, you are very far indeed from the Chelsea Hotel. The night is dark, the rain hits the roof, and the silence of the world is suddenly irrefutable. Things with feathers hoot in the distance. They never stop. For almost two years.

Krystal Burgers is what ended the dream, apparently. At least that's what Leonard later told a reporter. Like a true Judeo-Christian, he blamed the loss of Eden on woman's craving for the forbidden fruit. His claim is that an irrational passion for Krystal Burgers had seized Suzanne, forcing him to drive her to Nashville more and more often and, soon enough, every night. Twenty-five miles in. Twenty-five miles out. And that was it: the trees no longer protected him from the world. He no longer lived away from it all, knowing much too well that Nashville was only twenty-five miles away. He might as well go back to Montreal where his mother was hooting.[40]

In Franklin, however, the solitary angel had lived a rather comical existence. Or at least that's how he chose to talk about the period. The principle of all comedy is displacement: in the wrong context, any character becomes funny. In the stories Leonard later fed to the press about the Southern episode, he always cast himself as the comic anti-hero. A melancholy Jewish cowboy. A trickster who gives LSD to his closest neighbour Willie York, an ex-convict and moonshiner straight out of a William Faulkner novel, whose only comment the next day is "Leonard, these things just make you damn nervous." A bored poet who shoots icicles but is awed by the paramilitary arsenal brought by his friends to a shooting session on his grounds. A naïve guy who is sold "just the right horse for you, Leonard" by a rodeo champion named Kid Marley, actually a grey mare so wild that the poet could ride her only once, spending weeks trying to coax her with sugar cubes. Beside the self-deprecation, we recognize Leonard's talent for parables. An abandoned Jewish poet who tries to coax a wild mare with sugar cubes? That's one of his finest self-portraits.[41]

ECCE LEONARDO

So, let there be an artist who has vowed to be the servant of gravity. Let there be two successful albums and almost unanimous good reviews. Let there be a generation in need of a poet and a record company that is ready to invest. A Leonard Cohen tour must logically ensue. Whoever liked the records will love the concerts.

But still traumatized by his experience at the Village Theatre, Leonard has a very acute awareness of how serious that act is: taking the stage. Rockers and bluesmen come from the music hall tradition and, for them, the stage is not a problem. You play your songs, people dance and everybody's happy. Then comes the hard bit: getting paid, finding an open restaurant and a companion for the night. The next day, you start again. There's no business like show business.

Leonard sees it a little differently. He has observed in the synagogue how the priest reconnects each person to their heart with ritual and language and, what is more, he was told at an early age that this was his mission as a descendant of the kohanim. Having later experienced the stage's potential for humiliation, he also knows the true nature of the place: the stage is where what we usually keep hidden (the depth of our humanity) is put into the spotlight. The job of all actors, troubadours, griots, or jugglers is precisely this: to present their humanity to the crowd and make it exciting and mysterious. It's a huge responsibility. For the audience has a metaphysical deal with the artist; they offer their lives in chunks of two or three hours and say, "Take this life and live it now, dance it if you must, but probe its mystery and let me leave the place re-energized and a little wiser." Entertainment is just an aspect of it: we go to the theatre to be put into contact with that mysterious thing — the beating heart inside us that will soon stop beating. Hence the artists' true mission, a noble one: to use what is most singular about them — their living presence on stage — to create a moment that is throbbing with life. A dancer does it by dancing, a jazzman with his saxophone, Mick Jagger by wiggling his ass, and Johnny Rotten by spitting on the crowd disguised as a garbage can Richard III.

Leonard knows all this (except the bit about Johnny Rotten, which hasn't happened yet) and he is actually okay with it. His experience as a touring poet has brought him a good technical knowledge of the craft; he knows how to work an audience, how to organize a tempo. He also knows you can't sentimentalize your humanity or flatter an audience and feed them only what they want. An artist must be subversive and surprising, like life itself. All of this, Leonard knows very well. His problem is elsewhere.

His problem is that he now has to accomplish this task by singing. And he has read the same verdict everywhere: great poet, crummy voice. It's in the *Melody Maker*, in the *New Musical Express*, in *Beat*, in *The Saturday Night Review*, in *Maclean's*, *Rolling Stone*, *The Village Voice*, and the *Montreal Star* — it's in every newspaper Leonard has ever picked up, and he has come to believe the propaganda. It's official: he can't sing. Quoth the poet:

> I began to believe everything people said about my terrible singing. I hated the sound of my own voice. I thought it was weak and full of self-pity. My life was falling apart and I was not inclined to look at my work in a very charitable way. I had a deep sense of failure.[42]

Of course, having listened to a lot of flamenco and read the Bible, Leonard has set the bar very high. He knows that in the Book of Samuel, David cures Saul's melancholy with his harp and songs. Mending the broken heart. That's what it's all about. That was what his mother was doing when she sang Russian songs in the kitchen. That's what Ray Charles was doing on the jukeboxes of Montreal. What Orpheus could do even in the underworld. But how to do that with a voice like his? How dare he even try? He has no voice. He can't sing.

Of course, Bob Dylan had opened a door for bad singers, but Dylan was no balladeer and had a different aim: he was Ezekiel with a guitar and sought to give electric shocks. But Leonard sings ballads and ballads require good voices. And surely in 1970 that voice was not yet the powerful bass of the singer's late career, but a fragile baritone with a slight tremble, almost no range at all and a very low ability to project volume. Melodies were tricky affairs in the best of circumstances and, whatever Leonard did, he had to sing as little as possible. If he sang too loud, his voice broke. If he sang too high, his voice broke. A bird on a wire? Certainly not a nightingale. A hummingbird perhaps.[43]

But voice or no voice, what the market wants, God wants. Realizing that he could no longer hide behind his records, the singer finally agrees to tour in 1970. On two conditions, that is. One, Bob Johnston must play organ. "I'm not an organist," says Johnston but Leonard answers he is no singer, so no tour. One glass of bourbon and Johnston comes around. He even hires a band, organizes rehearsals, and holds auditions for backing singers. For that was Leonard's second condition: he wanted women on stage, so that he might imagine he was surrounded by angels. Not a problem, Leonard. We'll find a couple of chicks. And even a tour manager who will look after logistics and buy plane tickets. Leonard Cohen's first concert tour can begin. He doesn't know what he's letting himself in for.

TOUR OF 1970: A POET ON STAGE

For that first string of concerts, Leonard looks like he has just come back from the desert (or from a hotel room) with something important to say. With a three-day stubble, a wiry face, and longer hair, this is like a hip version of the biblical prophet: Eli, probably or maybe, on bad hair days, Jeremiah. His safari jacket and flared trousers show that hippie fashions in their Yves Saint-Laurent version have not gone unnoticed and expensive cowboy boots bought on the Champs-Élysées complete the silhouette.

The singer hits the road in late April for a dozen dates in Europe. Then come a few summer festivals in Forest Hills, New York (Dylan in the wings), in Aix-en-Provence, France (where his high fee was leaked, creating a scandal), and on the Isle of Wight (where the singer would check if you still feel alone in front of six hundred thousand people). In autumn, there's a tour of American campuses (then ablaze with protest), with a few added Canadian dates at the end of the year and, for good measure, Leonard has added a handful of free concerts in psychiatric hospitals, where he thinks his songs will find their ultimate resonance. But for the moment, he's in Europe where he sings to sold-out venues: Amsterdam, Hamburg, Frankfurt, Munich, Vienna, Leeds, London, and, as closure, the Olympia Hall in Paris. Ten dates only — that tour is a test. The record company wants to check if the singer is bankable, and Leonard if he really is the high priest of his generation.

So, what does a Leonard Cohen concert look like in 1970? A few bootleg recordings, an almost complete thirty-millimetre film of the Isle of Wight performance, and countless photographs and reviews make at least one thing clear: it's not your usual rock concert.[44] With the funerary country music concocted by Johnston, Cohen turns his shows into intimate rituals meant to reconnect people to their hearts.

The forces at work? Centre stage, in the spotlights, is Leonard with his guitar. In semi-circle behind him is his small army of musicians: four guys in denim and velvet (Ron Cornelius, Elkin Fowler, Charlie Daniels, and Bob Johnston *himself*). To his left: two backup singers in long see-through dresses — Corlynn Hanney and Susan Mussmano. They act like spies sent from on high and they translate Cohen's lyrics into the language of angels: whispers, murmurs, and moans.

The concerts per se consist of two equal-length parts (about ten songs each), each ending in a climax when the audience is invited on stage and asked to clap their hands. Things start quietly, though. To establish contact, Leonard sometimes begins the show alone on stage, usually with the untenable promise of "Bird on the Wire" (i.e., that the little ones will be consoled). Then the audience is given "So Long, Marianne" and, as people sing along to the catchy, bittersweet chorus, a community is created. Then comes a first journey through the night: a series of dark ballads with the odd recited poems, which culminates in the gravity of "The Stranger's Song" where Leonard (again alone on guitar) asserts our ontological solitude: "I told you when I came I was a stranger."

The first half closes with the evangelical joy of "Tonight Will Be Fine," played like a country-and-western barn dance, complete with fiddle and banjo. Cohen pushes his voice, shouting out his faith that "tonight will — indeed — be fine." For now, the promise is kept. Intermission.

The second part follows the same pattern but opens in darkness: in the angst-filled guitar loop of "The Partisan," and a paean to a freedom that can neither die nor be reborn.[45] "Sisters of Mercy" and a series of delicate ballads ("Suzanne" and the newly written "Famous Blue Raincoat") lead to more upbeat songs that end with the climax of "Let's Sing Another Song, Boys" and "Diamonds in the Mine." The finale is "Please, Don't Pass Me By," an epic anthem in which Leonard tells of his encounter with a blind man in the streets of New York. The man carries a sign that says:

Please don't pass me by,
I am blind but you can see,
I've been blinded totally,
So please don't pass me by.

With the repetition of that plea in a long finale, the song becomes a kind of Internationale for an underground nation of losers as the audience is again invited to join the singer on stage and sing along: the barriers between hall and stage have been lifted.

It's a beautiful journey: from "Bird on the Wire" and its refusal of consolations to the closing number, which transforms the venue into a vast choir repeating a prayer, with Leonard serving as coryphaeus. What he affirms? The infirmity that comes with our inexhaustible need for love.

At this point, the concerts resemble a collective celebration of the art of losing, as Cohen summons, from one song to the next, his gallery of broken characters: a saint who falls in love with fire, a triangle of disunited lovers, a young girl who commits suicide, an eternal stranger on his way to the next train station. The purpose: to connect every member of the audience to that nook in the heart where they know they have failed, and then to bring the solace of song. That's the spiritual mission Leonard has given his troops: to lay siege to every heart. During a long improvisation at the Royal Albert Hall, he explains who he sings for: the crippled, the broken, those who burn, the gypsies and the Jews, the freaks and the hunchbacks. He even sneaks in a tiny self-portrait: a "saviour with no one to save." Not a bad description of himself at that time.

Throughout the tour, the musicians feel that they are indeed on a mission. To avoid all ambiguity, their boss — actually, the poet-in-chief — has removed their civilian status and baptized his band "The Army." He travels with them, eats with them, and before each concert, they have a toast to the audience they are going to play for. Several rock journalists were struck by the sanctimonious atmosphere that reigned backstage, in sharp contrast with the extravagances then de rigueur in rock circles. Forty years later, band members would still speak of the tour as a defining moment in their lives: they were in Leonard's army for a while and warmed themselves at the fire of his vision. He was the "Moses of their little exodus" through Europe.[46]

Most nights, the concerts end with standing ovations and several encores, but what strikes even more on the bootlegs is the intensity of the silence during the shows. "You could hear a metaphor drop," is how an observer later put it.[47] It was not exactly the silence that had greeted Dylan's last acoustic concerts in 1965. For Dylan, the silence had been reverential: the silence of suspended speech, as audiences stood agape before that compound of Rimbaud, Ezekiel, and Hermes: the Zeitgeist himself passing through Manchester or London. In Cohen's case, the silence seemed more like the emergence of an inner silence, a silence that emerges from the silent zones inside you. Or the silence that naturally arises when you enter the night. For in 1970, Leonard had that talent already: to bring to the surface the secret parts of our lives.

Enveloped in light and silence, he could speak with the authority of the true lyrical poets. And, quite naturally, the atmosphere was reverential. Here was a hero of introversion who had explored the secret chamber of the heart and he simply told what he had found there: anguish, despair, and a little light. In the Middle Ages, some books were called "mirrors," because they "mirrored" their subject matter but also the readers, as they read the book, could see themselves turn into that subject. *The Mirror of Simple and Annihilated Souls*, written by the mystic poetess Marguerite Porete in 1290, is a good example: a treatise through which the reader is invited to discover in their soul an aspiration to exist only in love. We mention Porete not only because she was burnt by the Inquisition or because she talked to the seraphim of God (thus checking most of Leonard's criteria for the perfect woman) but also because the singer seemed to be on a similar path in 1970: he wanted to make his concerts "mirrors" where everyone could see their simple soul. With his stoop and that air of being eternally defeated, he himself resembled a simple soul annihilated by love. He looked like a bird that had been ruffled by wind and the rain. He looked like one of his songs.

JEANNE D'ARC, C'EST MOI

> *In the depths of every living being,*
> *suffering and suffering only*
> *bears witness to life*
> *(the only indisputable, universal, irreducible witness).*

— ROGER GILBERT-LECOMTE, *Testament*[48]

Musically, the tour showcases the country-and-western turn Leonard's music has taken. Surrounded by banjos and violins, Leonard sounds like a Jew exiled in a Babylon called Nashville. It's a far cry from flamenco, a far cry from Judaism, a far cry from the troubadours. With a few chords on the Hammond B3, Bob Johnston adds a deliciously funereal atmosphere to his friend's ballads, while Sue and Corlynn wrap Cohen's voice in a complex texture of humming and moans and countermelodies: the celestial art of backing singers. They sing with their eyes closed, amorously, looking angelic and childlike. Thanks to them, Leonard finds his place: he is the stowaway in the celestial choir or, as he once put it in poetry, a "parasite of heaven." The scenic formula invented during that tour will remain for decades: the singer explores the human predicament but two guardian angels stand behind him for protection. They translate what he says into the tongue of angels so that our misfortunes down here may be heard in high places.

Which doesn't mean that Leonard finds it easy to be on stage yet. First, he has not entirely given up singing at this stage and occasionally still strains his voice like the rock singer he will never be. Or he tries to reach notes that are clearly beyond his range. The result — though not necessarily unpleasant — often flirts with dissonance and occasionally makes him sound, quite interestingly as a matter of fact, like that "drunk in the midnight choir." The problem is elsewhere.

Leonard has often confessed that he was then on a heavy diet of methaqualone, a barbiturate widely prescribed at the time for insomnia and anxiety.[49] Whether he wished to get rid of stage fright or of the human condition is unknown, but the ensuing sedated states often amused the band, who had nicknamed their boss "Captain Mandrax" (after the British name of the product). The result was that on some nights, as bootlegs testify, Leonard sang and played very, very slow.[50] On the Isle of Wight, for example, the tempos were slowed down beyond measure, giving the performance an aura of torpor, with something numb in the singer's voice, and an overall lack of punch that made some songs lose their drive and, inevitably, part of their mystery.

Several reviews suggest that this was also the case at the Forest Hills concert and on a few other dates: ballads that became laments and people probably more hypnotized than bewitched. At various moments on the Isle of Wight, Leonard seems engulfed in his songs, baffled by their gravity, as if he were singing from the bottom of a well: songs from a hole.

Perhaps the poet's modus operandi — which he had revealed in a Paris interview — was also to blame. Some nights, to find the centre of gravity that would allow him to raise his voice, the singer (so he explained) chose to sing from the heart of what radiated most in him: suffering. To sing from the heart of suffering in order to dissolve the suffering: that was the rationale.[51] At least Leonard got his physics right: you cannot produce light unless a fire consumes you. Basically, he's saying, "Jeanne d'Arc, c'est moi."[52]

Obviously, the singer still felt quite lonely during concerts and, most nights, he took radical measures to dissolve that loneliness, often creating problems with security teams. He routinely asked the audience to join him on stage, extended some shows with impromptu performances in adjoining parks (in Copenhagen and Austin), interrupted at least one show to hug a fan (in Hamburg), suggested that people leave the concert with another person than the one they came with (in London), or asked — on an American campus — that the audience made love while he played. He exuded a Christ-like charm, but sometimes also a strange black light.

And of course, there were a few incidents. Like everyone in the counterculture, Cohen then felt that America was going through a very dark period. In Hamburg, on the second day of the tour, the band heard that the Federal Guard had opened fire on the protesting students at Kent State University, killing four and seriously injuring nine, an event that deeply affected the singer, as did the unexpected shock of performing in Germany. The Jew in him, who a few months back had confessed to a journalist that he sometimes dreamt he had to protect orphaned Holocaust survivors from Stuka attacks,[53] finds himself face to face with a crowd of German flower children, on the ground where the Final Solution was planned.

In Frankfurt, made paranoid by the uniformed police that have escorted the band from the airport, the singer felt like raising his fist. Arriving on stage, as the crowd still cheered, he slammed his heels and flashed a Nazi salute, before intoning a traditional Yiddish song called "Und As Der Rebbe Zingt" ("And as the Rabbi Sings"). The audience went crazy and booed. How dare he! Not to them, the generation that was reinventing Germany and looking the past in the eyes. But once again, Leonard charmed the crowd and, by the end of the concert, they refused to let the Jewish balladeer go.

In Aix-en-Provence and on the Isle of Wight, the roles were inverted: it was the singer's turn to be called a fascist. In both festivals, a number of protesters had decided they didn't have to pay for tickets. The festivals belonged to the people, didn't they? In

France, Leonard's fee (a significant part of the festival's budget) has leaked and when the poet who, as the audience knows, still took his vacation in Greece (despite the military regime), arrived on stage on the back of a white horse to sing a song about Joan of Arc (a figure commonly associated in France with patriotism and right-wing politics), a few insults were hurled, prompting Cohen's small clarification to the crowd (in demotic French):

> And one more thing: there never was *one* revolution. When someone talks about *the* revolution, it is *their* revolution. Leave the revolution to the owners of the revolution. They are like all owners. They are looking for a profit.[54]

At the end of the tour, Leonard was forced to concur with the poet Alexander Pope: "Fools rush in where angels fear to tread." Understand: mixed impressions. Of course, nothing beats a rock-and-roll tour: you storm a new city every night, girls fling themselves at you, and, on certain evenings, grace dissolves all doubts (as in the Olympia Hall concert on the last night, still legendary in France). But what with the *NME*'s insults, the tears on stage, the lunatics who don't want to let you out of their asylum (as happened several times in the "private" concerts), an allegedly frosty meeting with Dylan (who apparently didn't like the Forest Hills concert), the singer has the feeling that something is still missing from the equation. Perhaps the right attitude has not been found yet. So an appointment is taken for 1972 (Leonard's second tour) to see how things can be improved. But wherever he goes, the singer makes an impression and gets great reviews. He meets people from all walks of life and is now as comfortable having lunch with the young French Minister of Economy and future president of the republic, Valéry Giscard d'Estaing, in May as he is with the hippies of Dennis Hopper's commune in New Mexico in November. But then again, he's just a passenger. And he rides and he rides.

THE ISLE OF WIGHT AND THE THEOLOGY OF FIRE

Back on the Isle of Wight, August 1970. Six hundred thousand hippies meet for three days of peace, music, and nasty riots. A radicalized fraction of the public (Afghan caftans, cockney accents, Marxist speeches) considers that this festival has sold out to the Capital. They refuse to pay the entrance fee and decide they want a revolution. And they want it now. So, they burn the sandwich stands and boo the artists. The fire department intervenes when a fire spreads to the stage, and schoolmistress Joan Baez, here to teach English hippies about peace and love and protest, is not amused. Quite flustered, in fact.[55]

Now Leonard Cohen has a very special relationship with fire. He has learnt from Heraclitus that it is the primary force that animates all things, and from the Torah that it is one of the forms the Eternal takes when He manifests in our world: a bush that burns without consuming. So, he likes to see the world in flames. He has written several poems about pyromania, and regularly sets things on fire in his songs: trees, ships' sails, young girls' bodies. He also knows that love is a fire and our hearts are its favourite fuel. In a word, for him, fire deserves our deepest respect.[56] He is not so sure on the other hand whether he likes to see fires lit in vain, and so he sees fit, in the early hours of August 31, 1970, to give the hippie fire-starters a little lesson about the nature of the flames that burn inside us.

For three days, big acts — the Who, the Doors, Miles Davis, Joni Mitchell, Jethro Tull — have successively occupied the main stage. On the last night, Leonard was supposed to close the festival and take the stage just after Joan Baez, who came after Jimi Hendrix. Punctuality being the politeness of kings but not of guitar heroes, it is past three in the morning when the stage manager comes into the Canadian's trailer to wake him up. When he arrives on stage, looking haggard and plunged in infinite sadness, Leonard first tunes his guitar, and not too hurriedly either: he is not going to rush because six hundred thousand people are waiting. And, once he is ready, he does not sing immediately. He remembers he is a poet and suggests a game. Let everyone in the audience light a match, right? Shall we all play that game? Several thousand people do, and for a couple of minutes, you saw an immense cloud of sparks spread over the hill of East Afton Farm: tiny eruptions of fire, one or two seconds each. As if thousands of fireflies were coming to greet the singer. It was of course a poetic act — a poet made the dark night of the Isle of Wight sparkle for a moment. But it was also a lesson in humility via the Kabbalah of Isaac Luria: each of us is but a spark of light, a little flea and nothing more. Which means the great Inferno blaze of the revolution would probably have to wait. In the meantime, a single match held long enough was enough to burn the tip of your finger. The interest of the minor mode, once more.

During the concert, the poet repeatedly evokes the precariousness of the hippie moment, arguing in front of the crowd that "we are a very weak nation." To say that when you stand alone in front of half a million people is rather cheeky: you have to be Leonard Cohen. The singer had allies of course to silence the troublemakers: the late hour, the spellbinding songs, his unflappable calm (the Mandrax must have helped). But under the admiring eye of Kris Kristofferson and Joan Baez, the first of whom had been booed off the stage and the other hissed into silence, he had "tamed the beast."[57] With songs and a few matches.

SONGS OF LOVE AND HATE (1971) — AN ANTI-HIPPIE TEXTBOOK

> *Love is a fire*
> *It burns everyone*
> *It disfigures everyone*
> *It is the world's excuse for being ugly.*

— LEONARD COHEN, *The Energy of Slaves*[58]

Leonard and the hippies were at odds, however. A travelling companion and benevolent observer of flower power, Leonard was not ready to go the whole way. "Wight is Wight": no question about it — "Dylan is Dylan": more debatable already — "Hip-hip-hip Hippie": count him out.[59] First, he is fifteen years older and doesn't like the state the flower children leave the sites they have occupied.[60] Then, he disagrees with hippies on love and bohemia. Leonard likes the upmarket versions: the bohemia of the saint or the artist. Hippie bohemia is a mass phenomenon, often anti-intellectual and slogan-happy. Turn on, tune in, drop out. Make love, not war. We want the world and we want it now. As we know Leonard called the hippie propagandists the "flabby liars of the Aquarian age" (1–0 for the poet), but the real bone of contention was love. With hindsight, it's hard not to feel that, for all their talk about love, the hippies were actually not that interested. Their big idea was *peace*, and love was just what made peace possible. At best, it was what you did communally when you were out of acid. A decidedly untragic affair, hippie love set nobody's heart on fire (there were no hippie Romeo and Juliet) and perhaps hippie hearts (like extinguished joints) were hard to light up. What Leonard clearly saw was that hippies did not have the right concepts to really "get" love: no broken heart, no transubstantiation of matter, no flesh that becomes light, no Corinthians 13, no Song of Solomon. The word therefore became a fetish word: love child, love-in, free love, make love not war, love is all you need . . . During the riots on the Isle of Wight, one of the organizers, Rikki Farr, also MC for the event (and, as we saw, not a great fan of Cohen), decided he had to take the stage with his fetching fringe jacket to give the audience a lesson in love. Unfortunately, he was angry as hell and found himself yelling in the microphone:

> We put this festival on you bastards with a lot of love. We worked for one year for you pigs. And you want to destroy it? Well, you go to hell.[61]

So, a lesson in theology was clearly required and Leonard took care of it. The lesson was called *Songs of Love and Hate* and it began with a very simple equation: love is fire.

On this premise, Leonard develops his argument and unfolds it logically, as in a course in classical physics. Lesson number one: Fire is insatiable and spreads to all inflammable things — hearts, bodies, and the world itself.[62] Lesson number two: Fire consumes you and reduces you to ashes, but here is lesson number three: combustion gives off light and without it, there's only night. Leonard then adds a few pragmatic observations. There are forces at work that extinguish all fires: rain, drizzle, avalanches. And, inside us, some dark nights of the soul seem to stifle our ability to love. And that's lesson number four: love, for all its power, is a fragile thing — all it takes is a little rain or a little darkness to extinguish it.

Around these ideas, Leonard organizes a journey in eight songs that is a progressive revelation of the nature of Love, from the "Avalanche" that opens the record with intimations of self-hatred to the flames of Joan of Arc's pyre in the closing song. Of course, the record cover is another provocation in hippie time: no colour, just a black background and the title "SONGS OF LOVE AND HATE" in broad white letters, with Leonard's tired face squeezed next to the word *HATE*. With glistening eyes, he is grinning at something in front of him. He alone can see it, but we can hypothesize. He sees an avalanche coming his way. He sees the black sun of melancholy. Or, more simply, he sees the future. And in 1971, it's already an apocalypse.

THE INNER AVALANCHE

In the opening track, Leonard makes an avalanche speak. The dominant note is fear and the attack is pure Cohen: struck violently on the guitar, an E minor chord kickstarts the famous tremolo — an unflinching line of fast and tense arpeggios: the engine of the song. In *Bird on a Wire*, Tony Palmer found the perfect images for that music: low-angle shots of the elevators inside the metal structure of the Eiffel Tower and a travelling shot of Leonard swimming naked in a deserted Olympic pool: head under water, head out of water, head under water, head out of water. The guitar tremolo hangs over him like a threat — you feel that an avalanche is following him.

After a minute and a half (an eternity), you hear strings crescendo and fade out — something powerful had just visited you.[63] Then the voice, significantly lower than on the first two albums, opens the record with one of Leonard's most chilling declarations: "I stepped into an avalanche / it covered up my soul."

The world according to Leonard: you go for a walk; you meet an avalanche. And it swallows you whole. It's so sinister that it's almost funny. "A mass of snow that comes off a mountain with rocks and mud," says the dictionary. Go fight with that. Of course, the song is partly allegorical, and its subject is the inner catastrophe known as depression. The avalanche metaphor is fantastic because it reveals the true scope of the phenomenon, its cataclysmic nature. A true depression involves the total collapse of the world. Another stroke of genius of course is the colour: white. Perhaps in facetious answer to the critics who accuse him of seeing life in black, Leonard transforms the dark night of the soul into a white apocalypse, reminding us in passing of the formidable purity of the depressive state: a depression is by nature a wiping out of the self and a journey into the void. So, two lines into the song and everything is said. We could leave it at that.

But just as the violins start playing countermelodies, Leonard's voice calls out again. Who exactly is speaking is unclear, but we soon understand where the voice is coming from: from inside the avalanche. What does it say? That we have awakened it by striking the side of the mountain. That we must learn to "serve it well." That it belongs to a deformed hunchback who covets our flesh. At the end of the song, the voice has taken possession of us, and we understand who was speaking: the avalanche itself, the ugly thing inside us that extinguishes all fires.

Such is the precarious starting point of Leonard's theology of love circa 1970: we are inhabited by a white apocalypse that can suck us in at any moment. The journey towards the blazing fire that closes the record in "Joan of Arc" starts here: in the necessity to bow before everything that is dark and deformed in us — the hunchback inside, himself only "the pedestal for this ugly hump at which you stare."

We feel Carl Gustav Jung's influence here and Leonard probably presents a dramatized form of the psychoanalyst's "alchemy of the soul" — the (often painful) process of the integration of the "shadow" (i.e., the hunchback), a necessary step for anyone who is in search of the "gold" of spiritual completeness, the state where you can give true love.[64]

What follows is seven songs that carry out a systematic exploration of the nature of love, from snow to fire. We meet a few desperate beings along the way — a depressed ladies' man, a triangle of destitute lovers, a few vagrant soldiers — and we are treated with a few powerful self-portraits: Leonard as a serial lover who confines his mistresses in notebooks but lets solitude dissolve him in a movie theatre ("Love Calls You by Your Name"), Leonard as a burnt-out writer dreaming of biblical weddings and orgies ("Last Year's Man"), Leonard as a desperate man who shaves in his hotel room and sees in the mirror a razor-wielding Santa Claus ("Dress Rehearsal Rag").[65] We meet real couples and allegorical ones: a woman and Fire, a man and an avalanche. but although everyone seems hungry for love, a question recurs: is the heart of man still inflammable? Only women seem to know the answer, of course, and we meet quite a few on the record: some wait for Jesus, some wait for Cain, one is the whore of Babylon and another Joan of Arc, who appears first as a mighty warrior who plays all night with her army of lovers ("Last Year's Man"), then as a naïve shepherdess seduced by fire ("Joan of Arc").

At the end of the journey, the theologian songwriter delivers his diagnosis; a simple one. First, love is not an optional state — we are its subjects and love is our only light. Second, women have a head start in the matter; they always answer the calls of fire. A few metaphors illustrate the complexity of the phenomenon (perhaps overlooked by hippies). Love is an embrace and an Inferno. Love is the marriage of sin and innocence. Love is a war and a vast orgy that reveals, in the mingled flesh, a serpent biting its tail . . .

SISTER JOAN, BROTHER FIRE

Songs of Love and Hate opens with a frightening folk song; it closes with an apotheosis of light and a tiny, almost childlike waltz. Its subject: the wedding of Joan of Arc.

The language is simple, the meter swift and there's nothing heavy here as Cohen transforms an epic story — the passion of Joan of France — into a lyrical ballad about how a naïve virgin dreaming of a wedding dress was seduced by Fire and died in the flames. A song of courtly love, with a tragic end and a lesson known to all: love and death are one.

The narrator, probably a demobbed soldier from Joan's army, saw it all happen: Fire's approach, the flirtatious dialogue, the saint's surrender, the glory in her eyes as she burnt. He understands the stakes, but has a question:

> Myself I long for Love and Light,
> But must it come so cruel and, oh, so bright?

The song has the apparent naïvety of a medieval illumination: everything is colourful and clear. Joan is adorable and gullible; Fire is truly Fire and never lets go of its prey. We are obviously in troubadour territory and fin'amor deserves its name here as the poet delicately envelops Joan's tragedy in finely crafted quatrains of rhymed couplets. He is careful not to name the unnameable: the execution is a wedding, and the saint's death is evoked only with the perfect litotes:

And then she clearly understood
If he was Fire, then she must be wood.

Equally delicate is the guitar work, arpeggios plucked so gently you'd think you hear a lute, while the melody itself — as simple as melodies get — unfolds the definitive ritournelle in graceful la-la-las: exactly what the poet ordered for a little shepherdess from Lorraine. Of course, Leonard can't help it: he sings those la-la-las as off-key as he can, lest we forget how off-key life and love can get.

It's common knowledge that the song was largely inspired by Nico, of Velvet Underground fame, clearly alluded to in the second stanza with a coded word:

And something in me yearns to win
Such a cold and lonesome *heroine*.

The singer makes sure that whoever has ears hears: it's about Nico who, with her martial beauty and her ability to hear only what she wanted, was indeed like a sister to Joan of Arc. A junkie's life is by definition a life of martyrdom and passion and Nico (as we may remember) was not addicted to heroin alone, but to all the things that kill you slowly, poetry and love among them. A thousand reasons to have imagined Christa Paffgen as Joan of Arc. Like everyone else, Leonard had seen Nico wearing a medieval helmet in *La Dolce Vita* (perhaps where the idea originated) and we must assume he already had his ballad in mind when he asked his muse in 1967 if Joan of Arc ever fell in love. Nico's answer was perhaps what helped him finish the song: "Every day, Leonard, every day . . ."[66]

But identifying the model says nothing about the meaning of the song. "Joan of Arc" is ultimately an allegory, and the aim of every allegory is to instruct and teach. Thirty years later, for the benefit of those who still wondered what the marriage of Joan and Fire was all about, Cohen would reformulate his argument more explicitly in a song called "Boogie Street":

So come my friend, be not afraid
We are so lightly here.
It is in love that we are made,
In love we disappear.

Thirty years only to accept to disappear. Not a bad score.

FAMOUS BLUE WHAT?

Downtown New York

In many ways, "Famous Blue Raincoat" is the culmination of that first phase of Leonard's career. The song rests on a simple idea (you hear a letter being written) and its 280 words actually constitute the third novel that the poet never wrote. The pitch? Four o'clock in the morning, end of December, Clinton Street, New York: the city is cold and "L. Cohen" is writing to an old friend who once seduced his wife, Jane, and is now lost (in a desert). He has actually little to say: Jane is sleeping beside him, but she is not really here anymore. Hence his letter and his message: if the friend returns, the sleeping woman is his. Salutation, signature, end of text and end of song:

> Sincerely,
> L. Cohen.

With its non sequiturs and its conversational tone, the epistolary mode makes us hear a spontaneous, authentic voice which almost conceals the exquisite rhymes, the sophisticated use of meter, and an impressively complex narrative that combines four layers of the past.[67] The story is classic Leonard Cohen: a hostile metropolis in winter snow, an adulterous triangle, and a haunting loneliness. The husband has lost his wife, the wife has lost her lover, and the lover has lost himself. But grace persists in the form of a fragile waltz . . . All of it in a concise and precise form: a masterpiece.

As we know, Leonard likes to explore the adulterous triangle and its eternal geometry of cuckoldry, but adultery is not the real subject here, even if the poet reflects on the nature of the ties that bind lovers (do they belong to each other?). Adultery is just an excuse to present life as it is, New York as it is, winter as it is, the intrinsic frailty of things as it is. In the song, a snowflake — that most delicate and transient thing — is enough to destroy a relationship:

> And you treated my woman
> to a flake of your life
> and when she came back,
> she was nobody's wife.[68]

Bottom line: life is a waltz of impermanence, and lovers, whatever they do, are only stowaways in each other's lives.

To accept this, a certain heroism is necessary. Hence that second symbol: the raincoat. The ultimate Cohenian garment. Perfect for pessimists who think it's going to rain and for metaphysical private eyes who look for the meaning of life. So, just before it gets stolen (probably in 1970), Leonard immortalizes the Burberry coat he had acquired a decade before. Complete with belt, shoulder pads, multiple buckles, and flaps, a trench coat is like a modern armor. Wearing one reminds you that on the front lines of our respective lives, we are all heroes, even if our heroic act is just to go out and confront the rain.

Once more, the song is a waltz and, while the singer unfolds the lyrics in his trademark mournful tone, two female voices (Susan and Corlynn's) sing the tune with increasing insistence: da-da-da, da-da-da, da-da, da-da-da-da . . . A melody that mirrors the existential waltz of the characters who find and lose each other, but also one that reminds us, in its naïve clarity, that consolation comes in the smallest things. You can save someone with a flake of life, with a moment of attention or just with a lullaby. And in the song, it is with tiny acts of love and light that the three lovers accomplish their mutual salvation: the husband forgives the lover, the lover gives a lock of hair, Jane gives herself — and everyone is saved.[69]

Perhaps the ultimate meaning of "Famous Blue Raincoat" becomes apparent only when you realize that the Logos is circular here, like the waltz melody. Leonard writes, sings, and signs the song. He thus designates himself as the "husband."[70] But by virtue of the raincoat, he is also the lover, the eternal stranger. The letter is therefore — quite logically — a letter that Cohen sends to himself. Epistle of Saint Leonard to Leonard the Gypsy. To forgive himself, perhaps?

> I guess that I miss you, I guess I forgive you
> I'm glad you stood in my way.

Spiritually, forgiveness is no small matter. It is an aptitude that Leonard would later admire in his master Sasaki Roshi, and perhaps Buddhist awakening finally consists in that single and not so tiny act: to forgive yourself and others completely.[71] For "Famous Blue Raincoat" is ultimately a song about awakening. The awakening Leonard sought in the Moroccan desert and in Scientology. The one he sometimes found in letting go of things: a wife, a lover, himself. As for Jane, her awakening in the song is simpler still: she just wakes up, and "L. Cohen" seems surprised:

> Well, I see Jane's awake.
> She sends her regards.

A delightful moment when you interpret it in Buddhist terms: she awakes and says hello. Isn't that a nice little bodhisattva?

TURNING DARKNESS INTO LIGHT (TOUR OF 1972, ACT I)

A hit record in Germany, Northern Europe, and Canada, *Songs of Love and Hate* quickly rose to #4 in the English charts and #2 in the Netherlands, while in France, Cohenmania was still raging. So a new tour was announced on a larger scale this time. The previous one had taught Leonard what a good concert required — to face the darkness of the songs and locate in them a possibility of light — and what the dangers were — torpor and lamentation. For that second tour, he prepared like a boxer before a match.

First came a stay in the monastery that Reverend Joshu Sasaki Roshi had just opened in an old scout camp up Mount Baldy, in the San Gabriel mountains near Los Angeles. The poet arrived there in late November or early December, just before an intensive retreat called rohatsu.[72] On the menu: a very early rise (half past three in the morning), vegetarian meals, silent physical work, and up to ten hours of seated meditation every day. With a few sermons and Zen koans thrown in for good measure. While he sat in half-lotus, Leonard must have pricked up his ear when the roshi taught that "Buddha is the centre of gravity" (a frequent motif in Joshu Sasaki's early teaching). The theory is that awakening to our true nature requires locating a "centre of gravity" inside ourselves and realizing that this centre — the source of all authentic actions and words — is also the centre of gravity of the world. To locate that centre, Sasaki had a time-tested method: Zen life.

The first few days in the monastery were fine (Leonard even shaved his head), but during the rohatsu proper, the snow, the schedule, the hours spent contending with that wild monkey called the mind, as well as the generous administration of the kyosaku stick on the meditators' shoulders (a "stick of awakening" used to stimulate practice) proved too much for Leonard. Imagining he was taking part in "the revenge for World War II" (the Japanese master's assistant was German), he famously sneaked out of the camp in mid-retreat. Suzanne joined him in Los Angeles and the couple fled to Acapulco for a quick holiday.[73]

In late February, Leonard was back in Nashville for several weeks of rehearsals. There, Bob Johnston had gathered a band (with himself and Ron Cornelius as veterans of the previous tour), this time with a standing bass player and different instructions from Leonard, who was looking for a different sound than the country and western of 1970. Something more elegant perhaps, and the keyword for the rehearsals was "madrigal." Cohen was obviously craving for discipline and, while in Nashville, he visited the local YMCA at least once a day for a swim or a workout. As a result, the clean-shaven, short-haired Jewish singer who landed in Europe in late March looked sharp, energetic, and in great physical shape. No longer considering himself a civilian, he wore black, brown, and khaki shirts and was rarely seen offstage without a double-breasted suit, sometimes accessorized with a worker's flat cap bought in Greece. Not your average rock singer circa 1972.

Dublin, March 18. The tour is about to begin: forty days on the road and twenty-one concerts in eleven countries, from Ireland to Israel. The logistics are well-oiled: the buses are on time, the hotels first class and the venues sold out. Everywhere there are radio and press interviews and, here and there, television appearances. Marty Machat has even integrated a side project: a documentary film. Which means that a cinema crew, led by English filmmaker Tony Palmer (a rock critic, early Cohen enthusiast, and friend of the

Beatles), is following the tour with unlimited backstage access to immortalize the event and maximize profits.[74]

What makes Palmer's subsequent film — *Bird on a Wire*, released only two years later — so special is first his clever, fast-paced editing of airport arrivals, dressing room scenes, and concert footage, but also a true filmmaker's eye. The director, who considers himself a portraitist, shows us Leonard Cohen as he saw him: bright, funny, and on the verge of collapse. *Bird on a Wire* or the portrait of the rocker as holy depressive.

Some of the included footage is simply inconceivable in today's age of locked storytelling: we see Leonard swimming naked in a deserted pool; Leonard with dollar bills in hand, personally giving a refund to disgruntled spectators; Leonard skimming pebbles alone on the North Sea shore; Leonard licking an old LSD blotter before climbing on stage. We also see him studying how to become a bodhisattva, offering his full attention to all interviewers and signing pretty much anything that is handed to him (a program, a record, a poster, a pair of pants, a female bosom . . .) while politely denying in a noble fight against himself the solicitations of famous actresses and sexy groupies.[75] And everywhere, the singer exudes an undeniable dark sovereignty.

Palmer has that rare gift: he knows how to film music, and the documentary gives us a good idea of the intense beauty that seems to have inhabited the 1972 concerts. With a little help from the double bass and probably lighter doses of Mandrax, Leonard had indeed rediscovered the tempos that preserved the mystery of the songs. He obviously also had an incredible alchemy going with the two backing singers: Jennifer Warnes, the slender blonde, and Donna Washburn, the maternal brunette. Wrapped in the glorious splendour of 1970s womanhood, schoolteacher's glasses, romantic dresses, and *Charlie's Angels* hairdos, they were wonderfully filmed by Palmer. We see them sing and hum beside Leonard, and we understand they are doing more than singing; they are nursing the wounded child in him and, in the process, consoling the world. Not just backing singers then — women in love and earth mothers. And angels escaped from a Botticelli painting. Their vocalizations transform the whole range of vowels — the "ahs," the "oohs," the "ohs" — into outpourings of mercy and sweet complaints as they demonstrate on stage that redemption exists after all.[76]

Leonard often compared concert tours to military operations, and Palmer's film seems to prove him right: we follow a small group of storm troopers from town to town and watch them launch small incursions of grace into the audience's lives. As in the army, everybody's role is well-defined: Leonard is the general and strategist, Bob Johnston deals with troop morale, a very British road manager takes care of logistics and discipline, and a biker-looking sound engineer gets scolded a lot. In a velvet raincoat, the indispensable Marty Machat is in charge of money and public relations. A motley crew.

AND FIAT FIASCO (TOUR OF 1972, ACT II)

Melody Maker, June 8, 1974

How to resist grace when it is presented with military precision? Palmer's footage shows that everywhere audiences seemed delighted to look on as Cohen waged his war against darkness.

And it seems the whole operation was not just a concert tour but a ritual repeated night after night: on stage, a poet spoke about the heart (which no one can control), about the gravity of our lives, and about our common attraction to a fire called love.

Throughout the film, we follow the singer — then a dead ringer for the young Al Pacino — to the centre of the maelstrom, as he was looking for "a balance between standing up and falling down."[77] And indeed, he looks both wonderfully present and a little lost, seeming somewhat amused by the chaos around him.[78] But the dramatic force of *Bird on a Wire* comes from an inescapable fact: Leonard is struggling. With technology to begin with (several concerts are disrupted by persistent feedback). With rowdy audiences (it's a time of cheap tickets and easy protest). But mostly with himself. In Berlin's Sportpalast for example, the singer almost causes a riot when he decides to confront a few troublemakers with a question that a certain Joseph Goebbels had asked in the same venue, thirty years before ("Wolt ihr den totallen Krieg?"). In Tel Aviv, there was a riot and the concert had to be stopped — despite Cohen's calls for calm — when the security team started beating up the crowd in their attempt to keep the crowd away from the stage.

And Leonard was sometimes his worst enemy. Convinced he was incapable of returning with equal force the love offered by audiences, he felt — as he profusely explained in interviews — that he was betraying his mission. Often, he even found himself unable to penetrate the songs, as in Frankfurt, where he declared himself a "prisoner of songs," or in Copenhagen, where he claimed to be "a parrot chained to the microphone" who wrote "Suzanne" a "hundred years ago." In Manchester, he improvised a blues about his lack of talent and a made-up song about a "broken nightin-gale" who sang "songs full of anguish and despair." In Jerusalem, he famously left the stage and considered refunding the tickets.

Two shows in particular will strongly affect him. On April 6, as he took the stage in Frankfurt, he opened the concert with a confession: he was terrified. In German, the word for fear is *angst* and, in existentialist philosophy, angst is what you call the anguish that is inherent to our mortal condition. On stage, that evening, Leonard really looked like a refugee from Albert Camus's novel *The Stranger*. He even sought shelter for a moment in the arms of a female fan in the front row. We have mentioned the scene before: he lies collapsed on the boards surrounded by a group of loving fans who are all laying their hands on him, as in a strange ritual. "One man down," as they say in the American army. Of course, some members of the audience hiss and boo: they have not "paid to see him make love." Hence a sermon by Rabbi Cohen about love, money, and the Frankfurt banks. The footage filmed the next day would break your heart if it wasn't so funny: sitting in a dressing room, Leonard drinks orange juice from a bottle, looking absolutely contrite. With the saddest smile imaginable, he tells the director, "I've disgraced myself, Tony." He shakes his head and repeats the words, emphasizing each syllable: "dis-graced my-self."

In Jerusalem a few days later, there's an opposite temptation, but a similar result: Leonard is now the prodigal son back in his ancestors' country, Eretz Yisrael, the promised land. In the hall, young Israeli hippies rub shoulders with girls in military uniform and something in the air says the Messiah is back. It is the last night of the tour and the riot in Tel Aviv the previous night has left everyone on their knees. For good measure, Leonard has also passed around an old blotter of LSD at intermission. So, what could possibly go wrong? Back on stage, he plays a few songs, actually quite hesitantly, then stops. Maybe he was hoping to be saved in the town of David. But standing there on stage, he suddenly realizes that he remains a stranger even here. A stranger knocking on the door of songs that remain obstinately closed. *I told you when I came, I was a stranger*. Once more.

We have already mentioned the Kabbalistic theme of the exile of grace (the exile of shekinah). That evening, Leonard refers to it explicitly, reminding the audience that the Kabbalah claims that "If Adam and Eve do not stand face to face, God cannot ascend his throne." Such is, so he says, his inner state. Hence the following: he will go back to his dressing room and meditate. Perhaps he will return, perhaps not. And under his band's astonished gaze, Leonard Cohen leaves the stage like a sad old dog. It had to be that way: the last night of the tour had to be a return to square one, to the primitive scene five years before when he left the stage of the New York Town Hall after three chords of "Suzanne." Bis repetita in Jerusalem: God definitely had a sense of humour. And wasn't it a long way down?

In the dressing room Machat, Johnston, Cornelius, and the road manager besiege the singer; they want him back on stage, preferably now. The singer listens, smokes a cigarette, then another one. Then he decides it is urgent to shave. That's it, probably. Jerusalem is the holy of holies and the unworthy kohen has just entered the temple without purifying himself. And what Palmer's cameras capture next is a seemingly euphoric Leonard Cohen (the LSD is kicking in), shaving without soap in front of his mirror, surrounded by the band. At the end of the operation, he surreptitiously slips in a little joke to amuse the party: he pretends to slit his wrists with the disposable razor. It lasts no more than two seconds: a little joke in the middle of a fiasco. Two seats away, the manager wonders how he will repay the promoters and refund the audience. In the main hall, three thousand youngsters sing hymns to bring peace to Leonard's soul. But in the dressing room, the singer is busy exploring the art of being simultaneously depressed and in good spirits.

The scene that takes place when the poet finally returns to the stage defies description. Alone in the spotlight, Leonard Cohen finds himself in front of the most loving audience ever captured on film. Hundreds of young men and women clap their hands and sing for their tzadik. In Hebrew. Clutching his guitar, Leonard is standing, wearing the broadest child's smile you have ever seen on a thirty-eight-year-old face, his eyes full of tears. He has lost his bearings and, to be precise, at that very moment, he has lost everything. Everything except the love of two thousand adoring fans.

The crowd is beaming with happiness; the tzadik has returned and they sing for him so that he may sing for them. How to describe this moment without desecrating it? Perhaps by returning to Marguerite Porete's book *The Mirror of Simple and Annihilated Souls*. For that is indeed what it is all about: a game of mirrors. The crowd sees in Leonard what Leonard sees in the crowd: that pure love is pure light and that the true effect of love is to annihilate us absolutely and to make us simple, childlike, and luminous. Lambs. That's what everyone in the room was at that moment: the harmless lambs of God.

As Leonard starts singing again (he begins with "So Long, Marianne"), he has a decisive spiritual vision he will keep quiet about for forty-four years, then he goes back to the dressing room, where it's all hugs, tears, smiles, and tomb-like silence.[79] Four thousand miles away from his Forty-Second Street office, the seated manager remains speechless in his chair. Only Tony Palmer stays active and he gives Leonard no rest: he films the tears the singer keeps wiping away, and tries to assess, in successive close-ups, whatever defeat or victory can be read on the singer's face. More heartbreaking images follow; we see the band wade through the crowd on their way to the bus. Everyone tries to touch and comfort the holy man. The very last sequence of the film is almost allegorical: Leonard Cohen is sitting motionless on the floor of the coach's central aisle, clutching a seat with his right hand, as though he had just fallen. He is trying to regain his composure, but nothing helps: if he moves, he weeps; if he lifts his head and looks at the camera, he weeps; if he tries to speak, he weeps. The 1972 tour ends here and this could actually be the end of the singer's career: the troubadour is defeated by love. All is accomplished.

EXIT THE POET

Things could have ended there. Three records which helped the poet confirm in pop music the first noble truth of Buddhism: life is unease, desire, and suffering (*dukkha* in the original Sanskrit). Plus two tours that have taught him — the hard way and without a safety net — that the stage is the place where your full humanity is exposed and potentially turned to light.

By the summer of 1972, exhausted by the tour, burnt out, and drained of all inspiration, Leonard, who has rejoined Sasaki's monastery, finds himself unable to write and discouraged at the prospect of delivering two more albums to CBS as his contract stipulates. Less than two months after the end of the tour, Tony Palmer delivers a first version of *Bird on a Wire* and the singer is upset to see himself exposed so frontally. He wanted a different film.[80] After a first recut, Palmer is removed from the project and Leonard, who has decided to re-edit the documentary himself, spends the next six months with Henry Zemel in various studios in London, Montreal, and Los Angeles watching himself sing and cry and laugh. Until he can no longer bear to see his face. The re-edited film will finally be released in 1974 (two years too late) in a watered-down version of the first cut.

On February 23, 1973, in London, Leonard is awarded the first gold record of his career. The same afternoon, he has an appointment at the CBS offices with a British music journalist. The two men gather in a conference room and the content of their conversation suggests the singer is tired, disillusioned, and deeply depressed. There are reasons for this. He hasn't been writing for a while and a young artist named Daphne Richardson, whom he had commissioned to illustrate his latest poetry book, has just committed suicide in a psychiatric hospital where the doctors refused to believe she was really in contact with Leonard Cohen. On February 24, the front page of *Melody Maker* ran a sensationalist headline: "Cohen Quits."

Soon, rumours spread of a suicide attempt, but Leonard has already moved on. His first child has just been born and, as though to start everything over, he called him Adam. A few months later, Leonard will go to war.

CHAPTER 7

LEONARDO FURIOSO

COHEN VS. COHEN
1973-1977

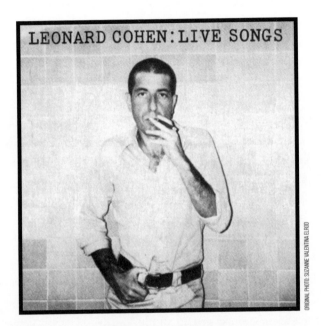

The CD cover of *Live Songs* (1973)

READY FOR WAR

In the early '70s, Leonard Cohen was fighting multiple wars. On stage, he waged a war against darkness and transformed the gravity of our lives into moments of fragile beauty. Fought in public, that war required absolute purity and did not leave the soldier unscathed. In the press, music critics waged their own war against Leonard, accusing him of the worst of crimes: being a poet. On the domestic front, a third war broke out with a wild and headstrong creature named Suzanne. Part concubine, part femme fatale, she seemed determined to teach her man that love was indeed, as Dylan had said, "just a four-letter word." Bent on making Leonard the perfect mate and father, she was ready to show him, when necessary, that she could be as sexually liberated as he was.

Hence a marital war fought for ten years in kitchens and bedrooms in Montreal, Los Angeles, and Hydra. Despite regular truces and armistices, it was actually a violent guerrilla war with an eternal return of crises, rows, and infidelities. The situation was probably quite banal, actually: a passionate but mismatched couple. Miami versus Montreal, a young woman who loved the joys of the world and a middle-aged poet who no longer knew what he loved. He aspired to be a saint; she aspired to be a Persian cat.[1] Cats are basically untameable and so was Suzanne, who knew how to fight back and return blow for blow, with an irony that is evidenced in her husband's mid-'70s lyrics:

> I live here with a woman and a child. The situation
> makes me kind of nervous. I rise up from her arms,
> she says, "I guess you call this love, I call it Room
> Service."[2]

For a while, determined to be a nice husband, Leonard also launched a war against the *stranger* in him, the one always ready to leave and seduce more women, but that was counting without the women themselves, who had started their own erotic blitz-krieg against the poet. Everywhere he went, an army of angels in fur coats and mascara laid siege to his dressing rooms and hotel rooms, impatient to be his. Some of them travelled thousands of miles and a few actually started stalking the singer in Montreal and Hydra, sometimes for years, imagining they were married to him or had special heavenly messages to deliver. Caught in that erotic campaign, Leonard, who used sex and seduction as ways to cope with anguish and depression, rather than being a mere ladies' man, became for a while a lady-killer who asked to see female interviewer's breasts before he agreed to start an interview or often asked for sex before he asked for names.

But four wars are hardly enough for the man who wanted to be all Jewish heroes at once. So, around the same time, he starts a fifth one — that one spiritual — under the leadership of General Sasaki: the war of Zen against the folly of the ego. At the beginning of the '70s, the poet famously begins a regime of regular Buddhist retreats: one or two months every year at monasteries. On Mt. Baldy Zen Center in the San Gabriel Mountains, sixty-five hundred feet above Los Angeles, or in Jemez Springs, New Mexico. At sixty-five, Joshu Sasaki was a great general — the double agent of the dharma, both the ally and the enemy of his disciples. Like Hakuin in the eighteenth century, he invited you to practise as if your head was on fire and warned that sanzen (the personal encounters where he gave students koans to solve) were open only to students who were ready to kill or be killed. Sometimes he offered you a boiled rice soup, sometimes a glass of ginger brandy: who wouldn't want to go to war with a general like that?[3]

Now, the first effect of zazen — sitting meditation — is to bring you face to face with your inner conflicts; you sit in silence, and soon realize that you are engaged in ten private wars at once, none of which has any real substance. You are like the Siamese fighting fish who fight their own reflection when faced with a mirror (sometimes until they die of exhaustion).[4] Leonard immediately loved the martial atmosphere of Rinzai Zen: the rise before dawn, the days spent in silence, meditating and working, the bells, the sutras, and the constant bows and prostrations. That rigorous structure is designed to break down the most hardened resistance, but the target of Zen is not so much the ego as the pedestal of rigidities and illusions that the ego rests on. The ego will dissolve on its own accord. In summer with the crickets; in winter with the crows. Leonard loved that disciplined life from day one: koans to enter the universe of non-duality; zazen as a gateway to the deeper life and direct transmission by a master who is both your drinking buddy and your best enemy. He must also have liked the clear contract of Zen: nothing to gain except a deep respect for all things — the bowl you eat from, the black cushion you sit on, and the limitless world you join. Sometimes, Zen clearly worked. Leonard's heart was unified and he found he was in the heart of life at last. He then left the mountain and returned to Babylon to resume his imaginary wars.

Wars, then, are the stuff that Leonard's '70s were made of. After years spent looking for perfect unions with women in alcoves and with God in his heart, the singer was now a soldier engaged on multiple fronts. And the cruelest war was perhaps the one he was waging with the Logos. By the end of 1972, he had indeed been facing a dry spell for at least eighteen months, with no new songs coming his way and every blank page a challenge. By 1973, the poet was almost ready to throw in the towel. Five years of songwriting was a short career, but it was better than nothing.[5]

But Leonard was not afraid of emptiness. Quite the opposite, in fact. Maybe he had been too openly mystical until now. Hence that new idea: a gigantic tabula rasa. A clean slate, with no angels, no troubadour, no Nashville. He was ready to start over with what Buddhism recommends: Zen mind, beginner's mind.[6] And for this, what better method than his favourite game: to describe what is in front of you. In that case, it was turbulences. He sits in zazen and is divided against himself. He sits in his new Montreal house (rue Saint-Dominique, just off the Boulevard Saint-Laurent) or in the garden in Hydra, and finds his marriage is an explosive union of opposites. He looks at the world and sees international terrorism and gender wars everywhere. For the year is 1972 and news programs are filled with radical feminism, terrorist attacks, and hostage takings. The PLO, the IRA, the Red Brigades, the Weathermen, and Baader Meinhoff are in the limelight and, in August, eleven athletes of the Israeli athletics team are massacred at the Olympic Games in Munich. That same year, audiences dig the ultra-violence of *Dirty Harry* and *A Clockwork Orange*, and the world gradually forgets what was left of "peace and love" to return to the more orthodox views of Hegel ("conflict is the engine of history") and Hume ("man is a wolf to man"). In keeping with that Zeitgeist, Leonard redefines his gesture with a new hypothesis: in the beginning was the War.

He enters his Hegelian period and, for a few years, his work will deal almost exclusively with dialectics, conflicts, and the energy of negativity. The '70s will not spare the poet and the decade will lead him to personal chaos, a Casanovian overkill, and to ever darker depression.

Artistically, it will be a time of redefinition, as his talent and vision are tested and put into play again. The period opens with a small book of hatred called *The Energy of Slaves* in October 1972 and culminates six years later with *Death of a Lady's Man*, a collection of poems in which the author submits his own poems to his own fierce criticism — Leonard deconstructs Leonard. In 1977, he will put himself in the hands of the most anti-Cohenian producer available (Phil Spector, then lost in megalomaniac excess) for a record called *Death of a Ladies' Man*. Unsurprisingly, the poet will end the period on his knees, without a wife and without much of a career, but ready once again to hear angels sing.

THE ENERGY OF SLAVES (1972)

> *Welcome to these lines*
> *There is a war on [. . .]*
> *The village will be taken soon*
> *I have removed whatever*
> *might give comfort to the enemy.*
>
> — LEONARD COHEN, *The Energy of Slaves*[7]

The opening lines are clear. *The Energy of Slaves* will provide no consolation. The poet is not here to reunify hearts. Instead, he declares war to his readers and sticks to the basic principle of guerrilla warfare: leave nothing to the enemy. Tabula rasa, act 1. The title itself is intimidating, especially when you remember what Nietzsche says about slaves: they are fed by resentment, and want only revenge.[8] Plus, there's that picture at the back of the book, which introduces Leonard's new persona and organizes a confrontation between the reader and the poet.[9]

Leonard is standing, staring straight at the lens while dragging on a cigarillo, apparently leaning against a bathroom wall. He is clean-shaven with cropped hair (tabula rasa, act 2), not exactly in an attitude of defiance, but looking perfectly determined. Is this still a "poet"? Not so sure. Just as likely a mercenary or an officer in an undetermined secret service. He also exudes the combination of pride and mild hostility that is professionally required of fashion models. And the picture could indeed be a fashion photograph. With a little help from a fitted shirt with rolled-up sleeves and a dangerously pointed collar (and that famous second unfastened button to reveal the torso), Leonard gives us a lesson in attitude: how to wear your shirt the manly way. As we know, the social function of the fashion model is to exclude us. Alone in a universe of luxury and beauty, fashion models hint that they are sexier than you, worth infinitely more and will never have to smile again. Leonard's version is "I'm tougher than you and no one will ever be able to take me down."[10] If he is a fashion model, he's working for your local army surplus. And where else but in the Marines could a poet have learnt to clutch his leather belt in such a manly way?

Roland Barthes defines a good photograph as the intrusion into a clearly defined subject (a studium, in Barthesian language) of one or more incongruous details (punctum, puncti) that reintroduce "play" and allow us to reinterpret the picture endlessly.[11] Here the studium is clear: a portrait of the poet as a man of action. But there are intriguing details, indeed: the determined stare that seems to probe our souls, the tiled bathroom wall (Why here? What has just happened in that bathroom?), and of course, totally at odds with the era's capillary extravagance, the cropped hair.[12] It's even slightly disquieting. The same goes for the posture: a very precise mixture of deep relaxation and perceptible tension: that guy (a slave, but whose?) can strike back at any moment.

So, with the cold title and the virile persona, Leonard announces the mood of the book: defiance and threat. He also shows the first effects of Zen on his person: it sharpens him. In contact with the purity of Rinzai, he has turned at least in his own eyes into a bushido who asks (in the middle of the book) the provocative question that Colonel Kurtz will ask again seven years later in *Apocalypse Now*:

> Why don't they make Vietnam
> worth fighting for?[13]

So, the intentions are clear. After years of investigating holiness and methods to turn lovers into angels, Leonard was now ready for war. In particular for the terrorist guerrillas extolled by the Viet Cong, the exiled Black Panthers, or the now underground Weathermen. For that was the big idea in the counterculture in 1972: to go *underground*, to disappear in order to subvert society and strike where you are least expected — from the heart of things. Leonard applies that program to poetry and the cover photograph is a manifesto and a confession: the poet is on the lam, he is hiding somewhere in a bathroom, but he is about to strike because he is (quite literally) up against the wall. The troubadour has gone underground.

The Energy of Slaves will therefore be a book of terrorist poetry: 127 poems that use derision, threats, insults, and a perpetual confession of unspeakable desires; 127 poems that take readers hostage and force them to witness Leonard's imaginary wars: the war against women — the opposite sex that is here the enemy sex. The war against the bogus revolutionaries and bleating propagandists of peace and love. The war against the establishment poets (who are merely "employees" while Cohen is a "slave"[14]). The war against the readers themselves, who are potential enemies if they expect consolation and understanding. And finally, the war against beauty, which is, as in Rimbaud's *A Season in Hell*, officially dismissed from the collection one-third into the book.[15] It's the tabula rasa principle once again: no poetic beauty here, no metaphor, nothing but raw language and hard feelings. All those wars are fought mercilessly and with no expectations of glory, making *The Energy of Slaves* a daunting, biting, and misogynistic book, albeit a hilarious and necessary one. In 1972, with terrorism on one side and radical feminism on the other, a poet had to speak up and Leonard Cohen did. So, Women's Lib, how many divisions?

THE MISOGYNIST SAMURAI

> *Speed is the essence of war. Take advantage of*
> *the enemy's unreadiness; take unexpected routes*
> *and attack unguarded spots.*
>
> — SUN TZU, *The Art of War*[16]

The Energy of Slaves is a military operation. After defining his targets (which is the easy part: all is takes is to take your resentments seriously), Leonard sets up a strategy. In *The Art of War*, Chinese general Sun Tzu (fifth century BC) defined the conditions for military victory: a good knowledge of the terrain, a good evaluation of the enemy, a good seizure of the kairos (the proverbial "right moment"), and a good use of spies — a point which seems to have particularly impressed Leonard. In each war, he does indeed present himself as an infiltrating spy: an enemy of beauty pretending to be a poet, a cynical Casanova masquerading as a lover of women, a traitor to all revolutions posing as a countercultural hero. Striking by surprise is not a problem; all it takes is sharpening your weapons, i.e., the poems. Not a very hard task, either: a few insults, a few threats and ultimatums, and you're well on your way.

> I will burn down your house
> and fuck you in the ass [. . .]
> Why don't you come over to my table
> with no pants on
> I'm sick of surprising you.[17]

For all its wry humour, the volume is certainly a little creepy. A silhouetted razor blade on the top of every page creates an interesting rhythm — a poem, a razor blade, a poem, a razor blade — that keeps us in touch with the poet's intentions to cut through to the brutal truth of our emotional lives and reveal the beauty of all things sharp. The beauty of radical rhetoric, of gestures that kill, and the beauty of war, which clarifies relationships. The beauty of resentment also, when resentment has become absolutely pure. In the middle of the book, Leonard presents an allegory of his own hatred with a scorpion that he imagines lodged in him, a "rare and perfect creature" that gnaws at his heart but makes him write with venom.[18]

Of course, it's all a radical reversal of Cohen's original gesture; the poet of love becomes "the angel of revenge" (the only winged being to appear in the book).[19] Rimbaud claimed that the hand on the pen was worth that on the plough; Cohen adds that the hand on the weapon is worth that on the pen. And clearly the fascination this new opus can exert is akin to that of firearms. Firearms, often little masterpieces of engineering and design, can be fascinating because their beauty wounds and kills. And this is what Leonard is aiming at in his new poems: a discourse so radical and precise in its insults that it could cause damage as surely as his Walter PPK. He admits it himself:

> I hate my music
> I long for weapons.[20]

LEONARD'S GRAND GUIGNOL

Caught in imaginary wars and in slanging matches so outrageous they become comical, the reader is invited to enjoy the ferocity of the poet's Grand Guignol show. How he dynamites love poetry and invents a lyricism of hatred. How he speaks to his tomahawk or inflicts torments on women (torture, rape, murder, enslavement, arson of their homes, arbitrary trials . . .). How he unfolds a list of conquests that one hopes is fictional: twenty-year-old girls, fifteen-year-old girls, a fourteen-year-old girl with round buttocks . . .[21] How he stages his suicide to let us know that the poet in him is dead. How he ironically signs a poem with the serial number of his personal weapon (Walter PPK-S, Serial No. 115142).[22] How he displays an impressive collection of weapons, with rifles, a saw, an axe, automatic machine guns, a bazooka, instruments of torture, a Second World War fighter plane, a DC-3 bomber, and a boa constrictor laced around his mistress's boots. How he tries to scare himself with his own gaze in the mirror. And, finally, how he declares his poetic bankruptcy in the middle of the collection:

> I have no talent left
> I can't write a poem anymore
> You can call me Len or Lennie now,
> Like you always wanted.[23]

WHY SO MUCH HATRED?

> *If you ever read this, think of the man writing it.*
> *He hated the world on your behalf.*

— LEONARD COHEN, *The Energy of Slaves*[24]

But why so much hatred? Leonard has often claimed to write with no pre-established plan, seized by sudden impulses to raise the voice in certain ways. In the present case, he was obviously set on provocation, as is evident in the joyful ways in which the poet inverts his public image as a woman-loving troubadour. Like striptease, provocation is an erotic art: the provocateur plays with taboo ideas and unacceptable words. Here, the poet explores limits and boundaries and tries to assess where poems stop being poems to become jokes, where jokes stop being jokes to become insults. Dark humour is central as Leonard exaggerates his provocations, gets a few laughs, and then attacks again with new outbursts of misanthropy or misogyny. It's hardcore flirtation: he plays with the reader's ability to catch fire. The central rule: never reveal if you're serious or not. Better still, never really know yourself. The result is a book that is certainly of dubious taste, but also authentically "alive," a quality that Leonard has mentioned every time he called *The Energy of Slaves* his favourite book.[25]

Of course, at that particular moment in history, such an explicitly misogynistic textual assemblage was bound to alienate many readers. But the extent to which the obvious irony in Cohen's posturing was ignored by critics is quite striking in retrospect. For simply reading the book shows that irony is everywhere. A Nazi war criminal comes to visit the poet in a silk parachute? The poet falls in love with a lizard who does push-ups? The poet, like Samson, crashes the pillars of traditional poetry and threatens to kill Norman Mailer and his whole family if the American writer ever "comes up" to him? Irony is definitely the only way into the book.[26]

Another fundamental impulse in the volume is the urge to desecrate. The heroes of *Beautiful Losers* wanted to "fuck a saint"; Leonard wants to mess up poetry. But he has an aim: to temporarily suspend the lyrical machine and send poetry to purgatory. Where it will be purged. Purged of its lies, of its accommodations with all things "poetic." For what right has the poet to speak "poetically" when he finds his throat stuck with cries of hate? What right does he have to promise that "the sisters of mercy, they are departed or gone" when he dreams of razor blades? And perhaps the omnipresent razor blades in the volume also indicate a desire to bleed poetry in the medical sense — an act of purgation which, of course, could kill the patient.[27]

A third direction in the volume is that Leonard explores the dark side of the masculine unconscious. The 127 poems examine not only the positive or negative stereotypes of masculine identity (the hero, the lover, the brute, the coward) but also the modalities of masculine action (parade, predation, physical coercion), their political extensions (tyranny, fascism), and the primitive impulses which underlie the masculine: to possess, to submit, to penetrate. In order to become the metaphysician of the broken heart and the poet of love that Leonard aspired to be — the equal of Rumi and Ovid — a detour through Casanova and the Marquis de Sade was necessary. It was necessary for a while to examine love from the exclusive point of view of masculinist sexual fundamentalism. Hence this *hardcore* lyricism reminiscent in its radicality of the confessional poets, through which Cohen bluntly exposes his obsessions:

> My own music
> Is not merely naked
> It is open-legged
> It is like a cunt.[28]

Obviously, the poet can no longer hold his tongue.

THE SLAVE OF TWO SUZANNES

But, as always, the final impulse in the book is much simpler: Leonard just confesses. He tells us quite frankly, with just enough exaggeration to keep us entertained, where he stands and, for this, the title is almost enough, clarifying as it does with a single word what he is in every way: a slave. The word comes from the Bible, of course, and it will never again leave Cohen's vocabulary. He wanted to be a saint; he ended up a slave. That is to say a creature of labour and a man who does not own himself.[29] And in 1972, slavery is an objective fact for Leonard in any way he looks at his life. He is a slave of women by appetite, a slave of beauty by vocation, the slave of his worktable by temperament, and probably also the slave of two or three psychotropic substances. Recently, he has also become the slave of a commercial system that transformed his songs into products and his name into a trademark. His role has actually been defined very precisely by his record company, tour operators, and by the rock press. He is *Leonard Cohen, Poet of rock music*. That's the sales pitch and his official title, actually printed on posters and tickets. In other words, as the poet himself puts it:

> A beautiful slave
> to make you cry.[30]

That status is familiar to Leonard, for it is that of the minstrels of Israel in Psalm 137. Deported to Babylon, they had to entertain their new masters with the songs of Zion. But how could they sing the Lord's song in a strange land? Of course, Leonard is faced with a slightly different version of the predicament. He is under contract to CBS-Columbia and has yet to produce two more albums, for which he doesn't have a single song yet. A live album or a compilation could be a solution, but Leonard knows that whatever happens, he is condemned to write a new "Suzanne" every year. In Frankfurt that April, he had ironically said it on stage:

> Yes, I am the man who wrote Suzanne
> I am the man who wrote Suzanne
> I am the man who wrote Suzanne
> A thousand years ago.[31]

And that's Leonard's real confession — he is the slave of Suzanne. To be precise, he is, at that particular moment, the slave of two Suzannes: one is an angel locked in a song whose publishing rights no longer belong to him; the other is that young woman with whom he is having a tumultuous affair and who has decided to make him a father. But the fundamental energy of the slave, as Nietzsche ceaselessly reminds, is his desire for revenge. And that's exactly what fuels *The Energy of Slaves*: the book is Leonard's effort to write an anti-Suzanne, something that is both desperate and cynical, but also strangely tonic in its irony. For the poet, the operation was also a test, whereby he could find out how far he was willing to go in the disclosure of his personal hell. Largely ignored by fans and predictably mocked and spurned by Canadian critics, *The Energy of Slaves* was the necessary hallali before the hallelujah.[32] Needless to say, the new moral order that has spread over North America as I write these lines has made the book subversive and delicious again — as it should be.

KIPPUR

We have said it already: by the early '70s, Leonard had seen all types of wars. Except, of course, a real one. Surely, he had heard bullets fly and seen some scuffles in Cuba, but that didn't count. In 1973, history comes to his rescue. Once more, it all begins in Greece where Suzanne, Leonard, and the little Adam have retired in early autumn. Still struggling with inspiration, the poet was back from New York where he had attended the rehearsals for an off-Broadway show based on his work with six actors declaiming or singing his lyrics around a non-existent plot. Not a great critical success; not a great show, either. It would close after a couple of weeks before briefly heading to Toronto and Paris.[33]

Immediately after opening night, Leonard flies back to the place where he had once lived with a Norwegian angel to resume in paradise the saga of his great disagreement with his wife.[34] They quickly come to a status quo: Suzanne on the terrace; Leonard in the cellar. There, he is sweating over the first draft of a book that will only see the light of day five years later in its fifth or sixth version, after many changes in title and form. For the moment, only the subject is clear: the marital bond. Or (to be precise) the thousand ways in which married couples mate: in rows and bacchanals, in interlockings and dislocations. But the conclusion was clear before the book was begun: marriage is a furnace, not for the weak-hearted. For the moment, Leonard takes detailed notes about the violent rows in the kitchen (in front of their baby child) and about the moments of truce and passion in the bedroom. He also observes that marital wars always bring out the worst in you. With hindsight, the situation is almost comical: the world sees him as a great poet of love while he, locked up on an island with his wife, experiences something that reminds one of Sartre's famous shock-phrases in *No Exit*: "Hell is other people." Another confirmation of God's sense of humour.

But history offers the poet a way out. On Yom Kippur Day, October 6, 1973, Egypt's infantry and the Syrian aircraft launched a combined assault on Israel, triggering the Fourth Arab–Israeli War. Three weeks of fighting ensue, with a catastrophic first week for the unprepared Jewish army and a total of twenty thousand casualties on both sides. Leonard apparently left Hydra the day after the attack. The following morning, he was sitting in a Tel Aviv café, examining his options: to join the war effort or join a kibbutz. On Hydra, the short trip from the house to the harbour was the occasion for a final vitriolic exchange with Suzanne, a poetic transcription of which would appear in *Death of a Lady's Man*: an argument about who carries more luggage. We understand why the poet wanted to see a real war up close: his private wars were so petty that there was no end or glory in sight.

In the Tel Aviv café, Leonard is recognized by Ilana Rovina and Oshik Levi, two Israeli singers who were putting together an entertainment section for the troops.[35] They invite him to join in but the

Canadian is unsure whether his songs — critics insisted they were depressing — could entertain anyone, let alone soldiers. But he agrees to sing the next day for a concert at the Hatzor air base north of Tel Aviv: luminous, according to Oshik. What will happen during the following three weeks will leave a lasting impression on the singer and probably breathe new life into his career: he joins a team that travels to the front lines in the Sinai. They travel by jeep, by troop transport planes, by truck, by helicopter. Leonard sees artillery guns, he sees soldiers pray in the desert, wounded soldiers, Egyptian prisoners and dead bodies. Everyone around him wears a uniform; everyone carries a gun. With the team, he gives six to eight brief concerts every day. The idea is to stop and sing as soon as you see troops. Eight soldiers around an artillery piece: you sing. Seventy soldiers resting in the shadow of their tanks: you sing.[36] For example, that heartfelt song that Leonard has just composed:

Yes, and lover, lover, lover, lover, lover, lover, lover,
Come back to me.

Some evenings, slightly more formal concerts are organized in warehouses, with a couple of spotlights set on oil cans. A handful of photographs taken by the war correspondents Uri Dan and Isaac Shokal have surfaced. In one of them, Leonard looks quite serene. We see him sing, one knee in the sand, with eyes closed. All around are troops: tired, bearded, hairy. They don't know whether they are winning the war or losing it. But in the picture, it seems like the songs have gotten their attention and, if you go by the smiles of some faces, perhaps a few hearts were touched. Oshik Levi would later recall, maybe with some exaggeration, that Leonard wanted to enlist everywhere: to join the paratroopers when he was with paratroopers; the air force when he met the air force.[37] Perhaps we should keep in mind that Leonard had a father and that father had served in the French trenches. Here, at last, was the son's war, a war that was much purer than the one he had been fighting everywhere with little Adam's mother. A war he could wage in his own way. By singing the infinite mystery of things to tired soldiers, discreetly slipping in the kohen's blessing:

> And may the Spirit of this song,
> may it rise up pure and free
> may it be a shield for you,
> a shield against the enemy.[38]

And, fatefully, when Leonard entered Sinai, he entered biblical land. Very far, once more, from the Chelsea Hotel. For, if you forget the technology, the Yom Kippur War was actually a replica of the Old Testament wars: chariots in the desert for the survival of Israel. And as they did with the young David in the Bible, many soldiers took a liking to the poet: one offers him a handgun; another gives him Egyptian money taken from a corpse (which Leonard buries in the sand); and General Ariel Sharon (a.k.a. "the lion of the desert") apparently shares a cognac with the poet, an anecdote transcribed in Leonard's diary with a laconic comment: *I want his job.*[39] Every night, the singer sleeps in warehouses or in sleeping bags under the starry sky. He eats military rations and, with only basic knowledge of Biblical Hebrew, doesn't speak the language. But for the first time in a very long while, perhaps stimulated by what Nietzsche called "the curative virtue of war,"[40] he starts composing again. For a year or two, he will shock journalists by saying it out loud: war is marvellous. He will speak of the palpable fraternity, the purity of the bond between adversaries, and the vitality of life when it is concentrated in an absolute point of urgency and confrontation.[41] Of course, soldiers die — friends and foes — and foes are men as well and — in this case — Semites, almost brothers who, for Leonard, just happened to be from the other tribe. This prompts the poet to be wanting to sing for both sides, which he will later claim to have done in the secret of his heart.[42] But let war be war. After that tour, he took on a habit that lasted way into the following millennium: giving his audience, and pretty much anyone he met, a military salute. To a Spanish journalist who asked why he did this, he answered quite frankly, "Because I don't consider myself a civilian."[43]

And clearly, the lyrics composed during those weeks have a new tone to them. "Lover, Lover, Lover," originally a blessing for the Tsahal soldiers, is gradually transformed into a letter of grievance sent to the Creator on behalf of us all. More ironic is "Field Commander Cohen," Leonard's self-portrait as an officer and spy who wins every war — the wars of the world and those of the heart. "There Is a War" is an homage to Hegel that reminds us that the world advances only by ceaselessly dividing itself against itself. Hence the war between rich and poor. Between the man and the woman. Between left and right, the Black and white, the odd and the even. The song claims that the energy of those multiple wars is the great tonic of existence. War keeps the world alive.

It seems that after two and a half weeks, Leonard returns to civilian life refreshed. At the end of the previous tour, he was ready to give up; he is now ready to start again. Still in Israel, after hesitating between a pilgrimage on foot from Tel Aviv to Jerusalem to atone for his lechery and a vast enterprise of seduction of every passing skirt, he decides (after stays in Montreal, Los Angeles, and Hydra again) to isolate himself from his wife and the crying baby to finish the new songs. Preferably in a quiet place — a country in the middle of a civil war, for example. Ethiopia? Perfect. In March 1974, Leonard locks himself up in a room at the International Hotel in Asmara, where he indulges in his favourite activity: to live in a hotel. He comes out after a couple of weeks with complete versions of the three songs composed in Israel, but also with "Chelsea Hotel #2" and a few others. The war had freed him. He was a songwriter again.

KIDNAPPING A PRODUCER

Back to Montreal, early 1974. A small house on rue Saint-Dominique that visitors describe as full of books and that will soon be full of children's laughs and cries — a second child, Lorca, will be born in September. Leonard is thirty-nine. A few months before, a short live album, *Live Songs*, was greeted with indifference and *Bird on a Wire* is still unreleased. For the new songs, Leonard is not going back to Nashville; he is looking for a more incisive sound. Exactly which sound, he doesn't know, at least not until January 1974, when he attends a concert in the harbour district of Montreal in a small club called L'Evéché. There, a twenty-five-year-old singer named Lewis Furey plays quirky little jazz songs and dissonant ballads with lyrics about underground Montreal and borderline states. In the room, Leonard hears the future of rock, and it sounds like a mix of Jacques Brel, Lou Reed, Kurt Weill, and David Bowie. Backstage, he kidnaps the band's musical director, John Lissauer, a multi-instrumentalist just out of Yale University where he has studied Bach, Stockhausen, and the history of jazz. His specialty? Sharpness and counterpoint. His strings are like razor blades; his brass and woodwinds like marching armies. Leonard arranges to meet Lissauer in Manhattan. He has a few songs he would like to play the young man.

The problem of course is that, as a producer-arranger, Lissauer is very young, very unknown, and hardly a producer-arranger at all, having actually produced no one yet. Not exactly what Cohen's manager had in mind. After two years of silence and an unnoticed record, the lawyer knows that his client's next move may be his last. So it's no time to take risks and let a fledgling nobody produce a major CBS star. Leonard Cohen a.k.a. "poet of rock." But the poet of rock insists and Machat reluctantly grants his seal of approval. CBS agrees to finance a few demos and thus begins the second act of Cohen's musical career. June 1974, the theatre district, New York City. Leonard starts work on his new album at a small place called Sound Ideas Studio with a producer sixteen years his junior.[44] His objective: to reinvent his music. Hence the title: *New Skin for the Old Ceremony*.

This time, there is no reaching after a specific "sound." On the basis of a trio — Leonard on guitar, John Miller on bass, Lissauer on piano — the appropriate arrangements are thought out track by track with only one instruction: to give each song an edge. Lissauer works scissors in hand, like a couturier. He cuts a new dress for each song, usually drawing his inspiration from contemporary classical music and New Orleans jazz.[45] With a love song from the Renaissance, an ode to war, an elegy for a lustful saint, an irreverent prayer, the story of the singer's trial, and a few caustic evocations of marital life, Leonard has brought the producer a vast range of material — enough to work in several directions.

The first thing Lissauer does is encourage the singer to accelerate the tempos. He then adds percussion (a kind of Ethiopian tabla on "Lover, Lover, Lover" and "There Is a War") and, here and there, a jazz trombone or a clarinet ("Is This What You Wanted?" and "Why Don't You Try?"). In addition to the necessary female harmonies — perhaps a little more soulful this time — he goes back to basics: strings. But not just any strings. Precise, efficient, modern strings. They emphasize melodic contours ("Field Commander Cohen," "Who by Fire"), define stages in the progression of songs ("A Singer Must Die"), and clarify their mood. The result? One of Leonard's finest records, with a sound that an inspired critic would call "cabaret funk."[46]

NEW SKIN FOR THE OLD CEREMONY (1974): AS BELOW, SO ABOVE

Thematically, Leonard starts (as always) with a simple idea: our insatiable need for love. We are all orphaned children and abandoned lovers who long for a "Lover, Lover, Lover" to "come back" to us. Hence our search for ideal unions, the perfect image of which is given by the heavenly coitus realized by the angels on the cover.[47] An "old ceremony" that ceaselessly renews the world, but for which a "new skin" is always required as Leonard the serial lover knew full well.

This image allows the poet to clarify a point: he thinks, as did Rilke and *Wings of Desire* director Wim Wenders, that angels imitate men. They have seen us mate and they, too — so it would seem — are hungry for flesh, duality, and coitus.[48] And if angels themselves embrace the great dialectical struggle, who are we, beings of flesh, to want to escape it? That seems to be the central question of the album and its ideological matrix, perfectly summarized in the manifesto-song "There Is a War": forget ideal unions and embrace, as fully, as resolutely as you can, the imperfection of your life. Embrace the conflicts and dualities of reality. Join existence as it is (i.e., perpetually divided against itself) and find in wars and coitus the energy which renews life. It's a dangerous invitation but one that is perfectly explicit:

> Why don't you come on back to the war?
> Don't be a tourist.
> Why don't you come on back to the war?
> Don't be embarrassed.

So the aim of *New Skin for the Old Ceremony* is to explore the wars that are fought down here, far from the angelic world: the conjugal wars of a couple (Leonard and Suzanne) that is present everywhere but never named and the inner conflicts of a poet who, like Shakespeare's Brutus, seems "with himself at war." There's also the new frontline that Leonard has just opened: that of a polemical dispute (a disputatio) with the Creator. For the time has apparently come for the singer to settle his accounts with his favourite opponents: women, God, and rock critics.

JE T'AIME, MOI NON PLUS

A self-portrait of the poet as a triple agent (at once a popular singer, a CIA agent, and an LSD propagator), the song "Field Commander Cohen" reminds us beneath its apparent self-deprecation that we are all spies infiltrated in our lives and that we necessarily import the wars of the world into our bedrooms. As an expert strategist, Cohen explains here how to conduct these bedroom wars: just play master-and-servant. I lie down, you obey, and we multiply masks until "love is pierced and love is hung and every kind of freedom gone."

The diagnosis here, as on the rest of the album, is the same Rimbaud had made a hundred years before: "Love must be reinvented."[49] Cohen's proposed method for this is dangerous but invigorating: to make the couple a battlefield, where love will either be reborn or killed for good. Interestingly, the starting point of the album is a declaration of emotional bankruptcy, as the poet ironically asks his lover:

> And is this what you wanted
> to live in a house that is haunted
> by the ghost of you and me?

To make sure we understand that all efforts to revive that love affair have failed, Leonard closes the record with a cover of the most famous sixteenth-century love song, "Lady Greensleeves," originally a pledge of allegiance to a disdainful woman; here an obvious parody of that pledge. The singer distorts the melody, adds his own cynical lyrics, and sings as off-key as possible:

> Greensleeves was all my joy
> Now there's nothing left
> not even the Lady Greensleeves.[50]

It's only when the song ends that we understand the shrieks we have just heard: Leonard has just slit the throat of the troubadour in him.[51] So while angels accomplish perfect unions on the cover, poets of love can't seem to seduce their mistresses anymore and sixteenth-century love songs are changed into parodies. Is that the "new skin for the old ceremony"?

Caustic. That is obviously the dominant note of the record, "causticity" being the character of that which attacks, corrodes, and bites — acid, soda, satire. Of course Leonard considers that the politeness of causticity is to be caustic with yourself first. Hence his self-portrait on the record as "patron saint of envy and grocer of despair" or as every lady's "favourite singing millionaire."[52] Hence also the constant organization of his conjugal humiliation: he is the grotesque and unworthy half of the couple — Steve McQueen to his wife's Marlon Brando, Rin Tin Tin to her Beast of Babylon, the dirty little boy to her "manual orgasm."[53]

But throughout the album, Leonard adds an undercurrent of lyricism to the caustic note. At the end of "Field Commander Cohen," for example, after love has been declared defeated, a very simple call arises, repeated in fade-out to a background of beautiful strings:

> And o my love
> o my love,
> o my love,
> o my love . . .

We note the beauty of that "o," repeated over and over, which opens the singer's mouth, as in an inexhaustible astonishment that it has all come to this. Equally touching is the lover's tender declaration in "I Tried To Leave You":

> The bed is kind of narrow,
> but my arms are open wide.

So the listener is caught, like Leonard and his lady, between two fires: the songs of hate and the songs of love. A familiar dilemma.

J'ACCUSE

And all the ladies go moist,
and the judge has no choice:
a singer must die
for the lie in his voice.

— LEONARD COHEN, "A SINGER MUST DIE"

If love is on trial, so is the singer. He meets his judges in "A Singer Must Die," a song that dramatizes the prosecution of a poet in a totalitarian regime on the model of the Moscow Trial, with a little nod at the arbitrariness of the music press.[54] But mostly he uses the song to accuse himself of the only crime that totally disqualifies the artist in his own eyes: falsity. *A lie in his voice*: this is what he cannot forgive himself.[55] Lissauer masterfully accentuates the song's dramatic character with a quiet beginning — just Leonard's guitar, with a discreet organ and a waltz tune worthy of Chopin — followed by strings: first a few isolated salvoes, then a whole battery of violins that transform the track into a twisted little music-hall number à la Kurt Weill. The dissonance brings out everything that is twisted in that world: the lies of the state, the lies of the artist, the lies of desire. A black waltz. A masterpiece.

But facing judges is one thing. Facing *the* judge is another. In "Lover, Lover, Lover," written in Israel and first sung as we remember to the Israeli soldiers, Leonard initiates a dialogue with the Creator with a petition sent to the great celestial boss.[56] His requests are frank (change my name, my face, my spirit) but so are God's answers: your body is a test (you decide what you do with it) and my so-called absence is your making. The famous refrain is more ambiguous than may first appear. For who is really speaking here? Who is it that speaks to whom? At first, the call seems to be that of the abandoned son, an eternal orphan deprived of the

Father's love. He calls on the one whose very nature it is to love and says to him:

> Yes and lover, lover, lover, lover, lover, lover, lover
> Come back to me.

But isn't it also the Father's call, as he calls back the prodigal son, the little Casanova and professional lover, in his vain pursuit of a love that can be found only in God?

> Yes and lover, lover, lover, lover, lover, lover, lover
> Come back to *Me*.

As in all prayers, the speaker speaks to God so that he may speak *in* God, so that God may answer in the same breath. But Leonard's real achievement is to conduct his theological dispute to a backbeat of a cool guitar riff and Ethiopian drums and get the result into the hit parades (#9 in Germany).

Another instant Cohen classic is "Who by Fire," unexpectedly inspired by an eleventh-century Hebrew prayer recited on the eve of Yom Kippur: the Unetanneh Tokef. The original prayer carries out the particularly solemn task of opening the *Book of Life* to unveil the list of the men and women who are to die in the coming year. In his song, Leonard sends God a universal appeal of his decision but, as he does, he reviews (as did the original prayer) the various ways in which death can occur. Twenty-four possibilities from the most elementary deaths ("Who by fire? Who by water?"), to political deaths ("Who by common trial?"), accidental deaths ("Who by avalanche?"), and sophisticated modern deaths ("Who by powder?" "Who by barbiturates?"), not to mention deaths for love ("Who by his lady's command?").

The song can be heard as a letter of condolences to mankind but one that contains an intimation of fraternity, hinting that our common status as the helpless sons and daughters of a loving

Death who, like Medea, forgets none of its children, makes us all siblings.

That alone would make it a great song. But as we know, Leonard loves to play the smart guy. So he introduces into the original prayer the opposite of a prayer: an expression of irreverence. He answers the solemn call of the *Book of Life* with an impertinent question that he chooses to ask with exquisite politeness: "And who, shall I say, is calling?" In other words, we will answer the call of death when the one who calls has explained himself. And it is a very good question actually: who is it that is calling? Or rather, what should we call the one who is calling? That supposed champion of love who kills us like flies?

So, for the moment, Leonard is adamant: he will not get reconciled. Not with the wife, not with God, not with the judges. And *New Skin for the Old Ceremony* is definitely an exploration of that disagreement. Loved in Europe, although not as much as the first three records,[57] the album was completely ignored in America, where the two angels on the cover were censored in favour of a less risqué carbon copy of the cover art on the first album: a medium close-up of a nicely besuited Leonard nicely leaning against the nice wall of a nice hotel lobby.[58] The change however was not enough to convince American record shops to actually stock the album. Except perhaps at Interesting Records, on the ground floor of the Chelsea, where Leonard could see it every day.

THE HEAVENLY CANARY (TOUR OF 1974)

The singer believed in the record though, and with John Lissauer as musical director, he chose to defend it on stage with thirty-four concerts in nine European countries, beginning in Belgium in September and ending two months later in Paris's Olympia Theatre. The summer release of *Bird on a Wire*, with premieres in New York and London, was meant to create a Leonard Cohen buzz before the tour, but the movie came two years too late and made little impression.

After the European tour, the singer took the pulse of the American market with two small residencies in late November and early December at the Bottom Line in Manhattan and the prestigious Troubadour in Los Angeles, where he sang to a hip crowd of glitterati and socialites (Dylan attended one of the Californian shows).[59] After a short break came a forty-day tour of Canada which kept the singer busy until early March 1975, by which time he had spent almost seven months on the road. In November, the band reconvened in more intimate venues: jazz clubs and folk cabarets in Chicago, Nashville, Atlanta, Syracuse, and Denver. The contrast must have been strange for the singer, with sold-out concerts at the Royal Albert Hall or the Vienna Opera House, but only a few hundred spectators in Nashville, who find the guy amazing but can't remember his name. Leonard who?

Evidence shows that the singer's stage act had clearly benefited from the collaboration with Lissauer. Often backed up by percussion or just by the pounding of a boot sole on the stage floor, the songs were played faster to the great benefit of their melodic properties: the waltzes whirled away and Cohen's guitar had never been that close to flamenco. On the bootlegs, "Bird on the Wire" takes on an incredible lightness while "Famous Blue Raincoat," played much faster, finds an airy perfection without abandoning an inch of gravity. The music often sounds like gypsy jazz or crooner jazz and, on at least two tracks, like a kind of acoustic reggae. Accompanied by Emily Bindiger and Erin Dickins, whom he calls on stage his "celestial canaries," Leonard sings wonderfully; the new tempos have helped him locate a swing in his voice. You can tell that the stage is no longer the place where he tries to dissolve his solitude, but a space where he seeks to keep the audience on the edge of their seats. Every night the concerts, now lasting three hours with an average of twenty-six songs, culminate with the new hits "Lover, Lover, Lover" and "Who by Fire." In 1970 and 1972, the singer sometimes exuded darkness. Everything now is swift and light and airy.

During the small US tour of November 1975, Leonard and Lissauer tested five new jazzy songs that they had just co-written in the summer at the Chateau Marmont. The album was meant to be called *Songs for Rebecca* and some of those tracks are among Leonard's finest. But fearing that such a close collaboration (the young man is now a partner in writing, not just an arranger) would damage his client's reputation as a singer-songwriter, Marty Machat disapproved of the project. And since *New Skin for the Old Ceremony* had been a relative commercial failure (peaking at #24 in the English charts), the manager, who was dreaming of more glorious collaborations, put an end to what he considered Leonard's extravagance. *Songs for Rebecca* was shelved and Lissauer fired without an explanation or a phone call. Not from Leonard. Not from anyone. An angel passes.

ACROSS EUROPE IN A BLACK BERET (TOUR OF 1976)

The Leonard Cohen who hit the roads of Europe again in the spring of 1976, now pairing his trademark raincoat with a black beret, had an undeniable bohemian panache. From April to July, he was back in the same old venues and the same old hotel rooms. A few smaller cities had been added to his usual stops — places like Strasbourg, Gothenburg, and Düsseldorf — making this his longest tour to date, with a total of fifty-six concerts in forty-six cities with, again, a stop at the Olympia Hall, this time for four days in a row (with twelve encores on the last night). Every day had its soundcheck, its share of interviews, and fifty to a hundred fans admitted to the dressing rooms for autographs. Obviously, Lissauer was gone, replaced as band leader by John Miller, a close buddy of Leonard's.[60] But the bass player had neither his prede-cessor's vision nor his authority and the bootlegs reveal a band that is not quite as tight, with a freewheeling pianist, unbridled backing singers, and occasional concessions to kitsch. "To get out there and boogie" — that was the purpose of the tour, as Leonard told a French magazine.[61] To boost his rock credibility, there was a drummer on stage for the first time — and not just any drummer actually but Luther Rix, who was still officiating on Dylan's *Rolling Thunder Revue* six months before — but the jury's still out as to whether "Who by Fire," "Famous Blue Raincoat," or "Suzanne" were much improved by his presence. As for Leonard himself, he seemed to have fallen back into some old habits: slowed-down tempos and stretched-out songs. Of course, the concerts included fantastic moments, like the raging "Store Room," resurrected from the *Songs of Leonard Cohen* sessions and an astonishing "Lover, Lover, Lover" transformed courtesy of a wah-wah pedal into a funky anthem à la Starsky & Hutch. And surely, with slicked-back hair and a grey double-breasted suit, Leonard looked great on French TV that June with a band that was ready to rock up Jacques Chancel's variety program *Le Grand Échiquier*. After the song, the host asked the poet what he thought of Dylan, and with a smile, the Canadian replied, "Il est jeune . . ." On stage, the band was playing a quasi-disco track that Leonard had just written, which quickly became the anthem of the tour. In it, Leonard evokes the excesses of his current rock-and-roll life, but the tongue-in-cheek chorus seems to contain a call for help:

> I'm forty-one, the moon is full,
> You make love very well,
> You touch me like I touch myself,
> I love you, mademoiselle[. . .]
> But tell me bird of paradise
> Do I have to dance all night?[62]

We are not sure who the girl was, but there were certainly antics and erotic shenanigans going on backstage. With no record to defend, however, except a *Greatest Hits* collection — which actually sold like hotcakes in Europe — the tour seemed to have been a wasted shot. But three months in hotel rooms is still three months in hotel rooms, and three months away from marital life. Despite another triumph at the Olympia, the reviews were mixed and, in France, *Rock & Folk*, usually strong supporters of Cohen, chose not to attend.

AGAINST THE TIDE

Rock & Folk had an excuse: they had seen Leonard in London two weeks before. Plus, they had better things to do: while the man who has just designated himself as "last year's man" performed at the Olympia, the Rolling Stones were on stage at La Villette in a venue just vacated by David Bowie. The English band had just started their disco crossover while Bowie, energized by Kraftwerk and dressed like a Gestapo agent, was inventing the ice-cold funk soon to be called *new wave*. He was on his way to Berlin, where he would record three albums of ambient electronic music.

That invisible crossing of paths is not without interest. On the right, an English dandy and a major star in America was fleeing the City of Angels after two years spent there in a cocaine daze. On the left, a Jewish poet with a European audience was dropping his bags in L.A. when everything seemed to indicate that the music scene there had drowned in soft rock and Brandy Alexanders.

Just before the tour, Leonard had indeed settled with wife and kids in a rented ranch house in Mandeville Canyon, Los Angeles. On the agenda: eucalyptus trees, serpentine streets, and millionaire neighbours. In New York and London, a new generation was waiting for its cue: December 31, 1976, midnight. Then, the great punk offensive would begin with a new paradigm: short hair, short songs, and a lot of spitting on *peace and love*. The avant-garde — Iggy and the Stooges, the Ramones, Patti Smith, Tom Verlaine — had already taken over the Chelsea Hotel and CBGB while Andy Warhol was inventing the '80s in his new white-walled factory. For once, Leonard was late.

In March, just before the tour, the singer had met his old crony Phil Ochs in New York, and their encounter had been like a warning. After several years of decline, the man who had once been Dylan's rival was now sleeping on the subway and fighting in bars. That evening, over a bowl of soup, he explained to Leonard that he had been murdered the year before at the Chelsea Hotel. Also that he was the secret FBI leader and, basically, that he was no longer Phil Ochs. On April 9, he hung himself. Sad as it was, the encounter confirmed what Leonard already knew from the Talmud: whoever marries the spirit of his generation will be a widower in the next.[63] By the mid-'70s, the veterans of the '60s, some clinging to their past glory, some evidently drifting, were going through a bad hangover and all of them — John Lennon included — seemed to have relocated in Los Angeles. The end of the decade would be very hard on them and for once, Leonard was no exception.

Of course, when he settled in L.A. in 1976, the singer was not looking for a *flower power* that had interested him so little the first time around. For him, the city was the city of Zen, where he was trying to deepen his practice with Sasaki Roshi. Perhaps it would also be — so he still hoped — the city where he and Suzanne could learn to get along. And perhaps in their new house, she would even like him as much as she liked the burgundy 1967 Mercedes-Benz coupé he had just bought her. At any rate, a new phase opens for the poet — one that would bring him what Master Sōkō Morinaga promises all Zen students: a lesson in the extent of their own stupidity.[64]

And after two unfocused years, Leonard seemed to need that lesson. In spite of the birth (in September 1974) of a daughter named Lorca, the union with Suzanne remained a tumultuous affair that the poet was trying to dissect in a book (he still called it a "novel" at this stage), of which he had just delivered a second draft to McClelland & Stewart in March 1976. He quickly withdrew his manuscript to deliver a third version five months later, which he would again withdraw.[65]

In all its successive versions, that book the poet couldn't seem to write was very explicit about how chaotic his conjugal life had become and about his increasingly uncontrolled bouts of woman-izing, which at this stage seemed to be escalating into a fully-fledged sex addiction. A careful reading of the final version (*Death of a Lady's Man*, 1978) reveals for example how the singer had transformed a quick solo tour of Italy in the summer of 1975 (to promote his newly translated 1960s novels) into a crazed sexual quest during which he bent over backwards to apply the program of "Lover, Lover, Lover" literally and become the lover of every Italian woman he met. The book actually helps you track itineraries and encoun-ters: there was Lori in Milan, Huguette in Florence, and Patricia in Rome (where Leonard saw the Holy Spirit come down on him, as he was sitting at the terrace of a café). Before that, still according to *Death of a Lady's Man*, came Danae in Athens — with whom the poet claims to have spent a week at the Hilton — Stephanie (aged sixteen) and Sherry (who loved him for "something [he] said ten years ago"). Not to mention Alexandra in New York, Iris in Munich, Barbara in Paris, Monica in various places . . .[66] In an unpublished diary consulted by Nadel, the poet bluntly admits he was at first "girl-crazy," then "simply cunt-crazy."[67]

Add to this a rising alcohol intake, conjugal rows galore, a few aborted projects, and you realize how adrift Leonard clearly was. It seems probable at this stage that the regime of sex and drugs and restless travelling was essentially a coping strategy that the poet used to curb increasingly severe depressive episodes. He clearly needed an anchor and Zen seemed to provide one that was maybe worth a try: sunyata — the great emptiness that pervades all things and, as Zen masters claim, is our true nature. In December 1975, Sasaki Roshi, who regularly took the singer to interconfessional sesshins in Catholic monasteries, invited his friend to Kyoto, where Buddhist rituals and visits to temples (among them Myoshinji and Ryoanji) alternated with drinking binges. Leonard returned the favour by inviting his friend to a recording session, at the end of which the maestro gave advice that, quite unsurprisingly, was the exact opposite of what everybody was telling the singer: "You should sing more sad." Perhaps the Roshi had guessed there was a fundamental sadness that his disciple was trying to avoid.

By the end of 1976, Leonard Cohen, now living in Los Angeles, visited the Zen Center almost daily. His manager took advantage of that geographical opportunity: there was someone in the city with whom he wanted his protégé to work. You could tell from this person's taste for guns and cocaine that he was not exactly a Zen master. In the following months, Leonard would gradually slip into his most chaotic period to date: a pandemonium or, to use a term taken from the book of Genesis, a tohu-bohu.

CHAPTER 8

DEATH AND REDEMPTION OF A LADIES' MAN

TOHU-BOHU AND SMOKEY LIFE
1977–1980

Tour book, 1974, from the collection of Jarkko Arjatsalo

ORIGINAL PHOTO: MICHAEL PUTLAND

L.A. BLUES

*D*eath of a Ladies' Man begins like a mafia movie circa 1976: a smart guy is trying to set up a heist. The smart guy in question is Marty Machat, who is faced with two problems: the artistic and financial bankruptcy of his client Phil Spector (who owes tons of money to Warner Brothers for a record he could not complete) and America's obstinate indifference to Leonard Cohen. The French post-structuralist philosopher Jean Baudrillard could have explained the latter phenomenon: America likes only simulacra and the surface of things — Andy Warhol's art or TV channels with nothing left to watch — making Cohen's investigation of depth a non-starter by definition. But, being unschooled in French philosophy, the manager thought he had to find a solution to Cohen's problem. And quickly, if possible. The last record had sold only 12,000 copies in the land of Uncle Sam (not a lot for a supposed rival of Bob Dylan[1]) and reputations are quickly lost in the music business. Hence an idea that must have seemed brilliant for at least five minutes: to team up the poet of grieving hearts and the creator of "Da Doo Ron Ron."

On paper, it works quite well: the Spector touch makes Cohen a mainstream star, Cohen's depth revives Spector, the record hits the tops of charts, the Warner debt is repaid and Machat, as agent of both artists, earns money from both sides of the equation: the heist of the century. What could go wrong? Nothing at all. Unless of course you chose to remember that both artists were not in the best of shape and that one of them was seriously unbalanced.

For the time being, Machat's task is to make sure the two misunderstood geniuses get on. Not exactly a problem: they are two middle-aged Jewish men with teenybopper hearts and a love of country music. What is more, Spector was uncharacteristically well-behaved during one of Leonard's appearances at *The Troubadour*: a good sign. Now that Lissauer was out of the picture, all it took was organizing a working session in the Beverly Hills mansion where Spector lived alone with 27 empty rooms and a white piano. Work begins in December 1976 with clear instructions from Machat: to write a hit record and aim high. They have three weeks. The studio is already booked.

In truth, Leonard can't have been that difficult to convince. Aware that a bold career move was required, he also knew — at least since he had seen Dylan's *Rolling Thunder Revue* rouse a packed Montreal Forum in December 1975 — that there was a potential future for 1960s singer-songwriters.[2] As for Spector's music, Leonard — who had always loved naïve piety and sweet devotions in all forms (Christian or pop) — had of course adored his early hits when he heard them on the jukeboxes of Montreal in 1958.

> To know, know, know her
> is to love, love, love her.

And at that time, Phil Spector had been a true visionary. Inspired by Wagner, his great idea was to inject momentum and scope into three-minute songs and turn them into "little symphonies for teenagers." The ingredients? Choruses in major mode, well-made bridges, echo chambers, girl bands, plus dozens of musicians and backup singers. Just add layers of sound to layers of sound — drums on drums, bass on bass, choirs, brass sections, string sections — saturate the result with reverb, mix it in mono, and Bob's your uncle: it's called the *wall of sound* and it's irresistible: "Be My Baby," "You've Lost That Lovin' Feelin'," "Unchained Melody," "River Deep Mountain High" — hit after hit after hit. The Beach Boys and the Beatles never recovered and stole from Spector the idea that the fundamental instrument of pop, the one that must absolutely be heard on the record, was the studio. But, as Francis Scott Fitzgerald once said, there are no second acts in American lives and since his early '60s heyday, Phil Spector had rested on laurels that were slightly less golden every year. Collaborations with John Lennon and

George Harrison in the early 1970s did not stop a well-known spiral of drugs, alcohol, artistic decline, and irremovable sunglasses. His life was now ordinary *rock-and-roll* boredom: Babylon in Malibu, Babylon in Bel-Air. Locked in his mansion with tyrannized valets and paid friends, the paranoid Phil now spent his days listening to Wagner at full volume, dreaming of the *Gesamtkunstwerk* he would never write. Not a good sign.

On his first visit that December, two things strike Leonard. First, the temperature. The producer, who likes to control everything, keeps it at 54 degrees. Then, there's Spector's eccentricity: the way he locks you in, for example. In case you may get tired of the Phil Spector Show and try to leave the place. So, on the first day, the poet and the mogul work all night as Suzanne sleeps on a sofa. And Leonard is happy. Face-to-face, Phil Spector is adorable and he lets you see the wounded child in him: a tiny, gifted Oliver Twist and puer aeternus who became too rich too fast and had the misfortune of having only one great idea. Now he lived surrounded by sycophants and toys: Rolls-Royces, revolvers and exuberant suits. And the palpable absence of all the women who left.

For the next writing sessions, Leonard recycles three old texts: "As the Mist Leaves No Scar" (a Zen pronouncement on the lightness of life originally published in 1961), "Fingertips" (a 1966 tale about a femme fatale who erases her many lovers' fingerprints), and "I Left a Woman Waiting" (a fragment of cruel dialogue between a lover and his mistress).[3] Two songs are recovered from the aborted project with Lissauer ("Don't Go Home with Your Hard-On" and "Iodine") and there's the last delivery from the front line of his marital life: a literary ballad about a woman who finds her suicided husband "hanging by a thread" ("Death of a Ladies' Man") and an evocation of a man's relief when he hears his wife making love to another man in the room next to his ("Paper-Thin Hotel," written during the previous tour). The pièce de résistance would be Leonard's foray into Spectorian territory: the epic tale of how he once approached the "tallest and blondest girl" during their high-school prom ball and begged, while they danced, to see "her naked body." For a couple of weeks, the two songwriting partners get on quite well: they work on melodies, get drunk on cocktails, talk about arrangements, and everything is fine and dandy. Then recording begins.

WAGNER IN MALIBU

Gold Star Studios, where Spector has home-court advantage — he has been working there for twenty years — is located on a stretch of Sunset Boulevard that comes straight out of the complete works of Charles Bukowski: a few palm trees, a couple of strip clubs, a military surplus and, everywhere, those liquor stores where Angelenos come to feed their collective amnesia. The credits of the album mention two local institutions as "official" suppliers: Piece O'Pizza and John & Pete's liquor store. It's again Cohen's caveat emptor principle: let the buyer beware and know exactly what record he's purchasing: one that was fueled by alcohol and pizza.

In that month of February 1977, the forces in the studio are unequal. On one side, a rather weakened Leonard Cohen: his marriage is on the verge of collapse, his career on the wane, his mother terminally ill, and he never refuses a drink.[4] On the other side, Phil Spector in full regalia: a bushy moustache, a star-studded tie on a striped shirt, black shades worn even at night, a silver belt buckle with his name on it, and a gun on the mixing table. His idea of glory: violent cops in TV shows. His daily fuel: cheap kosher wine and white powder. At the end of each session, he disappears with the tapes and keeps them under lock. Between the two men, an insurmountable barrier: twenty-seven musicians, fifteen backup singers, four sound engineers, an arranger, Phil's bodyguards, and a few tourists who have come to see the sessions that the whole city is talking about: Allen Ginsberg and Bob Dylan, Doc Pomus, the journalist Harvey Kubernick, the Ramones, and a few others. "I quickly realized," the former Hydra recluse would later say, "that I was entering a foreign country. I had rarely worked with twenty-five musicians in the room, including two drummers, three bassists and six guitarists."

On Spector's orders, the staff must be ready at 7 p.m. sharp, so that he may keep everyone waiting for at least an hour. Session musicians are paid double after ten and triple after midnight. So the project promises to be very expensive, all the more so as Spector likes to extend work until after dawn. Before midnight, it's the preparation phase: he divides the musicians into teams, decides who plays what, adjusts the microphones, distributes scores, confiscates scores, has bottles of red wine delivered, makes jokes, sings the chorus himself, prepares the room, orders pizzas, shouts his instructions from the control booth, plays playbacks at full blast, and — on occasion — gives the whole team lessons in step-marching. He also throws tantrums and occasionally fires a shot or two. He dreams of being Wagner but resembles Donald Duck. Now, Leonard's response to stress is usually to become even more quiet and melancholy. So much so that Spector quickly seizes total control of the operations. In the words of a studio employee: Phil was the artist and Leonard the subject of the painting.[5]

But the author of "Suzanne" is lucid: he knows that his access to the control room is purely honorary and that he is only an extra in Spector's project. He counts about as much as one of the three bass players and his role is to sing the lyrics when the boss tells him to, preferably at two in the morning and in a single take. Leonard will later sum up the Spectorian adventure with two words: "kid's stuff."[6] And it was probably a fair description: a spoiled kid had been given the keys to Gold Star Studios. Leonard must have shivered on the studio floor when he remembered the warning in Ecclesiastes:

> Woe to you, O land, whose king is a child and whose princes feast in the morning.[7]

It isn't hard to imagine the singer's contradictory feelings during the two weeks of the ordeal. First, there must have been anguish:

his music, his reputation and, ultimately, his career were at stake. But surely, Leonard was also amused, an amusement no doubt mixed with a kind of Stockholm syndrome for the man who had kidnapped his songs. And how not to love at least a little bit a man able to join you at the mike stand during a vocal, with a bottle of Manischewitz wine in one hand and a .45 in the other, and whisper, "I love you, Leonard" with the gun in your neck? The episode has been told many times, perhaps embellished for the great rock-and-roll saga that must be fed to journalists, but it rings true: tyrants are by nature great sentimentalists.

Then of course there must have been anger. The Phil Spector Show — a play by Phil Spector produced by Phil Spector starring Phil Spector — may have been interesting from a Buddhist point of view ("for four or five minutes" as Leonard would later say), but at the end of day, anger must have prevailed. And Leonard probably felt like a stowaway on a cheap rock-and-roll tour, one that had forgotten to go on the road, that made no money and that he was paying for. After a week, the extent of the shipwreck was getting clear: the producer produced nothing and the troubadour no longer believed in love. Klaus Kinski in the control room, Droopy the dog at the mike. And two careers on a road to nowhere.

Then one day, surprise: Spector has vanished. He is mixing the tapes in a secret place. Wagner is inspired. Panic in the Cohen clan: the singer had only recorded test vocals that were actually first takes. When the finished record is delivered several months later, Leonard and Machat are horrified. But the genius refuses to resume work. He has done his bit, can he please be paid now? For a while, Leonard considers hiring his own bodyguards to settle the matter with Spector on Sunset Boulevard, but he soon realizes that a megalomaniac like Spector couldn't tolerate someone else's talent and that he just "couldn't resist annihilating him."[8] So initially, Leonard refuses to release the record or to let his name be used.

In July, he retires to Mt. Baldy to compose summer haikus with Roshi and attempt to reattune himself to the infinite lightness of things. When he returns, he has better things to do than deal with a failed record: his mother is battling leukemia and the poet finds he must shuttle back and forth between Montreal and L.A., where he tries to save his family by living apart from them (Suzanne is often in France). Pressed by time and financial constraints (and with no plan B), he finally gives his assent to release the record, although he will pre-emptively disown it in the press and let every journalist know what he thinks of the end product.

Meanwhile, he has started work again on the book that has been plaguing him for five years now (of which he has just withdrawn the fourth version although it was already in press) and there happens to be a lot of talk in Canada about this book that Leonard Cohen is unable to write. As the year drew to a close, 1977 — with a stillborn record, a book that refused to be born, a marriage on the verge of collapse, and death lurking around the corner — was clearly developing into an annus horribilis of sorts. An entry into the tohu-bohu. In September, when *Death of a Ladies' Man* was finally released in Spector's original mix, the critics were not exactly adverse: they couldn't make head or tail of the object. A word often used in reviews had been suggested by Leonard himself: *grotesque*. Not a bad description.

DEATH OF A LADIES' MAN: ACT I

Initially, *grotesque* was a term used in aesthetics to designate the meeting of two incompatible things: a man with a cabbage-head for example.[9] On *Death of a Ladies' Man*, the grotesque effect comes from the discrepancy between the lyrics about sexual wars and psychological pain and Spector's wall-of-sound treatment: the choirs, the saxophones, the cascades of crescendos. But there is such a thing as grotesque beauty, as some critics perceived. And the reviews were often interesting. Under the title "Cohen's doo-wop nightmare," Paul Nelson's verdict in *Rolling Stone* was "a great album, but a failed one." In *Melody Maker*, Chris Bohn called it "Cohen's last tango" (in reference to Bertolucci's Marlon Brando movie about failed masculinity) and his "voyage to the bottom of his soul" but bemoaned the "skeleton tunes" and the overhanging bitterness, while in France, *Rock & Folk* put Leonard on the cover in an Elvis-like pose, with a title that facetiously asked "COHEN ROCKER?" An ecstatic five-page analysis inside the magazine presented the album as a marvel of ironic *muzak* and Cohen as the heir of decadent writers. A wee bit exaggerated perhaps, but again, not entirely false.[10] For, despite its irredeemable flaws (the weak vocal takes, the sluggish tempos on some tracks and an omnipresent flute), the record has aged surprisingly well.

It opens with a pop gem entitled "True Love Leaves No Traces," in which Leonard asserts that love leaves no more trace on lovers than mist on the hill, an idea strangely confirmed by Spector's *easy listening* treatment that conveys a faint pop thrill. With a furious saxophone "Iodine" is transformed by Spector into a ballad worthy of Scott Walker, while Leonard writes off his great love affair in two definitive lines:

> You let me love you till I was a failure
> Your beauty on my bruise like iodine.

At the end of the song, the singer lists all the things in his life that reek of medicine. The beauty of women, their kisses, and Love itself: all of it was just iodine. Equally cynical is "Don't Go Home with Your Hard-On," an overproduced salsa and the first peak of the album. In it, Leonard speaks as a manufacturer of lipstick and silicone whose father was a dresser of hair and whose mother (when you called) was "always there." And as trombones and saxophones compete for prominence with a male choir (that included Allen Ginsberg and Bob Dylan), Leonard celebrates the vulgar beauty of mass culture, exposing with untypical rage how it titillates but never satisfies. The song peaks with an unconventional battle-cry, which spelled out what was probably the only rule of conduct Leonard still stuck to in real life at this stage:

Don't go home with your hard-on,
It will only drive you insane.

Another highlight is "Memories," a piece of epic pop with thundering brass and funky guitars that will feature prominently in the tour of 1979. In an outré neo-'50s crooner act — an undecided mix of Tom Jones and Johnny Rotten — Leonard recounts his first defeat in love. How the girl he was dancing with at promball refused to show herself naked. The cascading crescendos and bold choruses ring true: they express the irrepressible nature of the attraction exerted on all men by that absolute fetish object: a woman's naked body. Bombastic as hell, the chorus is unforgettable:

So, won't you let me see,
I said won't you let me see,
I said won't you let me see,
your naked body?

So, track after track, the album returns to the heart of Cohen's dilemma: how male lust transforms women into idols, and how a ladies' man at various moments in his life finds himself confronted with an overpowering female goddess: the "naked angel in my heart / the woman with her legs apart" ("Paper-Thin Hotel.") And despite Spector's production, we remain entirely in Cohenian land as the singer unfolds, from one song to the next, the detailed history of his complete failure as a ladies' man, from that first rebuke at high school to the Pietà that closes the record in the title track ("Death of a Ladies' Man"), when an unfaithful woman finds her husband hanged and well-hung at last. Between these two moments, Leonard spares us nothing of the hostilities involved: the nasty quips of former lovers on their lost beauties, the violent desire that makes them unite "quick as dogs [. . .] and free like running water"

("I Left a Woman Waiting") or the great liberation that a husband feels when he hears his wife make love with another man in the adjoining room ("Paper-Thin Hotel").

On the album's release, Leonard did reclaim its autobiographical nature and it's tempting of course to see the album as a reflection of the singer's marital misadventures.[11] He mentions pell-mell his sense of a total failure, his cultish worship of his wife's beauty, a retinue of lovers and mistresses that they hurt each other with, the sense of imprisonment that came to Cohen with marriage and his wife's contempt for his religious moods. At the centre of the record are the two temptations of the failing ladies' man. One is cynical — to embrace the surrounding masquerade. The other is spiritual — to accept that love is beyond his control. Which seems to be the very crossroads that Leonard finds himself at. But by his own admission, he was not facing that dilemma in the best of shape:

> The album was the symptom of a man falling apart. [. . .] I was still putting on a mask, trying to be "Leonard Cohen," the poet who makes records, but I had lost my mind. Even in its mildest forms, insanity makes you lose perspective. You don't go "gee, I'm losing my mind here." Instead, the room just tilts and you fall to your knees and pray you'll make it to the next moment of your life.[12]

In 1977, *Death of a Ladies' Man* was snubbed by fans and, because his mother's illness required his presence in Montreal, Leonard refused to tour. It is unknown whether Cohen ever spoke to Phil Spector after the last session in February, but when the anger abated, he sent his producer red braces with a gun holster as a token of reconciliation. As though he was adding a line to the epigraph in his 1964 poetry collection:

Walls for Genghis Khan,
Sunshine for Napoleon,
Flowers for Hitler
. . . and a Holster for Phil Spector

This was the last time Leonard crossed paths with a dictator. Sadly, it was also the last time Spector met a poet. The decades that followed were not kind to the author of "Da Doo Ron Ron" and his inability to let go of his wild persona would eventually get the better of him. He died in 2021 in Stockton Penitentiary, California, where he was serving a nineteen-year prison sentence for the second-degree murder of Mrs. Lana Clarkson, an actress he had killed by firearm in gruesome circumstances in his Alhambra home. Perhaps she wouldn't let him see her naked body.

THE IMPOSSIBLE BOOK (*DEATH OF A LADIES' MAN*, ACT II)

> *Grease up your ass*
> *Let's tear our love to pieces*
> *Your beauty won't be anything*
> *When I take off my glasses.*
>
> — LEONARD COHEN, *Death of a Lady's Man*[13]

If cats have nine lives, ladies' men have at least two. Or at least, you must kill them twice — which is what Leonard Cohen was apparently doing at the end of the decade. After killing the ladies' man on record, he kills him again with a book. There are subtle differences, however: the "Ladies' Man" he kills with Spector in 1977 was the man of several women (hence the plural form), the one he kills in the autumn of 1978 with his publisher McClelland & Stewart is the man of a single wife — hence the singular: "Lady."

A devious and difficult book, *Death of a Lady's Man* took Leonard five years of efforts and it could not be completed before the separation proceedings with Suzanne were underway. But for the poet, it was a necessary book that probed further into the mechanisms that make husband and wife mutual slaves. What is immediately striking is the volume's fragmented nature: 184 texts grouped in 97 titled sections that lay out a seemingly random succession of confessional fragments, diary entries and prose or verse poems, most of them followed by a commentary. The driving principle beneath this apparent dispersion is that the book carries out a life audit. The examined life, which clearly resembles Leonard's, is caught in a triple impasse. That of a broken marriage with an insubordinate creature ("my wife," "Lilith," "my dark companion"[14]). That of an insatiable desire which leads the author into the throes of sex addiction. And that of a writing impulse that has gone berserk. The collection is therefore a triple logbook: the chronicle of an ailing marriage, the diary of a compulsive seducer, and the journal of an artist who is sick of his art.

"FUCK THIS BOOK AND FUCK THIS MARRIAGE"

From the first pages on, the succession of cities (New York, Los Angeles, Paris, Rome, Athens, Hydra, Tel Aviv . . .) and female names (Alexandra, Patricia, Barbara, Aleece, Iris, Monica . . .) introduces the central subject: the confusion of a life that has gone off-track.[15] Around a few activities that are ceaselessly repeated — sex, writing, travelling, domestic quarrels — the book examines the progressive disintegration of a "Lady's Man." Confronted with the misery of his desire and with archetypal female figures (the shrew, the angel, the woman in heat, the model that channels absolute beauty, the goddess . . .), the seducer discovers what he ultimately is: a ridiculous and actually useless appendage of the female body. And that's the real subject of *Death of a Lady's Man*: the poverty of the masculine, the ridiculousness of the penis, that small "archaic" organ that floats on the surface of the bath and makes the poet's mistress laugh.[16]

A few emblematic moments set the tone:

Section 86: Hollywood, summer of 1975, a balcony at the Chateau Marmont Hotel. At dawn, the poet feels that "the blossoming beauty" of the young pregnant mistress who sleeps in the adjoining room fills him with terror. He tells himself that he is living his last hours and decides to start smoking again.

Section 21: Hydra, summer of 1973, the walled garden of the famous house, among the daisies. A moment of grace with "the wife" who takes pictures of the poet surrounded by flowers. He finds her very beautiful and thinks that she will soon shoot him with a .22-caliber revolver. He tells her about the day when Adam and Eve tried to commit suicide.

Section 92: place and date not specified. A man contemplates the mutilated and desecrated corpse of a woman (breasts nailed to the wall and cigar stuck in the vagina): he realizes that he must re-enchant the world by singing the beauty of the Feminine.

Section 25: the poet has an attack of asthma. A voice seeming to be that of God unfolds the twenty-five causes — each one a sin — that hinder his breathing.

Finally, section 1, which is almost programmatic: an apartment above Central Park in the summer of 1975. The poet kneels before his mistress, who has just turned into a colossal golden statue holding a Gauloise cigarette. He worships her and is given a shield, a helmet and the mission to protect the widow and the orphan.

So, *Death of a Lady's Man* (as we can see) is a tortuous and illogical book that advances under the organic thrusts of two impulses: the desire (announced in the title) to put a ladies' man to death and the desire to desecrate all sanctuaries — marriage, the female body and poetry itself. "Fuck this book and fuck this marriage" is what the poet declares: you cannot be clearer.[17]

COHEN VS. COHEN

The major formal innovation of the book (much commented at the time) is that it contains its own critique, almost each of ninety-seven sections consisting of a primary text (poem, journal entry, narrative fragment) followed by one or several commentaries. The voice of the poet is thus doubled by a second, unidentified voice that has taken on the task of tracking down the lies, the insincerities and impostures in the primary texts. That voice warns us:

> When it comes to lamentations
> I prefer Aretha Franklin
> to, let's say, Leonard Cohen.[18]

Hence, unceasingly, indignant judgments ("How dare he? I hate him! [. . .] Never let him sing again" [199]), dismissive verdicts ("This fails" [53], "There is a lie here" [39]) and put-downs ("A middle-class mind flirting with terrorism" [25]). It's Cohen's struggle against Cohen. With explanatory notes, reading instructions, alternate versions, and texts culled from the poet's archives, "supplementary" texts are constantly added to the original poems and, in the inter-mingling of voices, the book loses its capacity to affirm anything clearly. Leonard thus mobilizes eleven different notebooks (dated from 1954 to 1978), a diary (California, 1977), mysterious "secret yellow pages" (Greece, July 1973), unpublished manuscripts (*My Life in Art*, summer 1976, and *The Final Revision of My Life in Art*, 1977) as well as an oral diary on magnetic tape (1978): a whole library that transforms the book into an autobiographical labyrinth where — quite fatally — the reader soon loses the thread of a life that has reached a point of no return.[19]

Written by a man who thinks he has "betrayed his calling,"[20] the book declares a triple bankruptcy. One that is simultaneously poetic (when as Cohen designates himself as a swindler and traitor to poetry), personal (when he poses as a traitor to women ready to prepare "a voodoo milkshake of semen and menstrual blood"[21]), and spiritual (when the poet discovers he has become a vulgar idol worshipper). For the coveted women in the book are just that: idols and nothing more. Just as their sex is an idol, so much so that the poet considers replacing the statuette on the radiator of his Buick car by a chrome vulva.[22] Even his own sexual desire is an idol, worshipped as a sign of manliness. So, what has to happen happens: the ex-troubadour, failed mystic, poor lover, and fallen poet Leonard Cohen is changed before our eyes into a grotesque juggler who lives upside down, walking on his hands so as to be constantly ready to provide his wife with oral sex: the man of desire in its most grotesque form.[23] On publication, *Death of a Lady's Man* was described by a critic as a "monologue on failure." He was right.[24]

GOD ENTERS STAGE LEFT

And yet. As claustrophobic as the book may seem,[25] it nevertheless postulates that desire — even in its degraded form — can channel a more radiant force. Mystics have described the process: desire tears us apart and, doing that, it opens cracks in us through which — as Leonard would later claim — light can "get in."[26] So, in the book, the poet of desire occasionally raises his voice to pray. Prayers are timid at first: a hymn in which the speaker admits he has no time for God, having "a pig to feed," or a psalm that confesses he likes God only when He manifests as a woman.[27] But soon, they unfold more boldly, with a praise of the Divine Name, a request for a godly blessing, the offering of sexual desire as a holocaust, and (at long last) a prayer to the Virgin Mary.[28] Then miracles happen: the enunciative system of the book cracks open and the voice of God makes incursions to speak to the poet as to a lost son, sometimes with infinite sweetness. There's a beautiful page for example where God offers Leonard a modest companion (the ladybug that crawls up the wall of the room he writes in) to teach him patience and brotherhood. And to remind him that he himself, the little poet of desire, is the ladybug that God chooses not to crush.[29]

On several occasions, spiritual words arise from unexpected places, even from the heart of conjugal quarrels. In "This Marriage" for example (a verbatim account of an altercation between husband and wife), the shouting voices overlap and, amid reproaches and insults, they merge and adopt a rhythm that is the breathing of the quarrel. With parallel structures, cadences and rhythmic games, the most degrading words ("Fuck you! Fuck yourself!") start dancing until the union of the two voices (a union of husband and wife) gives birth to a third voice: the voice of an angel — the angel of the quarrel — who takes over the end of the poem to reveal what holds the disunited couple together: the ardent desire of Adam for Eve and of Eve for Adam. A domestic quarrel in a kitchen leads us to the vivid centre of the divine plan: the great song of the desiring world.

Having spotted that metaphysical song in a quarrel, the poet will be able — in the last pages of the collection — to detect it everywhere: in the mating of birds, in the cries of children who constantly express their need for love, and even in the buzz of traffic in Montreal.[30] Desire is now simply an expression of the world's aspiration to change, the pure energetic manifestation of the impermanence of things (which Buddhists see as holy and precious because it is the essence of life). The man of specific desires — who was the subject of the book — gradually dissolves into a man who is attuned to the impersonal desire of the universe. This is, finally, the glorious death of the Lady's Man (after his infamous death as a Ladies' Man): his dissolution into the world's universal longing for change.

LOVE'S LABOUR'S LOST

Death of a Lady's Man is an important text. The chronicle of a war between three adversaries — Leonard, his erotomania, and the untamed angel that God has sent in the person of Suzanne[31] — it gives us a good idea of the texture of the poet's existence between 1974 and 1978: the restless travelling, the aborted attempts to be a husband, the nights spent writing in the garden in Hydra, the shame of behaving like an idolatrous debauchee, the vague hope to start over by marrying Suzanne in Jerusalem. . . . Despite its disconcerting form, the book is therefore charged with great dramatic tension as it ceaselessly reminds us that, sometime in the mid-'70s, in bedrooms and kitchens on a Greek island and in Montreal, the war of the sexes did take place. Almost on every page, Leonard insists: he has totally and unilaterally lost that war.

As spiritual testimony, the book also shows the pain that comes with desire, the pain of wanting to be everything at once: the perfect lover, God's favourite son, the hero of the people and the high priest of your generation. The ultimate lesson is perhaps just that: unchecked greed turns everything (the female body, the religious experience, the Logos itself) into an idol. And the unique function of idols is to make God and our true lives inaccessible.[32] On the lighter side, *Death of a Lady's Man* also contains a discreet birth announcement: the second face of Leonard's career starts here as he rediscovers the spiritual nature of his mission:

> This is the nature of your work [. . .]. You are to create an angel. Not an Angel of the High, obviously not one of the Host. An earthly Angel, the Shadow of an Angel. [. . .] It will move through the world in the service of _ _ _ [. . .] and nourish everything.[33]

So paradoxically, the book constitutes a first entry into the world of things without weight. The gateway was an unbearable marriage and everything that is heavy in desire. But Leonard emerges from the book (and from his failed marriage) with a new obsession for lightness, which will inspire the working title of his next album: "The Smokey Life."

Something will soon change in the songs as well. They will take on a more explicitly spiritual colour and gradually lose their elegiac tone to become outcroppings of light, angelic songs that — eventually — will change Leonard himself into an archangel, into the cherubic pilgrim of his late career.

But in late 1978, Canadian critics dislike the book and say so. Too difficult. Too hard to read. Too honest, probably. Was a little lyricism too much to ask? Did satire have to be that grim? It seems the critics (and the few readers who actually bought the volume) just didn't *get* what the book was about, despite its programmatic title: the poet's aim is to destroy his own mythologies, to put a Lady's Man to *death*, not to write media-friendly tales of Casanovian glory. So, with nothing too accessible to put their teeth into, the critics seemed happy to call the book a failure. In the fall of 1978, Cohen toured Canada to promote the volume and, early the following year, he appeared on a literary program called *Authors* on CBC. Everything in the interview seems to indicate that the host, Patrick Watson, had barely browsed through the book. In the footage, the poet, now equipped with a cigarette holder, looks quite depressed. Once again, he had desecrated the holy body of Poetry and nobody likes that very much. Interestingly, he speaks with a voice that is noticeably lower in pitch. His next record will be about a quest for absolute lightness, but he doesn't know it yet.

RECENT SONGS AND SMOKEY LIVES (1979)

> Say a prayer for the cowboy,
> his mare has run away.

— LEONARD COHEN, "BALLAD OF THE ABSENT MARE"

In the fourteenth century, long before psychoanalysis appropriated the term, the word *sublimation* still had its Latin meaning of elevation and, for alchemists, the word designated the purifi-cation of a solid body when heat turns it into vapor. Sublimation thus involved a vaporization and a volatilization and that is the main theme of *Recent Songs*, Leonard's next record: how things disappear, volatilize, and how their disappearance brings an unbur-dening, an elevation, and an entry into the sublime.

In early March 1978, the poet loses his mother Masha (who succumbs to leukemia) and, in the same month, Suzanne leaves him again, this time for good and without warning. One morning, she has just vanished with the children. Evaporated. Vaporized. Off to France. So, a new exile begins for Leonard, who will now have to live far from the thing which gave his existence its pulse: Suzanne's beauty. That spring of 1978, he therefore finds himself with plenty of time to think about the insubstantiality of things as he smokes alone, gazing at the distant L.A. smog from the terrace of the house he had just rented for his family in the Hollywood hills.[34]

He then goes through an experience that one never gets used to: a *privatio* — an absence that is also a deprivation, things or beings are taken away from you (you are deprived of them) and, volatil-ized, they become sublime. The disappearance of a loved one is an irremediably painful phenomenon, but it always begins with an astonishment. Where there was someone, there is now no one, just silence. Hence this fundamental question, which is the question of children and poets: *Ubi sunt?* Where are these things or beings? It is as old as François Villon and his snows of yesteryear, it is even older than that: it's in the Gilgamesh epic. On Leonard's new record, it begins with a stutter:

And where,
where, where
is my gypsy wife tonight?

Accompanied by a flamenco tune, the question breaks your heart. Zen says: disappearing objects reveal our true nature, which is impermanence and emptiness. Something we hold on to disappears: we lose our balance and find out what we really are. Which is actually not much. On the new record — decidedly more spiritual in tone than the previous one — Leonard will investigate what happens when you let go and decide to inhabit the privatio and dance with it.

Recent Songs therefore develops a pedagogy of emptiness as Leonard attempts to show how the disappearance of things dictates the kind of life we should live: a life that has the properties of smoke. Smoke has no weight, no definite form and an endless capacity to rise and disappear. Hence the title of one of the songs, which will be the official name of the following tour: "The Smokey Life."

GONE LIKE THE SMOKE

As is often the case on his records, Leonard explores one phenomenon (in this case, a disappearance) from multiple perspectives. A lover loses his wife and experiences it as the coming of the apocalypse — it's the lyrical loss of "The Gypsy's Wife." A desperate cowboy loses his mare — it's the mock-epic loss of "Ballad of the Absent Mare." A Canadian exiled in *mariachi* land has lost his home country — it's the tragicomic loss of "Un Canadien Errant." And of course there is the mystical loss that opens the album with "The Guests." In that song — a short fable about how man was left alone in Creation by the Creator — life unfolds like a feast without a host, and Man roams in a palace with other guests, in search of his benefactor, unsure of "why the wine is flowing" or "where the night is going."

Each time, the starting point is the privatio that Leonard examines in detail: how it always begins with tears and laments, like those of the guests in the empty palace:

> O Love, I need you, I need you,
> I need you oh!
> I need you now.

The simpler the lament, the more beautiful the song, and if you are as lucky as Leonard Cohen, an angel will lament with you in the voice of Jennifer Warnes (the backing singer on "The Guests"). But, whatever happens, the pain will not abate, because in that state of deprivation, anything can break you, even the most soothing sounds in the world. Which is what happens to the cowboy in "Ballad of the Absent Mare": he feels so lonely that even the crickets' song breaks his heart.[35] And that is the second step of a privatio and almost a formality: the heart breaks. As always. And that's the end of the preliminaries — absence has done its work. Now the losers must do their part and learn — if they survive — to let go of the absent thing.[36]

And that's the paradox of all privatios: the thing that has disappeared (the wife, the mare, the country, the meaning of life, God himself) never leaves us entirely. Which is why the cowboy sees the horse everywhere, why the husband sees the ghost of his gypsy wife dance on a table in a "tired old café," why the missing mistress leaves behind her soulless body for her lover to keep playing at love after she is gone ("The Traitor"). Now, in order to know what to do with these absent things that haunt you, you must first discover which tribe you belong to: "those who dance" or "those who weep." The distinction is introduced in "The Guests": at the feast, some guests lament and quote the psalms like Christ on the cross ("Oh, why hast thou forsaken me?"), others — probably more fortunate — dance.

And those who dance begin to dance
Those who weep begin.

And that's what Leonard is aiming for on *Recent Songs*: to teach us how to dance with what's missing in our lives. To teach us to open our hands, let go of our grip, and notice that, in the letting go, the hungry spirit in us evaporates and everything becomes lighter: a collective sublimation. For everything (this is the ultimate lesson of the record — no doubt inspired by Buddhism) is light:

the presence of the loved ones, their absence, our sorrows and even our joys. That's what Leonard sings here to a heavenly jazz tune:

It's light enough,
light enough
to let it go.[37]

In his previous book, the poet had referred to a Zen koan that gives a very accurate image of the egoistic Self that clings to things: a monk hanging by his teeth from the branch of a tree that extends above a cliff. If the monk loosens his jaw, he will fall into the abyss. So, he is clenching desperately and suffers unbearable anguish, wondering when he will fall. To free him, all it takes is to ask him a question, for he has vowed to answer everyone. For example, the favourite question of Zennists: What is Buddha-nature? The monk opens his mouth and disappears, with the branch, the abyss, and the question.[38] On the record, Leonard organizes similar volatilizations: a palace disappears in "The Guests," the whole world evaporates in "The Smokey Life" and, after the joy of their reunion, the cowboy and mare are vaporized in "Ballad of the Absent Mare," so that *Recent Songs* closes with a disappearance:

And they're gone like the smoke,
And they're gone like this song.

So, things appear and disappear. And, in the interval, the world breathes and God breathes with it. That is the ultimate lesson of "The Window": God is re-embodied from moment to moment — in "the continuous stutter / of the Word that was made into Flesh" — but, conversely, things constantly dissolve into God: the rose becomes fire, the fire becomes sun, the sun becomes splendour, and splendour reaches "The High Holy One," a Kabbalistic journey up the Tree of Life that confirms the intuitions of Zen: the ever-changing emptiness of things is also their plenitude and can only be experienced through the act of letting go, that is, through living the "smokey life."[39]

Interestingly, if *Recent Songs* inaugurates the theme of "travelling light," it also features Leonard's farewell to Suzanne, ten years after he met her. In "Came So Far for Beauty," he reveals one last time the details of how he failed to seduce her just as he summarizes their relationship with unforgettable words in "Humbled in Love":

> You will never see a man this naked
> I will never hold a woman this close.

Well said, poet.

THE INFINITE LIGHTNESS OF THE CROONER

The music mirrors this quest for light and lightness. After the Wagnerian kitsch of *Death of a Ladies' Man*, Leonard enlists Joni Mitchell's friend Henry Lewy as producer and, together, the two men opt for a return to simple acoustic folk. They add a Middle Eastern twist to the formula, with a little help from two Armenian musicians called Raffi Hakopian and John Bilezikjian, who bewitch four tracks with an Ashkenazi violin (straight out of a painting by Chagall) and (in delicious dialogue with Cohen's Spanish guitar) a Sephardic oud.[40]

But there is a second album within the album. For *Recent Songs* is also a jazz record, with four tracks recorded in the style of jazz crooners, courtesy of a Texas fusion band called Passenger. Sometimes (as in "The Smokey Life"), it's a delicious Sinatra-like swing with brush-drums, finger-snapping and electric piano. Sometimes it's a more *bluesy* sound with prominent bass and saxophone (on "Humbled in Love" and "Our Lady of Solitude"). And at least once it's a film noir mixture of piano, double bass and trumpets ("Came So Far for Beauty"). Often overlooked, that aspect of the record announces what will soon be central in Leonard's stage act: his reinvention as a full-fledged crooner.

And what a great crooner he already is on *Recent Songs*. With precise diction and a fuller, deeper voice, he does what crooners do: he carries the burden of our suffering and makes it clear that, when he suffered in love, he suffered for us. This he does as well as Sinatra, but he adds something that Sinatra never did: he gives crooner jazz a spiritual twist and, doing that, he makes us hear once again (like John Donne four centuries before) all that is sensual about the spiritual world. Listen again, for example, to the intertwining of Leonard's voice with Jennifer Warnes's in "The Smokey Life": was mysticism ever so sexy?

So, lightness is definitely the keyword this time, an impression reinforced by the discreet humour and a writing style that emphasizes clarity. Perhaps the gist of the record is simply that discovery: every mystic is a creature of desire who feels lonely as hell. And that loneliness needs not be dissolved — as Leonard has just learnt. What must be dissolved is the thing that feels alone: Leonard Cohen himself — who is "light enough" to be let go of.

The two preceding records were about flesh, desire, and the inferno that every couple has to go through. *Recent Songs* is about smoke, light, solitude, and about how to enter — alone — into the infinite lightness of life. Nobody noticed it at the time, but Leonard had just reinvented the crooner as a spiritual figure.

LAST YEAR'S MAN

Nobody noticed because nobody bought the record. Except in Germany, *Recent Songs* had no success whatsoever. And to be fair, Cohen's music and concerns were at odds with post-punk and new wave. But perhaps the singer knew he was only a few purgatories away from becoming a cult figure and hitting it big. That would happen, surely. Very soon: in ten years' time. For the moment, when an old friend from Hydra, the CBC filmmaker Harry Rasky, suggests a new documentary, Leonard warns him that the project may prove to be a film about "a man who is probably finished."[41]

At the end of 1978, the finished man bought a modest house on rue Vallière in Montreal, just off the St-Lawrence Boulevard, with a view on the small Parc de Portugal, two doorsteps away from where he used to live with Suzanne. When Leonard moved into a few unpretentious and not-too-comfortable rooms, the neighbourhood (formerly Jewish, now Portuguese) was still essentially working-class. The place would be his Canadian home for the rest of his life and he would live there (sometimes with a passing girlfriend) unless work, Zen, sunshine, or wanderlust called him to other places, often to L.A. In July of 1979, the singer also acquired a small house in the City of Angels, which he bought with two other disciples of Sasaki Roshi. Situated on South Tremaine Avenue (a mere seven minutes' drive from the Cimarron Street Zen Center), the house was a duplex of which Leonard originally occupied the first floor (for a few years, the ground floor was the home of Leonard's Zen buddy Eric Lerner). For two and a half years, one of the rooms downstairs also served as an office for a biannual art magazine called *Zero*. Edited by Lerner and financed by Leonard, the magazine (which became slightly trendy for a very short while) sought to cross bridges between Zen and the world of contemporary art.[42] Leonard, who himself aspired to lead the perfect life of the number zero, must have loved the title, and he certainly loved the house. By the mid-'80s, he had bought out his two comrades and occupied the whole house, now his L.A. home, which he always called (as though it was a first name) "Tremaine."[43] He later even defined a tiny nook in the upstairs kitchen (where you could see the palm trees on the horizon above the neighbouring roofs) as his "favourite corner" in the whole world.[44]

Meanwhile, back in late summer of 1979. After completion of the album and a stay in Hydra, Leonard returns to Montreal, where he is joined by Harry Rasky's film crew. We may remember that seven years earlier, Tony Palmer had followed Leonard on tour with a subjective camera and extensive backstage access. *The Song of Leonard Cohen* (Rasky's film) will be more conventional, alternating concert footage with sit-down interviews. Leonard sitting at his desk with a small glass of ouzo. Leonard sitting on his bed with a guitar. Leonard sitting on the tour bus. Leonard sitting at Solomon's (his favourite Jewish diner). Leonard doing a lot of sitting. Once more, the singer looks like a spitting image of a depressed Al Pacino, with a stoop that is a little more pronounced than in 1972. He seems worried about the upcoming tour and the yet-to-be-released album, but mostly (you can tell), he is still licking his wounds and living in the shadow of Suzanne's absence.

Despite great editing, Rasky's film has two shortcomings. First, the director is less gifted than Palmer in the difficult art of filming concerts and, second, Leonard seems to remain (despite their friendship) quite an enigma for the filmmaker. Which would not be a problem if Mr. Rasky (obviously an extrovert) wasn't trying so hard to obtain great pronouncements: what is the meaning of that song? And what about women? What about his divorce? What about God? What about Judaism? So, Leonard has a problem: how to answer a question that is too explicit? How to answer a question which, in its very formulation, violates the great mystery of things? So, the poet plays the cat: he refuses to come when called, says the opposite of what the director wants to hear or answers evasively, speaking for example about the small objects that adorn his house, like a three-dollar art deco statuette of a naked woman on his desk (he has bought twenty copies). When Rasky wants declarations about Evil Deutschland and the Holocaust, Leonard — who will play more than half of his upcoming tour dates in Germany (the last country where he is still a big star) answers with a Zen concept: the necessary dissolution of dualist categories. In the privileged moment of the concert, when the song is being played, there are no Germans and no Jews, only unified hearts. Back to *zero*.

But the film provides important information nonetheless. First, we learn that Leonard wears a fedora only inside his home and that he pairs three-piece suits with checkered shirts. Which proves that practising the smokey life and the dissolution of the ego is not incompatible with sartorial daring — good to know. Then, we see that, on tour, Leonard now travels with a Zen master in his luggage. One is indeed surprised to see Joshu Sasaki Roshi (in traditional robes, of course) in the dressing rooms, listlessly observing the hustle and bustle (the groupies, the journalists, the musicians, the cameras . . .) caused by the disciple he will always call Kone. And then, there's this amazing scene in the tour bus: a Latin hymn sung in canon by a delicate Jewish poet, two Armenian tough guys, four jazzmen from Texas, and two backing singers with angelic voices: *sum pauper ego, nihil habeo, cor meum dabo* — "I am poor. I have nothing. I give my heart."[45] A Zen master sits and listens approvingly. It is almost too good to have happened.

I AM THE PASSENGER (TOUR OF 1979)

From October to mid-December of 1979, Leonard was crossing Europe again, this time with a band called Passenger,[46] plus the two Armenian soloists Bilezikjian and Hakopian (bodies of bodyguards, souls of gypsies) not to mention his friends Sharon Robinson and Jennifer Warnes as backing singers. A few bootlegs, an official live album, and a filmed concert for German television give us a good idea of where Leonard stood artistically.

What strikes is the singer's stoic sobriety: he now sings several notes lower than on the previous tour (his voice has begun its great mutation) and his stage presence is draped in a beautiful gravity.[47]

Perhaps what is lacking is a clear musical direction: the songs seem at times buried in excessive musicality and, gifted as Raffi was, too much violin is too much violin. Plus, there's the synthesizers, the flutes, the saxophone solos: too many notes, as Joseph II allegedly once said to Mozart.[48] Not that anybody noticed — in the time of post-punk and nascent new wave, a Leonard Cohen tour attracted only the converted and the event was not exactly what rock critics dreamt of writing about.

An Australian tour follows — nine concerts in March of 1980 — with the same team minus Jennifer Warnes and, six months later, the band is back on duty for a second batch of concerts: thirty-two dates in Europe and Tel Aviv. And then, nothing. No record, no tour. Nothing on Leonard's schedule. He will not be seen on stage again for five years, and four years will be necessary for a new album, which the American branch of CBS will (quite unwisely) refuse to distribute. In the meantime, Leonard will travel a lot, he will occasionally live in monasteries or in a trailer. He will study in a Yeshiva in Jerusalem and stay in his Hydra house for almost a full year. When he returns, he will sing an octave lower, and all his songs will sound like prayers or jokes. Or like both at the same time.

CHAPTER 9

THE CROONER'S PRAYERS

LEONARD IN PURGATORY
1980–1985

Leonard Cohen sitting at his kitchen table, Hydra, January 1981

It took me a long time to shake off the seductive idea that
my voice mattered, that I had significance in the cosmos.
After enough nights alone, the idea that one might have
significance in the cosmos loses its appeal.

— LEONARD COHEN, INTERVIEWED BY MARK ROWLAND (1988)[1]

As Leonard had declared to Harry Rasky in the summer of 1979, a cycle was completed: his elegiac phase. So far, he had established diagnoses, determined the laws that govern our lives, and sung the great lament of the world. He was now aiming for *light*. "Mehr Licht," as in Goethe's famous last words. And why not? After the diagnosis, a pharmacopoeia. With a new mix of wisdom, lyricism, and humour, the poet would soon transform his songs into precious talismans against angst and his concerts into even deeper rituals of reconciliation. The goal: to reunify the heart. This of course required a rebirth, a new Leonard. A comforter of souls, someone capable of making the gravity of our lives so delicious that even the angels will stop and listen. But being reborn at forty-seven is no easy task.

The end of 1980 is a critical time. After his fifth tour, the inevitable postpartum moment[2] is amplified by the dearth of future projects: no record in sight, no book in the works, no new song coming. With his wife gone and his mother dead, Leonard also finds himself without ties — nothing really holds him anywhere. He therefore resumes his nomadic life on the binary rhythm that he knows so well: arrive and leave. A few new places are added to his list of favourite stops: the Luberon hills in Southeast France, where Suzanne has retired with the children, and pretty soon Paris, the home of a talented fashion photographer with whom the poet will maintain a secret transatlantic romance for almost a decade between New York, Los Angeles, Greece, and the fourteenth arrondissement. Her name is Dominique Issermann and her sharp eye for the essence of chic and the beauty of women, which she likes to show in black and white, will help Leonard redefine his style. But for the time being, the singer has not met her. First, he has to face the silence of his career and struggle once again with a dark angel.

At this stage, depression is something that Leonard still thinks he can handle. Zen, a little alcohol, and one-night stands usually get him back on the track, although the blue devils seem to get harder to overcome.[3] No, the tricky affair right now is his career, which is subjected to the laws of fashion that also rule the oceans: the ebb and the flow. For the time being, it's the ebb: like many '60s survivors, Leonard finds himself in purgatory with his audience reduced to a contingent of converts, his record sales plummeting, and his critical aura at half-mast.[4] So the poet will spend the beginning of the decade under the radar. On the menu, stays in monk cells, a deepening of his Zen practice, the study of the Talmud, and an inter-century dialogue with dissident Hasidim, like Nachman of Bratslav. But there is definitely a gap in his career — 1981: low profile, 1982: low profile, 1983: low profile. An absence that is so discreet that his record company gradually forgets his name. By his own admission, his career "evaporates."[5]

In the meantime, with a little help from Margaret Thatcher, Ronald Reagan, and a few neoclassical economists, a new decade — the '80s — was being born for which, as a prominent funk band had just sung, "le freak, c'est chic."[6] The punks, who had come to play Attila or Genghis Khan, had wiped out the '70s and, in their wake, the new wave was rearranging the territory around a trinity that inverted the '60s in every way: money, jet-set, and new wave cool. New York and the art market were once more on fire and a century after Rimbaud everyone believed again that you had to be "absolutely modern." The place to be was Studio 54 in Manhattan and Le Palace and Les Bains-Douches in Paris. There, cocaine was the drug of choice and everyone, boys and girls, wore the same designer clothes (Japanese, of course), the same dark glasses, the same asymmetrical fringe. The trendy middle class listened to white funk and worked in the advertising business while the masses danced to ice-cold electronica in warehouse-sized clubs. Synthesizers and drum machines made everyone forget all that was all too human about human presence:

> Sweet dreams are made of these
> Who am I to disagree?

So, quite logically, if there was one thing less fashionable than an acoustic guitar, it was the singer-songwriter holding it. Bob Dylan? Never heard of him. It would take Leonard a few more years to dissipate misunderstandings and prove that he had only been a stowaway in the '60s. Once that was done, he would infiltrate the decade that first snubbed him and turn the '80s over to his advantage. But he is not there yet — he has a desert to cross.

THE HUNDRED-FOOT POLE

For here comes a delicate moment. After fifteen years in the music business and almost twenty-five years since his first book, Leonard masters his craft. He knows how to write, how to handle an audience, and, having defined a territory, he has a very precise idea of what he has to say. To a large extent, he has even said it.

Now for an artist, that is a tricky position. Knowing how to do something is only a step away from faking it. Hence that vital rule: when you arrive somewhere, leave immediately. If possible, with an empty suitcase. Leonard knows the principle, of course. Judaism and a life in hotel rooms have taught him that every check-in is followed by a check-out. But the question remains: how — after a hundred departures — to still fall in love with the moment when you pack your suitcase? And how to resist the temptation of taking anything with you every time?

In a famous koan, Zen master Ekaï Mumon asked a similar question in the thirteenth century: how to keep climbing at the top of a hundred-foot pole?[7] A koan is not a poetic object that kindly familiarizes you with the principles of Zen. It's more like a violent trap to dispel the disciple's illusions. The master gives the student a koan, as Sasaki Roshi regularly does to Leonard, and it's like "a hot iron ball that you can neither swallow nor spit out."[8] Days, sometimes years, spent with an enigma or an obsessive image. How to keep climbing at the top of a hundred-foot pole? To keep the question alive, the master rejects all your answers: the timid answer, the philosophical answers, the answers that seek to please. And one day, if you're lucky, the koan opens and you jump from the hundred-foot pole.

For Leonard, three years pass without an answer. Silence. No more songs. Back to square one: a dry patch and a nervous breakdown, like eight years before, but more severe this time. A photograph taken by Dominique Issermann in 1982 shows him in an empty room in Los Angeles in front of the typewriter: a portrait of the writer at work, his guitar at hand, propped against the wall. In the Olivetti, a sheet of paper. You can make out the first words: a song that the singer will record twenty-two years later. A farewell to the nightingale, the symbol of inspiration for Greek poets and English romantics. The lyrics basically say, "I lived only for you, but I know you are gone now. So, fare you well, my nightingale."[9] It is simple and poignant. Goodbye, inspiration; goodbye, career; goodbye, Leonard Cohen. A year earlier, in December 1980, just after celebrating Hanukkah with his children in New York, the singer had jotted down a few words in a notebook in his hotel room, words that his fans would hear half a decade later:

If it be your will that I speak no more
and my voice be still as it was before
I will speak no more
I shall abide until I am spoken for
if it be your will.[10]

In such deep humility, koans do their work. So how do you keep climbing at the top of a hundred-foot pole? Nothing simpler, Roshi. You climb the sky. Good answer, Kone. And how do you do *that*? You lean on the void, Roshi. Or on Buddha's head, which is pretty much the same thing. In other words, you start from scratch. From *zero*.

For years now, Joshu Sasaki has taught Leonard to love *zero* above all else and to make every new breath a clean slate. And for an artist, a clean slate means reconsidering the original questions: who am I? what do I have to offer? what is my vision? So, Leonard reconsiders and answers the questions. I am the servant of gravity; I have this burning heart to offer; I see men fall and all things in black.

It's the three pillars of his work and his eternal points of departure and of arrival: the life of the heart, the law of gravity, and a passion for the colour black. But the poet knows he must now push further in each direction to probe the heart more deeply until he sees the comedy behind despair; to push gravity to the point where it loses all ponderousness; to accentuate blackness until "dull, matte black" (*ater* in Latin) becomes luminous black (*niger* in Latin). He has to become an alchemist again.[11]

For that new departure, the decade will provide Leonard with three unlikely allies. First, the electronic keyboards with integrated drum machines that will help him reinvent his art. Then, a voice that gets deeper and raspier every year (by the mid-'80s, Leonard often jokes it is "fifty thousand cigarettes and two pools of whiskey deeper" than when he started singing[12]). And finally, there's the era itself, a paradoxical ally, perfectly captured by Michael Mann's TV series *Miami Vice* — cops in sports cars and designer suits, coke dealers and funky guitars, girls escaped from a catwalk or a *Playboy* spread.

Years on that regime will naturally create a strong thirst for gravity and, since prophets of depth are not exactly abundant in '80s pop (think Prince or A-ha), all that Leonard has to do is be patient. Soon, he will become the man who whispers in the ears of the 1980s.

For this, he just has to make his message a little clearer. He will work twice as hard for texts that will be twice as minimal.[13] In the meantime, the cold reign of synthesizers has begun.

OUT OF THE HIATUS

For the moment, the singer's career is at a standstill and so is his inspiration. Living separated from his children with no clear project and a lot of time on his hands, apparently stuck in a losing strategy of compulsive seduction that brings solace only one night at a time, he finds himself faced with bouts of bleakness that are increasingly harder to snap out of.

It's the same old story: *midway along the journey of our life, I woke to find myself in a dark wood.* In other words, he sinks into depression again.

In an interview a few months before, he had facetiously listed the various levels of anguish he had to face — an art he called "chillilogy" — from concern about his laundry or a pervasive sense of guilt, right up to God's anger against mankind or the fear of the apocalypse.[14] Like Dante, however, Leonard knew that as a poet, his only weapon against anguish and darkness was the Logos. Perhaps there was something he needed to say that hadn't been said yet.

Two parallel projects will help him explore his options. The first is a matter of imperious necessity: a collection of psalms called *Book of Mercy* that Leonard begins to write around 1982. The second is a commission: the libretto for his friend Lewis Furey's rock opera, a revamping of the Faustus myth that anticipates Wim Wenders's *Wings of Desire*. The plot, delivered by Furey in the winter of 1981, seems tailor-made for Cohen:

> Consumed by ambition, the singer-composer Michael yearns for fame, adoration and money. One night, three female angels offer him what he has always

desired. One of them even decides to incarnate to give him a child and bring him love. Everything works for a while, but dissatisfaction resurfaces and leads the singer to destroy the idyllic world that he had so much longed for.

Happy to deal with familiar themes without actually having to sweat over a story, Leonard approaches the project as a writing exercise — a story he just has to put into verse. For this, he chooses the intricate nine-line stanza that Edmund Spenser developed three hundred years earlier for his *Faerie Queene*, which will ensure the lyrics a swift but dignified unfolding.

Finally released as a TV film called *Night Magic* in 1985, the opera, which got a few awards in Canada,[15] is certainly worth a view despite its bland title and a few concessions to 1980s fashion. Once described by Leonard as "Walt Disney meets Bertolt Brecht,"[16] it is well-produced and Furey's Kurt Weill–esque music and acid singing still gives you the creeps. A few distinctly Cohenian scenes are like opera versions of his biography (Walt Disney meets *Don Giovanni*). For example, when three female angels (Carole Laure among them) tempt the hero on the roofs of New York, when the same hero seduces eight women in a row, or when he finally sets fire to his house after probing his heart to find only despair in it.

For the project, Leonard recycles a few texts from his 1960s note-books and delivers an early version of "Anthem." And as it were, the libretto seems to unclog the machine and help him start writing again. There's even a fair dose of humour in much of the libretto, as though the opera form allowed the poet a playfulness that helped him to temporarily put his obsessions at ironic distance, as — for instance — when the angels interrupt yet another of the hero's mournful confessions with:

O Jesus, not the heart, the heart again
So boring. Everyone's like everyone

Your famous heart is like an onion,
All layers and layers of wild distress
All gathered into rings round nothingness.[17]

But humour is no guarantee against falling into abysses. Now nearing fifty, faced with a violent custody trial with Suzanne,[18] and living six thousand miles away from his children, Leonard was finding it increasingly hard to deal with his sense of shipwreck.

His usual coping strategies of sex and drugs and twenty-year-old girlfriends no longer seemed to work and, with a lot of time on his hands (empty days in Los Angeles; long winter nights in Montreal), he was bound to examine with a critical eye the complex and dysfunctional affair that his private life had become.

Clearly, women were for him the centre of a deep-rooted and incredibly volatile psychological complex that combined an unreasonable idealization of women (they had to bring salvation, no less[19]) and a true and sincere love of their company, with a pattern of compulsive seduction and an addiction to sex that fit badly with his spiritual aspirations.

For two decades, a strategy of multiplying partners (almost invariably much younger women) and making no commitments had helped him keep anguish at bay, but now, in L.A., as he flicked yet another time through the long lists of first names and phone numbers in his notebooks (sleeping alone was okay; dining alone was hell), it was getting harder to deny the gist of his problem: a deep inability to either truly receive or truly give real love. At least more than one night at a time. After what he called "ten years of hotel rooms and broken families," he was still *the stranger* in heartbreak hotel feeling so lonely baby, so lonely he could die.[20]

At the end of the decade, he would humorously summarize his problem on his record *I'm Your Man*. In the title song, he pines for his lost true love, makes promises, and implores her to take him back, but elsewhere on the album, he offers women "big bouquet[s] of cactus" while they stick little pins in Leonard Cohen–shaped voodoo dolls.[21] The satire is delicious but it can't have been that fun in real life on either side of the relationship.

So in the early '80s (as friends and diaries attest), there were many lonely nights, many breakdowns, and many panic attacks that often left the singer unable to function for days, if not weeks, an ailment that he later recognized as

> a clinical depression that [was] the background of
> [my] entire life, a background of anguish and anxiety,
> a sense that nothing goes well, that pleasure is unavail-
> able and all your strategies collapse.[22]

With his sixth decade just around the corner, Leonard started to accept that it was not just the human condition he was struggling with but an issue of mental health. Advised by friends, he saw doctors and had his first try at antidepressant medication. He knew, however, that no amount of Wellbutrin, Zoloft, Paxil, or Prozac, all of which he would try during the coming decade, would spare him a new confrontation with the avalanche inside and the black angel who lived in it.[23] He also knew from Jacob's story that when struggling with angels, your aim is not to win, but to be wounded and blessed in the morning. The problem was that every new encounter with the black angel seemed to strengthen the creature, while Leonard felt seriously weakened by years of struggle.

It was also getting increasingly clearer that the love Leonard really needed could not be given by twenty-year-old girlfriends, especially those you don't make promises to. Hence a deeper relationship, with Dominique Issermann, an artist and professional woman in her early thirties who fascinated Leonard. Hence also an increasing tendency to turn to another source of love. And somehow the poet knew that his next book — the one he was beginning to write — would include an avalanche and a love so vast it dissolves all your sins and fears.

A DYBBUK IN THE LUBERON

The next episode takes place in the Luberon mountains in Southeast France, where Suzanne has settled with the children in a town called Roussillon. When he visits, Leonard is tolerated at the edge of his ex-wife's orchard, but he is denied access to the stone house that was bought with his money. Adam and Lorca come to see him at the edge of the vineyards, where he lives — sometimes for several weeks in a row — in a caravan beside the cherry trees. Every morning, he takes his coffee at the village bistro, follows the local discipline of coffee-cum-brandy, answers the card players' greetings, and at least once is chased up a tree by a dog — once more, an allegorical episode: forgotten rock star versus angry dog.[24]

In addition to a Talmudic dictionary and a Bible that have been with him since a 1982 trip to a Yeshiva in Jerusalem,[25] Leonard studies the writings of Rabbi Nachman of Bratslav, a late eighteenth-century Hasidic sage who saw depression as a holy condition, life as a journey through the night, and naïve songs as antidotes to despair. Leonard had heard one of the rabbi's songs in Israel during the Yom Kippur War: "Kol haolam kulo, gesher tzar me'od," which roughly translates as "The world is like a narrow bridge. Make sure you are not afraid." A good tune for a night in the trailer, for sure.

So that's Leonard's brand of voluntary poverty, circa 1982: a small plot of land, a trailer caravan, the company of stray cats, and all the time in the world to listen to the silence of his career. Of course, whether here or in Hydra, where he spends a lot of time in the early 1980s, he writes every day to try and pierce the frozen zones of the heart and investigate why blackness is brewing in him once more. To his own amazement, his notebooks soon fill with expressions of bitterness, anger, and shame at having soiled his soul. Even the trees in blossom disgust the poet, who calls out to his Creator:

> You mock us with the beauty of your world. My
> heart hates the trees, the wind moving the branches.

[. . .] I pace the corridor between my teeth and my bladder, angry, murderous, comforted by the smell of my sweat [. . .] Find me here, you whom David found in hell.[26]

Ashkenazi folklore mentions "dybbuks," souls whose sins are so deep that they find no rest after death and must haunt a living person and take up residence in him. Leonard must have thought about this legend a lot. One can easily picture the scene: Leonard, his caravan, Suzanne's cherry blossoms, and his hatred of the world — 1983: the year of the Cohen dybbuk.

The only way out, of course, is to pray.[27] But when a poet prays, he is not just praying; he writes prayers. In that particular case, Leonard writes dozens of them. He seeks the right voice, the right language — one that will help him untie the knots in his viscera and turn the mud of the heart into light. Crying out is not enough. What he needs is a poetic form that retains the urgency of the cry but also connects him to what he calls "the source of all mercy." For months, he blackens pages with texts and more texts that try to coax the heart into opening. Texts that invent rhythmic journeys out of despair. Texts that curiously resemble psalms. Some of them will become songs ("Hallelujah" starts here). Others will stay on the page. But the result is a collection of fifty poems that Leonard will publish in his fiftieth year: *Book of Mercy*, a tribute to the Jewish tradition. Taken together, the fifty poems, containing desperate pleas but also hymns and acts of thanksgiving, form a spiritual diary that chronicles the author's game of hide-and-seek with an obstinately absent God. They also show us how, in the early 1980s, in a caravan by the vineyards, an old miscreant learnt to let go of his anger, rediscovering as he did the beauty of two words that you can't pronounce with an impure heart: "hallelujah" and "hosanna."

When the book was released in April 1984, critics in Canada were suddenly experts in biblical poetry, with opinions on how authentic Cohen's psalms were. The book was often seen as Leonard Cohen's new stunt (or in the words of one reviewer, the "audacious gambit" of his "return to the Bible"). But although some journalists tried to mute their admiration, it was clear that Leonard had impressed them again with what a shrewd observer called "the prayers of an unbeliever."[28] All critics had to admit it — this was not just a heart laid bare; it was a heart laid bare nailed to a barn door.

REDEMPTION: THE USER'S MANUAL – *BOOK OF MERCY* (1984)

> *It is all around me, the darkness.*
> *You alone are my only shield.*
> *Your name is my only light.*
>
> — LEONARD COHEN, PSALM 37, *Book of Mercy*

Page after page, it's the same scenario: in a barren world devoid of light — our world — a voice rises from the centre of a life that has collapsed to call out from a position of absolute poverty. It calls out to a Creator that it barely believes in and that it loves only half-heartedly. The call is usually accompanied by a confession, always the same: that of three sins (which are also our sins) that call for a triple punishment.

The first is vanity. The speaker admires himself, swells with pride, and usurps God's place. Hence, a first sanction: he gives birth to a monkey he must live with. Second sin: concupiscence and envy. Caught in the flames of desire, Leonard wants everything at the same time and finds himself deprived of his soul. He becomes a "ghost bathing and shitting" — his second punishment. Third sin: he plays the smart guy, trying to seduce God to obtain his love while offering only half his heart. Third punishment: the withdrawal of God, which leaves man absolutely alone, a deus absconditus harsher than any coitus interruptus.[29]

The person speaking here is a man divorced from everything — from his family, from language, from himself, from God. Armed with the Hebrew tradition and an icy lucidity, the poet takes the only route that seems open: to describe his misery as precisely as possible and ask for mercy. In so doing, he reminds us of what the Swedish writer Stig Dagerman calls our "unfathomable need for consolation," and invites us to seek refuge in prayer and Jewish theology "as a child at night breaks into its parents' room."[30]

Obviously, the poet's major source of inspiration is the biblical Book of Psalms, traditionally attributed to King David. God is therefore a "shield," a "rock," or a king on a throne; the Torah is a "sweet bride"; and the divine name has thaumaturgical properties. But the principal borrowing from Hebrew poetry is the famous "primacy of rhythm in writing" that French critic Henri Meschonnic has detected in the Old Testament. With each poem, Leonard creates a rhythmical journey with unpredictable changes in tempo or intensity and an original redistribution of the speech acts that form the basis of prayer: confession, lament, supplication, thanksgiving, and praise. In each case, rhythm is what provides escape out of the spiritual crisis.

THE CHEATER'S PRAYER

Book of Mercy is both the honest diary of a journey through a dark patch and a lesson in courage. It is therefore a useful book — as well as a poignant one — that will remind whoever may have forgotten it that a "spiritual technology" called "prayer" exists and that it is available when needed. The volume also includes explicit criticism of an era — hyper-liberal modernity — which, in its complete submission to the laws of the market, neglects divine mercy to the point of forgetting that such a thing even exists.[31]

But of course, this is not exactly the Old Testament. We remain in Cohenian land, and the spiritual vision presented here is distinctively Leonard Cohen's. From page to page, we recognize the poet's daily life as well as his fetish themes — concupiscence, the praise of the fall, or the idea of salvation through heartbreak. There are also a few delightful self-portraits: Leonard as a puppet fallen among its strings that only prayer can pick up again. Leonard as a slave who must carry God's throne. Leonard as an eternal charlatan who must entertain his Creator with a pet monkey who doesn't obey very well. Leonard as a monkey himself, unable to tie his tefillin straps.[32]

The collection opens what is perhaps one of Leonard's greatest poems and certainly the perfect summary of his spiritual journey so far. It evokes how a cheater is temporarily transformed into an angel. It begins in medias res with the words: "I stopped to listen, but he didn't come."

A man, presumably engaged in prayer or meditation, is anxiously waiting for an all-powerful being to manifest: God.[33] But the Creator seems intent on winning the game of hide-and-seek He has engaged with His creature. He will remain shrouded in absence until he is called with the absolute sincerity of a broken heart. So, out of pain, the speaker recognizes the true distribution of power: he is nothing, God everything, and the latter's mercy must be begged for, even if all one has to offer in exchange for his love is buttons. So, he begs. And God gives in. Slowly, reluctantly. He approaches his throne and the angels begin to sing. Then, for a brief moment, all is grace: the divine court appears in "beams of golden symmetry" and God takes his place on the throne and the cheater poet is once again "a singer of the lower choirs born fifty years ago to raise his voice this high and no higher."[34]

It's a pivotal text — Leonard's first portrait as an angel and a demonstration that spiritual literature is not incompatible with humour or self-deprecation. Good to know.

THE ORDER OF THE UNIFIED HEART

In 1982 and 1983, Leonard used a caravan and a book of psalms to reunite his heart, a spiritual feat he illustrates on the book cover with a deliberately naïve symbol that will later become his signature: two interwoven hearts modelled on the Star of David triangles (in Hebrew the "Magen David" or Shield of David).

The image invites us to accept the centrality of love in our lives and by crossing two hearts, Cohen insists that an isolated being is nothing and that everybody's heart is the meeting place between two loves: our own love, which rises towards Heaven, and another one that pours down on us. The reference to the Star of David is an obvious sign of Leonard's allegiance to his native Judaism, but the centrality of the heart also shows the influence of a quasi-Christian theology of love. Some observers will also have noticed that few things look more like a pair of female buttocks than a heart turned upside down, so that Cohen's newly designed shield of two hearts can also be seen as affirming the interlocking of spiritual and bodily love.[35]

For the moment, the symbol is merely a book cover, but it will soon become the emblem of a semi-fictional secret society: the Order of the United Heart, which Leonard creates, partly a joke: an order without members, dogmas, or meetings. But one that materializes whenever the invisible life of the heart dissolves your ego. When we listen to a song, for example. Or when we pray or make love. Whenever two hearts are unified.

During a signature tour of Canadian bookstores in the autumn of 1984, a black-suited Leonard in cowboy boots apologized for writing something that was so incompatible with the times (it "doesn't go well with your sunglasses," he told an interviewer[36]). He nevertheless claimed that the book had soothed his heart and expressed hope that it could do that for others. He was now ready to return to his other career and, in fact, he had already done so. Work on a new album had begun in the late summer of 1983. The record was not ready yet, and it wouldn't be released before long — his American record company will actually turn it down. To understand why, we need to go back in time and study what was happening in the music industry while Leonard Cohen was talking to God and being chased by dogs in Provence.

ANGELS AND CASIO KEYBOARDS

In 1982, during Leonard's stays in Hydra and the Luberon, the German group Trio placed their little pop gem "Da Da Da (Ich lieb dich nicht, du liebst mich nicht)" in the top ten in more than thirty countries on both sides of the Atlantic. With its Brechtian irony, the song was an anti-love song disguised as a love song. Or perhaps the opposite (it's hard to tell). What we know is that it is based on an extremely basic rhythmical pattern chosen among the ten preprogrammed loops on the Casio VL-1 toy synthesizer commonly known as Casiotone. The decade would not recover.

Put on the market two years earlier for $150, the Casiotone was a remarkable object. Beside five available sound textures ("piano," "violin," "flute," and "guitar"), it included a sequencer that could memorize ninety-nine notes.[37] And the fact was that anyone could now be a one-man band. As a lover of sonic architecture, Leonard was certainly interested, and it mattered little to him if the pre-recorded rhythms sounded like something dreamed up by Pac-Man or Super Mario Boss. They were haunting, modern, and funny. Something to occupy his sleepless nights with.

We don't actually know what Leonard thought of "Da Da Da" but, in the spring of 1983, when John Lissauer, who had not heard from Leonard in eight years, joined his former collaborator in a high-end hotel room near Times Square to hear the new songs, he was surprised to see the prince of black moods play the said songs with a grin on his face, not on a cedar-scented Spanish guitar but on the MT-65 Casiotone synthesizer, the flagship of the second generation of Casio keyboards. It had only four octaves but, like the VL1, it was equipped with a built-in sequencer and pre-recorded rhythms and basslines. The arranger was appalled. The man he considered the greatest songwriter of his generation was now composing on what any professional musician would have considered a toy and, what is more, he followed the chord changes the machine suggested whenever he pressed a key. Leonard, on the other hand, was ecstatic. Literally. The Casiotone (which he insisted on using for the upcoming record[38]) had made him join the world of angels — a world that is mathematical, perfect, and freed from human emotions.

Yet Leonard had no desire to follow Kraftwerk into a Warholian dream of men-machines. He simply wished to put emotions in their rightful place. Feelings exist (as every poet knows) and they provide a fundamental doorway into the truth of our existence. But they exist only in a wider landscape where they lose their absolute relevance. What is our sadness, what are our preferences in the face of the law of gravity or the laws of irrepressible attractions that constantly decentre us? Leonard had always insisted on that idea: you do not determine the circumstances of your existence any more than you determine the laws of the world, which are impersonal and absolute. It is therefore necessary for art — should art wish to mirror life — to integrate impersonality.[39] Hence Leonard's Casio obsession. If he now wished to place his voice — a voice that was increasingly charged with gravity and grit — in the impersonal landscape of sequencers and drum machines, it was because such is our true situation: we are placed at birth in a life that unfolds impersonally, without our consent. If the rhythms produced by those machines occasionally sounded cheap (boom, tchi-tchi, boom-boom / boom, tchi-tchi, boom-boom), so much the better. That is precisely our predicament — from a certain point of view, all our lives are cheap and all our feelings kitsch.[40]

So Casio Electronics came at the right time. With his last literary opus, Leonard had gotten closer to God — a first step towards the absolute. Casio technology offered a second step: an entry into mathematical soundscapes. With Zen, it's the second time in ten years that Japanese technology came to the poet's rescue. As Trio said in their hit song: "A-ha . . ."

KAMASUTRA CHAMELEON: *VARIOUS POSITIONS* (1985)

From the video "Moments of Old Ideas" (2012)

Complain, complain, that's all you've done
ever since we lost
If it's not the crucifixion,
then it's the holocaust.

— LEONARD COHEN, "THE CAPTAIN"

Although he was unsure of his friend's musical choices, Lissauer was blown away by the quality of the material Leonard played him: "Hallelujah," "Dance Me to the End of Love," "If It Be Your Will," and others. But the singer knew what he wanted — a blend of synthesizer and country music — and the producer would give it to him.

In terms of content, Cohen's vision was precise as well. His goal with this new album was to settle the question of love once and for all. Hence the idea — explicit in the title — to make the record a Kamasutra: a compilation of the positions we can take with our partners in love: with women, with God, and with life itself.

For each partner, the singer considers the same questions: how to approach them? how to love them? how to leave them? He opens his investigations to extreme positions, seeking not one point of view but nine (the number of songs). The record is therefore successively romantic, confessional, realistic, and cynical. Pious prayers and icy hallelujahs coexist with love songs, a couple of waltzes, and a lullaby, and Leonard reminds us in passing that love necessarily defeats us but that this defeat is a doorway into grace. Also central on the album are the three activities that make Leonard a Jew: prayer, lamentations, and twisted humour.

For, as is clear from the polaroid on the cover, *Various Positions* is a self-portrait, albeit a slanted and a blurred one. "I am the sum total of those nine songs," Cohen seems to say. Nine contradictory impulses; nine invitations to pray or complain, to believe or stop believing, to consort with angels, with women, or with the devil. And if he looks gloomy on the cover, it's probably the sign that he is about to burst out laughing. What does he laugh at? The world. Which is presented here as it truly is: unstable and unpredictable. A place where we fall with our angel ("The Law"). A place where our hearts must all break ("Hallelujah"). A garden of delights where unborn children ask to be let in ("Dance Me to the End of Love"). A butcher shop and a gigantic massacre ("The Captain").

The songs are carefully assembled. "Dance Me to the End of Love" opens the record with a wedding hymn and an ode to the end of things. To the sound of a Greek mandolin, a man woos a woman so that everything may begin: embraces, dances, the unpredictable flux of life. It's a love song and a manual for an enlightened life that teaches you how to fall in love with the ephemeral nature of all things. For in love as in all things (so the song says), the first step is already a step towards the end, and the end is what we should always aim for. It turns out that *Various Positions* ends with Leonard putting on his priestly robe, first with a blessing disguised as a country-and-western tune ("Heart with No Companion"), then with a prayer, in which he offers his silence if all hearts be soothed ("If It Be Your Will").

But Leviticus is very clear: whoever wishes to take up the priestly function must purify themselves. And that's what the rest of the album accomplishes: six songs where Leonard purges himself of the dross of ordinary moods with his spiritual Kamasutra. First step: to look back and reflect. Done with "The Night Comes On," where Leonard reviews his life and all the dark nights he had to cross. Second step: to repent. Done with "Coming Back to You," an apology to all the partners he has cheated on[41] and with "The Law," a Gainsbourg-like reggae (perhaps the hidden masterpiece of the record) in which the singer finally comes clean: yes, he is the unrepentant sinner whose stubborn heart stayed deaf to the repeated calls of the Father, but he knows at least that no one escapes the karma of divine retribution, for:

> There's a Law,
> There's an Arm,
> There's a Hand.

Third and last step: to accept one's fate. Done with "Hallelujah," the incandescent climax of the album. After one last cynical look at the butcher shop called the world and a flirtation with the devil's point of view ("The Captain"), Leonard can finally claim, at the end of the record, to sing the most delicate things: a lullaby ("Hunter's Lullaby"), a blessing ("Heart with No Companion"), and a prayer ("If It Be Your Will").[42] *Various Positions* indeed.

HALLELUJAH EUREKA

In "Hallelujah," one of the album's most solemn moments, Leonard reveals the hidden formula of our lives, no less. For there is (so the song claims) an invisible structure in our existence that we didn't choose or want, but that constantly leads us back to a place where only one action is possible: to say hallelujah. The speaker has detected this structure (which, as he claims, "pleas[es] the Lord") in the musical architecture of David's psalms and he reveals it head on, almost casually, knowing how little the modern world cares about hidden spiritual truths:

> I've heard there was a secret chord
> that David played and it pleased the Lord,
> but you don't really care for music, do you?
> It goes like this: the fourth, the fifth,
> the minor fall, the major lift,
> the baffled king composing hallelujah.

If we translate the musicology into practical theology, our lives become a little clearer. Every fall — even "minor" ones — contains the seeds of a "major" lift. In other words, every fall can turn your life into a living psalm of praise. Every fall is a potential hallelujah.

To back up this theory, Leonard offers us a few glimpses of his own life. Like King David, he watches a naked woman bathe in the moonlight and marvels at the beauty of the world — *hallelujah*. Like Samson, he is defeated by a partner who cuts his hair — *hallelujah*. Like us all, he is broken by successive failures — *hallelujah*. His breathing and his partner's merge in lovemaking — *hallelujah*. He roams alone in an empty apartment — *hallelujah*. Of course, Leonard says "you" not "I," presenting his life as if it were ours, just as he uses stories from the Old Testament (Samson, David) to remind us that all lives, including his own and ours, have the intensity of biblical lives and end with the same lesson: that defeat is salvation at hand.

> There's a praise of light in every word
> it doesn't matter which you heard,
> the holy or the broken hallelujah.[43]

Outside of Cohenian circles, no one will notice the song for almost ten years. From one cover version to the next, through multiple inclusions in movies and TV series, "Hallelujah" will then penetrate the culture, proving that Leonard has indeed risen to his own challenge: to write a hallelujah for an era that has forgotten the meaning of that word. In the song, he proceeds in the least proselytizing way possible, like a man who has objectively studied the secret resonances that these four syllables have in everyone's life: hal-le-lu-jah. A cry of assent to all things.

BROKEN PRAYERS AND COUNTRY RAGS

The strength of the song also lies in the poet's aesthetic decision: to keep it simple. Purged once again by contact with the Bible, Cohen's style appears here in a nakedness and simplicity that makes it luminous. And just as light instantly invades all available space in an empty room, so Cohen's clear language instantly invades the listeners' hearts. For some songs, one hearing is enough for what Zen calls "sudden enlightenment":

> If it be your will
> That I speak no more
> And my voice be still
> as it was before,
> I will speak no more.

Carried by swift clear metrics along sequences of simple but deeply moving words, "If It Be Your Will" draws us in until we're frontally hit by the psalmist's solemn promise (which immediately becomes ours): to sing songs of praise from the heart of a broken life. The song closes with a perfect description of our predicament, and some of Leonard's boldest lyrics: we are lost children "dressed to kill" in "rags of light." Not bad, poet. You can almost hear David, Milton, and John Donne nod in assent. When asked a few years later by a music magazine what song he would have loved to have written, the poet answered, "If It Be Your Will and I wrote it." We see what he means.[44]

With a little help from Lissauer and a group from Texas called Slow Train (John Crowder on bass; Richard Crooks on drums; Ron Getman on harmonica), Leonard made the album a new tribute to his favourite musical genre: country and western. Once more, he explores its multiple poles: crooner ballads à la Ray Charles, gospel-flavoured hymns, and upbeat barn dance tunes. In that sonic landscape, his vocals are reminiscent of Johnny Cash, but — this was the bone of contention for some critics — the music was not "pure" country. Treated with a strong emphasis on the clarity of sound (sometimes almost clinically so), the guitars share the stage with synthesizers meant to evoke the presence of something absolute and impersonal.

It is routinely argued today that the arrangement of *Various Positions* has "aged" or that the album is only preparatory work for the full electronica of *I'm Your Man*. But listen to the record again and almost every track is irreproachable. The problem was the slick synthesizer on "Hallelujah" and the shoddy Casiotone sound that almost spoiled the enchanting melody of "Dance Me to the End of Love." Of course, the two tracks were the ones Leonard chose to represent the album on the airwaves. Not that many stations actually played the songs.

NO GOOD LEONARD

In his 1967 book *The Society of the Spectacle*, French situationist Guy Debord made a famous prediction about the future of capitalism: the more the market would prevail, the more it would sell only images, and the more we would become the passive spectators of our lives. As the '80s unfolded, the diagnosis seemed more correct every day. The question seemed therefore valid: what use was a record like *Various Positions* in 1984?

In the field of rock, the rules of the game had changed some time around 1982, when it became clear the decade would be that of MTV (i.e., visual content) and the absolute reign of the market, which for artists meant two things: a) aim high and think big (to be Madonna, Michael Jackson, or nothing) and b) have a gimmick and a cool haircut. Nothing reveals the '80s better than the sight of a stranded Bob Dylan in a white sleeveless leather jacket with mittens to match and trinket earrings. It was a lost cause, of course. Dylan was a mirror that reflected two centuries of American folk culture and the '80s liked only images. Think Duran Duran. Think Tears for Fears. Think A-ha. So, we imagine Leonard's concern: in a market now divided into a niche of synthetic pop (Depeche Mode, Eurythmics, and Pet Shop Boys), a niche of arrogant funk-pop (Prince and Bowie), and a niche of world music pop (Boy George or Peter Gabriel), the poet was definitely *out*. Out of style, out of date, and incurably off topic. And the low sales of the coming record would only confirm a simple fact: video killed the radio stars. In late 1984, the cheap synthesizers of "Dance Me to the End of Love" and its obscure lyrics puzzled the few listeners who gave the song a chance, starting with the new CEO of CBS-Columbia, Walter Yetnikoff.

A party animal and a former corporate lawyer, Yetnikoff was in tune with the '80s. His goal was to win the war with Warner Music. For that, he was gathering a stable of artists who sold exclusively in millions of units: Michael Jackson (his personal friend — twenty-nine million units for "Thriller"); George Michael (ten million units for "Faith"); Bruce Springsteen (eighteen million units for "Born in the USA"); Barbara Streisand (twenty million units for "Guilty"); not to mention the Rolling Stones or Paul McCartney, lured to CBS with offers they couldn't refuse. It is almost hard to believe that Yetnikoff found time for a meeting with the man he called "the poet from the North" and that he probably considered as a cumbersome heritage of the '60s.[45] Let's talk figures. Leonard's previous album, *Recent Songs*, peaked five years earlier at #54 in the

German charts, selling only a few tens of thousand units in total. Leonard who? Leonard what?

The fact remains that when no release date was looming on the horizon for *Various Positions* months after its completion, it became hard to hide to its author how little efforts were made to promote his career. Since Yetnikoff seemed too busy to take his phone calls, Leonard was forced, at the age of fifty, to repeat the stunt that had earned him a publishing contract with McClelland & Stewart twenty-five years earlier: he laid siege to Yetnikoff's office unannounced until the CEO received him. The scene took place in Midtown Manhattan, at Fifty-Second Street and Sixth Avenue, 150 metres above the ground, on the top floor of a black granite building known to New Yorkers as "Black Rock Tower" and to Leonard as "the tomb of the forgotten record." Cohen and Yetnikoff are the same age; they share Jewish roots and a love of music. The meeting is therefore cordial — Leonard's suit is praised — but the boss does not mince his words. After Leonard had played him a few songs, Walter was not convinced. Grievance number one: the time spent since the last record. Grievance number two: he doesn't like the mix of "Dance Me to the End of Love" (quoth Leonard, "You mix it, Mr. Yetnikoff"). Grievance number three: he thinks that the album is not attuned to the realities of the market. Conclusion: CBS-Columbia will not release the record in the United States and Yetnikoff has that famous line soon declared "refreshingly frank" by the poet, "Leonard, we all know you're great, but we don't know if you're any good." In other words, you may be a genius, but we're not sure you're worth a dime.[46]

Just imagine the elevator ride back to Fifty-Second Street. Leonard exits the lift, crosses the lobby, and finds himself in Midtown amid smoke, yellow cabs, horns, and distant sirens. The noisy symphony of the new world. That's probably when he gets it. He is nowhere; he no longer has any market value. It's official: his record company has just told him so. What do you do in such a moment? Do you go to the Royalton a couple of blocks away for a whisky in the famous mahogany bar of Dorothy Parker fame? Do you take a cab to the Machat & Machat offices to devise a strategy? Do you remember the destruction of the Temple and the Jewish art of exile? What Cohen does that day is he doesn't lose his sense of humour. Then he insists, because he believes in an album that contains "Hallelujah" and "If It Be Your Will." With some difficulty, Marty Machat finds an independent publisher for the American market, Passport Records. The name of the company must have made Leonard smile. In January 1985, he had his own passport ready. In a frozen Manhattan, he was rehearsing for a tour that would keep him on the road for almost six months. Wearing a beret and a charcoal suit, he looked like a modern Jeremiah. But the prophet was back with a vengeance and none of the concerts would sound like a lamentation. For the moment, however, Leonard is looking for a tour manager. The one he had been working with for the last thirteen years is not so sure about the project. He has promised to call back.[47]

AM I A HOTEL?

Back a few years to 1982. It is already clear to Leonard that he would not leave his mark on the '80s without sharpening his image. He also knows that videos are now mandatory. At the cocktail party that year for a television pay-channel launching, C-Channel, he mentions an idea to the future program director: a short film that would retrace the memories of a hotel with a few of his songs. A hotel? But Leonard, what a great idea! An appointment is taken, the financing raised, and before the poet can finish his champagne and his cheese cracker, he finds himself at a table with a writer from the channel, and a mission: to turn five of his songs into a film script and call the result "I Am a Hotel."[48] The following March and April, between two Zen sessions and three stays in France, Leonard was made to shoot what was in fact a twenty-seven-minute video. He was coaxed onto the Toronto set with his guilty pleasure: a luxury hotel, actually one of his favourites: the King Edward, 298 rooms and a decrepit Empire ballroom on the seventh floor with a good view of the city. During the six days he spent on location, the producers apparently tried to hide that C-Channel, still supposedly the producer, has gone bankrupt.

The result is so kitsch that Leonard will consider pulling out several times, but new producers, including his friends Moses Znaimer and Barrie Wexler, were brought in and, besides, he had better things to do — he was writing "Hallelujah." Hence the release of *I Am a Hotel* in 1983, a product that shows a watered-down version of Leonard's universe, somewhere between Chekhov, MTV, and early-'80s soft porn. The pitch? A chambermaid and a bellboy undress while dancing on the service stairs of a hotel as a doo-wop orchestra plays just for them in the ballroom (a nod to Alan Parker's *Fame*, which was still in everybody's mind). Haunted by the memory of his inconstant gypsy wife, the hotel manager meets her ghost in the lobby while an elderly couple reminisces about the youth they spent here. Leonard plays the coryphaeus: a poet in a black suit who roams the corridors and the grand staircase, perceiving in the guests' comings and goings the poetic vacuity of a life in which he is only passing through. He chain-smokes cigarettes and receives a certain Suzanne in his room, whose true nature (a woman of flesh? an ethereal being?) is unclear.

That the film got a prize at the Montreux Television Festival says more about the times than about the movie, and its complete submission to '80s aesthetics saw to it that it was outmoded before anyone had actually seen it. In short, a wasted effort; just an exploitation of the poet's back catalogue and a reminder that Leonard Cohen was still alive and that he still liked hotel rooms. Nothing new, therefore, except perhaps a sharper silhouette: a chalk-striped black suit, slicked-back hair, and trendy sunglasses. Leonard had a new French girlfriend and it showed. Watch this space.

TAILORED SUITS AND DEADPAN JOKES

Back to 1985. It is a bad habit since childhood: Leonard learns his lessons really fast. Which means he now knows what not to do with videos. For his new single, "Dance Me to the End of Love," he has placed himself in the hands of an artist who shares his sense of humour and knows how to look at things: Dominique Issermann. With just the right balance of poetry and irony, her video is a black-and-white portrait of Leonard as a depressed ghost. The first sequence sets the tone. A young woman comes to pay her last respects to her dead lover Leonard Cohen. There he lies, lifeless on a hospital bed. She covers his face with a sheet and moves on. Direction: the rest of her life. Except that Leonard now follows her as a ghost, guiding her from beyond the grave to the "end" of their particular "love": he surreptitiously takes off her wedding ring, follows her into a maternity hospital (where they watch premature babies in incubators), and looks on as she poses naked for dozens of nuns in the grand amphitheatre of the Paris Beaux-Art School. Looking pensive on the stairs, he seems to consider the deep meaning of the phrase "end of love." Or maybe he ponders why the CEOs of big record companies never get it right. For the video can certainly be read as a subtle warning to the thirty-eighth floor of the Black Rock Building. Leonard Cohen, dead singer, is not done haunting you. Either way, it's stylish, sinister in a cute sort of way, and — depending on your sense of humour — circuitously funny.

Beside the video, Leonard has another weapon to promote the tour: himself. During his media exile, he has become increasingly telegenic. With a deeper voice, a few Armani suits,[49] and an omnipresent cigarette, he now cuts a sharp and self-assured figure, half jaded rock star, half defrocked monk able to mention the Flood, the glory of the female body, and the hallelujahs that save your soul in the same breath. He is also — as wrinkles attest — the first rock artist to have reached the age of fifty alive. Hence the privilege of being interviewed as a veteran and survivor. The perfect customer for questions about free love, drugs and bohemia. You can tell from his answers that the Zen retreats, the women who have come and gone, the decades spent writing have left their mark. He is now able to approach any subject with the right mix of humour and depth. He usually answers the questions about the '60s with the tone of a former CIA director who is not at liberty to say but hints that the secret wars that you didn't fight, young man, were even more exciting than you imagine. He always has a few wisecracks in the pockets of his double-breasted suits. His answer to a Swiss journalist who asked about his wishes for mankind? "May everyone get through the winter without a cold." The profession on his passport? "Sinner." To a female journalist asking about women: "You are a much better authority on the subject." Why he has more success in Europe? "They don't understand the lyrics." Not bad. In January 1985, Leonard will bring that persona to the TV sets of Europe. Not everybody will get his jokes.[50]

THE BLACK SWAN (1985 TOUR)

Leonard Cohen, Kalvøya Festival, June 1985

Owing to the singer's supposedly lost prestige, the 1985 tour was a low-profile affair: a single backup singer; young jazz pianist Anjani Thomas, who inaugurates a long collaboration with Leonard; and a small band: three Slow Train members and, as veteran of the 1979 tour, Mitch Watkins on guitar. Basically a drummer, a guitarist, a bassist, and basta. Add two engineers, a roadie, and a bus driver, and you're ready to go — a secret tour of Europe in February and March 1985. This time, it's fifteen countries and forty-three concerts in fifty-five days, with an eventful stop behind the Iron Curtain in Jaruzelski's Poland. April brings new dates in Philadelphia, Boston, and New York, after which the tour reaches Canada. At the end of the month, the band flies to Australia before closing that second wing with three dates in San Francisco and Los Angeles (where the record is not yet available): nineteen concerts in forty days and quite a few plane rides. After ten days of rest, the team hits European summer festivals with a brief incursion to Israel — sixteen concerts in three weeks in June and July,[51] totalling eighty concerts in six months. Stakhanovism.

But to his great surprise, Leonard plays to full houses and relatively young audiences everywhere (including a packed Carnegie Hall in New York). Plus, the reviews tend to be excellent. Good news for the artist, but this is only fair. The audio and video recordings show that concerts were both delicate and energetic. A reduced band enables the singer to reconnect with the kernel of the songs — their inexhaustible gravity — and Getman's slide guitar and harmonica envelop the concerts in delicious mystery. An expurgated "Dance Me to the End of Love" (with no Casiotone but a lot of guitar) takes on the lightness it didn't have on the record, while "Lover, Lover, Lover" finds what is perhaps its ultimate version, not to mention a sepulchral "Avalanche" played solo on a black Chet Atkins Gibson. In Copenhagen, Leonard fell in love with a particularly warm audience to whom he explained that in a former life he was a "black swan on the Baltic Sea," now returning in human form. The image is quite accurate. He sings on this tour with the majesty of a black swan, seeming perfectly at ease on stage. Perhaps the systematic practice of his favourite sacrament (French Bordeaux wine) or the frequent presence of Dominique Issermann in the wings is not unconnected to the singer's relaxed stance, but part of it is also due to the evolution of his voice — the gravity of the timbre now opens new sonic territories where murmured talk-overs alternate with clever jazz scansion. Little Gainsbourgian exercises.[52]

The only tricky moment was Poland. If we go by the leaked videos and bootlegs, Leonard was not comfortable. First, he was in the land of the Holocaust and had to play in Wrocław in a hall where Hitler had given a speech. Then, he was entering a country that was almost in a state of insurrection and where he had become, unbeknownst to him, an underground hero of dissidence. In Warsaw, his local promoter, a Solidarność supporter, had asked him to invite Lech Wałęsa (then under house arrest) to the stage.[53] In front of a weird audience, tuxedoed party officials on the floor and dissidents on the balcony, Leonard was visibly unsure of where to stand. Solidarność was counting on him but despite a deep distrust of communism inherited from his mother, he had no desire to interfere with local politics. So, with a little help from the Bordeaux wine, he starts speaking to the audience. Quite profusely in fact. Several times, he is tempted to take the plunge: with jokes about five-year plans, with greetings to the authorities that are so solemn that you can't tell whether he is being ironic or not. A standing ovation after "The Partisan" almost brings down the regime, but the singer also speaks about Auschwitz and the songs' ability to dissolve distinctions. About the necessity of having two legs: a right one and a left one. Listening to the tapes decades later, we feel that Leonard was lost that night, in the midst of a superb concert. Another Polish problem was that the band was paid in zlotys, a currency that could not be converted or taken out of the country. It was probably just enough to cover the bar bill anyway.

TWO SAMURAI IN PARIS

Unsurprisingly, the wandering resumes as soon as the tour ends. As always. Between one city and the next, Leonard meets an old friend and that's lucky — he has a confession to make. The scene takes place in Paris, on Monday, July 2, 1984, in a café of the fourteenth arrondissement, rue d'Alésia. We can imagine the zinc countertop, the hustle and bustle of the café, and the ballet of the Parisian street outside: 4L Renault vans, 103-type mopeds, and a ceaseless flow of passersby. In a corner, two men have met for coffee. They have a lot to say, and each has drawn his cigarette pack: Marlboro on one side; Peter Jackson on the other. They know the moment is precious. You don't meet another Samurai every day. Because they speak English, some of the patrons raise their eyes from time to time, but the two strangers don't look like tourists. They look like an elegant clergyman and a middle-aged gypsy. They look like Leonard Cohen and Bob Dylan.

The previous night, Leonard had joined the forty thousand faithful who attended Dylan's outdoor concert at Parc des Sceaux. On stage, the singer had mentioned "he whose face no one can see without dying" and closed the show, where he was joined by Van Morrison, Joan Baez, and Hughes Aufray, by knocking on heaven's door. The following afternoon, something unprecedented happens. Dylan is alone with the colleague that he thinks most highly of, the one he is reported to have said that yes, if he could be someone else, he wouldn't mind being Leonard Cohen for fifteen minutes.[54] Picasso and Matisse are having coffee. Kasparov and Bobby Fisher meet without their entourage.

So, while their guardian angels guard the door, the two men talk. Maybe they mention old fallen friends, but mostly they talk shop. Singing. Writing. Guitar technique. We can imagine the dialogue. "How do you write?" "What about you?" "And *that* song?" "And *that* one?" For Leonard, this is the opportunity to confess. Here is a man who will no doubt understand. Maybe he will even confirm.

But Dylan is quicker and asks the question first: "How long did it take to write 'Hallelujah'?" Leonard is walking on a tightrope. He must not make a fool of himself. Not in front of Bob Dylan. So he lies and says, "Almost two years." It actually took him five. The American is shocked. "Two years!" But it's Cohen's turn. "What about you, 'I and I,' how long?" Predictable as it was, the answer almost made the Canadian fall off his chair: "Fifteen minutes."

The constant cheeriness with which Leonard told and retold that anecdote in the following years says a lot about the depth of the confession the story enabled him to make.[55] The moment was indeed decisive. That day, in Paris, rue d'Alésia, in front of Bob Dylan, he must have understood. That there was no way out. That he had no choice. Some people are born under the protection of Mercury and dance beneath the diamond sky with one hand waving free; others are the sons of Saturn and to them, everything is slow, heavy, and graceless. As if Dylan's answer had brought home the true meaning of the phrase Leonard had invented ten years before to describe himself: "the energy of slaves."

So, having confessed to the pope, he will now say it loud to whoever asks (or doesn't ask): he's slow and not so proud. No, he doesn't write songs in fifteen minutes in the back of taxicabs. Yes, he is "a scavenger who scrapes the bottom of the barrel," a deep-pit miner who must sweat over every word and "hits his head against the hotel carpet in search of rhyme for orange." Yes, he is a man who climbs Mount Baldy with a grand piano made out of concrete strapped on his back because he fell in love with the unbearable lightness of Mozart.[56] Soon, he will even get specific. "Anthem" was not ready after nine years of work; "Secret Life," almost complete in 1988, was polished until 2001; "Democracy" originally had fifty completed verses as opposed to five in the released recording.[57]

So back in Los Angeles, vain hopes are cast aside. Leonard sits down at his kitchen table with a mug of coffee. He starts work on his new songs and knows that it's going to take him years. One is about a songwriter that angels have locked in a tower — a confession. Another will remind the world that in the days of HIV, love is still a disease for which there is no cure. A third investigates the allure and seduction of fascist postures. As the poet blackens pages, a record slowly takes shape. In Leonard's head are synthetic sounds and a relentless desire to take over the great capitals of the world. He had always seen himself as a double agent — a poet infiltrated in rock music and a warrior disguised as a poet. He will now act the part and launch an assault on the 1980s. His strategy is a little stingy with details, but it goes straight to the point: first to take Manhattan, then to take Berlin.

CHAPTER 10

BANANA CASANOVA

THE FALL OF MANHATTAN
1986–1988

From the video for "First We Take Manhattan" (1988)

A PHILOSOPHER AT THE HEAD OF THE ARMY

Leonard listened to the '80s and got their essential lesson: boys don't cry and girls just wanna have fun. Recorded on the sly in Montreal, Paris, and Los Angeles throughout 1987, the upcoming record is a secret weapon designed to make Cohen a rock star again. The title is a challenge to the entertainment industry (*I'm Your Man*) and everything about the album — the cover, the tone, the music, incorporating cold wave, electro-pop, and funk — is sharp and incisive. As for Leonard's personal assets (the voice, the inexhaustible gravitas, the precise knowledge of the human heart), he turns them into a formidable strike force.

In *The Art of War*, Sun Tzu defines the best moment to attack — when the enemy least expects it, preferably just before dawn. In 1985, when Leonard began writing the songs, it was closer to midnight in his career. But there were encouraging signs: a few mavericks named Nick Cave, Ian McCulloch, Suzanne Vega, and Sisters of Mercy kept referring to his work. An even surer sign of turning tides was in 1986 when the singer, like Miles Davis or Frank Zappa, was offered a cameo in Michael Mann's TV series *Miami Vice*. Against all odds, Leonard said yes and found himself playing François Zolan, the fictional French head of Interpol in an episode called "French Twist." From his Parisian office with rococo armchairs and contemporary furniture, Zolan orders murders over the phone and his key line, "Il doit être assassiné," lets us see the James Bond villain he could have been had he known how to act.[1]

The following year, his friend Jennifer Warnes, now a top-selling pop star in her own right,[2] teams up with the independent label Olympia Records for an album of Cohen covers that everybody has warned her against. Immensely touched, Leonard gets involved. He travels to Los Angeles, supervises recordings, works on visuals, offers three unpublished lyrics, helps shoot a video, and records a duet. He knows what should be avoided at all costs (a nostalgic celebration) and insists that *Famous Blue Raincoat*, the chosen title for the record, should be absolutely contemporary in sound and aesthetics. The songs are therefore morphed into '80s blues-pop and the result, complete with showy guitar solos and saxophone cries, is full of stamina, albeit a little slick. Perfect at any rate for the decade of Phil Collins and Tina Turner. Against all odds, the record is a hit on both sides of the Atlantic, ensuring Warnes a prolonged presence in the charts and Leonard the praise of *USA Today* and *People*, not to mention the cover of the professional magazine

Music Connection. MTV pushes the album and constantly plays the peppy video Paula Walker has concocted for Warnes's first single, a new song yet unrecorded by Leonard with a programmatic title: "First We Take Manhattan."

In the video, Stevie Ray Vaughan plays brilliant blues-rock solos on the Brooklyn Bridge while a team of young dancers tears through the streets of Midtown in designer clothes. Windows explode on their way and we suddenly understand: they are taking Manhattan. In alternating editing, Jennifer Warnes in a black coat and sunglasses acts as coryphaeus to this pop tragedy: she sings the song in an empty warehouse, clenching her fists. Behind her, the stormy rehearsals for a fashion show. Filmed in crane shots, Leonard appears several times for a few Hitchcockian seconds. Dressed in black, he stands on the high balcony of an unfinished building and looks at the New York skyline, while a hot Italian woman dances around him in full *Flashdance* mode. The crane shots make us dizzy, but things are clear: ecce homo. Here is the brain that planned the whole operation. The video closes with a vision of the maestro in an elevator; the grid finally opens but we don't know where. François Zolan is coming to claim his due. An army of models have paved the way and taken Manhattan for him. Berlin must follow. Where are you, Mister Bond?

It's pure 1980s kitsch, of course — a story told in fragmented images, a singer who acts as narrator, and all the visual clichés the director could think of. But at the end of 1987, one and a half million copies of *Famous Blue Raincoat* have been sold and the entire MTV generation has seen Leonard in black shades in a cool video, which must have helped restore the man's credibility in the Black Rock Tower, where his name was no longer a joke. His next album would be released with maximum publicity. Just to be on the safe side, the singer has personally sent each CBS executive in charge of promoting an envelope with three one-dollar bills. The accompanying letter specified the artist name, record title, and release date: Leonard Cohen, *I'm Your Man*, February 1988.

LEONARD'S BLITZKRIEG

A Talmudic legend claims that it took God twenty-seven tries to create the world we live in now. Twenty-six attempts failed, which is an encouragement to all creators: nothing great was ever done on first try.[3] Leonard (who asserts in "Tower of Song" that twenty-seven angels have tied him to his worktable) probably found comfort in that legend when he recorded the album, for it was once again a painful process. The singer worked with many arrangers (among them Jeff Fisher and Roscoe Beck) in six different studios in Montreal, Paris, and Los Angeles, often producing the sessions himself. It took him more than a year.

Once more, there was a nervous breakdown involved and a familiar situation: the singer unable to sing in front of the microphone when he realizes the lyrics are not true enough, which meant postponing the release date, withdrawing for several months to Roshi's monastery in Jemez Springs, and starting some songs over. From scratch.[4]

In January 1988, the secret weapon is finally ready and Leonard's media blitzkrieg can be unleashed. It will unfold in three successive salvos. The objective: to impress upon everyone's mind that Leonard Cohen is back and that he is the most original survivor of the '60s. The first salvo comes in January. The singer storms the television studios of no less than nine European countries to present his chilling new single "First We Take Manhattan" with a surprising but stylish playback act. Behind a desk, the poet impassively recites his plan to take the great capitals of the world, speaking into an art-deco microphone, as though he was the news anchor of a nondescript fascist country. Backing vocalists dolled up as aggressive call girls (red nails, red lips, and hairdo in major mode) dance in front of him and repeat his words with a sexual charge inversely proportional to the singer's restraint. When he explains that he is "guided by the beauty of [his] weapons," we take his word for it.[5]

The second salvo comes in mid-February. While the singer conducts auditions and rehearsals in Los Angeles for his forthcoming tour, CBS releases the album and the accompanying single, paired with an impressive video by Dominique Issermann. It features the poet in a black coat on the beach of Trouville (Normandy), lip-syncing his Napoleonic ambitions in front of the ocean while an army of women and young ephebes joins him, each with a suitcase in hand. A philosopher at the head of the army.

At the beginning of April, the album is #1 in Norway and Spain. Time for the third salvo: backed by a solid promotion campaign, Leonard kicks off his most important tour to date in Mainz, Germany, the first of fifty-six concerts that will take him from Iceland to Greece. With twenty-nine dates in North America the following summer and autumn, this means eighty-five stays in eighty-five high-class hotels — enough to keep the singer busy until late November. Everywhere, there are radio and television interviews, press conferences, profiles in magazines, album reviews, and, of course, a massive video broadcast. The BBC shows a new ninety-minute documentary about the singer and there are TV specials in Finland, Iceland, Spain, and Italy, often with concerts broadcast live. In France, Leonard is in every magazine you pick up and once on two competing TV channels the same night. In Iceland, his visit culminates in a reception by the president of the republic. Leonard Cohen is a star again.

THE SPY WHO CAME FROM THE GRAVE

Everywhere, the double-breasted suits, the irony, and the depth in the voice work miracles and no one escapes the singer's charm. It's as if the society of the spectacle belatedly recognized Leonard Cohen for who he is: a professional of depth. Now routinely asked the questions about the meaning of existence that he has been waiting for since 1967, he is happy to answer, often doing so with a single word. For example, the *flood*. Everywhere he goes,

Leonard claims that the flood has already taken place and that our lives are unfolding in what is, in fact, the apocalypse. Another word he uses a lot is *emptiness* — the supposed emptiness of an era where consumption and entertainment have organized our collective amnesia and eliminated death and unhappy consciousness. Another fetish word is *broken*: the state of our hearts and of our societies that the singer claims we must accept and cherish. He also speaks about fire, about prayers, about the heart that burns like shish kebab in our breasts, and about the devil who laughs when we make plans. Not bad for words exchanged with journalists in nightclubs or TV studios or in the bed of a Swedish television sexologist. Not bad for the head of Interpol.[6]

Of course, what makes those answers work is the voice, now an octave and a half deeper. A perfect alchemist, Leonard has spent fifteen years impregnating it with very exact doses of smoke, alcohol, and prayers. Now stronger, warmer, and infinitely more relaxed, the voice oscillates with the singer's moods between demonstrations of stoicism (the gravity according to Lee Marvin), displays of manly sexiness (the gravity according to Barry White), or prophetic authority (the gravity according to Ezekiel).

By the late '80s, the voice has also taken on almost seismic properties — Leonard speaks, and the room shakes. And everything he says (bad jokes and anecdotes about his childhood dog included) becomes deep, grave, and vibrant.[7] He speaks, and we are convinced (deep voices are more persuasive), but we also realize that nothing compels us to stay on the surface of our lives. Like him, we can make the deepest things vibrate in us and speak with our lowest voice. It happens in almost every interview: Leonard uses the words "monastery," "burning heart," or "naked body" in the same sentence and the TV babble is suddenly suspended — the delicious gravity of our existence is restored for a second or two. Hallelujah.[8]

But of course, that lower register is infinitely modulable, and prophetic authority cohabits in Cohen's gravity with seduction and infinite irony. Hence the poet's acrobatics as he jumps from one inflection to the next — from the gravity of the prophet to that of the seducer and immediately to that of the joker who lets you know that being deep does not mean being serious. So when he explains to the TV sexologist with just the right amount of croakiness that he has never seduced a single woman, or when he reminds an Icelandic journalist that in Judaism, sin can erase you from the book of life, it's all part of Cohen's great dramaturgy of gravity. Everything in him says, I am an absolute expert of the heart (my voice attests to that), but everything in him adds, I dissolve my own seriousness at will and make the most serious matters the lightest (and vice versa). He is at the top of his game.

So in 1988, in TV studios around Europe, Leonard Cohen reinvents himself as a double agent of gravity, both a poet-spy who subverts television rituals from within and subjects them to his poetic project (to inform every man about the state of his heart — broken — and the state of the culture — the Flood) and a star who uses the hegemonic instruments of rock culture (the video clip, synthesizers, and the rock-star interviews) to remind the world that the Logos has a power of its own. Evidently, the poet was back. His new song — a chilling one that seemed as grave as him — would take everyone by surprise.

TERRORIST CHIC

With its drum machines and synthetic bass lines, "First We Take Manhattan" opens with a geometry of intersections and perfect sounds. It's called "automatic polyrhythm": five, six, and seven layers of elastic rhythms and counter-rhythms arranged by Montreal-based musician Jeffrey Fisher. Combined with the chilling rhetoric in the lyrics and its apparent apology of war, this sonic envelope, reminiscent of the then extremely popular Pet Shop Boys, is almost a terrorist act in itself. As though Cohen was disowning his acoustic past and his status as poet of the heart. As if he was erasing "Suzanne" for the song's twenty-first birthday.

The speaker is the leader of an undefined and perhaps imaginary armed group returning from exile and the lyrics contain his political and spiritual manifesto. After "twenty years of boredom" for trying to "change the system from within," he launches his revenge with a very explicit plan of action:

> First, we take Manhattan,
> Then we take Berlin.

Everyone will have noted the economy here. In less than fifty words, Cohen has created a character, a revenge tragedy scenario, and a paranoid universe where the destinies of the great capitals are subjected to the moods of one man. Guided by "a signal in the Heavens" and the "beauty of [his] weapons," the speaker is convinced that nothing can stop him, just as nothing can stop the sequencers and drum machines which, once programmed, mechanically add rhythm to rhythm and sound to sound.

To a great extent, the strength of the song lies in what the lyrics refuse to say. Who is that man? What exactly is this armed group he claims to control? What structure are they fighting? And what does it mean to condemn someone to "twenty years of boredom"? Is it exile or something more sinister? Cohen cleverly places his clear scenario in a universe that is so elliptical it becomes almost abstract; as a result, his song intrigues durably. What is it about? Pure science fiction? Red Brigades vs. Big Business? Dissidents vs. totalitarian state? Poets vs. mass culture? A modern Moses avenging the Jews? Whatever the situation the listener chooses, the song points to the seduction of fascist positions and puts us in touch with the inner fascist who sleeps in every heart and dreams there of radical speeches and final solutions.[9]

Of course, "First We Take Manhattan" is also an ironic self-portrait through which Leonard dramatizes his professional ambitions (the conquest of new markets) and his fantasized revenge against the music business. From this perspective, the allegory is almost transparent. Condemned to twenty years of boredom (the time passed since the singer's first record), a poet has infiltrated the entertainment industry and turns it against itself. As he proceeds, he shrugs off the by-products of '80s culture ("fashion business" and "drugs that keep you thin") and slips in a personal message to the CEO of Columbia:

> You loved me as a loser but now you're worried that
> I just might win. You know the way to stop me, but
> you don't have the discipline.

It has been said since that with his terrorist dream of attacking Manhattan, Leonard was foreseeing in 1988 the ways in which the postmodern "age of emptiness" invited radical responses like 9/11.[10] Maybe he was just being attentive to the radical responses that decade invited in his own heart. Once a prophet, always a prophet.

MOSES REVISITED

From the video for "First We Take Manhattan" (1988)

With shades of Magritte and Hitchcock, Dominique Issermann's highly cinematic video for the song — a key element in Leonard's media plan — presents in black and white a poetic narrative of great formal beauty.

Once more, a simple idea. Winter on a beach in Normandy, a stormy sea, and happy seagulls. A man dressed in a black coat arrives alone. He is captured in a very wide shot that endlessly unfolds the massive horizontality of the ocean. The man is Leonard Cohen, a terrorist in exile. Facing the waves, he takes out a crumpled piece of paper from his pocket with two words on it (his to-do list): "Manhattan" on one side, "Berlin" on the other.

Still in front of the ocean, he sits down on his suitcase and waits. He is soon joined by a black-coated young woman who sits next to him. Similarly dressed young men and women arrive in trains. By mid-song, a dozen faithful have joined the prophet, suitcase in hand, leaving behind them in the sand the broken lines of their footprints. Then the camera spins around Leonard as he calls out the rulers of the modern world:

> I don't like your fashion business, mister. I don't like these drugs that keep you thin. I don't like what happened to my sister. First, we take Manhattan, then we take Berlin.

But in the end, the ocean never opens, the great departure doesn't take place, and the faithful depart from the beach, leaving the prophet alone with the seagulls and a collection of abandoned suitcases. End of the clip.

Undeniably one of the most stylish videos of the period, "First We Take Manhattan" keeps us on the edge of our seats, in part thanks to the superb alternation of close-ups (of seagulls, hands, necks, suitcases, Leonard's face), mid-frame portraits of the singer (who mimes the lyrics impassibly), and very wide shots of small silhouettes on a desolate landscape. Issermann shows the prophet's army less as an armed group than as a metaphysical army of men and women in transit. Combined with the heavy winter coats, the vintage suitcases, the use of black and white, the train platforms, her images evoke the Holocaust. Hence a new interpretation of the song — that of the Jewish prophet's revenge against Berlin: first, he takes Manhattan and then he gets even.[11] There are also traces of Cohenian humour in the video. The prophet is a loser, not a glorious Moses who opens the ocean, but a pilgrim in front of whom the sea remains obstinately closed and hostile. The last shot shows Leonard alone with abandoned suitcases, his feet in the water. The tide, to be sure, is rising.

THE SIGNIFYING BANANA

Presumably, it's the same character on the cover of *I'm Your Man*. In a black-and-white picture with perfect lines of flight, the singer poses in three-quarter profile in that most emblematic locus of urban chic: a warehouse.[12] The dark glasses signal his star status and the suit evokes the classic combination of male dandyism since George Bryan Brummel: a dominant colour of ascetic elegance (the double-breasted pinstriped suit and its strong 1930s connotations) matched with a touch of indomitability and contemporary cool (the white T-shirt and black sunglasses).[13] Only one detail disrupts the heroic posture: Leonard is caught red-handed in a non-iconic activity — he is eating. And what is more, he is eating that curved and slightly ridiculous fruit, the favourite of monkeys and children: a banana. And the picture comes alive. That coolest of characters — the male dandy — is dismissed. Exit Casanova. Enter instead a much more stimulating mock-heroic figure: Banana Casanova. One more example of Leonard's favourite sport: self-deprecation.

When asked on Belgian television why he was eating a banana on his record cover, the singer greeted the question as "highly metaphysical" and he was only half-joking. When he saw the picture, there was an instant and deep recognition — he saw who he really was. "I said: 'Yes, that's me. I am a man eating a banana.'"[14] In Zen, the experience of suddenly seeing into your own nature has a name. It is called kensho, and by definition, it is an experience of emptiness. The great illusion of the ego is suddenly seen through and you realize that your ego is but a fiction that is actually the source of most of your suffering. Later he would explain to the *Toronto Star* how that fortuitous banana revealed to him the vanity of all poses:

> Here's this guy looking cool, in shades and a dark suit. He seems to have a grip on things and a very precise idea of who he is. The only thing wrong is he holds a half-eaten banana. And it suddenly occurred to me that this was everybody's dilemma. At the time we think we're coolest, what everybody else sees is a guy with his mouth full of banana.[15]

So a signifying banana disrupts the production of heroic signs. Obviously a phallic symbol, the banana is also a feminine fruit whose consumption (as opposed to that of the apple, for example) requires a certain delicacy and patience. A banana must be undressed before you consume it. Just like a woman for a ladies' man. Which means the picture shows Casanova at work: an expert con artist eating the forbidden fruit, which in this case happens to look like his phallus. As the point of entry into the album, Cohen thus presents a ritual suicide of sorts, albeit a comical one: another symbolical death of himself as ladies' man. It's all in tune with the central theme of the album — the highs and lows of Casanovian life.

But of course, black shades and a banana on the cover of a rock album is also a nod to the Velvet Underground's first record, with Andy Warhol's famous banana cover. As if Leonard wished to declare that after "twenty years of boredom," he was picking up the torch of sophisticated urban rock.[16] Obstinately undecidable and endlessly ambiguous, the cover is at once heroic, hilarious, and philosophically challenging — you can look at it for twenty years and not be bored.

Ditto for the album title. We don't know who it's addressed to. Is Leonard speaking to the women in his life (i.e., "I'm your man, but don't expect too much in terms of phallic prowess"), to God ("I'm your man, but obviously only one step away from the monkey"), to the mass audience he has in mind, or his record company ("I'm your man and I'll put on black shades if that's what it takes to sell albums")?

The ambiguity is also a way for Cohen to announce that two moods of equal strength will compete on *I'm Your Man*: there will be irony in gravity and lyricism behind every laugh.

Unsurprisingly, the record will be #1 in Norway (where Leonard will outsell Michael Jackson that year) and Spain, but it will not quite make the American charts. The author had warned us in "Hallelujah," "I did my best, it wasn't much."

NEW WAVE TROUBADOUR

Love is the record's first theme. Nothing new under the sun. It's Leonard's eternal relationship with women — he longs for them; he idealizes them; he leaves them. A three-step waltz. On *I'm Your Man*, twenty years after *Songs of Leonard Cohen*, the poet returns to the troubadour ideology. Once again, he declares himself the subject of love: love is his master and women are his mistresses.[17] He confessed it in May to the Swedish television sexologist: men have "puppy-dog hearts" and "fall in love every second."[18] On the slow song that gives its title to the record, the singer blindly accepts any games his mistress might invent. He will be her driver, her boxer, her pimp, or her doctor. But for the time being, there is that pesky little detail: the woman in question has left and although the singer knows he can't win her back by "begging on his knees," the song culminates in a comical but pathetic plea ("please!") and in Leonard's self-portrait as a "dog in heat," howling at his lady's beauty. A puppy dog, perhaps, but still a dog in heat — the splendours and humiliations of masculinity. All along, the voice overplays the crooner's virility, but that is only fair game. Leonard's message to women is brief: "I'm your man," which means "I'm yours" but also "I'm a man." As though he could locate an identity only in that gendered game of love that he either wins (rarely) or loses (often).

Throughout the record, of course, you feel the presence of a troubadour who is initiated into the pains of love, but also that of a rake who calls the women "baby" and keeps Ovid's *Art of Love* in his pocket and Sun Tzu's *The Art of War* under his pillow. In the end, the poet reveals himself for what he still is and has always been: a creature of desire. In the album's second song, the angels finally reveal the key to the koan that women have always been for him. The scene takes place in a deserted church, to a backdrop of outré saxophone and the lesson, once again, is short: "There ain't no cure for love," the great revelation of the record disguised as a gaudy pop song. Morality: the synthesizers are only a scam. They would have us believe that the album is a *cold* record. But the singer's fiery voice betrays the true nature of *I'm Your Man* everywhere: it is a smoldering record that picks up the great love song initiated in Languedoc in the twelfth century. It's just that Leonard's troubadour has become an ironic gravelly-voiced crooner who does his little masculine schtick — a poor little mating dance:

> Ah, the moon's too bright
> The chain's too tight
> The beast won't go to sleep
> I've been running through these promises to you
> That I made and I could not keep.

But a mating parade is a tribute, however clichéd, to women and to the unremitting calls of love.

IRONIC, MOI?

Situationist philosopher Guy Debord had based his critique of the society of the spectacle on a rigorous succession of 221 theses. In

"Everybody Knows," Leonard follows suit: twenty-six axioms to review the true state of the world on the supposed good side of the Berlin Wall. He reviews our social, spiritual, and sentimental lives and the diagnosis is severe: the social contract is broken; man and woman are strangers; and the triumph of capitalism and big money is complete. Goodbye, '60s.

The first objective of "Everybody Knows" is to administer twenty-six therapeutic injections of pessimism. Leonard knows that we are all diabetics of hope and with the help of his black insulin, he has made up his mind to keep us in good spiritual shape: lean, lucid, and without illusions. The second objective is to update Jeremiah and write the definitive 1980s lamentation. A successful operation:

> Everybody knows the dice are loaded
> Everybody rolls with their fingers crossed
> Everybody knows the war is over
> Everybody knows the good guys lost.

But unlike Jeremiah, Leonard unfolds the great dirge for the world's misfortunes without a trace of pathos. It is necessary to lament (our hearts seem programmed for it), but it should always be done with a tinge of irony. And beneath its apparent flirtation with despair, "Everybody Knows" is indeed oddly funny. The poet plays with slogans, satire, nursery rhymes, and pop culture, and he adopts a tone that combines the lucidity of Ecclesiastes with the amused fatalism of the blues and the ironic wisdom of a jaded bartender. The world is going badly and love is dead, but no need to be alarmed — it's nothing special: just the ordinary apocalypse.

Perhaps the core of the song is elsewhere. Maybe in its discreet teaching of compassion. At the height of the Algerian war, French President De Gaulle had cajoled the crowd in Algiers with a blaring ""Je vous ai compris!" Leonard does the same here, with the difference that he is not bluffing. He *has* understood us.

He makes us see that the suffering in Malibu equals that of the cotton fields equals that of Golgotha, for that is the great lesson in "Everybody Knows":

> Everybody's got this broken feeling
> Like their father or their dog just died.

Which is actually good news because that shared heartbreak is a firmer foundation for universal brotherhood than Kant's categorical imperatives or your average moral abstraction. Your heart is broken, so is mine. We are brothers.

Mishima claimed in *The Temple of the Golden Pavilion* that a Zen master's only positive quality is humour. Leonard goes further. He shows that gallows humour is pure compassion, for gallows humour proves that you know the world's pain — *Weltschmerz* — but also that laughing at your misfortunes is often possible. And that is what Leonard tries to do. From one stanza to the next, he seeks for the most exaggerated expression for our predicament (a sinking ship? a rigged game? a crucifixion?) to get us to laugh at whatever is dark in our lives.[19]

From a social point of view, "Everybody Knows" also describes a society whose social contract has collapsed. And on the whole album Leonard explores the soft totalitarianism of postmodern America: how its cult of the cool, its worship of the market, and its omnipresent television screens destroy everything that resembles an inner life. Perhaps the album boils down to that: with a couple of crooner ballads, and a plastic waltz, a Jewish prophet in an Armani suit and cool shades crashes the 1980s, hyper-liberal party to reveal its lack of joy. The prophet's verdict is bleak: the rich have got their channels in the bedrooms of the poor, and nobody is quite sure if it's them living their lives or a double. Smile. You are in America.[20]

PRISONER OF ANGELS

DOMINIQUE ISSERMANN

From the video for "First We Take Manhattan" (1988)

The record opens with a fantasy of the poet as a metaphysical terrorist; it ends with a quasi-realistic self-portrait — Leonard as a songwriter held captive by angels. "Tower of Song," an ironic lament haunted by the ghost of the blues, describes Leonard's profession as he experiences it: as a calling that is both sacred and utterly devoid of glory.

The song starts almost in comedy, with a quirky bass groove, a cowbell, and a rumba rhythm on synthesizer. Then comes the lament in deadpan tone:

> Well, my friends are gone, and my hair is grey
> I ache in the places where I used to play.
> And I am crazy for love but I am not coming on,
> I am just paying my rent every day
> in the Tower of Song.

It's sung with little jazz modulations that confirm the outstanding vocalist the singer has become. But casual as they may sound, the lyrics contain a pledge of allegiance and an ode to his craft. Leonard tells us his profession, shabby as it may seem, is practised in a tower — the ultimate *locus* of lyrical poetry — and (even better) a tower where you hear "funny voices" from Heaven. The tower in question is a mix of the Brill Building on Forty-Second Street, where teams of songwriters used to write love songs on office hours, and the Black Rock Building, the poet's administrative home as a Columbia Records artist.[21] It's a prison where the guardians are angels and the inmates, geniuses. On the top floor is the founding father and early martyr of modern country music, Hank Williams, the poor man's King David, and first Elvis. One hundred floors below him, Leonard Cohen who hears the maestro coughing all night long. Between them, the whole history of modern American song.

We said it before: *I'm Your Man* is a smoldering record. With "Tower of Song," Leonard closes it on a declaration of love to his craft. Written by slaves under angelic watch, the songs we listen to in bars, kitchens, or bedrooms are sacred. Their simplicity mirrors the truth of our inner life and invites us to a greater purity. Which is why we are never done with Hank Williams. And why we will never be done with Leonard Cohen, who daringly asserts his entry into posterity:

> You'll be hearing from me baby
> long after I'm gone
> I'll be singing to you sweetly from my window
> in the Tower of Song.

But that poetical manifesto is also an unpretentious doo-wop rumba, the kind of songs he used to listen to on jukeboxes in Montreal in the early '50s. Songs that went:

Doo-dom-dom-dom
Da-doo dom-dom.

The album's perfect last words.

ELECTRONIC GEOMETRIES

A gold record in Canada that went quintuple platinum in Scandinavia, *I'm Your Man* was an instant classic, although its soundscape that Leonard himself called "postmodernist disco" shocked some purists.[22]

The sonic textures of *I'm Your Man* are almost entirely synthetic, but this time, Leonard had upgraded to a new (and much better) keyboard: the Technics SXK530. That instrument was basically used to streamline the songs and expose what a song truly is: just a beat that sets the tempo, a minimal melody, an elementary solo — if possible on no more than four notes — and (when it's absolutely necessary) a touch of oud or saxophone, as a reminder that there once were such things as musical styles.

Thus reduced and protected from the musicians' virtuosity (i.e., their ego[23]), songs become pure, geometric, and timeless, as sharp today as they were in 1988. The neutral musical textures also happen to be the perfect shrine for a voice now full of grit and gravel and fire. Undistracted by instruments, we are free to enjoy Leonard's jazzy scansions, which are now full of swing and surprise — the perfect art of the *talkover*.[24]

The texture of the songs also mirrors our predicament: we are beings whose hearts still beat in an automated world; beings who live real lives surrounded by TV simulacra and virtual hyper-realities.

But despite Leonard's conversion to electronica (or maybe because of it), the record — like *Songs of Leonard Cohen* twenty years before — sold like hotcakes, especially in Europe. Five of its eight songs would never again leave Cohen's stage repertoire. Somewhere in northeast France, the video to "First We Take

Manhattan" and its gravelly voiced singer got the attention of a thirteen-year-old who barely spoke English (he is now writing these lines) and soon the strippers in the Canadian film *Exotica* would be seen pole-dancing to the slow beat of "Everybody Knows." Was despair ever so sexy?[25]

Today, *I'm Your Man* is still among the singer's most accessible records. It is also paradoxical as hell: chilly synthesizers and fire of the voice; poppy texture and sophisticated lyrics; inexhaustible gravity and irony everywhere. A masterpiece.

THE THOUSAND FACES OF GRAVITY (TOUR OF 1988)

For the subsequent tour, Leonard has created a structure for his live shows that would remain unchanged until the end of his career: a first set of eight or nine songs (opening with "Dance Me to the End of Love"; closing with "First We Take Manhattan") followed after an intermission by a short acoustic section with Leonard alone on stage, before a second set of eight songs (opening with "Tower of Song"; closing with "Take This Waltz") and a few (inevitable) encores usually beginning (in tongue-and-cheek fashion) with "I Tried to Leave You." For the first time, the concerts often end with the biblical hymn "Whither Thou Goest" (Ruth 1:16) sung by the whole band holding hands.[26]

Particularly striking in 1988 is the band's efficiency. For once, the two backing singers, a Valkyrie with ember in the voice (Julie Christensen) and a petite brunette with the power of an opera singer (Perla Batalla), do not look like angels but like two executive women straight out of a Helmut Newton photo shoot. His celestial task force. John Bilezikjian is back to bewitch "Who by Fire," "Story of Isaac," and "The Partisan" with his oud, while a newly joined blues guitarist, Bob Metzger (he will stay twenty years) will illuminate many songs with soulful solos played in the Clapton style (slow hand, deep feeling). Thanks to him, "Bird on the Wire" — now complete with Hammond organ and angelic moans — becomes the ultimate hymn to accompany late night drinks in hotel lobbies.[27]

And of course, there's Leonard himself. At the age of fifty-three, he has taken a decisive step towards the lighter side, at least on stage. His deeper and more relaxed voice allows for a much greater tonal range, so that the shows now feature laid-back crooner numbers ("I'm Your Man" and "Tower of Song"), moments of strong passion ("Hallelujah," where Cohen tries his hand at screaming), and exercises of pure sepulchral beauty ("The Stranger Song," "Avalanche," and "Suzanne," sung alone to the accompaniment of an acoustic Gibson). Now convinced that the stage calls for drama and entertainment, the singer also adds comedic doubles to his usual masks of high priest of the heart and the prophet of gravity.

So, he successively operates during the concerts as a prophet who announces the apocalypse, the leader of a metaphysical army, and an ironic crooner who knows the heart too well, but also as a deadpan joker who reveals how light things can get when you've accepted your defeat. Hence concerts that constantly change tonality and cover the whole range of the life of the heart. A very seductive dramaturgy of gravity. One moment, Leonard is on his knees, his face turned to Heaven, reminding us that only failure teaches us to say "hallelujah"; the next he rises to reassure women that he is still ready to do anything to be their "man" before making fun of himself as a loser or evoking the mystery of Christ's last words.

The French word *doublure* designates both the inner lining of a jacket (its hidden side) and an actor's body double: he who takes your place in case of danger. Leonard's new ironic masks are doublures in both senses. When the high priest pulls the concert towards excessive solemnity, the joker steps in; when the prophet is through revealing the extent of the catastrophe, the crooner takes over and reminds us love still exists. Throughout, Leonard demonstrates that for all its tragedy, life is also a slapstick comedy where God has us constantly slipping on the banana peels of love, failure, and depression. So in 1988, Leonard laments, Leonard jokes, and

Leonard gives the audience the ritual blessing of the kohens, the solemn birkat kohanim. And, every night, as he had announced in one of his recent songs, he greets us

> from the other side of sorrow and despair
> with a love so vast and shattered
> it will reach [us] anywhere.[28]

That year, American concert reviewers all seemed to ask how it could be they had never noticed what a class act this man was. The poet knew the answer and he had given it on the album: "I know this can't be me / must be my double."

CHAPTER 11

THE CROONER'S PROPHECIES AND THE APOCALYPSE FOR LAUGHS

1989–1993

There are very few things I do well:
prophecies and cleaning the dishes.

— LEONARD COHEN, INTERVIEW FOR *LE CERCLE DE MINUIT* (1992)[1]

Leonard Cohen at home in Los Angeles, 1991

PROFESSION: STOWAWAY

So 1988 was a pivotal moment in Leonard's career: his return from exile and the year of his commercial and critical rehabilitation. Rid of the misunderstandings that associated him with the '60s, he imposed a new persona — that of an über-cool poet with the authority of the prophet and the aura of the rock star.[2] A double agent infiltrated in rock music to teach us that the gravest of life is where the true fun is. Everybody suddenly seemed to get that he had only been a stowaway in the '60s and that his anti-war songs were also anti-peace. For the first time, he himself seemed to know exactly who he was:

> I am not a novelist. I am not the light of my generation. I am not the vanguard of a new sensibility. I am a songwriter living in Los Angeles.[3]

Some observers, like *Chatelaine*, who had included him in 1986 among the "ten sexiest men" in Canada, had foreseen this resurrection; others were joining the Cohen bandwagon, like *Entertainment Weekly*, which gave seven reasons why Leonard Cohen was "the next best thing to God," but gone were the days when the singer could be simply laughed off.[4] He now hung out with Iggy Pop, duetted with Sonny Rollins on *Saturday Night Live*, and recorded a quasi-hip-hop song about Elvis Presley's Rolls-Royce with the Detroit band Was (Not Was). For a while, Leonard had kudos in spades. He talked the talk and walked the walk and was the coolest songwriter around.[5]

In the offices of the hip Parisian magazine *Les Inrockuptibles*, Leonard, together with Morrissey, was the highest figure on the totem pole and the staff did a lot to convert young French hipsters to his work. They conducted a few remarkable interviews with him and turned the singer into a convincing cult figure: Leonard Cohen, godfather and precursor of sombre indie rock. For their September

1991 issue, they produced a remarkable album of Cohen covers by the cream of alternative rock — Nick Cave, the Pixies, R.E.M., John Cale, Ian McCullough, Bill Pritchard, and Dead Famous People — all of which claimed a secret kinship with the gravelly-voiced Canadian, as artists now routinely did.[6] Times were changing, obviously, and definitive recognition came in 1993 when Oliver Stone chose three recent Cohen tracks for the *Natural Born Killers* soundtrack and the following year, when St. Kurt Cobain himself, the up-and-coming martyr and patron saint of grunge, called for

> a Leonard Cohen afterworld
> so I can sigh eternally.[7]

This homage was quickly followed by Jeff Buckley's now classic cover of "Hallelujah," which made "Leonard Cohen" a household name for Generation X.

With the singer's rock credibility thus restored, Canadian institutions, sensing that they had perhaps lost track of a poet who was now increasingly vocal about his attachment to Los Angeles,[8] launched a takeover bid over all things Cohen. It was urgent to remind the world that the Montreal-born poet was a national treasure. For this, there was nothing like official accolades. So, after three successive television specials on the CBC in 1989,[9] the singer was made an Officer of the Order of Canada in October 1991, an honorary doctor of McGill University in May 1992, and a Canadian Music Hall of Fame member in 1991. In 1993 and 1994, he obtained an almost indecent shower of Juno Awards as well as a Governor General's Award for his entire career.[10] He was also made the subject of two biographies,[11] of yet another stage musical (Bryden MacDonald's *Sincerely, A Friend*, 1991), of an exhibition at the National Library (1993), and of several scholarly publications as well as an academic conference at Red Deer College in October 1993.[12] In 1994, his sixtieth birthday was celebrated (in his absence, as we will see) with countless articles in the Canadian press as well as a tribute book, *Take This Waltz*, with testimonies and wishes from the cream of the Canadian literary scene. Had there been a Mount Rushmore in Canada, Leonard's profile would no doubt have been added, squeezed between Pierre Trudeau, Jacques Cartier, and Chief Crowfoot. Which didn't stop Cohen from staying in Los Angeles for longer and longer periods of time. *A singer-songwriter living in L.A.*

BACK IN THE CITY OF ANGELS

With other people busy working at his posterity, Leonard did something he had always done very well: he vanished. CBS was asking for *I'm Your Man* opus II, but after his televised duet with Sonny Rollins in February 1989, the poet went AWOL again.

Probably still licking his wounds from a painful separation with his friend Dominique, the poet kept a low profile for two and a half years, moving swiftly from city to city, as though to check where he wrote the slowest. But he could often be spotted in the food marts of Mid-Wilshire, Los Angeles, or in Sasaki Roshi's monasteries. If we believe subsequent interviews, he also saw a few doctors (some of whom diagnosed bipolarity) but gave no sign of life to his record company. His next engagement with public life would not take place before November 1992, for the release of the next record *The Future*.

Until that date, the poet resumed his pursuit of many angels: the angels of poetic inspiration (he wrote every day and obsessively polished the same texts); the angels of spiritual awakening; and any female angel that would nurse (or break) his heart. He allegedly had brief affairs with an Egyptian woman from Paris, a Canadian actress of Asian origin, a Puerto Rican model he had been dating since 1980, and — with fateful consequences, as we shall see — his new manager Kelly Lynch. It's the eternal return of the same starting point: women, writing, and religious practice as quintessential ways of reconnecting with the world.

And it so happens that the state of the world in 1989 was something that Leonard was interested in. The fall of the Berlin Wall and the collapse of the Soviet bloc seemed to confirm his old diagnosis: the Flood had begun. The old post-war status quo was collapsing with nothing to replace it except twenty-four-hour television channels and the war of all against all and of Burger King against the rest. Hence a series of new songs concerned with the current hyper-liberal apocalypse, and Los Angeles, where the collapse of Western culture and what French philosopher Jean Baudrillard called "the perfect crime" (the complete disappearance of reality and its replacement by television images[13]) could be observed in real time, was once more the ideal city to write them in. Other advantages the city offered Leonard were the regular seismic episodes, the disintegrating social contract, and the nascent gangsta rap scene which kept the prophet's paranoia at just the right level.

Like every Angeleno, Leonard owned a car. He knew, therefore, that you could pick up few angels in the streets of L.A., but that the future was waiting at every corner. In April 1992, the future finally materialized after four police officers who had been filmed brutalizing a Black man named Rodney King were acquitted. Several neighbourhoods were set ablaze and for five days, riots and looting took place on a very large scale until the Republican Guard was sent in. Leonard spent those days watching his favourite Korean shops go up in smoke on television and his nights watching the fires from his balcony while a thin layer of ash slowly invaded his front lawn. His formal verdict, delivered a year later, was unsurprisingly ambiguous. On the one hand, it was:

> I've seen the Future, brother
> It is murder.

On the other:

> Democracy is Coming to the U.S.A.

But one thing was obviously becoming clearer: someone had to pick up the lyre of St. John the Revelator to determine what revelation was hidden in the Angeleno apocalypse and what part love had to play in it. Hence, the next record, understandably more American and more political than the previous one: *The Future*.

ACUTE COHENITIS

But the twenty-seven angels in charge of the artist's production didn't wait for the riots: they had found the fugitive immediately after the previous tour as he tried to escape and chained him once again to his kitchen table in Los Angeles. There, Leonard had started work on "Democracy" — his ode to the impossible but ever reinvigorating American democracy — and on "The Future," a detailed evocation of the global collapse that would follow the fall of the Berlin Wall. As for "Waiting for the Miracle" or "Anthem," fragments had started to appear in the poet's notebooks almost ten years before.

The green Olivetti was now stored in a cupboard, replaced in 1988 by a Macintosh computer,[14] but fundamentally very little had changed. Writing was still writing. For Leonard, as we know, it was a slow and painful process, one he had once called "the continuous stutter / of the Word that was made into Flesh."[15] The gist of the operation is that what you truly feel is not immediately accessible; it must be distilled from the mass of slogans and approximations that come first. So, Leonard relapses: he moves from room to room, writes the same words a hundred times, no longer answers the phone, bangs his head against carpets in search of a rhyme. The splendours and miseries of a songwriter's life. And it lasts for two and a half years: he writes, crosses out, rewrites, writes again, always the same stanzas with incremental changes. He takes drugs, drinks heavily, stops drinking, quits smoking, starts smoking again, writes and rewrites, takes Prozac, changes girlfriends — whatever the situation requires. In other words, the usual crisis of acute Cohenitis. Explanation:

> I tend to fall apart when I'm working on a record, and
> I think it's necessary. To get to that point where I can
> defend every line and every word, I have to annihi-
> late and kill those versions of myself that whisper lies,
> slogans or easy solutions. And every time, it's a carnage
> [that] involves the collapse of the personality.[16]

Nadel mentions the story of a friend who, after coercing the poet into leaving his apartment for coffee, found herself sitting in front a "little zombie" who mumbled fragments of lyrics to himself.[17] Quite the atmosphere.

In the summer of 1990, work is interrupted when Adam Cohen, aged eighteen, is involved in a very serious motorcycle accident in Jamaica. Leonard immediately joins his son in the North York hospital where he has been transferred and apparently put into a coma. Instinctively, he starts to read out the Bible to him. The story goes that when Adam finally regained consciousness, his first words were to beg his famous dad to "please, read something else."[18] Leonard thanked the Lord but, back in Los Angeles, he realized he had once more lost contact with the songs. The writing had been difficult — it was now almost impossible. And neither Zen, nor women or Prozac, nor the best hotel rooms in the country made any difference. As he often did in such circumstances, the poet collapsed. Back to square one. The black square. Clinical depression.

Not everything was black, though, in 1990. The year closed with the secret arrival of a new angel in Leonard's life. She would remain there for thirty-six months. The creature is actually a bright young lady who will soon terrorize America in the role — she's an actress — of a psychopathic babysitter. Her name: Rebecca De Mornay, an ex-girlfriend of Tom Cruise. Leonard, who had apparently met her when she was a child,[19] had more recently bumped into her at social events, so much so that a romance quickly developed, to the astonishment of the celebrity press. For a while, the two lovers were often seen together: he escorted her to film sets or to the Academy

Awards; interviewed her for *Interview*; she accompanied him on tour or in recording studios, even once presiding over a session for a song she was tired of hearing him rehearse in her living room.[20] In that young woman's radiant beauty, there was a clarity that would have made any man fall in love, but Leonard, as the reader may remember, had a history with Rebeccas. A previous Rebecca was an old flirtation to whom he had dedicated his unfinished 1975 record *Songs for Rebecca*; another was a character in the book of Genesis: Isaac's wife. Long after he had been offered in sacrifice or fought with angels, Isaac fell in love with a certain Rebecca who offered him water from a well. It quenched his thirst forever.[21]

Like the biblical character and like many twenty-five-year-olds who have just gotten rid of their exes, Rebecca De Mornay was looking for a husband and, for a while, she thought she had found one. As for Leonard, he knew — being quite the connoisseur — that this was the perfect woman. But that was precisely the problem. How can you say, "I told you when I came I was a stranger" to the perfect woman? So, Leonard almost takes the plunge: he offers the girl a ring and — at least in a song lyric — proposes to marry.[22] But the heart has reasons that neither Montreal poets nor Californian actresses can understand — the singer is quickly caught up by his karma. He goes on tour, drinks far too much, and remembers that in life, there are some things you're good at (exploring the darkness of the soul and working to excess) and others that you will never learn (writing *Blonde on Blonde* in five minutes in the back of a cab or being a good husband). So, at the end of 1993, exhausted by three months of touring and fifty years of semi-comical melancholy, the singer retires to a monastery without exactly warning Rebecca, which was not that much of a problem because she had actually just left him. The following year, on morning television in England, Leonard explained — quite sheepishly in fact — that the actress had "wised up to [him]" and left, adding, however, that "in a damp corner of the heart, our love is alive and flourishes."[23]

THE FUTURE (1992): USES AND REFRACTIONS OF THE APOCALYPSE

November 1992. Leonard puts on a black coat and hits the road again. His destination: Toronto, New York, and seventeen European cities. His assignment: forty days of promotion for the new album and the forthcoming concert tour.

It begins with a cocktail party at a former punk club on the first floor of Toronto's Spadina Hotel and goes on with full days of interviews in New York and across Europe, with photoshoots, television shows, and radio programs everywhere.[24]

As he sits down with journalists in a succession of great hotel rooms (the Mayflower in New York, the Raphael in Paris, the Palace Hotel in Madrid, Home House in London . . .), Leonard knows that the resulting articles (in the *New York Times*, the *Wall Street Journal*, *Rolling Stone*, *NME*, *The Globe and Mail*, *Details for Men*, *Vox*, *L'Express* or *Maclean's* . . .) will have similar clichéd titles ("Lord Byron of Rock-and-Roll," "Prophet of Love," "Rebirth of a Ladies' Man," "Troubadour of Gloom" . . .) but he makes sure every journalist gets his message: the apocalypse has begun. The evidence, he says, is everywhere. In the streets, on television, in our hearts. And that happens to be the subject of the new album: eight songs designed as a lesson in practical things. The subject? How to spot an apocalypse and what to do with it.

In principle, an apocalypse is easy to spot; everything — borders, walls, hierarchies, certainties — collapses. With the opening track, "The Future," Leonard provides his version of the Los Angeles riots and a general recap: an apocalypse is destruction on an epic scale (i.e., a city in flames) and the end of something (i.e., Western civilization).

The rest of the album introduces apocalypses that may be harder to spot. Those hidden in the heart when all certainties collapse ("Waiting for the Miracle"), those that gradually claim our lives when our defeat becomes inescapable ("Anthem"), those that purify society and contain secret beginnings ("Democracy").

There are also apocalypses that only a mystical lecher like Leonard can see when you kneel before a woman and her beauty erases the world (it's the erotic apocalypse of "Light as a Breeze") or when a bar owner turns on the lights and kills an evening that music, flirtation, and alcohol had made sublime (it's the revellers' apocalypse in "Closing Time"). In each case, a revelation takes place, which is actually what the Greek word ἀποκάλυψις means (revelation[25]), but what is revealed can hardly be put into words and, when it is, it's rarely popular. It's "the awful truth which you can't reveal to the ears of youth."[26]

No doubt that truth is the truth that we all have a hard time accepting that all things — good or bad — have an end: your youth, your love affair, or Western civilization. Hence, Leonard's second great theme on the album. It's actually a question, an ethical one: how to put those small and large apocalypses to good use? In other words, how to behave in the apocalypse? The answer, of course, is a reformulation of the Leonardian code of conduct: keep calm and ironic but show compassion for all men.

In an exciting crossing of voices, the eight new songs contain as many lessons in courage, with emergences of prayer and black humour at every turn.

THE STAND-UP PROPHET: CROONING IN THE RAIN

That year, the video for "The Future" got a lot of airplay on MTV. To the background of a boogie-woogie tune and a gospel choir, Leonard reinvents the rhetoric of biblical prophecy for cable television: Ezekiel on CNN. His imagination fuelled by the recent riots and William Butler Yeats, he chronicles the details of the apocalypse with the enthusiasm of your average televangelist launching the commercials.[27]

With riots, destroyed fetuses, and burning cities, not to mention "your woman hanging upside down," the day of doom comes in the guise of the ultimate television-friendly *spectacle*. There is irony here, of course, but also good faith: the prophet Cohen makes us see the apocalypse as he has seen it in Los Angeles (give or take a couple of hyperboles) and as he believes it will happen everywhere. In the early '70s, the proto-rapper Gil Scott Heron had announced that "the revolution [would] not be televised." He was right, but only because the revolution didn't happen at all. Cohen says instead that, from now on, *everything* will be televised, especially the apocalypse, which will even be broadcast live via satellite and commented in real time by the devil.[28] For a few seconds in the song, Leonard turns the Berlin Wall into the wall of lamentations, but he soon snaps back from Jeremiah to Ezekiel, explaining to his "baby" that the future he has seen is just "murder."

But here's the surprising bit (and the song's big discovery): even in the era of generalized spectacle, announcing the end of times still requires a professional voice. A voice much more charged in gravitas than the voices of the "lousy little poet" who try to "sound like Charlie Manson." As a Jew, as a kohen, as an expert in catastrophes, Cohen considers himself more credible. To be on the safe side, he even states his pedigree in every interview. He was announcing the flood when the hippies sang "Let the Sunshine In" and still mourning his dog (dead circa 1951) when the Reagan-era yuppies partied on champagne and cocaine. So why not puff up his résumé a little bit and say what is literally false but metaphysically true: he has been in the apocalyptic business not just for twenty-five years, but for three thousand.[29] Or, to put it his way: "I'm the little Jew who wrote the Bible."

So that was it. The chronicle of the first flood, the visions of Ezekiel, the walls of Jericho tumbling down — it was all Leonard Cohen. As was the apocalypse in Daniel and the revelation in John. So obviously, there's no way the bigwigs of gangsta rap will impress him and Leonard even challenges L.A. rappers on their home ground, providing as he does the definitive answer to a question that seemed to obsess everyone in African American music: "Who's bad"? So, who's bad? Ezekiel, of course. Or in that case,

Leonard Cohen, who reconfigures the Jewish prophet as rock-and-roll desperado. He even briefly goes *gangsta* in the second stanza:

> Give me crack and anal sex
> Take the only tree that's left
> And stuff it up the hole in your culture.[30]

The verdict? "The Future" is a brilliant opening for the album, even if only in the way it refocuses the debate on the real situation: the end of time is not to come; it has already happened. The question of "hope" is therefore resolved (there is none) and Leonard has great fun riding his pessimistic hobbyhorse in every interview, repeating to every journalist that in the face of the inevitable, his only advice was to make ourselves "strong and cheerful" and "duck."[31]

But with its quasi-rockabilly backbeat and its gospel feel, the song — bleak as the lyrics are — is also full of humour. In the video, Leonard's prophet announces the apocalypse with a couple of dance steps on a cheerful little boogie (a prophet with a twist, so to speak) and he ironically explains the obsolescence of the Christian concept of repentance ("When they said 'repent,' I wonder what they meant") to the background of a cool gospel choir. The scene, besides, takes place in what seems to be a hotel lobby, where rain starts to fall on the prophet, at first just a drizzle, then harder. His suit soon gets soaked, and the water rises to his ankles, but he stands poker-faced: a fatalist, singing in the rain. QED: the end of the world is serious stuff, but it's also funny as hell. He told us so: it is *murder*.[32]

On the album, that great epic apocalypse is balanced with "Anthem," a discreet chronicle of interior collapses. To the backdrop of another church choir, he reminds us that freedom is impossible ("The dove is never free") and that every day is a day of defeat. The voice, now cracked and husky, is in tune with the message and brings to the sonic surface of the song everything that is cracked in our lives. But the grit gives the singer the authority that is required to pronounce the two poetic formulas that will seal the Cohenian credo once and for all. Formula number one: "Every heart to love will come, but like a refugee." Formula number two (the famous one): "There is a crack in everything, that's how the light gets in." It's as if the concerts had just been waiting for that song (in the works for ten years) to gain once more in poignant force.

LOVE ACTUALLY

Seemingly unconnected to the prophet's eschatological declarations are two suave covers of classic crooner songs: Frederick Knight's "Be for Real" and Irving Berlin's "Always." Arguably an odd choice for an album concerned with the apocalypse. On those tracks, Leonard plays — with some irony — with the codes of crooning, exaggerating the gravity and manliness of his voice in an attempt to out-Barry-White Barry White. He nonetheless transforms the stereotypical speech of the popular love song (love lasts forever, love never lies) into a profound teaching about our true predicament. Yes, love lasts forever, for it is our true condition (we fall in love every minute). Yes, love is our point of entry into reality (without it our lives atrophy and wither). And yes, love is a serious matter; it is even a very, very serious matter, as the gravity in Leonard's voice makes abundantly clear.

So that's the second idea on the record: we are programmed to love. The apocalypse is just the thing that compels us to do it now. In the seventeenth century, the great reformer of Rinzai Zen, Hakuin, wrote that monks must practise Zen as if their heads were on fire.[33] Leonard says here that is also how we must love: with absolute urgency. So, at the end of the day, Frederick Knight and Irving Berlin were absolutely right (and so was Julio Iglesias): love never dies, love never lies.

Hence this unexpected conclusion for an album about the apocalypse: a flirtation in a bar at closing time is worth a psalm

("Closing Time") or, to say it another way, love (which redeems our lives) is never cheap. That's how far ahead of ordinary crooners Leonard is. Like St. John at Patmos, he understands the essential role that love must play in the ultimate ends:

> I've seen the nations rise and fall
> I've heard their stories, heard them all
> but love's the only engine of survival.[34]

That's perhaps another truth that you can't reveal to the ears of youth.[35]

TOUR OF 1993: ACROSS THE WORLD IN A SHERMAN TANK

Built on the two pillars of love and the apocalypse, *The Future*, which earned Leonard almost unanimous praise, is a staunch and solid record that erased the distinctions between Cohen the crooner and Cohen the high priest. The songs, which also include an ode to cunnilingus disguised as a mystical prayer ("Light as a Breeze") and a melancholic tango about impossible salvation ("Waiting for the Miracle"), are solid and powerful: "Sherman Tanks rather than butterflies," according to the singer.[36] Based on a mix of electronic rhythms, country music, and crooner blues, the production aims at efficiency, in keeping with an era when the American market (Leonard's chief target with this album) liked solid, flawless records. Like Nirvana's *Nevermind* or Eric Clapton's *MTV Unplugged*, for example.

As for the singer's voice, it has again — while still filled with fire — gained in depth and, with an added huskiness and a slight warp inherited from decades of smoking, it now grates and rasps and is charged with the extra authority that comes with grit. Ever more noticeable also are the vibratory qualities of the timbre — it is not yet the voice of God, but already that of a battered archangel. One that's back from yet another raid against the dark side.

Some might be tempted to bemoan the record's slightly over-produced quality (the singer has worked in twelve different studios with four producers over a period of two years), which sometimes smooths off the songs' rough edges, but what is that reproach when everything in Leonard's voice is fire and rough edges? And indeed, *The Future* was a greater success than *I'm Your Man* in the United States and Canada (a platinum record there and #7 in the charts) and the record got Leonard his best sales in the United Kingdom since *New Skin for the Old Ceremony*.[37] Solidity pays, apparently.

At the end of April 1992, Leonard opens a new world tour with a test concert in Los Angeles. The band is tight, the voice sepulchral, and a widely available bootleg of the show is one of Leonard's best live albums ever. With twenty-eight European dates, followed by thirty-eight concerts in the United States and Canada in June and July, the tour is Cohen's largest stunt in the Land of Uncle Sam yet. It's a frenetic pace, a sum total of sixty-seven three-hour shows in sixty cities in slightly over three months, with countless plane rides, coach rides, taxi rides, limousine rides, and elevator rides. With waits at airports and customs every other day. Waits in hotel lobbies and in backstage areas. A different language every week, sometimes two. New journalists every day. And hangers-on. A television show here, a radio interview there. A nap if you're lucky, a soundcheck in the afternoon. And every night, the ritual: the songs, some of them old, some of them new — waiting to be performed. And a crowd in the dark, waiting for the songs, waiting to be saved, waiting for Leonard Cohen.

> All your children here,
> In their rags of light.

And every night, after the show, there's a dressing room, a few smiles, a few old friends, and a couple of celebrities to greet; a few drinks, probably. And the day ends with an elevator ride, a hotel corridor, and a window looking on a city that sleeps. And your hotel bed. Breakfast in six hours. Or five hours. Airport at nine.

The band is the same as five years before: Perla and Julie plus the ever-excellent Bob Metzger. Missing is John Bilezikjian's oud, replaced this time around by Paul Ostermayer's saxophone (already present in the 1979 tour). Overall, the sound is a little more severe, perhaps. At fifty-eight, Leonard looks his age, with a marked stoop in the shoulders and flashes of silver in the hair. The dark Armani suits and charcoal-grey shirts plus the severe razor cut remind everyone that Leonard isn't exactly a civilian. And indeed, a lot about him — the weightier physical appearance, the husky voice, the military salutes, the caustic solemnity of the exchanges with the audience — suggests the presence of an old soldier: Leonard Cohen, jagged veteran of many wars. Wars against despair. Wars against himself. Wars against love that comes too fast or love that comes too slow. Wars against songs that refuse getting written.

In 1992, every critic seems to have joined the Cohenian cause, and the poet confirms the success of the 1988 tour: every article he picks up on both sides of the Atlantic is full of praise, which is not really surprising. At this point, Leonard is the perfect anti-singer. He keeps the crowd on the edge of their seats with little scansions that are ever more charged with swing and meaning, impressing even a seasoned poet and performer like Allen Ginsberg:

> I was amazed at his gritty realistic voice, relaxed
> in the abdomen and the elegant ease of irony. The
> language bitter, disillusioning as befits a practiced
> Yankee Canadian Buddhist, always surprising [. . .]
> A kind of Bodhisattva Shambhogakaya was behind
> his strength.[38]

Once more, the fiery centre of the concerts is the voice: a voice that overplays "Leonard Cohen," overplays virility, overplays stoicism, creating in the process a fascinating tension between gravity and derision. And for three hours, Leonard thus takes his audience into exile, into a land where grace and the higher registers seem to be forbidden, sacred territories that you observe from afar. Of course, he smuggles grace back into the shows with his sense of humour. He thanks the Royal Albert Hall audience for the flowers they have sent for twenty-five years, specifying that "they didn't help," and writes off the '60s as "an intoxicating time of about eleven or twelve minutes." In Boston, while the band sings a hymn, he imitates a televangelist and pretends to dissolve the audience's existential anxiety — and to replace it with "a mere daily terror."

The prominence of caustic humour on that tour may partly be due to the fifty-eight-year-old singer's recent discovery of 1982 Château Latour, a Bordeaux wine that had made him invent a new concept: sober drunkenness. Convinced that the wine in question favoured contact with the songs, Leonard introduced a new sacrament: the band's sharing of Château Latour before going on stage. The only problems were the price of the bottle (US$250) and the singer's tendency, perhaps fuelled by his ever-present stage fright, to drink a little more every day. So, by Cohen's own admission, a few glasses at the beginning of the tour quickly led to a regime of three bottles a day, sometimes four. Although miraculously protected (or so he said) from inebriation, the singer nevertheless ended the tour on his knees. Apparently unhappy about the way the concerts turned out, he also put on a lot of weight — probably at least twenty pounds if you believe the pictures — and came out of the operation physically, emotionally, and spiritually exhausted, all the more so as the tour apparently marked the end of his romance with Rebecca.[39] And then of course came the usual post-tour blues:

> It's like being dropped off in a desert. You don't know where you live anymore, or what a driver's license is for, or if you still have a car or a girlfriend or a wife and kids: you're lost.[40]

After the tour, Cohen's media profile is at an all-time high. Kurt Cobain and his Nirvana bandmates had come to pay their respects in Cohen's dressing room at the Seattle concert and President Clinton asked for "Democracy" to be played at his inauguration. But in late 1993, the singer starts feeling worse every week. He is clearly not recovering from three months of touring and heavy drinking. Nor from the fifty-eight years that preceded the tour. Soon, he hit rock bottom. He would later diagnose what he was suffering from with a metaphor: he no longer believed in his alibi. That was it. Eureka. The songwriter's career, the movie-star girlfriend, the poetic life, the travelling, and the superb gravity — it was all a vast alibi. In other words, "a circumstance that allows one to exonerate oneself or to create a diversion." And an alibi means there's a hidden crime. Leonard has a definite idea of the hidden crime that makes him suffer; there is an abyss inside him that he still refuses to look into. Now, he happens to know a place where looking into abysses is an activity that is not frowned upon. It's even encouraged, so to speak. What is more, that place even invites you to do it with a certain elevation and elevation seems quite indicated when you hit rock bottom. So very early one morning in the autumn of 1993, Leonard drives his car up Mount Baldy — sixty-five hundred metres high — with no specific intention of coming back. For the next few years, his career will indeed continue without him. Up there, in a small log cabin, he will have time to write many epistles — actually mea culpas — to Rebecca. One of them, which will become a song, sheds light on the comical side of the situation:

> I was never any good at loving you
> I was just some tourist in your bed looking at the
> view.

Another one, written after several years in the lotus position, is more poignant. In substance, it says: when you looked at me,

I could never bring myself to believe that you were looking for a husband. But look at me now: "married to everyone but you."[41]

Maybe there was another Nirvana waiting for him up Mount Baldy. Without Kurt Cobain.

CHAPTER 12

WAITING FOR THE MIRACLE

LIFE OF MONK COHEN, THE LAST ALIBI
1993–1999

Leonard Cohen's cabin at Mt. Baldy Zen Center

THE MAGIC MOUNTAIN

> *To study the Buddha is to study oneself,*
> *To study oneself is to forget oneself,*
> *To forget oneself is to be enlightened by the myriad dharma.*
>
> — DOGEN ZENJI[I]

Zen dissolves everything, especially the distinctions between the Self, the world, and emptiness — an experience called mu-ga or

334

"no-Self." Then everything returns to its rightful place (the Self here, the world there, and emptiness all around) but everything has been revived and refreshed. Lovers of mysticism and of shoveling snow, here we go — Leonard Cohen joins a Zen monastery.

When the singer left his civilian life to settle full-time in a cabin at more than sixty-five hundred feet up Mount Baldy in Joshu Sasaki Roshi's Rinzai-ji Zen Center, joining the small community of full-time monks, he already had twenty years of practice behind him. Not exactly a beginner. He therefore knew that his only friends up there would be rocks and boulders of all sizes, shriveled old fir trees, and an equally ancient Zen master with little English and a strongly marked taste for cognac and fondling the naked breasts of his female students. For Leonard, it was now or never — his children were adults, his songs were engraved in the hearts of hundreds of thousands of fans around the world, and he himself was tired of hotel rooms and Château Latour. A monk's cabin must have seemed like a nice change. At eighty-six, Joshu Sasaki Roshi, a cunning old fox, was beginning to look more and more like an old turtle. The roshi just had a major health scare and now was time — before it was too late — to go and listen a little closer to what he'd been whispering in Leonard's ear for two decades in a strange Japanese-flavoured pidgin-English Buddhist mumbo-jumbo that Shakyamuni Buddha himself would have had a hard time understanding, and to check whether or not enlightenment was indeed waiting on the other side of the mountain.

When he shaved his head and took up his quarters on Mount Baldy (in Greek "Golgotha"), Leonard's semi-official function was to be the master's cook, driver, and drinking buddy. Together with the shika (vice-abbot), the shoji (work manager), the shikijitsu (keeper of discipline), the tenzo (cook), and the translator, he would be part of the roshi's close guard.[2] The only privilege granted to the rock star was a double cabin originally meant for guests, where he could move in his synthesizer and his antediluvian computer. A sum total of almost fifteen square metres just for him, with his own stove and a small bathtub — a billionaire's luxury given the standards of the place. He would stay there, with the occasional holiday or promotional break, for more than six years and observe through the shed's three small windows the slow passing of the seasons: Mount Baldy in winter (the world is covered with snow); Mount Baldy in summer (the world belongs to crickets); Mount Baldy in spring (the world is a flower). Every morning, to remind himself why he was here, he recited the four vows of the Buddha in ancient Japanese:

> Shujo muen seigan do
> Bonno mujin seigan dan
> Homon muryo seigan gaku
> Butsu-do mujo seigan jo.[3]

HAVE YOU EATEN? THEN WASH YOUR BOWL

> *Ten years of joy spent in brothels; now I'm in the mountains:*
> *the fir trees are like a prison and only the wind caresses my skin.*

— IKKYŪ SOJŪN (1394–1481)[4]

Sasaki Roshi's method was to constantly throw his students into the icy water of Zen. His aim? To dispel the veil of illusions that separates you from clear and limpid life. His weapons? Zazen, koans, and a fierce sense of humour. His strategy? Never to give you a moment's rest. In his monasteries, life therefore unfolded like nowhere else in the world, except of course every other Zen monastery.[5] Days begin with an early rise (several hours before dawn), followed by formal tea in the zendo plus an hour of sutra chanting (on a single note), followed by zazen: you sit on a black cushion and stop moving for two hours. Throughout the day, bells and gongs of all kinds, knocks on wood or metal signal more zazens, more kinhins (walking meditation), more rituals, more silent meals until the monks retire to their cabins — around nine — for a few hours of sleep. Every day, there's collective work or samu, practised in silence of course. When he is composing, Leonard is sometimes exempted from the latter, but he never abuses that privilege. So, he shovels snow and polishes floors, he cooks meals and paints sheds. If asked, he sweeps the pine needles from a whole side of the mountain with his toothbrush. Nothing special: Zen life.

At least once a month there is a dai-sesshin, a week of intensive silent practice to refocus the monks on their "body-mind." You get up at three to meditate more and sleep less, you attend teishos (or teachings) every day as well as four very short face-to-face interviews with the master — called sanzen — to check if the koans he has given you are working well. Three times ten minutes of free time allow you to smoke a cigarette and the day ends with five hours of sleep unless the roshi has decided to extend the last zazen until late at night. The regime is exhausting, but it's meant to be. The purpose is to loosen everything rigid about you: your preferences, your opinions, and that old donkey head called the ego.[6]

Every December, to celebrate the Buddha's awakening, the centre organizes a rohatsu sesshin, seven days of constant meditation from 4 a.m. to late at night. Traditionally, on the last night you don't sleep or leave the dojo; you stay on your cushion and play Buddha. This sesshin has a bad reputation among Zennists — it is nicknamed the "monk killer."[7] In the '90s, the rohatsu will kill Leonard six times in a row. Luckily, he had seven lives.

Rinzai Zen, therefore, is hardcore Buddhism. Its ambition is to generate vigorous breakthroughs into awakening and to radically emancipate you from the fear of death or — even better — from the fear of life. Hence that necessary flavour of military academy that made Leonard repeat everywhere that he had joined the "marines of spirituality." And in truth, there's little difference between your average paratrooper and a Zennist. Both train to jump into the void; the Zen marine just does it without a parachute and the void he jumps into is called sunyata, the marvellous emptiness and impermanence of things which is life itself. Like your average marine, a Zen monk is also taught a thousand ways to kill: he must kill every Buddha and patriarch he meets, and — like every soldier in the world — become an expert in the art of sweeping barracks.[8]

After years of "sitting in the fire" and "sleeping with the wind" (as Leonard once summarized practice at Mount Baldy[9]), the student usually starts to perceive the intrinsic emptiness of things and sees that this emptiness includes him. He has reached the other shore: awakening.[10] Then he returns to self-based living and reaches the other shore again. And again, and again, and again. A thousand times, until he no longer knows on which side of enlightenment he stands. He has then crossed what Master Mumon called the "gateless gate" of Zen: he is free at last and fully awake.

A long time before leaving civilian life, Leonard had reminded an English journalist that "we can be destroyed by mindless frivolity as surely as by obsessive depression."[11] We stand reassured: there's little risk of that on Mount Baldy. Speaking to an unnamed girlfriend, he had joked about it on the last record:

> You wouldn't like it, baby,
> you wouldn't like it here
> There's not much entertainment
> and the judgements are severe
> The maestro says it's Mozart,
> but it sounds like bubble-gum.
> When you're waiting for the miracle
> for the miracle to come.[12]

BEWARE OF THE FOX[13]

Rinzai Zen is not an abstraction. You live it in the flesh, in direct transmission from a master who, for the most part, is there to kick your ass. And to be fair, the love story between Leonard and

Buddhism is mostly a story between him and an old man about whom he had often said, perhaps with a wee bit of exaggeration, that he just *happened* to be a Zen master. Had he been a physics teacher in Heidelberg, Leonard (so he liked to say) would have learnt German and studied quantum physics.

Born in a peasant family in 1907, Kyozan Joshu Sasaki entered novicehood at the age of fourteen under the tutelage of Joten Soko Miruwa Roshi and was ordained priest at twenty-one. When he arrived in the United States without too much luggage in July 1962, just in time to guide baby boomers on the path to enlightenment, he had already taught for thirty years, been the chief abbot of two temples (one in Tokyo, one in the Japanese Alps), and received dharma transmission or inka shomei, which certified he was not just a teacher but a fully-fledged roshi, the equal of past masters, in direct link with Rinzai, Hakuin, and the other patriarchs, all the way to Bodhidharma and Shakyamuni Buddha. Before he left Japan for the United States, where a small Buddhist group was asking for a teacher, he formally vowed to die abroad, spreading Zen. Fully credible rumours later circulated that his masters actually wished to get rid of an uncontrollable maverick.

Firmly rooted in the tradition of irreverence and crazy wisdom specific to Rinzai, Sasaki's iconoclastic teaching quickly attracted many American students. For a few years, he taught in a small private house in Gardena, California, with the garage as the zendo. By 1968, he had bought a 1930s villa and turned it into a temple, Rinzai-Ji on Cimaron Street, Los Angeles, which he ran in traditional Rinzai fashion. In 1970, he added a retreat camp (a former scout camp in the San Bernardino Mountains, soon to be known as MBZC or Mt. Baldy Zen Center) and another one called Bodhi Mandala in Jemez Springs three years later. Disciples soon started opening their own Zen centres (where the roshi was often asked to teach) in Santa Monica, San Diego, Vancouver, as well as on the East Coast (Princetown and Ithaca). Later, centres were opened in Puerto Rico, Montreal, and Europe.

By all accounts, Joshu Sasaki was an unpredictable, iconoclastic old fox who could be your best friend or your worst enemy. Able to rent a coach to drive his students to the nearest McDonald's to cure them of their attachment to vegetarianism, to prescribe tennis lessons to Leonard (he knew how to work, but not how to play), or to tell the American Buddhist magazine *Tricycle* in an interview for his hundredth birthday, "I'm a hundred and I no longer hear stupid questions,"[14] Sasaki Roshi was also an intellectual of sorts who for fifteen years organized seminars on the Sutras, led interreligious retreats with Christian monks, and developed modelizations of Buddhist concepts that combined mathematics and erotic metaphors. He particularly insisted on two ideas: the Self is only a moment of Non-Self (it is therefore not necessary to actively reject it) and the impermanence of things is a perpetual contraction and expansion of the world. A *zero* that constantly manifests as one, two, three, four, five, six, seven, eight and nine, before going back to zero. He also routinely warned his disciples not to let themselves be fooled by "this old fox."

For many years, actually decades, the old fox also used sanzen — the personal meetings with disciples — to extract sexual favours from young female students under the guise of teaching them true love, letting go, and selflessness, something which, when a Zen website first published testimonies in November 2012 under the loaded title "Everybody Knows," caused a major scandal that all but ruined Sasaki's reputation when the scandal hit the *New York Times*. More damage ensued when further investigations established not only the pervasiveness of the master's behaviour (it concerned dozens if not hundreds of young women over several decades) but also the repeated efforts of senior monks to silence and ostracize whoever objected or spoke up. So the roshi was right: beware of the fox. Foxes are predatory creatures — what they love, they seize.[15]

As for Leonard, the fox regularly bit his ass, but they were on friendly terms. Leonard loved Sasaki the way you love a teacher, a father, a grandfather, a friend, a baby, a puzzle, and a pet. In the years they spent together on the mountain, often drinking cognac, the master would fire questions at his most famous disciple.

Question number one: Leonard Cohen tries to catch the moon reflection in the water. Can he catch it? Question number two: Leonard the ox goes through a window. His head, legs, and body have gone through. Why can't his tail pass? Question number three: One Leonard Cohen went to Mount Baldy; another one stayed in L.A. Which is the real one? And — the most essential question of all — does Leonard Cohen have Buddha-nature?

So, little by little, Leonard allowed himself to be polished by the wisdom of his master, which was also his own. Zen claims there is a great intuitive natural wisdom called hannya shingyo, i.e. "a great wisdom," that inhabits us all and can never be completely obscured. It just needs to be awoken and that's what the practice is for. In his years up the mountain, Leonard understood that if Zen practice is hard, it is also secretly funny and that it is inhuman only to make your humanity blossom.[16] He also got that it is entirely normal to be desperately waiting (like he was) for the end of every zazen or for a miracle to happen in the zendo (for example, that a lithe young woman burst in to deliver him from this hell). But since such things never happen and given zazen's well-known capacity to be interminable, the waiting usually dissolved, and Leonard sometimes found he was just where he needed to be — right in the heart of life, singing the praises of his master:

> Roshi cared so deeply about who I was, or he deeply
> didn't care — I was never quite sure. Let's just say he
> so passionately didn't care that 'who I was' began to

dissolve, to be replaced by much more interesting versions of myself.[17]

But although Mount Baldy is at the right altitude to meet angels — a famous French magazine cover claimed the singer, who was shown on the cover in black robes and Nike sneakers against the blue sky and snowy peaks, lived "between Heaven and Earth"[18] — angels are rare in Zen. During his six-year-long stay, Leonard had therefore many opportunities to ponder on what another maverick poet-monk called Ikkyū had declared six centuries before:

> I would have loved to give you sweets,
> but alas, the Zen school offers nothing.[19]

And yet, Zen in high doses inevitably makes everything vast. Your breathing, your suffering, your joy, your gratitude, the brotherhood you feel for the other monks. At some point, each of these things takes on the size of the world. Then it dissolves again into the great emptiness of things, which is also their full accomplishment.

Zen also makes all things clear: the seasons become clear, as do the contours of each day — ideally shaped out by the schedule. So does the taste of green tea or ginger cognac. Also clear, in their indisputable *suchness*, are the owl's hoot or the icy rain that pierces your heart now and then. And as you sit in silence for hours on end, what structures your inner life becomes very clear, indeed. You cannot escape it and you *really* get to know "what's going on below" and how tiresome the ego's favourite games can be. Hence, for Leonard, great moments of clarity: Mount Baldy exhausts him; Mount Baldy bores him; Mount Baldy fills him with joy or anger. Some nights, Mount Baldy has him howl for love with the coyotes or wax comical when, for example, the old shaven-headed rock star ironically notes that:

It's dismal here
the only thing I don't need,
is a comb.[20]

In his lonely cabin, Leonard writes a lot — mostly satirical poems about the monastery and its incongruous life. Or poignant poems about the persistence of desire or the temptation to pull your brain out through your nose with a knitting needle.[21] He also writes a few songs, in particular "A Thousand Kisses Deep" which goes through a thousand incarnations up the mountain. Meanwhile, life goes on: young nuns fall in love with him; he gives advice to beginners (basically, kill both spiders and mystics for both are poisonous);[22] he beats the cook at arm wrestling and almost dies of laughter when the roshi declares after falling asleep in front of a pornographic movie Leonard wanted to show him that

study human love interesting
but not so interesting.[23]

He also receives a few visits: a journalist or two, his daughter, his son (now a fully-fledged songwriter), his manager Kelly Lynch who needs some papers signed, and a couple of orthodox Lubavitcher rabbis who turn up one day to save him from Buddhism and leave the place puzzled but reassured after finding a menorah in the cell of the most Jewish Zen monk in the world.

HOSPITAL OF DESIRE

For Sasaki Roshi, a monastery is a hospital where the master cures the illusion that you are sick.[24] In the case of "Kone," the diagnosis was made years before: "needs more Buddhism." His sickness? Multiple obsessions, especially about female bodies (a condition obviously shared by the Roshi[25]) and his depressive tendencies (doctors in L.A. had apparently diagnosed bipolarity), but mostly

Leonard had an unwholesome taste for burdens. Hence the need to return again and again to square one: the Buddha's four noble truths. Truth number one: unease and suffering permeate every life. Truth number two: selfish desire is the cause of all suffering. Truth number three: it is possible to put an end to this desire and therefore to suffering. Truth number four: there is a method for doing that, which is called the "eightfold path," which in Rinzai Zen consists essentially of an uninterrupted succession of zazens, kinhins, and koans. On August 6, 1996, halfway through Cohen's stay up the mountain, an important ceremony took place. The author of "Suzanne" took the monk's vows and, for the first time, he put on the kolomo, an impressive black robe with impossibly long sleeves. Inspired by a twelfth-century archer's costume, the garment made him look strikingly like a Jedi knight. As for Sasaki Roshi, who had just entrusted Leonard with the honour of conducting his future funeral, he looked like Master Yoda, but then he usually did. That day, he also acted the part and gave his disciple a new name, his dharma name: "Jikan," which, despite many journalists' claims does not mean "the silent one," but (according to the roshi's reluctant explanations) "ordinary silence." Not a bad choice for a poet and a singer — the old fox obviously had a sense of humour.[26]

As funeral executor, Jikan would be allowed to keep (should he wish to) one of his master's bones as a souvenir. Now who said the Zen School offered nothing? Perhaps this was to remind Leonard that he had the same Buddha nature as Joshu's dog, the most famous dog of Buddhism.[27] So, does Leonard Cohen have Buddha-nature? The answer was given fifty years before by the poet's childhood dog: Mu! Mu! Mu! Mu!

THE PHOTOGENIC MONK

As season followed season, Leonard gradually put his artistic activities on hold. For a while, he had considered writing an album of eight lightweight songs but called it quits after the second title.[28] Meanwhile, his manager Kelly Lynch made sure his career continued without him, with a Leonard Cohen–stamped product for sale almost every year. In 1993, it was a long-overdue anthology called *Stranger Music*.[29] In 1994, it was *Cohen Live*, a record covering the last two tours. The year 1995 was devoted to Lynch's pet project *Tower of Song*, a dispensable tribute album on which the likes of Elton John, Billy Joel, and Bono sing transparent M.O.R. versions of the master's classics.[30] And 1997 couldn't end without a modest compilation poetically called *More Best Of*— enough to keep his name alive.

Each time, the singer took time off from the monastery for a week or two of promotion on both sides of the Atlantic and, each time, the news spread a little more: Leonard Cohen had left the world. The proof? He had just been seen in Paris or London but was only passing through. At the beginning, his absence was discreet (he had never made his retirement official) but, little by little, journalists sniffed out the trail and, intrigued by the romantic idea of a sixty-year-old Casanova in a monk's robe, they finally drove up the mountain to interview the ex-singer.

The first to arrive were the American Buddhists of the *Shambhala Sun* in January 1994 but in France, the news broke out in March 1995 with the aforementioned cover of *Les Inrockuptibles* and an announcement: a Zen monk was born; his name was Leonard; he was sixty years old, about 130 pounds and in very good health. *Elle* followed suit, speaking of a "singing monk," while the Italian weekly *La Nazione* described a "virtue-less monk." As for Sylvie Simmons, she wittily called Leonard "felonious monk" in a later interview for *Mojo Magazine*.[31]

After the press came film crews. First for a French documentary that Leonard couldn't say no to. The director — a Parisian femme fatale called Armelle Brusq — had recorded a pop song entitled "Couché contre toi" and *that* alone deserved an interview. Shot in the fogs of Mount Baldy and in the glare of the Los Angeles sun, her brilliant film *Leonard Cohen: Spring 1996* featured the poet successively enjoying an ice cream cone, declaring his faith in military education, and brilliantly explaining how a love that doesn't settle on a single object can illuminate the world.[32]

The following year, Swedish journalist Stina Lundberg Dabrowski spent two autumnal days up Mount Baldy in Leonard's company. He served her whisky, called her "sweetheart," and gave one of his best interviews ever and a splendid performance as hardened monk, proud to show the kyosaku or "awakening stick" that is struck on the shoulders of sleepy monks during zazen. Soon after, in October 1997, the poet was again interviewed for Canadian, French, and Polish television,[33] but the highlight of that autumn was a program called *Beautiful Losers* for the French-German channel *Arte*. It featured a shaven-headed Leonard interviewed in his sparse L.A. kitchen in black suit and tie. Sitting in front of a glass of ouzo and fiddling with a komboloi, he explained that unless we rebuilt the hospitality of the world from moment to moment, we could not truly inhabit our lives. Judging by the grim smiles he gave that day, he was not quite there yet.[34]

Each time though, there was plenty of humour and Leonard, then in his mid-sixties,[35] was in great dialectical form, improvising on his pet themes (the broken heart, the consolation of song) with ease and grace. His rare smiles were irresistible but, watching him, you felt that this man was not spending every minute in what Saint Francis had called "the perfect joy." There was anguish in his eyes and a tightness about the jaw. Jikan didn't know it yet, but in a little over a year he would leave the monastery in a state of panic. In the meantime, he had decided to give up all antidepressants. "If I am going to go down," he told Sylvie Simmons, "I am going to go down with my eyes open."[36]

LAST PANIC ATTACK BEFORE AWAKENING

If you don't cross the barrier of Zen, you will be like a ghost
clinging to grass and tree branches.
— MUMON EKAI, *The Gateless Gate*

"Did you ever go clear?" is what the speaker asks his friend in "Famous Blue Raincoat." In Scientology vocabulary, it roughly means, "Have you dissolved the opacity of your existence?" All unhealthy curiosity about the spiritual state of others aside, the question may seem relevant in view of the serenity of Cohen's next album *Ten New Songs*: did the man actually go clear on Mount Baldy?

Like every Zen concept, enlightenment is both a very simple notion and one that radically resists language.[37] The explicit aim of Rinzai Zen is to vigorously bring students to the realization that they are already — and have always been — the equals of all the Buddhas of the past, of the present, and of the future, "Buddha" meaning "awakened one." In other words, they are already awake. Which doesn't mean they don't need alarm clocks or regular wake-up calls. A good way to grasp the concept of "awakening" is to examine what sleep it is supposed to interrupt. There's of course the sleep of selfish desire, which makes us crave for objects that are incapable of satisfying us, and the sleep of illusion, which prevents us from seeing our lives and the world as they truly are, everybody's favourite illusion being the "ego," a series of fixed beliefs about ourselves that we seem to strangely cling to although they isolate us from our true selves, from others and, ultimately, from our lives.

Traditional Buddhist texts claim that maintaining that fiction of a substantial and separate "ego" whose originality must be recognized by all and celebrated at all costs is what keeps us in a perpetual cycle of rebirths through the six realms of illusion and desire (also known as *samsara*), making our life a constant journey from greed to contentment to anger to fear. A cyclical journey that is just a way of avoiding the only question that really matters: not "what am I?" but "what am I not?"[38]

In Zen, awakening is said to come first through a series of kenshos, moments when our true nature (emptiness, impermanence, and interdependence) is abruptly revealed. In traditional stories, it happens to monks when they hear an owl screech, or when they bump into a hard rock, or the full moon on the way to the zendo at four in the morning, as must have happened countless times to Leonard. Then comes satori, the enlightenment that makes everything clear and brings true emancipation. The reaching of the other shore. Leonard loved to play — as he did in an interview for a Canadian news program — with the connotations of the English term: how *enlightenment* gracefully hangs in English between "light" and "lightness":

> That's what enlightenment means: to lighten up. You've lightened up. Don't hold yourself so solid. Don't take the predicament so seriously, don't fixate yourself in relation to some problem.[39]

So, Leonard says, awakening is basically that you get the joke. The big cosmic joke God played on you. And the still bigger joke that you have played on yourself: the joke of the ego. And when you get the joke, the face lights up, you smile again and it's instant illumination. You look ten years younger — you've lightened up.

But although everyone is free to believe the traditional Zen tales about awakening that seizes you with a summer breeze or a stroke of lightning, satori — which is a very radical form of letting go — is not something that just happens; it takes some serious spiritual training. Plus, there's something of ourselves that we must give up on the way and giving up anything — especially what we think we are — involves its share of fear. This is why Zen masters sometimes compare awakening to a poisonous snake: when it bites you, something must die.[40] Now, as Leonard has often said in interviews, "Everybody wants to go to heaven, nobody wants to die" and that includes him, of course. So, although the poet went from one feeling to another at Mount Baldy, from euphoria to boredom to gratitude to unfathomable serenity, his stay on the mountain ended with a new scary plunge into the night. Apparently, so Leonard later confided to Sylvie Simmons, everything fell apart in the autumn of 1998. Leonard was sixty-four and no Beatles song was going to cheer him up. The night was dark and he no longer knew what he was doing up there or understood what the roshi was saying. Maybe he was just tired. Tired of pretending to be a marine, tired of getting up at 3 or 4 a.m., tired of Roshi's pidgin English and of the way he played with his mind, tired of sleeping in Sasaki's closet to take better care of him (as he had lately come to do[41]). Dark night of the soul, act five. After a few weeks of dismay comes a radical decision: Jikan would leave the mountain and return to civilian life. Permission was reluctantly granted by the Roshi, who later told the singer that half of him died when his famous disciple left. But in January 1999, the poet left Mount Baldy in a state of intense anxiety. "I couldn't breathe" is what he told his friend Eric Lerner.[42]

RAMESH

I know your burden's heavy
as you wheel it through the night
the guru says it's empty
but that doesn't mean it's light.

— LEONARD COHEN, EARLY VERSION OF "THE STREET"[43]

A few hours after hanging his kolomo on the peg of his shed, Leonard was on a plane. Direction: the other side of the world. To be precise: Mumbai. He was looking for Ramesh S. Balsekar, a former bank manager who had become a guru in the Vedanta tradition and whose books intrigued him. As soon as he arrives, he settles in the Kemps Corner Hotel, a discreet two-star hotel near the Arabian Sea and for a few months attends the teachings (or sastangs) that the guru delivers every morning at his home. A disciple of Nisargadatta Maharaj, Balsekar teaches a form of Hindu non-dualism called Advaita, which is largely compatible with the Buddhist worldview, but his methods and metaphors are very different from Joshu Sasaki's.[44] Balsekar's great credo is that existence is a play written, staged, and produced by God — we are just the actors who unfold the fable to keep him entertained.[45] Which means that free will is an illusion and that we must radically abandon the very notion of "personal action" — we do things, but we are not "doers." Actions are done through us. Once we have fully accepted this (so the guru claims), we can finally relax and enjoy life as it is with spontaneous humility and natural compassion for ourselves and others. A motto? No pride when the world asserts you, no shame when the world lets you down. In other words: relax, this is God's world.[46]

The path set forth by Balsekar requires no hard discipline: just sit silently for a few minutes every day, attend a few of his one-hour lectures and Q&A sessions which are usually conducted with a lot of humour, and perhaps chant a mantra or two now and then. The guru deters you from following his teaching for too long. After a while, just go home and live your life. But Leonard has nothing special to do in L.A. So he stays for eleven or twelve weeks. Every morning, he walks to the guru's home and sits on cushions with other students in Balsekar's living room. The rest of the day, he reprises his role a Baudelairean flâneur, enjoying the crowds, sounds, and smells of Mumbai, visiting synagogues, taking a daily swim in the Arabian Sea, and eating vegetarian meals. He also starts smoking again. He ends the day with some lightweight reading (the *Baghavad Gita* with Ramesh's commentaries) and perhaps some writing. And relatively quickly, a miracle happens. At first, like all miracles, it is undetectable. But soon, there's no denying it: Leonard feels lighter. Then lighter still. He sits in front of the ocean with no anguish at all — he actually likes what he sees, likes where he is. Then, one day, he understands. He has stopped resisting life. The burden has lifted. So, in his small nondescript room, he grabs a sheet of Kemps Corner Hotel note-paper and writes a letter to his Japanese master:

> Dear Roshi,
> I am dead now
> I died before you
> Just as you had predicted
> in the early '70s.[47]

A short and precise report. It's done. I finally got it and I am dead. Thank you for everything.

Two years later, when Leonard reappeared in public with what was his brightest record to date, there was a constant smile on his face, a smile which surely had not been seen that frequently since he was nine. Hence an interesting conclusion: in Eastern religions, the dead smile. Which makes sense: they die only as individuals that were struggling with existence and are immediately reborn as sparks of divine light. Leonard would often joke about it in interviews — it took him six years in the monastery and months of listening to a guru in India to understand that he had no aptitude for religious life (oops!).

The same year, Leonard visits his Hydra house for the first time since God knows when and spends a couple of weeks there, writing. Writing lyrics that would appear on his next album. Lyrics about people who never stop disappearing ("Alexandra Leaving") or about how God uses the suspended dust in beams of light to give a name to people who have lost theirs ("Love Itself"). Back in Los Angeles, he proposes a game to his friend Sharon Robinson (the co-writer of "Everybody Knows"): what about writing a record together? Master Sōkō Morinaga mentions something he calls the "samadhi of play," which is basically a state of liberation that comes when you consider every activity (no matter how mundane and ordinary) as a game.[48] This is how Leonard will choose to live for a while. The rules of the particular game he wants to play with Sharon Robinson are the following: let's pretend there's no need to actually come up with the goods. Let's have delicious lunchbreaks and work as slowly as we wish and in optimum conditions. For example, in the luminous home studio full of Indian carpets that the singer has just set up above his garage, a place he will soon baptize "still-life studio." In that room in 2000 and 2001, Leonard and Sharon will put ten miraculous songs on tape.

The work will often be interrupted. But not by breakdowns this time; by travels. For at the age of sixty-six, Leonard has indeed resumed his old career as a voyageur sans bagage. So, he's in L.A., he's in Mumbai, he's in Montreal, he's in Japan. He's back. He starts Zen again, but no longer as a self-punishing monk, but like a passerby who just wished to sit in the temple and enjoy the breeze. And interestingly — another miracle — his voice changes again: still vibrant enough to shake the earth, but now integrating a slightly unvoiced quality — the meeting in the voice of Heaven and Earth. Graf Durckheim, a German scholar with a passion for Buddhism, had once defined enlightenment as "an altitude that places you simultaneously above everything and in the heart of life."[49] That's the place that Leonard is starting to inhabit. And it feels like going home.

C. LEBOLD

this guy's getting too tough
for us
we're not going to
be able to call him
a poet much longer

I'm afraid he's
leaving everything
behind

and he's wearing
his Star Trek uniform

I don't think
he's coming back

02/08/03

"Too Tough for Us," self-portrait, 2003.

The Cohen family home, 599 Belmont Avenue, Westmount, Montreal.

LADIES AND GENTLEMEN ... MR. LEONARD COHEN (1965) | NATIONAL FILM BOARD OF CANADA

"This guy is getting too tough for us . . ." A young Cohen on his tricycle, circa 1938.

C. LEBOLD

The Shaar Hashomayim synagogue (Westmount, Montreal), where, as a child, Cohen shivered when the rabbi lifted up the Torah.

ECCO | AUTHOR'S COLLECTION

The medal below combines the singer's signature seal of intertwined hearts with the "birkat kohanim," the Jewish priestly blessing from the *Book of Numbers*.

AUTHOR'S COLLECTION

Let Us Compare Mythologies (1956). The title of Cohen's first book defined a spiritual program that he carried out his whole life, and that helped him combine a deep attachment to his native Judaism with a lifelong love of the Virgin and his later forays into Zen Buddhism, Sufi, and Advaita traditions.

"Our Lady of the Harbour." A seventeenth-century Virgin Mary at Notre-Dame-de-Bon-Secours Chapel (Montreal), where the poet liked to sit in the 1960s.

AUTHOR'S COLLECTION

Credit: Harry Hess
Leonard Cohen, author of "The Favorite Game,"
which Viking will publish September 12.

Publicity shot for Cohen's first
novel, *The Favourite Game.*

"And Jesus was a sailor . . ."
Montreal street scene
featuring Dunn's Delicatessen
on Sainte-Catherine Street,
where the young Cohen
performed his poetry to the
accompaniment of jazz music
in 1958.

The first edition of *The Spice-Box of Earth* (1961), featuring Frank Newfeld's artwork (insert).

Hydra landscape
(Charles Gurd,
early 1970s).

A smiling Leonard by
Ralph Gibson, circa 1973.

Leonard arrived on the
Greek island of Hydra in
the spring of 1960. There,
he joined the bohemian
crowd and spent the next
eight years commuting
between Montreal and
Greece. He would stay
on the island frequently
until the mid-1980s.

Hydra: paradise regained and a cubist masterpiece.

LEONARD COHEN

Flowers for Hitler

Above: House #764, bought by Cohen for $1,500 two days before his twenty-sixth birthday.

Left: The poet's provocatively titled fourth book (1964).

Above: The necessary angel. Leonard's companion and lover Marianne Ihlen-Jensen with the poet's Olivetti typewriter, early 1960s (back cover of *Songs from a Room*).

Right: Vegetables and paper sheets: Leonard caught shopping in 1975.

BEAUTIFUL LOSERS

LEONARD COHEN

Above: Leonard, Marianne, and their French friend Lisette captured in a happy moment by Leonard's Hydra friend and neighbour, Dinnie Blair (1964).

Right: The first edition of *Beautiful Losers* (1966). Leonard's hallucinated masterpiece follows the spiritual quest of three beat characters in love with Kateri Tekakwitha, a seventeenth-century Iroquois saint. Fuelled by amphetamine and despair, Leonard wrote the book in Hydra in 1965.

Sainte-Catherine Street, 1964.

Back in Montreal, Leonard —
who had taken up songwriting
in Hydra — writes an ode
to the bohemian dancer
Suzanne Verdal in lyrics about
an undercover angel who
exposes the world's deep
thirst for love. The song got
Leonard some attention when
versions by Judy Collins and
Noel Harrison hit the U.S.
charts in 1967, paving the way
for his debut album.

"And you want to travel blind . . ." Suzanne Verdal at the
Montreal café Le Bistro in 1967.

In Cohen's peripatetic life as a singer-songwriter, hotel rooms were sanctuaries but also places of courtship and introspection where much writing was done.

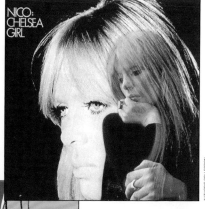

AUTHOR'S COLLECTION

Above: *Chelsea Girl* (1967) by Nico. Cohen's painful passion for the German singer inspired several songs on his debut album.

SLAIGHT FAMILY POLARIS HERITAGE PRIZE

LEONARD COHEN

SONGS of LEONARD COHEN

© LAUREN TAMAKI

In her 2016 poster for *Songs of Leonard Cohen*, Lauren Tamaki captures the poet in his favourite position: as a philosopher observing life from a hotel room window — the metaphysical private eye.

For the poet, Manhattan was first a compendium of solitude he had to confront. Here, the New York Telephone Company building on West Street.

NEW YORK PUBLIC LIBRARY

The Chelsea Hotel on 23rd Street, New York. Together with the Henry Hudson and Penn Terminal, the Chelsea was one of Cohen's haunts in the late 1960s.

Angels mating in a sixteenth-century alchemical treatise — an image that fascinated the poet.

The man who saw the angels fall — Leonard in a Montreal hotel room, November 1964.

A sleepy Marianne by Nick Broomfield (UK, 1969).

"So Long, Marianne." Cohen's first album established his early persona as a romantic poet and existential troubadour. It also marked the twilight of his relationship with Marianne.

He says he's bored. Isn't that just beautiful?

*"TEAR" REPRODUCED COURTESY OF McCLELLAND & STEWART LTD AND COLUMBIA RECORDS (MONO 473, 84982 [PLEASE NOTE THAT THERE IS NO STEREO REFERENCE NUMBER AS THE POEMS WON'T ALLOW IT]).

Leonard as Lord Byron, drawn by Terry Mosher, 1969.

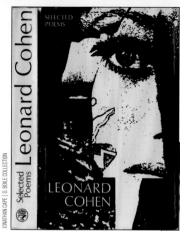

The success of Cohen's first opus established him as an international pop star. In 1969, he was awarded (and famously declined) a Governor General's Award for *Selected Poems*.

Selected Poems (1956–1968). Spurred by the singer's success, the book would sell 200,000 copies. Right: "Did you ever go clear?" In 1968, Cohen had a brief fling with Scientology. He can be seen here at a Dianetics course in New York.

Around 1969, Cohen relocated to a log cabin in Big East Fork, fifteen miles outside Nashville, Tennessee (exact location pictured above). He recorded two albums in that city with producer Bob Johnston and a band, The Army, that toured with him in 1970 and 1972 (see ad).

GESSER ENTERPRISES & PAUL SALTZMAN PRESENT

LEONARD COHEN
and
THE ARMY
WED. DEC. 9 at 8.30 p.m.
$3, 4, 5, 6
COLUMBIA RECORDING ARTIST
– now on sale –

SALLE WILFRID-PELLETIER
PLACE DES ARTS, Montreal 129 (Quebec) Tel 842-2112

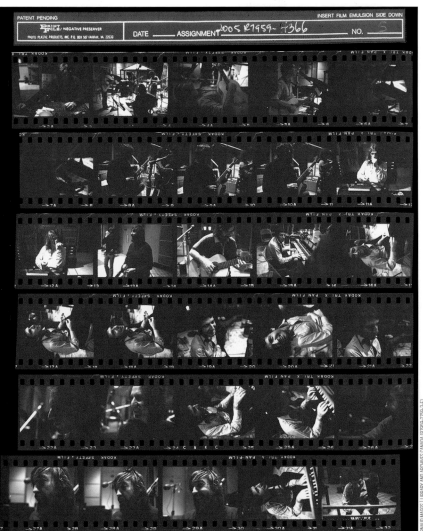

ARNAUD MAGGS | LIBRARY AND ARCHIVES CANADA (R7959-2759-3-F)

Rehearsal for the 1972 tour with
Bob Johnston and Ron Cornelius
(Nashville, March 1972).

Samstag, 19. Juni 1976, 20 Uhr · Schwarzwaldhalle Karlsruhe

The Poet of Rock-Music

LEONARD COHEN

Durchführung: Concert Management Schleifer, Karlsruhe

| DM 9.– zuzügl. Vorverk.geb. | Block G | Reihe 29 | Sitz 377 * |

Kontrollabschnitt   LEONARD COHEN   377 *

So. 19. 6. 76, 20 Uhr. Schwarzwaldhalle Karlsruhe
Karten ohne Kontrollabschnitt sind ungültig !
Kein Rückerstattungsanspruch, außer bei Absage !

D. BOLE COLLECTION

Ticket stub for a German concert featuring "The Poet of
Rock Music" (1976).

Suffering for fun and profit

The return of Leonard Cohen.
By MICK BROWN.

THE POSTER outside the Colston Hall, Bristol announced the appearance that evening of 'The Poet of Rock and Roll'.

Inside a girl takes photographs of the road-crew setting up equipment on stage — for an art-project, she explains. She really wanted to photograph the concert, so she'd scrimped, saved, begged and borrowed enough to buy a couple of tickets. Now she can't make it on account of the revision she has to do for tomorrow's exams. She'd sold the tickets to friends in a matter of hours. She's all of sixteen years old.

LEONARD COHEN is clearly bemused by it all. He sits back in his dressing-room, issues a slight smile and says isn't it amazing that some of these people were only *eight years old* when he wrote his first song? Cohen is forty-one.

On stage, illuminated by

Backstage he looks strangely vulnerable; a thin, slight figure dressed in pressed slacks and a brown leather jacket, a cigarette burning between his fingers. One has heard that Cohen can be reserved to the point of being *difficult*. In fact he's extraordinarily charming, polite, approachable.

It is a rule of the road that he never gives interviews or holds audience before a performance, using those couple of hours before going on stage to summon-up reserves of energy and concentration for the task at hand.

After a performance he will talk, sign photographs and scraps of paper, receive gifts, kisses, handshakes. Gladly. He says he cherishes the attentions of his audience.

In Montreal he lives in an immigrant-worker neighbourhood where he's known only as a guy who has two kids and a small house and who never seems to be around very much.

In the small village in Greece where he also spends

in droves, thrusting programmes at the road-manager who brings them back signed. In the inner-sanctum Cohen holds court with a tribunal from a local college newspaper, hunched in a chair wreathed in cigarette-smoke, ringed by earnest, enquiring faces; a scatter of papers on the floor — Cohen's poems, which one of his inquisitor's has painstakingly copied by hand.

"What I'd *really* like to know is why your poetry is so stark, so incredibly blunt — a poem like for instance . . ." Cohen takes the proffered sheet, glances at the writing. "Yeah — I like that poem . . . If it didn't have the word 'cunt' in it I'd probably read it out loud on stage. But I'm not ready to say that word *well* enough yet. There are some things that are designed to rest on the page and not be spoken . . ."

"Do you use the same technique then for writing songs and poetry?"

"Yeah — just one word at a time . . ."

"To what extent then

forever is a long time . . ."

Leonard Cohen hasn't come back. He's never been away. While other performers tend to move, or even stand still, in a blaze of publicity, Cohen just keeps on toiling away quietly in what he calls his little corner — writing songs, sometimes; poems, sometimes; books, sometimes — all at his own pace.

Travelling . . . He's always been peripatetic — trace his career from Montreal, to New York, to Nashville, to Greece — but more so in the last six or seven years, "since I could afford the air-fares". He was in Ethiopia when "I just got to a place, check into a hotel and hit the streets." The Wandering Jew.

"But to tell you the truth I'm getting a little tired of all that now. A tour'll cure that for you for a while." Not that he tours often; he says he needs the nourishment of a private life more than anything touring can give him. But, for whatever reasons, this year he's been back on the road — a brief round of club dates in the southern American states, and now Europe, where he seems to enjoy a larger and more loyal following than anywhere else.

So far it's been sold-out houses all the way, and Bristol is no exception — a lot of older faces in the audience, people for whom 'Songs From A Room' was no doubt a soundtrack for sorrowful bedsit dramas all those years ago; a surprisingly large number of younger people who can't have been aware of Cohen first or second time around, but who've tuned into that finely-honed *angst* somewhere along the way; and a man in elfin boots, long hair and a cloak who stands up in one of those moments of pregnant, reverential silence which punctuate a Cohen performance and shouts out 'God bless you, Leonard' to crackle of sympathetic applause from the rest of the audience; an audience which, in short, substantiates the tag 'The Poet' more than the description 'Of Rock and Roll . . .'

The tour publicist says it's been like this everywhere Cohen has played, and it'll no doubt be the same tomorrow night when he plays the Albert Hall, even though he's

The four sides of Lenny . . . upended

Above: Cohen's radical change of perspective in the 1970s as he discovered the joys and servitudes of marital life, Zen Buddhism, and a new persona as a warrior/slave (*Sounds Magazine*, July 3, 1976).

THE ENERGY OF SLAVES LEONARD COHEN

The back and front cover of Cohen's 1972 collection of ironic masculinist anti-poems.

Left: The Smokey Life. Leonard's "dark lady," Suzanne Elrod, is also the mother of his children, Adam and Lorca.

As Cohen redefined his vision in the early to mid-1970s — and now sang songs of love *and* hate — two key players in his life were both partners and fierce adversaries. One was a Zen master, the other a ferociously independent young woman.

LEONARD COHEN
SONGS OF LOVE AND HATE

Above: "Me not Japanese. You not Jewish." Leonard's maverick Zen master, Joshu Sasaki Roshi (1907–2014).

Left: Songbook for Cohen's third album (1971).

"A shield against the enemy." In October 1973, Cohen sang for Israeli troops during the Yom Kippur War. He wrote several songs in the desert, including "Lover, Lover, Lover." Photographer Isaac Shokal was covering the war.

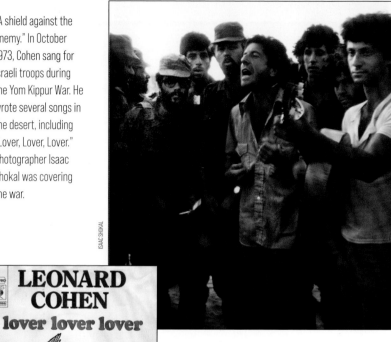

ISAAC SHOKAL

LEONARD COHEN
lover lover lover

who by fire

D. BOILE COLLECTION

Left: A debate with God and a hit single in Germany.

Below: With his personal life in shambles, Cohen fought an artistic war with psychopath producer Phil Spector in 1977. The baroque result — the aptly titled *Death of a Ladies' Man* — almost put an end to his career.

PHOTOGRAPHER UNKNOWN | AUTHOR'S COLLECTION

"And where is my gypsy wife tonight?" In 1978, as Suzanne leaves him for good, Leonard loses his mother. He starts work on *Recent Songs*, a noticeably more spiritual album that explores the themes of loss, transience, and dissolution. [Arnaud Maggs, Montreal, December 1977.]

"Zazen instruction series," Hydra, circa 1972, by Charles Gurd. Throughout the 1970s, Leonard intensified his Rinzai Zen practice. The second noble truth of Buddhism famously states that suffering is caused by selfish desire and belief in the Self, ideas that Cohen explores in his 1978 book, *Death of a Lady's Man* (top right).

Framed prints of the complete zazen instruction sequence (five images) are available at www.bmzc.org and sold for the benefit of Bodhi Manda Zen Center.

As his career gradually evaporates, Cohen settles in the late 1970s in a little house on rue Vallière (above) and starts commuting between Montreal, Hydra, Sasaki's American monasteries, and trips to France to see his children.

Above: Sainte-Catherine Street at night (undated).

Left: A happy moment with friend and lover Céline La Frenière in Los Angeles, 1977.

After his 1979–1980 tour, Cohen vanishes once again into avalanches and skirmishes with the dark angels of depression. He will not be seen on stage again until 1985 (as pictured above in Kalvøya, Norway).

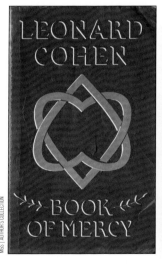

Hallelujah starts here. Written in a period of intense self-doubt, *Book of Mercy* (1984) celebrates the poet's half-century with fifty prayers that a critic called "psalms for unbelievers."

The Smokey Life, Act II. Leonard backstage by Christof Graf (Germany, 1979).

Portrait of a Lady. In the early 1980s, Leonard met French photographer Dominique Issermann on Hydra. Sharing a devotion to beauty, a strong work ethic, and a fierce sense of humour, they lived a transatlantic passion for seven years and remained friends and collaborators for life (picture by Leonard Cohen, Hydra, circa 1982).

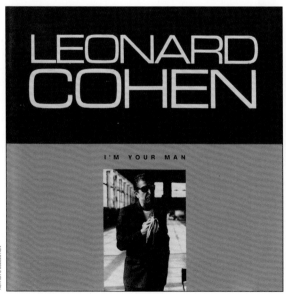

"All these songs are for you D.I." In 1988, the poet dedicated *I'm Your Man* to Dominique. With its decidedly chic and ironic cover featuring the Casanovian singer eating a banana, the album renews the troubadour theme of the first album with synthesizers, Buddhist satire of the ego, and what Cohen called "postmodern disco." It went #1 in Norway.

A poet at work (Dominique Issermann, circa 1982).

Lleida, Spain, 1988.

LEONARD COHEN
FIRST WE TAKE MANHATTAN

FOR PROMOTION ONLY - NOT FOR SALE

PRO 431

Thanks to a strong album, superb concerts, and a great music video, Leonard's 1988 world tour revitalized Cohen's art. His career plan — made explicit in the single "First We Take Manhattan" — was working well.

Eyes like ice, heart on fire. Cohen in his Los Angeles home by Renaud Monfourny (South Tremaine Avenue, 1991).

LEONARD COHEN

THE FUTURE

Barcelona, 1993. With a voice now toughened by a very strict diet of cigarettes, whisky, and looking into the abyss, Cohen's stage act was now both playful and deep as the singer alternately embodied a prophet of doom, a high priest of the heart, and an ironic crooner.

Famous Blue What? Cohen by Ron Watts, 1983.

"Teach us to care and not to care. Teach us to sit still" (T.S. Eliot). On the cover of his 1994 anthology of poems and lyrics, the singer prepares for zazen.

At the end of 1993, Cohen packed up his bags and joined Sasaki Roshi on Mt. Baldy. Formally ordained as "Jikan," he stayed as a resident monk for five years, acting as his master's personal assistant, cook, and drinking buddy.

Joshu Sasaki Roshi nearing his hundredth birthday in 2007.

Leonard Cohen on Mt. Baldy by Dana Lixenberg, 1995.

With depression never far from the picture, Leonard spent five years in the monastery honing his ability to observe the Self appear and disappear. Precious spiritual insights ensued: spring is sweet, winter cold.

Self-portrait, 2004.

Meditation hall at the Mt. Baldy Zen Center in winter.

DANA LIXENBERG

"Sleep, baby, sleep . . ." Leonard portrayed in a restful moment in his cabin by Dana Lixenberg.

After five years up on Mt. Baldy, Cohen finally escaped with a bunch of satirical poems and lyrics about love manifesting in sunbeams. Within days, he was in India studying Advaita spirituality with Ramesh S. Baslekar.

C. LEBOLD

"First, there is a mountain, then there is no mountain, then there is" (Donovan Leitch). A view of Mt. Baldy from the San Bernardino freeway.

"Enlightened, Moi?" Leonard Cohen at home in Montreal (Charla Jones, 2006). After his depression lifted in India, Cohen pursued his career with *Ten New Songs* (2001), an album of luminous beauty and a careful study of the nature of enlightenment. By the early 2000s, the poet seemed to have left the flames of purgatory and embraced the quiet fire of perfect joy.

The Anima Sola, an allegory of the souls in purgatory, as featured on the back cover of *Songs of Leonard Cohen*.

'Awe-inspiring ... Cohen emerges as the wry, sensual mystic his champions have always known he was'
SUNDAY TELEGRAPH

book of longing

LEONARD COHEN

Book of Longing, Cohen's first collection of new poems in twenty years featured a small bird that seemed ready to fly away. No wire this time.

OLYMPIA
BRUNO COQUATRIX

MUSIC - HALL
GERARD DROUOT PRODUCTIONS PRÉSENTE

LEONARD COHEN

Paris's Olympia music hall, 2012.

Soundcheck in Wiesbaden, Germany, 2010. Defrauded by his manager, Cohen was forced to start touring again in 2008. The following 367 concerts combined musical excellence with humour and spiritual depth. The show was universally celebrated as one of the best rock performances ever.

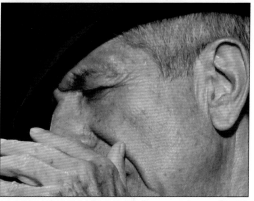

On stage in Lörrach, 2008.

If he is fire, then we must be wood. Cohen's posthumous volume, *The Flame* (2018), featured the poet's drawing of the burning bush.

As a born kohen, the singer had always considered his concerts spiritual experiments, but to the collective exploration of the dark night of previous tours, he now added a celebration of the fires of divine presence.

Fedoraed bodhisattva and Jewish high priest. Cohen reinvents the crooner as a spiritual figure on stage in Vigo, Spain, 2009.

D. BOILE COLLECTION

DANI DAPENA | FLICKR CC

Vigo, Spain, 2009. Now in his seventies, the singer engaged with the deeper dynamics of life and death and acted on stage both as a grocer of darkness and a bringer of light. He would soon learn that God wanted it darker.

POINTS | AUTHOR'S COLLECTION

Top: A merchandise box with Cohen's signature seal and totem hummingbird.

Bottom: Cohen giving the blessing on the French edition of *The Flame*.

CÉCILE CLAUSS

Soundcheck in Lörrach, 2008.

"Hineni, my Lord." Leonard on stage in Portland, 2010.

Left: Leonard Cohen's L.A. home.

Strong ties — the author and Leonard Cohen in Los Angeles, 2015.

Portrait of the artist as an archangel (Rino Noto, Toronto, 1992). Theologically, an archangel is a warrior angel sent to war by God. Leonard's wars — wars against all things dark — were fought as a poet, with the sword of the Logos.

CHAPTER 13

FEDORA BODHISATTVA

THE MAN CHANGED INTO AN ANGEL
2000–2013

The way of Heaven that acts without hindrance completes all beings. The virtue of the saint that operates without hindrance wins all hearts.

— ZHUANG ZHOU, *THE WAY OF HEAVEN*[1]

Leonard Cohen, Konstanz, May 1993

A MAN CHANGED INTO AN ANGEL

B enedictine monks aspired to live an angelic life. Constant prayer and chanting — plus a little wine at every meal — was supposed to help them become, as far as is humanly possible, the delegates of angels on Earth.[2] In October 2001, when Leonard Cohen reappeared with his new album, there was definitely something angelic about him. Journalists were struck by a certain extra radiance about him and felt that they had crossed paths, if not with an angel (an event theologians call "angelophany"), at least with someone who had spent time with them.

The extra radiance is obvious if we compare the previously mentioned interview by Diethard Küster in Leonard's kitchen in November 1997 and the one conducted in the Hotel Raphael in Paris by Stina Lundberg Dabrowski in October 2001.[3] It's obviously the same man, the same voice, the same grammar of gestures — the dialectician's hands that punctuate sentences, the frowning eyes that peer into the distance. And it's basically the same sense of humour and the same ideas: the broken heart; the irrepressible nature of desire; the need to dissolve the self. But there's a detail that changes everything: a tiny surplus of light. The man who speaks in 1997 is a general at war. Sipping a glass of ouzo at some distance from the front, he's obviously a brilliant strategist, but he isn't sure who's winning the war. He constantly mentions the intrinsic gravity of things and the prospect of a possible defeat. In 2001, the mood has lifted. It's almost imperceptible at first. It's in the tempo of the delivery, in the energy of the gestures, but mostly it's in the face: a sparkle in the eyes, an overall sense of brightness, and an almost irremovable smile that illumines every answer.

Religious iconography has always represented the inner light of saints and angels with a halo behind their heads, just as it has symbolized the angels' spiritual nature with wings. In 2001, the new Leonard, often equipped with a komboloi as though his life was now an uninterrupted prayer, has no visible wings, but there's a lightness about him. A burden has obviously lifted. Gone are the anguished eyes, the clenched jaw, and there's nothing heavy in the voice. Perhaps this is still a general, but one who commands cohorts of angels.

So, at least for a while, he has indeed become the cherubic pilgrim he had always aspired to be: a creature of light. For the moment, that creature travels from country to country to speak with journalists and spread clarity around him — the clarity of his carefully chosen word, the clarity of his mere presence, the clarity of his new electro-pop album. With its transparent title, the record *Ten New Songs* resembles him. It is sophisticated and relaxed and an act of light. Its subject: the unfathomable depth of our existence and our marvellous aptitude to disappear. Exactly what you would expect from a man who has just spent six years in a monastery and many months taking tea in India.

TEN NEW SONGS (2001): LEONARD'S DOUBLE LIFE

> *So come my friend, be not afraid.*
> *We are so lightly here*
> *It is in love that we are made,*
> *in love we disappear.*

> — LEONARD COHEN, "BOOGIE STREET"

Ten New Songs is the album of all awakenings. The monk formerly known as Jikan comes down from the mountain with ten songs and no commandments, determined to teach us a couple of things that will change our lives. But he will operate so discreetly that we will hardly notice. It's the politeness of Roshi Leonard — to awaken us surreptitiously.

On this album, he has two things to say. First, he was always right: love is an epiphany of light; resisting it is useless. Second, he was always wrong: the process is not a glorious pyre that illuminates the night, but a dissolution that happens a hundred times every day. There's nothing special about it. You embrace your beloved, you dissolve. You embrace your children, you dissolve. You experience the totality of life in one way or another, you dissolve.[4] But — and this is actually the real subject of the record — every time, you're back. Without delay. After twenty-five years of Zen practice and half a century of spiritual quest, Leonard is ready to explore the mechanism that gives the true tempo of our lives. It's a simple, binary pattern: you disappear, and you return. Nothing more.

We always know more or less what spiritual literature is going to tell, and *Ten New Songs* is no exception: the presence and absence of God, eternity in the moment and infinity in the flesh, the grip of love on our hearts. What else is there to say? Leonard's contribution is that his poetry and vision bend those ideas just enough to make them stimulating again. What's more, he has the honesty to say where he is speaking from — from the heart of a life that is filled with desire, delight, and disappointment. A life very similar to ours.

To understand the record, a detour via Singapore is necessary. There, the poet has discovered a street, perhaps during his recent bouts of travelling, called Bugis Street (a.k.a. "Boogie Street" for the Yankee soldiers during the Vietnam war). In the daytime, it's a market with cheap shops of all kinds. At night, the commerce is love with prostitutes and transvestites. And Leonard says this: like that street, we live two parallel lives. On the surface, our daytime existence: we wait in traffic jams, we carry burdens, we unfold our alibis — our small victories, our small defeats, and the whole gamut of the usual social comedy. But inside us, a secret life unfolds. As fluctuating as the social life, but more vibrant: the life of the heart. On *Ten New Songs*, Leonard studies collisions between the two existences — the collisions of *samsara* and *nirvana* — and he has three things to say, which is just enough to make his album luminous.

First, he claims that the second life — the hidden life — is in fact the first but that the mundane life is not less irreducible. We always return to it. We're always back to our conditioned selves, our obstinate opinions, our waits in traffic jams. Second idea: our mundane life, however cumbersome, is also incredibly light, since all it takes is a stirring in the deeper life — a tiny pain, a tiny joy — for it to disappear. Someone smiles at you and your social self is gone. You have once again joined the world of angels. Third idea: there is a divine force which gives us no rest and constantly moves us from one life to the other. The objective: to make us cross the barriers between surface and depth so many times that we can no longer tell what existence we are in. We can then live each life as if it was the other — the life of the heart with the lightness it requires, the futile life "as if it [was] real."[5]

BIRTH OF A BUDDHIST COOL

Organized according to a perfect geometry, *Ten New Songs* opens with "My Secret Life," the confession of a renegade who has abjured the life of the heart. He cheats and lies and smiles when he is angry. It closes with a universal prayer meant to announce the triumph of light and console the world ("Land of Plenty"). Halfway through, at the exact centre of the album, Leonard offers a theology of light disguised as a crooner's ballad, which is also a teisho (a Zen teaching) on the nature of love ("Love Itself").[6] Between these three cardinal points, the poet puts on many spiritual masks and uses the classic forms of spiritual literature — prayers, sermons, parables — to help us explore our secret lives. He is successively a Zen master who teaches the beauties of paradox, a kohen who reminds us that delving deep is our duty, and a bad monk who expounds on the comedy of his spiritual failure.

So we stand reassured. Leonard has not yet become a saint who frequents only angels. The record constantly takes us back to true life, to the fire of desire and the dizziness of falls. Hence Leonard's numerous self-portraits as someone who's still struggling: a stubborn monk reluctant to love; an inveterate erotomaniac; an inhabitant of Babylon in conflict with God; and an incurable drunk who agrees to "fight against the bottle" but only if he is allowed to "do it drunk."[7] It's part of his message: don't pay too much attention to signs of awakening — Zen and life dissolve everything, including the awakening of the wise. He's still a walking bordello. He's still puzzled by this God who raises us in grace but immediately makes us fall. The difference is that he now gets the joke. God is having fun with us. And if we release our grip, we can have fun with him. That's the good news on the album. "Gospel" means "good news" and *Ten New Songs* — Leonard's new gospel — is replete with good news, small and big. Examples? You can study the mystery of the world in a traffic jam ("Boogie Street"). You can be embraced by a God you no longer believe in ("You Have Loved Enough"). You can understand everything but still enjoy the mystery of each moment ("Love Itself"). And most importantly, there's this old Buddhist idea which tirelessly recurs — that ultimately nothing has any real substance (especially not ourselves) and that all things are very light. Life. Death. Our misfortunes. Our burdens. Our egos. All of them, light enough to let them go. Good to know? Good to know.

PARADISE EXISTS: IT'S AN ELECTRO BEAT

A question remains: how do you make a mystical record sound good? *Ten New Songs* is so perfect that the answer seems obvious: you use electro-pop. When the album was released, most reviews celebrated the happy marriage between Leonard's metaphysical lyrics and a suave soundscape that discreetly integrated trip-hop and electro-jazz in the spirit of Portishead, Goldfrapp, or Shade. You wanted a Zen master? You get a hypermodern crooner. Explanation:

> The virtue of these songs is to caress and comfort
> the listener. It is not necessary to go deep into what
> they whisper to you. You can let yourself be carried

by the groove, the general feeling. But the songs also have doors and windows and, if you feel like it or have the time, you can push a door and enter another room. I hope you like the furniture you will find there.[8]

It all began with a simple wish: that each song opens a space of consolation where the listener will feel protected for as long as the track lasts. A space where all is order, light, and beauty. A sonic utopia. An ephemeral paradise. In other words, a pop song. How is that done? Easy: a backbeat, a waltz melody, a voice as warm as fire and you're pretty much on your way.

Struck by the ways in which Leonard's voice now seemed to affirm the possibility of redemption, Sharon turned to the only music that seemed to fit: the one they call "soul," hence the strong bass lines, the combination of jazz and trip-hop, and those delicious, deeply relaxing ritournelles. In addition to the backing singers' usual grammar of "oohs" and "ahs," Sharon also sings in duet with Leonard on almost every track. God the Father speaks, a soulful angel accompanies him: a sonic cocktail called paradise.

The rest is just work — months spent in 2000 and 2001 on the Persian carpets of Leonard's home studio to find the shape of every song with a little help of a software program called Pro Tools. The singer would usually record vocals between 3 a.m. and 4 a.m. (before the dawn chorus of urban traffic and birds) and Sharon joined him a few hours later to work on arrangements. The result lived up to their expectations: ten pop gems, ten breakaways to heaven. We are in lounge territory throughout with a fine mix of electronic pop ("Here It Is," "By the Rivers Dark"), pure soul ("You Have Loved Enough"), hip-hop grooves ("Boogie Street"), soaring gospel ("Boogie Street"), suave blues-pop ("My Secret Life," courtesy of Bob Metzger's guitar), and, of course, crooner songs like "Alexandra Leaving," where Leonard sings like Frank Sinatra — words that Frank Sinatra would never have dared sing.

Defined by its author as "a little pop tune about death,"⁹ "Here It Is" encapsulates the spirit of the record. In the lyrics, Leonard, like Saint Francis of Assisi before him, invites us to welcome death as a friend, but he does it to the backdrop of a groovy bassline and female voices that make everything sweet. The message — an important one — is received as though it was the sweetest news ever: death is real, friends, but there's nothing to fear. *Ten New Songs* is the record no one expected anymore — a record defined by spiritual joy and endless humility.

It is said in Zen that it's important to eliminate the traces of your awakening. An awakening that you still notice is not awakening yet.¹⁰ Like a true bodhisattva, Leonard wraps his teaching (we are just ephemeral sparkles of light) in sweet sounds and makes it all sound very easy: gentle pop songs that are so angelic that they need no longer mention angels.

Launched in the autumn of 2001 with a vast promotional campaign and supported by an intriguing video for "My Secret Life" that featured a stylish fedora-wearing Leonard in a DS Citroën car observing the secret life of ordinary families (in this case, strange egg-headed creatures) in the concrete structures of the Habitat 67 housing complex in Montreal,¹¹ *Ten New Songs* met with great critical and commercial success. It went platinum and reached #4 in Canada, #3 in Sweden, #5 in Austria, and hit the top of the charts in Norway. Even in the United States, the album did not go entirely unnoticed, receiving, for example (it's never too late), an enthralled review by John Bauldie in *Rolling Stone*. But that is only fair — you can't resist a man who sings crooner songs about the similarity between our lives and the particles of dust in sunbeams.

Logically, this would be the right moment for a return to the stage, but 9/11 had killed that idea. After the attacks, Leonard disappeared once more, and since he now had the same nature as light, disappearing was easy. He intermittently grew a Hemingway-like beard (perfect for Starbucks, perfect for Hydra), exchanged his fedora for a newsboy cap (as a sign of mourning), and hit the road again, this time as an anonymous traveller constantly commuting between L.A., India, and Montreal. For a whole year in 2003, wherever he was, he drew a (beardless) self-portrait every morning to closely study everything he was not. Living an understated quiet life with a "new" girlfriend, jazz musician, singer, and old collaborator Anjani Thomas, he would not be heard of again until three years later for a record with an incomprehensible title that made everyone believe he was saying goodbye for good.

THE HEATHER MYSTERY (2004)

An intriguing and disparate assemblage of songs and spoken texts, *Dear Heather* was released without warning or after-sales service in October 2004 in Leonard's absence, so to speak. The album resembles a recapitulation of the previous thirty-five years and a crash course in all things Cohenian for anyone who might have missed the singer's career. Dark waltzes stand cheek to cheek with poems declaimed to jazz, country music ballads, and electro minimalism. There's also a Jew's harp, an oud, and drum machines. Nothing is missing. References to the 1950s and the poet's early career are fused with a valedictory colour and constant evocations of ultimate ends: farewells, things done for the last time, and Death as a guest star. At seventy, as he was entering what he then routinely called (using Tennessee Williams's phrase) the "third act," Leonard seemed to be looking back for the first time.

He also played the elementary game that the Beatles had learnt from children: Hello-Goodbye. The principle is known to every toddler: you hide and pretend not to be here, as Leonard does here when his lyrics are reduced to a few words or when the crooner's voice seems to evaporate in an unearthly whisper, and you suddenly reappear to say "Hello!" or "Goodbye!" What really matters is who you play the game with. The Beatles had played with their entire generation and transformed the '60s into a vast school playground, teaching everyone the virtues of innocence. Leonard's chosen partners change the tonality — he plays with death, with women, and with his past.[12]

The record explores the countless ways the singer can disappear as though he was staging his future absence. He is not on the cover; the title is incomprehensible and the female voices are sometimes more prominent than his own. He also hides behind other people's lyrics (there are more covers here than on any previous albums[13]), or behind an unlistenable one-line ditty ("Dear Heather" with its grinding barrel organ) but reappears for a revealing confession made to a backdrop of cool-jazz vibraphone and double bass:

> No words this time, no words
> Is it censorship?
> No, it's evaporation.[14]

So poetry evaporates and the poet re-materializes only to say goodbye. Again and again. To Irving Layton ("Go No More A-Roving"), to the teachers of his youth ("To a Teacher"), to the peace that 9/11 made impossible ("On That Day"), to the nightingale he had loved so much before she flew away ("Nightingale"), and to women, of course ("Because Of"). He says "hello" only once: to God (or Death — he isn't sure) to whom he declares, to the backdrop of another hip-hop groove, that he has finally got it: he was (and had always been) *there for you* ("There for You"). "The Letters" is like a testament sent to his audience that contends that his old letters about the Flood were right after all and "Because Of," a soulful lullaby, is perhaps the album's masterpiece and Leonard's farewell to the fair sex.

In it, Leonard humorously lists the benefits you reap in old age when you have written "Suzanne" in your youth. It's a short list, but a substantial one: women are "exceptionally kind" to your old age. To be precise, they take turns at your bedside to show themselves naked, imploring, "Look at me, Leonard! Look at me one last time."

While a xylophone or one of those music boxes that put the little ones to sleep plays, Leonard evokes — with ember in the voice — the only way his lifelong idyll with women could end: by a reversal of role that reveals the true nature of things. For thirty years, he had called his women "baby" (at least in songs) — now he finally appears as a shivering old man lying in bed who has morphed back into the only truly irresistible male: the little baby that every woman wants to pamper and console. He has become the "baby."[15] Unlike a baby, however, he gets the consolation of erotic visions (such is the advantage of old crooners over ordinary men), as Anjani Thomas invents the perfect jazz lullaby climaxing with Marylin Monroe–like vocalizations ("doo-be-doo" and "doo-da-doo") to repeatedly offer the beatific vision of her body:

> Look at me Leonard, look at me Leonard,
> look at me one last time,
> one last time.[16]

The funniest thing is of course how Leonard "owns" the song with sharp scansions and a swing in every sentence, transforming it into a manifesto. Yes, he will be addicted to women until the end. Yes, he congratulates himself for having cheated them one last time. Yes, he is adamant and remains the thing he has never stopped being — a walking bordello.

So at least the old Ladies' Man mask is still there, if only as a joke. But when the album was released in October 2004, Cohen's audience had plenty to worry about. The record was filled with sighs, nostalgia, and a credo that seemed surprisingly bleak ("The Faith").

As they listened to a voice now so whispery that it almost dissolved into pure vibration ask "O love aren't you tired yet?" in an infinitely sad Québécois ballad, fans could legitimately wonder whether their man was still really here. You could feel on the record a pervasive poignancy and the sadness of true farewells. And the complete lack of promotion that accompanied the album (not a single interview) was in no way reassuring. *Dear Heather* seemed the portrait of a man who wished to take his leave for good.

Things could have ended there. The year 2004 is another instance of the many narrowly missed endings of Leonard Cohen's career. There was the sunstroke in 1965, which could have crushed the poet's mind and made him a Canadian Rimbaud or a Canadian Artaud — a poet gone mad or silent. There was the overwhelming tour of 1972, which almost made him quit because he was defeated by love, and heart-wrenching concerts like Jacques Brel in 1965. The Phil Spector debacle was another fitting end — an ex-star of the '60s survives for a while, disappoints, and disappears. Or he could have never come down from Mount Baldy or just said in 2004, "I'm seventy, I quit." It almost happened. But it didn't. Something came up.

JUDAS, L.A. STYLE

For there is that pesky little thing that Lenin called "the eternal return of the concrete," which in Leonard's case, to no one's surprise, turned out to be the eternal return of theology. God apparently disliked Leonard's grandfather beard and wouldn't let him retire. He evidently wanted the world to enjoy his angelic presence for a few more years. A coup de théâtre was called for. Something that would reshuffle everything. A betrayal, for example. As in the Gospels. The Son of Man cannot accomplish our redemption if he is not betrayed, and the betrayer has to be one of the twelve. Ditto for Leonard. Except that in the singer's case, Judas — quite logically — had to be a woman. One of the inner circle, one of the apostles. Necessarily.

Flashback to four years earlier. The year 2000: Leonard lives in Los Angeles, surrounded by female angels. His daughter, Lorca, had joined him there almost ten years before. She runs an art deco antique shop downtown and lives with her dogs on the ground floor of his duplex house. Sharon Robinson, his close collaborator and soul sister, is an almost daily visitor, as is Leanne Ungar, the poet's friend and sound engineer since 1974. There is of course Anjani Thomas, his ex-chorist of 1985 and backing singer on "Hallelujah," who is now his life partner. He cooks for her, she cooks for him. And finally, there's Kelly Lynch, the brilliant, determined manager, loyal to him for fifteen years, a former flirtation, now the necessary interface between the poet, the outside world, and the music industry.

For *Ten New Songs* and *Dear Heather*, this tight group meets several times a week and works in the best understanding. A team. A tribe. A loving little group. But as in the Gospels, one of them will betray. Brutally. Irreparably. And actually, it has already happened and, from a karmic point of view, it makes complete sense. From a karmic point of view, it was even entirely predictable. For the laws of karma are very simple: you are punished where you sinned. So here comes the karmically simple, the theologically complex, and the judicially inextricable story of Kelly Lynch's betrayal. The pitch is depressingly banal: a rock star with a gift for depression and a penchant for the weaker sex retires to a monastery with a wise old man (who he knows is half-crazy, but that's why he wants to be there), leaving the management of his career and fortune to his manager. He trusts her completely and for good reason: they have remained excellent friends after a brief sexual fling and the manager in question practises Tibetan Buddhism (the kind of people you trust, right?). But that was reckoning without the wounded heart of a desperate woman.

In the second half of the '90s, the monk Leonard had apparently been persuaded by Lynch and financial advisers to carry out two major financial operations (they actually took place in 1997 and 2001) meant to secure his retirement: the selling of his copyrights to Sony Music in two successive transactions of five and eight million dollars, respectively. The sums were placed in three different trust funds, one of them interestingly called "Charitable Day Sabbath Trust," designed and run by a prominent investment company from Boulder, Colorado, that specializes in creating "tax-efficient-investment-products."[17] The company happens to be run by another

Tibetan Buddhist who became Cohen's financier. The only hitch in the plan: Lynch had signing power on everything, controlled the chequebooks, and — allegedly unbeknownst to Cohen — owned 99.5 percent of the third trust fund. Being under the impression that the money belonged to her (or that it should), Lynch soon started to methodically siphon off the accounts in many successive hidden "loans" that paid for designer clothes, gigolos, and — one suspects — cocaine bills. How she managed to intercept the emails and letters that might have tipped off her boss, how said boss still got a monthly report that told him his accounts were safe, is not entirely clear. But the truth is that it couldn't have been too difficult to organize. Not for someone intelligent, determined, and mad with rage like Kelly Lynch. Caught as he was between monasteries, depressions, trips to India, and months spent writing or recording, Leonard was not the type to check his accounts too often or call the office to make sure things were okay. His kingdom was not entirely of this world. The shock came in October 2004, a few days after his seventieth birthday, when his daughter, Lorca, was apparently warned by one of Lynch's employees that massive acts of embezzlement had taken place. It must have been a strange weekend for Leonard: to fly back from Montreal and find out in a few hours that all you have left is $150,000 and taxes to be paid on huge sums you no longer own. A disaster. A catastrophe. A wipeout, but not of the usual psychic kind. A financial wipeout — the complete disappearance of your life's savings. So, no, there was no time for promoting the new record. Instead, Leonard had a few meetings with lawyers. Then a few meetings with police officers. Then a few meetings with tax experts.

Eighteen months of legal proceedings ensued (for which the singer mortgaged at least one of his famous houses) as well as a tragicomical imbroglio worthy of your average television series. Three interlocked parties sued each other: Leonard, who has hired a lawyer named Robert Kory (Anjani's former husband), accuses Lynch of embezzlement and the investment company of misconduct and breach of contract. The company accuses Leonard and his lawyer of defamation and attempted extortion. Lynch accuses Cohen of tax evasion and hypocrisy. More peripeteia lead to the ex-manager's arrest in her bathing suit by an LAPD SWAT team and to the seizure of the poet's archives held hostage by the manager who was selling them piecemeal on eBay. The result? Two full years spent in the company of lawyers and chartered accountants that led the poet to surmise (as he told me) that God wanted him to die of boredom. The first trial ends in May 2006 with Lynch (now officially guilty) ordered to refund $7.3 million to her former client and lover of a season. Of course, she was insolvent and even for a while without a home and, of course, she began a strategy of multiple appeals and contests that would last till after Leonard's death.[18] The singer came up with a couple of witty quips to feed the media ("I do not recommend losing everything as a spiritual exercise," "I discovered money has a habit of disappearing if you don't watch it closely"), but in spite of his displayed phlegm, he was indeed devastated and ruined. At the age of seventy, he was compelled to relaunch his career.

And that is one of the central tenets of Catholic theology: the devil always unwittingly works at his own downfall and serves the divine plan. The very light that Lynch had sought to extinguish would be sent into the world again and Leonard's comeback would indeed be an act of light.

BOOK OF LONGING (2006): "MY SHABBY LITTLE STORY"[19]

Leonard had no choice. The years 2006 and 2007 were his return to the market, with reissues of his first three albums, a record by Anjani Thomas (with nine new Leonard Cohen songs), a collaboration with Philip Glass, a travelling exhibition of drawings, and lithographs (in galleries in Toronto and Manchester), not to mention a popstar-laden tribute show given on three continents and a documentary film (*I'm Your Man* by Lian Lunson). Of course, that upsurge of activity was just a way to postpone the singer's only viable option to restore his financial health: go on tour again. But the first act of the comeback had to be a return to square one. A book.

Originally announced in the late '90s as a collection of satirical poems about the monastery and postponed many times, *Book of Longing* was finally published in May 2006. Augmented by 120 sketches and drawings (most of them self-portraits and female nudes), the volume is a kind of lyrical exercise book that can be read as a fragmented diary of the 1994–2004 decade and a vast investigation of the absolute mystery of being an aging Leonard Cohen.[20] From page to page, we see a waggish sixty-year-old monk who dies of loneliness in a bleak Zen camp turn into a seventy-year-old traveller without luggage who falls in love with every moment of his life and every female face he sees in the streets of Mumbai.

The book contains literature of very different densities. On the one hand, highly elaborate spiritual manifestos (often song lyrics[21]). On the other hand, short ironic pronouncements on the nature of awakening or the destinies of the world, as well as rhymed hoaxes and doggerel, poetic grumbles, or innumerable "snapshot" poems that record one specific moment: a moment of clarity in the kitchen in Hydra, a call for help sent from Mount Baldy, a memory that resurfaces during a plane ride or in a hotel bar. To accompany these snapshots of the poet's soul, sixty-seven self-portraits try to capture versions of the poet's constantly changing face. The book's conclusion? "Leonard Cohen" does not exist. He is — like us all — just a succession of scattered moods and miens.

Book of Longing is therefore another Zen lesson. What does it say? That we are all travellers. Travellers from place to place but also from mood to mood and from thought to thought. From empty day to bright day to medium day. Life, therefore, is an uninterrupted journey through multiple versions of ourselves, each moment being an invitation for the Self to dissolve. With that sunset. Or that plane ride. Or that heartbreak.[22] The book also says (it will surprise no one) that desire, irreducible as it may be, comes in various densities and under several names. One of them gives its title to the volume: "longing."

PEDAGOGY OF DESIRE UNDER DESIRE

> *Only one thing made him happy*
> *and now that it was gone*
> *everything made him happy.*

— LEONARD COHEN, *Book of Longing*[23]

Twenty years prior, *Book of Mercy* was a case study of how a poet torn apart by desire turned to prayer for survival. In 2006, Leonard seems to have come to terms with his lot: he is a "desiring machine" and not much can be done about that.[24] But he now knows you can survive in the fire and even relax. In his old age, the persistence of desire is even something he would find rather amusing. The reason? The twelve thousand hours he has just spent cross-legged in silence. An ideal time to carry out a few observations about the mechanics of desire — all of which are recorded in the book.

Observation number one: the infinite variations of desire transform us into comedy characters: the Buster Keatons of desire. Seen from the outside, it's actually quite funny. Leonard Cohen wants a cigarette. Leonard Cohen wants a woman's body. Leonard Cohen wants to reform his life. Leonard Cohen wants an interview with God. Observation number two: desire varies in intensity. Some days it burns; others, it's a hardly perceptible tension, a desire without object that the poet calls pure "longing," the desire beneath desire. "A kind of fuel that keeps our interest in the world alive."[25] Observing this "longing" carefully (as the book urges us to do) will teach us one thing, which happens to be the thesis of the book: we are not the owners of our desire. It happens to be one of the central tenets of Balsekar's teaching: someone else — someone that can be called God — desires through us. In other words, we are the vehicles of God's desire for His creation; we are attracted to people and things only because God desires His creation through us. Consequently, joining your desire is joining God.[26]

It's easy to see why that idea must have fascinated Leonard. What had been pestering him his whole life — desire — could actually be an expression of his divine nature. So be it. It is also an excellent theological excuse to keep an eye on the daughters of Eve and nobody will be surprised that the book is indeed replete with allusions to female partners, whether platonic, real, or imaginary. There's a "young nun" called Seisen, a communist girl met fifty-five years earlier — probably Freda Guttman; a woman called "Sahara"; a French woman crossed in the bar of a luxury hotel; a certain "Sheila" summoned from childhood; a certain "Marianne" summoned from the '60s; a mysterious "Shirley"; the "most beautiful girl on the religious left"; the speaker's mother; someone called "Jana," now in love with another man; a couple of Québécois girls who turn out to be angels; a lover who, having spotted a cheater in the poet, teaches him new sexual techniques; not to mention a gigantic celestial woman who seems to take the poet to Heaven and leads him to surmise that his "redeemer" is a woman.[27] Nothing new under the sun, therefore, except perhaps the general mood. All these women are now partners in a very innocent game — the poet flirts with them out of sheer courtesy, the way you drop grains of salt on the tails of sparrows to keep them in your world for a moment or two. And then let them go.

LAUGHTER AND GRAVITY

The drawings in the book, essentially self-portraits and female nudes, are sketched in clear lines around simple artistic questions: how many lines does it take to make a female body or Leonard Cohen's face appear? The nudes — girls and women in various positions — are essentially a reminder that grace and joy exist in the world and that creating man as male and female — that is, as sexual beings — was God's stroke of genius.

Cohen explained to the *Shambhala Sun* that although he was no great artist, the women in the book had (like medieval saints and Virgins) absolute beauty and youth. He added (with a lie) that he never drew from life but selected the images from *Playboy* or suchlike magazines and performed "a rescue operation" to put the girls back "in their true place: the twelfth century."[28] The purpose? To remind us of the promise that comes with incarnation and make us see the world as a garden of delights. No need to look for salvation elsewhere, the book seems to say: it waits in the audacity of that eyelash, in the oval of that cheek, or the curve of that breast.

Is darkness therefore defeated? Not at all. But in *Book of Longing*, the poet's black moods seem to have considerably gained in lightness, as if the volume itself were a vast alchemical operation that turned burning desires into the pure joy of being alive, anguish and despair into occasional nostalgia, and heavy-handed sexual adventures into short and pleasant flirtations. How did that general lightening of life come about? Nothing simpler, says the poet:

> As soon as I understood
> (even to a limited degree)
> that this is G-d's world
> I began to lose weight
> immediately
> At this very moment
> I am wearing
> my field hockey uniform
> from the Sixth Grade.[29]

Self-deprecation is the default position of bodhisattvas, without which you cannot teach the infinite lightness of being. Nowhere in the book is that attitude more evident than in the self-portraits.

We have described elsewhere how those drawings combined an art of funny faces (incredible wrinkles, interminable ears, sagging dog eyes) and verbal irony to debunk the ego's claim to be centre stage. But the portraits are also great memento mori that explore the myriad ways age and the law of gravity organize the collapse of Leonard Cohen's face. But there's gravity that pulls you down and gravity that picks you up. And the artist's face also ceaselessly recomposes itself around dignified airs, sulking mugs, and wrathful glances. The inspiration, of course, is the art of Zenga and in particular the portraits of Zen masters. Like Hakuin in the eighteenth century or Sengaï in the nineteenth, Leonard uses scowls and grim faces to express both the ferocious determination that is required to reach enlightenment and the weight of Dasein — our being in the world — as well as our limitless capacity, which the poet had indeed studied very closely, to scowl at life as it is.[30]

With almost seventy versions of a face (few actually resembling each other), the book also demonstrates that the Leonardess of Leonard Cohen cannot be captured. And for good reason — there is no such thing. In French, *souvent Leonard Cohen varie, bien fol qui s'y fie.*

The Buddhist virtue illustrated here is non-attachment. Our face is not any more reliable or stable, not any more *ourselves* than the many moods that we go through every day. In a poem called "Titles," Leonard reviews his famous public identities and declares them as insubstantial as the snow that falls on Montreal. "Poet," "singer": he is none of these things, and in retrospect, the "Ladies' Man" label seems just a joke to amuse him "the ten thousand nights I spent alone." Elsewhere, he even seems to have forgotten the actual circumstances of his existence:

Children, roshi, songs, Greece, Los Angeles,
what was that all about?[31]

Moral of the story: to live happy, travel light. And to travel light, just slip out of your life and live outside it — you will be better off. This is what the poet declares to his guru Ramesh at the end of the book: "Peace did not come into my life / My life escaped / and peace was there." He adds that he bumps into his life from time to time and hastens to report that "my life [is] doing just fine without me."[32]

Book of Longing is ultimately a long apology for the disposable nature of all things. It basically says, let's abandon all the things that seemed so heavy and were actually quite light — our illusions, our attachments, our dark moods — and see if our life lifts off. In an interview for Norwegian television, Cohen invites the reader to throw away the book itself. Sitting in his Montreal kitchen, he explains he had just read what he thought was his best review. It's short:

> I read Leonard Cohen's book. It was very good. I threw it away.[33]

HIDDEN IN THE PUBLIC SQUARE

In 2007, twenty-two of the book's poems were set to music by Philip Glass for a small orchestra and a quartet of operatic voices. Together with projections of drawings and recordings of Leonard reciting the texts, this became *Book of Longing: A Song Cycle*, a recital that premiered in Toronto in June and travelled to festivals in New York, Austin, Los Angeles, London, Cardiff, and Milan . . . As is often the case with Glass, the result is alternatively sublime and somewhat pompous.[34] Some listeners may express doubt that the poems, some of which are light as air, are best served by operatic treatment, nor is it absolutely clear that classically trained tenor voices do full justice to the poems' humour.

Glass's piece is not the first time that Cohen's songs were sent on tour without him. After stage tributes to Walt Disney, Bertolt

Brecht, and — who else? — Le Marquis de Sade, producer Hal Willner had decided in 2003 that Leonard Cohen should be the next recipient of his magic touch. Hence, an exciting four-hour show called *Came So Far for Beauty*, with the upper crust of alternative rock, Nick Cave, Beth Orton, Antony and Laurie Anderson, playing the master's classics accompanied by strings, brass, and an energetic rock band. Created in Brooklyn, the visually and sonically striking show was reprised in Brighton in 2004 with Jarvis Cocker, in Sydney the following year, and Dublin in 2006 (with Lou Reed and Anjani joining), each time to full houses and astounding reviews and with rumours that the man himself might be present.[35]

One thing was clear: people rushed in en masse to any event labelled "Leonard Cohen" and the artist's new agent Robert Kory, a fan as well as a lawyer, had another argument when suggesting that it was perhaps time the man himself toured. In the age of massive illegal downloading, touring was the only profitable business, period. But still traumatized by his last tour, not to mention his first professional concert in 1967, Leonard had a thousand arguments to refuse: his age, his vocal cords, his lack of practice, his vanishing audience . . . Two small syllables, "Dy–lan," were counterarguments each time, but the old swan was just not ready for the swan dive yet. For a little while more, he would hide behind other artists.

In the meantime, the singer's first three albums were reissued with bonus tracks and his status as a living national treasure was confirmed when he was inducted into the Canadian Songwriter Hall of Fame in early 2006 in a televised ceremony complete with a tribute concert and hyperbolic speeches of panegyric praise.[36] Then came Anjani Thomas's album of unpublished Cohen songs, *Blue Alert*,[37] during the promotion of which the old warrior popped up on stage in Oslo, London, and Warsaw for a couple of duets. The tension rose a couple of notches and soon the music press spoke of nothing but the impending return of Saint Leonard Cohen.

In late 2007, it became harder for the artist to continue playing hard-to-get when a crazy music promoter and Cohen devotee called

Rob Hallett offered to finance rehearsals with no engagement from the singer — *Let Leonard rehearse and then decide . . .*[38] Studios were booked in Los Angeles in January 2008 for rehearsals that would last four months. Cohen's 1979 band leader Roscoe Beck, also a collaborator on *I'm Your Man*, was appointed musical director and put in charge of gathering a band. The first names were obvious: the now indispensable Bob Metzger and big names like the flamenco virtuoso Javier Mas or the dandy of Hammond organ, Neil Larsen. Anjani joined the rehearsals for a while but left. So did a female violin player. But everyone in the room was impressed by the power in Leonard's voice and presence. When the drummer Rafael Gayol, later dubbed "the prince of precision," arrived, followed by the faithful Sharon Robinson, the band started to click. And when God sent two young English vocalists called Hattie and Charley Webb to the SIR studios, miracles of grace started happening. Counting Leonard and the multi-instrumentalist Dino Soldo with his plethora of wind instruments, it would be a nine-piece band (ten counting Leonard), the biggest group the singer ever played with live.

In the meantime, promoters were doing their job and soon venues and festivals were outbidding each other to hire what was announced as the rock event of the year. Soon, a major tour seemed in the offing, but at that point no one could imagine what would follow. No one knew that Leonard would stay on the road for two and a half years, with a six-month break halfway through, for a triple round-the-world trip and 256 concerts in thirteen successive parts. No one knew that to the venues he had often visited in the past (the Olympia, the Royal Albert Hall, New York's Radio City Music Hall, and Vienna's Opera House), Leonard would add more exotic destinations like Bratislava, Istanbul, Moscow, or Kansas City. No one expected open-air concerts in front of the Kremlin, on Venice's Saint Mark's Square, at the foot of Edinburgh Castle, Helsingborg Castle, or Copenhagen Castle. Or in Roman amphitheatres in Zagreb, Nimes, and Lyon. In the medieval city centres of Ghent, Granada, or Florence. Or shows in the Red Rocks Amphitheatre in Denver, at the Glastonbury Festival (with an audience of 150,000), in the Olympic Stadium of Berlin (built by Albert Speer), the Sydney Opera House, a stadium in Tel Aviv, or — perhaps weirdest of all — in a Las Vegas hotel. There would also be dozens of anonymous modern arenas: 7,000-seaters, 10,000-seaters, sometimes 15,000-seaters. No one knew that when the tour was over, Leonard would have celebrated three birthdays on stage: in Bucharest (he was seventy-four); Barcelona (he was seventy-five); and Marseille (he was seventy-six). And no one expected exactly how ecstatic the reviews would be, with accolades like "miraculous," "unhoped for," "immaculate." *Mojo Magazine* would even steal the title of a Nick Cave song to claim that "God [was] in the house." No one knew that in the first two years, the artist would have generated $20 million of net profit (without counting the merchandising or album sales) and Leonard himself had not anticipated that in the process, he would fall in love with performing more than ever before. He didn't know he would hit the road again in August 2012 for a new tour to promote an album of original material called *Old Ideas*, and of course, no one in that rehearsal room knew that at least on one occasion, the old pilgrim would cross paths — in the same city the same night — with a slightly younger artist also caught in an endless tour. That one was travelling incognito, under an alias: Bob D.

TOUR OF 2008: DRAMATURGY OF PARADISE

Hear the voice of the bard
Who present past and future sees
Whose ears have heard
The holy word
That walked among the ancient trees.

— WILLIAM BLAKE, "INTRODUCTION," *Songs of Experience*

Leonard Cohen at soundcheck, Lörrach, July 2008

A few minutes before 8 p.m. on May 11, 2008, as Leonard Cohen and the band were harmonizing in Latin in the dressing room of the Playhouse Theatre in Fredericton, New Brunswick,[39] everyone in the hall — reporters included — was holding their breath. Later that night, Leonard would joke to the audience that when he had last appeared on stage, he was sixty years old, "just a kid with a crazy dream." That was a long time ago. Fourteen years on, no one knew exactly what to expect.

But at the end of the show, the 709 spectators refused to leave the hall without the poet's blessing, and the beatitude on everyone's face was a sign that a small miracle had taken place. In the coming two years, hundreds of reviewers would confirm that miracle: never had this man been draped in such light. As though transfigured.

We know that Leonard's concerts had always been "spiritual experiments" around the kohen's eternal mission: to reconnect us to our hearts and to the mysteries buried in it — mysteries called

God, love and desire. This time, something in the singer's presence made him move beyond the M.O. of the High Priest to join the realm of angelic action. Saint Thomas Aquinas thought that angels silently intervened in our lives every day. They exhorted our hearts, uplifted our souls, and illuminated us in a thousand ways: Leonard Cohen's very agenda in 2008.[40]

What is for sure is that every night, when the frail singer frisked onto the stage in beams of gold and blue with a levity that would almost make us forget he was the sole author of the Bible (indeed just a joyful kid), heartbeats would accelerate in the theatre halls as crowds invariably greeted the singer with cheers, often offering standing ovations before the concerts even began. As swiftly as he had appeared, the old man would then grab the mic, bend his knees, and instantly recreate the world with a waltz tune and a gravelly voice. The liturgy always began with a plea:

> Dance me to your beauty with a burning violin
> Dance me through the panic till I'm gathered safely in.

Then started what must be called — in strict etymology — a *rapture*: everyone in the hall was "rapt," taken away, kidnapped by the kid and his crazy dream, and relocated for a moment in paradise, the world of perfect forms. Indeed, for three hours every night, everything on stage — from the Persian carpets to the tailored suits, the sumptuous lights and the Hammond organ — was pure order and beauty. Light and luxury. And beatitude.[41]

In its combination of pure soul, crooner ballads, bewitched flamenco, and neo-'60s pop-jazz, the music — always precise, always perfect — traced a very strict path to a spiritual place where the full human condition could be celebrated. But for that band, perfection was evidently not an objective but just a starting point. The necessary condition for Leonard to accomplish the liturgical act he had come to perform: reconcile the darkest of existence with the most luminous. The great alchemical operation. The *Magnum Opus*.

So, every night, with precise diction and the authority of a voice that shook every seat in the auditorium, the man in the double-breasted suit targeted his lyrics straight at every spectator, transforming his stage act into a form of action poetry meant to revive our hearts.

And, suddenly, the songs appeared once again for what they were: small concentrations of truth and metric force intended to defeat us absolutely. And the wet eyes, the delighted faces, clenching hands, and tight throats that you saw everywhere proved how effective Leonard's war was against all that is hard and rigid in us. Every night, with elegies and hallelujahs (and with a little Hammond organ), he reminded the audience of the truths that form the core and kernel of his work: that this heart in our chest does not belong to us, and that the heart's cracks are indeed how the light gets in.

But angels will be angels and the singer made sure we got comforted as well. And he had tools for that. The strength of conviction with which the man declared himself our brother. The perpetual outpouring of shekinah in the female voices. A whole liturgy of light that Ryan Murphy had designed with Leonard's soul in mind, with strong contrasts that alternately plunged the stage into darkness and flooded it with light. With warm golds, subtle silvers, or mysterious blues.

And of course, there was the music. Fervent. Intense. Glorious. A voice of fire and grit (Leonard's) vs. voices of velvet and crystal (Sharon's and the Webb Sisters'). "Hallelujah" magnified by an organ solo. "Bird on the Wire" illuminated by Bob Metzger's guitar. "Who by Fire" bewitched by Javier Mas's oud, so evocative that you could almost smell the smoke of biblical holocausts or see the burning bush itself.

And centre stage was Leonard Cohen. An old crooner and an old warrior. Watching him, as he bowed — Japanese style — to his musicians, or as he followed a guitar solo with closed eyes, fedora on his heart, was like watching an old samurai listen to the sound of crossing swords. Or an old alchemist preparing for the ancient task: distilling light from black.

There was the singing, of course, more vibrant, more fervent than ever. But Leonard — who had become a great, authentic, awe-inspiring crooner — wasn't just presenting songs during that tour. With closed eyes and bent knees, his face turned to the sky, he was presenting a whole dramaturgy of inner life: how to face love, how to face God, how to face death. He was a man on a mission, waging a war on our behalf against the darkness of our lives.

The now almost unbelievable depth in the voice was — as always — the sign of a major covenant with gravity, and the crack in the voice instantly lodged us in the heart of everything that's broken in us. But of course, Cohen also *played* with gravity, exploring with the crowd every degree that separated the metaphysician's high seriousness from the levity of those who have penetrated that cosmic joke we call existence. In turn solemn, mock-serious, or clearly ironic, the singer kept reminding his audiences that, in his company, we were always invited to celebrate in equal measure the intrinsic gravity of our lives and the lightness of our anchorage in this world. He was both the high priest of the heart and an ironic crooner with angels at his beck and call. He was a beautiful loser and just a sparkle of light.

To keep us entertained, the poet also brought onto the stage every Leonard we have come to love. The unrepentant sinner. The prophet of doom. The inept monk. The wandering Jew. The Zen master. The high priest of the heart. The compulsive seducer. And all of them gathered in that one figure: "Leonard Cohen," great connoisseur of earthly love and divine plans. The expert in all things that fall. The crooner of the apocalypse.

During the three hours spent in his company, each spectator was bound to realize, if only for a few moments, that the man on stage was not just a teacher, or a wise old man. As he sang and unfolded the great secrets, he somehow became every spectator's guardian angel come here to teach them about abysses and avalanches. As he navigated from song to song and mask to mask, his spiritual strength was palpable even for his band, leading Charley Webb (one of the chorists) to speculate that "it's almost like he could part the Red Sea."[42] Hence, of course, the incredible gamut of emotions in the audience: the gratitude for being in that man's company, the reverence at the solemnity of the occasion, the joy of being reconnected to one's heart, and the sheer thrill of seeing a rock-and-roll crooner at the top of his game. Talk about "late style."

Of course, every angel is a messenger. And during that long tour, Leonard finally came clean. After almost six decades of studying religions, philosophies, and Kamasutra positions, he was ready. Ready to publicly reveal the key to the great mysteries of life. It took place every night towards the middle of the show, at the end of "Tower of Song" after teasing the audience a little ("Are you ready? Are you truly hungry for the answer?"). Then he made his announcement. The key to the mystery?

> Doo-dom-dom-dom,
> da-doo dom-dom.

That little thing that Sharon and the Webb Sisters had been singing for five minutes. It's a hoax, of course, but almost a koan, not unlike the Buddha's non-speech at Vulture Peak that famous day when, instead of teaching, the enlightened one just offered his favourite disciple a flower. Like the Buddha, Leonard pointed with his little joke to what was already there — a humble, little melody that was unfolding for us. It's what the Hasidic Jews call a niggun, a song without words, just a little tune, a ritournelle. But one that secretly carries a blessing and a benediction. One that makes everything sweet. The secret chord:

> Doo-dom-dom-dom,
> da-doo dom-dom.

If there is such a thing, the task of a Zen master is to show us that we are already awake, already comforted, already able to enjoy life. Or the little melodies that move from heart to heart and lip to lip.

So, we understand why, night after night, crowds around the world gave Leonard the longest standing ovations in the history of rock. Because the concerts were rituals that reunified their hearts. They were mirrors that revealed the metaphysical side of their lives.[43] It was therefore not rolling arpeggios and guitar tremolos that the audience heard in "The Stranger Song," but their own anguish, made precise and splendid by flamenco. It was not female voices that they heard climbing the melody in "If It Be Your Will," but their own aspiration to rise, finally clear. It was not sad tunes, but their infinite capacity to perceive the poignancy of life, not funky groove (as in "First We Take Manhattan") but their own ability to engage with joy.

An even simpler reason why crowds gave the poet so many encores is that you simply don't let an angel go. Not if you have the choice. Saint Thomas said the passage of angels could be proven in hindsight by the traces they left on people: enlightened intellects, revived imaginations, sudden bouts of courage — the very symptoms listed in a thousand concert reviews by witnesses as cynical and blasé as professional rock critics. They finally saw Leonard Cohen for what he was: an archangel in a double-breasted suit.

Of course, even during those shows, the angel of Montreal was an angel only metaphorically.[44] But metaphors are sometimes necessary to decipher the true nature of things. Angelic or not, Leonard was at this stage a bringer of light, someone who made us clear-sighted and luminous for a moment. And, as I left the many concerts I attended, I certainly had the feeling of coming back to the front line of my life better armed. Wiser, funnier, more generous. I also felt an old friend had just spoken to me and I am pretty sure I was not the only one.

In acute cases of *angelophobia*, you could of course use other metaphors. The Buddhist metaphor of the bodhisattva would be just as appropriate to describe the singer's M.O. For three hours, Leonard took us to the other shore of enlightenment (or, as he put it, "the other side of sorrow and despair") to let us experience life from the perspective of pure acceptance and compassion. He then took us back with a blessing: a fedora bodhisattva.

From a purely showbiz point of view, the concerts were amazing as well. The scenic impact was worthy of Brel or Dylan, but with an elegant Gainsbourg-like detachment, not to mention the fire, depth, and visionary power of first-rate literature. This was as good as Rumi or William Blake, no less. And that had been Leonard's great provocation, of course, from his first days as a songwriter: depth.

So, if I had to remember this or that moment of that first European tour, it would be in Dublin on Father's Day, when fifteen thousand huddled Irish people sang along to "Hallelujah" in an ice-cold rain (rain was dripping down my face), a song that seemed, for a moment, to have been written especially for that shivering Irish crowd. Moved to tears, Cohen knelt for a few seconds to thank the audience ("Thank you, Ireland, for still baffling the world"). It would be in the Manchester Opera House, in the first row of the balcony, when I saw tears in grown men's eyes everywhere around me, or when my next-seat neighbour declared during "First We Take Manhattan," with the poshest accent ever heard outside Buckingham Palace: "This is just *too* exciting." It would be in Frankfurt when Cohen left the stage with a blessing: "It's getting chilly out there. Listen to your mum and be as lucky as Volkswagen." Or it could be in Dublin again, in a pub near the Royal Hospital, two hours after the show. I stand at the bar with dozens of fans, all of us singing and raising our glasses to Leonard Cohen. An angel had passed, and I was chasing that angel across Europe. For fourteen luminous concerts.

ANGELOPHANY IN LIVERPOOL

To be able to conduct such intimate conversations with five or ten thousand people every night, a strict discipline is necessary: you must stop speaking altogether. Apparently, the 2008–2010 tour was fuelled by silence. Leonard had stopped smoking and drinking (his taste for alcohol, he said, had just "evaporated") and he did avoid speaking between concerts, which meant no interviews, no backstage access, no meet-and-greet sessions with friends or celebrities. Instead, a lot of rest, a lot of zazen, and macrobiotic food. Maybe a glass of wine or whisky here and there or a good meal with the band from time to time.

In the morning, it was not uncommon to see the singer visit a cathedral or order a Filet-O-Fish in the local McDonald's. He was very easy to spot, always dressed exactly as on stage: a double-breasted suit and a fedora hat. That's how he appears to you when you meet him near the docks in Liverpool one day in July 2009. You feel depleted for some reason; you look up after crossing the crosswalk and the angel is in front of you. "Leonard!" You have just called him. He spots you and stops. You shake hands. You exchange a few sentences — he never stops smiling and he compliments you on your work (you're this young academic writing about him). A few steps behind him, an assistant is panicking. The cherubic pilgrim has stopped and he must never cease walking. But, strangely, no one else on that busy street seems to notice him, as if he had come there only for you. He promises to continue the dialogue by email — you have been exchanging messages with him for a few years already — and, with your blessing, he leaves. You just can't hold back someone who is just passing through — he taught you that. You don't even try. But you do the opposite of what Dylan had advised: you look back. But the crowd has already closed in on the angel. He is already somewhere else. *I told you when I came I was a stranger.*

For a few years, Leonard Cohen will thus lead a very pure life, a miraculous life, the life he had coveted in the '60s: that of a saint who moves from town to town to give birth to a few ephemeral angels and who blesses the crowd every night after teaching them a few spiritual tricks. Along the way, there were a couple of peripeteia: the poet collapsed on stage in Valencia; raised some criticism when he performed in Israel. Then one day it's over and after a last appearance at The Colosseum of Caesar's Palace in Las Vegas (of all places), the discharged angel returns to civilian life. I don't know what he did the next day, but very quickly he was at work on a new record, which would be ready less than a year later. Angels work faster than slaves.

OLD IDEAS AND NEW VISIONS

Immediately after the tour, the singer retires to Los Angeles to record new songs — some of which have already been played live — for a new album that will be the next episode in Leonard Cohen's never-ending comeback: *Old Ideas*. Five songs have words and music by Leonard, one is a collaboration with Anjani, and four tracks were co-written with a newcomer and regular Madonna collaborator named Patrick Leonard, but the title is a warning — it is all a recapitulation and the eternal return of the fundamentals of the Cohenian position: defeat as a non-negotiable fact of life, the impossibility of controlling the heart, and invincible calls from women, God, and the abyss. As usual, the poet serves as M.C. and makes sure all Leonard Cohens — the lover, the slave, the melancholic, the priest, the visionary — get equal floor time to play their favourite language games (prayer, complaints, courtship, and consolation of the world). And, as usual, the poet settles a few scores. He admits to women he had to go crazy to love them ("Crazy to Love You"), confesses to a former lover that he still dreams of her "wearing half her dress" ("Anyhow"), and reminds God how dark the world that he has created is ("Amen," "Come Healing").[45]

Despite its popish coating, *Old Ideas* actually strikes by its darkness: breathless angels are "scratching at the door to come in," the butcher's filth is "washed in the blood of the lamb," an old man stands "naked and filthy" while a Kabbalist who loves his creator "like a slave" declares that the only thing he ever saved was "a thread of light, a particle, a wave." In "Darkness," Leonard renews the feat of "Avalanche" and finds another perfect image for depression. Not a white apocalypse that swallows you whole, but a black disease caught by drinking from someone's cup. One sip and everything turned black: the past, the present, the rainbows, the early morning.[46] But there's no trace of moaning in the song. Quite the opposite, in fact: the fierce, sexy little blues groove turns the refrain into a manifesto and a profession of faith as Leonard demonstrates once again that you can wear your inner darkness like a badge of honour.

> I caught the darkness, baby,
> and I got it worse than you.

So the record is like a warning. Although he is in cahoots with angels, Leonard the Obscure is still here, but he has realized that darkness is the twin sister of light and that both share our hearts in equal measure. Hence that fine balance on the record between seductive blues ("Darkness" and "Banjo"), infectious jazz ("Anyhow," "Different Sides"), and pure church hymn ("Come Healing"). Balance is actually a key word here — a poignant psalm that petitions the Lord about what French philosopher Cioran called "the inconvenience of being born" ("Show Me the Place") is answered by a lullaby that consoles a little child with the evocation of a love story between a cat and a mouse ("Lullaby").[47] Ultimately, the accomplishment of *Old Ideas* is this reciprocal contamination of darkness and light, gravity and weightlessness. Each becomes the indispensable flipside of the other. Yin and Yang. That kind of thing.

"Banjo," which Leonard had premiered on stage, could be mistaken for a minor little ditty, but it contains what is perhaps the most decisive image of the record. It's an adorable upbeat blues in which the singer reveals a recurring vision that "means a lot" to him.

> A broken banjo bumping
> on a dark infested sea.

It is an allegory, of course. This banjo is what each of us is: a broken vehicle of harmony that is still light enough to float in the Flood.

The boldest gesture on the record is probably the first track — "Going Home" — which opens the record by granting the floor to God the Father who speaks to us. And God the Father, as it were, has nothing better to do than speak about Leonard Cohen. A portrait of the artist by God. Not a bad opening for a pop record. And it so happens that God is just like the rest of us: he is very fond of Leonard, a man he calls a "sportsman," a "shepherd," and a "lazy bastard living in a suit." But He warns us: Leonard has got it all wrong. He thinks he has to write "love songs," "anthems of forgiving," and "manuals for living with defeat." So God reminds his son Leonard of his true mission (which is ours as well): drop the burden, abandon the vision, and come back home with a lighter heart. Can you imagine a more adorable scene? God announces that one of his favourite sons — the eternal passerby — is finally "going home without a burden."

So Leonard's new credo could be stated as follows: "I believe in the One and Indivisible Lightness of all Things, and I believe in Leonard, its messenger." Is this the announcement of a next act in the poet's drama? Will the singer become light enough to simply disappear?

Experiences of enlightenment, as we know, have consequences. It is even a principle in physics: whoever drops ballast gains in altitude. Supported by a chorus of unanimously good reviews and launched with maximum publicity, including a huge poster in Times Square the week of its release, *Old Ideas* was an immediate hit and Leonard's quickest-selling album to date. Very quickly, the record was #1 on both sides of the Atlantic — in Canada as well as in Finland, Norway, and the Netherlands — a first in Leonard's career, but seventy-seven is perhaps the best age for first times. In England, it reached only second place and a modest third in the United States, finally converted to the Cohenian dialectic of gravity and grace. Patrick Leonard's pop production was certainly a key factor in that success, but the fiery centre of the record remains the encounter of superbly written texts with that sepulchral voice as credible when it speaks for the Celestial Father as when it tells you about its erotic dreams. Pure Leonard, through and through. The singer then discovers the advantage of having finished an album so fast: you can go back on tour immediately. So, he sets off again, a seventy-eight-year-old kid. With the same crazy dream: to illuminate the world.

In the sixteenth century, Isaac Luria had taught the Jewish world that sparks of divine light were buried in the universe and that it was the Kabbalist's task to collect them. Two hundred years later, Hasidism asserted that sparks were also hidden in the human heart. In the summer of 2012 and for more than a year, Leonard became a traveller again, and he searched everywhere for those buried sparks. He knew, however, that you cannot hold a spark in your hand, so he just blew long warm outbreaths of poetry over the crowd every evening to check if the sparks were still there and if the hearts of men were as inflammable in 2012 as they were in 1970. Tikkun is the Kabbalistic name of the enterprise: the redemption of the world through the gathering of sparks, which (as some Kabbalists assert) is the mending of God himself. That year, the Kabbalist's gross profit apparently amounted to $44 million.

CHAPTER 14

EVIDENCE OF DARKNESS

2014–2016

*L'incessante contemplation
d'une évidence noire.*

— ROGER GILBERT-LECOMTE & RENÉ DAUMAL, *LE GRAND JEU*[1]

Edinburgh, July 2008

POPULAR PROBLEMS

Leonard's conversion to pop through Phil Spector had ended badly. But the former lover of Montreal jukeboxes, who has just introduced an old doo-wop hit into his stage act (the Drifters' "Save the Last Dance for Me"), has always had a penchant for simple songs. Hence the project, given how successful the previous record had been, of a new Cohenian incursion into pop paradise. In the role of Dante: Leonard Cohen. In that of Beatrice: a genius named Patrick Leonard, the creator — among other things — of some of Madonna's greatest hits.[2]

After being introduced by Adam (who had himself hired the producer's services), the two Leonards joined forces on four tracks for *Old Ideas* and hit it off immediately. Hence, the idea of extending their collaboration. Why not a full album? A hit record, for example? One they could call *Popular Problems*. "Popular" like "pop music" and "Problems" like "Pro Tools," the music software that Patrick L. would like best had he not discovered Logic 9. So, the two men set up a song factory in their respective home studios: Leonard & Leonard, a century of combined musical experience. The jobs are well defined: one writes the lyrics and makes the sandwiches, the other composes, arranges, and mixes. The result? A poppy record created by pros that deals with problems so popular they tend to be universal — our tendency to burn when our hearts catch fire, our tendency to fall when we want to rise.

But this time, the Montrealer wishes to speed up his process. He sends his lyrics more or less as they get written and sometimes receives a demo with a proposed melody and arrangement in less than two hours. Leonard has veto power: "Yes" (sometimes) or "No" (often). When a demo is agreed on, serious work begins. Voices are recorded in Leonard number one's studio, and Leonard number two vanishes in the mysterious world of samples, session musicians, and computers with a lot of RAM. There, it's trial-and-error time: he adds a bass, a chorus, some keyboards, a bridge, a countermelody, a synthetic saxophone, a little echo and sometimes, a wee bit of pop candy. If Mr. Veto, who has a strong tendency to like demos better than finished products, says "Yes," mixing begins and that is that. If he says "No," the process starts again. After nine tracks, you have a record. You let the manager know, who lets Sony Music know, who sells a few million copies. It's as simple as that: *Popular Problems*.

It's an easy collaboration between two professionals: one of the deeper reaches of the human heart; the other of the formatted pop song. What they want to avoid at all costs: three weeks in the studio, marathon late-night sessions, and full ashtrays. They're too old for that.

The resulting album is remarkable in many respects and the dream record to hit the top five. The context has never been more favourable. The year 2014 is the warmest in the century, and Leonard's reputation is at its highest. Hence, an album designed for efficiency: lethal blues tunes ("Slow," "A Street"); hymns disguised as country-pop or love ballads ("Did I Ever Love You?" "You Got Me Singing"); and the usual batch of sexy, subversive, and humorous lyrics. In "Almost Like the Blues," the first single, Leonard is in top shape. Between complaints about the Holocaust, his Jewish mother, and his bad reviews, he claims (trigger warning: gallows humour) that all things considered, those old stories "about the gypsies and the Jews," although entertaining, were only "*almost* like the blues." The deadpan tone is used to best effect and Jewish humour functions at full regime:

> I let my heart get frozen
> To keep away the rot
> My father says I'm chosen
> My mother says I'm not.

So, humour and a popish coating give the record an unusually buoyant quality and *Popular Problems*, as it were, is not unlike a

Leonard Cohen equivalent to *The Adventures of Tintin: Flight 747 for Pop*, *Leonard in the Land of Pro Tools*, or *Destination: Black*.

PUBLIC WARS, PRIVATE WARS

And yet, in keeping with the Descartes motto, Leonard advances masked on the album.[3] Beneath its suave soundscape, *Popular Problems* examines the state of the world and our hearts in 2014. The verdict will surprise no one: could do better. With recurring references to burning villages, paramilitary groups, and secret wars, it conjures up a universe caught in various states of disarray.

"Samson in New Orleans," for example — the closest thing Cohen ever wrote to a protest song — evokes Hurricane Katrina and portrays Leonard as a modern-day Samson eager to destroy the Temple of America to avenge its abandoned holy city. "A Street" and "Nevermind," originally poems inspired by 9/11, reappear as two war songs with electro beats and a definite thriller quality.[4] The former claims that the world is entering a cycle of wars and proposes a toast to a peace that will come only with ruins — Leonard as the stoic philosopher of the clash of civilizations. The latter presents the poet as the sleeper agent of a clandestine group ready to subvert the country and our souls with tactics known only to himself. The Arabic words sampled in the chorus ("Salaam, Salaam") give the track a decidedly Middle Eastern flavour, but Cohen (as he explained) has aimed for "complete political illegibility."[5]

For ultimately, the conflicts dealt with here are the secret and clandestine wars fought in our hearts rather than those that rage in the world. So we shall never know what specific militia is joined by the femme fatale in "A Street" or what civil war she fights in, but war — as Leonard explains — makes her sexy as hell. Likewise, what disruption exactly the poet claims to cause in "Nevermind" is not revealed, but the song suggests we can all be spies and double agents in our own lives. Like a good Heraclitean, Cohen has always believed that peoples and sexes are by nature caught in an eternal conflict, just as we all are (in some dark corner of the heart) at war with ourselves, love, and God. *Popular Problems* just reminds us what a fantastic ally our inner warrior is to keep sharp and alert.

And Leonard C. seems very sharp and alert, indeed even bouncy during the sessions, as he croons his lyrics into Patrick L.'s Neumann U47. When the singer wants a hand mic instead, the producer suggests an MS105, but the two home studio Ho Chi Minhs agree on a strategy confirmed by every treatise on the art of war: record fast and mix slow.

POP PARADISE

Operation *Popular Problems* is a success. Unanimously lauded by rock critics who have now all jumped on the Cohenian bandwagon, the album quickly gains silver, gold, and platinum certifications and reaches the top-five slot in seventeen countries, including a very respectable #4 in the United States. Surely, a few pop gems on the record have helped, like "My Oh My," a discreet goodbye to a lover that may be a young woman but also life itself. With less than forty words and a little slide guitar, the track attains the poignant beauty of the pop ballads that all the McCartneys in the world no longer know how to write. It is refreshing like a summer breeze and deep like the blues — Leonard in Los Angeles and a masterpiece of simplicity.

Some of the musical choices are perhaps more debatable and maybe "Nevermind" had a sharper ring as it stood silent on the pages of the *Book of Longing*.[6] But at the end of the day, the record is as voluptuous as it gets and it is obvious to anyone with ears that Leonard's voice, now so deep that Adam Cohen will soon compare it to an A320 airliner, is surreptitiously taking us to pop paradise. If Leonard is a double agent here, he is working for Heaven, an incognito archangel. He says it on the record:

> I live among you
> Well-disguised.

No wings on the cover, however, but the perfect Leonard Cohen: sharp suit, cool stubble, piercing eyes. Please hide that cane that nobody wants to see and focus instead on the colourful shadows that surround him.[7] Not exactly Sgt. Pepper in terms of graphic revolution, but who minds the package when the psalmist goes pop?

THE SHOESHINER AND THE ALCHEMIST

More important perhaps are the nine portraits featured in the CD booklet. Leonard in boxer shorts, Leonard in a suit, Leonard in his shirt sleeves or in a hotel bathrobe. Each time caught in his nightly ritual during the tour: shining his shoes.[8] Some may see here an allusion to an album that is slightly too cosmetic, but they would be wrong — it is a crucial allegory.

Flashback to Toronto, May 1966. In the CBC studios, the poet is being interviewed by a very young and slightly condescending Adrienne Clarkson, who pretends to find the young provocateur amusing. Twenty-two years later, they will briefly collaborate on an anthology of his poems and thirty-seven years later, Clarkson, as Governor General, will make him a Companion of the Order of Canada. But on that day in 1966, the matter at hand is more trivial: Leonard expounds on the art of shoeshining and claims he doesn't know whether the poet is any more important than the shoeshiner.

Forty-eight years later, a CD booklet seems to imply he has finally decided. The world sees him as a high priest of the heart, part ladies' man, part archangel; Leonard suggests he is above all a shoeshiner. Or an alchemist (what is the difference?). Transformation of matter is the nature of both activities and the shoeshiner's job is to turn dull black (*ater* in Latin) into shiny black (*niger* in Latin) to extract from black the properties of light. Leonard was doing it in 1971, when he turned attacks of black bile into avalanches and avalanches into epiphanies of light. He still does it on *Popular*

Problems. The pictures even suggest that alchemy is his favourite hobby. It's there in the louche blues about Jewish mothers and the Holocaust or in the country music songs that teach you to let go of all things. The alchemist knows the method: turn darkness into gravity, gravity into irony, irony into love, and love into a beauty that redeems the world.

And yet, when the album was released in October 2014, Leonard knew that as pleasant as it had been, his little excursion in pop territory would not last. He was already at work on the next project, which would turn out to be a much darker record. He claimed on *Popular Problems* that he "likes it slow," but the truth was he was in a hurry. He was about to die.

THUNDER

Any pop song foreshadows Paradise. For three minutes, you feel the promise of an existence that is more intense and more beautiful. Your heartbeat quickens, the melody lifts up your soul, and you hear a harmony that does not exist on earth. A sonic utopia.

Despite the bleak outlook and wry humour, there is no shortage of mercy on Cohen's albums: a waltz here, three unforgettable chords there, or, there again, a woman's voice (or is it an angel's?). On *Popular Problems*, female voices abound and, in the way they surround his throaty growl, they carry out (as always) a reunification of the world: the marriage of masculine and feminine that the Kabbalah presents as a prerequisite to any manifestation of the divine.[9]

So one might have expected that as a purveyor of grace, Leonard would be paid back in kind, but then again, there's this small detail in Judaism: "The Lord your God is a consuming fire" (Deuteronomy 4:24). Which means God's mercy is not always kosher and he likes to burn the things he creates. A fact that the Montrealo-Angelian poet will experience once more, this time in his flesh.

On the scale of your average melancholic rock singer, Cohen had until then shown — give or take a few mental collapses — an almost insolent good health, displaying in his early seventies an amazing and luminous energy. Zen in high doses is good for the body, as could be seen for example in how he recently still frisked onto the stage of Europe. In Sharon Robinson's 2014 book of photographs of the tour, Leonard is shown in airports and buses, in backstage areas and hotel laundromats. Two things stand out: a) he is constantly carrying something — a suitcase, a guitar, a pressed suit, or a bag of dirty laundry; b) he seems to exert a natural sovereignty over things, as if the centre of gravity of the world was also his.[10]

But, as an ex-Beatle once said, all things must pass, and no place is safe from thunder. And it is precisely in that radiant and slim body that thunder will strike so that Leonard Cohen may experience brokenness again.

It is not necessary to be a Buddhist or a great theologian of impermanence to have noticed that the seventy-three-year-old man who started the tour in May 2008 is not the seventy-nine-year-old who ended it in December 2013. Five busy years, several round-the-world trips, 372 concerts and soundchecks, hundreds of plane rides, and months on end spent in hotel rooms have left their toll on the singer's body. The silhouette has gone from slim to thin and the hair is noticeably whiter. To the trained eye, a little fatigue is even perceptible at the end of some concerts, but of course, Leonard is an old fox and a Zen master — he knows how to inhabit tiredness with grace. Besides, what is a drop of tiredness in an avalanche of light? And yet, on the cover of his last album to date, the singer has chosen to appear leaning on a cane, just as the previous one had showed him (not that anybody noticed) facing a black shadow that seemed to be taking aim. A confession? Better than that: an allegory.

The secret was then well kept: a disease, diagnosed a while ago, possibly the one he was alluding to in 2012 when he called for the rejuvenation of body and soul in "Come Healing":

O longing of the branches
To lift the little bud
O longing of the arteries
To purify the blood.

Three decades before, his mother — as we remember — had died of leukemia. The same disease will now impose on Leonard a radical change of routine. No more tours, obviously, plus treatments, and regular and often unpleasant trips to the hospital. The last act is on. As in classical tragedies, it will be governed by a single rule: the rule of three unities. Time, place, and action.

1033 SOUTH TREMAINE AVENUE

Unity of place, therefore. A life reinvents itself on a restricted perimeter: the house on South Tremaine Avenue. The street is wide, unbelievably quiet, and lined with trees that uproot the paving stones, as they do everywhere in Los Angeles. They could easily be mistaken for maple trees, but they are actually *Liquidambar styraciflua*, American sweetgums, imported from the East Coast with star-shaped leaves. Dark green in summer and purple and gold in autumn. The house is a duplex and Leonard lives on the first floor with four rooms and a kitchen. Modesty itself. A flight of stairs leads to the tiniest of terraces with a wrought-iron balcony that overlooks a small front lawn with two sturdy garden chairs, green in colour, where the poet likes to sit at all hours and where I sat with him. At the back of the house, the garage was converted (a while ago now) into a home studio, with a guest room upstairs. Nothing more.

No social apocalypse in sight here after 1992 and the quietness is such that you could easily imagine yourself a thousand miles away — and not five, as it was — from Sunset Strip. Only the occasional LAPD helicopter will interrupt silence. Or a passing car. Or a neighbour pruning the hedges.

Leonard takes his quarters here at the beginning of 2014. Of course, he keeps his suitcase at the foot of his bed and starts living here as he has lived everywhere, as if he were just about to leave.[11] Except that he will no longer leave. He has a better plan: to disappear. Soon. In two years. Two times eternity.

Behind him is a distinguished career as a part-time Angeleno. He has lived here at the Landmark Hotel (of rock and roll and junkie fame), at Joni Mitchell's Laurel Canyon house, and in a Brentwood farmhouse where he tried to save his non-marriage. He recorded seven albums in the city (one of them with a madman), played at the Troubadour, in nightclubs, and, more recently, at the Nokia Theatre for an audience of seventy-one hundred. He stayed countless times at the Chateau Marmont — not always sober, not always alone — but found himself alone in an improbable villa in Hollywood Hills after Suzanne had left for good. Exactly thirty-five years ago. Then came that house on South Tremaine that he bought with two other Roshi followers in a district that no one, including its inhabitants, had ever heard of: Mid-Wilshire. The date? July 25, 1979. Since then, Los Angeles has been one of his operational bases, but he has never really felt he lived there for good. Or for real. There was always a monastery, a woman, or an apocalypse to join, a tour to do, a hotel room to visit urgently. Somewhere else.

But now, there is unity of place. Every day, the poet sits on that front lawn where from noon to night, the sun describes a perfect semi-circle. He makes friends with the neighbourhood cats,[12] ponders on the mysterious succession of days and takes notes in his five thousandth black notebook. Sometimes he stops and listens to the sound the world will make without him: wind filtered by trees.

FLIRT AT DUSK

That vita nuova is not so much an orderly life as a regulated one. In monastic culture, "regulated" means organized according to a rule. The purpose of all monastic rules is to make life sharper and more focused. In Leonard's case, it just happens that the rule in question is no longer imposed by an old Japanese monk but by treatment protocols and a very strict diet. The aim: to stabilize the disease and preserve the poet's forces.

The first year, everything seems under control. The slim-looking Leonard recorded — as we saw — an album with Patrick Leonard and the album rose to #5 in the British charts and #4 in the United States. Not as high as *Old Ideas*, but high enough to convert a few souls to Leonard's dialectics of shadows and light.

Since, routine galore. Leonard lives upstairs, his daughter downstairs, and Adam a couple of blocks away. A few close friends regularly drop by and hang around, but every morning, the poet does what he has always done: he slips on a dark suit, prepares a black coffee — or buys one in the local Starbucks on Wilshire Boulevard — and scribbles away in black notebooks. The same lyrics, over and over, until they are ready. He once called the process "the continuous stutter / of the Word that is made into Flesh"[13] and he knows how that works: alchemy and black ink, again and again. Sharpness of Truth, again and again. *A busy bastard living in a suit.*

On Friday evenings, the family gathers at dusk to celebrate the Sabbath. Upstairs in the study, a statue of the Virgin keeps watch, not far from a picture of Roshi, who has just died at age 107. Leonard was very present during his friend's final days and, in July 2014, he sat vigil at his death. Two months later, his sister Esther died and in early 2015 it was his old friend Steve Sanfield's turn. Death was apparently closing in. Nothing special, of course — when was it not? As Cohen said a thousand times in interviews, his own death was never a great concern. A few years back, he even told Jian Ghomeshi that were it not for "the preliminaries," he would be looking forward to the experience.[14] Hence, perhaps the poetical flirt he has started with the grim reaper. He observes her, teases her, as he did in one of his finest love songs ("There for You") or on the *Old Ideas* cover, which shows Leonard Cohen in a black suit, looking cool as hell on his front lawn, writing. Few people have noted that tiny detail: a very visible shadow facing him and taking aim. It's obviously the shadow of his assistant Kezban as she takes the picture, but the allegory is no less obvious: a black shadow lurks around the poet. As he says on that record, hilariously kidnapping an old punk slogan, "I've got no future / I know my days are few."

On *Popular Problems*, the singer had used a voluptuous blues ("Slow") that seemed the perfect soundtrack for a couple of Whisky Sours in the lounge bar of your favourite hotel to discreetly remind a partner that may be a woman, God, or Death of his erotic preferences. In a word, he likes to make love the way he likes to do everything: slowly. Very, very slowly. The tone is ironic, but we get the message: Leonard is asking for a little extension.

> I am slowing down the tune
> I never liked it fast
> You wanna get there soon
> I wanna get there last.

To a Hammond organ background, the crooner hams it up like he rarely did, but he would be a fool not to try. Make God or Death or the angels laugh and there might be five minutes to gain. Or a year or two.[15] So Leonard likes it slow? It's rather that he's got a couple of things to do: a house to put in order, six decades of old notebooks to transcribe,[16] and, perhaps more urgently still, a life to live in Los Angeles. As if it were real. As if it were his.

THE PASSION OF ANGEL LEONARD

But death had not read the *Song of Solomon* in the standard version. No milk and honey this time; no Hammond organ, either. Like a praying mantis, death wants everything and grants nothing. She will now brutalize Leonard for a while.

So peripeteia number one. Of a type that the poet of gravity knows well: a worsening. To be precise, Leonard suffers a compression fracture. And then another. It takes more than that of course to clip an archangel's wings, but the poet will now have to live with pain radiating through his whole body whenever he moves. Vertebra number one, vertebra number two: a crack in everything, and three words that come with each pang: Memento mori, Leonard. *Memento mori.* Surgery and painkillers will not help much: the foreplay has begun. But the game remains the same — a record to finish, a house to set in order, and a life to live.

Order in the house was always Leonard's passion. And for good reason: he found the advice in the book of Isaiah. Interestingly, he will praise house cleaning in his last two interviews. To unclutter space, he explains, is to clear your mind and the best painkiller in the world, especially when one is allergic (as he is) to opium, which might have alleviated his back pains better than medicinal cannabis. What Cohen does not mention in the interviews, however, is that in the Bible, Isaiah wraps up his feng-shui advice with a solemn reminder: "Put your house in order, because you are going to die; you will not recover" (Isaiah 38:1). Those words did not fall on deaf ears. Since the end of the tour, Leonard has started work on a selection of unpublished texts and he made arrangements to organize his archives, his estate, and his legacy. He puts his house in order.

The record turns out to be more resistant. The singer knows the process well: 1) Get the lyrics to the required level of completion; 2) Find the adequate sonic formula — maybe not the poppy sound of the previous record; 3) Have a nervous breakdown and stand in front of the mic. But art is long, time is short, and energy is dwindling. So, changes are made in the M.O. The poet decides to skip the nervous breakdown and to record the voice tracks (still under Patrick Leonard's guidance) bit by bit, as the texts are being completed. But his intention with the record is clear: to say goodbye and bear witness. He wants us to see the twilight as he saw it: lit by a black torch. As for saying goodbye, fifty years of practice have brought him a certain expertise in the matter. His swan song promises to be superb. It will just be a little darker than planned. *Hey, that's no way to say goodbye.*

FAR MORE REAL THAN YOU

One imagines that the episode must have been arranged in the higher spheres, as was the case for Job, perhaps with a "Dialogue in Paradise" along the line of:

> THE TEMPTER: Let me test your son Leonard who serves you well and whom you changed into an angel.
> GOD THE FATHER: Hmm . . . Okay.

What is sure is that at eighty years of age, Leonard walks into a new avalanche whose name is pain. A pain that is such that some days it sweeps away everything in its path, including deep convictions. In the song "Steer Your Way," the poet will soon describe it with great precision.

> Steer your way through the pain
> That is far more real than you
> That smashed the Cosmic Model
> That blinded every View.

A pain in whose embrace Leonard will now have to accept to dissolve, as he once dissolved in love. And yet that pain impacts the poet's body according to the laws of a strange alchemy. On the one hand, it exhausts it. On the other, it intervenes on it creatively, almost like a sculptor, to clarify and sharpen the angles and lines — the stoop is more pronounced, the silhouette noticeably thinner, the face now almost gaunt, and the elegant eagle profile a little sharper. And, strangely, caught as he is in the spiral of weight loss, Leonard, who will soon weigh less than 104 pounds and describe himself on the coming record as "broken and lame," is in no way diminished.

Whoever has seen him in those days knows he lost nothing in terms of inner fire. The voice is pure ember, the humour intact, and the bearing nothing short of imperial — a battered archangel who walks with a cane but (to quote Lord Byron) "walks in beauty / beauty that must die." His gait is elegance itself, lines in movement. Leonard as an angular bird, sometimes an old ibis, sometimes a sparrow in a double-breasted suit. So, pain was a sculptor that transformed Leonard Cohen into a work of art: a Giacometti silhouette, a head by Brancusi. He had announced that transformation as early as 1961: "I'm turning into gold, into gold."[17] It's done.

In the emails he then sends to his friends, he mentions his health as an amusing prank the body is playing on him, and he seems to appreciate every moment of a life that goes by (as he will soon explain)

> Year by year
> Day by day
> Thought by thought.[18]

But back to the predicament: a record to make, lyrics to polish, and declining forces. Which means? Which means nothing special. Leonard knows full well that life takes us again and again to ground zero: the nakedness, the crack, the avalanche. But a battered archangel is still an archangel and Leonard does not — like Job — ask, "Why Me?" Quite the contrary, in fact: why not indeed? To die is but a trifle. Has he ever done anything else?

> I have to die a little
> Between each murderous thought
> And when I'm finished thinking
> I have to die a lot.[19]

So he eats and he doesn't eat. He sleeps and he doesn't sleep. He writes all night; he writes all day. He puts on weight and loses some. He is ready to die and ready to live. He wants to finish the record, but the songs have stalled (they always do). Actually, Leonard is looking for the specific hallelujah that befits his situation: one that is harsh, elegant, and secretly funny. He cannot be certain he will find the strength or have enough time. He is eighty years old. And suddenly, eighty-one.

DISCOURSE ON THE METHOD

Nevertheless, it would seem — at least this is what I could observe — that Cohen goes through the avalanche with a sharp mind and in a relatively good mood. His method? Nothing simpler. First, a few decades of austere Zen practice, if possible, with a master whose compassion is sharp as a razor blade. Long retreats in monasteries and koans to bash your skull against: not optional. At the outset, you can (so says a twelfth-century Zen master) "amaze the heaven and move the earth" and feel — even on the brink of death — "like a tiger in the mountain."[20] Second, develop a poetic vision where the brokenness of man, of the world, and of God is the key to all things and let the facts prove you right.[21] And for good measure, use your sense of humour to track down the comedy in every situation. The comedy of the body that breaks. The comedy of the record that has stalled. The comedy of the producer who quits (faced with personal problems, Patrick Leonard did indeed throw in the towel at the end of 2015). And of course, the comedy of the disappearance of a Leonard Cohen who never really existed in the first place. If all that is not enough, start smoking again, preferably luxury Greek cigarettes: George Karelias & Sons, for example (Leonard's favourites). There's nothing quite like smoking to relearn how to set fire to the world — all smokers are de facto arsonists — and make friends with combustion, ashes, and the taste of smoke.

With that training, Leonard is at this stage fully equipped to walk through avalanches and he is not afraid of the dark or white apocalypses. Perhaps we should also mention his secret weapon.

As it turns out, it was a fragrance and (more precisely) an incense. One, incidentally, that is rather expensive and not so easy to find: oak moss. The little boy from the Shaar Hashomayim synagogue, the tireless visitor of Catholic churches who once lived on a Greek island and was later addicted to Zen rituals, had tried a few incenses in his life. The one he was using now had the specific virtue of plunging you into the delights of this world while suggesting those of the next. Its fragrance is close to myrrh and yet more subtle — an olfactive utopia that awakens the archangel in you. And given that the archangel has just started smoking again, the conditions are indeed gathered for the record to be completed. With or without Patrick Leonard. With or without a hallelujah.

Meanwhile, Leonard pursues his efforts and works as much as his health permits. A few very close friends come to visit, among them Dominique Issermann, who spends several months by his side. She takes magnificent photographs of her friend, some of which will remain among the most potent portraits ever taken of him. They document the intensity and depth with which life followed its course at 1033 South Tremaine Avenue. Fire in black and white.

THE PARADOX AND THE LULLABY

So, from the top: Tragedy in Los Angeles. Unity of place, time, and action, plus one sacred rule: to face the facts, as dark as the facts may be. Let there be Leonard Cohen sitting at his post on the front lawn of South Tremaine, a black notebook on his knees and a crack inside his body. In front of him, the world of perfect shapes. Or to be specific, trees. The sweetgum in front of the house, a sycamore, and a blue cedar across the street plus a cypress a little further down the lane. And of course, everywhere on the horizon, the Los Angeles palm trees reaching for the sky.

Leonard closes his eyes to listen. To what? A white noise of inexhaustible harmonic richness: the wind in the branches. Filtered silence, rustling, and swishing, the sonic form that trees give to the eternal flux of things. In one of the *Old Ideas* hidden gems, he had described that sound as an ordinary Pentecost and the sweetest of lullabies:

> Sleep baby sleep
> The day's on the run
> The wind in the trees
> Is talking in tongues.[22]

At night, the wind comes with crickets. And with the smell of grass and dew. Perhaps a waft of incense on Sabbath night. All of this in the quasi-supernatural sweetness of the Californian climate, a sweetness that anyone who spent but one night in Los Angeles has noticed. The world of perfect forms. Paradise. But for one detail: the endless pain in the body. And therefore, hell.

The next record starts here. In the paradox that Leonard is trapped in day after day, night after night — the last koan. A contradiction, an aporia. On the one hand, the obvious signs of divine mercy: the wind like the spirit of God (ruach) rustling in the branches and the absolute sweetness of life (shekinah). On the other, the body at war with itself, irretrievably broken, irretrievably painful. Some days, it must be what all koans are supposed to be: a red-hot iron ball stuck in the throat that you cannot swallow or spit out.

And the mystery of existence must indeed have been gaining in intensity in South Tremaine, like all things that are about to cease. What, exactly, *is* "existence"? To what degree do things really exist? The trees, the wind, that suffering body exist. Undeniably. Leonard Cohen, on the other hand . . . He has a habit of dissolving. He is doing so now, with the sound of the wind in the branches. He has always known that. You dissolve. He has even recently explained it to a woman who happened to be driving past, a street away from his home. On January 23, 2016, recognizing the singer, the woman had stopped her car and stepped out to give him a kiss. When she asked if he was really "Leonard Cohen," he had answered, "I used to be."

The game of being this or that had stopped a good while ago. Zen training had seen to that. But soon all things will stop for good, and maybe the ultimate mystery will be solved. Leonard will have gone like that wind he had once said you could not tell him apart from:

> You don't know me from the wind
> You never will, you never did.[23]

But the breeze has abated and, on the lawn, the poet has opened his eyes. An old Hebrew word has just come back to him with a decisive insight. When you are broken like he is, *hallelujah* is pronounced "hineni." *I am here, I am ready.* So Leonard Cohen opens his little black notebook and jots down a sentence that will give the tone of the coming record, a record that he has just understood will reek of metaphysics the way only a film noir can. Speaking to his Creator, he writes:

> You want it darker?
> We kill the flame.

From the video "Moments of Old Ideas" (2012)

BACK TO BLACK

With hindsight, nothing seems more logical and more consistent than *You Want It Darker*. Let there be Leonard Cohen facing his own extinction and a life that insists within him and without him. Let there be his usual conversations with God, with women, and with himself. Let there also be a lucidity that is sharper than ever. And this very record must necessarily ensue. A record structured around a colour (black, as one may have guessed) and three motifs: a heart more broken than ever; farewells that are now urgent; and a love so strong that it just won't die. Nothing new under the sun? Maybe, maybe not. Leonard adjusts his vision once more with a few decisive details.

About darkness, for example (the first theme), he has three things to say: that it can always be darker; that God likes it very dark, indeed (an idea he borrows from Isaiah — God sometimes craves for black); and that this darkness willed by God makes our lives a very thrilling film noir. Quite an agenda already, which makes the album not so much a new journey through the night (because "night" means "dawn"), but a fully-fledged jump into a black hole that Leonard knows only one thing about: it will eat him alive.

About death (the second theme), Leonard reminds us that it is no big deal — just our irrevocable extinction. A touch of stoicism, a few adjustments, and all will be well. This, to a great extent, sums up the record: a Kaddish, a few goodbyes, and off we go. In passing Leonard offers a few clarifications on the subject of existence (his third theme): life is fragile and without substance but savouring every moment is the only way to travel light as long as you travel. And that's all. An ever-increasing blackness, death as a formality, and a life that requires infinite delicacy. A Leonard Cohen record. Of marmorean frivolity. The ideal soundtrack for your last cigarette, in a voice now so deep that it leaves you charred.

That voice was actually recorded by Leonard's son. Patrick Leonard had composed most of the tunes, but after his departure, there was no producer left. Adam, who lived nearby, stepped in and directed the sessions with great gusto, leaving his mark on the record. He had to operate quite fast — the vocal tracks took place in his father's front room, production and mixing in a downtown studio.[24]

Somewhere along the way, Leonard has a brilliant idea: a synagogue choir as guest star. And while they are at it, why not the Shaar Hashomayim choir where he had his bar mitzvah seventy years earlier? Maybe they still have that style of traditional and slightly atonal cantillation. Their address can be found easily: Westmount, Montreal, a stone's throw from his grandfather's house. God wants it darker? Awesome! So does Leonard.

SMOKEY LIFE, SCHMOKEY LIFE

A good way to enter *You Want It Darker* is through the front cover picture. Signed Adam Cohen, it shows his father smoking a cigarette, wearing a tie, and observing the world — three times a heretic and three times great: Leonard Trismegistus. The cigarette — in this case, the proverbial condemned man's last cigarette[25] — is central to one of the album's themes (the brevity of life) and seems like a belated answer to the banana on *I'm Your Man*. Leonard no longer embodies human comedy as he did on the 1988 album cover. He observes it from afar with the gravity of old masters. A moment in a smoker's life, a moment in a life made of smoke:

> The Smokey Life is practiced
> everywhere.

Some details speak for themselves: the silhouette and allure, the solemn beauty of the face, the sovereignty of that elbow on the banister — all suggest a "wise guy" (as they say in mafia movies), a man "freed from life and death" (as they say in Zen). At this stage, Leonard's elegance — both manly and angelic, dark and luminous —

had little to do with the suit (as well-cut as it may be) or with the fedora (a mere accessory); it was now just a way of inhabiting the moment, without insisting, but with an acute sense of the exact form that each moment, be it a cigarette break, must take.

So, a gaze, a cigarette, and the right attitude — there seems to be a teaching here.[26] Of the gaze, concealed as it is by dark glasses, little can be said, but in those glasses, we see the world returning to its true nature: a collection of dim reflections. As if Leonard were confirming the lesson of the old baroque masters: life is a dream and men shadows that pass.

As for the cigarette (a George Karelias, no doubt), it is obviously the incandescent centre of the picture, a sign that something here — life itself — is consuming. What is Leonard telling us? That one may still, should one wish to, rub shoulders with fire and smoke and with one's own mortality. That one may still, with the adequate ritual (and smoking a cigarette is exactly that), combine the very mechanism of life (breathing) and that of death (cremation). And that one may still choose to remember that we are kept alive by "a mere breath" (Psalm 69:02), but that this breath does not belong to us, although tobacco makes it visible in the smoke rings that rise in the air. All cigarette breaks are therefore little holocausts that send our breath back to God, charged with nicotine and tar.[27] You can choose to remember all that, Leonard seems to suggest. If you accept, that is, that life is not a walk in the park but a constant cremation. Leonard on his balcony; Joan of Arc in the furnace: where is the difference?

As that picture illustrates, *You Want It Darker* re-explores a principle that Cohen had spelled out in the mid-'70s: life is made of smoke. As such, it is opaque and fleeting, but also incredibly light, "light enough to let it go."[28] You can also, as Leonard's attitude suggests, make each moment a tiny festival, what Milan Kundera called a "festival of insignificance," a celebration of the joyful insignificance that is life itself.[29]

So, this is it. A quick lesson in elegance and stoicism by an old singer living in L.A., but also an ordinary moment: a cigarette break during a recording session. Captured by the camera, it has the poignancy of the things that will not return — our last moment with Leonard.

> A cup of wine,
> A cigarette,
> And then it's time to go.[30]

THE CELESTIAL CORLEONE

But as always, there's humour behind the straight face. With his black fedora and shirt, his matching tie and charcoal suit, Leonard Cohen seems dressed for a gangster movie financed by the Jewish mafia. And the cover therefore also illustrates the idea that if God is indeed — as Isaiah claims — a purveyor of darkness as well as light, who will plot against his creatures whenever he sees fit, then life must indeed regularly become a film noir, with dirty tricks, double-breasted suits, and massacres galore.

So *that* is the story: Leonard Cohen, perfect goodfella and Los Angeles consigliere of the Heavenly Corleone (a.k.a. God the Father, a.k.a. Yaveh Sabaoth) casts one last glance over his shoulder and finally understands that his life — the women, the hotel rooms, the endless search, the years spent in silence at Mt. Baldy Zen Center, the disease — all of it was just a film noir scripted by the big boss and adequately caught in the smoke of cigarettes and holocausts. "You want it darker?" Leonard asks his maker with some irreverence. A legitimate question, it seems, as his body disintegrates while his heart still burns like kebab meat. But the Lord's answer is the same as to us all: "You're talking to me?"[31]

It's clear at first listening: the album is as dark as films noirs go. To signal the debt to another dark opus, Adam's photograph was reframed to make the cover look like *Songs from a Room*. As in 1969, Leonard is placed inside a white square framed by a black square. He thus seems to be smoking his cigarette sitting at an abstract window, casting out one last glance into this world from the other side of things. Has he forgotten something out there? His life, perhaps? Does he want it back? No, thanks. No. It will surprise no one that Leonard looks much more relaxed in his white square than forty-seven years earlier — the last of the great smokers.[32]

NOIR REALISM

On its release in late October 2016, the record caused quite a stir. Partly because of a message to Marianne a few weeks before, that had leaked to the press and gone viral. Leonard's old friend was dying of leukemia and the poet claimed to be "so close behind [her]" that "if you stretch out your hand, I think you can reach mine," an implicit statement about his health which he confirmed in an October interview with *The New Yorker*. Although Leonard joked one week later that he now intended "to live forever," a context was set for the album, which was unanimously received as a swan song and an anthology of farewells.[33]

And indeed, alongside the trappings of a film noir (with the mandatory guns, poker games, and stoicism), what strikes on the record is how it insistently returns in more-or-less covert ways to the poet's present circumstances. "Treaty" in particular presents a chilling parable about a snake poisoned by his own blood, while "Seemed the Better Way" imagines life as a cup of blood that must be drunk after saying grace. And indeed, the album is (among other things) Leonard's last Kamasutra: a list of the various positions you can take in the face of death: imperial detachment, despair, courage, or kamikaze defiance.[34] And everywhere on the record, gritty realism: life as it is (without consolation); death as it is (without folklore); and Leonard as he is at this stage: elegant, broken, and very honest about the pain, the anguish, and the temptation of despair.[35]

Ceaselessly, the record goes back to the paradoxes that reconcile the Bible, Buddhism, and gangster movies: death exists, but hardly matters; life is fragile, but demands the softest touch and human beings are paradoxes on legs: fragile creatures looking for mercy, but also the formidable spies of a God who wants it darker.

And many will indeed have noted that the poet's distrust of consolations seems more acute than ever before. Of course like Boethius in the fifth century, Leonard seeks the support of philosophy, but this time it seems that, chased as he is by that great metaphysical avalanche called death, he has to ascend Mount Wisdom by the steep side.[36] The fundamentals of his philosophy are still the same (there is no cure for love and cracks are where the light gets in) but a postscript was necessary: love is still lethal and a crack is still a crack. So, no poetical candy on *You Want It Darker*, no handy formula to tattoo on your arm, no dance to the end of love. As if Leonard's last alchemical experiment were to turn what is black into something blacker still.

The result is songs that haunt you from the get-go and invite you into a black hole. A hole where a voice of granite and fire (as gritty as it will ever get) awaits. Listening to Leonard at this stage is like walking on embers — an initiatory experience that connects you to the great gravity within. It suggests Ezekiel breathing down your neck or Isaiah whispering in your ear, to prepare you for what comes next, something that doesn't look too good. And yet the fire in that voice also rekindles you like a swig of liquor.

But gravity is not the whole story. For understandable reasons, people have somehow missed how musically diverse the record is. Thanks in part to Adam's brilliant production, *You Want It Darker* is a recap of all the musical idioms that Leonard has ever loved. As bouzouki succeeds to blues or crooner ballad, as an Ashkenazi violin completes a synagogal chant, the singer becomes all the Leonards he ever was one last time: the prophet announcing a flood of darkness ("You Want It Darker"); the mystical sex addict convinced that the bodies of women are made of beatific light ("On the Level"); the crooner who sings his millionth goodbye ("Leaving the Table"); and the eternal passerby who lets a Greek ritournelle demonstrate how light life can be when you have given everything up ("Travelling Light").[37] He whispers a last goodbye to women, to God, and to his own heart; lets a string quartet close the record — e basta![38]

Determined to sing his own Kaddish but also ours, he explains — with a final joke — that he is ready to die, but not to save all men "to make things cheap" ("Steer Your Way"). In case you were wondering, there's nothing wrong with his sense of humour.

IN HINENI, HALLELUJAH

With a "million candles burning," with the water "changed into wine" (and into water again), with blessings pronounced over a glass of blood and the presence of angels, there is something resolutely sacramental on *You Want It Darker*.[39] As though Leonard, in his testimony from death row, was smuggling fragments of psalms under the table and thus secretly delivering a sumptuous liturgy for precarious days.

And indeed prayers abound on the record, sometimes fragmented, sometimes disguised as agnostic statements: little acts of praise, petition, or thanksgiving. Broken hallelujahs once more. The irreverent "You Want It Darker" is in many ways a psalm of praise (as we will see) and "On the Level" is a hymn to all the women the poet has ever loved. "If I Didn't Have Your Love" celebrates love as the great redeeming force and, to some degree, every song on the record works at opening our hearts to the great mercy that (so the poet claims) can be found everywhere: in the sky, in your lover's eyes, in the flow of existence. And, if you're lucky and if God's in the right mood, even in your own heart.

Three strategically placed texts have a special spiritual resonance. Taken together, they form a triptych about existence as a perpetual vanishing act. Three major contributions to the Cohenian canon. Their titles? "You Want It Darker," "Travelling Light," and "Steer Your Way."

Some will consider the eponymous song as the masterpiece of Cohen's late career — they will not necessarily be wrong. Released by Sony Music three weeks before the album, "You Want It Darker" is an impressive appetizer: a compendium of Jewish liturgy and crime thriller dialogue used by the poet to deliver what may well be his spiritual testament — a pledge of allegiance to a God who wishes to make our lives the ultimate film noir. Anyone interested?

The production is breathtaking: with the sweetest dirge, a synagogue choir serenades us for ten seconds and — bem-bam, bem-bam — a groovy bassline plus an electronic pulse set the number going at 109 beats per minute, keeping us just an itch away from dancing for the whole song. Then, introit Leonard, who opens fire by denying God a poker game:

> If you are the dealer,
> I'm out of the Game.
> If you are the healer,
> I'm broken and lame.

There's some important spiritual advice there: how to adjust our egos to God's moods and the divine will. Namely, fold when He raises you, confess when He's in a better mood but never — never — forget who the boss is. After ninety seconds, the choir hesitates between traditional cantillation and Ennio Morricone and we are caught in a crime thriller with God as villain and Leonard as guest star. Fans are in Heaven. So are we.

What comes next is a liturgical act: Leonard pronounces his own Kaddish. Once a kohen, always a kohen. He sanctifies the Holy Name, makes us see "a million candles," and seems to have a whole synagogue at his beck and call. But once a renegade, always a renegade. Leonard's prayer is decidedly unorthodox as he adds to the Kaddish's first words ("Magnified, sanctified / Be Thy Holy Name"[40]) a heterodox reference to Christ's passion:

> Vilified, crucified
> In the human frame.

Nothing unfamiliar here — just the old Cohenian habit of spicing up his Judaism with a drop of Catholicism or Zen, but also a theological reminder: when the Name takes Flesh, things tend (as in every film noir) to end badly. It's interesting to note that Leonard leaves out the sections in the Kaddish about the hopeful expectation of the Messiah. In his song, the Messiah has come and died (oops!) and the moral of the story so far is:

> A million candles burning
> For the help that never came.

In other words, sanctify all things but prepare for the worst, for God does strictly what He wants. And right now, He apparently wants it darker.

So, less than two minutes into the record, something is clear already: Leonard insists. With that syncopated bass line, with the throaty voice and the electro beat, he invents an alternative liturgy that says, "My kaddish is sexier than yours." And although dancing to "You Want It Darker" would require some guts, the song would not exactly be out of sync with a late-night whisky in the bar of your favourite luxury hotel. You can almost hear the barman's voice, as he dims the lights just before closing time: *You want it darker?*

But Leonard's Kaddish is not just sexier, it's also more subversive than ours. It promises nothing — no Messiah, no realm, no redemption — and finds its sources in obscure biblical places (in Ezekiel, Isaiah, or Deuteronomy) that claim that he who is pure light and burning bush sometimes gets the munchies for darkness.[41] And Leonard confirms what the Torah says and what every prophet knows: to serve God, you must be ready for dirty tricks and funny business. And God's next move is a dirty trick indeed — the termination of the earthly journey of his son Leonard Norman Eliezer Cohen.

Twenty-five years earlier, "Closing Time" portrayed God as a bar owner who wanted to close his establishment while the patrons were having the time of their lives. Here, God is a bluffer in the "holy game of poker" who claims He can heal us but tolerates massacres, broken vertebra, and lethal diseases. There's only one answer to that God and Cohen steals it from Abraham, Moses, and Isaiah:

> Hineni, Hineni
> I'm ready, my Lord.[42]

Conclusion of the song: God is like Don Corleone and Leonard is his messenger. His last mission (should he accept it): to enter darkness for good and turn the light off when he leaves. And that's it. Enough for a masterpiece, exciting like a crime thriller, deep like a psalm. With a cool bassline and synagogal chant. Leonard reminds us that God is great, whatever He does. When He heals us. When He wipes us out. Glory to Him, therefore. For ever and ever. Amen.

The song, of course, makes no extravagant claim. The inescapability of death, the silence of God, and the gap between His will (which will be done) and ours (which will not) are not exactly theological novelties and we didn't need Leonard to understand that. But the poet's aim is to remind us (like David once did) that prayer is a subversive act. With prayer, we can speak to our Creator in any way we choose. Like a child to his father, a sinner to his saviour, or a mafioso to his padrino. In all cases, it's just safer to remember that he might be in a rotten mood.

So, not a bad start for an album recorded from a medical chair in a small living room on South Tremaine Avenue, Los Angeles. I remember shivering (and smiling actually) when Leonard first recited the lyrics to me, impromptu as it were, over appetizers across the table in a small Italian restaurant in Larchmont, L.A. But God had warned us as early as 1974, "Field Commander Cohen, he was our most important spy." We had a hunch, indeed.

NIGHTS CLEARER THAN DAYS

"Travelling Light" is the ideal companion piece to "You Want It Darker," but also its polar opposite. Instead of a prayer, a farewell. Instead of gravity, an infinite lightness. Instead of a synagogue choir, a mandolin, female voices, and a bouzouki. With a rebetiko tune and a klezmer violin, Cohen joins Greece again — where he will no longer set foot — to look back on his life one last time.

Something to declare? Yes, sir. That he is, at long last, travelling light, even though he is stranded in L.A. Nothing weighs him down any longer — no suitcase, no illusion, no expectation of any kind. All is light now and, under the protection of a backing singer called "Athena" (the kind of thing you can't make up), Cohen goes through his life again in four minutes and twenty seconds:

> I'm travelling light
> It's au revoir
> My once so bright
> My fallen star.

The key to his unburdening? Just stop believing the myths that weigh you down. The myth of the "you and me," for example, one of the ego's favourite tricks: to make you believe you exist autonomously and substantially. There's "me"; there's "you"; and there's "Me and You." Stop this and you start relaxing, as Leonard does here:

> I'm just a fool
> A dreamer who
> Forgot to dream
> Of the Me and You.

He just "forgot": that's how lucky he is. And the result is that all things, at long last, his past lives and memories, dissolve into a Greek waltz and into the joyful insignificance of things. Who am I? No matter. I no longer play guitar? No matter. They're closing the bar? Slightly more annoying but actually, no matter. Light, therefore, is the song's nostalgia for the taverns and bars of Hydra where Leonard used to reinvent the games of love and chance. Light is the song's farewell, so light it has to be in French: au revoir.

Not much darkness in that song, therefore, and few reviewers have indeed noted the double entendre in the title. Of course, like Billie Holiday and other blues artists, Leonard declares that he is travelling *lightly*, but he also issues a little esoteric clarification about his true nature: he is *light* that travels for a while before returning to the source of all light. And in a vacuum, as we know, light travels swiftly. Last time someone checked, it was 186,282 miles per second. Au revoir, indeed.

So, with its mandolin and jazz organ, "Travelling Light" smuggles in a sweet little waltz and a nasty little groove on Cohen's darkest album. It comes with one last Buddhist lesson, as lighthearted as Buddhism gets: your life happened to nobody, and it weighs less than a sunny day on a Greek island. Did someone *really* want it darker?

THOUGHT BY THOUGHT

A secular prayer disguised as an Irish pub song, "Steer Your Way" exhorts the heart to cheer up, stay on course, and walk the line. There again, Leonard's instructions are simple: drop all useless things and you'll be well on your way. Used-up myths and religions, used-up truths you no longer believe in, used-up pain, and used-up loves. Drop everything until there is nothing left but what is mortal in you, until you have reached

> The one who was never,
> never equal to the task

Who knows he's been convicted,
who knows he will be shot.

From that position, live. And then — says the poet — mountains will weep, ancient stones whisper, and the world will be re-unified around a chorus and a violin that will warm your heart better than three pints of Guinness and a shooter of whisky. Somewhere between Hank Williams and King David, Leonard invents here the country music mantra as he reminds us in that chorus to greet life as a succession of tiny miracles that come:

Day by day
Thought by thought.

So Leonard finally answers the favourite question of smart alecks, "Is there a life before death?" It's clearly a "No." There's not *a* life, but a hundred thousand. A hundred thousand lives, a hundred thousand deaths that make us all professionals in these matters who have no reason whatsoever to fear one more disappearance. To live, to die, say no more. Are you Leonard Cohen? *I used to be.*

LUX AETERNA

You Want It Darker, therefore, is as black as a pitch-black night but also light as a breeze. On it, an archangel about to depart testifies one last time: how he dived into a darkness which, willed by God, may have been divine, may have been God itself, or just another black hole. He also invites us one last time to dissolve into the joyful lightness of things and to cheer our hearts. A great record, there-fore, that Cohen will present to the world during a press conference at the Consulate General of Canada to the United States, in Los Angeles, 550 South Hope Street, a fifteen-minute drive away from his house. It will be his last public appearance — October 13, 2016. As he entered the reception rooms that Thursday and sat down on a high stool facing a pool of international journalists, he had exactly twenty-five days left to spend on this earth. He was magnificent.

We said earlier that through a secret and strange alchemy, pain had changed Leonard's body into a work of art. Giacometti, Brancusi, that kind of thing. The footage of that day confirms that. At the end of the *Old Ideas* tour, a joke about aging men's decline in sex appeal was added to the show. The process, Leonard claimed, takes place in six decisive steps and as many quantum leaps. Starting off "irresistible," men soon become "resistible," then "transparent" and "invisible," and — eventually — "repulsive." But then came the strangest alchemical transformation, which makes everyone "cute," a stage the singer claimed to have reached.[43] As the press watched him enter the room that October day accompanied by his son, and as he sat down on the high stool, with a drink of water in one hand and his walking cane in the other, it was clear that Leonard Cohen, eighty-two years and three weeks of age, grossly underestimated himself. He was nothing short of imperial.

With a dark-toned three-piece suit and a black tie on a charcoal grey shirt — a perfect match for the salt and pepper hair and the luminous black of the polished Oxford shoes — Cohen was as dapper as ever, maybe slightly more formally so than in the past, but the waistcoat may have been there to keep King David warm or mask his thinness. Fifty shades of elegance, at any rate. And clearly the man had passed master in the art of being stylish and frail at the same time. His stooped, asymmetrical, and incredibly thin body was energetic and bouncy while the face — now wrinkled, gaunt, and battered — seemed to come straight out of one of his self-portraits. There had always been a tragicomic feel to that face, with its gift for looking askance: it now also had the beauty that is prized in Japan, the beauty of things that carry the three marks of existence: impermanence, suffering, insubstantiality. A wabi-sabi face.[44]

What does Leonard say that day? The same as usual. A paradox, one or two wisecracks, a piece of spiritual advice, a couple of well-honed anecdotes. The songs come to him by "trickles and drops"; he values uncluttered spaces but has no "spiritual strategy"; he says "Hineni" but "intend[s] to live forever." He speaks of his children with irony and tenderness; he congratulates Dylan on his Nobel Prize; he elegantly thanks his son. He does the job.

But one has to be deaf not to notice the slowness of the delivery and (perhaps more alarmingly) the persistent wheeze in the voice. Plus the poet occasionally pauses in mid-sentence and, despite his graceful manner, seems visibly in pain. And yet, another transformation — perhaps less immediately visible — has taken place. One so subtle that it could easily be missed. Unless you turn off the sound of the footage, in which case it becomes obvious. Something in Leonard that day transcends the banal questions, the clever answers, and the predictability of the exercise. Quite simply put, Mr. Cohen is now pure light. He smiles, shakes his head, raises his eyebrows, laughs, opens his eyes, closes them, and laughs again. He switches from papal gravity to the suggestion that all this is but a cosmic joke. He is both an archangel and a *muppet*, sometimes an old tortoise. He is more alive than he has ever been, and his lightness is absolute. He is unburdened of everything. Everything except that extraordinary thin body that now weighs almost nothing. He has no mission, no burden, no ego. By embracing it fully, he has vanquished — at least for a day — what his old friend Irving Layton had called "the inescapable lousiness of growing old." So, here he is, presenting his last record to the world with exquisite courtesy.[45] Then he salutes, stands up, and leaves the room, whispering a compliment in Sharon Robinson's ear on his way to the door. He takes the elevator and he is gone. *Leonard has left the building.* He will carry on living, of course. He will still take care of business, of course. He will still write, change moods, speak to friends and family. But, on a deeper level, all is accomplished. In Greek, Tetelestai.

MY ONLY FRIEND, THE END

Death and passing are two completely unrelated things. Death accompanies us throughout life and gradually gains density. Death is the unknowable unconscious of existence and, potentially, a vivifying force. The grain of salt of life and Leonard, like most poets, had started a dialogue with her very early in his life (he was nine, as we remember). Since, he had told her a thousand times that he was "there for you," warning her, however, that he was "never any good" as a lover. I know from a reliable source that he was not afraid for one moment — he told me so. For I visited the archangel and walked with him a while. To see him in the days we spent together negotiate so gracefully and humorously with life and death changed me forever. For this as well, my gratitude is eternal.

Unlike death, *passing* is only an event. As such, it is subject to chance and circumstances (or to a higher will, if you lean that way) and most often, we have no grip on it. In an attempt to teach us to live with the required humility, Montaigne made an inventory of foolish famous deaths,[46] while the *Unetaneh Tokef* features a more solemn list:

> And who by fire,
> Who by Water,
> Who in the sunshine,
> Who in the nighttime . . .

So what about Leonard? Nighttime. The official version that I make a point of honour not to doubt, is that he died at home in his sleep in the night of November 7–8 after falling in his apartment. A death that the official announcement described three days later as "sudden, unexpected, and peaceful." In the last email we exchanged, three weeks earlier, Leonard had mentioned, like an amusing detail, that his body was "fiercely insisting on gravitational rights." He knew I had abundantly studied his work in the context of falling angels.

I know almost nothing of his last day. Did he write? Did he sit on the lawn? Did he listen to a conference of his friend, neo-Kabbalist Yakov Leib HaKohain, as he loved to do? What is sure is that the Los Angeles weather report for that day indicated glorious weather, as had been the case since the beginning of the month, with sunshine the whole day — sixty degrees at night and average highs of seventy-nine degrees that afternoon. The sweetgum in front of the house probably still looked like a maple tree, and in the late Californian autumn, its foliage must have ranged from copper to bright yellow and purple. It's a safe bet also to assume that less than twelve miles away, the sound of the ocean waves was a splendid white noise. I wouldn't be surprised to learn that at some point during the day, Leonard had put pen or pencil to paper. But maybe he didn't. I am told he was writing emails.

For somebody who loved him dearly revealed to me the true circumstances of his passing. I will repeat them now, without divulging everything: Leonard Cohen did die of a fall. He slipped on the banana peel he was eating in that 1988 picture, which God had picked up and placed in front of him. Because it was time. And to teach him a lesson. As a payment, so to speak, for befriending angels, for playing with gravity, and for turning everything into hallelujahs. God then erased all traces. I am pretty sure it was premeditated.

EPILOGUE

"We are so lightly here." The archangel in plain clothes,
London, 2006

SAY A PRAYER FOR THE ANGEL

Throughout his life, Leonard Cohen displayed a unique talent for the delicate art of dissolving opposites. He embraced bohemia with the energy of slaves, hid an angel's soul beneath a sinner's life, sought the sacred in the profane but wanted to sleep only with saints. All along the way, his uninterrupted dialogue with women, God, and the abyss made his oeuvre a pressing invitation to join the gravity of existence, with the promise that true light was awaiting us there.

As the many lives lived by the poet attest, Leonard Cohen clearly had a plan: to be Casanova and to be a monk. To be a joker and a melancholic. To be a poet, a rock star, and an angel — to be Leonard Cohen.

As we followed him, we have encountered women in love and femmes fatales, mysticism and despair, avalanches, angels, and a passion for darkness, as well as a few dogs and a Zen master. We have examined all the things that Leonard once was and ceased to be: a little boy on a tricycle, an outrageous poet who collected exiles, an existentialist troubadour, an unconvincing monk, and the dapper pilgrim who crisscrossed the world to teach crowds that darkness is just the flipside of light.

Like that of ancient philosophers, his oeuvre (thirteen books and some 130 songs) engages both with the physical laws of the world (gravity, gravitation, and the irrepressible attraction of bodies) and with the metaphysical side of life (our hidden falls, our games of hide-and-seek with God). But it teaches us two things only: to play with gravity and to surrender to love. A humble program, but one carried out with a depth of vision and a theological creativity that allow us to finally assert that Leonard has indeed joined the likes of John Donne or Jalal al-Din Rumi in a very small club: that of the great spiritual poets. Rabbi Leonard Cohen. Roshi Leonard Cohen.

It is no coincidence therefore if the concepts we have used to describe his work — the beautiful loser, the ephemeral angel, the shish-kebab heart, the hotel room as a darkroom, the pop song as talisman and sanctuary — invariably highlighted the persistence of light even in the darkest of existence. Today, everybody agrees that Cohen's work is luminous and that the grocer of despair was also a smuggler of light.

Of course, the metaphysical poet wore double-breasted suits, he had a contract with Sony Music and had backing singers that — one suspects — would not be welcome in every synagogue. But so what? The poet was in tune with the times and so was his oeuvre: syncretic and subversive, profound, sexy, and secretly funny.

In tune with the Zeitgeist, Leonard has also played a central role (like Bob Dylan or Lou Reed) in establishing a new international form of oral literature — the art of the singer-songwriter, an art that throws the Logos into the world in small doses of three or four minutes, with backbeats and cool basslines. He has thus helped rekindle a very old way of experiencing literature: in direct contact with oral poets.

As our investigation draws to a close, we are quite understandably tempted to conclude with a vindication and a praise, but maybe also with a temporary answer to the question, "What was Leonard Cohen?" And — if we be so bold — we might perhaps suggest that "Leonard Cohen" was first the name of a skill — the ability to see men and angels fall — and the name of that literary alchemy which turns what is darkest in out lives into light.

Perhaps "Leonard Cohen" could also be the name of a virtue — the elegance he practised both in life and art — and the name of a grace — the grace of being constantly in motion. For although he struggled with that truth for a long time, he taught that, if the law of gravity does indeed govern our lives, we are ultimately weightless beings who are meant to travel light.

And perhaps finally, "Leonard Cohen" is the name of an attitude. Deeply concerned with soteriology (the theology of salvation), the poet seemed to suggest in his later work that salvation (or enlightenment, for that matter) is but a small, ordinary thing: a dissolution of self that occurs when the circumstances (an embrace, a sunbeam) or the attitude are right. We could be tempted to describe that "correct attitude,"[1] the "Leonard Cohen attitude" (very evident in the last phase of the poet's life) as a mix between a fundamental acceptance of life as it is (which conferred him such grace) and an ardent compassion for all beings coupled with an irony for all things, including himself. Grace, compassion and humour. At the end of *The Wanderer and His Shadow*, Nietzsche reminds us that "it requires beings more spiritual than men to fully appreciate the humour of man's view of himself as the ultimate goal of the world's existence." Leonard Cohen was clearly one of those beings and, if he famously tried — in his way — to be free, he mostly tried to be free not of gravity (gravity he accepted and cherished) but of himself. In one of his very last poems, he very elegantly proposed we free ourselves from Leonard Cohen as well. No one at this stage will be surprised that a bird (what is more a bird of the smallest kind) is again the key to that liberation:

> Listen to the hummingbird
> Whose wings you cannot see
> Listen to the hummingbird
> Don't listen to me.

FROM LEONARD COHEN TO CHRISTOPHE LEBOLD AND BACK

But it's not that easy to let go of Leonard Cohen. In my case, he is never far away. He regularly appears in my dreams. Like an old master, like a spiritual friend. The days I spent with him in Los Angeles were of such scorching nature that I need only close my eyes to still feel the warmth and fire of his presence.

It all began, as I remember, when I was probably fifteen, with two LPs (*Greatest Hits* and *New Skin for the Old Ceremony*) that my father had taken out of the closet to test my budding English. I remember getting caught in the flamenco of "The Stranger Song" and sensing that the voice was calling me.

I had no idea then, of course, that I would follow that man's tracks to Los Angeles, Montreal, Tennessee, or Toronto. I had no idea that I would recover his steps in New York, Mt. Baldy, Greece, or Paris's fourteenth arrondissement. Or that I was going to write a doctoral thesis about him or the book you're now reading. I could not imagine that I would one day bump into him on the street in Liverpool or open Sabbath in his company in Los Angeles. I didn't know any of that. But after listening to those first two LPs, I knew one thing: I would buy every record this man had recorded. And when I later discovered he was a poet, I bought every book.

I remember buying *Beautiful Losers*. A French paperback. Four sevenths in size. It's a clear memory: I am eighteen; I open the book; and I disappear. Put another way, I stepped into an avalanche of snow and fire, which is what that book was for me.

I also remember an eleven and a half square metre room with just a table, a bed, a couple of shelves, and a sink. Not unlike a cheap hotel room, actually. The room where I would conduct my quite successful university studies and my much more modest studies of the feminine sublime. As I was entering that small room at nineteen, I was also entering a larger landscape: the universe of Leonard Cohen, where I could finally breathe, for that universe, although poetical, was entirely realistic. I had finally found that rare thing: a poet who described life exactly as it is — a genius, therefore. Men fall, they speak to avalanches, the apocalypse is underway, angels visit just for one night and God is absent: real life, absolute realism. Thank you, Leonard.

I remember deciding at one point that the only thing that would adorn the white walls of my room would be a tiny portrait of Leonard Cohen in a black frame — a picture by French photographer Renaud Monfourny I had photocopied from a 1991 French magazine. With grey hair, piercing eyes, and a pinstriped tailored jacket on a black T-shirt, he looked on that picture like a defrocked Jansenist priest. Hello, sir.

I would take the portrait with me in several rooms and several countries (I still have it). I remember that one day two friends on LSD had a bad trip because they thought Leonard Cohen was observing them (I mercifully turned the portrait against the wall).

I remember a 1995 magazine cover (I was twenty) with Leonard in a monk's robe and Nike sneakers and an interview inside the magazine where the singer defined Zen Buddhists as the "Marines of spirituality." I liked the expression and the black robe, and soon discovered that I actually lived ten streets away from a Zen centre. There, at the age of twenty-two, I began to sit cross-legged with monks and nuns to explore the great silence of things and the joyful emptiness that is our true nature. That was twenty-five years ago, and it changed my life. I still practise Zen but have never looked for a master, because I somehow knew when I started that I already had one. He was living in Los Angeles. I just hadn't met him yet. But I knew that would happen. Some day. Somehow.

I then became an academic, the way you become wet in the fog: very gradually. First with a master's studies dissertation on *Beautiful Losers*, then a postgraduate dissertation on Leonard Cohen's songs, followed by journal articles and a PhD dissertation on the use of voices and masks in the work of Leonard C. and Robert Z. At thirty, I became a senior lecturer at the University of Strasbourg (bingo!), where I have since been trying to teach students how to study literature, poetry, performance, and pop songs, and where I have created two courses on Leonard.

It was only around that time that I began to realize that I hadn't come out entirely unscathed from years of looking at the dark fire that burns in Cohen's work. Nobody comes out of Cohen's work entirely unscathed because, like other poets before him, he reminds us that *in girum imus nocte et consumimur igni.*

We go round in circles in the night
and are consumed by fire.[2]

Except that in the case of Leonard, he also says that the fire that burns us is love and that, as we burn, we give off intense light for a while and illuminate the whole world. Like Joan of Arc. Like us all.

In our rags of light,
all dressed to kill.

In 2005, a Finnish gentleman named Jarkko Arjatsalo had given me the poet's address. I sent him my PhD dissertation with a letter of thanks and — almost as a joke — a proposition: let's have a drink, Leonard.

I was busy with work and theatre and not really expecting an answer, but a couple of months later, a message labelled "from Leonard Cohen" popped up in my mailbox and I almost fell off my chair. The great man was thanking me, saying he was looking forward to that drink. It would actually take a few more years, but we began emailing each other. He sent me pictures. Or jokes. I sent him my articles. Or pictures and jokes. Little things. Nothing at all.

Years went by and we couldn't seem to meet — he was constantly on the move and I didn't want to seem insistent or rude. Then he went back on tour. One rainy day (as I have mentioned in his book), feeling depleted on the streets of Liverpool, I looked up after crossing the street and there he was. In front of me. Three yards away. We shook hands; talked for three minutes. He smiled a lot, and he was gone. Bye-bye, poet. Nice suit.

There were more emails. I had decided to write a book that would be part biography, part analysis, part ode. For the original French edition, I worked in a one-hundred-room palace every day for three years. And that is literally true: a kind person had given me the keys to a one-hundred-room palace with marble columns and baroque angels. At some point I sent Leonard the detailed outline of the book, with titles and a few puns. He answered, "We are kindred spirits." *Kindred spirits*. That made my day, but I knew it was true. We are all kindred spirits with Leonard Cohen — someone who digs that deep is everybody's soulmate.

This was confirmed to me when I saw him on stage in France, Germany, England, Switzerland, and Ireland (I followed him on tour for a while). I watched him night after night operate like that high priest, an old ironic crooner who became every spectator's guardian angel. Draped in silver and golden lights, he was also an elegant shaman who took audiences though dark nights of the soul but regularly relocated them in Paradise. The first edition of my book was published in French in late 2013 to good reviews and few readers.

Then came 2014. Leonard tells me that if we must meet, it should be soon. He tells me why. A few months later, I am on a plane to Los Angeles with a medal he has sent me with the kohen's blessing, the birkat kohanim. The purpose is for me to look at his personal archives. That's the excuse, anyway, for master and disciple to finally meet face to face and for me to shake hands with the old archangel again.

In 1970, Jean-Pierre Melville had started his movie *The Red Circle* with a made-up quote by the Buddha:

> When men are to meet one day, whatever the diverging paths, on the said day, they will inevitably meet in the red circle.

Here I was on a night flight, finally on my way to meet Leonard in a red circle. It was going to be a circle of fire.

I was planning to stay in a cheap motel near his home, but, insisting that I would "check in but not check out," he put me up instead in a small house in front of one of his best friends' swimming pool. On a Friday evening I was brought to his house for Sabbath, and for a few fiery days, I entered the world of perfect forms again.

Perfect courtesy, absolute elegance, and — of course — that vibrant, seismic, golden voice. Except that the voice was now speaking to me in private and calling me by my first name.

"Hello, Christophe."

From the first minute, we spoke like old friends, sometimes until late at night. Although he was not well, he let me watch him live for a little. He opened his archives. I spent my days with transcriptions of his notebooks and diaries.

And we talked. About our lives and women. About God and our mothers. About death and *Hamlet* (I was rehearsing the part), and about our favourite kinds of tailored jackets. We smoked cigarettes, looked at pictures, offered incense to the Virgin Mary. And he cooked for me, inviting me to sit in a little corner in his Los Angeles kitchen — a corner he had called his "favourite corner in the whole world" in an interview for a French TV channel eighteen years earlier. A very nice place with a view of distant palm trees.

I wish I was still sitting there.

He made sure I could work and, from time to time, served me a glass of alcohol. We said things to each other that I can't repeat. It is not that they are secret; they are just very delicate. Like butterflies or hummingbirds. To repeat them would destroy them. We spoke man to man and Buddha to Buddha. In Zen we say "Ishin-denshin," or heart to heart. And for a few days the two little Buddhas were the best of buddies.

All I can say now is that I finally know what happens when master and disciple meet: they bow to each other as in feudal Japan and smile and smile.

One night, sitting late alone with him in that tiny living room (actually smaller than mine) on South Tremaine Avenue, I suddenly realized that I was not just sitting with Leonard Cohen — I was in the company of an archangel. I could feel his fire and the strength of his love. An archangel, as theologians explain, is a warrior angel and this one had fought his whole life against all things dark. And here I was, sitting under his protection.

And today, as I said, all it takes for me is to close my eyes to feel the fire of his presence.

He introduced me to a few of his friends. I travelled to Montreal, Greece, and a Zen monastery where I studied with a close friend of his. Everywhere I went, I lit candles for him — especially in the churches of Paris that I knew he liked so much — and I would send him a message: "There's a light burning for you in that church in Paris." "There's a light burning for you in a chapel in Hydra."

We met again in Los Angeles two months later (he seemed in much better shape). I shivered when he recited some lyrics to me over drinks in a restaurant. They contained the line:

A million candles burning
for the help that never came.

He looked me in the eyes.

We spent a last afternoon together; we hung out; we had a laugh; smoked a cigarette. And it was time to go. His last words to me were "Christophe, you're a Zen monk. I am not afraid for you."

Later that same night, as I sat alone in the Chateau Marmont bar listening to a Carla Bruni song which, in this particular venue, seemed incredibly voluptuous, I understood that the circle was complete.

Since the first spin of that first LP twenty-five years earlier, I understood that the great man had taught me four major lessons. Lesson number one: We are just passing through and must try to enjoy every second and be at peace with every mood, every place, every thought. Lesson number two: We should not be afraid of avalanches. Lesson number three: We should never be just one thing, but always a thing and its opposite: a melancholic and a joker, a lover of the flesh and a monk, a liberal and a conservative, a loser and a master, and just a passerby. Lesson number four, perhaps the most important one — especially today, when all the forces in society seem determined to make courtesy, elegance, and kindness impossible: we should be the alchemists of our own lives and every day transform what is heavy inside us into what is light, what is dark into what is bright. Or maybe we should just shine our shoes. Shoeshiner, alchemist. No difference.

We stayed in touch. We were now friends. In his emails, he always talked about his health as an amusing detail, a little whim of the body. There were talks that I should travel over again, but two weeks before his death, I got a last, humorous, loving email warning me that the "body ferociously insists on gravitational rights." A little nod at my theme of the fall of men and angels. And then, he left.

It broke my heart, of course, but that's what hearts are for. They break again and again until we break or become creatures of pure light. After his death, for a few weeks, I had a little ritual every morning over coffee. I solemnly gave him the Nobel Prize for Literature in my modest kitchen. It's hard to say if he liked the ceremony. He had that undecided ironic look on the old picture. But I am pretty sure he found the intention charming. And in my dreams, he smiles and smiles.

The author's bookcase
(original picture by Renaud Monfourny)

ACKNOWLEDGEMENTS

While a book is always the result of a plotting that takes place deep in the heart, getting it published and sending it off into the world is a process that involves many people. I cannot begin to express how grateful I feel to all who helped me in small and great ways.

My first thanks of course go to Mr. Leonard Cohen, whose friendship and generosity blew my mind and warmed my heart. For everything you did, Leonard, for your work and the shared moments, thank you! I will never forget your laugh and your kind heart.

I want to thank my French publishers Dominique Revolon and Sébastien Raizer, who, with Dominique Franceschi, published the first version of this book in French in 2013 for Camion Blanc and an extended version in 2018. They are true rock-and-rollers, may God bless them!

I want to thank Jack David from ECW Press, a true gentleman, who spared no efforts to make this English version happen, with a unique mix of buoyant good humour, brief emails, and deadpan wisdom. I enjoyed every conversation we had and hope there are many still to come. I want to thank the whole team at ECW Press, chief among them Samantha Chin, who was in charge of keeping the book and me on schedule. Her diligence, competence, and good spirits impressed me deeply. Thank you, Sammy! I also want to thank Jessica Albert, Emily Ferko, Claire Pokorchak, and everyone else who worked hard on this book. I am proud to have collaborated with such great professionals. As long as publishing houses like ECW Press exist, the battle against darkness is not entirely lost. They are like beacons of joy and culture in a dark age. We need them.

I want to thank Dominique Issermann, who was so generous to me and this book. Seeing the passion, astuteness, and good humour with which she and her great team (thank you, Olivier!) worked on the photographic material that she kindly allowed me to use was a sight to see, and I cannot begin to articulate how proud it makes me that the cover of my modest book is a picture of an artist and servant of beauty that I admire so much. Thank you, Dominique, for your kindness, your sense of humour, and being so relentlessly yourself.

I also want to thank the great photographers and artists Nick Broomfield, Michael Donald, Charla Jones, Ralph Gibson, Christof Graff, Charlie Gurd, Dana Lixenberg, Renaud Monfourny, Rino Noto, Isaac Shokhal, Lauren Tamari, and Ron Watts for allowing me to reproduce their work. I am proud their images are featured in these pages and, in each case, I have been impressed by their artistic vision and integrity: they are all great visual poets and, as such, they renew our ability to see the world, to see human faces and to enjoy life. God bless them for that!

I extend my thanks to the Estate of Arnaud Maggs for providing images by the late and great photographer, to the late Jeremy Taylor, and to the NFBC for providing film stills of *Ladies and Gentlemen . . . Mr. Leonard Cohen*, the University of Manitoba, and Les Archives de la Ville de Montreal for providing images of the poet's beloved hometown through Flickr.

From the depth of my heart, I also want to thank the many talented, non-professional photographers who honoured me with their images of Leonard Cohen. This book prides itself on featuring live pictures of the singer by Ivan Giesen, Hermina Sirvent, Hans Arne Nakrem, and Cécile Clauss, as well as images that Dana Dapena and Hollywata kindly made available through Flickr and

Creative Commons. As for Céline La Frenière, Candy Swanson, Dinnie Blair, and Alberto Manzano, they were immensely generous in sharing memories and pictures that meant a lot to them. I will not forget their authors' kindness. Thank you also to Francesco Vives for his image of Leonard's Montreal house and to Arsène Ott for his breathtaking views of New York.

I also want to thank Maarten Massa for his assistance and my friend the indefatigable Dominique Boile, who gave me access to his great Leonard Cohen archive on countless occasions. His diligence, ruthless efficiency, and passion for all things Cohenian were an inspiration throughout.

In years of research and travel, many people have helped me along the way and showed a kindness that I barely deserved. I think of the great Michael Posner, who was immensely supportive and opened so many doors. His own work on Leonard Cohen is a joy to read and of immense value to all Leonard Cohen fans and scholars. I think of the admirable Kezban özcan, who was my guardian angel in L.A. and helped me in a thousand ways, and Robert Faggen, who kindly guided me through Leonard's archives in Larchmont.

I think of the great Denise Beaugrand-Champagne and Morton Rosengarten, who joyfully showed me around Montreal, shared their stories and good humour, and introduced me to smoked meat. I think of Hazel Field, whose sharp eye and quick mind I admire a lot, and of Victor Schiffman and François LeTourneux, who royally received me and other Cohen scholars at the Musée d'Art Contemporain in Montreal (Hi François!). I think of Jennifer Toews and the team at the Thomas Fisher Rare Books Library, who made sure I spent a wonderful and fruitful week in the archives at the University of Toronto.

I must also thank my good friend Shozan Jack Haubner, who welcomed me and made me feel at home at the Rinzai-ji Zen Center and later helped me so kindly with that open heart of his. I warmly recommend his books and his YouTube channel *Zen Confidential* and am a great admirer of his many talents. I also

e

want to thank Dr. Harold Roth of Brown University for helping me understand Joshu Sasaki Roshi's teachings and for the pictures of Sasaki he provided as well as Dokan Charles Martin for showing me around an ice-cold Mt. Baldy and for a great night at the lodge. I thank the kind guitar player of Dead Miners Union who took me to the very grounds where Leonard lived in Big East Fork and then provided a campfire, food, and music. I thank the Hydriot poet Roger Green and the cats and donkeys of Hydra for keeping the island so quiet and clean.

I am of course indebted to the work, research, and passion of many Cohen scholars of the past and present: Jarkko Arjatsalo, Marie Mazur, and Allan Showalter among them, whose incredible online work was endlessly inspiring for me and all Cohen scholars. Thank you, Jarkko and Allan, for your good hearts and kind support!

I want to thank Professor Ira Nadel (of the University of British Columbia) who read an early English chapter of this book and offered heartfelt encouragement: discovering his biography of Leonard thirty years ago was a great treat and I never got tired of the volume. I want to thank Gilles Tordjman as well as Sylvie Simmons for her book on Leonard, her work in *Mojo*, and her kindness and inquisitive rock-and-roll spirit.

I must also mention here the groundbreaking work (both on Leonard Cohen and Bob Dylan) of Professor Stephen Scobie, which has inspired me deeply. There are so many other Leonard Cohen, performance studies, or pop music scholars whose ideas have intrigued and inspired me, chief among those Richard Schechner, Claude Chastagner, Deshaye Joel, Jiří Měsíc, Francis Mus, Kait Pinder, Alexandra Pleshoyano, David Shumway, and Chantal Ringuet.

I want to thank my research laboratory SEARCH at the University of Strasbourg for their kind support and all my colleagues at the Department of Anglophone Studies. Professor Andrew Eastman, who didn't yawn once in two years as I endlessly entertained him with the minutiae of the development of this book certainly deserves special thanks.

On a more personal note, I want to thank Professor Bernard Genton and Professor Jean-Marie Husser, as well as Lucien Koeppel and all the angels of Palais Universitaire for their help and support in the early stages of writing, not to forget Sandra Zemor for her great friendship as well as Nicolas, Huguette, and Gérard Fleurentdidier for their royal hospitality. I also want to thank Joan Ott and David Muller for their early rereadings, the wonderful Kankyo Tannier, who helped me in more ways than I can say, Master Olivier Reigen Wang-Genh and all the people at Ryumonji monastery, plus all the readers of the French edition who were kind enough to write to me. Thank you all.

Of course, this book wouldn't exist if my father, one fateful day, had not taken out the right record from his cupboard: an LP he bought the year of my birth called *New Skin for the Old Ceremony*. You got my attention, Dad: thanks a lot, and thanks for the ride.

Finally, I want to thank the great Yoshin David Radin for his teaching and his immensely kind heart (a thousand *gasshos* to you, my friend) and his daughter Yoshi for her kind help.

More than anything, I want to send a thousand thanks and kisses to Cécile and to my tabby four-footed Zen master, who has no idea who Leonard Cohen is.

NOTES

PROLOGUE

1. *Book of Longing*, 212.
2. Malena Ivarsson, interview for *Fancy Friday*, SVT, April 28, 1988.
3. See Tony Palmer, *Bird on a Wire*, DVD, 2010 [1974].
4. Although spectacular, it was a benign incident and Cohen was back on stage two days later.
5. "The Law," *Various Positions*, 1985.
6. See Jon Pareles, "At Lunch with Leonard: Philosophical Songwriter on a Wire," *New York Times*, October 11, 1995, and Anjelica Huston, "Leonard Cohen," *Interview Magazine*, November 1995.
7. "Dress Rehearsal Rag," *Songs of Love and Hate*, 1971.
8. "Waiting for the Miracle," *The Future*, 1992.
9. See Curtis Wehrfritz, "The Future" (video), Sony Music, 1992.
10. See *The Favourite Game*, 243–244. In Cohen's world, "gravity" is essentially a game that a mischievous God plays with us to turn our lives into slapstick comedy (see *infra,* Chapter 4, "Imaginary Satori").
11. A mythological figure in Mahayana Buddhism, the bodhisattva embodies the ideal of compassion. Unlike the arhat, who stands alone in enlightenment, he suspends his entry into nirvana until all sentient beings are saved. See Helen J. Baroni, *The Illustrated Encyclopedia of Zen Buddhism* (New York: Rosen Publishing, 2002), 27–29.
12. *Book of Mercy* (1984), psalm 1.
13. Michel de Certeau, *La faiblesse de croire* (Paris: Seuil, 1987), 266.

14. The 1947 song "Passing Through" (featured on Cohen's *Live Songs*) portrays Jesus, Adam, and George Washington as hobo-like pilgrims who are "only passing through."

15. Leon Wieseltier, "The Art of Wandering," CD Booklet, *Leonard Cohen: Songs for the Road*, 3.

16. See Baudelaire's premonitory portrait of Leonard as "man of the world and man of crowds" in *Le Peintre de la vie moderne* (Paris: Mille et Une Nuits, 2010), 22.

17. See André Neher, *L'Identité juive* (Paris: Petite Bibliothèque Payot), 20–30. The author insists that the name Abraham derives from the term *ivri*, which means "to pass."

18. On a deeper level, of course, we are all exiles from the Celestial Garden, and Leonard has often mentioned his Judaism as a cultural heritage that simply portrayed the dilemmas of humanity with the required intensity.

19. Interview in *Ladies and Gentlemen . . . Mr. Leonard Cohen* (1965)

20. Filmed in his parents' house for *Ladies and Gentlemen . . . Mr. Leonard Cohen*, Leonard immortalized his Greek house on the back of *Songs from a Room* and in the inner sleeve of *I'm Your Man*. A memorable sequence in Bob Portway's BBC documentary *Songs from the Life of Leonard Cohen* (1988) features a hilarious tour of the house, with the singer perched on a chair in an attempt to locate the tiny fraction of sea visible from the second floor.

21. His passion for empty spaces must be linked to his favourite philosophical act: undressing. Cohen the interior decorator undresses rooms the way the writer removes useless words in poems, or the way the ladies' man undresses his mistresses. The purpose: to defeat opacity, to reveal the inherent light of things, and get rid of everything that weighs us down.

22. See for example the pictures taken in his Los Angeles home by Dominique Issermann (from the early 1980s to 2016) and by Renaud Monfourny ("Comme un guerrier," *Les Inrockuptibles*, no. 30, July–August 1991), or James Cassimus ("Cohen's Nervous Breakthrough," *Musician*, July 1988).

23. See William Styron, *Darkness Visible: A Memoir of Madness* (London: Vintage, 2001).

24. See David Sheppard, *Leonard Cohen: Kill Your Idols* (New York: Thunder's Mouth Press, 2000), 129.

25. It was probably an ironic response to the critics who accused Cohen of writing "songs to slit your wrists by."

26. "So Long, Marianne" (1967).

27. For more scalpels and razor blades, see "Teachers," *Death of a Lady's Man* (54, 85) and "Dress Rehearsal Rag," a song in which the dejected poet (who is shaving) is confronted (in his mirror) with a cream-covered, razor-wielding, suicidal Santa Claus.

28. Cohen usually uses the word *heart* in the biblical sense, to designate not just the seat of emotions, but a person's spiritual centre, their "inner synagogue" where the spiritual life is led.

29. Some books — like *The Energy of Slaves* (1972), a semi-ironical study of misogyny, *Death of a Lady's Man* (1978), which chronicles an impossible marriage, or *Book of Mercy* (1984), a book of modern psalms — are specific lyrical experiments.

30. The great title of an otherwise unreadable book by L.S. Dorman and C.L. Rawlins (London: Omnibus Press, 1990).

31. In that context, the scene in *The Favourite Game* (60–64) that shows the drunken hero dissecting the heart of a frog on the Montreal pavement (before trying to revive that heart with salt water in a Chinese restaurant) is quite programmatic.

32. In many ways, Cohen's work is a vast commentary on Genesis 1:27 ("male and female He created them") and Genesis 2:24 ("and they shall be one flesh").

33. Never actually used in poems or songs, the "shish kebab" metaphor (first used in "The Great Ones Never Leave," *Melody Maker*, November 20, 1977) is omnipresent in Cohen's interviews. Its staggering description of desire anticipates the poet's last words on the subject in 2016: "It ain't pretty, it ain't subtle, what happens to the heart" (*The Flame*, 3).

34. Very present in the book of Psalms (for example in 50:17, "A broken and a contrite heart, O God, thou wilt not despise"), the motif of the

"broken heart" was later developed by Christians with Jesus's "sacred heart" (which Cohen shows to explode in "Everybody Knows").

35. Many commentators explain Luria's theology as a mystical answer to the Jews' expulsion from Spain (1492): the task was now to travel the world and gather the lost sparks of God's love. See Neher, *op. cit.*, 95–96; Gershom Scholem, *Major Trends of Jewish Mysticism* (New York: Schocken Books, 1995), 284–326; and Marc-Alain Ouaknin, *Tsim-Tsum* (Paris: Albin Michel, 1992), 30–36.

36. Cohen mentions Luria's Kabbalah in several interviews, including the very last one two weeks before his passing (*The New Yorker*, October 17, 2016) in which he summarized Luria's theology as, "We basically live in the ruins of God." See *infra*, Chapter 14.

37. Cindy Bisaillon, "Leonard Cohen: The Other Side of Waiting" (*Shambhala Sun*, January 1994) and Paul Zollo, *Songwriters on Songwriting* (Boston: Da Capo Press, 2003), 348.

CHAPTER 1

1. The poem is "What I'm Doing Here," *Flowers for Hitler*, 13. For the mirror anecdote, see the 1988 interview for KCRW Radio (Burger, 237).

2. Fifty of them appear in *Book of Longing* (2006), sixty-nine in *The Flame* (2018), and about a hundred more were on display in the 2018 exhibit *A Crack in Everything* at the Museum of Contemporary Art of Montreal. For Leonard's Zen sources, see for example the drawings of Hakuin (1686–1768) or Sengaï (1750–1837).

3. One caption (for a portrait dated August 2, 2003) goes, "This guy is getting too tough for us. We're not going to be able to call him a poet much longer" (see the "Blackening Pages" section of Jarkko Arjatsalo's website, www.leonardcohenfiles.com/mirror.html).

4. The term *theory* comes from the Greek verb *theorein*, which simply means "to look."

5. Michael Posner's amazing oral biography *Leonard Cohen: The Untold Stories* (Toronto: Simon & Schuster, 2020 and 2021), compiled from

interviews of 500 friends and acquaintances) does a very good job in proving me wrong. Essential reading.

6. The French philosopher Paul Ricoeur argues that our true identity is narrative and that we are ultimately the sum total of the stories we tell about ourselves.

7. To a great extent, Leonard's whole oeuvre is an invitation into his "secret life," which — influenced as he was by the American school of confessional poetry — he often discloses with brutal honesty in his poetry books.

8. The French word for a "stand-in" (in cinema) is *doublure*, a term which also designates the inner lining of a garment (something that waits to be turned inside out). As a lyrical artist, Cohen has always presented his artistic personae as doublures of his true self, often also showing several competing personae that were indeed doublures of each other: a melancholy poet that hides an inner joker, a Casanova who is also a loser, a spiritual master who cohabits with a desperate seeker, and a believer who is also a radical skeptic.

9. See Nadel, 1996, 9–14.

10. See Tim Footman, *Leonard Cohen: Hallelujah: A New Biography* (London: Chrome Dreams, 2009), 7.

11. The footage can be seen in Owen and Brittain's documentary *Ladies and Gentlemen . . . Mr. Leonard Cohen* (CBC, 1965).

12. See "The Rose," *Death of a Lady's Man*, 121.

13. Described in *The Favourite Game* (5), the home movies are used in several documentaries. *Ladies and Gentlemen . . . Mr. Leonard Cohen* (1965) successively shows little Leonard on his tricycle, Leonard waving in front of the family car with his sister and the chauffeur, the uncles in dinner jackets, the baby poet and his dog, grandfather Lyon, Leonard in a balaclava, and — finally — the boy on skis.

14. See for example Nadel, 1996, photographic insert, 2.

15. Salman Rushdie, *Imaginary Homelands: Essays and Criticism 1981–1991* (London: Granta Books, 1991), 11.

16. *The Favourite Game*, 6.

17. *Mike Walsh Show*, Australia, May 20, 1985.

18. The headline appeared in the *Canadian Jewish Chronicle* the day after a symposium on the future of Judaism where Cohen spoke. See Nadel, 1994, 126, and — for a full transcript of the speech — Winfried Siemerling, "Leonard Cohen, 'Loneliness and History: A Speech Before the Jewish Public Library,'" in Fournier and Norris (eds.), *Take This Waltz* (Montreal: Muses' Company, 1994), 143–153.

19. An institution created in 1927 to defend the civil and political rights of Canadian citizens of the Hebrew faith.

20. After pogroms in the Russian-Polish area, the Jewish population of Quebec increased from 16,000 to 156,000, stabilizing at about 6 percent of the population (see *Encyclopedic Dictionary of Judaism*, 1424–1432).

21. "The Genius," *The Spice-Box of Earth*, 86–87.

22. For the quote, see *The Favourite Game*, 22.

23. *The Favourite Game*, 4.

24. Fleeing pogroms and the Russian Revolution, the Klonitzki-Kline had sought help from the unofficial godfather of Montreal Jews: Lyon Cohen. Nathan was born in 1891 and Masha in 1908.

25. Aviva Layton, interviewed for Nick Broomfield's documentary *Marianne & Leonard: Words of Love* (2019).

26. "The Genius," *The Spice-Box of Earth*, 86–87.

27. See Posner, 2020, 43.

28. Cohen had proclaimed his love for Christ his whole career, to the point where he actually became a Jewish tourist in Christianity and a kind of surrogate Christian, puzzling both his Jewish and his Christian friends. Influenced by the ideas of the German mystic Franz Rosenzweig (who saw Christianity as the armed wing of Judaism and the instrument of its popular dissemination), he spoke to Mark Rowland of his "Christological infatuation" (*Musician*, July 1988) and explained that Christ seemed the perfect symbol to express the need to die in order to be reborn.

29. For the photograph, see for example Nadel, *op. cit.* (1996, central insert, 2). *The Gateless Gate* or *Mumonkan* is a collection of koans

compiled by the Chinese master Mumon Ekai in the thirteenth century, which Leonard would later study thoroughly. A classic translation in English was made available when Paul Reps and Nyogen Senzaki published their influential 1957 anthology of Buddhist texts, *Zen Flesh, Zen Bones* (London: Penguin, 2000).

30. See Rufus Wainwright's interview in Lian Lunson's documentary *I'm Your Man* (Lionsgate DVD, 2005).

31. The Judaism passed on to Leonard is very much imbued with the idea that the Jews are not the people of "the Book," but the people of the commentary, of infinite speculation, and theological dispute. In one word, the people of the intertext. See for example Marc-Alain Ouaknin's *Lire aux éclats* (Paris: Seuil, 1998) or his *Invitation au Talmud* (Paris: Flammarion, 2001).

32. "The Genius," *The Spice-Box of Earth*, 86–87.

33. Simmons, 1. In "Going Home" (*Old Ideas*, 2012), the singer also defines himself as "a lazy bastard living in a suit."

34. In Élisabeth Quin and François Armanet's *The Killer Detail: Sartorial Icons from Cary Grant to Kate Moss* (Paris: Flammarion, 2016), Dominique Issermann reveals that Leonard's '80s suits — although some were sent by Giorgio Armani — were still hand-made by Greek tailors in Athens.

35. In the original French: "Là, tout n'est qu'ordre et beauté / Luxe, calme et volupté." "L'Invitation au Voyage," *Les Fleurs du mal* (1857).

36. Every day of his life as a Zen monk, Leonard recited the Heart Sutra (or Hannya Shingyo), which famously contains a line that says: "Form is Emptiness, Emptiness is Form" (In Japanese: "Shiki fu i ku, ku fu i shiki"). Forms can be abandoned and replaced by other forms.

37. *The Tibetan Book of the Dead* (CBC, 1994, vol. 1, "A Way of Life").

38. In 1990, the poet confided the details of that day's proceedings to his biographers Dorman and Rawlins: the rows of cars parked in front of the house, the factory workers who came to attend the funeral, the exposed coffin, the bagels at the reception, and the immense loneliness that invaded the house as the last guests were leaving. He also mentioned his mother's cries and, finally, the secret celebration of his

sister's birthday, which everyone had forgotten but occurred that very day (Dorman and Rawlins, 27–28).

39. Mentioned in *The Favourite Game* (15), this revolver (actually Nathan's .38-caliber officer gun) inaugurates a long fascination with weapons, confirmed by Joni Mitchell in her song "Rainy Night House" (1970) that later made Leonard an NRA member. To the poet's great embarrassment, a Canadian journalist even spotted a gun in an open drawer of his Chelsea Hotel room (see Marci McDonald, "Leonard Cohen Is a Poet Who Is Trying To Be Free," *Toronto Daily Star*, April 26, 1969). *The Energy of Slaves* mentions the author's Walter PPK and gives it a serial number (42), and the 1983 poem "My Honour" (*Stranger Music*, 394) explains how that weapon was confiscated by his manager.

40. Dorman and Rawlins, *op. cit.*, 362.

41. Cohen 1961, *The Spice-Box of Earth*, 86–87.

42. Morton (fictionalized as "Krantz" in *The Favourite Game*) appears in two Cohen documentaries: he consults the *I Ching* with his friend in *Ladies and Gentlemen . . . Mr. Leonard Cohen* (1965) and has breakfast with him fifteen years later at Mr. Solomon's Delicatessen (for Harry Rasky's film *The Song of Leonard Cohen*, 1980).

43. See Nadel, 1996, 25. In his tenth-grade class photograph in 1950 (Dorman and Rawlins, 209), Leonard is exactly the same height as the two shortest girls in the group. For most of his adult life, Cohen wore Cuban-heeled boots that added two inches to his size.

44. See Nadel, 21 (1996), Simmons, 16–17, and Posner, 42 (2020).

45. For the "Sun-Maid girl," see Posner, 2021, 102. For the high-school flirts, see Nadel, 27, and the song "Memories" (1977), in which Cohen recalls asking the blonde girl in the middle of prom ball if she would let him "see her naked body" (she refused). The episode of the maid is recounted in Posner, *op. cit.*, 43.

46. About Freda Guttman, see Posner, 2020, 111–115. Fictionalized as Tamara in *The Favourite Game* (78–79, et al.), she also inspired several of Cohen's love poems in his first book (also illustrated by her), among which a gruesome "Ballad" (52–53) that evokes her body (assembled,

the poet says, from Ingres, Rossetti, Botticelli, and Goldwyn-Mayer) mutilated in a boarding house and buried among flowers.

47. See "Hey, That's No Way to Say Goodbye" (1967) and "Beneath My Hands" (*The Spice-Box of Earth*, 65).

48. Cited in Nadel, 29.

49. In "I'm Your Man" (1988).

50. See Brian D. Johnson, "Life of a Lady's Man: Leonard Cohen Sings of Love and Freedom," *Maclean's*, December 7, 1992.

51. In *The Favourite Game*, the first naked body seen by the teenage hero was that of the hypnotized family maid, a country girl from Alberta (51–55). The story was later authenticated by Leonard (see Posner, 2020, 42) with the nuance that the maid may have just *pretended* to be hypnotized.

52. TV Interview for *Intérieur Nuit*, RTBF, September 18, 1994.

53. "Paris Model," *Stranger Music*, 391.

54. In the short film *Hallelujah in Moll* (1985), Leonard declares that this "category does not exist," a belief confirmed by the poet's proclivity to proclaim his own "death" as a "ladies' man." "Death of a Lady's/Ladies' Man" being the title of a poem, a song, a record, a book and (perhaps ultimately) of a whole chapter of his life (see *infra*, Chapter 8).

55. For the troubadour connection, see *infra*, Chapter 5, as well as Jiří Měsíc's study *Leonard Cohen, The Modern Troubadour* (Olomouc: Palacký University Press, 2020).

56. Anyone familiar with Cohen's 1970s poetic output (*The Energy of Slaves* and *Death of a Lady's Man*) is aware of the obsessive and at times uncontrollable nature of Cohen's passion for the opposite sex. The neurotic extent of his womanizing — which Leonard was fully aware of — also comes across in Posner's *Leonard Cohen: Untold Stories* (three volumes), which includes the point of view of many of Cohen's female companions.

57. "When the cantor would catalogue the various ways we sinned and died, that moved me very much" is one comment (Reynolds, 6). In *The Favourite Game*, the hero is angered by the way the rabbi and his

uncles failed, for lack of gravity, to take adequate care of the fragile synagogue ritual (126–127).

58. Leonard would later define poetry as language inhabited by a joint resonance of "truth and rhythm and authority and music" (interview for *The Jewish Book News*, January 1994).

59. See Marc-Alain Ouaknin, *Les mystères de la Kabbale* (Paris: Assouline, 2006), 167 and 171.

60. After clarinet and ukulele lessons, Leonard had his first serious taste of guitar practice in the summer of 1950, at Irving Morton's (socialist-leaning) summer camp, where he was working as a trainee counsellor (see Posner, 2020, 48–50) and discovered the recently published *People's Songbook*, soon to be the quasi-official bible of the folk revival movement. Among the tunes that caught his attention was a French resistance song called "The Partisan."

61. In his reception speech for the 2011 Prince of the Asturias Prize, Cohen placed that anecdote in the early '60s, when he was trying to improve his guitar skills. Earlier interviews (see for example Fevret, 99) always placed the episode in Cohen's late teenage years (in the very early '50s).

62. See *Beautiful Losers*, Diethard Kuster's filmed interview for the French and German cultural TV channel *Arte* (1997).

63. Cohen, *The Spice-Box of Earth*, 86–87.

64. See "The Circus Animals' Desertion" in John Kelly (ed.), *Yeats, W.B.* (London: Everyman, 1997), 88–89.

65. *The Spice-Box of Earth*, 28.

66. "Everybody Knows" (1988).

67. See Charles Mopsik, *Le Zohar. Lamentations* (Paris: Verdier, 2000), 6.

68. *The Favourite Game*, 90.

69. Cohen, 1961, 86–87.

70. The poem in question ("The Sparrows," *Let Us Compare Mythologies*, 26–27) will seem a little mannered today, but it is quite accomplished technically and impersonal enough to impress a Pound devotee.

CHAPTER 2

1. See "Howl" and "Footnote to Howl" in Allen Ginsberg, *Howl and Other Poems* (San Francisco: City Lights Publishing, 1956).

2. The term *beat*, which meant "beaten up" in the slang of drug addicts, was hijacked by the Catholic Kerouac to evoke the "beatitude" of angelic visions. To a great extent, the whole beat ethos lies in the tension between the three meanings of "beat": rhythm, defeat, and *beatitude*.

3. Christian Fevret, "Comme un Guerrier," *Les Inrockuptibles*, no. 30, July–August 1991, 100.

4. See Dudek's poetic manifesto in the first issue of *CIV/n* quoted in Nadel, 39, and Dorman and Rawlins, 61–62.

5. See respectively E.J. Pratt, *Towards the Last Spike* (1952) and Dudek, Layton, and Souster, *Cerberus* (1953).

6. On account of an unfortunate tendency to connect Western decadence to usury and Judaism, and after hosting a radio program in Mussolini's Italy that was not exactly politically correct, the fascist Pound was placed in a Washington psychiatric hospital after the war to avoid the death penalty.

7. Fevret, 100.

8. See respectively "Every Pebble" (*Stranger Music*, 399), *Beautiful Losers* (173–180) and *Book of Mercy* (psalm 2).

9. See Harry Rasky, *op. cit.*, 31–47.

10. For the quotes, see respectively Paul Zollo, *Songwriters on Songwriting* (Boston: DaCapo Press, 2003), 322, and Antony DeCurtis, "Leonard Cohen's Tales from the Dark Side," *Rolling Stone*, January 21, 1993.

11. See Allan Donaldson, "Let Us Compare Mythologies by Leonard Cohen," *The Fiddlehead* (November 1956), reprinted in Gnarowski, *Leonard Cohen: The Artist and His Critics* (Whitby: McGraw-Hill Ryerson, 1976), 11–12.

12. See, for example, the poem about a stillborn eaglet whose death is a victory that saves him from future arrows ("Item," 28) or the one that presents Jesus as a lonely loser in a boarding room ("City Christ," 29).

13. See respectively "Pagans" (44–45), "Halloween Poem" (62–63), "Sainte-Catherine Street" (50–51), "Ballad [My Lady Was Found Mutilated]" (52–53), "Lovers" (40), "Ballad [He Pulled a Flower]" (46–7), "Summer Nights" (54) and "Saviours" (73–74).

14. Early in his career, the Canadian Broadcasting Corporation (CBC) took an instant liking to Cohen, supporting him in many ways. They even started negotiations in 1966 to hire the poet as cohost of a current affairs news show (see Nadel, 140, and Posner, 2020, 318–323).

15. Fevret, 99.

16. *The Favourite Game*, 128.

17. In late September 1961, Cohen would again spend a couple of days with Ginsberg, who was stopping over in Hydra on his way to India. Much later, the beat poet would attend one of Leonard's recording sessions with his friend Bob Dylan and provide backing vocals to a song (see *infra*, Chapter 8). By that time, both poets had watched each other's work very closely. In the early '60s (still in Greece), Cohen would also befriend beat poets Kenneth Koch and Harold Norse.

18. "The Gift," *The Spice-Box of Earth*, 11. Leonard was really in love apparently, and Marianne once claimed he had never really recovered from the break-up with Ann Sherman (Posner, 2020, 225).

19. See *The Favourite Game*, 110–111.

20. Don Owen, "The Poet as Hero. Part 2. Cohen Remembered," *Saturday Night Review*, June 1969.

21. Fevret, *op. cit.*, 99–100.

22. In keeping with Rimbaud's instructions ("The poet makes himself a seer through a long, vast and methodical derangement of all the senses"), Leonard enthusiastically participated in his generation's great chemical adventure. His involvement with a CIA-financed research program on LSD that did take place at the Allan Memorial Hospital in McGill University is uncertain, but Nadel notes that by the late '50s the poet had tried hashish and peyote (1996, 49) and that, he was familiar with all available substances by late 1963 (opiates, LSD, barbiturates, and amphetamines). As we shall see, Cohen's relationship to drugs remained mostly

either sacramental (hallucinogens to open the doors of perception) or functional (amphetamines to write all night and ward off depression).

23. Among those are a few gems like "Luggage for Sale," "Diary of a Montreal Lecher," and "The Juke-Box Heart."

24. Written in 1960, published in *Parasites of Heaven* (18).

25. See Doug Beardsley, "On First Looking into Leonard Cohen" in Stephen Scobie (ed.), *Intricate Preparations, op. cit.*, 5–8.

26. A year later, on November 18, 1959, Leonard (accompanied by Layton) will read to 800 people at the New York YMHA (Young Men's Hebrew Association). His first crowd.

27. Nadel, 69.

28. See Gnarowski, 10.

29. The publisher gives his version of the episode in Fournier and Norris (eds.) *Take This Waltz* (Montreal: Muses' Company, 1994), 111–112.

30. For more details on the long love affair between Leonard and his Olivetti, see "Leonard Cohen: My Old Flame" in Scott Cohen, *Yakety Yak: Midnight Confessions and Revelations of 37 Rockstars and Legends* (London: Simon & Schuster, 1994), 123. For the picture, see photo insert, p. 12.

31. A 1974 interview for the British countercultural magazine *Zigzag* reveals that the young woman was actually a Shakespearean actress (see Robin Pike, "September 15, 1974," in Burger, 59).

32. Born Michael de Freitas in the West Indies, Michael X (1933–1975) was the leader of the Black Power Movement in London. After his commune burnt down and a short stay in prison, he left the UK for Tobago, where he recreated a revolutionary organization and was arrested again, this time for the murder of two members of his group. After a highly publicized trial and despite the support of many voices in the American counterculture (including John Lennon's and Leonard's), he was convicted and hanged in 1975.

33. *Flowers for Hitler*, 63.

34. Fevret, *op. cit.*, 105.

35. Back cover of *The Spice-Box of Earth* (1961).

36. From a 2005 interview with Kari Hesthamar for NRK radio. For a transcript, see "Leonard Cohen Looks Back on the Past" at www .leonardcohenfiles.com/leonard2006.html.

37. See "St. Francis," *Death of a Ladies' Man*, 124–125, and Saint Francis's "Canticle of Creatures."

38. Fevret, *op. cit.*, 105.

39. For a mystical (and humorous) reading of Leonard Cohen's Greek garden as hortus conclusus, see the Hydriot Roger Green's excellent *Hydra and the Bananas of Leonard Cohen* (London: Basic Books, 2003), 114–115.

40. Leonard's second volume would be published only six months after his arrival.

41. The expression is borrowed from the American poet Wallace Stevens (1879–1955) who speaks of "the necessary angel of reality." See Stevens, *Complete Poetry and Prose* (Boston: Library of America, 1997), 637.

42. See Mark Rowland, "Leonard Cohen's Nervous Breakthrough," *Musician*, July 1988.

43. The first quote is from the back cover of *The Spice-Box of Earth* (1961), the second from a letter Leonard wrote to his sister in October 1961 (Thomas Fisher Rare Book Library, Ms. Coll. 122, Box #11, Folder 2).

44. Leonard described Marianne's "transfigurations" in a 2005 interview: "The wonderful thing about Marianne is that there were two Mariannes. There was the Marianne of some nights [. . .] and it had nothing to do with wine: a thimble could be enough to transfigure her into another kind of being [that was] bold, menacing, beautiful in some ways, but frightening if you were the man beside her." Cf. Kari Hesthamar, "Leonard Cohen Looks Back on His Past." Full transcript is available on Jarkko Arjatsalo's website, www.leonardcohenfiles.com /mirror.html.

45. See "Tower of Song," *I'm Your Man* (1988).

46. Hesthamar, *op. cit.*

47. A former war reporter and army buddy of George Johnston, Burke stopped over in Hydra in October 1960 on his way back from India. He took hundreds of pictures for a photo-reportage on the expat

community meant for *Life Magazine*. Although the reportage was never published at the time, the pictures are now widely available on the internet.

48. Also of interest are the many testimonies by the couple's entourage in Michael Posner's *Leonard Cohen: Untold Stories, The Early Years* (2021), Kari Hesthamar and Helle V. Goldman's book-length memoir of Marianne's life (*So Long, Marianne: A Love Story*, ECW Press, 2014), as well as Fabien Greenberg and Bård Kjøge Rønning's poignant movie *Little Axel* about Marianne's son (Antipode Films, 2021).

49. In *Ladies and Gentlemen . . . Mr. Leonard Cohen.*

50. See Fevret, 106.

51. *Flowers for Hitler*, 42.

CHAPTER 3

1. For the quote, see Marc-Alain Ouaknin, *Les secrets de la Kabbale*, 27. The limited 1961 edition of *Spice-Box* featured high-quality paper, incredible craftsmanship and thirteen illustrations by Frank Newfeld. These included stylized flowers, a cricket, Hasidic dancers, naked women with allegorical trumpets (to evoke the glory of the poet) and a vision of the poet asleep beneath a mountain.

2. See respectively "A Kite is a Victim" (9), "After the Sabbath Prayer" (10), "Good Brothers" (where Cohen depicts himself dancing on Van Gogh's grave with the yellow skeletons of Vincent and Theo), or "Out of the Land of Heaven" (79, which evokes the poet's entry into Paradise with Marc Chagall) and "When I Uncovered Your Body" (39).

3. *The Spice-Box of Earth*, 77.

4. "As the Mist Leaves No Scar," 64. The poem will become a song on the album *Death of a Ladies' Man* (1977).

5. The title is ambiguous, however, for it may designate either a box "made of earth" or Earth itself as a metaphorical spice box.

6. See *Flowers for Hitler*, 52, and Posner, 2020, 184–186.

7. In her memoir of Hydriot life, *Leonard, Marianne, and Me* (Guilford: Backbeat Books, 2021), Judy Scott reports Marianne's confidence that

Leonard self-medicated his depression with Ritalin, then available over the counter (44). Leonard described amphetamine to Christian Fevret as "a very bad drug for depressed people. It took me ten years to fully recover: I had blackouts and ended up completely burnt out, unable to get out of bed. [. . .] Amphetamines tap into future resources: in my case, they had eaten ten years" (Fevret, 108). The singer also regularly insisted in later life that many substances, including hashish, were actually harmful (see *Zigzag*, "October 1974," Burger, 71–72). In the 1980s with the growing popularity of cocaine, the singer adopted a very aggressive position, supporting the republican "war on drugs" (see "Leonard Cohen. A Portrait in the First Person," CBC, 1989).

8. See *Parasites of Heaven*, 69.

9. *Ibid.*, 11. After seeing the place where lambs were slaughtered for the Easter celebration, Leonard remained a vegetarian for two years, eventually giving up when he realized he was becoming sectarian. He would practise occasional fasting most of his life (see Paul Grescoe, "Poet, Writer, Singer, Lover, Cohen," *Canadian Magazine*, February 10, 1968).

10. See Nadel, 132, and Green, 82.

11. See Thomas Cleary and Lieou Yi-Ming, *Yi-King* (Paris: Éditions du Rocher, 1994), back cover.

12. Nadel, 104.

13. See, for example, the lesson on the art of falling in love in the Manhattan snow (170–174) or the incredible dissection of a frog in the middle of the street by two drunken students, followed by their remorseful attempt to revive the animal's heart in a Chinese restaurant (60–64).

14. Gilles Tordjman, "Histoire sans morale. Cohen entre Ciel et Terre," *Les Inrockuptibles*, no. 1, September 1995, 23.

15. In an era when D.H. Lawrence's *Lady Chatterley's Lover* had been legal in the UK for only two years, one critic compares the book to a "peep show" (Gnarowski, *op. cit.*, 23).

16. See "Playing the Favourite Game," interview for the CBC, 1963.

17. *The Favourite Game*, 230–231.

18. Milton Wilson, "Poetry," *Letters in Canada: 1964* (Gnarowski, 20–23).

19. In both appearances at the Jewish Public Library, large sections of the audience were alienated by Cohen's contrary and provocative attitude.

20. The remarks respectively come from a letter to his editor (Nadel, 119), the poem "Montreal, 1964" (*Flowers for Hitler*, 39), a television interview for the CBC on May 23, 1966, and the two aforementioned symposiums at the Jewish Public Library.

21. The final cover featured sketches in the poet's hand: a friendly dog, a warplane, and (of course) a baby's face with a Hitler moustache. As for the cover of the 1970 UK edition of *The Favourite Game* (Avon Press), it featured a teenage girl in a high school uniform brazenly staring at the reader under the inscription: "The daring world of the new love where SEX is THE FAVOURITE GAME." It sold like hotcakes.

22. The "Mahatma" reference is mentioned by Grace Lichtenstein in her profile for the *New York Times* ("Leonard Cohen Muses on New Stage," September 8, 1973). The quote by Leonard is from "Priest of God," *Parasites of Heaven*, 68.

23. At this stage, the poet's fame has actually reached the trendy circles of New York. Warhol's assistant Gerard Malanga (a poet himself) collected Cohen's books and dedicated one of his own texts to him. See Andy Warhol, *Popism: The Warhol Sixties* (London: Pimlico, 1996), 82, and Gerard Malanga, *Ten Poems for Ten Poets* (Avon: Derringer Books, 2000), 14–18.

24. Originally intended to be a portrait of the four McClelland & Stewart poets who did the tour (Cohen, Layton, Earle Birney, and Phyllis Gotlieb), the film became a solo portrait of Leonard when it appeared his readings were the only ones that retained their impact on screen. Stylistically, the film echoes Robert Frank's beat generation classic *Pull My Daisy* (1959), presenting Cohen's beatnik life as an interweaving of jazz, poetry, and urban bohemia.

25. See the November 6, 1964, review of the performance (quoted in Nadel, 1996, 129).

26. Just days before the reading, Cohen had indeed visited his interned poet-friend Henry Moskovitch (see Posner, 2020, 247–49).

27. We have learnt in the meantime that the friend was not insane, but "did this instead of College."

28. The asylum in question foreshadows the hospital in "Teachers" (1967), where patients are given scalpels to dig their own flesh. Psychiatric hospitals were not terra incognita for Cohen: he had had several opportunities to visit his mother there (as well as several friends) and, each time, he could see the damage done by contemporary drug treatments and electroshocks. Hence the singer's deep affection for the insane, which led him to give several free concerts in mental institutions (in 1970 and 1974).

29. For the quote about the inner KZ, see Michael Ondaatje, *Leonard Cohen, Canadian Writers, no. 5* (McClelland & Stewart, 1970), 61, n. 1. For the poem, see *Flowers for Hitler*, 49. We may note in that couplet how, to the backdrop of stuttering b's ("brain / boils / bowels") and g's ("Goering / ingots /gold") and a beautiful inner rhyme ("boils / bowels"), the eternal recurrence of an "o" is dramatized, to open our mouths again and again in amazement at the horror of the foul beasts within us.

30. "Leviathan" (55).

31. The first occurrence of this (then much quoted) pronouncement is in *Dialektik der Aufklärung* (Berlin: Suhrkamp, 1981 [1947]), 30.

32. See "Congratulations" (15).

33. "All There Is to Know About Adolf Eichmann" (66) notes that everything about the criminal is "average"; "The Failure of a Secular Life" (53) evokes the loneliness of the executioners when they come home after work and "A Migrating Dialogue" (72) describes the sexual intimacy of Hitler and Eva Braun and transforms characters from American comics into assistants of the SS brutes.

34. "What I'm Doing Here" (13).

35. See respectively "Montreal 1964," "Portrait of the City Hall," and "Business as Usual"; "Opium and Hitler" and "The Drawer's Condition on November 28, 1961"; "I Wanted to Be a Doctor," "The Music Crept by Us," and "The Suit"; and "Hydra 1963," "The New Step," "Style," and "Millennium."

36. "Leonard Cohen: Black Romantic," originally published in *Canadian Literature* (fall 1967) and reprinted in Gnarowski, 94–105.

37. See, for example, the outré ode to fellatio in "The Celebration" (*The Spice-Box of Earth*, 63) or "Dead Song" (*ibid.*, 56), where the dead poet makes love to an angel, or "Inquiry into the Nature of Cruelty," about a moth drowned in the poet's urine (*ibid.*, 36).

38. In the words of George Bowering, "Keep looking at that belly button, Leonard Cohen. [It's] got angel dust in it." (Gnarowski, 34)

39. See *Parasites of Heaven*, 35, and *The Spice-Box of Earth*, 37–38.

40. A vast movement of popular mysticism initiated in eighteenth-century Ukraine led by the famous rabbi Israel Ben Eliezer (or Baal Shem Tov), Hasidism was propagated by tzadiks, spiritual masters that had courts of disciples and were sometimes itinerant. Often miracle workers, they disseminated Kabbalistic themes and ideas and advocated a joyful practice of prayer rather than Talmudic scholarship. See, for example, Gershom Scholem, *op. cit.*, 244–366.

41. For Cohen's interventions, see Jon Ruddy, "Is the World (or Anybody) Ready for Leonard Cohen?" *Maclean's*, November 1, 1966, and *This Hour Has Seven Days* (CBC TV), May 1, 1966.

42. For the anecdote, see *This Hour Has Seven Days*, CBC TV, May 1, 1966. For the quote, see *The Favourite Game*, 10.

43. The koan (often called the "koan of Sozan's dharma body") is "Case 52." See Wick Gerry Shishin, *Book of Equanimity: Illuminating Classic Zen Koans* (Somerville: Wisdom Publications, 2005), 161.

44. "A Thousand Kisses Deep" (2001).

45. Although Balaam is a seer and a visionary, his donkey sees the angel of the Lord three times before he does (Num. 22).

46. Quoted in Susan Lumsey, "Leonard Cohen Wants the Unconditional Leadership of the World," *Weekend Magazine*, no. 37 (1970), reprinted in Gnarowski, 69–73.

47. We are spared no detail of the saint's mortifications or her successive rapes (see pp. 86–89 and 200–201).

48. Writing also regularly dissolves into shouting, prayer, or pornographic delirium.

49. For a systematic analysis of those two forces (a *diabolic* and a *symbolic* one) see C. Lebold, "Fragmentation and Unity in Leonard Cohen's Beautiful Losers," *Canadian Studies*, no. 46, 1999 (143–153).

50. To give the volume an "art book" feel (and increase the price to avoid censorship), the original M&S edition has two Edvard Munch–like lithographs by Harold Town printed in black and gold on the dust jacket and imprinted in the black velvet underneath.

51. Quotes from the positive reviews of the *New York Times*, the *Dallas Times*, and by the influential critic Leslie Fiedler were printed on the back cover of the American paperback edition (Viking Press, 1966). The opening of the *Boston Sunday Herald* review is still famous: "James Joyce is not dead. He lives in Montreal as Leonard Cohen." The Canadian reactions are quoted in *Take 30* (CBC TV, May 23, 1966) and in Robert Fulford, "Cohen's Nightmare Novel," *Toronto Daily Star*, April 26, 1966.

52. The "God Is Alive, Magic Is Afoot" section (often read by Cohen in public readings) was later set to music by Buffy Sainte-Marie for her album *Illuminations* (1969). For the original text, see *Beautiful Losers*, 157–158.

53. Accounts of the event — including Leonard's many versions — differ considerably. Marianne mentioned a hospital in Athens.

54. He finished the song at the Henry Hudson Hotel in New York in early 1966. The movie that inspired him (whose title appears in the lyrics) is Otto Preminger's *The Man with the Golden Arm* (1955) in which Sinatra plays a heroin-addicted card dealer.

55. All of which will be recorded as songs, some very soon.

56. As Posner explains, he even contacts Dylan's management (295).

57. "The Stormy Clovers," *Toronto Star*, June 26, 1966.

58. The band would record, probably in the early fall of 1966, the first existing version of "Suzanne," as was revealed by Allan Showalter's defunct website: 1HeckOfAGuy.com.

CHAPTER 4

1. *The Spice-Box of Earth*, 19.

2. It is hard to pinpoint exactly when the singer settled in New York. After a series of successive stays in 1966, Leonard — who still lived in Montreal with Marianne in an unhappy attempt to rekindle their relationship — stayed in Mexico in the summer for a shamanistic initiation with the mystic John Starr Cook and seems to have stayed in New York again in autumn. He presumably took "permanent" residence there shortly after Marianne's departure for Greece by late January 1967.

3. The first songs — often begun in Montreal or Hydra — are apparently "Teachers" (completed in 1965), "The Stranger Song," "Tonight Will Be Fine," "Store Room," and "Everybody's Child" (as well as the unreleased "Rivers"). While in New York, Leonard wrote "Dress Rehearsal Rag," "The Master Song," "Love Calls You by Your Name," as well as an early version of "Take This Longing" (i.e., "The Bells"). "Suzanne" (underway since 1965) was probably completed in Montreal in the summer of 1966.

4. The Virgin is mentioned by Richard Goldstein, who interviewed Cohen for the *Village Voice* ("Beautiful Creep," December 28, 1967, reproduced in Gnarowski, 40–46). "Aubades" were literally "songs of dawn," farewells addressed to mistresses after nights of love.

5. The "424" is sometimes referred to as the "Cohenian" room. As of the late '70s, Leonard will also upgrade to the Royalton Hotel (less bohemian, more luxurious) and later to the Mayflower.

6. Interestingly, the title was originally "Come On, Marianne."

7. Marianne had joined her lover in January 1964, only to return to Hydra the following April, when it was clear their North American cohabitation had failed.

8. The quote is from Barrie Wexler (Posner, 2021, 180).

9. The culprit was apparently Steve Sanfield, and the episode led to a great bout of Cohenian jealousy recorded in "What did I do with my breath?" (*Parasites of Heaven*, 36–37), where the poet — appointed "detective of love" — comically tries to "reconstruct / every one of your nights" at five thousand miles of distance.

10. Probably the several abortions that seem to have taken place (at a time when abortions were illegal and required "contacts" in London

or Norway) must have taken their toll of tears, as Marianne was gradually brought to accept she would never have children with Leonard, being unable to give him Jewish kids (see Posner, 386–387), and Nick Broomfield, *Marianne & Leonard: Words of Love* (2019).

11. See "New Poems" in *Selected Poems: 1956–1968* (Toronto: McClelland & Stewart, 1969).

12. Reading Leonard's letters to Marianne at that time is a rather disheartening experience. It's hard to read how the poet — whose energies are obviously elsewhere — gives just enough signs of love not to let Marianne off the hook. Apparently, he saw her more as a Penelope than a Calypso but it's not clear whether he enjoyed having a woman waiting for him in his Greek house. Two years later, although Leonard had already met the mother of his future children, Marianne will again try to live near him in New York in an apartment at Stanton and Clinton Street in the Lower East Side, with Leonard as a frequent visitor and occasional companion and provider.

13. A legacy of the building's first two decades (when it housed only private residential apartments), the leased apartments were sometimes occupied by tenants who had not stepped out of the hotel for several decades, like Alphaeus Philemon Cole, a portrait painter who died here at the age of 112 after 35 years of residence.

14. This is actually Arthur Miller's description of his friend Stanley Bard. See Sherill Tippins, *Inside the Dream Palace: The Life and Times of New York's Legendary Chelsea Hotel* (New York: Houghton Mifflin Harcourt, 2013), 141.

15. Spoken introduction to "Chelsea Hotel," Nuremberg, October 5, 1988.

16. The music manager and factory regular Danny Fields told Edie's biographers that Leonard had warned the actress that the candles' arrangement on her mantelpiece heralded bad luck. See Jean Stein and George Plimpton, *Edie: An American Biography* (New York: Grove Press, 1994), 326. He also remembers that Cohen's immoderate use of incense infuriated the management.

17. Quoted by Nick Walsh, "I Never Discuss My Mistresses and My Tailors," *The Guardian*, October 14, 2001.

18. See Maurice de Gandillac (ed.), *Œuvres complètes du Pseudo-Denys l'Aréopagite* (Paris: Aubier, 1989), 207–219.

19. The episode, narrated in detail in a 1972 interview for *Melody Maker*, most likely took place in the autumn of 1967 (see also Nadel, 168). The woman in question was later immortalized as "Lady Midnight" (*Songs from a Room*, 1969), an allegorical woman whose body was made of wind and was eaten by stars.

20. The anecdote usually served as a comedic counterpoint to the tragic and raw song during the 1980, 1985, and 1988 tours.

21. See Tony Palmer, *Bird on a Wire*, DVD, Machat Company, 2010 [1974].

22. See respectively "The Gypsy's Wife" (*Recent Songs*, 1979), the poem "The Language of Love" (*Death of a Lady's Man*, 142–143), and "Paper-Thin Hotel" (*Death of a Ladies' Man*, 1977).

23. A 1963 poem entitled "Suzanne Wears a Leather Coat" describes the young woman striding the streets with such grace that the traffic comes to a halt, motorists fall out of cars, and crowds find salvation. (*Parasites of Heaven*, 31).

24. Whoever likes details will be glad to know the brand of tea ("Constant Comment") revealed by Cohen — himself a lover of details — in a radio interview for BBC One (August 7, 1994).

25. Cohen often mentioned that given how splendid the couple was, even to want to kiss Armand Vaillancourt's wife was inconceivable (BBC One interview, July 8, 1994).

26. Bonino, *Les anges et les démons. 14 leçons de théologie* (Paris: Parole et Silence, 2007), 120–130.

27. Turning tea flavoured with orange peels into "tea and oranges" is one of the song's great poetic insights. The orange, a fruit in obvious metonymic connection with the sun, opens at the outset of the song, a paradigm of light which reappears at the end, with the reflection of the setting sun in Suzanne's mirror.

28. According to Thomas, the presence of an angel, not necessarily perceptible in real time, can be proven in retrospect by the traces they leave in the world and in ourselves. Unusual stimulation of our intelligence,

our imagination, or our courage can thus be signs of angelic action (see Bonino, *op. cit.*, 81–82).

29. Bonino, *op. cit.*, 120–130.

30. A belief expressed in an interview for the BBC One radio program *Kaleidoscope*, August 7, 1994.

31. "Beneath My Hands," *The Spice-Box of Earth*, 65.

32. This is how the poet describes the young girls imitating Bardot in "One of the Nights I Didn't Kill Myself" (*Flowers for Hitler*, 120).

33. "I couldn't get a date. By the time that first album came out, I was in such a shattered situation that I found myself living at the Henry Hudson Hotel on Fifty-Seventh Street, going to the Morningside Café on Eighth Avenue, trying to find some way to approach the waitress and ask her out. I would get letters of longing from around the world, and I would find myself walking the streets of New York at three in the morning, trying to strike up a conversation with women." (Wayne Robins, "The Loneliness of the Long-Suffering Folkie," *Newsday*, November 22, 1992.)

34. Leonard celebrated the automaton in a poem about the moments of mystical grace that came to him while buying industrial pancakes there ("The Old 23rd Street Automat," *Book of Longing*, 77). Patti Smith, another tenant of the Chelsea, mentions meeting Allen Ginsberg there. See *Just Kids* (New York: HarperCollins, 2010), 91–93.

35. *The Energy of Slaves*, 116.

36. We are still surprised that the episode hasn't yet joined Rosa Parks and the students of Tiananmen Square in the annals of modern protest. For the anecdote see John Walsh, "Research, You Understand . . . ," *Mojo Magazine*, September 1994, 58.

37. For the picture, see Nadel, 1996, photographic section.

38. Buffy Sainte-Marie, "Leonard Cohen: His Songs," *Sing Out!* 17, no. 4 (August–September 1967), 16–17.

39. In 1967, Julie Felix recorded three more Cohen songs for her follow-up album, while Buffy Sainte-Marie transformed one of *Beautiful Losers*'s prayers into a song. The financial benefit of the "Suzanne" covers was nil for the Jew Cohen, who had just been conned by a goyish Shylock, the arranger and publisher Jeff Chase. Presented with what he naïvely

believed was "the standard contract," Leonard actually signed away the rights of three songs ("Suzanne" among them) that he would not get back until 1988 (see Nadel, 153–154, and Simmons, 176–177).

40. Bridget "Polk" Berlin had compiled a book, where every artist she met was invited to draw a penis. Pressed to comply at Max's, Cohen apparently graced his page with the (signed) inscription, "Let me be the shy one in this book."

41. Regarding their relationship, he writes — always blowing hot and cold: "I hope we can repair the painful spaces where uncertainties have led us. I hope you can lead yourself out of despair, and I hope I can help you."

42. Research by Allan Showalter and Michael Posner has shown that the two girls were actually local students, not travellers (see Posner, 2020, 323–328).

43. The melody, one of Leonard's mother's favourites, was ready before the song (see *Greatest Hits*, liner notes).

44. Of course, "Sisters of Mercy" is also the English name of the religious order founded by the French St. Vincent de Paul to bring hospitality to travellers and pilgrims.

45. Cohen's abundant use of "you" and narratives featuring us as protagonists explains in part his songs' hospitality and their power to affect us (see also "Suzanne" or "The Stranger Song").

46. Of course, the song also evokes a sexual situation: two passing girls and a man who touches "the dew on their hem" after having been tied up by them. In his first recorded concert in England (BBC, August 1968), Cohen joked that the sisters' main act of "mercy" was "to introduce the miniskirt to Edmonton" (not likely in a November blizzard).

47. The expression is used by George Bowering in his review of *Parasites of Heaven* for *Canadian Literature* (see Gnarowski, *op. cit.*, 32).

48. See "You Live Like a God" in *Selected Poems: 1956–1968*, 84–85.

49. For a more detailed presentation of the treatise, see Renée de Trion-Montalembert, *La cabbale et la tradition judaïque* (Paris: CELT, 1974), 197–199.

50. See Wigoder, *The Oxford Dictionary of the Jewish Religion* (Oxford: Oxford University Press, 1997), 74.

51. Accounts (including his own) diverge as to when Leonard first saw Nico. She was booked for solo shows at the Dom in October 1966 and again from early February to late April 1967.

52. The poem in question ("Beauty"), which depicts a daunting, sphynx-like femme fatale who keeps poets prisoner and combines "the cygnet's whiteness with a heart of snow," seems written with Nico in mind. See Roy Campbell, *Poems of Baudelaire* (New York: Pantheon Books, 1952), 47.

53. Those cracks will strike all of Nico's men, especially perhaps French filmmaker Philippe Garrel, who will show her screaming and howling in the desolate splendour of Icelandic and Egyptian landscapes in *La cicatrice intérieure* (1972), a movie whose medieval aesthetics — a monk's robe and a horse for Nico, often shown surrounded by fire — will be a direct nod to Leonard's "Joan of Arc."

54. See "You Do Not Have to Love Me" (*Selected Poems: 1956–1968*, 83) and "Take This Longing" (*New Skin for the Old Ceremony*, 1974). In his savoury chronicle of Nico's last tours, keyboardist James Young mentions the singer's claim that Cohen had squeezed her hands so hard he had broken her wrist (*Nico: Songs They Never Play on the Radio*, Bloomsbury, 59).

55. One of these prayers was published five years later in the aptly named *The Energy of Slaves* ("How we used to approach *The Book of Changes*: 1966," 65).

56. Nadel, 148.

57. Certeau, *op. cit.*, 313.

58. Quoted in Samuel Rosenberg and Hans Tischler, *Chansons des Trouvères, Chanter M'estuet* (Paris: Livre de Poche, 1995), 579.

59. "You Live Like a God," *Selected Poems: 1956–1968*, 84–85.

60. According to James Young, Nico became a serious heroin addict only in the early 1970s (*op. cit.*, XI), a claim contradicted by John Cale, who mentions in his autobiography the arguments "due to opiates" during the recording of *The Marble Index* in September 1968. See *What's Welsh for Zen?* (London: Bloomsbury, 1999), 90. A recent biography attests that when Nico crossed Leonard's path, she was

probably not the determined junkie she would soon become but was certainly familiar with heroin. See Jennifer Otter, *You Are Beautiful and You Are Alone* (London: Hachette UK, 2021), 296.

61. "Last Year's Man" (1971). We may note John Cale's tongue-in-cheek response to Leonard when he portrayed Nico as "Helen of Troy" on his eponymous album in 1975.

62. The Eskimo who shows the narrator a movie may well be Warhol, who had done multiple screen tests of Nico. The "saint who had loved you" could be Lou Reed, unless we choose to see in that saint's death by drowning a premonition of the sad ends of Brian Jones and Jim Morrison, two lovers of Nico, both of whom were found dead in water, one in a pool in 1969 and the other in a Paris bathtub in 1971. Didn't Leonard claim he could "see the future" and that the future "was murder"?

63. For the quotes, see Nadel, 147, and John Walsh, "Research, You Understand . . . ," *Mojo Magazine*, September 1994, 58.

64. See *infra*, Chapter 1.

65. Andy Warhol and Patricia Hackett, *op. cit.*, 208.

66. "On hearing of a name long unspoken," *Flowers for Hitler*, 25.

67. In 1970, Cohen will later explain to his Isle of Wight audience that he was "coming off amphetamines" during that early New York period, a withdrawal that must have amplified his depressive streak.

68. See respectively *Greatest Hits* (1975, liner notes), Dorman and Rawlins, *op. cit.*, 142; Paul Grescoe, "Lover, Poet, Singer, Priest," *Canadian Magazine* (February 1968); Nadel, 148 (journal entry); spoken prologue to "Please Don't Pass Me By" (*Live Songs*, 1973).

69. In the poem "Picture of the Artist in His Room" (*The Energy of Slaves*, 60), Leonard describes the exercise: to name what lies before you (a bed, a cup, a window) and then check if you yourself are still here.

70. "Field Commander Cohen" (1974).

71. Those (meta)physical laws are of course supplemented by the law of cause and effect, a little thing also known as karma. Leonard knew the moral corollary of that law quite well: sin sends you to hell, an opinion that has dismayed several countercultural journalists (see,

for example, Graham Lock, "Love Me, Love My Barrel Gun," *NME*, March 23, 1980).

72. "Tower of Song" (1988).

CHAPTER 5

1. Most of the action took place in the various studios of CBS's Fifty-Second Street building near St. Patrick's Cathedral, but a couple of sessions occurred under the cathedral ceiling of the mythical Thirtieth Street studio in a former Armenian church.

2. Leonard ended up directing the last sessions himself.

3. See Cohen's interview for "The John Hammond Years: Leonard Cohen," BBC Radio, September 20, 1986.

4. Obviously, the idea behind using female backing singers is a central contribution to the creation of Cohen's musical identity.

5. See Paul Grescoe "Poet, Lover, Singer, Priest: Cohen," *Canadian Magazine*, February 1968.

6. This is what sets Cohen apart from the likes of Tim Hardin, Tim Buckley, or Jackson Browne. His art is not just about poetry and intimate confessions; it also provides a very precise theological landscape (the world of the fall, compulsory wanderings, and irrepressible attractions).

7. Described by Leonard as "fragile things that have a disarming life of their own" (Rowland, *op. cit.*), the melodies, sometimes so simple you barely notice them, are no less haunting.

8. Cohen's guitar playing, which producer Bob Johnston would later compare to the movement of "a gigantic black spider" (*Leonard Cohen Under Review, 1934–1977*, DVD, 2007) is an art of convolutions. Inspired by the basic flamenco tremolo, his trademark loop of repeated chords creates in many songs both a rush and a sense of going round in circles (cf. "Master Song," "Story of Isaac," "You Know Who I Am," "Teachers," "The Partisan," or "Avalanche").

9. Until the end of Cohen's career, female voices in the songs will make us hear the shekinah at work.

10. On the exile of the shekinah, see for example Gershom Scholem, *On the Kabbalah and its Symbolism* (New York: Schocken Books, 1977), 105–107.

11. For the quote, see Nadel (1994), 82.

12. Ruptures, re-readings, and complex negotiations with syntax and other pleasures of silent reading are forbidden.

13. The charm also operates on men. Apparently, in his Algerian exile, the Black Panther Eldridge Cleaver would listen to "The Stranger Song" for days on end. See Robert Greenfield, *Timothy Leary: A Biography* (San Diego: Harcourt, 2006), 406.

14. "Master Song."

15. Several years before, Leonard had already praised '60s girls for "wearing their mouths like Bardot" (*Flowers for Hitler*, 120).

16. As was then customary, the names of the session musicians were not mentioned in the credits, but ironically the photo booth is ("Photo by Machine").

17. Roland Barthes, "Tels," *Œuvres complètes V* (Paris: Seuil, 2002), 299.

18. See also Richard Goldstein's comment (*Village Voice*, December 1967) that the singer looked so distressed in the Henry Hudson Hotel room that you wanted to "tuck him in and put him to bed" (see Gnarowski, 45).

19. In the words of Brian Cruchley in the *Toronto Daily Star*, "Leonard poured out his philosophy in soft, almost monotone tones" ("Mariposa," August 14, 1967). For the dates, see Jim Devlin, *In Every Style of Passion* (London: Omnibus Press, 1992), 27.

20. No one is a prophet in their own land, however. Most of the Canadian press seems to consider the record as their favourite poet's latest bizarre extravagance.

21. His attempt to kick his speed habit during a prolonged stay at his mother's house at the end of the year was successful, indeed: he switched to barbiturates.

22. That version appears in Tony Palmer's *Bird on a Wire* (2010).

23. Joni Mitchell, "A Case of You," *Blue* (1971).

24. Interview with Richard Avedon, August 13, 1969, NYC. See Avedon, *The Sixties* (New York: Random House, 1999), 167.

25. Paul Grescoe, "Poet, Lover, Singer, Priest: Cohen," *Canadian Magazine*, February 10, 1968.

26. William Kloman, "Leonard Cohen," *New York Times*, January 28, 1968.

27. See Marci McDonald, "Leonard Cohen is a poet who is trying to be free," *Toronto Daily Star*, April 26, 1969.

28. Carl Gustav Jung, *Aïon. Études sur la phénoménologie du Soi* (Paris: Albin Michel, 1982), 26.

29. *Ibid.*, 26.

30. Anjelica Huston, "Leonard Cohen," *Interview Magazine*, November 1995.

31. For the first and third quote, see "That Song About the Midway," and "Gallery" for the second quote. Both songs are from *Clouds* (1969).

32. See *Take This Waltz*, 182.

33. Nadel, 160.

34. "Suzanne takes you down to listen to mermaids," Graeme Allwright, *Le jour de clarté* (LP, Mercury, 1968).

CHAPTER 6

1. *Op. cit.* (Paris: Gallimard, 1955), 43.

2. Leon Wieseltier, "Prince of the Bummers," *The New Yorker*, July 26, 1993, 40–45.

3. An idea most coarsely put in a 1971 review for *Songs of Love and Hate*: "If you want to be depressed, this is for you." See Allan Evans, "Songs of Love and Hate," *NME*, May 22, 1971, reproduced in *Bob Dylan and the Folk Rock Boom, 1964–1974*, *NME Originals*, 2005, 95.

4. See C.G. Jung, *Psychologie et Alchimie* (Paris: Buchet-Chastel, 1970), 53 and 299, et al.

5. René Daumal, "Poésie noire et poésie blanche," *Le Contre-Ciel* (Paris: Gallimard, 1990 [1936]), 188.

6. See respectively "Lady Midnight" (1969), "Avalanche" (1971), and "Teachers" (1968).

7. The quote, often attributed by Leonard to *Melody Maker*, which did feature a negative review of his Isle of Wight performance, was actually a comment made a few months later (December 5, 1970) to *The Globe and Mail* by Rikki Farr, who was disgruntled with Leonard's high fee.

8. About the dark side of the American counterculture, see Joan Didion's seminal essays "Slouching Towards Bethlehem" (1967) and "The White Album" (1970).

9. The gallery owner was the man who first took Leonard to the Chelsea Hotel (see *Book of Longing*, 125–127). About the *black photograph*, see also Nadel, 148–149.

10. See Nadel, 157, and Cohen, *Yakety Yak*. The film was *Hell in the Pacific*, about the cohabitation on a drifting raft of an American G.I. (Lee Marvin) and a Japanese soldier (Toshiro Mifune). Leonard was asked to compose the lullaby sung by Marvin.

11. It was there (in room #105) that the diva died in October 1970.

12. Interestingly, the picture on the postcard features a statue of Saint Francis and the saint's famous prayer for universal peace.

13. Interview with Ron Cornelius in *Leonard Cohen Under Review 1934–1977* (DVD, 2007).

14. Interview for the English magazine *Zigzag*, no. 10 (March 1970), quoted in Jacques Vassal, *Leonard Cohen* (Paris: Albin Michel, 1974), 122–123.

15. See Richard Robert, "Justesse sans limite," *Les Inrockuptibles*, no. 308, October 9–15, 2001, 23–27.

16. See Louis Black, "First, We Take Berlin," *Austin Chronicle*, November 16, 2007.

17. Hence the absence of female voices on the record which appear only on "The Partisan."

18. As for the melody of "Tonight Will Be Fine," it was clearly borrowed from Johnny Cash's "I Walk the Line" (as could not have gone unnoticed in that studio).

19. Nancy is actually Nancy Challies (1943–1965), the daughter of a Toronto judge and a close friend of Morton's who, as Cohen would explain

during his first tour, spent time in psychiatric care and committed suicide when her illegitimate child was taken from her (see Burger, 25).

20. Despite its ambivalent conclusion ("I will kill you if I can"), "Story of Isaac" was interpreted at the time as Leonard's condemnation of the conflict. Elsewhere on the album ("The Old Revolution"), the poet declares himself engaged in "search and destroy" operations, using (like Iggy and the Stooges) the official US army terminology.

21. Michel Houellebecq, "Le Libertaire Impossible," *Les Inrockuptibles*, no. 1, March 15, 1995, 20.

22. See Pascal, *Pensées*, 358.

23. See "Going Home," *Old Ideas* (2012).

24. Daumal, *op. cit.* (Paris: Gallimard, 1990 [1936]), 25.

25. We can connect this to the concept of salutary "inespoir" put forth by the French Buddhist philosopher Fabrice Midal in *Auschwitz, l'Impossible regard* (Paris: Seuil, 2012).

26. Extracted from the 1947 *People's Songbook*, "The Partisan" is an adaptation (by Hy Zaret) of "La Complainte du partisan" (music by resistance fighter Anna Marly and lyrics by Emmanuel d'Astier de la Vigne), written in London in 1943. Not to be confused with the quasi-official anthem of the French Resistance "Le Chant des Partisans (Ami, entends-tu?)," composed by the same Anna Marly (with lyrics by J. Kessel and M. Druon).

27. For the footage, see *Arpèges sur Joe Dassin*, May 13, 1970, where Cohen appears as Joe Dassin's guest star (he knew the singer — another former fling of Marianne — from Hydra).

28. For the quote by Cornelius, see *Leonard Cohen Under Review 1934–1977* (DVD, 2007). Shelley's definition of the poet is the last sentence of his *Defense of Poetry* (1821).

29. Quoted in Gnarowski, 69.

30. Their association, which will last until the manager's death in March 1988, was obscured in later years by the usual setbacks, each partner thinking the other one owed him tons of money.

31. For the birds, see "St. Francis," *Death of a Lady's Man*, 124. To make amends and inspire the Scottish songwriter, Leonard will send him

an envelope with a medallion of the Virgin, a catalog of plastic holy trinkets, and a printing of the Anima Sola. See Donovan Leitch, *The Hurdy-Gurdy Man* (London: Arrow Books, 2005), 362.

32. To "improve man spiritually" and help him "handle people and the environment." That is the declared aim of Dr. Hubbard's controversial institution. Defined as "the modern science of mental health," the doctrine (or "Dianetics") is based on concepts and practices borrowed from psychoanalysis, Buddhism, Hinduism, and various esoteric traditions. Through successive "audits," the practitioner goes "clear" (i.e., he frees himself from all conditionings) and learns to connect to the immortal part of his soul (the "thetan"). Although Cohen — who received a diploma sanctioning "grade IV" of spiritual awakening on June 17, 1968, and apparently met Ron Hubbard in Copenhagen (Posner, 2020, 378) — took his distance after 1969, he claimed that the sect's spiritual system had some value.

33. That's Suzanne's version of the story as told to the American magazine *People* 13, no. 2, January 14, 1980, 53–64.

34. Daniel 13:08.

35. Michael Posner details a rumour that Susanne Valentina Elrod had gallicized her first name (supposedly "Susan") to fit the song. In my conversations with Leonard (who always had a lot to say about her), she was always "Suzanne."

36. See "Leonard par Dominique," *Le Nouvel Observateur*, January 26, 2012, 126–129.

37. See Guy Lobrichon, *Les moines d'Occident. L'éternité de l'Europe* (Paris: Gallimard, 2007), 45.

38. *People Magazine* 13, no. 2, January 14, 1980, 53–64.

39. Five years later, he explained to a journalist that he had not spent a month in a row in the same place since 1968 (Jack Kapica, "The Trials of Leonard Cohen," *Montreal Gazette*, August 25, 1973).

40. From a 1975 interview with William Conrad (Nashville, Autumn 1975) reproduced in Burger, *op. cit.*, 103–107.

41. See respectively William Conrad, *op. cit.*, and Nadel, 166. He would later remember the horse in "Ballad of the Absent Mare" (1979), a

western adaptation of an allegorical Buddhist poem about a herdsman and his lost ox.

42. Fevret, *op. cit.*, 110–111. In the interview, the poet adds that his lack of confidence was also the sign of "severe damage" caused by years of amphetamine use.

43. In 1970, the singer Cohen had not yet understood that the higher registers — the sky — were forbidden territories and that a microphone is the crooner's best friend: one whisper and everyone in the Albert Hall hears the voice of God. He was not forty yet; gravity still had to do its work on him. I find his later fondness for the hummingbird (who appears on the cover of *Recent Songs* and *The Future*, as well as in several poems) an adorable confession: as a singer, he is not only a featherweight — some hummingbirds weigh two or three grams — but also one who should stick to humming. Hilarious.

44. See Murray Lerner, *Leonard Cohen: Live at the Isle of Wight* (Sony Music DVD, 2009).

45. Most nights, he will dedicate that song to the students killed at Kent State University on the second day of the tour and to "all who refuse to die."

46. See Johnston's testimony in *Austin City Limits*, and Ron Cornelius's in *Leonard Cohen Under Review 1934–1977* (as well as in *Leonard and Marianne, Words of Love*) and Charlie Daniels's in the *National Examiner*, May 23, 2009. The "Moses" quote is how F. defines himself in *Beautiful Losers* (167).

47. Dean Jensen, "Poetical Cohen: A Rare Find in the '70s," *Milwaukee Sentinel*, February 26, 1975.

48. *Op. cit.*, 91.

49. The drug in question — known as quaaludes in America and mandies in the UK — also increased sexual desire. It became the middle classes' favourite recreational drug in the '70s.

50. The version of "The Stranger Song" played at the Isle of Wight is twice as slow in tempo as the one played on May 23, 1966, for the TV show *Take 30*.

51. Interview with Susan Lumsden for *Weekend Magazine*, quoted in Gnarowski, 73.

52. A nod to Flaubert's explanation of his famous heroine: "Mme Bovary, c'est moi."

53. Michael Harris, "The Poet as Hero 2," *Saturday Night Review*, June 1969, quoted in Gnarowski, 55–56.

54. Leonard has often said in interviews that he was sure he was shot at in Aix-en-Provence (someone had apparently shot at a spotlight with a firearm).

55. See Murray Lerner, *op. cit.*

56. A few years before his art gallery burnt down (see *infra*), Leonard had invited his young sister-in-law Roz to see a house on fire in downtown Montreal (Posner, 2020, 47) and almost set his mother's house on fire when burning love letters in the fireplace (*ibid.*, 359). In Hydra he allegedly cursed the Ghikas family house, which later burnt down (a fact the poet exploited a lot in conversation), and he publicly predicted ill luck to Edie Sedgwick a mere three days before her room burnt down at the Chelsea Hotel (in 1967).

57. The quote is from Kristofferson in Murray Lerner, *op. cit.*

58. *Op. cit.*, 105.

59. "Wight is Wight / Dylan is Dylan / Wight is Wight / Viva Donovan [. . .] And hip-hip-hip hippy" were the first words of Michel Delpech's 1969 hit single "Wight Is Wight," a chronicle of the festival and one of the few French hippie hymns. An English version was released the following year by Sandie Shaw.

60. Sylvie Simmons, "Felonius Monk," *Mojo Magazine*, no. 96, November 2001, 49.

61. See Murray Lerner, *op. cit.* For all the irony of his position, I have to admit Mr. Farrar actually had a point.

62. Of course, the Buddha's *Fire Sermon* states that everyone (and everything) is constantly on fire.

63. Impressed by Paul Buckmaster's orchestral arrangements for Elton John's second album, Leonard and Johnston flew to London in

December 1971 to add strings on four songs they had recorded in autumn.

64. See Nathan Schwar-Salant, *Jung on Alchemy* (London: Routledge, 1995), 99–116.

65. See respectively "Love Calls You by Your Name," "Last Year's Man," and "Dress Rehearsal Rag."

66. For the anecdote, see Sylvie Simmons, "Felonious Monk," *Mojo Magazine*, no. 96, November 2001, 48. Interestingly, Leonard's song inspired later portraits of Nico. Philippe Garrel's filmic portrait of her in *La cicatrice intérieure* (1972) is almost an illustration of the song, with Nico on horseback in a monk's robe, surrounded by rings of Fire in deserted landscapes. As for John Cale, he facetiously dismisses Joan of Arc from the first lines of a song that revamps Nico as "Helen of Troy" (1975).

67. We see the lover in Grand Central Station looking for an absent "Lily Marlene," the wife coming home with a lock of hair, the lover in the desert, and the constant return of the present moment when the letter is being written: New York, late December, four o'clock in the morning.

68. Of course, the poet chooses his words carefully: the "flake of life" is there to remind us that our lives have the texture of snow: try to seize them and they melt in your hands.

69. As for Leonard, he saves us from an irrepressible sadness by organizing three brief incursions into C major when the melody lifts off ("and Jane came / by with a lock of your hair . . ."). Each time, for fifteen seconds, everyone is saved: the lovers by love; the listeners by grace.

70. Cohen's friends have seen in the song an allusion to one of Marianne's late '60s affairs in Hydra and New York (see Posner, 2020, 434–437).

71. About his master's talent for forgiveness, see "Montreal Interview" by Helle Vaagland (Swedish TV, NRK1, 2006): "He has forgiven himself, he has forgiven the world, and he forgives you. Automatically. Impersonally."

72. Held in early December in every Zen monastery, the rohatsu is an eight-day retreat (sometimes known as "monk-killer") that commemorates the Buddha's awakening.

73. Evoked in a poem (*The Energy of Slaves*, 111) the escape has been recounted many times (see for example Lian Lunson, *I'm Your Man*, DVD, Lionsgate, 2005). In Acapulco, Suzanne took the famous photograph of a cropped-headed Leonard smoking a cigarillo in the bathroom of the hotel suite (see *infra*). Nine months later, Adam was born.

74. By the early '70s, the cinéma vérité tour documentary (on the model of D.E. Pennebaker's *Don't Look Back* about Dylan's tour of 1965) was a well-established genre and a necessary step to establish your status as a rock star. While cameras followed Cohen in Europe, Elvis Presley was being filmed for *Elvis on Tour* and so were the Rolling Stones (for the never released *Cocksucker Blues*).

75. What happened off camera is unclear, but *Death of a Lady's Man* (141) and *The Energy of Slaves* (97) are quite explicit about the sexual antics during the tour (and their medical consequences).

76. The collaboration with Jennifer Warnes will last for decades and, according to interviews with Howard Sounes, Jenny and Lenny apparently lived together for a short while in the late '70s. See *Down the Highway: The Life of Bob Dylan* (London: Black Swan Press, 2001), 392.

77. See Dorman and Rawlins, *op. cit.*, 243.

78. *Bird on a Wire* seems to have captured both a rock star and the schlimazel of Jewish folklore: an anti-hero who comically carries the weight of the world, and never stops lamenting.

79. In the singer's last interview forty-four years later (*The New Yorker*, October 17, 2016), he reveals what happened to him that night. As he was singing "So Long, Marianne" with the crowd, the band and himself in tears, Leonard saw the entire audience turn into "one Jew, one gigantic being" that signified to him how unimpressed he was. Start again, Cohen-boy!

80. Cohen is also dissatisfied with some of Palmer's heavy-handed editing (i.e., footage of Nazi meetings and Auschwitz camps to illustrate some songs). See "Cohen: Haunted by Spector" (interview with Chris Bohn), *Melody Maker*, May 1, 1980.

CHAPTER 7

1. The "Persian cat" description is by Leonard's old Hydra crony, the painter Antony Kingsmill, who saw Marianne as a "puma" (Nadel, 164). Roger Green — Suzanne's neighbour on the island — evokes "a Sibyl, a Pythia and a Cassandra" and a mistress of irony (*Hydra and the Bananas of Leonard Cohen*, London: Basic Books, 2003, 100) while Harry Rasky more prosaically calls her a "Miami Beach Princess" (*The Song of Leonard Cohen*, Oakville: Mosaïc Press, 2001, 20). As for Leonard, he described her to me (among more picturesque evocations) as having "the personality of Catherine the Great."

2. "There is a War" (1974). Domestic turbulence is a central theme of Cohen's mid-'70s output and *Death of a Lady's Man* (1978) actually invents a lyrical form that transforms marital quarrels into poems (see *infra*, Chapter 8).

3. Answer: many women. It was later revealed that Sasaki Roshi regularly used *sanzen* to extract sexual favours from unsuspecting female students (see *infra*, Chapter 11). For the quote by Hakuin, see *The Essentials Teachings of Zen Master Hakuin* (Boston: Shambhala, 2010), 63. For the quote by Sasaki Roshi, see Joshu Sasaki Roshi, *Buddha Is the Center of Gravity* (San Cristobal: Lama Foundation, 1974), 44.

4. The *Betta splendens*, put to wonderful cinematographic use by Francis Ford Coppola in *Rusty James* (1983).

5. See Andrew Furnival, "The Strange, Sad, Beautiful World of Leonard Cohen," *Petticoat*, December 30, 1972.

6. Such is the title of Shunryu Susuki's classic book, *Zen Mind, Beginner's Mind* (London: Weatherhill, 1970).

7. *Op. cit.*, 9.

8. See for example *Genealogy of Morals*, first essay, §10.

9. Leonard used the picture again for the cover of *Live Songs* in 1973.

10. Thirty years later, an ironic Leonard wrote the following caption for another self-portrait: "This guy is getting too tough for us. I'm afraid we won't be able to call him a poet much longer" (see the photo insert

in this book or the "Blackening Pages" section on Jarkko Arjatsalo's website, www.leonardcohenfiles.com/mirror.html).

11. See Roland Barthes, *Camera Lucida* (New York: Vintage Books, 1981), 25–27.

12. In 1972, an abundant mane of hair was de rigueur for every rebel, from Led Zeppelin to Jacques Mesrine. Leonard's razor cut could only evoke the Marines, the elite troop at work in Vietnam. As we remember, the poet had just shaven his head for his first (interrupted) sesshin at Mt. Baldy and soon enough, he tellingly started to refer to Zen Buddhists as "the marines of spirituality."

13. *The Energy of Slaves*, 91.

14. *Ibid.*, 95.

15. See Arthur Rimbaud, *A Season in Hell & Illuminations* (Paris: NRF, 1998), 123. In *The Energy of Slaves*, Beauty returns the poet's blows: she speaks in the middle of the book and declares that she leaves the volume to seek refuge among younger authors ("Beauty Speaks in the Third Act," 59).

16. *Op. cit.* (Paris: Mille et Une Nuits, 2000).

17. *The Energy of Slaves*, 82.

18. *Ibid.*, 43.

19. *Ibid.*, 59.

20. *The Energy of Slaves*, 74. Fifteen years later, Leonard explored that rhetoric again in songs like "First We Take Manhattan" (1988), in which he exposes a megalomaniac plan to conquer the world. The famous video by Dominique Issermann shows him, on a beach in Normandy, as the leader of an underground (and maybe imaginary) terrorist group.

21. We should keep in mind the libertarian climate of the '70s, a time when artists almost unanimously celebrated adolescent sexuality, from French sulfurous writers to film directors like Fassbinder, Pasolini, or Bertolucci. The latter's *Last Tango in Paris* (also released in 1972) shares with *The Energy of Slaves* an atmosphere of fallen virility and fascination for brute force.

22. *The Energy of Slaves*, 42.

23. *Ibid.*, 112.

24. *Ibid.*, 13.

25. See for example Fevret, *op. cit.*, III.

26. See respectively 127, 123, 19, 117.

27. The purging of Cohen's poetry will last until the end of the decade. Until then, he will confront the inner scorpion with books and records that are essentially collections of dark moods and bad jokes (see in particular *New Skin for the Old Ceremony* and *Death of a Ladies' Man*).

28. *Ibid.*, 42.

29. Leonard still claims his identity as slave in his "Ladies' Man" cycle (1977–1978) as well as in "Tower of Song" (1988) and "Show Me the Place" (2012).

30. *The Energy of Slaves*, 46.

31. See Palmer's *Bird on a Wire*.

32. The hallali is the trumpet cry that excites the hounds in fox hunting. For examples of dismissive critics, see Tom Wayman's "Cohen's Women" (*Canadian Literature* 60, Spring 1974, 89–93) or Eli Mandel's "Cohen's Life as a Slave" in *Another Time (Three Solitudes: Contemporary Literary Criticism in Canada)* (Erin, Ontario: Porcupine's Quill, 1977), 124–136.

33. Directed by Sam Gesser, the show (one of Machat's pet projects) was called *Sisters of Mercy: A Musical Journey into the Words of Leonard Cohen*. I still consider my victory over boredom when attending the reprise of a similar show in Manhattan in 2008 as one of the high feats of my heroic secret life.

34. Although they were never formally married, Cohen consistently referred to Suzanne as his "wife," once telling an interviewer the relationship was "a marriage with everything but the document." See Alan Twigg, *For Openers: Conversations with 24 Canadian Writers* (Madeira Park: Harbour Publishing, 1981), 55. In her memoir, Judy Scott remembers that Leonard had actually spent time in the house with Marianne a mere two months before he stayed there with Suzanne (Scott, *op. cit.*, 33–57).

35. Also part of the team were the comedian Mordechai "Pupik" Arnon and the folksinger Matti Caspi (see Simmons, 272).

36. A detailed account of Leonard's experience in the Yom Kippur War is available in Matti Friedman's excellent *Who by Fire: War, Atonement, and the Resurrection of Leonard Cohen* (New York: Penguin Random House, 2022).

37. *Yedihot Aharonot*, May 28, 2009.

38. "Lover, Lover, Lover" (1974).

39. See Nadel, 1996, 193.

40. See Friedrich Nietzsche, *Crépuscule des Idoles* (Paris: Gallimard, 1992), 9.

41. See for example the September 1974 interview with Robin Pike for the British countercultural magazine *Zigzag*: "War is wonderful. They'll never stamp it out" (Burger, 62).

42. That's what he said as introduction to "Lover, Lover, Lover" in a French TV program (*Le Grand Echiquier*, June 2, 1976) and during several concerts in 1974.

43. See Burger, 79.

44. The sound engineer there, Leanne Ungar, aged 24, will never again leave Leonard's entourage.

45. Two tracks only — "Chelsea Hotel #2" and an old ode to Nico ("Take This Longing") once recorded as "The Bells" by Judy Collins — will stick to Cohen's old minimal formula.

46. Graham Lock, "Love Me, Love My Gun Barrel," *NME*, February 23, 1980.

47. The illustration, found by Cohen in a book by C.G. Jung (*Psychology and Alchemy*, Princeton University Press, 1968) originally appeared in an anonymous alchemical treaty (the *Rosarium Philosophorum*, 1593), where it illustrates the coniunctio spirituums, the alchemical marriage of the male and the female principles.

48. Quite the opposite in fact of the old esoteric motto "as above, so below."

49. The exact quote is "Love must be re-invented, as we know." In the "Vierge Folle" section of *A Season in Hell*.

50. Among the added lyrics are the lover's confession that he lied "to lie between [his mistress's] matchless thighs" and his desire "to end [their] exercise."

51. A perfect echo of the end of the first album, which also ends with screams as a lover enters the snowstorm of his mistress's body.

52. "Field Commander Cohen."

53. "Is This What You Wanted?"

54. Leonard's evocation of police brutality is probably also a nod to the Greek Colonels' regime, of which at least one of his close friends was a victim (on the subject, see also *The Energy of Slaves*, 10–11).

55. Interestingly, the verdict provokes an upsurge of tears (or libido?) among the ladies in the assistance as the "ladies go moist."

56. Martin Buber (whom Leonard had read attentively) defines personal dialogue with God (in the "I-Thou" form) as the only authentic religious experience. See *I and You* (New York: Scribner's, 1970).

57. *New Skin for the Old Ceremony* reached #2 in Austria, #17 in Germany, #18 in the Netherlands, and a weak #24 in the UK.

58. For those keeping score, the Hotel Raphael in Paris, and the picture is by Erica Lennard.

59. Dylan actually gave Leonard a guided tour of his L.A. mansion the next day.

60. Anthony Reynold mentions their shared passion for sushi and sake in *Leonard Cohen: A Remarkable Life* (London: Omnibus Press, 2010), 122.

61. See *Rock & Folk*, no. 114, 72.

62. A version recorded on stage in Paris was issued as a single during the European tour.

63. For the anecdote about Phil Ochs, see *Leonard Cohen: Live in San Sebastian* (Spanish TV, June 1988).

64. See Sōkō Morinaga, *Novice to Master: An Ongoing Lesson in the Extent of My Own Stupidity* (Boston: Wisdom Publications, 2004).

65. In the summer of 1977, a fourth version (called *The Final Revision of My Life in Art*) was once again delivered and withdrawn.

66. See *Death of a Lady's Man* (the entire volume). The first names are all pseudonyms.

67. See Nadel, 193.

CHAPTER 8

1. The figure is mentioned by Leonard in a conversation recorded by Larry Sloman in *On the Road with Bob Dylan* (London: Helter Skelter, 2002), 385.

2. The ex-prophet of Greenwich Village was back in the charts with "Hurricane," and he had relaunched his career with two gigantic tours in 1974 and 1975. Although Cohen refused to join him on stage in Montreal, he must have been quite impressed by the scale of the operation.

3. The three texts originally appeared in *The Spice-Box of Earth*, *Parasites of Heaven*, and *The Energy of Slaves*.

4. Plus the '70s were entering their final phase: that of long-point collars, exaggeratedly fitted one-button jackets and bell-bottom pants. No man with an even remote sense of style could feel too good.

5. See *Leonard Cohen: Under Review, 1934–1977* (DVD, New Malden: Sexy Intellectual, 2007). Also of note is the extensive interview Cohen gave to *Melody Maker* for the album's release: "The Great Ones Never Leave," November 26, 1977.

6. See Stephen Holden, "Leonard Cohen Obscured . . . A Haunting by Spector," *Rolling Stone*, January 26, 1978.

7. Ecclesiastes 10:16.

8. Holden, *op. cit.*

9. As in Serge Gainsbourg's contemporary concept album, *L'Homme à la Tête de Chou* (1976).

10. See François Ducray, "L'adieu aux larmes" (*Rock & Folk*, no. 131, December 1977, 95–99), Chris Bohn, "Cohen: Haunted by Spector" (*Melody Maker*, January 5, 1980, 29–30) and Paul Nelson, "Leonard Cohen's Doo-Wop Nightmare" (*Rolling Stone*, February 9, 1978).

11. "Paper-Thin Hotel" was apparently inspired by an episode that took place in Germany during Cohen's previous tour.

12. Quoted in Cliff Jones, "Heavy Cohen," *Rock CD*, no. 6, December 1992.

13. *Op. cit.*, 14.

14. The last expression obviously refers to the mysterious *dark lady* that haunts Shakespeare's sonnets, Suzanne becoming here the Shakespearean heroine's double.

15. The book is also full of anonymous women, among them a waitress of Stockholm's Crazy Horse Bar who apparently passed on a venereal disease to the author (141).

16. *Death of a Lady's Man*, 114.

17. *Ibid.*, 20.

18. The poem adds: "Needless to add, he hears a different drum," 79.

19. For a detailed reading of the volume through the prism of the "supplement" (a concept borrowed from Jacques Derrida), see Stephen Scobie's "The Doubled Text" (in *Signature Event Cantext*, Edmonton: Newest, 1989, 63–70). Scobie argues that, because texts refer to commentaries and commentaries to texts, *Death of a Lady's Man* loses all center and meaning, a valid argument. But, as a Canadian advocate of French post-structuralism, Scobie probably over-invests the supposed absence of meaning and it seems that for him (as for many academics of his generation), texts never really refer to anything but their own textuality. Quite obviously here, Cohen writes from the front line of a life that he had actually lived, placing us in a chaos that is spiritual and emotional and not just textual.

20. *Death of a Lady's Man*, 91.

21. *Death of a Lady's Man*, 136.

22. *Ibid.*, 100.

23. *Ibid.*, 105.

24. See "Leonard Cohen: A Much Bigger Man Than He Appears," *The Province*, October 27, 1978.

25. "Claustrophobia! Bullshit! Air, air! Give us air!" (129).

26. See "Anthem" (1992).

27. See 99 and 18.

28. See (respectively) 162, 11, 151, 167.

29. *Ibid.*, 44.

30. See 163, 200, 173.

31. That's what God tells the poet: Suzanne is a test he has prepared for him: "You wrestle with an angel. I made her for you out of everything you hate" (133).

32. As explained by François Lecercle in "Des yeux pour ne point voir. Avatars de l'idolâtrie chez les théologiens catholiques du XVIe siècle" in *L'Idolâtrie*, Rencontres de l'École du Louvre (Paris: La documentation Française, 1990), 35–53.

33. *Death of a Lady's Man*, 57.

34. The house was on Woodrow Wilson Drive, a haven for millionaires and celebrities (Harry Nilsson lived just round the corner and Ringo Starr was a frequent guest).

35. The song is actually an adaptation of the *Ten Bulls*, a twelfth century poem by the Chinese Zen master Kakuan about a herdsman who has lost his ox (an allegory for his true nature) and goes, while looking for her, through the ten supposed stages of awakening, disappearing when he finds her. (For the classic English translation that made the text famous in the West, see Paul Reps, *op. cit.*, 133–147.)

36. Leonard will come back to this task twenty-three years later in his adaption of Constantine P. Cavafy's poem "The Gods Abandon Antony" for the song "Alexandra Leaving" (*Ten New Songs*, 2001), a song that states that we must always say goodbye twice to the things we love. We must say goodbye "to Alexandra leaving," then say goodbye "to Alexandra lost."

37. See "The Smokey Life."

38. The koan in question (alluded to in *Death of a Lady's Man*, 193, actually a transcription of a sanzen session with Sasaki Roshi) is the fifth case in the collection *The Gateless Gate* ("Kyogen Mounts the Tree" in Paul Reps, *Zen Flesh, Zen Bones* (Penguin, 2000 [1957]), 99–100.

39. There is a prominent spiritual turn in the lyrics: inspired by the Sufi poets Rumi and Attar, Leonard uses prayers for refrains ("The

Guests," "The Window"). He also quotes the Kabbalah, the scriptures, and a thirteenth-century Dominican treatise called *The Cloud of Unknowing*, which theorizes a mystical union with God through emptiness of mind that is strangely close to Zen. He had actually discovered the treatise through Thomas Keating, the abbot of St. Joseph's Trappist Abbey, where the singer stayed with Roshi for inter-religious Zen sesshins.

40. Both musicians would feature prominently in the upcoming tour and the two instruments would never again durably leave Leonard's stage act. The world music quality of *Recent Songs* has often been interpreted as an homage to the singer's mother, who had (as the liner notes specify) reminded him "shortly before she died" of the kind of music she liked.

41. Rasky, *op. cit.*, 24.

42. After a first issue in the autumn of 1978, *Zero* will be published twice a year until March 1981.

43. For two decades, the ground floor would later be occupied by his daughter, Lorca.

44. See Leonard's interview with Diethard Küster's for *Beautiful Losers* (Arte TV, 1997). I had the privilege to sit in that corner several times as Leonard cooked for me. I wish I was sitting there still.

45. This Catholic hymn, then popular with boy scouts, was apparently sung nightly by the band before they went on stage (a ritual reprised in 2009, with variations in the third line).

46. On bass: Roscoe Beck; on drums: Steve Meador; on wind instruments: Paul Ostermayer; on guitar: Mitch Watkins; on keyboards: Bill Ginn.

47. The shows also feature a few moments of comic relief, like the chorists' doo-wop routine in "Memories" and Leonard's ironic "Blues for the Jews," which reveals the great secret of God's anger against us (i.e., he hates our bodies).

48. The mix of flute, violin, and drums is perhaps most lethal on "The Partisan," "Suzanne," and "Famous Blue Raincoat," three songs which were not particularly well served on the tour.

CHAPTER 9

1. In "Leonard Cohen's Nervous Breakthrough," *Musician*, July 1988.

2. In a 2009 interview, Jennifer Warnes explained how the end of the tour left everyone feeling exiled from light. "After the Passenger tour, everyone went into depression. There were two or three divorces. Our personalities had changed. Roscoe started wearing three-piece suits and we were all drifting. We would phone each other and say, 'Now what do we do?' The heart opening throughout the tour had broken us" (see Brad Buchholz, "Touring with Cohen," *Austin American-Statesman*, March 31, 2009).

3. Cohen's condition will worsen significantly in the early '80s, as we will see.

4. It had not escaped the poet's notice, for example, that very few people had actually turned up at the CBS cocktail party for the release of his last album (see Steve Lake, "Cohen Plays a Timeless Game," *Melody Maker*, December 11, 1980, 12).

5. See the 1988 interview for KCRW-FM in Burger, *op. cit.*, 241.

6. With a triple pun ("freak" / "fric" / "Afrique") perceptible only in French ("fric" means "dough"), Chic's somewhat cynical slogan "Le Fric, C'est Chic" was in many ways the battle cry of the yuppie years.

7. Case no. 46 of the already quoted *Gateless Gate* (Paul Reps, *op. cit.*, 128).

8. *Ibid.*, 95.

9. "Nightingale," *Dear Heather*, 2004.

10. "If It Be Your Will," *Various Positions*, 1985. For the anecdote, see Nadel, 233.

11. For that distinction see Michel Pastoureau, *Black: The History of a Color* (Princeton University Press, 2008), 28–29.

12. For the quote see "Leonard Cohen at 50," *Morningside*, interview with Peter Gzowski, CBC Radio, 1984.

13. He would soon begin to confess (the way you confess a shameful illness) how hard he had to work: the years spent polishing lyrics; the perpetual rewrites; the nights spent "in his pajamas banging his head against the carpet in his Royalton Hotel room trying to find a

rhyme for orange" (Adrian Deevoy, "Porridge? Lozenge? Syringe?" *Q Magazine*, October 1991).

14. See Graham Lock, *ibid.*, *NME*, February 23, 1980.

15. It got four Genie Awards in 1985 but made no impression at the Cannes Film Festival.

16. Nadel, 234.

17. "Wishing Window," *Night Magic* (Cinémusique), CD booklet, 5.

18. Nadel mentions proceedings that lasted from 1978 to 1984 (230).

19. In *Night Magic*, the hero realizes he is "dead except in their company" ("The Throne of Desire," *op. cit.*, 6).

20. Although not interested in psychological analysis per se, Leonard was quite aware of the neurotic aspect of his relation to women. I am not betraying our conversations if I say it had not escaped him that his behaviour could be linked to an impaired relationship with a traumatized mother.

21. See respectively "I'm Your Man," "I Can't Forget," and "Tower of Song."

22. Dorian Lynskey, "Leonard Cohen: All I've got to put in a song is my own experience," *The Guardian*, January 19, 2012.

23. In 2008, the singer would joke in his live shows about the impressive list of antidepressants that were prescribed to him, a list that also includes Effexor as well as experimental anti-seizure drugs. About the extent of the singer's depression, see also Mark Rowland, "Leonard Cohen's Nervous Breakthrough," *Musician*, July 1988, "Leonard Cohen on Depression," *Valerie Pringle Show* (CTV 1997) and Mireille Silcott, "Leonard Cohen: A Happy Man," *Saturday Night*, September 15, 2001.

24. For the anecdotes, see *Book of Mercy*, psalms 18 and 23, and also *Stranger Music*, 393.

25. For the stay in Jerusalem, see Paul King, "Montreal Poet Working on TV Project, But His Heart Belongs to Buddha," *Montreal Gazette*, July 16, 1983. On Nachman of Bratslav, see Dorman and Rawlins, 355.

26. *Book of Mercy*, psalm 12.

27. As Leonard explained on CBC Radio when the book was released, "there are no atheists in the fox's den" ("Leonard Cohen at 50," *Morningside* with Peter Gzowski, 1984).

28. See "Prayers" by Rowland Smith in *Canadian Literature*, no. 104, spring 1985. Also revealing are "Cohen's Audacious Gambit" (Norman Snider, *The Globe and Mail*, April 21, 1984) or "Cohen Seeks Spiritual Solace Not Perfect Love" (Marianne Ackerman, *The Gazette*, April 14, 1984).

29. See in particular *Book of Mercy*, psalms 2, 7, and 12.

30. Psalm 31.

31. In one of the most moving texts, Leonard pleads for the salvation of his twelve-year-old son, who is at the mercy of TV merchants who "want him with no soul" (psalm 33).

32. See respectively psalms 40, 6, 2, and 22.

33. Practitioners of seated meditation will perhaps recognize in the speaker's mix of expectation, hope, disappointment, and release the emotional dynamics of zazen.

34. Psalm 1.

35. How that symbol, which also adorned a medal that Leonard liked to give to friends in later life with the kohen's blessing on the back, turned up in the mid-'80s on a stained-glass window in the thirteenth-century church of Bourg-Lastic in the highlands of central France remains a mystery to this day.

36. See Nadel, 239.

37. The textures were actually hard to tell apart. For their four-note chorus, Trio had chosen "piano" (the rhythm was Rock #1).

38. To Lissauer's dismay, it was on "Dance Me to the End of Love."

39. T.S. Eliot had reached the same conclusion in the 1920s, but sadly no Casiotones were available to accompany his readings of *The Waste Land*.

40. A secondary benefit is that this electronic turn preserves Leonard's songs from the two great temptations of musicians: expressiveness and virtuosity. The singer always considered that both tendencies needlessly heroize our little human situation.

41. God or women, he can't tell. *Various Positions* is the record where Leonard reaches the point of maximum confusion between the two. In 1985, he explained to a German documentary maker that he refused to distinguish between things that emit the same light (see Georg Stefan Troller, *Hallelujah in Moll*, ZDF). He also told a journalist friend that his one obsessive idea was "to create the ultimate confusion between woman and God" (Posner, 2022, 185).

42. The lullaby, rescued from the *Night Magic* project, contains Leonard's apology to his children for their father's absence: he has "gone a-hunting" (being a hunter of absolutes). Of course, the Father in the song is also the Father to us all, whose absence is enveloped in the musical wails of Getman's slide guitar: a fine piece of spiritual country and western.

43. In the second volume of Michael Posner's oral biography (2022, 335), one of Leonard Cohen's '80s girlfriends tells how she has indeed cut Leonard's hair on a kitchen chair in Hydra and made love with him. A moving testimony.

44. For the quote, see "Leonard Cohen: The Questionnaire," *Q Magazine*, September 1994.

45. Leonard's latest German release, *Liebesträume*, a hastily done compilation of hits with a über-kitsch cover (beach, guitar, and setting sun), can't have served his prestige too well.

46. The anecdote, told many times, can be heard in "Mixed Bag," interview with Pete Fornatale, WNEW-FM, April 28, 1985, on *Leonard Cohen, The Classic Interviews* (CD, Chrome Dream, 2007).

47. See "German Interview," March 1985, *Leonard Cohen, The Classic Interviews* (CD, Chrome Dreams, 2008).

48. The songs will be "The Guests," "Memories," "Chelsea Hotel," "The Gypsy's Wife," and "Suzanne."

49. The trend of power-dressing had not gone unnoticed by the former Freedman Company employee. His '80s suits were either made to measure by Greek tailors or sent to him by Giorgio Armani.

50. See respectively *Karussel* (DRT, Basel, March 5, 1985), *Mixed Bag* (New York, WNEW-FN, April 28, 1985) *Mike Walsh Show* (Sydney, May 20, 1985), Danny Fields, December 5, 1974 (*Soho Weekly News*).

the answer on women comes from a later source: "Leonard Cohen on Depression and Relationships" (*Buskin' Trail*, Canadian TV, 1997).

51. In Brittany, France, Leonard meets the punk singer Daniel Darc, who made the poet laugh by asking him to sign a book that was not one of his. Darc later confessed that it was during that day's concert, in front of Leonard Cohen, that he decided he would go on living.

52. Now often living partly in Paris, Cohen was aware of Gainsbourg's jazzy talk-over style, and he had met the French singer several times.

53. Founded in 1980 in the Lenin shipyard in Gdansk, Solidarność (named after the Polish word for "solidarity") was an originally illegal independent workers' trade union that soon gathered a third of the working population of Poland. It played a major role in the downfall of Communist rule.

54. See Scott Cohen, "A Few Things About Bob Dylan as Told to Scott Cohen," *Interview Magazine*, February 1986.

55. This particular version of the story is from a brief Cohen interview in the Dylan fanzine *The Telegraph* (Winter 1991, no. 41, 30).

56. For the image, see "His Master's Voice," *Book of Longing*, 3.

57. I was lucky to see transcriptions of notebooks that contained several dozens of unpublished verses — many of them incredibly good — for "Hallelujah."

CHAPTER 10

1. The singer has often explained how his role was drastically cut after his first day of shooting. It may also be noted that accepting that the Parisian head of Interpol speaks with Cohen's thick Canadian accent requires considerable suspension of disbelief from the French viewer.

2. In 1982, Warnes's duet with Joe Cocker, "Up Where We Belong," the title song of the romantic comedy *An Officer and a Gentleman*, was a worldwide hit, confirmed in 1987 by an even more successful "(I've Had the) Time of My Life," the title song for *Dirty Dancing*.

3. "Twenty-seven" is most likely a tribute to the twenty-two letters of the Hebrew alphabet with their five variants.

4. It was the case in particular for "I Can't Forget," originally a psalm about spiritual liberation called "Out of Egypt," refashioned into a song about Leonard's inexhaustible perplexity in front of existence. The reappearance of the original lyrics in "Born in Chains" is perhaps not one of the high points of *Popular Problems* (2014). About the rocky recording sessions, see Mark Rowland, "Leonard Cohen's Nervous Breakthrough," *Musician*, July 1988.

5. See *Mike* (Belgium, February 16), *Na-Siensie* (Germany, February 17), *À la folie* and *Lahaie d'Honneur* (respectively TF1 and A2, February 21), *Champs-Élysées* (May 14).

6. See respectively *À la folie* (France, TF1, January 1988), *Bains de Minuit* (France, La Cinq, December 11, 1987) and *Fancy Friday* (Sweden, SVT, April 29, 1988).

7. Linguists would speak here of the "performative" quality of Leonard's gravity; he says something and, automatically, that thing becomes "grave."

8. What Cohen's voice ultimately demonstrates is that there are a chosen people of gravity who seem inherently qualified to speak about the meaning of things because they inhabit the heart of life: people with deep voices.

9. In many ways, the song echoes the study of the psychology of fascist impulses inaugurated in *The Energy of Slaves*.

10. Although Leonard himself had no such problems, Jennifer Warnes told the *Austin American-Statesman* (see Buchholtz, *op. cit.*) she could no longer sing that song after 9/11. For the "age of emptiness," see Gilles Lipovetsky's brilliant essays *L'Ère du vide* (Paris: Gallimard, 1993), in many ways the perfect companion (with Jean Baudrillard's philosophy) for *I'm Your Man*.

11. For this interpretation, see Dominique Issermann in "Leonard par Dominique," *Le Nouvel Observateur* (January 26, 2012), 126–129.

12. The photograph was taken in 1987 by Leonard's assistant Sharon Weitz during the shooting of Jennifer Warnes's video in New York.

13. It is also a fashionable look popularized by Don Johnson and Philip Michael Thomas in *Miami Vice*.

14. See *Cargo de Nuit*, RTBF1 (Belgian TV), March 16, 1988.

15. Greg Quill, "Cohen Finds Humour in Being Taken Seriously," *Toronto Star*, May 4, 1988.

16. Or maybe he just meant it as a discreet message to Nico, to confirm just before she joined Jim Morrison that she was right after all — he was too ridiculous to be her lover.

17. Significantly, the record is dedicated to a woman, a first in Leonard's career ("All these songs are for you, D.I.").

18. *Fancy Friday* (SVT, Sweden, May 29, 1988).

19. From then on, Leonard will unceasingly look both in his song lyrics and interviews for hyperbolic images for our predicament. We are survivors in the Flood clinging to a crate of oranges; we are people fallen on the highway; we are snowmen waiting for spring; we are poets looking for a rhyme for "orange" . . .

20. For the quotes, see respectively "Tower of Song" and "I Can't Forget."

21. Leonard is also referring to the takeover of CBS-Columbia by Sony Music ("They're moving us tomorrow to that tower down the track"), which takes the singer's record company from the Black Rock Tower on Fifty-Ninth Street to the Sony Building on Fifty-Fifth.

22. *Offbeat*, TV5 (Germany, January 1988). For some fans Cohen's metamorphosis into an electro-pop crooner on this album was an equivalent to Bob Dylan's going electric in 1965: a major betrayal.

23. That's what Leonard likes best about his Technics SXK530 — it doesn't have an ego.

24. In the previous ten years, Leonard has gradually learnt to stay just below the limits of singing, with only a ghost of melody in the voice. For this, the influence of French singer-songwriter Serge Gainsbourg is patent. Much has been said about the impact of the Pet Shop Boys on the album's soundscape but listening to the French singer's *Love on the Beat* (1985), where vocals are unfurled against a background of sequencers and funky guitars, back to back with *I'm Your Man*, is a revealing experience.

25. See Atom Egoyan, *Exotica* (1994).

26. The hymn is a farewell but also a promise: "Wherever thou goest, I will go / Wherever thy lodgest, I will lodge / Your people shall be my people / Wherever thou goest, I will go."

27. "First We Take Manhattan," not easy to reproduce on stage, has not yet found the funkier turn it will begin to take in 1993. As for "Joan of Arc," it was butchered every night by cheesy duets, as it would be in every succeeding tour.

28. "Heart with No Companion" (1985). The expression "the other side of despair" was borrowed from an essay title on Christian existentialism by monk and theologian Thomas Merton.

CHAPTER 11

1. Interview for *Le Cercle de Minuit* (French TV program), France2, December 10, 1992.

2. As any media analyst will confirm, imposing a new persona is no mean feat for an artist. After the provocative golden boy poet of the '60s and the existentialist troubadour of his early songwriting career, the stylish gravelly voiced ladies' man of the late 1980s was actually Cohen's third media incarnation. Two more personae will follow.

3. Quoted in Mark Rowland, "Leonard Cohen's Nervous Breakthrough," *Musician*, July 1988.

4. See respectively Nadel, 220, and *Entertainment Weekly*, January 8, 1993.

5. The Sonny Rollins duet was for *Saturday Night Live* (NBC, February 13, 1989). "Elvis's Rolls-Royce" was for Was (Not Was)'s album *Are You Okay?* Set to a hip-hop groove, Leonard narrates in another ode to the impossible transcendence of kitsch how he bought Elvis's Rolls-Royce at an auction in London before driving it across the Atlantic, guided by the King's voice. The song ends on Cohen's emotional arrival to the holy homeland of Memphis, Tennessee.

6. The CD was called *I'm Your Fan*. For the interviews see *Les Inrockuptibles*, no. 1 (March–April 1986), no. 10 (February–March 1988), and no. 30 (July–August 1991).

7. Nirvana, "Pennyroyal Tea," *In Utero*, 1993.

8. Though a Canadian patriot, Cohen had always refused to dip his pen in maple syrup and agreed to contribute in 1996 to a celebration of Contemporary American poetry for PBS with a narration of "Democracy" against the backdrop of a US flag shaped in a barcode (see *The United States of Poetry Part 3*, "The American Dream," PBS, [DVD, 1996]).

9. Namely *An Evening with Leonard Cohen* in March, about the Canadian leg of the previous tour, Adrienne Clarkson's *Summer Festival* in September with an hour-long interview in his Montreal home, and Moses Znaimer's *Leonard Cohen: A Portrait in the First Person* in December.

10. Having completely missed *I'm Your Man*, the Juno academy had some catching up to do. For *The Future*, Leonard won best vocalist, best album, best video, best production, and "songwriter of the year." A roman triumph.

11. The unreadable *Leonard Cohen: Prophet of the Heart* by Dorman and Rawlins (London: Omnibus Press, 1991) and *A Life in Art* by Ira B. Nadel (Toronto: ECW Press, 1994), later expanded into *Various Positions* (New York: Random House, 1996).

12. The papers were published in *Canadian Poetry Series* (Fall/Winter 1993, vol. 33) by Professor Stephen Scobie, then author of a groundbreaking study *Leonard Cohen* (Vancouver: Douglas and McIntyre, 1978) and the champion of Cohen's work in academia.

13. Jean Baudrillard, *Mots de Passe* (Paris: Livre de Poche, 2002), 63–67.

14. In a vast publicity stunt, Apple had offered computers to twelve famous Canadian authors.

15. "The Window," *Recent Songs* (1979).

16. See *Talkshowet*, December 5, 1992 (DR1, interview with Jarl-Friis Mikkelsen) and Alan Jackson, "Growing Old Passionately" (*The Observer*, November 22, 1992).

17. Nadel, 254.

18. For the anecdote see, for example, Cohen's 1997 interview with Stina Lundsen Dabrowski (Burger, 422–423).

19. In 1967, Leonard had given an impromptu concert at little Axel's alternative school in Summerhill, where Rebecca happened to be a boarder. The singer later claimed to remember the girl, a fact that Rebecca, who was eight years old in 1967, understandably found hard to believe ("Knowing Rebecca De Mornay Like Only Leonard Cohen Can," *Interview Magazine*, June 1993).

20. See Simmons, 389.

21. In coded dedication, Leonard will print the biblical extract (Genesis 24:11–12) in the booklet of his next album, *The Future*.

22. "Waiting for the Miracle," *The Future* (1992).

23. "In Bed with Paula Yates," *The Big Breakfast* (Channel 4), April 1, 1994.

24. Among which an incredibly good-humoured one-hour interview by Jarl Friis-Mikkelsen for Denmark's *Talkshowet* (DR1, December 5, 1992) where Cohen prepared cocktails for the host and himself.

25. Leonard had referred to that etymology in several apocalyptic passages of *Beautiful Losers* (see especially 98–99).

26. "Closing Time," *The Future* (1992).

27. The singer has often mentioned the influence of Yeats's poem "The Second Coming" about the climate of impending doom between the two world wars. Some of its opening lines are still among the most well-known in modern poetry: "Things fall apart / The center cannot hold / Mere anarchy / is loosed upon the world." See John Kelly (ed.), *Yeats, W.B.* (London: Everyman, 1997), 39.

28. One of the key ideas of the song, already present on *I'm Your Man*, is that what Debord called "the generalized spectacle" (in other words, the absolute triumph of the televised image) is actually the apocalypse. Many cultural analysts (Baudrillard and Bourdieu among them) emphasized TV's ability to instantly *de-realize* whatever appears on the screen and accomplish — at least symbolically — the disappearance of the world.

29. Cohen started describing apocalypses in his first book, *Let Us Compare Mythologies* (see "Letter," 42–44).

30. Cohen's taunt earned him a response by Ice Cube and Dr. Dre in their song "Natural Born Killaz," an inside account of the riots in which the narrator declares (with two explicit references to Leonard's text) "Fuck Charlie Manson, I'll snatch him out of his truck, hit him with a brick and I'm dancing" ("Natural Born Killaz," *Death Row Records*, 1994).

31. See, for example, Cohen's interview for the Swedish TV program *Primetime* ("Leonard Cohen Special," April 29, 1993).

32. Whenever his pessimism was mentioned that year, Leonard explained in direct reference to the video that "a pessimist waits for rain, I'm already soaked to the skin."

33. See Hakuin, "The Difficulty of Repaying the Debt to the Buddha and the Patriarchs" in *The Essential Teachings of Zen Master Hakuin* (Boston and London: Shambhala, 2010), 63.

34. Bob Dylan apparently considered "The Future" an "evil" song that channels the point of view of the devil. Without that line, it would.

35. For further remarks about the theological consistency of the album and about the presence of naked female bodies in every apocalypse, the reader might want to consult the chapter entitled "The Apocalypse in Leonard Cohen's Pop Theology" in Joel Deshaye and Kait Pinder (ed.), *The Contemporary Leonard Cohen* (Waterloo: Wilfrid Laurier University Press, 2023).

36. In comparison, "Suzanne" or "Sisters of Mercy" sound like very fragile things indeed. For the quote, see Gilles Médioni, "Leonard Cohen : La culpabilité est dévaluée," *L'Express*, December 11, 1992.

37. In the rest of Europe, it's a step back from the previous record (#5 in Austria and Sweden, #3 in Norway).

38. Allen Ginsberg, "Leonard Cohen" in *Take This Waltz*, 93.

39. See Simmons, 405–406.

40. "Leonard Looks Back on His Past," interview with Kari Hesthamar (Norwegian Radio, 2005).

41. For the two quotes, see "Never Any Good" (*More Best Of*, 1997) and "Looking Away" (*Book of Longing*, 165).

CHAPTER 12

1. In Yasutani Hakuun, *Flowers Fall: A Commentary of Zen Master Dogen's Genjokoan* (Boston: Shambhala, 1996), 102.
2. When Leonard lived at Mt. Baldy Zen Center in the mid- to late '90s, five to ten monks and nuns lived there full-time. During retreats, population would rise to about forty students of both sexes. As personal assistant to the Roshi, Leonard followed his master as he moved to teach, sometimes sojourning in Jemez Springs, New Mexico, Ithaca, New Jersey, or even Puerto Rico or Vienna.
3. "Men are numberless, I vow to save them all / Delusions are numberless, I vow to end them all / The dharma gates are numberless, I vow to enter them all / The Buddha's path is unsurpassable, I vow to realize it perfectly." In *Sōtō Zen: An Introduction to Zazen* (Tokyo: Sotochu Shumucho, 2016), 101.
4. See Ikkyū Sojūn, *Crow with No Mouth: Fifteenth Century Zen Master* (Port Townsend: Copper Canyon Press, 2000), 58.
5. Joshu Sasaki was reputed to have stuck to traditional methods to an extent that was hard to find even in modern Japan.
6. Aside from the regular sesshins, ordinary time is divided between the seichu seasons of intense practice (winter and summer) meant for monks-in-training like Cohen to toughen up, and the seikan seasons of more leisurely practice (spring and autumn), with less than four hours of meditation a day.
7. See Arnaud Desjardin, *Le zen ici et maintenant* (Documentary film, ORTF, 1971).
8. The instruction to "kill the Buddha," a reminder that students should break free even from their teachers, is common in Zen and first introduced by Rinzai himself. See Imgard Schloegel, *The Zen Teachings of Rinzai* (Berkeley: Shambhala, 1976), 39.
9. See Jon Pareles, "At Lunch with Leonard: Philosophical Songwriter on the Wire," *New York Times*, October 11, 1995.
10. Sung at least once a day in every Zen monastery, the Heart Sutra ends with a martial call to seek awakening the way you invade a territory:

"Gya tei, gya tei, Hara gya tei, Hara so gya tei, Bo ji so wa ka!" ("To the other shore, To the other shore, All the way to the other shore. Awakening! Hurray!").

11. Elizabeth M. Thompson, "Leonard Cohen: Thoughts of a Ladies' Man," *Woman's Journal*, January 1980, 102.

12. "Waiting for the Miracle," *The Future* (1992).

13. That injunction is taken from Sasaki Roshi's commentary on a famous koan (i.e., "Hyakujo's fox") about a Zen master who, having deceived his students, was reincarnated as a fox five hundred times. See Sasaki Roshi, *Buddha Is the Center of Gravity*, 44, and (for the original koan) Reps, *op. cit.*, 96–97.

14. See Sean Murphy, "Sasaki Roshi, a founding father of American Zen, turns a hundred," *Tricycle*, April 2007.

15. The public apologies of the Rinzai-Ji Temple did little to restore the sangha's prestige. When I spent time there not long after Sasaki's death, there was ample evidence of denial and disarray. Speaking to Leonard and to many monks made clear to me that Sasaki Roshi was deeply loved but also that, as well as teaching a very radical form of Zen, he had established (perhaps unwittingly) a pervasive personality cult.

Approaching the man with a knowledge of Cohen's work, it's hard not to note the similarities with the Nietzschean guru F. in *Beautiful Losers*, as though F. had actually jumped out of the book, put on black robes, and forgotten the English language. A charismatic teacher beaming with crazy wisdom, Sasaki was also (apparently) a deeply flawed man who ruled over a deeply dysfunctional community with a blend of charismatic authority, cognitive dizzying, and emotional blackmail.

That for decades, senior monks and nuns sat in the lotus position in MBZC or Bodhi-Mandala, many of them proudly convinced that their practice was the "real thing" (they got up at 3 a.m., didn't they?) and that milder forms of Zen were basically for wimps, while a couple of partitions away, their sensei was asking the girl (sometimes fifty or sixty years his junior) who had joined him for koan practice for hugs, handjobs, or blowjobs (sometimes getting them) is just beyond belief. So many monks and nuns chose either to deny their Roshi's behaviour or to rationalize it (as did Leonard) as "skillful means" teaching of *selflessness* and *letting go*.*

Of course, things are never black or white and it's perhaps fair to remind that Sasaki Roshi's behaviour started in California in the 1960s and 1970s — a time when promiscuity and casual sex were largely considered as paths of emancipation (and often experienced as such). Perhaps it's also fair to say that, as a monk born in Japan in 1907, Sasaki came from a culture that approached sexuality very differently from the Judeo-Christian–Freudian West. For him, sex would most likely have been an activity that had a little to do with romantic love, nothing to do with sin, and a lot to do with nature. He would probably also have considered geishas empowered women, the female equivalent of samurai. Cohen once said that the Eastern teachers who arrived in the West in the 1960s had to go crazy when faced with emancipated women beaming with sexual charisma. Sasaki Roshi obviously did.

Yet, that the master's harassment of his injis (personal assistants) and female students could carry on for decades despite complaints, resignations, and even scissions in the community says a lot about the extent of his charismatic hold over his disciples. A moving and very precise testimony of the moral agonies of dealing with someone who could be at once an exceptional teacher manifesting love, a vulnerable old man, and an immoral sex fiend is provided by Shozan Jack Haubner (Roshi's assistant in his later years) in *Single White Monk: Tales of Death, Failure and Bad Sex* (Boulder: Shambhala, 2017). But not everyone seemed to have had Haubner's scruples. In his later years, Sasaki's behaviour seemed to have been considered by some as the benign habit of a harmless old man. So maybe rising at 3 a.m. isn't everything after all, and maybe it's fair to ask, "did they ever go clear?"

Unverifiable rumours say that Sasaki was once signalled to an L.A. district attorney and/or to a rape centre in New Mexico in the early 1970s, but no charges were ever officially pressed and the dozen women who did testify in 2013 to an Independent Buddhist Investigations

Commission also expressed their admiration for their teacher (as well as their anger and dismay).

As for Leonard, who famously had a soft spot for larger-than-life characters like Irving Layton or Anthony Kingsmill, he never judged other people and loved Sasaki Roshi deeply. In our conversations, his tenderness for his master was evident and an hour never passed without an anecdote about "Roshi," often about his complete disregard for social conventions and the way he never stopped kicking his ass.

In the climate of the 1970s, Sasaki's behaviour must have seemed quite innocuous to Leonard. In view of some female journalists' accounts of the singer's habit at that time of asking to see their naked breasts before interviews (or bluntly asking for sex afterwards), its even possible that some of the master's habits had rubbed off on his famous disciple. But if, in Leonard's eyes, there was at first nothing wrong with Roshi, his behaviour must have become more embarrassing as the master aged, and increasingly harder to reconcile with the ideals of compassion and detachment so prominent in Zen. After the scandal erupted Leonard was more prone to acknowledge that his friend was "quite flawed as [a] human being" (as he did in an unfinished documentary about Sasaki), but he always added that he cherished that craziness. The only time in our conversations when I felt he was on the defensive was when I asked about the sex scandal. After justifying Sasaki's behaviour as teaching, he finally said, "Roshi was not a yoga teacher. He was a ball of fire running down Mt. Baldy. If you didn't want to get charred, you shouldn't have approached. But he was a sight to see." Perhaps his final thoughts on the matter are featured in a thinly veiled portrait in the posthumous song "Happens to the Heart":

> I studied with a beggar
> he was filthy, he was scarred
> by the claws of many women
> he had failed to disregard

no fable here no lesson
he wasn't all that smart
just a filthy beggar blessing
what happened to the heart.

* In Buddhism, "skillful means" (*upaya* in Sanskrit) designates the teacher's ability (highly prized in Rinzai Zen) to adapt his teaching to the needs of specific students with unconventional and surprising methods.

16. As Gilles Tordjman elegantly put it in "Une Histoire sans morale. Leonard Cohen entre Ciel et Terre," in *Les Inrockuptibles*, no. 1, March 15, 1995 (21).

17. Interview by Lian Lunson in *I'm Your Man* (Lionsgate, 2005).

18. See the famous cover (with a picture by Eric Mullet) of the first issue of *Les Inrockuptibles*, no. 1, March 15, 1995.

19. Quoted in Christian Gaudin, *Histoires zen pour chats* (Paris: Sources La Sirène, 1997), 9.

20. "The Lovesick Monk," *Book of Longing*, 13.

21. "This Is It," *ibid.*, 28.

22. "The Luckiest Man in the World," *ibid.*, 24.

23. See "Early Questions," *ibid.*, 45.

24. Sasaki Roshi, *Buddha Is the Center of Gravity*, 62.

25. Sasaki Roshi had once told Leonard that — a sentence the poet liked to repeat — "the older you get, the more lonely you feel, and the deeper your need for love."

26. In ordinary Japanese, *jikan* means "interval of time" (or just "time"). The term also (apparently) designates the (silent) interval between two thoughts or, in the words of Cohen himself, "normal silence, don't-sweat-over-it silence." Dharma names are often chosen randomly and their function is essentially to remind monks of their commitment, not to express secret truths about their individual nature. A simplified version of the two Chinese characters that form this name (時間) was soon adopted by Cohen to form — when combined with his inter-twined-hearts symbol — his seal and artistic signature.

27. See *infra* (Chapter 1, "The Dog Kelef and Buddha Nature").

28. The only survivor was "Never Any Good," with its hilarious confession of inadequacy.

29. He was already working on it (quite reluctantly it seems) with Adrienne Clarkson in early 1989 (*Summer Festival*, CBC, September 9, 1989) and apparently got seriously depressed during preparation by what he perceived as the "thinness" of his work.

30. Sting's cover of "Sisters of Mercy" as an Irish pub ballad stands out, though.

31. See Cindy Bissailon, "Leonard Cohen: The Other Side of Waiting," *Shambhala Sun*, January 1994; Sacha Reins, "Le Moine qui chante," *Elle*, January 27, 1997, 94–99; Elona Comelli, "The Virtueless Monk," *La Nazione*, November 25, 1998; Sylvie Simmons, "Felonious Monk," *Mojo Magazine*, November 2001, 46–54. Also of note is Pico Iyer's profile of the monk-star in "Several Lifetimes Already," *Shambhala Sun*, September 1998. Leonard himself named his new publishing company Bad Monk Publishing.

32. See Armelle Brusq, *Leonard Cohen: Spring 1996* (Les Films du paradoxe, 1996). He also describes writing (borrowing again an image from W.B. Yeats) as the unglamorous job of a "ragpicker of the heart."

33. Stina Lundberg Dabrowski, *Stina Möter Om Leonard* (1999). Also of note is Laurie Brown, "Leonard Cohen interview on depression and spirituality" (*On the Arts*, CBC, 1997).

34. See Diethard Kuster, *Beautiful Losers* (Arte TV, 1997).

35. He had celebrated his sixtieth birthday on duty in a plane to Vienna, accompanying the roshi to a local branch of Rinzai-Ji, where he was filmed by Austrian television speaking of Zen.

36. Simmons, 416.

37. In a famous essay called *Genjokoan*, thirteenth-century Zen master Dogen affirms in the same paragraph that awakening and illusion exist, that they don't exist, but that they exist without existing. He concludes with an aphorism: "Flowers, though loved, fall. Weeds, while hated, grow." A way of saying, "Wake up, but know that awakening is no absolute state: weeds will still enter your garden and your

favourite flowers wither." See Dogen Zenji, *Shobogenzo* (Woods Hall: Windbell Publications, 1994), 33.

38. Contemporary interpretations of the six-realm doctrine suggest that we are reincarnated several times every day: as envious individuals when we feel we must compete with others; as self-satisfied demigods when all goes well; as hungry spirits who run from one desire to desire; as frightened animals who refuse to open their eyes and — thirty times a day — in the flames of our inexhaustible anger against life. See Chogyam Trungpa, *Cutting Through Spiritual Materialism* (Boston: Shambhala, 2002), 138–48, or Anagarika Govinda, *Foundations of Tibetan Mysticism* (New York: Samuel Weiser, 1969), 234–41 and 247–52.

39. Laurie Brown, *On the Arts*, CBC Newsworld, November 20, 1997.

40. For the snake, see "Hsueh Feng's Turtle-nosed Snake," a.k.a. "Case 22" of the twelfth century koan compilation *Blue Cliff Record*. See Thomas Cleary, *Blue Cliff Record* (Boston: Shambhala, 2005), 144–154. That symbolic death is also why Japanese masters traditionally gave novices "nirvana money" when they left their home monastery for their spiritual grand tour, in case they "died" on the way (see Sōkō Morinaga, *op. cit.*, 62–63).

41. That detail was revealed by Leonard's friend Eric Lerner in his great memoir of their forty-year friendship, *Matters of Vital Interest* (Boston: Da Capo Press, 2018), 20.

42. For this episode, see Simmons, 416–419, and Eric Lerner, 188–190.

43. Published in the "Blackening Pages" section of Jarkko Arjatsalo's website, leonardcohenfiles.com.

44. Balsekar's Advaita was resolutely modern and had little to do with Indian mythology and a lot to do with spiritual relaxation and Socratic dialogue. Interestingly, Cohen did not discover Advaita through Balsekar and in a 1992 interview, he mentions his careful study of a classic of modern Advaita: *I am That* by Sri Nisargadatta Maharadj (actually Balsekar's guru). See Robert O. Connor, "Not Boring, Nor Old, Nor Depressing. Rather Mighty and Lucid," *Downtown*, February 1992.

45. This is a variation on the traditional Vedantic idea of *lila*, life is a dream of God. As alternative words for "God," Ramesh uses "Source," "Totality" or "Consciousness" . . . A synthetic account of his philosophy can be found in Gautam Sachdeva, *Pointers to Ramesh Balsekar* (Mumbai: Yogi Impressions Books, 2008).

46. In Advaita man is by nature "being-consciousness-beatitude," a consciousness not entirely distinct from God. See Jacques Brosse, *Les grands maîtres de la spiritualité* (Paris: Larousse-Bordas, 1998), 231.

47. "The Wind Moves," *Book of Longing*, 170.

48. Sōkō Morinaga, *op. cit.*, 152–154. This is often defined as a symptom of enlightenment.

49. Quoted in Frédéric Lenoir, *La rencontre du Bouddhisme et de l'Occident* (Paris: Albin Michel, 2001), 286.

CHAPTER 13

1. Tchouang-Tseu, *Joie suprême* (Paris: Gallimard, 1969), 35.

2. See Guy Lobrichon, *Les moines d'Occident. L'éternité de l'Europe* (Paris: Gallimard, 2007), 97–99.

3. See respectively *Beautiful Losers* (Arte TV, 1997) and *Stina Om Leonard Cohen* (Stina Lundberg Produktion, 2001).

4. That's Leonard's description of the experience in "Thoughts on *Ten New Songs*" (filmed interview), VHS, Sony Music, 2001.

5. "A Thousand Kisses Deep."

6. According to Shinzen Young, a Buddhist scholar and one of Sasaki Roshi's translators, "Love Itself" is a quasi-verbatim adaptation of one of the master's teishos on the universe as contraction and expansion. In the song, Leonard explains that love manifests our true selves the way sunbeams manifest grains of dust.

7. See respectively "A Thousand Kisses Deep," "Love Itself," "That Don't Make It Junk," "You Have Loved Enough," and "By the Rivers Dark."

8. See "Justesse sans limites," interview by Richard Robert for *Les Inrockuptibles* (no. 308, October 9–15, 2001), 25.

9. "Thoughts on *Ten New Songs*."

10. The man who achieves perfect enlightenment is like the bird that leaves no trace in the sky or the fish that leaves no trace in the water. Mosshôseki (to leave no trace) is the Zen name of that game. See "mosshôseki" in *The Encyclopedia of Eastern Philosophy and Religion* (Boston: Shambhala, 1989), 230–231. On a blog called "Somathread," filmmaker and Ram Dass disciple John Krishna Bush remembers a Mount Baldy sesshin in the early '80s where Cohen, acting as *shoji* (i.e., responsible for discipline), brought out a cognac bottle at the outcome of the retreat "to wash away the stench of enlightenment."

11. See Floria Sigismondi, "My Secret Life," Music Video, Sony Entertainment, 2001.

12. For once, God seems to have been entirely left out of the operation.

13. Two poems by Lord Byron and F.R. Scott, a traditional Québécois ballad, and a country-and-western standard.

14. "Morning Glory."

15. Old Testament readers will also have recognized Leonard's reference to his biblical hero, the psalmist and ladies' man King David who was warmed, in his old age, by a young Virgin slave called Abishag (1 Kings 1:1–10).

16. To a great extent, this is the ironic inversion of the teenager's failure to convince the blonde girl to let him see her "naked body," recounted in *Death of a Lady's Man*, "Memories." A last-minute Pyrrhic victory for the Ladies' Man, so to speak.

17. At its height, the company apparently managed $1.4 billion of private money, 90 percent of which allegedly disappeared in the subprime crisis.

18. Two ricochet trials, one about his stolen archives, another about harassment, kept Leonard busy in 2008 and 2012. After her conviction, Lynch ceaselessly broke her restraining order and sent Leonard as well as his family and friends voice messages and hundreds of rambling emails that mixed supposed revelations about his "true life" with threats and conspiration theories about the Phil Spector trial or Leonard's supposed identity as an undercover CIA agent. A mere glance at that prose, which Lynch also generously poured on the

internet, shows a literal inversion of the singer's quest for light and an ardent desire to besmirch someone who had evidently been her idol. After years of harassment, Lynch was sued again and had to appear in court gagged and tied to her chair. She was sentenced in 2012 to eighteen months of incarceration and mandatory anger treatment.

19. The expression is used by Leonard to refer to the content of *Book of Longing* in an interview for Swedish television (cf. "Montreal Interview," Helle Vaglaand, NRK1, 2006).

20. The past sometimes bursts in with evocations of his mother, of Hydra or the Chelsea Hotel, not to mention about twenty texts and drawings taken from Cohen's 1970s and 1980s archives.

21. A good example is the long version of "A Thousand Kisses Deep," a manifesto on the persistence of love in our broken lives that teaches to accept the necessary constant death of ego (see 56–57).

22. A central idea for Sasaki Roshi and Balsekar, presented here as two masters who taught Leonard the joy of emptiness. In the "afterword," the poet claims that his grasp of his teachers' ideas was so poor that he can't be accused of plagiarizing them (*Book of Longing*, 232).

23. *Op. cit.*, 206.

24. The expression, of course, is from French post-structuralist philosophers Gilles Deleuze and Félix Guattari in their book *Anti-Oedipus* (1972).

25. "Montreal Interview," Helle Vaglaand (TV interview) NRK1, 2006.

26. See "The Centre" and "Your Relentless Appetite for New Perspectives," *Book of Longing*, 218 and 220.

27. Attentive readers may recognize Rebecca De Mornay, and Dante fans will see Beatrice in Paradise leading Dante to a vision of the Virgin. See, respectively, allusions to partners in the *Book of Longing*: "Seisen" (14), "Freda" (25), "Sahara" (44 and 220), "a French woman" (71), "Sheila" (163), "Marianne" (131), "Shirley" (140), "the most beautiful girl on the religious left" (98), "the speaker's mother" (137–39), "Jana" (177), "Québécois girls" (183), "a lover" (228), "a celestial woman" (37 and 121).

28. Sarah Hampson, "He Has Tried in His Way to Be Free," *Shambhala Sun*, November 2007.

29. "A Limited Degree," *Book of Longing*, 65.

30. Zen art is, by nature, humorous. A century apart, Hakuin (1685–1768) and Sengai (1750–1837) organized a competition of grim faces, as they represented themselves or the patriarchs (Bodhidharma in particular) with ever more wrathful and closed miens. On this subject, see D.T. Suzuki, *Sengaï: The Zen of Ink and Paper* (Boulder: Shambhala, 1999) and Kazuaki Tanahashi, *Penetrating Laughter: Hakuin's Zen and Art* (London: Overlook, 1987).

31. *Book of Longing*, 172.

32. "Report to R.S.B.," *Book of Longing*, 204.

33. Helle Vaagland, "Montreal Interview," NRK1, 2006.

34. Wonderful for example is the way the Ashkenazi violin that haunts Glass's entire work amplifies the Jewishness of the texts.

35. A 2005 DVD documentary called *I'm Your Man* by Lian Lunson combined excerpts from the Sydney concert with a superb interview and, as climax, the master duetting with U2.

36. Among the panegyrists were Governor General Adrienne Clarkson and Bono, who described Cohen's songs as "conversations" he wished to have "with Christ, Judas, Yahweh, all the women in the world and Buddha."

37. Some of the tracks are stunningly beautiful, but the note-perfect jazz treatment will seem to some a little too sleek: music that is perhaps hard to appreciate outside a fancy hotel cocktail bar . . .

38. See Simmons, 480.

39. About the pre-stage ritual (actually a revival of a ritual from the 1979 tour) see Elisa Bray, "Leonard Cohen: Before the gig, a chant in Latin" *The Independent*, September 6, 2012. The Latin song is the canon "Pauper sum ego, Nihil habeo, Cor meum dabo" (see *infra*, Chapter 8, "Last Year's Man," and Harry Rasky's movie, *The Song of Leonard Cohen*, 1980).

40. See Bonino, *op. cit.*, 221.

41. Thanks in part to the efforts of twenty-six technicians, including a light designer, a costume designer, and four sound engineers.

42. "Come On, Friends, Let's Go," interview by Michael Bonner, *Uncut*, December 2008, 58–60.

43. And Leonard "held the mirror." Of course.

44. The Kabbalah claims that men have the capacity to create angels. Through Mitzvot (ritual actions), they create channels for angels to enter the world to enlighten, console, or protect us (see Marc-Alain Ouaknin, *Mystères de la Kabbale*, 167–168). This might be a poetical way to point to what happens truly on stage: like any person who performs rituals — like any kohen — the crooner Cohen creates ephemeral angels who stay with us for a while and disappear again. He had long professed that women could manifest angels: he proves crooners can do the same. In an interesting 1984 interview with Robert Sward, he expounded on the "migratory gift" that people have to manifest angels (see Burger, *op. cit.*, 165–166).

45. He incidentally also mocks his own addiction to carrying burdens ("Going Home").

46. A contamination that inverts the famous epiphanic passage in *Beautiful Losers*, when Saint Kateri spills a glass of wine to see the purple stain spread to everything, people, landscape, and moon included (*Beautiful Losers*, 97–98).

47. Leonard was then the grandfather of a little Cassius (son of Adam) and a little Viva (daughter of Lorca).

CHAPTER 14

1. Translation: "The incessant contemplation of black evidence." In Claudio Rugafiori, *Le Grand Jeu. Collection complète* (Paris: Jean-Michel Placé, 1977), 68.

2. Among them "Who's That Girl?" and "La Isla Bonita." Other collaborations include Pink Floyd, Bryan Ferry, Elton John, and Marianne Faithfull.

3. Larvatus prodeo, in the original Latin. Descartes's aim was to avoid persecution because of his scientific activities and unorthodox religious views.

4. They were first published in *The New Yorker* in 2009 and in *Book of Longing* (144), respectively.

5. London press conference, October 13, 2014.

6. As for "Born in Chains," anyone still awake after the second verse will understand why the song had been dropped from *I'm Your Man* twenty-five years earlier.

7. The shadows are borrowed from the previous album. We will soon understand why.

8. The pictures were taken by his beloved assistant Kezban Özscan.

9. See for example Gershom Scholem, *Le Zohar* (Paris: Seuil, 1980), 31–35, and Marc-Alain Ouaknin, *Mystères de la Kabbale* (Paris: Assouline, 2006), 133–135.

10. *On Tour with Leonard Cohen* (New York: Power House Books, 2014).

11. For those keeping score a Centenary model Globe-Trotter suitcase given by his dear friend Dominique Issermann.

12. As it turns out, two quasi-identical cream-coloured tabbies that help the poet in one of his favourite games: spotting imperceptible differences.

13. "The Window" (1979).

14. *Q*, TV interview, CBC, April 16, 2009.

15. We may note that Leonard is very candid: the lyrics say the count-down has begun ("It's not because I am old / It's not what dying does") and that there's something in his blood: ("Slow is in my blood"). So, Leonard's dying? Rest assured, so are we.

16. He has asked an academic friend of his, Dr. Robert Faggen, to do the job.

17. See the poem "Cuckold's Song" (*The Spice-Box of Earth*, 42–43) or the song "A Bunch of Lonesome Heroes" (1969). In 2015, Morton Rosengarten, the childhood friend that Leonard considered a genius sculptor, was working on a superb bust of the poet that I was lucky to see: an oblong face, piercing eyes, and that enigmatic old mug: Leonard as a kingly pharaoh.

18. "Steer Your Way" (2016).

19. "Almost Like the Blues" (2014).

20. See again Wumen's commentary on the first koan in the *Gateless Gate* (Reps, *op. cit.*, 95–96) and for the tiger image (a classic metaphor for

enlightenment), many passages (89, 230, 278, etc.) in Thomas Cleary, *The Blue Cliff Record* (Boston: Shambhala, 2005).

21. In his last known interview (*The New Yorker*, October 17, 2016), Cohen reminds the listeners, while warning them against an exclusively Jewish vision of his work, of the impact on his poetic imagination of the idea in the Lurianic Kabbalah that the world as we know it is a catastrophe born out of the explosion of God. As Cohen explains in the interview, "We basically live in the ruins of God" and each prayer is an attempt to rebuild Him. No doubt such a vision helps deal with broken backs and terminal illnesses.

22. "Lullaby" (2012).

23. "The Future" (1992).

24. A touching detail: that father-and-son collaboration finally fulfills a contract signed in one of Leonard's 1990 notebooks as Adam was lying in hospital after a serious motorcycle accident. Leonard had committed to hire his son to produce "at least half a record" of "songs or rap." Gentlemen always keep their word.

25. Interestingly, the record mentions several firing squads and executions.

26. See "The Correct Attitude," *Book of Longing*, 155.

27. Fans will remember that on the back cover of *Greatest Hits* (1975), a picture by Giuseppe Pino showed Leonard making smoke rings.

28. See "The Smokey Life," *Recent Songs* (1979).

29. See Milan Kundera, *A Festival of Insignificance* (London: Faber & Faber, 2015), a book that suggests the meaningless of life is the great uncluttering and unburdening we need and the locus of true emancipation.

30. "Boogie Street," *Ten New Songs* (2001).

31. Like *I'm Your Man* thirty years earlier, the title of the album is ambiguous. Besides being Leonard's question to his maker, it could be God's question to us all, a challenge to a humanity that seems addicted to darkness in all domains. It could also be Leonard's final caveat emptor, an ironic question to his audience that warns them to buy the record only if they like their Leonard Cohen albums really dark.

32. That expression is stolen from chapter 12 of Tom Wolfe's 1988 novel *Bonfire of Vanities*.

33. The joke was made during Cohen's last press conference (see *supra*).

34. Nothing is missing except fear, inconceivable for an old Zen master. Also echoing the singer's predicament is the evocation of wine that is changed into water or radios that pick up only static (in "Treaty"), although the "static" lyric was written in the late '70s, possibly an evocation of depression.

35. The album's carnival of crucifixions and executions requires no comment and "If I Didn't Have Your Love" borrows from Byron's 1816 poem "Darkness" (Levine, *op. cit.*, 245) the hypothesis of a world plunged into eternal night.

36. Originally published as a poem refuting Christ's ethics of tenderness in the wake of 9/11 (*Book of Longing* 190), "Seemed the Better Way" is reshaped here as a recusation of all philosophical systems in the face of acute suffering.

37. Only flamenco seems to be missing, but Leonard's back problems forbid the use of guitar.

38. On "String Reprise/Treaty," Leonard takes a 2'40" leave of absence and comes back in extremis for two heart-rending sentences about brokenness and how hard it is to give true love.

39. See respectively "You Want It Darker," "Treaty," "Seemed the Better Way," and "On the Level."

40. In ancient Judaism the Kaddish, a major source of the Christian Lord's Prayer, was a proclamation of faith and exaltation of God that accompanied daily liturgical acts. It progressively took on a specific form, the *Kaddish Yatom* or *Kaddish Avellim* (literally the Kaddish "for orphans and bereaved") now reserved for funeral services.

41. "It's written in the Scriptures / And it's not some idle claim" says Leonard to justify God's love of darkness. Among the sources he may have in mind here are the famous "Day of Doom" passage in Ezekiel 30:3 or Isaiah 45:07, where God warns his prophet that he deals out light *and* darkness, grace *and* persecution. He insists in Deuteronomy

32:39, "I kill and I make alive. I wound and I heal." How do you say "don't fuck with me" in Hebrew?

42. "Hineni" is the patriarchs' and prophets' answer to God when he calls on them (see Genesis 22:11, Exodus 3:4, and Isaiah 6:8), but also the word that Adam no longer dares to use after the Fall.

43. The routine is included as "Stages" on *Can't Forget: Souvenir of the Grand Tour* live album (2015).

44. For an introduction to the Japanese aesthetics of wabi-sabi, the beauty of things imperfect and impermanent, the reader may want to consult the wonderful short treatise of the amazingly named Leonard Koren (sic), *Wabi-Sabi for Artists, Designers, Poets and Philosophers* (Point Reynes: Imperfect Publishing, 2008).

45. Layton's phrase, which Leonard has often cited, is taken from his 1961 poem "Keine Lazarovitch 1970–1959" about his dying mother. See *Selected Poems* (New York: New Directions Publishing, 1977), 21.

46. See Montaigne's *Essays*, Book I, "That to philosophize is to learn to die."

EPILOGUE

1. See the poem "The Correct Attitude" (*Book of Longing*, 157).

2. There's nothing like a Latin palindrome to impress people at parties.

SELECTIVE DISCOGRAPHY

STUDIO ALBUMS

Songs of Leonard Cohen. CBS-Sony, 1967/1968.

Songs from a Room. CBS-Sony, 1969.

Songs of Love and Hate. CBS-Sony, 1971.

New Skin for the Old Ceremony. CBS-Sony, 1974.

Death of a Ladies' Man. CBS-Sony, 1977.

Recent Songs. CBS-Sony, 1979.

Various Positions. CBS-Sony, 1985.

I'm Your Man. CBS-Sony, 1988.

The Future. CBS-Sony, 1992.

Ten New Songs. CBS-Sony, 2001.

Dear Heather. CBS-Sony, 2004.

Old Ideas. CBS-Sony, 2012.

Popular Problems. CBS-Sony, 2014.

You Want It Darker. CBS-Sony, 2016.

Thanks for the Dance. CBS-Sony, 2019.

LIVE ALBUMS

Live Songs. CBS-Sony, 1973.

Cohen Live: Leonard Cohen in Concert. CBS-Sony, 1994.

Live at the Isle of Wight 1970. CBS-Sony, 2009.

Field Commander Cohen. Tour of 1979. CBS-Sony, 2001.

Live in London. CBS-Sony, 2009.
Songs from the Road. CBS-Sony, 2010.
Live in Dublin. CBS-Sony, 2014.
Can't Forget. A Souvenir of the Grand Tour. CBS-Sony, 2015.

COMPILATION ALBUMS

Greatest Hits. CBS-Sony, 1974.
So Long Marianne. CBS-Sony, 1989.
More Best Of. CBS-Sony, 1997.
The Essential Leonard Cohen. CBS-Sony, 2002.
Greatest Hits. CBS-Sony, 2009.

SIDE PROJECTS

Furey, Lewis. *Night Magic.* RCA, 1985 (CD reissue by Cinémusique, 2004).
Glass, Philip. *Book of Longing: A Song Cycle.* Orange Mountain Music, 2007.
Thomas, Anjani. *Blue Alert.* Sony BMG, 2006.

BIBLIOGRAPHY

ORIGINAL WORKS BY LEONARD COHEN (IN CHRONOLOGICAL ORDER)

Let Us Compare Mythologies. Toronto: McClelland & Stewart, 1956.

The Spice-Box of Earth. Toronto: McClelland & Stewart, 1961.

The Favourite Game. Toronto: McClelland & Stewart, 1963.

Flowers for Hitler. Toronto: McClelland & Stewart, 1964.

Beautiful Losers. Toronto: McClelland & Stewart, 1966.

Parasites of Heaven. Toronto: McClelland & Stewart, 1966.

Selected Poems: 1956–1968. Toronto: McClelland & Stewart, 1968.

The Energy of Slaves. Toronto: McClelland & Stewart, 1972.

Death of a Lady's Man. Harmondsworth: Penguin, 1977.

Book of Mercy. Toronto: McClelland & Stewart, 1984.

Stranger Music. London: Jonathan Cape, 1993.

Book of Longing. Toronto: McClelland & Stewart, 2006.

The Flame. Edinburgh: Canongate, 2018.

BIOGRAPHICAL WORKS

Burger, Jeff. *Leonard Cohen on Leonard Cohen: Interviews and Encounters.*
    Chicago: Chicago Review Press, 2014.

Devlin, Jim. *In Every Style of Passion: The Works of Leonard Cohen.*
    London: Omnibus Press, 1996.

———. *Leonard Cohen: In His Own Words.* London: Omnibus Press,
    1998.

Dorman, Loranne, and Clive Rawlins. *Leonard Cohen: Prophet of the Heart*. London: Omnibus Press, 1990.

Footman, Tim. *Leonard Cohen: Hallelujah: A New Biography*. London: Chrome Dreams, 2009.

Fournier, Michael, and Ken Norris. *Take This Waltz: A Celebration of Leonard Cohen*. Montreal: Muses' Company, 1994.

Friedman, Matti. *Who by Fire: War, Atonement, and the Resurrection of Leonard Cohen*. New York: Penguin Random House, 2022.

Green, Roger. *Hydra and the Bananas of Leonard Cohen*. New York: Basic Books, 2003.

Hesthamar, Kari. *So Long, Marianne: A Love Story*. Toronto: ECW Press, 2014.

Lerner, Eric. *Matters of Vital Interest: A Forty-Year Friendship with Leonard Cohen*. New York: Da Capo Press, 2018.

Nadel, Ira B. *Leonard Cohen: A Life in Art*. Toronto: ECW Press, 1994.

———. *Various Positions: A Life of Leonard Cohen*. London: Bloomsbury, 1996.

Posner, Michael. *Leonard Cohen: Untold Stories, The Early Years (vol. 1)*. Toronto: Simon & Schuster, 2020.

———. *Leonard Cohen: Untold Stories, From this Broken Hill (vol. 2)*. Toronto: Simon & Schuster, 2021.

———. *Leonard Cohen: Untold Stories, That's How the Light Gets In (vol. 3)*. Toronto: Simon & Schuster, 2022.

Rasky, Harry. *The Song of Leonard Cohen*. Oakville: Mosaic Press, 2001.

Reynolds, Anthony. *Leonard Cohen: A Remarkable Life*. London: Omnibus Press, 2010.

Robinson, Sharon. *On Tour with Leonard Cohen*. New York: Powerhouse Books, 2014.

Scott, Judy. *Leonard, Marianne, and Me*. Guilford: Backbeat Books, 2021.

Sheppard, David. *Leonard Cohen*. New York: Thunder's Mouth Press, 2001.

Simmons, Sylvie. *I'm Your Man: The Life of Leonard Cohen*. New York: HarperCollins, 2012.

Tordjman, Gilles. *Leonard Cohen*. Paris: Le Castor Astral, 2006.

DOCUMENTARY MOVIES

Anonymous. *Leonard Cohen Under Review, 1934–1977.* DVD. New Malden: Sexy Intellectual, 2007 (90').

Anonymous. *Leonard Cohen Under Review, 1978–2006.* DVD. New Malden: Sexy Intellectual, 2007 (87').

Brittain, Donald, and Don Owen. *Ladies and Gentlemen . . . Mr. Leonard Cohen.* DVD, 1999. Toronto: National Film Board of Canada, 1965 (45').

Broomfield, Nick. *Marianne & Leonard: Words of Love.* Roadside Attractions/Dogwoof, 2019 (109').

Brusq, Armelle. *Leonard Cohen: Spring 1996.* DVD, 1997. Paris: Les Films du Paradoxe, 1996 (56').

Greenberg, Fabien, and Bård Kjøge Rønning. *Little Axel.* Antipode Film, 2021 (53').

Hayashi, Yukari, Barrie McLean, and Hiroaki Mori. *The Tibetan Book of the Dead, Part 1 & 2.* Narrated by Leonard Cohen. CBC, 1994.

Kuster, Diethard. *Beautiful Losers.* Features Willy DeVille, Marianne Faithfull, and Leonard Cohen. France-Germany, Arte TV, Dockland Production, 1997 (60').

Lerner, Murray. *Leonard Cohen: Live at the Isle of Wight 1970.* Sony Music, 2009 (64').

Lundberg Dabrowski, Stina. *Stina Möter Leonard Cohen.* Stina Lundberg Produktion, 1997 (50').

———. *Stina Om Leonard Cohen,* Stina Lundberg Produktion, 2001 (50').

Lunson, Lian. *Leonard Cohen: I'm Your Man.* DVD. Metropolitan Video/ Lionsgate, 2005 (103').

May, Derek. *Angel.* Short film. NFBC, 1966 (6'55").

Nicholls, Alan. *I Am a Hotel.* Musical movie. CBC, Toronto, Canada, Blue Memorial Video Ltd., 1983 (24').

Troller, Georg Stefan. *Hallelujah in Moll.* ZDF, 1985 (30').

Palmer, Tony. *Bird on a Wire.* DVD. The Machat Company, 2010 [1974] (106').

Portway, Bob. *Songs from the Life of Leonard Cohen*. BBC, 1988 (70').

Rasky, Harry. *The Song of Leonard Cohen*. CBC, 1980 (90').

Znaimer, Moses. *Leonard Cohen: A Portrait in the First Person*. CBC, 1989 (28').

RADIO AND TV INTERVIEWS (IN CHRONOLOGICAL ORDER)

"Cohen Playing the Favourite Game." Interview. CBC TV, Canada, 1963 (12'20").

This Hour Has Seven Days. Interview by Beryl Fox. CBC TV, Canada, May 1, 1966 (9'26").

Take 30. Interview by Adrienne Clarkson. CBC TV, Canada, May 23, 1966 (19').

Once More with Julie Felix. Songs. BBC, UK, January 27, 1968 (12').

Arpèges sur Joe Dassin. Songs. ORTF1, France, June 10, 1970 (6').

Le Grand échiquier. Interview by Jacques Chancel. Antenne 2, France, February 6, 1976 (2'37").

Authors: LC, Part I & II. Interview by Patrick Watson. CBC, Canada, February 8, 1978 (40').

Morningside. "Leonard Cohen at Fifty." Interview by Peter Gzowski. CBC Radio, Canada, 1984.

Karussel. Interview. DRS-TV, Switzerland, March 5, 1985 (15').

Mixed Bag. Interview by Pete Fornatale. WNEW-FN, New York, April 28, 1985.

Mike Walsh Show. Interview by Mike Walsh. Nine Network, Australia, May 20, 1985 (6'45").

The Midday Show with Ray Martin. Interview by Ray Martin. Nine Network, Australia, May 24, 1985 (15').

The John Hammond Years. Radio interview. BBC, UK, September 20, 1986.

Offbeat. Interview. Tele 5, Germany, January 1988 (10').

Cargo de Nuit. Interview. Belgium, RTBF1, March 16, 1988 (7').

Fancy Friday. Interview by Malena Ivarsson. SVT, Sweden, April 28, 1988 (5').

Leonard Cohen: Live in San Sebastian. Concert and interview. Spain, RTE-TV, May 20, 1988.

Summer Festival Series. Interview by Adrienne Clarkson. CBC TV, Canada, September 21, 1989 (56').

Talkshowet. Interview by Jarl Friis-Mikkelsen. DR1, Denmark, December 5, 1992 (60').

Le Cercle de minuit. Interview by Michel Field. France 2, France, December 10, 1992 (17').

Primetime TV/Leonard Cohen Special/The Future. Concert and interview. Finland, April 29, 1993 (35').

Leonard Cohen Special. BBC Radio 1, UK, July 8, 1994.

"In Bed with Paula Yates." *The Big Breakfast.* Interview by Paula Yates. Channel 4, UK, 1994 (6').

Valerie Pringle Show. Interview by Valerie Pringle. CTV, Canada, 1997 (6'20").

"On The Arts" / "Buskin' Trail." Interview by Laurie Browne. CBC, Canada, 1997 (12').

"Ten New Songs." EPK, filmed interview. VH-1, Sony Music, 2001 (17').

"If It Be Your Will: Leonard Cohen Looks Back on His Past." Interview by Kari Hesthamar. NRK, Norway, January 2006 (44'22").

Montreal Interview. Interview by Helle Vaagland. NRK, Norway, 2006 (27').

Q with Jian Ghomeshi. Interview by Jian Ghomeshi. CBC Radio, 2009 (42').

Popular Problems Q&A. Press conference, London. September 16, 2014 (16').

You Want It Darker Press Conference. Press conference, Los Angeles. October 13, 2016 (9').

PRESS ARTICLES AND INTERVIEWS

Anonymous. "The Stormy Clovers." *Toronto Star,* June 26, 1966.

Anonymous. "Leonard Cohen: A Much Bigger Man Than He Appears." *The Province,* October 27, 1978.

Anonymous. "The Face May Not Be Familiar, But the Name Should Be: It's Composer and Cult-Hero Leonard Cohen." *People Magazine* 13, no. 2 (January 14, 1980): 53–64.

Anonymous. "Knowing Rebecca De Mornay Like Only Leonard Cohen Can." *Interview Magazine*, June 1993.

Anonymous. "Leonard Cohen: The Questionnaire." *Q Magazine*, September 1994.

Ackerman, Marianne. "Cohen Seeks Spiritual Solace Not Perfect Love." *The Gazette*, April 14, 1984.

Bier, Jennifer, and Hervé Muller. "Leonard Cohen. Paroles et musique." *Rock & Folk*, no. 114, July 1976, 62–74.

Bisaillon, Cindy. "Leonard Cohen: The Other Side of Waiting." *Shambhala Sun*, January 1994.

Black, Louis. "First, We Take Berlin." *The Austin Chronicle*, November 16, 2007.

Blaine, Hal. "The Great Ones Never Leave." *Melody Maker*, November 26, 1977.

Bohn, Chris. "Cohen: Haunted by Spector." *Melody Maker*, May 1, 1980.

Bonner, Michael. "Come On, Friends, Let's Go." *Uncut*, no. 139, December 2008, 58–60.

Buchholz, Brad. "Touring with Cohen." *Austin American-Statesman*, March 31, 2009.

Bray, Elisa. "Leonard Cohen: Before the Gig, a Chant in Latin." *The Independent*, September 6, 2012.

Browne, David. "7 Reasons Why Leonard Cohen Is the Next Best Thing to God." *Entertainment Weekly*, January 8, 1993.

Cohen, Scott. "A Few Things About Bob Dylan as Told to Scott Cohen." *Interview Magazine*, February 1986.

———. "Leonard Cohen: My Old Flame." In *Yakety Yak: Midnight Confessions and Revelations of 37 Rock Stars and Legends*, London: Simon & Schuster, 1994.

Conrad, William. "Suzanne and Other Confessions: A Leonard Cohen Interview." Nashville, Autumn 1975 (in Burger, *op. cit.*, 103–107).

Cruchley, Brian. "Mariposa: A Battle Between Electric and Acoustic Guitar." *Toronto Daily Star*, August 14, 1967.

Dallas, Karl. "Cohen: Songwriter Who Got into Folk by Accident." *NME*,

February 17, 1968. In *Bob Dylan and the Folk Rock Boom, 1964–1974*, edited by Steve Sutherland, *NME Originals*, series 2, issue 5, 2005, 58.

DeCurtis, Antony. "No Mercy: Leonard's Tales from the Dark Side." *Rolling Stone*, January 21, 1993.

Deevoy, Adrian. "Porridge? Lozenge? Syringe?" *Q Magazine*, October 1991.

Ducray, François. "L'adieu aux larmes." *Rock & Folk*, no. 131, December 1977, 95–99.

Evans, Allan. "Leonard Cohen: Songs of Love and Hate." *NME*, May 22, 1971 (in Sutherland, *op. cit.*, 95).

Fevret, Christian. "Comme un guerrier." *Les Inrockuptibles*, no. 30, July–August 1991, 92–114.

———, ed. *Leonard Cohen : Folksinger moderne, Les Inrockuptibles Hors-série*. Paris: Éditions Indépendantesp, 2017.

Fulford, Robert. "Cohen's Nightmare Novel." *Toronto Daily Star*, April 26, 1966.

Furnival, Andrew. "The Strange, Sad, Beautiful World of Leonard Cohen." *Petticoat*, December 30, 1972.

Goldstein, Richard. "Beautiful Creep." *Village Voice*, December 28, 1967 (in Gnarowski, *op. cit.*, 40–46).

Grescoe, Paul. "Poet, Writer, Singer, Lover, Cohen." *Canadian Magazine*, February 10, 1968.

Hampson, Sarah. "He Has Tried in His Way to Be Free." *Shambhala Sun*, November 2007.

Harris, Michael. "The Poet as Hero 2." *Saturday Night Review*, June 1969 (in Gnarowski, *op. cit.*, 55–56).

Hilburn, Robert. "Telling It on the Mountain. R.H. Interviews Leonard Cohen." *L.A. Times Sunday*, September 24, 1995.

Holden, Stephen. "Leonard Cohen Obscured. A Haunting by Phil Spector." *Rolling Stone*, January 6, 1978.

Houellebecq, Michel. "Le libertaire impossible." *Les Inrockuptibles*, no. 1, March 15, 1995, 20.

Huston, Anjelica. "Leonard Cohen." *Interview Magazine*, November 1995.

Hubbard, Rob. "First, He's a Poet." *Pioneer Press*, June 21, 1993.

Issermann, Dominique. "Leonard par Dominique." *Le Nouvel Observateur*, January 26, 2012, 126–129.

Iyer, Pico. "Several Lifetimes Already." *Shambhala Sun*, September 1998, 50–60.

Jackson, Alan. "Growing Old Passionately." *The Observer*, November 22, 1992.

Jensen, Dean. "Poetical Cohen. A Rare Find in the 70s." *Milwaukee Journal Sentinel*, February 26, 1975.

Johnston, Brian D. "Life of a Lady's Man: Leonard Cohen Sings of Love and Freedom." *Maclean's*, December 7, 1992.

Jones, Cliff. "Heavy Cohen." *Rock CD*, no. 6, December 1992.

Kapica, Jack. "The Trials of Leonard Cohen." *Montreal Gazette*, August 25, 1973.

King, Paul. "Montreal Poet Working on TV Project, But His Heart Belongs to Buddha." *Montreal Gazette*, July 16, 1983.

Kloman, William. "Leonard Cohen." *New York Times*, January 28, 1968.

Kurzweil, Arthur. "I'm the Little Jew Who Wrote the Bible: A Conversation with Leonard Cohen." *Jewish Book News*, November 23, 1993.

Lake, Steve. "Cohen Plays a Tireless Game." *Melody Maker*, December 11, 1980.

Lichtenstein, Grace. "Leonard Cohen Muses on New Stage Musical." *New York Times*, September 8, 1973.

Lock, Graham. "Love Me, Love My Barrel Gun." *NME*, February 23, 1980.

Lumsden, Susan. "Leonard Cohen Wants the Unconditional Leadership of the World." *Weekend Magazine*, no. 37, 1970 (in Gnarowski, *op. cit.*, 69–73).

Lynskey, Dorian. "Leonard Cohen: All I've Got to Put in a Song Is My Own Experience." *The Guardian*, January 19, 2012.

Mandel, Eli. "Cohen's Life as a Slave." In *Another Time (Three Solitudes: Contemporary Literary Criticism in Canada)*. Erin, Ontario: Porcupine's Quill, 1977, 124–136.

McDonald, Marci. "Leonard Cohen Is a Poet Who Is Trying to Be Free." *Toronto Daily Star*, April 26, 1969.

Médioni, Gilles. "Leonard Cohen : la culpabilité est dévaluée." *L'Express*, December 11, 1992.

Nelson, Paul. "Cohen's Doo-Wop Nightmare." *Rolling Stone*, February 9, 1978.

Owen, Don. "The Poet as Hero. Part 2. Cohen Remembered." *Saturday Night Review*, June 1969.

Pareles, Jon. "At Lunch with Leonard: Philosophical Songwriter on the Wire." *New York Times*, October 11, 1995.

Pike, Robin. "September 15, 1974." *ZigZag*, October 1974 (in Burger, *op. cit.*, 57–74).

Quill, Greg. "Cohen Finds Humour in Being Taken Seriously." *Toronto Star*, May 4, 1988.

Remnick, David. "Leonard Cohen Makes It Darker." *The New Yorker*, October 17, 2016.

Robins, Wayne. "The Loneliness of the Long-Suffering Folkie." *Newsday*, November 22, 1992.

Robert, Richard. "Justesse sans limite." *Les Inrockuptibles*, no. 308, October 9–15, 2001, 23–27.

Rowland, Mark. "Leonard Cohen's Nervous Breakthrough." *Musician*, July 1988.

Ruddy, Jon. "Is the World (or Anybody) Ready for Leonard Cohen?" *Maclean's*, November 1, 1966.

Silcott, Mireille. "Leonard Cohen: A Happy Man." *Saturday Night*, September 15, 2001.

Simmons, Sylvie. "Felonious Monk." *Mojo Magazine*, no. 96, November 2001, 46–54.

———. "Quiet Revolution." *Mojo Magazine*, no. 220, March 2012, 83–84.

Snider, Norman. "Cohen's Audacious Gambit." *The Globe and Mail*, April 21, 1984.

Snow, Mat. "Cohen's Way. There's a New Comic Touch of Bedsit Angst." *The Guardian*, February 22, 1988.

Sward, Robert. "Leonard Cohen as Interviewed by Robert Sward. Montreal, 1984" (in Burger, *op. cit.*, 163–172).

Tordjman, Gilles. "Histoire sans morale. Cohen entre ciel et terre." *Les Inrockuptibles*, no. 1, March 15, 1995, 16–24.

Twigg, Alan. "Garbage and Flowers. Leonard Cohen." In *For Openers: Conversations with 24 Canadian Writers*. Madeira Park: Harbour Publishing, 1981, 53–68.

Walsh, John. "Research, You Understand . . ." *Mojo Magazine*, September 1994.

Walsh, Nick. "I Never Discuss My Mistresses and My Tailors." *The Guardian*, October 14, 2001.

Wieseltier, Leon. "Prince of Bummers." *The New Yorker*, July 26, 1993, 40–45.

———. "The Art of Wandering." CD booklet, *Leonard Cohen: Songs from the Road*, Sony Music, 2010.

Williams, Paul. "Leonard Cohen: The Romantic in a Ragpicker's Trade." *Crawdaddy Magazine*, March 1975.

Wilson, Milton. "Poetry." *Letters in Canada: 1964*, In Gnarowski, *op. cit.*, 20–23.

Zollo, Paul. "Leonard Cohen." In *Songwriters on Songwriting*. Boston: Da Capo Press, 2003, 329–349.

CRITICAL BOOKS AND ARTICLES ON LEONARD COHEN

Deshaye, Joel, and Kait Pinder. *The Contemporary Leonard Cohen*. Waterloo: Wilfrid Laurier University Press, 2023.

Gnarowski, Michael, ed. *Leonard Cohen: The Artist and His Critics*. Toronto: McGraw-Hill Ryerson, 1976.

Herold, Christoph. "Famous Blue Raincoat: An Approach to an Integrated Analysis of a Song." In *Intricate Preparations: Writing Leonard Cohen*, edited by Stephen Scobie. Toronto: ECW Press, 2000.

Lebold, Christophe. "The Traitor and the Stowaway: Persona Construction in the Trajectories of Bob Dylan and Leonard Cohen." *IASPM Journal* 1, no. 2, January 2011, 1–17.

———. "I'm The Little Jew Who Wrote the Bible: A Reconfiguration of the Devotional Poet for the Age of the Mass Media." In *Interdisciplinary*

Approaches to Spirituality in Science and Arts. London: Peter Lang, 2013, 133–147.

———. "Confessions d'un Prophète. Notes sur la tournée européenne de Leonard Cohen 2008–2009." In *Transatlantica* 1, 2009, transatlantica .revues.org/4326.

———. "Canadian Matter and American Manner: Leonard Cohen's *Beautiful Losers* between Pastoral and Pop." *Études canadiennes*, no. 54, 2003, 163–173.

———. "Fragmentation and Unity in Leonard Cohen's *Beautiful Losers*." *Études canadiennes*, no. 46, 1999, 143–153.

Mandel, Eli. "Cohen's Life as a Slave." Essay in *Another Time (Three Solitudes: Contemporary Literary Criticism in Canada)*. Erin, Ontario: Porcupine's Quill, 1977, 124–136.

Měsíc, Jiří. *Leonard Cohen: The Modern Troubadour*. Olomouc: Palacký University Press, 2020.

Mus, Francis. *The Demons of Leonard Cohen*. Translated by Laura Vroomen. University of Ottawa Press, 2020.

Ondaatje, Michael. *Leonard Cohen*. Toronto: McClelland & Stewart, 1970.

Pacey, Desmond. "The Phenomenon of Leonard Cohen." *Canadian Literature*, Autumn 1967, no. 34, 5–23.

Powe, B.W. "The Endless Confessions of a Lady's Man." In *A Climate Charged: Essays on Canadian Writers*. Oakville: Mosaic Press, 1984, 117–129.

Rabinovitch, Gérard, and Chantal Ringuet. *Les révolutions de Leonard Cohen*. Québec City: Presses de l'Université du Québec, 2016.

Scobie, Stephen. *Leonard Cohen*. Vancouver: Douglas & McIntyre, 1978.

———. *Signature Event Cantext*. Edmonton, Alberta: Newest Publishing, 1989.

———. Keynote address. "The Counterfeiter Begs Forgiveness." In *Canadian Poetry: The Proceedings of the Leonard Cohen Conference*, edited by E.F. Dyck. *Canadian Poetry* series, no. 33, 1993.

────, ed. *Intricate Preparations: Writing Leonard Cohen*. Toronto: ECW Press, 2000.

Sheppard, David. *Leonard Cohen: Kill Your Idols*. New York: Thunder's Mouth Press, 2000.

Siemerling, Winfried. "Leonard Cohen, 'Loneliness and History: A Speech Before the Jewish Public Library.'" In *Take This Waltz: A Celebration of Leonard Cohen*, edited by Michael Fournier and Ken Norris. Montreal: Muses' Company, 1994, 143–153.

Smith, Rowland. "Prayers." *Canadian Literature*, no. 104, spring 1985.

Vassal, Jacques. *Leonard Cohen*. Paris: Albin Michel, 1974.

Wayman, Tom. "Cohen's Women." *Canadian Literature*, no. 60, Spring 1974, 89–93.

PHILOSOPHY, LITERATURE, PSYCHANALYSIS, AND CULTURAL STUDIES

Adorno, Theodor. *Dialektik der Aufklärung*. Frankfurt: Suhonkamp, 1981 [1948].

Aromatico, Andrea. *Alchimie : le grand secret*. Paris: Gallimard, 1996.

Avedon, Richard. *The Sixties*. New York: Random House, 1999.

Bachelard, Gaston. *La psychanalyse du feu*. Paris: Gallimard, 1949.

Baudelaire, Charles. *Le peintre de la vie moderne*. Paris: Mille et Une Nuits, 2002 [1863].

Baudrillard, Jean. *Mots de passe*. Paris: Le Livre de Poche, 2002.

Barthes, Roland. *Camera Lucida*. New York: Vintage Books, 1981.

────. "Tels." *Œuvres complètes Vol. V*. Paris: Seuil, 2002, 299–303.

Buber, Martin. *I and You*. New York: Scribner, 1970.

Burton, Robert. *An Anatomy of Melancholy*. New York: New York Review Books, 2001.

Cale, John. *What's Welsh for Zen?* London: Bloomsbury, 1999.

Campbell, Roy. *Poems of Baudelaire*. New York: Pantheon Books, 1952.

Dagerman, Stig. *Notre besoin de consolation est impossible à rassasier*. Le Méjan: Actes Sud, 1981.

Daumal, René. *Le Contre-Ciel*. Paris: Gallimard, 1970 [1936].

Debord, Guy. *La société de spectacle*. Paris: Gallimard, 1992 [1967].

———. *Commentaire sur la société du spectacle*. Paris: Gallimard, 1992.

Deleuze, Gilles et Guattari, Félix, *Mille plateaux*. Paris: Editions de Minuit, 1980.

Dyer, Richard. *Stars*. London: Palgrave-Macmillan, 2009.

Gilbert-Lecomte, Roger. *Testament*. Paris: Gallimard, 1955.

Ginsberg, Allen. *Howl and Other Poems*. San Francisco: City Lights, 1992 [1956].

Greenfield, Robert. *Timothy Leary: A Biography*. San Diego: Harcourt, 2006.

Grimbert, Philippe. *Psychanalyse de la chanson*. Paris: Les Belles Lettres, 1996.

Jung, Carl Gustav. *Psychologie et alchimie*. Paris: Buchet-Chastel, 1970.

———. *Aïon : études sur la phénoménologie du soi*. Paris: Albin Michel, 1983.

Kelly, John, ed. *Yeats, W.B.* London: Everyman, 1997.

Kundera, Milan. *The Festival of Insignificance*. London: Faber & Faber, 2015.

Leitch, Donovan. *The Hurdy-Gurdy Man*. London: Arrows, 2005.

Layton, Irving. *Selected Poems*. New York: New Directions, 1977.

Lipovetsky, Gilles. *L'Ere du vide : essais sur l'individualisme contemporain*. Paris: Gallimard, 1993.

Malanga, Gerard. *Ten Poems for Ten Poets*. Avon: Derringer Books, 2000.

Midal, Fabrice. *Auschwitz, l'impossible regard*. Paris: Seuil, 2012.

Millett, Kate. *Sexual Politics*. London: Rupert Hart Davis, 1971.

Nietzsche, Friedrich. *Le Gai savoir*. Paris: Gallimard, 1982.

———. *Crépuscule des idoles*. Paris: Gallimard, 1992.

———. *Humain, trop humain II*. Paris: Gallimard, 1988.

Otter, Jennifer. *You Are Beautiful and You Are Alone*. London: Hachette UK, 2021.

Ovide. *L'Art d'aimer*. Paris: Gallimard, 1974.

Pascal, Blaise. *Pensées*. Paris: Garnier-Flammarion, 1976.

Pastoureau, Michel. *Black: The History of a Color*. Princeton University Press, 2008.

Prigent, Hélène. *Mélancholie : Les métamorphoses de la dépression*. Paris: Gallimard, 2005.

Quin, Élisabeth, and François Armanet. *The Killer Detail: Defining Moments in Fashion: Sartorial Icons from Cary Grant to Kate Moss*. Paris: Flammarion, 2016.

Rimbaud, Arthur. *Poésies. Une saison en enfer. Illuminations*. Paris: NRF, 1984.

Rugafiori, Claudio. *Le Grand Jeu. Collection complète*. Paris: Jean-Michel Placé, 1977.

Rushdie, Salman. *Imaginary Homelands: Essays and Criticism, 1981–1991*. London: Granta Books, 1991.

Schechner, Richard. *Performance Theory*. London & New York: Routledge & Kegan, 2003.

Schwar-Salant, Nathan. *Jung on Alchemy*. London: Routledge, 1995.

Servier, Jean. *Dictionnaire critique de l'ésotérisme*. Paris: PUF, 1998.

Sloman, Larry. *On the Road with Bob Dylan*. London: Helter Skelter, 2002.

Smith, Patti. *Just Kids*. New York: HarperCollins, 2010.

Sounes, Howard. *Down the Highway: The Life of Bob Dylan*. London: Black Swan Press, 2002.

Stein, Jean, and George Plimpton. *Edie: An American Biography*. New York: Grove Press, 1994.

Styron, William. *Darkness Visible: A Memoir of Madness*. London: Vintage, 2001.

Tippins, Sherill. *Dream Palace: The Life and Times of New York's Legendary Chelsea Hotel*. New York: Houghton Mifflin Harcourt, 2013.

Tzu, Sun. *L'Art de la guerre*. Paris: Mille et Une Nuits, 2000.

Warhol, Andy, and Pat Hackett. *Popism: The Warhol Sixties*. London: Pimlico, 1996.

Young, James. *Nico, Songs They Never Play on the Radio*. London: Bloomsbury, 1993.

Zink, Michel. *Chansons des trouvères*. Paris: Livre de Poche, 1995.

CHRISTIAN SOURCES

Anonymous. *The Cloud of Unknowing and Other Works*. Harmondsworth: Penguin, 2001.

Angelus, Silesius. *Le Pèlerin chérubinique*. Paris: PUF, 1964.

Benedict (Saint). *Rule of Saint Benedict*. New York: Vintage Books, 1998.

Bonino, Thomas. *Les anges et les démons : Quatorze leçons de théologie*. Paris: Paroles et silence, 2007.

Certeau, Michel de. *La faiblesse de croire*. Paris: Seuil, 1987.

Denys l'Aréopagite (saint). *Œuvres complètes*. Edited by Maurice de Gandillac. Paris: Aubier, 1989.

Faes de Motoni, Barbara. "Ange." In *Dictionnaire encyclopédique du Moyen-Âge*. Paris: Cerf, 1997, 64–66.

Faure, Philippe. "Ange: Occident médiéval." In *Dictionnaire critique de l'ésotérisme*. Paris: PUF, 1998, 85–88.

François d'Assise (saint). *La joie parfaite*. Paris: Le Point, 2008.

Jean de la Croix (saint). *La nuit obscure*. Paris: Cerf, 1992.

Jossua, Jean-Pierre. *Seul avec Dieu : L'aventure mystique*. Paris: Gallimard, 1996.

Lecercle, François. "Des yeux pour ne point voir. Avatars de l'idolâtrie chez les théologiens catholiques du XVIe siècle." In *L'Idolâtrie*. Paris: La Documentation française, 1990, 35–53.

Lobrichon, Guy. *Les moines d'Occident; L'éternité de l'Europe*. Paris: Gallimard, 2002.

Porete, Marguerite. *Le miroir des âmes simples et anéanties*. Paris: Albin Michel, 2011.

Wirth, Jean. *L'image à l'époque romane*. Paris: Cerf, 1999.

JUDAISM

Avril, Anne-Catherine. *Prières juives*. Paris: Cerf, 1989.

Baumgarten, Jean. *La naissance du hassidisme : Mystique, rituels et société*. Paris: Albin Michel, 2002.

Bratslav, Nachman de. *Songes, énigmes et paraboles*. Paris: Bibliophane, 2002.

Goetschel, Roland. *La Kabbale*. Paris: PUF, 1985.

Maïmonide, Moïse. *Le Guide des égarés*. Paris: Maisonneuve et Larose, 1970.

Meschonnic, Henri. *L'utopie du juif*. Paris: Desclée et Brower, 2001.

Mopsik, Charles, ed. *Le zohar : lamentations*. Paris: Verdier, 2000.

Müller, Ernst. *Histoire de la mystique juive*. Paris: Petite Bibliothèque Payot, 1976.

Neher, André. *L'exil de la parole : du silence biblique au silence d'Auschwitz*. Paris: Seuil, 1970.

———. *L'Identité juive*. Paris: Petite Bibliothèque Payot, 1994.

Ouaknin, Marc-Alain. *Mystères de la kabbale*. Paris: Assouline, 2006.

———. *Les symboles du judaïsme*. Paris: Assouline, 1999.

———. *Tsim-Tsoum*. Paris: Albin Michel, 1999.

———. *Invitation au Talmud*. Paris: Flammarion, 2001.

Scholem, Gershom. *Le Zohar : Le livre de la splendeur. Extraits choisis*. Paris: Seuil, 2011.

———. *Major Trends of Jewish Mysticism*. New York: Schocken Books, 1995.

———. *On the Kabbalah and Its Symbolism*, New York: Schocken Books, 1977.

Steinsaltz, Adin, and Josy Eisenberg. *Introduction à la prière juive*. Paris: Albin Michel, 2011.

Trion-Montalembert, Renée de. *La kabbale et la tradition judaïque*. Paris: Cerf, 1974.

Wigoder, Geoffrey, ed. *The Oxford Dictionary of the Jewish Religion*. Oxford: Oxford University Press, 1997.

ZEN BUDDHISM AND EASTERN THOUGHT

Balsekar, Ramesh. *Tout est conscience*. Paris: Editions Accarias, 2012.

Baroni, Helen J. *The Illustrated Encyclopedia of Zen Buddhism*. New York: Rosen, 2002.

Brosse, Jacques. *Les grands maîtres de la spiritualité*. Paris: Larousse-Bordas, 1998.

Cleary, Thomas, and Lieou Yi-Ming. *Yi King*. Paris: Éditions du Rocher, 1994.

Cleary, Thomas, ed. *Blue Cliff Record*. Boston: Shambhala, 2005.

Friedrichs, Kurt, Ingrid Fischer-Schreiber, and Michael Deiner. *The Encyclopedia of Eastern Philosophy and Religion*. Boston: Shambhala, 2002.

Gaudin, Christian. *Zen pour chats*. Paris: Sources la Sirène, 1991.

Govinda, Anagarika. *Les fondements de la mystique tibétaine*. Paris: Albin Michel, 1960.

Hakuin. *The Essential Teachings of Zen Master Hakuin*. Edited by Norman Waddell. Boston and London: Shambhala, 2010.

Hakuun, Yasutani. *Flowers Fall: A Commentary of Zen Master Dogen's Genjokoan*. Boston: Shambhala, 1996.

Herrigel, Eugen. *The Method of Zen*. London: Routledge & Kegan, 1960.

Hoffmann, Yoel. *The Sound of the One Hand: 281 Zen Koans with Answers*. New York: Bantam Books, 1975.

Izutzu, Toshihiko. *Le kôan zen : Essais sur le bouddhisme zen*. Paris: Fayard, 1978.

Koren, Leonard. *Wabi-Sabi for Artists, Designers, Poets & Philosophers*. Point Reynes: Imperfect Publishing, 2008.

Lenoir, Frédéric. *La rencontre du bouddhisme et de l'Occident*. Paris: Albin Michel, 2001.

Masui, Jacques. *L'exercice du Kôan*. Paris: Fata Morgana, 1994.

Merton, Thomas. *Mystics and Zen Masters*. New York: Farrar, Straus & Giroux, 1967.

Miura, Isshu, and Ruth Fuller Sasaki. *The Zen Koan: Its History and Use in Rinzaï Zen*. New York: Harvest Book, 1965.

Morinaga, Sōkō. *Novice to Master: An Ongoing Lesson in the Extent of My Own Stupidity*. Boston: Wisdom Publications, 2004.

Reps, Paul, *Zen Flesh, Zen Bones*. London: Penguin, 2000 [1957].

Sachedeva, Gautam. *Pointers to Ramesh Balsekar*. Mumbai: Yogi Impressions Books, 2008.

Sasaki Roshi, Kyozan Joshu. *Buddha Is the Center of Gravity*. San Cristobal: Lama Foundation, 1974.

Schloegel, Imgard. *The Zen Teachings of Rinzai*. Berkeley: Shambhala, 1976.

Shishin Wick, Gerry, ed. *Shoyoroku Book of Equanimity*. Somerville: Wisdom Publications, 2005.

Sojūn, Ikkyū. *Crow with No Mouth: Fifteenth Century Zen Master*. Translated by Stephen Berg. Port Townsend: Copper Canyon Press, 2000.

Suzuki, D.T., *Sengaï: The Zen of Ink and Paper*. Boulder: Shambhala, 1999.

Suzuki, Shunryu. *Zen Mind, Beginner's Mind*. New York & Tokyo: Weatherhill, 1994 [1970].

Taikan, Jyoji. *L'art du kôan zen*. Paris: Albin Michel, 2001.

Takuan, Soho. *The Mystery of Immovable Wisdom*. Tokyo & New York: Kodansha, 1987.

Tanahashi, Kazuaki. *Penetrating Laughter: Hakuin's Zen and Art*. London: Overlook, 1987.

Tchouang-tseu (Zhuang Zhou). *Joie suprême*. Paris: Gallimard, 1969.

Trungpa, Chogyam. *Cutting Through Spiritual Materialism*. Boston: Shambhala, 2002.

Zenji, Dogen. "Genjokoan." In *Shobogenzo*. Woods Hall: Windbell Publications, 1994, 33–39.

INDEX

Note: Page numbers in italics indicate a figure.

TITLES

This book is also available as a Global Certified Accessible™ (GCA) ebook. ECW Press's ebooks are screen reader friendly and are built to meet the needs of those who are unable to read standard print due to blindness, low vision, dyslexia, or a physical disability.

At ECW Press, we want you to enjoy our books in whatever format you like. If you've bought a print copy or an audiobook not purchased with a subscription credit, just send an email to ebook@ecwpress.com and include:

- the book title
- the name of the store where you purchased it
- a screenshot or picture of your order/receipt number and your name

A real person will respond to your email with your ePub attached. If you prefer to receive the ebook in PDF format, please let us know in your email.

Some restrictions apply. This offer is only valid for books already available in the ePub format. Some ECW Press books do not have an ePub format for us to send you. In those cases, we will let you know if a PDF format is available as an alternative. This offer is only valid for books purchased for personal use. At this time, this program is not offered on school or library copies.

Thank you for supporting an independently owned Canadian publisher with your purchase!